the LIONS of AL-RASSAN

GUY GAVRIEL KAY

VIKING

VIKING
Published by the Penguin Group
Penguin Books Canada Ltd, 10 Alcorn Avenue, Toronto, Ontario,
Canada M4V 3B2
Penguin Books Ltd, 27 Wrights Lane, London W8 5TZ, England
Viking Penguin, a division of Penguin Books USA Inc.,
375 Hudson Street, New York, New York 10014, U.S.A.
Penguin Books Australia Ltd, Ringwood, Victoria, Australia
Penguin Books (NZ) Ltd, 182–190 Wairau Road, Auckland 10,
New Zealand

Penguin Books Ltd, Registered Offices: Harmondsworth,
Middlesex, England

First published 1995
1 3 5 7 9 10 8 6 4 2

*Publisher's note: This book is a work of fiction. Names, characters,
places and incidents either are the product of the author's
imagination or are used fictitiously, and any resemblance to actual
persons living or dead, events, or locales is entirely coincidental.*

Printed and bound in Canada on acid free paper ∞

Canadian Cataloguing in Publication Data

Kay, Guy Gavriel
The Lions of Al-Rassan

ISBN 0-670-85896-X

I. Title.

PS8571.A935L5 1995   C813'.54   C94-932846-4
PR9199.3.K38L5 1995

American Library of Congress Cataloguing in Publication Data
Available
British Library Cataloguing in Publication Data Available

For Harry Karlinsky and Mayer Hoffer,
after thirty-five years.

Acknowledgments

～

Those of us with the temerity to walk a line—or create one—between history and the imagined are profoundly in the debt of the historians, whose delving among the fragmentary records of our past becomes a more creatively challenging labor the further back they go.

For the groundwork and the inspiration of my invented Al-Rassan, I am indebted to the scholarship of many people. Among them I wish to particularly note Richard Fletcher, David Wasserstein, T.F. Glick, Nancy G. Siraisi and Manfred Ullmann (on medicine), S.D. Goitein, Bernard Reilly, Pierre Riché and the sweeping, impassioned writings of Rheinhart Dozy.

In the verses and songs herein, those familiar with the period that serves as my source will find motifs derived from some of the most eloquent voices of the peninsula. It is appropriate that I pay tribute here to the art of al-Mu'tamid, ar-Rundi, ibn 'Ammar and ibn Bassam, among others.

My first introduction to the complexities and the power of the Iberian Peninsula came by way of two people who have embodied, for much of my life, the idea of a civilized existence: Gladys and David Bruser. It is a great pleasure to be able to acknowledge them here.

I continue to be the beneficiary of the talent and experience of a number of people. Dr. Rex Kay, always of assistance, was more so than ever in helping to research the medical elements of this book, and in carefully reviewing the manuscript in progress. Sue Reynolds offered another lucid, necessary map. In France I was abetted by the friendship and stimulation of Stan Rodbell and Cynthia Foster, and of Mary and Bruno Grawitz. In Toronto, my old friend Andy Patton continues to offer me the benefits of an uncompromising intelligence and an equally unflagging support. And finally, both at home and abroad, I am sustained by three people I love: my mother, my son, and my wife.

Guy Gavriel Kay

The evening is deep inside me forever.
Many a blond, northern moonrise,
Like a muted reflection, will softly
remind me and remind me again and again.
It will be my bride, my alter ego.
An incentive to find myself. I myself
am the moonrise of the south.

Paul Klee, *The Tunisian Diaries*

Principal Characters

∾

In Al-Rassan
(*All these are Asharite, worshippers of the stars of Ashar, except where noted*)

King Almalik of Cartada ("The Lion of Cartada")
Almalik, his eldest son and heir
Hazem, his second son

Zabira, his favored courtesan

Ammar ibn Khairan of Aljais, his principal advisor, guardian of the king's heir

King Badir of Ragosa
Mazur ben Avren, his chancellor, of the Kindath faith

Tarif ibn Hassan of Arbastro, an outlaw
Idar ⎫
        ⎬ his sons
Abir ⎭

Husari ibn Musa of Fezana, a silk merchant

Jehane bet Ishak, a physician in Fezana, of the Kindath faith
Ishak ben Yonannon, her father
Eliane bet Danel, her mother
Velaz, their servant

In the Three Kingdoms of Esperaña
(*All these are Jaddites, worshippers of the sun-god, Jad*)

King Sancho the Fat of Esperaña, now deceased
King Raimundo of Valledo, Sancho's eldest son, now deceased

In the Kingdom of Valledo (royal city: Esteren)
King Ramiro, son to Sancho the Fat
Queen Ines, his wife, daughter of the king of Ferrieres

Count Gonzalez de Rada, constable of Valledo
Garcia de Rada, his brother

In the Kingdom of Valledo (*continued*)

Rodrigo Belmonte ("The Captain"), soldier and rancher, once constable of Valledo

Miranda Belmonte d'Alveda, his wife

Fernan ⎱ his sons
Diego ⎰

Ibero, a cleric, tutor to the sons of Rodrigo Belmonte

Laín Nunez ⎫
Martín   ⎬
Ludus   ⎬ members of Ser Rodrigo's company
Alvar de Pellino ⎭

In the Kingdom of Jaloña

King Bermudo, brother to Sancho the Fat

Queen Fruela, his wife

Count Nino di Carrera, the king's (and the queen's) most-favored courtier

In the Kingdom of Ruenda

King Sanchez, youngest son of Sancho the Fat, brother to Ramiro of Valledo

Queen Bearte, his wife

In the Majriti Desert

(*Across the southern straits; home of the Muwardi tribes*)

Yazir ibn Q'arif, of the Zuhrite Tribe, Lord of the Majriti

Ghalib, his brother, war leader of the tribes

In Countries East

Geraud de Chervalles, a High Cleric of Jad, in Ferrieres

Rezzoni ben Corli, a Kindath physician and teacher; of the city of Sorenica, in Batiara

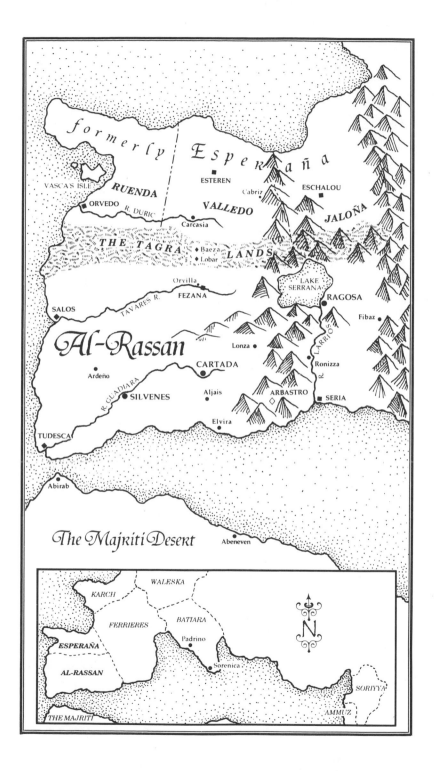

the
LIONS
of
Al-Rassan

PROLOGUE

It was just past midday, not long before the third summons to prayer, that Ammar ibn Khairan passed through the Gate of the Bells and entered the palace of Al-Fontina in Silvenes to kill the last of the khalifs of Al-Rassan.

Passing into the Court of Lions he came to the three sets of double doors and paused before those that led to the gardens. There were eunuchs guarding the doors. He knew them by name. They had been dealt with. One of them nodded slightly to him; the other kept his gaze averted. He preferred the second man. They opened the heavy doors and he went through. He heard them swing closed behind him.

In the heat of the day the gardens were deserted. All those still left within the dissolving magnificence of the Al-Fontina would have sought the shade of the innermost rooms. They would be sipping cool sweet wines or using the elaborately long spoons designed by Ziryani to taste sherbets kept frozen in the deep cellars by snow brought down from the mountains. Luxuries from another age, meant for very different men and women from those who dwelt here now.

Thinking such thoughts, ibn Khairan walked noiselessly through the Garden of Oranges and, passing through the horseshoe arch, into the Almond Garden and then, beneath another arch, into the Cypress Garden with its one tall, perfect tree reflected in three pools. Each garden was smaller than the one before, each heartbreaking in its loveliness. The Al-Fontina, a poet once had said, had been built to break the heart.

At the end of the long progression he came to the Garden of Desire, smallest and most jewel-like of all. And there, sitting quietly and alone on the broad rim of the fountain, clad in white, was Muzafar, as had been pre-arranged.

Ibn Khairan bowed in the archway, a habit deeply ingrained. The old, blind man could not see his obeisance. After a moment he moved forward, stepping deliberately on the pathway that led to the fountain.

"Ammar?" Muzafar said, hearing the sound. "They told me you would be here. Is it you? Have you come to lead me away from here? Is it you, Ammar?"

There were many things that could be said.

"It is," said ibn Khairan, walking up. He drew his dagger from its sheath. The old man's head lifted suddenly at that, as if he knew the sound. "I have, indeed, come to set you free of this place of ghosts and echoes."

With the words he slid the blade smoothly to the hilt in the old man's heart. Muzafar made no sound. It had been swift and sure. He could tell the wadjis in their temples, if it ever came to such a thing, that he had made it an easy end.

He laid the body down on the fountain rim, ordering the limbs within the white robe to allow the dead man as much dignity as could be. He cleaned his blade in the fountain, watching the waters swirl briefly red. In the teachings of his people, for hundreds and hundreds of years, going back and away to the deserts of the east where the faith of the Asharites had begun, it was a crime without possibility of assuaging to slay one of the god's anointed khalifs. He looked down at Muzafar, at the round, wrinkled face, sadly irresolute, even in death.

He has not been truly anointed, Almalik had said, back in Cartada. _All men know this._

There had been four puppet khalifs this year alone, one other here in Silvenes before Muzafar, one in Tudesca, and the poor child in Salos. It was not a situation that could have been allowed to continue. The other three were already dead. Muzafar was only the last.

Only the last. There had been lions once in Al-Rassan, lions upon the dais in this palace that had been built to make men fall to their knees upon marble and alabaster before the dazzling evidence of a glory beyond their grasp.

Muzafar had, indeed, never been properly anointed, just as Almalik of Cartada had said. But the thought came to Ammar ibn Khairan as he stood in his twentieth year in the Garden of Desire of the Al-Fontina of Silvenes, cleansing his blade of a man's red blood, that whatever else he did with his life, in the days and nights Ashar and the god saw fit to grant him under the holy circling of their stars, he might ever after be known as the man who slew the last khalif of Al-Rassan.

"You are best with the god among the stars. It will be a time of wolves now," he said to the dead man on the fountain rim before drying and sheathing his blade and walking back through the four perfect, empty gardens to the doors where the bribed eunuchs waited to let him out. On the way he heard one foolish bird singing in the fierce white light of midday, and then he heard the bells begin, summoning all good men to holy prayer.

PART I

Chapter I

༄

Always remember that they come from the desert.
Back in the days before Jehane had begun her own
practice, in that time when her father could still talk to her,
and teach, he had offered those words to her over and
again, speaking of the ruling Asharites among whom they
dwelt on sufferance, and labored—as the scattered tribes
of the Kindath did everywhere—to create a small space in
the world of safety and a measure of repose.

"But we have the desert in our own history, don't we?"
she could remember asking once, the question thrown
back as a challenge. She had never been an easy pupil, not
for him, not for anyone.

"We passed through," Ishak had replied in the beautifully modulated voice. "We sojourned for a time, on our
way. We were never truly a people of the dunes. They are.
Even here in Al-Rassan, amid gardens and water and trees,
the Star-born are never sure of the permanence of such
things. They remain in their hearts what they were when
they first accepted the teachings of Ashar among the
sands. When you are in doubt as to how to understand
one of them, remind yourself of this and your way will
likely be made clear."

In those days, despite her fractiousness, Jehane's
father's words had been as text and holy guide for her. On
another occasion, after she had complained for the third
time during a tedious morning preparing powders and
infusions, Ishak had mildly cautioned that a doctor's life

might often be dull, but was not invariably so, and there
would be times when she found herself longing for quiet
routine.

She was to sharply call to mind both of these teachings
before she finally fell asleep at the end of the day that
would long afterwards be known in Fezana—with curses,
and black candles burned in memory—as The Day of the
Moat.

It was a day that would be remembered all her life by
Jehane bet Ishak, the physician, for reasons over and above
those of her fellow citizens in that proud, notoriously
rebellious town: she lost her urine flask in the afternoon,
and a part of her heart forever before the moons had set.

The flask, for reasons of family history, was not a trivial matter.

The day had begun at the weekly market by the
Cartada Gate. Just past sunrise, Jehane was in the booth
by the fountain that had been her father's before her, in
time to see the last of the farmers coming in from the
countryside with their produce-laden mules. In a white
linen robe beneath the physician's green and white
awning, she settled in, cross-legged on her cushion, for a
morning of seeing patients. Velaz hovered, as ever, behind
her in the booth, ready to measure and dispense remedies
as she requested them, and to ward off any difficulties a
young woman might encounter in a place as tumultuous
as the market. Trouble was unlikely, however; Jehane was
well-known by now.

A morning at the Cartada Gate involved prescribing
mostly for farmers from beyond the walls but there were
also city servants, artisans, women bargaining for staples
at the market and, not infrequently, those among the high-
born too frugal to pay for a private visit, or too proud to
be treated at home by one of the Kindath. Such patients
never came in person; they would send a household
woman bearing a urine flask for diagnosis, and sometimes
a script spelled out by a scribe outlining symptoms and
complaints.

Jehane's own urine flask, which had been her father's, was prominently visible on the counter beneath the awning. It was a family signature, an announcement. A magnificent example of the glassblower's art, the flask was etched with images of the two moons the Kindath worshipped and the Higher Stars of divination.

In some ways it was an object too beautiful for every-day use, given the unglamorous function it was meant to serve. The flask had been made by an artisan in Lonza six years ago, commissioned by King Almalik of Cartada after Ishak had guided the midwives—from the far side of the birthing screen—through the difficult but successful deliv-ery of Almalik's third son.

When the time had come for the delivery of a fourth son, an even more difficult birth, but also, ultimately, a successful one, Ishak of Fezana, the celebrated Kindath physician, had been given a different, controversial gift by Cartada's king. A more generous offering in its way, but awareness of that did nothing to touch the core of bitter-ness Jehane felt to this day, four years after. It was not a bitterness that would pass; she knew that with certainty.

She gave a prescription for sleeplessness and another for stomach troubles. Several people stopped to buy her father's remedy for headache. It was a simple compound, though closely guarded, as all physicians' private mixtures were: cloves, myrrh and aloes. Jehane's mother was kept busy preparing that one all week long in the treatment rooms at the front of their home.

The morning passed. Velaz quietly and steadily filled clay pots and vials at the back of the booth as Jehane issued her directions. A flask of urine clear at the bottom but thin and pale at the top told its tale of chest conges-tion. Jehane prescribed fennel and told the woman to return the next week with another sample.

Ser Rezzoni of Sorenica, a sardonic man, had taught that the essence of the successful physician's practice lay in inducing patients to return. The dead ones, he'd noted, seldom did. Jehane could remember laughing; she had laughed often in those days, studying in far-off Batiara, before the fourth son of Cartada's king had been born.

Velaz dealt with all payments, most often in small coin, sometimes otherwise. One woman from a hamlet nearby, troubled by a variety of recurring ailments, brought a dozen brown eggs every week.

The market was unusually crowded. Stretching her arms and shoulders as she glanced up briefly from steady work, Jehane noted with satisfaction the respectable line of patients in front of her. In the first months after she'd taken over her father's weekly booth here and the treatment rooms at home the patients had been slow to come; now it seemed she was doing almost as well as Ishak had.

The noise level this morning was really quite extraordinary. There had to be some cause for this bustling excitement but Jehane couldn't think what it might be. It was only when she saw three blond and bearded foreign mercenaries arrogantly shouldering their way through the market that she remembered. The new wing of the castle was being consecrated by the wadjis today, and the young prince of Cartada, Almalik's eldest son, who bore his name, was here to receive selected dignitaries of subjugated Fezana. Even in a town notorious for its rebels, social status mattered; those who had received a coveted invitation to the ceremony had been preening for weeks.

Jehane paid little attention to this sort of thing, or to any other nuances of diplomacy and war most of the time. There was a saying among her people: *Whichever way the wind blows, it will rain upon the Kindath.* That pretty well summed up her feelings.

Since the thunderous, echoing fall of the Khalifate in Silvenes fifteen years ago, allegiances and alignments in Al-Rassan had shifted interminably, often several times a year, as petty-kings rose and fell in the cities with numbing regularity. Nor were affairs any clearer in the north, beyond the no-man's-land, where the Jaddite kings of Valledo and Ruenda and Jaloña—the two surviving sons and the brother of Sancho the Fat—schemed and warred against each other.

It was a waste of time, Jehane had long ago decided, to try to keep track of what former slave had gained an ascendancy here, or what king had poisoned his brother there.

It was becoming warmer in the marketplace as the sun climbed upwards in a blue sky. Not a great surprise; midsummer in Fezana was always hot. Jehane dabbed at her forehead with a square of muslin and brought her mind back to the business at hand. Medicine was her training and her love, her refuge from chaos, and it was her link to her father, now and as long as she lived.

A leather worker she did not recognize stood shyly at the front of the line. He carried a chipped earthenware beaker to serve as a flask. Placing a grimy coin on the counter beside her he grimaced apologetically as he proffered the beaker. "I'm sorry," he whispered, barely audible amid the tumult. "It is all we have. This is from my son. He is eight years old. He is not well."

Velaz, behind her, unobtrusively picked up the coin; it was considered bad form, Ser Rezzoni had taught, for doctors to actually touch their remuneration. That, he had said waspishly, is what servants are for. He had been her first lover as well as her teacher, during her time living and studying abroad in Batiara. He slept with almost all his women students, and a few of the men it had been rumored. He had a wife and three young daughters who doted upon him. A complex, brilliant, angry man, Ser Rezzoni. Kind enough to her, however, after his fashion, out of respect for Ishak.

Jehane smiled up at the leather worker reassuringly. "It doesn't matter what container you bring a sample in. Don't apologize."

By his coloring he appeared to be a Jaddite from the north, living here because the work for skilled artisans was better in Al-Rassan, most probably a convert. The Asharites didn't demand conversions, but the tax burden on Kindath and Jaddite made for a keen incentive to embrace the desert visions of Ashar the Sage.

She transferred the urine sample from the chipped

beaker to her father's gorgeous flask, gift of the grateful king whose namesake heir was here today to celebrate an event that further ensured Cartadan dominance of proud Fezana. On a bustling market morning Jehane had little time to ponder ironies, but they tended to surface nonetheless; her mind worked that way.

As the sample settled in the flask she saw that the urine of the leather worker's son was distinctly rose-colored. She tilted the flask back and forth in the light; in fact, the color was too close to red for comfort. The child had a fever; what else he had was hard to judge.

"Velaz," she murmured, "dilute the absinthe with a quarter of mint. A drop of the cordial for taste." She heard her servant withdraw into the booth to prepare the pre-scription.

To the leather worker she said, "He is warm to the touch?"

He nodded anxiously. "And dry. He is very dry, doctor. He has difficulty swallowing food."

Briskly, she said, "That is understandable. Give him the remedy we are preparing. Half when you arrive home, half at sundown. Do you understand that?" The man nodded. It was important to ask; some of them, especially the Jaddites from the countryside in the north, didn't under-stand the concept of fractions. Velaz would make up two separate vials for them.

"Feed him hot soups only today, a little at a time, and the juice of apples if you can. Make him take these things, even if he does not want to. He may vomit later today. That is not alarming unless there is blood with it. If there is blood, send to my house immediately. Otherwise, con-tinue with the soup and the juice until nightfall. If he is dry and hot he needs these things, you understand?" Again the man nodded, his brow furrowed with concentra-tion. "Before you go, give Velaz directions to your home. I will come in the morning tomorrow to see him."

The man's relief was evident, but then a familiar hesita-tion appeared. "Doctor, forgive me. We have no money to spare for a private consultation."

Jehane grimaced. Probably not a convert then, sorely burdened by the taxes but refusing to surrender his worship of the sun-god, Jad. Who was she, however, to question religious scruples? Nearly a third of her own earnings went to the Kindath tax, and she would never have called herself religious. Few doctors were. Pride, on the other hand, was another matter. The Kindath were the Wanderers, named for the two moons traversing the night sky among the stars, and as far as Jehane was concerned, they had not travelled so far, through so many centuries, only to surrender their long history here in Al-Rassan. If a Jaddite felt the same about his god, she could understand.

"We will deal with the matter of payment when the time comes. For the moment, the question is whether the child will need to be bled, and I cannot very well do that here in the marketplace."

She heard a ripple of laughter from someone standing by the booth. She ignored that, made her voice more gentle. Kindath physicians were known to be the most expensive in the peninsula. As well we should be, Jehane thought. We are the only ones who *know* anything. It was wrong of her, though, to chide people for concerns about cost. "Never fear," she smiled up at the leather worker. "I will not bleed both you and the boy."

More general laughter this time. Her father had always said that half the task of doctors was to make the patient *believe* in them. A certain kind of laughter helped, Jehane had found. It conveyed a sense of confidence. "Be sure you know both the moons and the Higher Stars of his birth hour. If I am going to draw blood I'll want to work out a time."

"My wife will know," the man whispered. "Thank you. Thank you, doctor."

"Tomorrow," she said crisply.

Velaz reappeared from the back with the medicine, gave it to the man, and took away her flask to empty it into the pail beside the counter. The leather worker paused beside him, nervously giving directions for the morrow.

"Who's next?" Jehane asked, looking up again.

There were a great many of King Almalik's mercenaries in the market now. The blond northern giants from far-off Karch or Waleska and, even more oppressively, Muwardi tribesmen ferried across the straits from the Majriti sands, their faces half-veiled, dark eyes unreadable, except when contempt showed clearly.

Almost certainly this was a deliberate public display by Cartada. There were probably soldiers strolling all through town, under orders to be seen. She belatedly remembered hearing that the prince had arrived two days ago with five hundred men. Far too many soldiers for a ceremonial visit. You could take a small city or launch a major raid across the *tagra*—the no-man's-land—with five hundred good men.

They needed soldiers here. The current governor of Fezana was a puppet of Almalik's, supported by a standing army. The mercenary troops were here ostensibly to guard against incursions from the Jaddite kingdoms, or brigands troubling the countryside. In reality their presence was the only thing that kept the city from rising in revolt again. And now, of course, with a new-built wing in the castle there would be more of them.

Fezana had been a free city from the fall of the Khalifate until seven years ago. Freedom was a memory, anger a reality now; they had been taken in Cartada's second wave of expansion. The siege had lasted half a year, then someone had opened the Salos Gate to the army outside one night as winter was coming, with its enforced end to the siege. They never learned who the traitor was. Jehane remembered hiding with her mother in the innermost room of their home in the Kindath Quarter, hearing screams and the shouts of battle and the crackle of fire. Her father had been on the other side of the walls, hired by the Cartadans a year before to serve as physician to Almalik's army; such was a doctor's life. Ironies again.

Human corpses, crawling with flies, had hung from the walls above this gate and the other five for weeks after the taking of the city, the smell hovering over fruit and vegetable stalls like a pestilence.

Fezana became part of the rapidly growing kingdom of Cartada. So, already, had Lonza, and Aljais, even Silvenes itself, with the sad, plundered ruins of the Al-Fontina. So, later, did Seria and Ardeño. Now even proud Ragosa on the shores of Lake Serrana was under threat, as were Elvira and Tudesca to the south and southwest. In the fragmented Al-Rassan of the petty-kings, Almalik of Cartada was named the Lion by the poets of his court.

Of all the conquered cities, it was Fezana that rebelled most violently: three times in seven years. Each time Almalik's mercenaries had come back, the blond ones and the veiled ones, and each time flies and carrion birds had feasted on corpses spread-eagled on the city walls.

But there were other ironies, keener ones, of late. The fierce Lion of Cartada was being forced to acknowledge the presence of beasts equally dangerous. The Jaddites of the north might be fewer in number and torn amongst themselves, but they were not blind to opportunity. For two years now Fezana had been paying tribute money to King Ramiro of Valledo. Almalik had been unable to refuse, not if he wanted to avoid the risk of war with the strongest of the Jaddite kings while policing the cities of his fractious realm, dealing with the outlaw bands that roamed the southern hills, and with King Badir of Ragosa wealthy enough to hire his own mercenaries.

Ramiro of Valledo might rule a rough society of herdsmen and primitive villagers, but it was also a society organized for war, and the Horsemen of Jad were not to be trifled with. Only the might of the khalifs of Al-Rassan, supreme in Silvenes for three hundred years, had sufficed to conquer most of the peninsula and confine the Jaddites to the north—and that confining had demanded raid after raid through the high plateaus of the no-man's-land, and not every raid had been successful.

If the three Jaddite kings ever stopped warring amongst each other, brother against uncle against brother, Jehane thought, Cartada's conquering Lion—along with all the lesser kings of Al-Rassan—might be muzzled and gelded soon enough.

Which would not necessarily be a good thing at all.

One more irony, bitterness in the taste of it. It seemed she had to hope for the survival of the man she hated as no other. All winds might bring rain for the Kindath, but here among the Asharites of Al-Rassan they had acceptance and a place. After centuries of wandering the earth like their moons through heaven, that meant a great deal. Taxed heavily, bound by restrictive laws, they could nonetheless live freely, seek their fortunes, worship as they wished, both the god and his sisters. And some among the Kindath had risen high indeed among the courts of the petty-kings.

No Kindath were high in the counsels of the Children of Jad in this peninsula. Hardly any of them were left in the north. History—and they had a long history—had taught the Kindath that they might be tolerated and even welcomed among the Jaddites when times were prosperous and peaceful, but when the skies darkened, when the rain winds came, the Kindath became Wanderers again. They were exiled, or forcibly converted, or they died in the lands where the sun-god held sway.

Tribute—the *parias*—was collected by a party of northern horsemen twice a year. Fezana was expensively engaged in paying the price of being too near to the *tagra* lands.

The poets were calling the three hundred years of the Khalifate a Golden Age now. Jehane had heard the songs and the spoken verses. In those vanished days, however people might have chafed at the absolute power or the extravagant splendor of the court at Silvenes, with the wadjis in their temples bemoaning decadence and sacrilege, in the raiding season the ancient roads to the north had witnessed the passage of the massed armies of Al-Rassan, and then their return with plunder and slaves.

No unified army went north into the no-man's-land now, and if the steppes of those empty places saw soldiers in numbers any time soon it was more likely to be the Horsemen of Jad the sun-god. Jehane could almost convince herself that even those last, impotent khalifs of her childhood had been symbols of a golden time.

She shook her head and turned from watching the mercenaries. A quarry laborer was next in line; she read his occupation in the chalk-white dust coating his clothing and hands. She also read, unexpectedly, gout in his pinched features and the awkward tilt of his stance, even before she glanced at the thick, milky sample of urine he held out to her. It was odd for a laborer to have gout; in the quarries the usual problems were with throat and lungs. With real curiosity she looked from the flask back up at the man.

As it happened, the quarryman was a patient Jehane never did treat. So, too, in fact, was the leather worker's child.

A sizable purse dropped onto the counter before her.

"Do forgive this intrusion, doctor," a voice said. "May I be permitted to impose upon your time?" The light tones and court diction were incongruous in the marketplace. Jehane looked up. This was, she realized, the man who had laughed before.

The rising sun was behind him, so her first image was haloed against the light and imprecise: a smooth-shaven face in the current court fashion, brown hair. She couldn't see his eyes clearly. He smelled of perfume and he wore a sword. Which meant he was from Cartada. Swords were forbidden the citizens of Fezana, even within their own walls.

On the other hand, she was a free woman going about her lawful affairs in her own place of business, and because of Almalik's gifts to her father she had no need to snatch at a purse, even a large purse, as this one manifestly was.

Irritated, she breached protocol sufficiently to pick it up and flip it back to him. "If your need is for a physician's assistance you are not intruding. That is why I am here. But there are, as you will have noted, people ahead of you. When you have, in due course, arrived at the front of this line I shall be pleased to assist, if I can." Had she been less vexed she might have been amused at how formal her own language had become. She still couldn't see him clearly. The quarryman had sidled nervously to one side.

"I greatly fear I have not the time for either alternative," the Cartadan murmured. "I will have to take you from your patients here, which is why I offer a purse for compensation."

"*Take* me?" Jehane snapped. She rose to her feet. Irritation had given way to anger. Several of the Muwardis, she realized, were now strolling over towards her stall. She was aware of Velaz directly behind her. She would have to be careful; he would challenge anyone for her.

The courtier smiled placatingly and quickly held up a gloved hand. "*Escort* you, I ought rather to have said. I entreat forgiveness. I had almost forgotten I was in Fezana, where such niceties matter greatly." He seemed amused more than anything else, which angered her further.

She could see him clearly now that she was standing. His eyes were blue, like her own—as unusual in the Asharites as it was among the Kindath. The hair was thick, curling in the heat. He was *very* expensively dressed, rings on several of his gloved fingers and a single pearl earring which was certainly worth more than the collective worldly goods of everyone in the line in front of her. More gems studded his belt and sword hilt; some were even sewn into the leather of the slippers on his feet. A dandy, Jehane thought, a mincing court dandy from Cartada.

The sword was a real one though, not a symbol, and his eyes, now that she was looking into them, were unsettlingly direct.

Jehane had been raised, by her mother and father both, to show deference where it was due and earned, and not otherwise.

"Such 'niceties,' as you prefer to call simple courtesy, ought to matter in Cartada as much as they do here," she said levelly. She pushed a strand of hair back from her eyes with the back of her hand. "I am here in the market until the midday bells have rung. If you have genuine need of a private consultation I will refer to my afternoon appointments and see when I am available."

He shook his head politely. Two of the veiled soldiers had come up to them. "As I believe I did mention, we have not time for that." There still seemed to be something amusing him. "I should perhaps say that I am not here for an affliction of my own, much as it might gratify any man to be subject to your care." There was a ripple of laughter.

Jehane was not amused. This sort of thing she knew how to deal with, and was about to, but the Cartadan went on without pausing: "I have just come from the house of a patient of yours. Husari ibn Musa is ill. He begs you to come to him this morning, before the consecration ceremony begins at the castle, that he might not be forced to miss being presented to the prince."

"Oh," Jehane said.

Ibn Musa had kidney stones, recurring ones. He had been her father's patient and one of the very first to accept her as Ishak's successor. He was wealthy, soft as the silk in which he traded, and he enjoyed rich foods far too much for his own good. He was also kind, surprisingly unpretentious, intelligent, and his early patronage had meant a great deal to her practice. Jehane liked him, and worried about him.

It was certain, given his wealth, that the silk merchant would have been on the list of citizens honored with an invitation to meet the prince of Cartada. Some things were becoming clear. Not all.

"Why did he send you? I know most of his people."

"But he didn't send me," the man demurred, with easy grace. "I offered to come. He warned me of your weekly market routine. Would you have left this booth at the behest of a servant? Even one you knew?"

Jehane had to shake her head. "Only for a birth or an accident."

The Cartadan smiled, showing white teeth against the tanned, smooth features. "Ibn Musa is, Ashar and the holy stars be thanked, not presently with child. Nor has any untoward accident befallen him. His condition is the one for which I understand you have treated him before. He swears no one else in Fezana knows how to alleviate his sufferings. And today, of course, is an...exceptional day. Will you not deviate from your custom this one time and permit me the honor of escorting you to him?"

Had he offered the purse again she would have refused. Had he not looked calm and very serious as he awaited her reply, she would have refused. Had it been anyone other than Husari ibn Musa entreating her presence...

Looking back, afterwards, Jehane was acutely aware that the smallest of gestures in that moment could have changed everything. She might so easily have told the smooth, polished Cartadan that she'd attend upon ibn Musa later that day. If so—the thought was inescapable—she would have had a very different life.

Better or worse? No man or woman could answer that. The winds blew, bringing rain, yes, but sometimes also sweeping away the low, obscuring clouds to allow the flourishes of sunrise or sunset seen from a high place, or those bright, hard, clear nights when the blue moon and the white seemed to ride like queens across a sky strewn with stars in glittering array.

Jehane instructed Velaz to close and lock the booth and follow her. She told all those left in the line to give their names to Velaz, that she would see them free of charge in her treatment rooms or at the next week's market. Then she took her urine flask and let the stranger take her off to ibn Musa's house.

The stranger.

The stranger was Ammar ibn Khairan of Aljais. The poet, the diplomat, the soldier. The man who had killed the last khalif of Al-Rassan. She learned his name when they arrived at her patient's house. It was the first great shock of that day. Not the last. She could never decide if she would have gone with him, had she known.

A different life, if she hadn't gone. Less wind, less rain. Perhaps none of the visions offered those who stand in the high, windy places of the world.

Ibn Musa's steward had briskly admitted her and then greeted her escort unctuously by name, almost scraping the floor with his forehead in obeisance, strewing phrases of gratitude like rose petals. The Cartadan had managed to interpose a quiet apology for not introducing himself, and then sketched a court bow of his own to her. It was not customary to bow to Kindath infidels. In fact, according to the wadjis, it was forbidden to Asharites, subject to a public lashing.

The bejewelled man bowing to her was not likely to be lashed any time soon. Jehane knew who he was as soon as she heard the name. Depending upon one's views, Ammar ibn Khairan was one of the most celebrated men or one of the most notorious in the peninsula.

It was said, and sung, that when scarcely come to manhood he had single-handedly scaled the walls of the Al-Fontina in Silvenes, slain a dozen guards within, fought through to the Cypress Garden to kill the khalif, then battled his way out again, alone, dead bodies strewn about him. For this service, the grateful, newly proclaimed king in Cartada had rewarded ibn Khairan with immediate wealth and increasing power through the years, including, of late, the formal role of guardian and advisor to the prince.

A status which brought a different sort of power. Too much so, some had been whispering. Almalik of Cartada was an impulsive, subtle, jealous man and was not said, in truth, to be particularly fond of his eldest son. Nor was the prince reputed to dote upon his father. It made for a volatile situation. The rumors surrounding the dissolute, flamboyant Ammar ibn Khairan—and there were always rumors surrounding him—had been of a somewhat altered sort in the past year.

Though none of them came remotely close to explaining why this man should have personally offered to summon a physician for a Fezanan silk merchant, just so the merchant could be enabled to attend a courtly reception. As to that, Jehane had only the thinly veiled hint of amusement in ibn Khairan's face to offer a clue—and it wasn't much of a clue.

In any event, she stopped thinking about such things, including the unsettling presence of the man beside her, when she entered the bedchamber and saw her longtime patient. One glance was enough.

Husari ibn Musa was lying in bed, propped on many pillows. A slave was energetically beating a fan in the air, trying to cool the room and its suffering occupant. Ibn Musa could not have been called a courageous man. He was white-faced, there were tears on his cheeks, he was whimpering with pain and the anticipation of worse to come.

Her father had taught her that it was not only the brave or the resolute who were deserving of a doctor's sympathy. Suffering came and was real, however one's constitution and nature responded to it. A glance at her afflicted patient served to focus Jehane abruptly and ease her own agitation.

Moving briskly to the bedside, Jehane adopted her most decisive tones. "Husari ibn Musa, you are not going anywhere today. You know these symptoms by now as well as I do. What were you thinking? That you would bound from bed, straddle a mule and ride off to a reception?"

The portly man on the bed groaned piteously at the very thought of such exertion and reached for her hand. They had known each other a long time; she allowed him to do that. "But Jehane, I *must* go! This is the event of the year in Fezana. How can I not be present? What can I do?"

"You can send your most fulsome regrets and advise that your physician has ordered you to remain in bed. If you wish, for some perverse reason, to offer details, you may have your steward say that you are about to pass a stone this afternoon or this evening in extreme pain, controlled only by such medications as leave you unable to stand upright or speak coherently. If, anticipating such a condition, you still wish to attend a Cartadan function I can only assume your mind has already been disjointed by your suffering. If you wish to be the first person to collapse and die in the new wing of the castle you will have to do so against my instructions."

She used this tone with him much of the time. With many of her patients, in truth. In a female physician men, even powerful ones, often seemed to want to hear their mothers giving orders. Ishak had induced obedience to his treatments by the gravity of his manner and the weight of his sonorous, beautiful voice. Jehane—a woman, and still young—had had to evolve her own methods.

Ibn Musa turned a despairing face towards the Cartadan courtier. "You see?" he said plaintively. "What can I do with such a doctor?"

Ammar ibn Khairan seemed amused again. Jehane found that irritation was helping her deal with the earlier feeling of being overwhelmed by his identity. She still had no idea what the man found so diverting about all of this, unless this was simply the habitual pose and manner of a cynical courtier. Perhaps he was bored by the usual court routine; the god's sisters knew, *she* would have been.

"You could consult another physician, I suppose," ibn Khairan said, thoughtfully stroking his chin. "But my guess, based on all-too-brief experience, is that this exquisite young woman knows exactly what she is doing." He favored her with another of the brilliant smiles. "You will have to tell me where you were trained, when we have greater leisure."

Jehane didn't like being treated as a woman when she was functioning as a doctor. "Little to tell," she said briefly. "Abroad at the university of Sorenica in Batiara, with Ser Rezzoni, for two years. Then with my father here."

"Your father?" he asked politely.

"Ishak ben Yonannon," Jehane said, and was deeply pleased to see this elicit a reaction he could not mask.

From a courtier in the service of Almalik of Cartada there would almost have to be a response to Ishak's name. It was no secret, the story of what had happened.

"Ah," said Ammar ibn Khairan quietly, arching his eyebrows. He regarded her for a moment. "I see the resemblance now. You have your father's eyes and mouth. I ought to have made the association before. You will have been even better trained here than in Sorenica."

"I am pleased that I seem to meet your standards," Jehane said drily. He grinned again, unfazed, rather too clearly enjoying her attempted sallies. Behind him, Jehane saw the steward's mouth gape at her impertinence. They were awed by the Cartadan, of course. Jehane supposed she should be, as well. In truth, she was, more than a little. No one needed to *know* that, however.

"The lord ibn Khairan has been most generous with his time on my behalf," Husari murmured faintly from the bed. "He came this morning, by appointment, to examine some silks for purchase and found me...as you see. When he learned I feared not being able to attend the reception this afternoon he insisted that my presence was important"—there was pride in the voice, audible through the pain—"and he offered to try to lure my stubborn physician to my side."

"And now she is here, and would stubbornly request that all those in this room save the slave and your steward be so kind as to leave us." Jehane turned to the Cartadan. "I'm sure one of ibn Musa's factors can assist you in the matter of silk."

"Doubtless," the man said calmly. "I take it, then, that you are of the view that your patient ought not to attend upon the prince this afternoon?"

"He could die there," Jehane said bluntly. It was unlikely, but certainly possible, and sometimes people needed to be shocked into accepting a physician's orders.

The Cartadan was not shocked. If anything, he seemed once more to be in the grip of his private source of diversion. Jehane heard a sound from beyond the door. Velaz had arrived, with her medications.

Ammar ibn Khairan heard it too. "You have work to do. I will take my leave, as requested. Failing an ailment that would allow me to spend the day in your care I am afraid I must attend this consecration in the castle." He turned to the man in the bed. "You need not send a messenger, ibn Musa. I will convey your regrets myself with a report of your condition. No offense will be taken, trust me. No one, least of all Prince Almalik, would want you to die passing a stone in the new courtyard." He bowed to ibn Musa and then a second time to Jehane—to the steward's visible displeasure—and withdrew.

There was a little silence. Amid the chatter of marketplace or temple, Jehane unexpectedly remembered, it was reported that the high-born women of Cartada—and some of the men, the whispers went—had been known to seriously injure each other in quarrels over the companionship of Ammar ibn Khairan. Two people had died, or was it three?

Jehane bit her lip. She shook her head as if to clear it, astonished at herself. This was the sheerest, most idle sort of gossip to be calling to mind, the kind of talk to which she had never paid attention in her life. A moment later Velaz hurried in and she set to work, gratefully, at her trade. Softening pain, prolonging life, offering a hope of ease where little might otherwise lie.

∞

One hundred and thirty-nine citizens of Fezana assembled in the newest wing of the castle that afternoon. Throughout Al-Rassan, not long after, what ensued became known as The Day of the Moat. This was the way of it.

The newly finished part of Fezana's castle was of a most unusual and particular design. A large dormitory for quartering the new Muwardi troops led to an equally large refectory for feeding them and an adjacent temple for prayers. The notorious Ammar ibn Khairan, who accompanied the guests through these rooms, was much too polite to make specific mention of the reason for further military presence in Fezana, but none of the assembled dignitaries of the town could possibly escape the significance of such extensive facilities.

Ibn Khairan, offering undeniably witty and impeccably courteous commentary, was also too discreet to draw anyone's attention, particularly during a celebration, to the ongoing indications of unrest and subversion in the city. A certain number of those passing through the castle, however, exchanged wary, sidelong glances with each other. What they were seeing, clearly, was meant to be intimidating.

In fact, it was a little more than that.

The odd nature of the new wing's design became even more apparent when they passed—a magnificently dressed herd of prosperous men—through the refectory to the near end of a long corridor. The narrow tunnel, ibn Khairan explained, designed for defensive purposes, led to the courtyard where the wadjis were to perform the consecration and where Prince Almalik, heir to Cartada's ambitious kingdom, was waiting to receive them.

The aristocracy and most successful merchants of Fezana were individually escorted by Muwardi soldiers down that dark corridor. Approaching the end of it each, in turn, could discern a blazing of sunlight. Each of them paused there, squinting, almost sightless on the threshold of light, while a herald announced their proffered names with satisfying resonance.

As they passed, blinking, into the blinding light and stepped forward to offer homage to the hazily perceived, white-robed figure seated on a cushion in the midst of the courtyard, each of the guests was sweepingly beheaded by one of two Muwardi tribesmen standing on either side of the tunnel's arch.

The Muwardis, not really strangers to this sort of thing, enjoyed their labors perhaps more than they ought to have done. There were, of course, no wadjis waiting in the courtyard; the castle wing was receiving a different sort of consecration.

One by one, through the course of a scorching hot, cloudless summer's afternoon, the elite of Fezanan society made their way along that dark, cool tunnel, and then, dazzled by the return to sunlight, followed the herald's ringing proclamation of their names into the white court-yard where they were slain. The Muwardis had been care-fully chosen. No mistakes were made. No one cried out.

The toppling bodies were swiftly seized by other veiled tribesmen and dragged to the far end of the courtyard where a round tower overlooked the new moat created by diverting the nearby Tavares River. The bodies of the dead men were thrown into the water from a low window in the tower. The severed heads were tossed carelessly onto a bloody pile not far from where the prince of Cartada sat, ostensibly waiting to receive the most prominent citizens of the most difficult of the cities he was one day to rule, if he lived long enough.

As it happened, the prince, whose relations with his father were indeed not entirely cordial, had not been informed about this central, long-planned aspect of the afternoon's agenda. King Almalik of Cartada had more than one purpose to what he was doing that day. The prince had, in fact, asked where the wadjis were. No one had been able to answer him. After the first man appeared and was slain, his severed head landing some distance from his top-pling body, the prince offered no further questions.

Part of the way through the afternoon's nearly silent, murderous progression under the blazing sun, around the time the carrion birds began to appear in numbers, circling above the water, it was noted by some of the soldiers in the increasingly bloody courtyard that the prince seemed to have developed an odd, disfiguring twitch above his left eye. For the Muwardis, this was a contemptible sign of weakness. He did stay on his cushion though, they noted. And he never moved, or spoke, through the entirety of what was done. He watched one hundred and thirty-nine men die doing formal obeisance to him.

He never lost that nervous tic. During times of stress or

elation it would return, an infallible signal to those who knew him well that he was experiencing intense emotion, no matter how he might try to hide the fact. It was also an inescapable reminder—because all of Al-Rassan was soon to learn this story—of a blood-soaked summer afternoon in Fezana.

The peninsula had seen its share of violent deeds, from the time of the Asharite conquest and before, but this was something special, something to be remembered. The Day of the Moat. One of the legacies of Almalik I, the Lion of Cartada. Part of his son's inheritance.

The slaughter did not end until some time after the fifth bells had called the pious again to their prayers. By then the number of birds over the river and moat had made it evident that something untoward was taking place. A few curious children had gone outside the walls and circled around to the north to see what was bringing so many birds. They carried word back into the city. There were headless bodies in the water. Not long after that the screaming began in the houses and the streets of Fezana.

Such distracting sounds did not penetrate the castle walls of course, and the birds could not be seen from within the handsome, arcaded refectory. After the last of the assembled guests had made his way from there along the tunnel, Ammar ibn Khairan, the man who had killed the last khalif of Al-Rassan, went alone down that corridor to the courtyard. The sun was over to the west by then, the light towards which he walked through a long, cool darkness was gentle, welcoming, almost worthy of a poem.

Chapter II

ༀ

After somehow coping with the disastrous incident at the very beginning of their ride south, Alvar had been finding the journey the most exhilarating time of his life. This did not come as a surprise; he had nourished dreams of this for years, and reality doesn't invariably shatter a young man's dreams. Not immediately, at any rate.

Had he been of a slightly less rational nature, he might even have given fuller rein to the fantasy he briefly entertained as they broke camp after the dawn invocation on their fifth morning south of the River Duric: that he had died and arrived, by the grace of Jad, at the Paradise of Warriors, and would be allowed to ride behind Rodrigo Belmonte, the Captain, through the plains and steppes of summer forever.

The river was far behind them, and the walls of Carcasia. They had passed the wooden stockade forts of Baeza and Lobar, small, fledgling outposts in emptiness. The company rode now through the wild, high, bare sweep of the no-man's-land, dust rising behind and the sun beating down upon them—fifty of Jad's own horsemen, journeying to the fabled cities of the Asharites at the king of Valledo's command.

And young Alvar de Pellino was one of those fifty, chosen, after scarcely a year among the riders at Esteren, to accompany the great Rodrigo—the Captain himself—on a tribute mission to Al-Rassan. There were miracles in the world, truly, bestowed without explanation, unless his mother's prayers on her pilgrimage to holy Vasca's Isle had been answered by the god behind the sun.

Since that was at least a possibility, each morning now at dawn Alvar faced east for the invocation and offered thanks to Jad with a full heart, vowing anew upon the iron of the sword his father had given him to be worthy of the god's trust. And, of course, the Captain's.

There were so many young riders in the army of King Ramiro. Horsemen from all over Valledo, some with splendid armor and magnificent horses, some with lineage going back to the Old Ones who had ruled the whole peninsula and named it Esperaña, who first learned the truths of the sun-god and built the straight roads. And almost every one of those men would have fasted a week, would have forsworn women and wine, would have seriously contemplated murder for the chance to be trained by the Captain, to be under the cool, grey-eyed scrutiny of Rodrigo Belmonte for three whole weeks. To be, if only for this one mission, numbered among his company.

A man could dream, you see. Three weeks might be only a beginning, with more to follow, the world opening up like a peeled and quartered orange. A young horseman could lie down at night on his saddle blanket and look up at the bright stars worshipped by the followers of Ashar. He could imagine himself cutting a shining swath through the ranks of the infidels to save the Captain himself from danger and death, being saluted and marked by Rodrigo in the midst of roaring battle, and then after, victorious, drinking unmixed wine at the Captain's side, being honored and made welcome among his company.

A young man could dream, could he not?

The problem, for Alvar, was that such immensely satisfying images had been giving way, in the almost-silence of night, or the long rhythms of a day's hard riding under the god's sun, to the vivid, excruciating memory of what had happened the morning they set out from Esteren. To a recollection of the moment, in particular, when young Alvar de Pellino—heart's pride and joy of his parents and three sisters—had chosen the wrong place entirely to unbutton his trousers and relieve himself before the company mounted up to ride.

It ought to have been a perfectly reasonable thing to do.

They had assembled at dawn in a newly built sidecourt of the palace at Esteren. Alvar, almost giddy with excitement and the simultaneous effort not to reveal it, had been attempting to remain as inconspicuous as possible. He was not a shy or diffident young man by nature, but even now, at the very moment of departure, a part of him feared, with lurid apprehension, that if someone noticed him—Laín Nunez, for example, the Captain's lean old companion-at-arms—they might declare Alvar's presence an obvious error of some kind, and he'd be left behind. He would, of course, have no choice but to kill himself if such a thing happened.

With fifty men and their horses and the laden pack mules in the enclosed space of the courtyard it was easy enough to keep a low profile. It was cool in the yard; something that might have deceived a stranger to the peninsula, a mercenary from Ferrieres or Waleska, say. It would be very hot later, Alvar knew. It was always hot in summer. There was a great deal of noise and men were hustling back and forth carrying planks of wood, tools, wheeling barrows of brick: King Ramiro was expanding his palace.

Alvar checked his saddle and saddlebags for the twentieth time and carefully avoided meeting anyone's eye. He tried to look older than his years, to convey the impression that he was, if anything, a trifle bored by a mission as routine as this one. He was intelligent enough to doubt he was fooling anyone.

When Count Gonzalez de Rada walked unannounced into the courtyard, dressed in crimson and black—even at dawn among horses—Alvar felt his feverish anxiety rise to an even higher level. He had never seen the constable of Valledo before, except at a distance. A brief silence fell over Rodrigo's company, and when their bustle of preparation resumed it had a subtly altered quality. Alvar experienced the stirrings of inescapable curiosity and sternly tried to suppress them.

He saw the Captain and Laín Nunez observe the count's arrival and exchange a glance. Rodrigo stepped a little aside from the others to await the man who'd replaced him as constable when King Ramiro was crowned. The count's attendants stopped at a word and Gonzalez de Rada approached alone. He was smiling broadly. The Captain, Alvar saw, was not. Behind Rodrigo, Laín Nunez abruptly turned his head and spat deliberately into the dirt of the yard.

At this point, Alvar decided that it would be ill-mannered to observe them further, even out of the corner of his eye—as he noticed the others doing while they pretended to busy themselves with their horses or gear. A Horseman of Jad, he told himself firmly, had no business concerning himself with the words and affairs of the great. Alvar virtuously turned his back upon the forthcoming encounter and walked to a corner of the yard to attend to his own pressing business in private, on the far side of a hay wagon.

Why Count Gonzalez de Rada and Ser Rodrigo Belmonte should have elected to stroll together, a moment later, to the shade of that same wagon would forever after remain one of the enduring mysteries of the world Jad had created, as far as Alvar de Pellino was concerned.

The two men were known throughout the three Jaddite kingdoms of Esperaña to have no love for one another. Even the youngest soldiers, new to the king's army, managed to hear *some* of the court stories. The tale of how Rodrigo Belmonte had demanded at the coronation of King Ramiro that the new king swear an oath of noncomplicity in the death of his brother before Ser Rodrigo would offer his own oath of allegiance was one that every one of them knew. It was a part of the legend of the Captain.

It might even be true, Alvar had cynically murmured to some drinking companions one night in a soldier's tavern. He was already becoming known for remarks like that. It was a good thing he knew how to fight. His father had warned him, more than once back on the farm, that a quick tongue could be more of a hindrance than it was an asset in the army of Valledo.

Clever remarks by young soldiers notwithstanding, what *was* true was that although Rodrigo Belmonte did swear his oath of fealty and King Ramiro accepted him as his man, it was Gonzalez de Rada who was named by the new king as his constable—the office Rodrigo had held for the late King Raimundo. It was, therefore, Count Gonzalez who was formally responsible, among other things, for overseeing the selection and promotion of young men throughout Valledo to posts in the king's army.

Not that many of the younger horsemen had been observed to deviate greatly from the collective view that if you wanted to be properly trained you did whatever you could to ride with the Captain. And if you wanted to be numbered among the elite soldiers of the peninsula, of the world, you offered money, land, your sisters, your own young body if need be, as a bribe to whomever could get you into Rodrigo's band.

Not that anyone *could* get you in, for any of those offerings. The Captain made his own choices, often unexpected ones, with gap toothed old Laín Nunez his only counsellor. Laín was manifestly uninterested in the alleged pleasures of boys, and the Captain...well, the very thought was near to sacrilege, besides which, Miranda Belmonte d'Alveda was the most beautiful woman in the world. So all the young men in Esteren agreed, though almost none of them had ever seen her.

On the morning he stood pissing against a wagon wheel in a sidecourt of Esteren's palace and overheard certain things he ought not to have heard, Alvar de Pellino was one of those who had never met the Captain's wife. He hadn't met anyone, really. He was less than a year in from a farm in the northwest. He still couldn't believe they were going to let him ride with them this morning.

He heard footsteps and voices approaching from the far side of the wagon; that was not of great concern. Some men might have to be alone to empty their bladder or bowels; they didn't last long in an army. But then, on that very thought, Alvar's groin muscles clenched in a spasm so hard they cut off the splashing flow of his water. He gasped, recognizing the Captain's wry tones, and then realized that the second man's voice—the one that sounded like slow honey being poured—belonged to Count Gonzalez.

With a decision to be swiftly made, Alvar de Pellino made what turned out to be the wrong one. Panic-stricken, irrationally preoccupied with remaining unnoticed, Alvar almost injured himself holding in the last of his water and kept silent. He hoped, fervently, that the two men were only here to exchange parting pleasantries.

"I could arrange to have your sons killed and your ranch burned," Gonzalez de Rada said, pleasantly enough, "if you make any trouble about this."

Alvar decided that it was by far the wisest course not to breathe for a time.

"Try it," the Captain said briskly. "The boys could use some practice against assault, however incompetent. But before you leave, do explain how I would be the one making trouble and not your pig of a brother."

"If a de Rada chooses to go raiding in Al-Rassan, what business is it of yours, Belmonte?"

"Ah. Well. If such is the case, why bother asking me to close my eyes and pretend not to see him?"

"I am merely trying to save you an embarrassing—"

"Don't assume *everyone* else is a fool, de Rada. I'm collecting tribute from Fezana for the king. The only legitimacy to such a claim is that Ramiro has formally guaranteed the security of the city and its countryside. Not only from brigands, or his brother in Ruenda, or the other petty-kings in Al-Rassan, but from buffoons in his own country. If your brother wants to play at raiding games for the fun of it, he'd best not do it on my watch. If I see him anywhere in the country around Fezana I'll deal with him in the name of the king. You'll be doing him a kindness if you make that clear." There was nothing wry or ironic, no hint of anything but iron in the voice now.

There was a silence. Alvar could hear Laín Nunez barking instructions over by the horses. He sounded angry. He often did. It became necessary, despite all his best efforts, to breathe. Alvar did so as quietly as he could.

"Doesn't it cause you some *concern*," Gonzalez de Rada said in a deceptively grave, an almost gentle tone, "to be riding off into infidel lands after speaking so rashly to the constable of Valledo, leaving your poor wife alone on a ranch with children and ranch hands?"

"In a word," said the Captain, "no. For one thing, you value your own life too much to make a real enemy of me. I will not be subtle about this: if any man I can trace to your authority is found within half a day's ride of my ranch I will know how to proceed and I will. I hope you understand me. I am speaking about killing you. For another thing, I may have my own thoughts about our king's ascension, but I believe him to be a fair man. What, think you, will Ramiro do when a messenger reports to him the precise words of this conversation?"

Gonzalez de Rada sounded amused. "You would actually try your word against mine with the king?"

"Think, man," the Captain said impatiently. Alvar knew that tone already. "He doesn't *have* to believe me. But once word of your threat does reach him—and in public, I promise you—what can the king do should any harm befall my family?"

There was a silence again. When de Rada next spoke the amusement was gone. "You would really tell him about this? Unwise. You might force my hand, Belmonte."

"As you have now forced mine. Consider an alternative, I beg of you. Act the part of an older, wiser brother. Tell that bullying man-child Garcia that his games cannot be allowed to compromise the king's laws and diplomacy. Is that really too much authority to ask of the constable of Valledo?"

Another silence, a longer one this time. Then, carefully, "I will do what I can to keep him from crossing your path."

"And I will do what I can to make him regret it if he does. If he fails to respect his older brother's words." Rodrigo's voice betrayed neither triumph nor concession.

"You will not report this to the king now?"

"I will have to think on that. Fortunately I do have a witness should I have need." With no more warning than that he raised his voice. "Alvar, finish doing what you have to, in the god's name, you've been at it long enough to flood the yard. Come let me present you to the constable."

Alvar, feeling his heart suddenly lodged considerably higher than it was wont to be found, discovered that he had gone dry as the desert sands. He fumbled to button his trousers and stepped gingerly out from behind the wagon. Crimson with embarrassment and apprehension, he discovered that Count Gonzalez's features were no less flushed—though what he read in the deep-set brown eyes was rage.

Rodrigo's voice was bland, as if he was oblivious to the feelings of either of them. "My lord count, please accept the salute of one of my company for this ride, Pellino de Damon's son. Alvar, make a bow to the constable."

Confused, horribly shaken, Alvar followed instructions. Gonzalez de Rada nodded curtly at his salute. The count's expression was bleak as winter in the north when the winds came down. He said, "I believe I know of your father. He held a fort in the southwest for King Sancho, did he not?"

"Maraña Guard, yes, my lord. I am honored you are so good as to call him to mind." Alvar was surprised his voice was working well enough to manage this. He kept his gaze lowered.

"And where is your father now?"

An innocuous question, a polite one, but Alvar, after what he'd heard from the far side of the wagon, seemed to catch a feathery hint of danger. He had no choice, though. This was the constable of Valledo.

"He was allowed to retire from the army, my lord, after suffering an injury in an Asharite raid. We have a farm now, in the north."

Gonzalez de Rada was silent a long moment. At length

he cleared his throat and said, "He was, if memory serves, a man famous for his discretion, your father."

"And for loyal service to his leaders," the Captain interjected briskly, before Alvar could say anything to that. "Alvar, best mount up before Laín blisters you raw for delaying us."

Gratefully, Alvar hastily bowed to both men and hurried off to the other side of the yard where horses and soldiers awaited, in a simpler world by far than the one into which he'd stumbled by the wagon.

Late in the morning of that same day, Ser Rodrigo Belmonte had dropped back from his position near the front of the column and signalled Alvar with a motion of his head to join him.

His heart pounding with the apprehension of disaster, Alvar followed his Captain to a position off one flank of the party. They were passing through the Vargas Hills, some of the most beautiful country in Valledo.

"Laín was born in a village beyond that western range," the Captain began conversationally. "Or so he says. I tell him it's a lie. That he was hatched from an egg in a swamp, as bald at birth as he is today."

Alvar was too nervous to laugh. He managed a feeble grin. It was the first time he'd ever been alone with Ser Rodrigo. The slandered Laín Nunez was up ahead, rasping orders again. They would be taking their midday break soon.

The Captain went on, in the same mild voice, "I heard of a man in Al-Rassan years ago who was afraid to leave the khalif's banquet table to take a piss. He held it in so long he ruptured himself and died before dessert was served."

"I can believe it," Alvar said fervently.

"What *ought* you to have done back there?" the Captain asked. His tone had changed, but only slightly.

Alvar had been thinking about nothing else since they had left the walls of Esteren behind. In a small voice, he said, "I should have cleared my throat, or coughed."

Rodrigo Belmonte nodded. "Whistled, sung, spat on a wheel. Anything to let us know you were there. Why didn't you?"

There was no good, clever answer so he offered the truth: "I was afraid. I still couldn't believe you were bringing me on this ride. I didn't want to be noticed."

The Captain nodded again. He gazed past Alvar at the rolling hills and the dense pine forest to the west. Then the clear grey eyes shifted and Alvar found himself pinned by a vivid gaze. "All right. First lesson. I do not choose men for my company, even for a short journey, by mistake. If you were named to be with us it was for a reason. I have little patience with that kind of thing in a fighting man. Understood?"

Alvar jerked his head up and down. He took a breath and let it out. Before he could speak, the Captain went on. "Second lesson. Tell me, why do you think I called you out from behind the wagon? I made an enemy for you—the second most powerful man in Valledo. That wasn't a generous thing for me to do. Why did I do it?"

Alvar looked away from the Captain and rode for a time thinking hard. He didn't know it, but his face bore an expression that used to induce apprehension in his family. His thoughts sometimes took him to unexpected, dangerous places. This, as it happened, was such a time. He glanced over at Ser Rodrigo and then away again, uncharacteristically cautious.

"*Say it!*" the Captain snapped.

Alvar suddenly wished he were back on the farm, planting grain with his father and the farm hands, waiting for one of his sisters to walk out with beer and cheese and bread, and gossip from the house. He swallowed. He might be back there, soon enough. But it had never been said that Pellino de Damon's son was a coward or, for that matter, overly shy with his thoughts.

"You weren't thinking about me," he said as firmly as he could manage. There was no point saying this if he sounded like a quavering child. "You pulled me out to be a body between Count Gonzalez and your family. I may be nothing in myself, but my father was known, and the constable now realizes that I'm a witness to what happened this morning. I'm protection for your wife and sons."

He closed his eyes. When he opened them it was to see Rodrigo Belmonte grinning at him. Miraculously, the Captain didn't seem angry. "As I said, there was a reason you were chosen to be tested on this ride. I don't mind a clever man, Alvar. Within limits, mind you. You may even be right. I may have been entirely selfish. When it comes to threats against my family, I can be. I did make a possible enemy for you. I even put your life at some risk. Not a very honorable thing for a leader to do to one of his company, is it?"

This was another test, and Alvar was aware of it. His father had told him, more than once, that he would do better if he thought a little less and spoke a great deal less. But this was Ser Rodrigo Belmonte himself, the Captain, asking questions that *demanded* thought. He could dodge it, Alvar supposed. Perhaps he was expected to. But here they were, riding towards Al-Rassan through the pine-clad hills of Vargas, which he had never seen, and he was in this company for a reason. The Captain had just said so. They weren't going to send him back. Alvar's customary nature seemed to be returning to him with every passing moment.

Alvar de Pellino said, "Was it an honorable thing to do? Not really, if you want my true thought, my lord. In war a captain can do anything with his men, of course, but in a private feud I don't know if it's right."

For a moment he thought he had gone too far. Then Ser Rodrigo smiled again; there was real amusement in the grey eyes. The Captain stroked his moustache with a gloved hand. "I imagine you caused your father some distress with your frankness, lad."

Alvar grinned back. "He did caution me at times, my lord. Yes."

"Cautioned?"

Alvar nodded. "Well, in fairness, I don't know what

more he—"

Alvar was not a small man, and there had been nothing easy about life on a northern farm, and even less that was conducive to softness during a year of service with the king's army in Esteren. He was strong and quick, and a good rider. Nonetheless, the fist he never saw coming hit the side of his head like a hammer and sent him flying from his horse into the grass as if he'd been a child.

Alvar struggled quickly to a sitting position, spitting blood. One hand went feebly to his jaw, which felt as if it might be broken. It had happened: his father's warning had just come true. His imbecilic habit of speaking whatever he thought had just cost him the opportunity any young soldier would die for. Rodrigo Belmonte had opened a door for him, and Alvar, swaggering through like the fool he was, had just fallen on his face. Or on his elbow and backside, actually.

Holding a hand to his face, Alvar looked up at his Captain. A short distance away the company had come to a halt and was regarding the two of them.

"I've had to do that to my sons, too, once or twice," Rodrigo said. He was, improbably, still looking amused. "I'll doubtless have to do it for a few years yet. Third lesson now, Alvar de Pellino. Sometimes it is wrong to hide as you did by the wagon. Sometimes it is equally wrong to push your ideas forward before they are complete. Take a little longer to be so sure of yourself. You'll have some time to think about this while we ride. And while you are doing so, you might consider whether an unauthorized raid in Al-Rassan by a band of Garcia de Rada's cronies playing outlaw might take this affair out of the realm of a private feud and into something else. I am an officer of the king of Valledo, and while you are in this company, so are you. The constable attempted to suborn me from my duty to the king with a threat. Is that a private matter, my young philosopher?"

"By the god's balls, Rodrigo!" came an unmistakable voice, approaching from the head of the column, "What did Pellino's brat do to deserve that?"

Ser Rodrigo turned to look at Laín Nunez trotting his horse over towards them. "Called me selfish and unfair to my men. Guilty of exploiting them in my private affairs."

"That all?" Laín spat into the grass. "His father said a lot worse to me in our day."

"Really?" The Captain seemed surprised. "De Rada just said he was famous for his discretion."

"Horsepiss," said Laín Nunez succinctly. "Why would you believe anything a de Rada said? Pellino de Damon had an opinion about anything and everything under the god's sun. Drove me near crazy, he did. I had to put up with it until I wangled him a promotion to commanding a fort by the no-man's-land. I was never as happy in my life as when I saw his backside on a horse going away from me."

Alvar goggled up at both of them; his jaw would have dropped if it hadn't hurt so much. He was too stunned to even get up from the grass. For most of his life his quiet, patient father had been gently chiding him against the evils of being too outspoken.

"You," Ser Rodrigo was saying, grinning at the veteran soldier beside him, "are as full of horsepiss as any de Rada I've ever met."

"That, I'll tell you, is a deadly insult," Laín Nunez rasped, the seamed and wizened face assuming an expression of fierce outrage.

Rodrigo laughed aloud. "You loved this man's father like a brother. You've been telling me that for years. You picked his son yourself for this ride. Do you want to deny it?"

"I will deny anything I have to," his lieutenant said sturdily. "But if Pellino's boy has already driven you to a blow I might have made a terrible mistake." They both looked down at Alvar, shaking their heads slowly.

"It may well be that you have," said the Captain at length. He didn't look particularly concerned. "We'll know soon enough. Get up, lad," he added. "Stick something cold on the side of your face or you'll have trouble offering opinions about anything for a while."

Laín Nunez had already turned to ride back. Now the Captain did the same. Alvar stood up.

"Captain," he called, with difficulty.

Ser Rodrigo looked back over his shoulder. The grey eyes regarded him with curiosity now. Alvar knew he was pushing things again. So be it. It seemed his father had been that way too, amazingly. He was going to need some time to deal with that. And it seemed that it wasn't his mother's pilgrimage to Vasca's Isle that had put him in this company, after all.

"Um, circumstances prevented me from finishing my last thought. I just wanted to say also that I would be proud to die defending your wife and sons."

The Captain's mouth quirked. He was amused again. "You are rather more likely to die defending yourself *from* them, actually. Come on, Alvar, I meant it about putting something on your jaw. If you don't keep the swelling down you'll frighten the women in Fezana and ruin your chances. In the meantime, remember to do some thinking before next you speak."

"But I *have* been thinking—"

The Captain raised a hand in warning. Alvar was abruptly silent. Rodrigo cantered back to the company and a moment later Alvar led his own horse by the reins over to where they had halted for the midday meal. Oddly enough, despite the pain in his jaw, which a cloth soaked in water did only a little to ease, he didn't feel badly at all.

And he *had* been thinking, already. He couldn't help it. He'd decided that the Captain was right about Garcia de Rada's raid taking the matter out of the area of a private feud and into the king's affairs. Alvar prided himself that he had always been willing to accept when someone else made a shrewd point in discussion.

All that was days in the past. A swollen but not a broken jaw had assisted Alvar in the difficult task of keeping his rapidly evolving thoughts to himself.

The twice-yearly collection of the *parias* from Fezana

had become something close to routine now, more an exercise in diplomacy than a military one. It was more important for King Ramiro to dispatch a leader of Ser Rodrigo's stature than to send an army. They knew Ramiro *could* send an army. The tribute would not be refused, though it might be slow in coming and there was a kind of dance that had to be performed before they could ride back with gold from Al-Rassan. This much Alvar learned during the shifts he rode ahead of the party with Ludus or Martín, the most experienced of the outriders.

They taught him other things too. This might be a routine expedition, but the Captain was never tolerant of carelessness, and most particularly not so in the no-man's-land, or in Al-Rassan itself. They were not riding south to give battle, but they had an image, a message to convey: that no one would ever *want* to do battle with the Horsemen of Valledo, and most particularly not with those commanded by Rodrigo Belmonte.

Ludus taught him how to anticipate from the movements of birds the presence of a stream or pond in the windswept plateau. Martín showed him how to read weather patterns in the clouds—the clues were very different here in the south from those Alvar had known in the far north by the sea. And it was the Captain himself who advised him to shorten his stirrups. It was the first time Ser Rodrigo had spoken directly to Alvar since flattening him with that blow on the first morning.

"You'll be awkward for a few days," he said, "but not for longer than that. All my men learn to ride like this into battle. Everyone here knows how. There may come a time in a fight when you need to stand up in the saddle, or leap from your horse. You'll find it easier with the stirrups high. It may save your life."

They had been in the no-man's-land by then, approaching the two small forts King Ramiro had built when he began claiming the *parias* from Fezana. The garrisons in the forts had been desperately glad to see them, even if they stayed only a single night in each, to leave letters and gossip and supplies.

It had to be a lonely, anxious life down here in Lobar and Baeza, Alvar had realized. The balance in the peninsula might have begun to shift with the fall of the Khalifate in Al-Rassan, but that was an evolving process, not an accomplished reality, and there had been more than a slight element of provocation in the Valledans placing garrisons, however small, in the *tagra* lands. These were a handful of soldiers in a vast emptiness, perilously near to the swords and arrows of the Asharites.

King Ramiro had tried at the beginning, two years ago, to encourage settlement around the forts. He couldn't *force* people to make their way down there, but he'd offered a ten-year tax exemption—given the costs of a steadily expanding army, not a trivial thing—and the usual promise of military support. It hadn't been enough. Not yet. Only fifteen or twenty families, clearly leaving hopeless situations in the north, had been brave or rash or desperate enough to try making lives for themselves here on the threshold of Al-Rassan.

Things might be changing year by year, but the memory of the Khalifate's armies thundering north through these high plains was a raw one yet. And everyone with a head above the ground knew the king was too fiercely engaged by his brother and uncle in Ruenda and Jaloña to be reckless in support of two speculative garrisons in the *tagra* and the families who huddled around them.

The balance might be shifting, but it was still a balance, and one could ignore that only at peril. Thinking, as they continued south, about the narrowed eyes and apprehensive faces of the men and women he'd seen in the fields beside the two forts, Alvar had decided there were worse things for a farmer to contend with than thin soil and early frosts in the north by the Ruenda border. Even the fields themselves down here had seemed pathetic and frail, small scratchings in the wide space of the otherwise empty land.

The Captain hadn't seemed to see it that way, though.

Ser Rodrigo had made a point of dismounting to speak to each of the farmers they saw. Alvar had been close enough to overhear him once: the talk was of crop rotation and the pattern of rainfall here in the *tagra* lands.

"We aren't the real warriors of Valledo," he'd said to his company upon mounting up again after one such conversation. "These people are. It will be a mistake for any man who rides with me to forget that."

His expression had been unusually grim as he spoke, as if daring any of them to disagree. Alvar hadn't been inclined to say anything at all. Thinking, he'd rubbed his bruised jaw through the beginnings of a sand-colored beard and kept silent.

The flat, high landscape of the plateau did not change, and there were no border markings of any kind, but late the following afternoon old Laín Nunez said aloud to no one in particular, "We're in Al-Rassan now."

Three days later, nearing sundown, the outriders caught a glimpse of the Tavares River and, not long after, Alvar saw for the first time the towers and walls of Fezana, tucked into a northward bend of the river, honey-colored in the westering light.

It was Ludus who first noticed the strange thing. An astonishing number of carrion birds seemed to be circling and swooping above the river by the northern wall of the city. Alvar had never seen anything like it. There had to be thousands of them.

"That's what happens on a battlefield," Martín said quietly. "When the battle's over, I mean."

Laín Nunez, squinting to see more clearly, turned after a moment to look at the Captain, a question in his eyes. Ser Rodrigo had not dismounted, so none of them had. He stared at Fezana in the distance for a long time.

"There are dead men in the water," he said finally. "We'll camp here tonight. I don't want to go closer, or enter the city, until we know what's happened."

"Do you want me to take two or three men and try to

find out?" Martín asked.

The Captain shook his head. "I don't think we'll have to. We'll light a good fire tonight. Double the guards, Laín, but I want them to know we're here."

Some time later, after the evening meal and after the sunset prayer for the god's safe night journey, they gathered around the fire while Martín played his guitar and Ludus and Baraño sang under the brilliant stars.

It was just after the white moon had risen in the east, almost full, that three people rode into their camp, with no attempt at concealment.

They dismounted from their mules and were led into the glow of the firelight by the posted guards and, as the music and the singing stopped, Rodrigo Belmonte and his company learned what had happened in Fezana that day.

Chapter III

∽

From within Husari ibn Musa's chamber late in the afternoon they heard the screaming in the streets. A slave was sent to inquire. Ashen-faced, he brought back word.

They did not believe him. Only when a friend of ibn Musa, another merchant, less successful—which appeared to have saved his life—sent a servant running with the same tidings did the reality become inescapable. Every man who had gone to the castle that morning was dead. Headless bodies were floating in the moat and down the river, carrion for the circling birds. Only thus, the very efficient king of Cartada appeared to have decided, could the threat of a rising in Fezana be utterly dispelled. In one afternoon virtually all of the most powerful figures left in the city had been eliminated.

Jehane's patient, the luxury-loving silk merchant who was, however improbably, to have been among the corpses in the moat, lay on his bed with a hand over his eyes, trembling and spent in the aftermath of passing a kidney stone. Struggling, not very successfully, to deal with her own churning emotions, Jehane looked at him closely. Her refuge, as ever, was in her profession. Quietly, grateful for the control she seemed to have over her voice, she instructed Velaz to mix a further soporific. Ibn Musa surprised her, though.

"No more, Jehane, please." He lowered the hand and opened his eyes. His voice was weak but quite clear. "I need to be able to think carefully. They may be coming for me. You had best leave this house."

Jehane hadn't thought of that. He was right, of course. There was no particular reason why Almalik's murderous desert mercenaries would allow an accident of ill-health to deprive them of Husari's head. And as for the doctor—the Kindath doctor—who had so inconveniently kept him from the palace...

She shrugged. *Whichever way the wind blows, it will rain upon the Kindath.* Her gaze met Husari's. There was something terrible in his face, still growing, a horror taking shape and a name. Jehane wondered how she must look herself, weary and bedraggled after most of a day in this warm, close room, and now dealing with what they had learned. With slaughter.

"It doesn't matter whether I stay or go," she said, surprised again at how calmly she said this. "Ibn Khairan knows who I am, remember? He brought me here."

Oddly, a part of her still wanted to deny that it was Ammar ibn Khairan who had arranged and achieved this wholesale massacre of innocent men. She couldn't have said why that had any importance to her: he was a killer, the whole of Al-Rassan knew he was. Did it matter that a killer was sophisticated and amusing? That he had known who her father was, and had spoken well of him?

Behind her, Velaz offered the small, discreet cough that meant he had something urgent to say. Usually in disagreement with a view she had expressed. Without looking back at him, Jehane said, "I know. You think we should leave."

In his subdued tones, her grey-haired servant—her father's before her—murmured, "I believe the most honorable ibn Musa offers wise counsel, doctor. The Muwardis may learn who you are from ibn Khairan, but there is no great reason for them to pursue you. If they come for the lord ibn Musa, though, and find us here, you are a provocation to them. My lord ibn Musa will tell you the same thing, I am sure of it. They are desert tribesmen, my lady. They are not...civilized."

And now Jehane did wheel around, aware that she was

channelling fear and anger onto her truest friend in the
world, aware that this was not the first time. "So you
would have me abandon a patient?" she snapped. "Is that
what I should do? How very civilized of us."

"I am recovering, Jehane."

She turned back to Husari. He had pushed himself up
to a sitting position. "You did all a physician could be
asked to do. You saved my life, though not in the way we
expected." Amazingly, he managed a wry smile. It did not
reach his eyes.

His voice was firmer now, sharper than she could ever
remember. She wondered if some disordered state had
descended upon the merchant in the wake of overwhelming horror; if this altered manner was his way of reacting.
Her father would have been able to tell her.

Her father, she thought, would not tell her anything
again.

There was a good chance the Muwardis would be coming for Husari, that they might indeed take her if they
found her here. The tribesmen from the Majriti were not
civilized at all. Ammar ibn Khairan knew exactly who she
was. Almalik of Cartada had ordered this butchery.
Almalik of Cartada had also done what he had done to her
father. Four years ago.

There are moments in some lives when it can truly be
said that everything pivots and changes, when the branching paths show clearly, when one makes a choice.

Jehane bet Ishak turned back to her patient. "I'm not
leaving you here to wait for them alone."

Husari actually smiled again. "What will you do, my
dear? Offer sleeping draughts to the veiled ones when they
come?"

"I have worse than that to give them," Jehane said darkly, but his words forced her to pause. "What do *you* want,"
she asked him. "I am running too fast, I'm sorry. It is possible they are sated. No one may come."

He shook his head decisively. Again, she registered the
change in manner. She had known ibn Musa for a long

time. She had never seen him like this.

He said, "I suppose that is possible. I don't greatly care. I don't intend to wait to find out. If I am going to do what I must do, I will have to leave Fezana, in any case."

Jehane blinked. "And what is it you must do?"

"Destroy Cartada," said the plump, lazy, self-indulgent silk merchant, Husari ibn Musa.

Jehane stared at him. This was a man who liked his dinner meat turned well, so he need not see blood when he ate. His voice was as calm and matter-of-fact as it was when she had heard him talking with a factor about insuring a shipment of silk for transport overseas.

Jehane heard Velaz offer his apologetic cough again. She turned. "If that is so," Velaz said, as softly as before, his forehead creased with worry now, "we cannot be of aid. Surely it will be better if we are gone from here...so the lord ibn Musa can begin to make his arrangements."

"I agree," Husari said. "I will call for an escort and—"

"I do not agree," Jehane said bluntly. "For one thing, you are at risk of fever after the stones pass and I have to watch for that. For another, you will not be able to leave the city until dark, and certainly not by any of the gates."

Husari laced his pudgy fingers together. His eyes held hers now, the gaze steady. "What are you proposing?"

It seemed obvious to Jehane. "That you hide in the Kindath Quarter with us until nightfall. I'll go first, to arrange for them to let you in. I'll be back at sundown for you. You ought to be in some disguise, I think. I'll leave that to you. After dark we can leave Fezana by a way that I know."

Velaz, pushed beyond discretion, made a strangled sound behind her.

"We?" said ibn Musa carefully.

"If I am going to do what I must do," said Jehane deliberately, "I, too, will have to leave Fezana."

"Ah," said the man in the bed. He gazed at her for a disquieting moment, no longer a patient, in some unexpected way. No longer the man she had known for so long.

"This is for your father?"

Jehane nodded. There was no point dissembling. He had always been clever.

"Past time," she said.

There was a great deal to be done. Jehane realized, walking quickly through the tumult of the streets with Velaz, that it was only the mention of her father that had induced Husari to accept her plan. That wasn't a surprising thing, if one looked at the matter in a certain light. If there was anything the Asharites understood, after centuries of killing each other in their homelands far to the east, and here in Al-Rassan, it was the enduring power of a blood feud, however long vengeance might be deferred.

No matter how absurd it might appear—a Kindath woman declaring her intention of taking revenge against the most powerful monarch to emerge since the Khalifate fell—she had spoken a language even a placid, innocuous Asharite merchant could understand.

And, in any case, the merchant was not so placid any more.

Velaz, seizing the ancient prerogative of longtime servants, was blistering her ears with objections and admonitions. His voice was, as always, appreciably less deferential than it was when others were with them. She could remember him doing this to her father as well, on nights when Ishak would be preparing to rush outside to a patient's summons without properly clothing himself against rain or wind, or without finishing his meal, or when he drove himself too hard, reading late into the night by candlelight.

She was doing a little bit more than staying up too late, and the frightened concern in Velaz's voice was going to erode her confidence if she let him go on. Besides which, she had a more difficult confrontation waiting at home.

"This has nothing to do with us," Velaz was saying urgently, in step with her and not behind, which was completely uncharacteristic, the surest sign of his agitation. "Except if they find a way to blame the Kindath for it, which I wouldn't be surprised if—"

"Velaz. Enough. Please. We are more than Kindath. We are people who live in Fezana, and have for many years. This is our home. We pay taxes, we pay our share of the filthy *parias* to Valledo, we shelter from danger behind these walls, and we suffer with others if Cartada's hand— or any other hand—falls too heavily on this city. What happened here today *does* matter to us."

"We will suffer no matter what they do to each other, Jehane." He was as stubborn as she was and, after years with Ishak, as versed in argument. His normally mild blue eyes were intense. "This is Asharite killing Asharite. Why let it throw our own lives into chaos. Think what you are doing to those who love you. Think—"

Again she had to interrupt. He sounded too much like her mother for comfort now. "Don't exaggerate," she said, though he wasn't, actually. "I am a physician. I am going to look for work outside the city. To expand my knowledge. To make a name. My father did that for years and years, riding with the khalif's armies some seasons, signing contracts at different courts after Silvenes fell. That's how he ended up in Cartada. You know that. You were with him."

"And I know what happened there," Velaz shot back.

Jehane stopped dead in the street. Someone running behind them almost crashed into her. It was a woman, Jehane saw, her face blank, a mask, as at the spring Processional. But this was a real face, and what lay behind the appearance of a mask was horror.

Velaz was forced to stop as well. He looked at her, his expression angry and afraid. A small man, and not young; nearly sixty years of age now, Jehane knew. He had been with her parents for a long time before her own birth. A Waleskan slave, bought as a young man in the market at Lonza; freed after ten years, which was the Kindath practice.

He could have gone anywhere then. Fluent in five languages after the years abroad with Ishak in Batiara and Ferrieres, and at the khalifs' courts in Silvenes itself, trained flawlessly as a physician's aide, more knowledge-able than most doctors were. Discreet, fiercely intelligent, Velaz would have had opportunities all over the peninsula or beyond the mountains east. The Al-Fontina of the khalifs, in those days, had been largely staffed and run by former slaves from the north, few of them as clever or versed in nuances of diplomacy as Velaz had been after ten years with Ishak ben Yonannon.

Such a course seemed never even to have been contemplated. Perhaps he lacked ambition, perhaps he was simply happy. He had converted to the Kindath faith immediately after being freed. Had willingly shouldered the difficult weight of their history. He prayed after that to the white and blue moons—the two sisters of the god—rather than invoking the images of Jad from his boyhood in Waleska or the stars of Ashar painted on the domed temple ceilings of Al-Rassan.

He had stayed with Ishak and Eliane and their small child from that day until this one, and if anyone in the world besides her parents truly loved her, Jehane knew it was this man.

Which made it harder to look at the apprehension in his eyes and realize that she really couldn't clearly explain why the path of her life seemed to have forked so sharply with the news of this massacre. Why it seemed so obvious what she now had to do. Obvious, but inexplicable. She could imagine what Ser Rezzoni of Sorenica would have said in response to such a conjunction. She could almost hear her father's words, as well. "An obvious failure to think clearly enough," Ishak would have murmured. "Start at the beginning, Jehane. Take all the time you need."

She didn't have that much time. She had to get Husari ibn Musa into the Kindath Quarter tonight, and do something even harder before that.

She said, "Velaz, I *know* what happened to my father in Cartada. This isn't a debate. I can't explain fully. I would do so if I could. You know that. I can only say that past a certain point accepting the things Almalik has done feels like *sharing* in them. Being responsible for them. If I stay here and simply open the treatment rooms in the morning and then the next day and the next, as if nothing has happened, that's how I'll feel."

There was a certain quality to Velaz, one of the measures of the man: he knew when what he heard was final.

They walked the rest of the way in silence.

At the heavy, unadorned iron gates that marked the enclosed Kindath Quarter of Fezana, Jehane breathed a sigh of relief. She knew both of the men posted there. One had been a lover, one a friend for much of her life.

She was as direct as she could afford to be. There was very little time. "Shimon, Bakir, I need your help," she said to them, even before they had finished unlocking the gates.

"You have it," Shimon grunted, "but hurry up and get inside. Do you know what is *happening* out there?"

"I know what *has* happened, yes, which is why I need you."

Bakir groaned as he swung the gate open. "Jehane, what have you done now?"

He was a big, broad-shouldered man, undeniably handsome. They had begun to bore each other within weeks of their liaison's beginning. Fortunately they had parted soon enough for affection to linger. He was married now, with two children. Jehane had delivered both of them.

"Nothing I could avoid, given my doctor's Oath of Galinus."

"Burn Galinus!" Shimon said bluntly. "They are killing people out there."

"That's why you have to help me," Jehane said quickly. "I have a patient in the city to whom I *must* attend tonight. I don't think I'm safe outside the Quarter—"

"You most certainly aren't!" Bakir interrupted.

"Fine. I want you to let me bring him in here in a little while. I'll put him to bed in our house and treat him there."

They looked at each other.

Bakir shrugged. "That's all?"

Shimon still looked suspicious. "He's an Asharite?"

"No, he's a horse. Of *course* he's an Asharite, you idiot. Why else would I be asking permission of the stupidest men in the Quarter?" The insult, she hoped, would distract them enough to end the questioning. Velaz was blessedly silent behind her.

"When will you bring him?"

"I'll go fetch him immediately. I have to ask my mother's permission first. Which is why I came ahead."

Bakir's dark eyes narrowed further. "You are being awfully proper about this, aren't you. That isn't like you, Jehane."

"Don't be more of a fool than you have to be, Bakir. You think I'm going to play games after what's happened this afternoon?"

Again they looked at each other.

"I suppose not," Shimon said grudgingly. "Very well, your patient can come in. But you aren't leaving the Quarter again. Velaz can bring him, although I certainly won't be the one to order him to do it."

"No, that's fine," said Velaz quickly. "I'll go."

Jehane had thought that might happen. It was all right. She turned to Velaz. "Go now, then," she murmured. "If my mother makes a fuss—I'm certain she won't—we'll put him in one of the travellers' inns. Go quickly."

She turned back to the two guards and offered her best smile. "Thank you, both of you. I won't forget this."

"I'd rather you did," said Shimon virtuously. "You know how irregular this is."

He was being pompous. It *was* irregular, but not greatly so. Asharites often came quietly into the Quarter, on business or in pursuit of pleasure. The only trick—and not a hard one—was to make sure the wadjis didn't know about it outside, or the Kindath high priests inside the gates. Jehane didn't think it was an appropriate time to get into a dispute with Shimon, however.

Among other things, the longer they talked the more it

was possible that he might inquire as to the identity of her patient. And if he asked and she had to tell, he might know that Husari ibn Musa was one of those who was to have been in the castle that day. If Shimon and Bakir discovered this was a man the Muwardi assassins might be seeking there was no way under the moons that Husari would be allowed into the Kindath Quarter.

She was putting her own people at risk with this, Jehane knew. She was young enough to have decided the risk was an acceptable one. The last Kindath massacres in Al-Rassan had taken place far to the south, in Tudesca and Elvira years before she was born.

Her mother, as expected, raised no objection. Wife and mother of physicians, Eliane bet Danel was long accustomed to adapting her home to the needs of patients. The fact that this disruption was occurring during the most violent day Fezana had known in a long time was not something that would ruffle her. The more so, because in this case Jehane made a point of telling her mother that the patient was ibn Musa. Eliane would have recognized him when he came. Husari had had Ishak as a dinner guest on several occasions and more than once the silk merchant had discreetly entered the Quarter to grace their own table—defying the wadjis and the high priests, both. Fezana was not a particularly devout city.

Which had probably done nothing but add to the pleasure of the fiercely pious Muwardis as they killed innocent men, Jehane thought. She was standing on the upstairs landing, one hand poised to knock on a door, a burning candle in her other hand.

For the first time in this long day she trembled, hesitating there, thinking of what she was about to do. She saw the flame waver. There was a tall window at the far end of the corridor, overlooking their inner courtyard. The rays of the setting sun were slanting through, reminding her that time mattered here. She had told her mother she would be leaving later that night and had braced herself for the fury of a storm that never came.

"It is not such a bad time to be out of this city," Eliane had said calmly after a moment's thought. She'd looked at her only child thoughtfully. "You will find work elsewhere. Your father always said it was good for a doctor to have experience of different places." She'd paused, then added, without smiling, "Perhaps you'll come back married."

Jehane had grimaced. This was an old issue. Nearing her thirtieth year she was past prime age for marrying and had essentially made her peace with that. Eliane had not.

"You'll be all right?" Jehane had asked, ignoring the last remark.

"I don't see why not," her mother had replied briskly. Then her stiffness was eased by the smile that made her beautiful. She had been wed herself, at twenty, to the most brilliant man among the brilliant Kindath community of Silvenes, in the days of the last bright flowering of the Khalifate. "What should I do, Jehane? Fall to my knees and clutch your hands, begging you to stay and comfort my old age?"

"You aren't old," her daughter said quickly.

"Of course I am. And of course I won't hold you back. If you aren't raising my grandchildren in a house around the corner by now, I have only myself and your father to blame for the way we brought you up."

"To think for myself?"

"Among other things." The smile again, unexpectedly. "To try to think for almost everyone else, I fear. I'll pack some things for you and order a place set for Husari at table. Is there anything he shouldn't eat tonight?"

Jehane had shaken her head. Sometimes she found herself wishing her mother would give vent to her emotions, that there might be a storm, after all. But mostly she was grateful for the nearly unbroken control that Eliane had displayed since that terrible day in Cartada four years ago. She could guess at the price of that restraint. She could measure it within herself. They weren't so very different, mother and daughter. Jehane hated to cry; she regarded it as a defeat.

"You'd better go upstairs," Eliane had said.

She had come upstairs. It was usually like this. There was seldom any pain in talking with her mother, but it never seemed as if the things that needed to be said *were* said. This afternoon, though, was not the time to be addressing such matters. Something very hard was still to come.

She knew that if she hesitated too long her resolve to leave might yet falter on this, the most difficult threshold of the day, of all her days. Jehane knocked twice, as was her habit, and entered the shuttered darkness of her father's study.

The candle lent its necessary glow to the books bound in leather and gold, the scrolls, the instruments and sky charts, the artifacts and mementos and gifts of a lifetime of study and travel and work. Its light fell, no longer wavering in her hand, upon a desk, a plain northern-style wooden chair, cushions on the floor, another deep chair—and the white-bearded man in the dark blue robe sitting motionless there, his back to the door and his daughter and the light.

Jehane looked at him, at the spear-like rigidity of his posture. She noted, as she noted every single day, how he did not even turn his head to acknowledge her entry into the room. She might as well not have entered, with her light and the tale she had to tell. It was always this way, but this afternoon was different. She had come to say goodbye and, looking at her father, the long sword of memory lay in Jehane's mind, hard and bright and terrible as the knives the Muwardis must have used.

Four years ago, the fourth son of King Almalik of Cartada had been twisted around his own birth cord in the womb of his mother. Such infants died and, almost invariably, the mother did as well. Physicians knew the signs well enough to be able to warn of what was coming. It happened often enough; no blame would attach. Childbirth was one of the dangerous things in the world. Doctors could not do the miraculous.

But Zabira of Cartada, the musician, was the favored

courtesan of the most powerful of all the city-kings in Al-
Rassan, and Ishak of Fezana was a brave and a brilliant
man. After consulting his charts of the heavens, and sending word to Almalik that what he was about to try offered
only the slimmest hope, Ishak had performed the only
recorded delivery of a child through an incision in the
mother's belly while preserving the life of the mother at
the same time.

Not Galinus himself, the source and fount of all medical knowledge, not Uzbet al-Maurus, not Avenal of Soriyya
in the Asharite homelands of the east—not one of them,
or any who had followed after, had reported successfully
doing such a thing, though these three had noted the procedure, and each of them had tried.

No, it was Ishak ben Yonannon of the Kindath who first
delivered a living child in such a way, in the palace of
Cartada in Al-Rassan in the second decade after the fall of
the Khalifate. And then he had healed the mother of her
wound and tended her after, so that she rose from her
bed one morning, very pale but beautiful as ever, to
reclaim her four-stringed lute and take her accustomed
place in Almalik's reception hall and his gardens and private chambers.

For this act of courage and skill on a scale never before
known, Almalik of Cartada had gratefully offered a quantity of gold and a gift of property such as to leave Ishak
and his wife and daughter secure for the rest of their lives.

Then he had ordered the physician's eyes put out and
his tongue cut off at the root, that the forbidden sight of
an Asharite woman's nakedness be atoned for, that no
man might ever hear a description of Zabira's milk-white
splendor from the Kindath doctor who had exposed her to
his cold glance and his scalpel.

It was an act of mercy, of a sort. The ordained punishment for a Jaddite or a Kindath who feasted lecherous
eyes on the unclothed figure of an Asharite woman who
was bride or concubine to another man was, as everyone
knew, the death between horses. And this woman

belonged to a king, the successor to khalifs, the Lion of Al-Rassan, from whose presence all lesser kings fled.

The wadjis, seeing an opportunity, had begun demanding that death in temple and marketplace the moment the story of the birth escaped the palace. Almalik, however, was genuinely grateful to his Kindath physician. He had always disliked the wadjis and the demands they made of him and he was—by his own assessment, at any rate—a generous man.

Ishak lived, blind and mute, sunken far into the stony depths of an inwardness his wife and only child could not reach. Not in those first days, not after, could he be roused to any response.

They brought him home from Cartada to their house in his long-since chosen city of Fezana. They had more than enough to sustain themselves; indeed, by any measure at all they were wealthy. In Silvenes, in Cartada, in his private practice here, Ishak had been hugely successful, and as much so in business ventures with Kindath merchants trading east in leather and spices. Almalik's last bounty merely set the seal on their worldly success. They were, it could have been said, blessed by the moons with great good fortune.

Jehane bet Ishak, child of such fortune, walked into her father's room, laid her candle down on the table and pulled back the shutters of the eastern window. She pushed opened the window as well, to let the late afternoon trace of a breeze come in with the soft light. Then she sat in the wooden chair at the table as was her habit.

The book she was in the midst of reading to Ishak—the text of Merovius on cataracts—lay open by her elbow. Each afternoon, at the end of her day's work, she would come into this room and tell her father about the patients she had seen, and then read aloud from whatever text she was studying herself. Sometimes letters came, from colleagues and friends in other cities, other lands. Ser Rezzoni wrote several times a year from Sorenica in Batiara or wherever else he was teaching or practising. Jehane would read these to her father, as well.

He never responded. He never even turned his head towards her. It had been so from the night he was marred. She would tell him about her day, read the letters, read her texts aloud. She would kiss him on the forehead when she left to go down for dinner. He never responded to that, either.

Velaz brought Ishak his meals in this room. He never left this room. He would not—unless they forced him— ever leave this room, Jehane knew. His voice had been deep and beautiful once, his eyes clear and blue as the river in sunlight, bright doorways to a grave depth of thought. The grace of his mind and the skill of his hands had been bestowed without stinting or hesitation upon all who asked or had need. He had been proud without vanity, wise without trivial wit, courageous without bravado. He was a shell, a husk, a blind, mute absence of all these things in a room without light.

In a way, Jehane thought—looking at her father, preparing to say goodbye—pursuing this vengeance, however belated, against Almalik of Cartada was the most obvious thing she had ever done.

She began. "Market day today. Nothing too difficult. I was about to see a quarry laborer with what looked to be gout—if you can believe it—when I was called away. I wouldn't have gone, of course, but it turned out to be Husari ibn Musa—he was passing another stone, the third one this year."

There was no movement in the deep armchair. The handsome, white-bearded profile seemed a carving of a man, not the man himself.

"While I was treating him," Jehane said, "we learned something terrible. If you listen you may be able to hear shouting in the streets beyond the Quarter." She did this often, trying to make him *use* his hearing, trying to draw him from this room.

No movement, no sign he even knew she was here. Almost angrily, Jehane said, "It seems that Almalik of

Cartada sent his oldest son and the lord Ammar ibn Khairan to consecrate the new wing of the castle today. And they have just murdered all those invited. That's why we can hear noise in the streets. One hundred and forty men, Father. Almalik had their heads cut off and threw the bodies in the moat."

And there, quite unexpectedly, it was. It could have been a trick of the light, slanting in through shadows, but she thought she saw him turn his head, just a little, towards her. *I don't think I've ever spoken Almalik's name to him*, Jehane realized suddenly.

Quickly, she went on, "Husari was meant to be one of them, Father. That's why he wanted me to come so quickly this morning. He'd hoped to be able to attend at the castle. Now he's the only one who wasn't killed. And it's possible the Muwardis—there are five hundred new troops in the city today—may come after him. So I've arranged to have him moved here. Velaz is bringing him now, in disguise. I asked Mother's permission," she added.

No mistaking it this time. Ishak had turned his head perceptibly towards her as if drawn against his will to hear what was being said. Jehane became aware that she was near to crying. She swallowed, fighting that. "Husari seems...different, Father. I hardly know him. He's calm, almost cold. He's *angry*, Father. He plans to leave the city tonight. Do you know why?" She risked the question, and waited until she saw the small inquiring motion of his head before answering: "He said he intends to destroy Cartada."

She swiped at a treacherous tear. Four years of monologues in this room, and now, on the eve of her going away, he had finally acknowledged her presence.

Jehane said, "I've decided to leave with him, Father."

She watched. No movement, no sign. But then, slowly, his head turned back away from her until she was looking, again, at the profile she had watched all these years. She swallowed again. In its own way, this, too, was a response. "I don't think I'll stay with him, I don't even know where he's going or what he plans. But somehow, after this afternoon, I just can't pretend nothing has happened. If Husari can decide to fight Almalik, so can I."

There. She had said it. It was spoken. And having said this much, Jehane found that she could say nothing more. She was crying, after all, wiping away tears.

She closed her eyes, overwhelmed. Until this very moment it might have been possible to pretend she was about to do nothing more than what her father had done many times: leave Fezana to pursue contracts and experience in the wider world. If a doctor wanted to build a reputation that was the way to do it. Declaring a course of vengeance against a king was a path to something entirely different. She was also a woman. Her profession might ensure her some measure of safety and respect, but Jehane had lived and studied abroad. She knew the difference between Ishak going into the world and his daughter doing so. She was acutely conscious that she might never be in this room again.

"Ache ve'rach wi'oo."

Jehane's eyes snapped open. What she saw stupefied her. Ishak had turned sideways in his chair to face her. His face was contorted with the effort of speech, the hollow sockets of his eyes trained on where he knew her to be sitting. Her hands flew to her mouth.

"What? Papa, I don't..."

"Ache ve'rach!" The mangled sounds were anguished, imperative.

Jehane hurtled from her chair and dropped to her knees on the carpet at her father's feet. She seized one of his hands and felt, for the first time in four years, his firm strong grasp as he squeezed her fingers tightly.

"I'm sorry. I'm sorry! Again, please. I don't understand!" She felt frantic, heartbroken. He was trying to speak clearly, his whole body twisting with effort and frustration.

"Ve'rach! Ve'rach!" His grip was fierce, willing her comprehension, as if sheer intensity could make the tragically distorted words intelligible.

"He is telling you to take your servant Velaz with you,

Jehane. Under the circumstances, a wise suggestion."

Jehane wheeled as if stabbed, springing to her feet as she turned to the window. Then she froze. She could feel the blood leave her face.

Sitting sideways on the broad window ledge, regarding them calmly, knees bent and both hands wrapped around them, was Ammar ibn Khairan. And of course if he was here they were already lost, because with him he would have brought—

"I am alone, Jehane. I don't like the Muwardis."

She fought for control. "No? You just let them do your killing for you? What does liking have to do with it? How did you get here? Where is—" She stopped herself just in time.

It didn't seem to matter. "Husari ibn Musa should be approaching the Kindath Gates just about now. He's dressed as a wadji, if you can imagine it. An eccentric disguise, I'd say. It's a good thing Velaz is there to vouch for him or they'd never let him in." He smiled, but there was something odd about his eyes. He said, "You have no reason to believe me, but I had nothing to do with what happened this afternoon. Neither did the prince."

"Hah!" Jehane said. The most sophisticated rejoinder she could manage for the moment.

He smiled again. This time it was an expression she remembered from the morning. "I am duly refuted, I suppose. Shall I fall out of the window now?"

And just then, for Jehane the most utterly unexpected event of an appalling day took place. She heard a gasping, strangled noise behind her and turned, terrified.

To realize, after a moment, that what she was hearing was her father's laughter.

Ammar ibn Khairan swung neatly down from the window and landed softly on the carpeted floor. He walked past Jehane and stood before her father's heavy chair.

"Ishak," he said gently.

"Ammar," her father said, almost clearly.

The murderer of the last khalif of Al-Rassan knelt

before him. "I had hoped you might remember my voice," he said. "Will you accept apologies, Ishak? I ought to have been here long ago, and certainly not in this fashion, shocking your daughter and without leave of your wife."

Ishak reached out a hand by way of reply, and ibn Khairan took it. He had removed his gloves and rings. Jehane was too stunned to even begin to formulate her thoughts.

"Muwaari? Wha happ?"

Ibn Khairan's voice was grave. "Almalik is a subtle man, as I think you know. He wanted Fezana quelled, obviously. He also seems to have had a message for the prince." He paused. "And another for me."

Jehane found her voice. "You really didn't know about this?"

"I wouldn't bother lying to you," Ammar ibn Khairan said precisely, without even looking at her.

Flushing, Jehane realized that it was, of course, quite true. Why would he care what she thought? But in that case, there was another obvious question, and she wasn't especially inclined to accept rebukes from men who climbed in through the windows of their home: "What are you doing here then?"

This time he did turn. "Two reasons. You ought to be able to guess at one of them." Out of the corner of her eye Jehane saw her father slowly nodding his head.

"Forgive me, I'm not disposed to play at guessing games just now." She tried to make it sting.

Ibn Khairan's expression was unruffled. "It isn't a game, Jehane. I'm here to ensure that Husari ibn Musa is not killed by the Muwardis this evening, and that the physician, more brave than intelligent perhaps, who is assisting him to escape, is likewise enabled to live beyond tonight."

Jehane felt suddenly cold. "They *are* coming for him, then?"

"Of course they are coming for him. The list of invited guests was known, and *some* of the Muwardis can read. They were instructed to execute every man on that list. Do you think they'd forgo the pleasure of killing even one, or risk Almalik's reaction to failure?"

"They'll go to his house?"

"If they aren't there by now. Which is why I went before them. Husari had already left, with Velaz. The servants and slaves had been sent to their quarters, except the steward, who was evidently trusted. A mistake. I demanded of him where his master was and he told me he'd just left, disguised as a wadji, with the Kindath doctor's servant."

She had been cold before; she was as ice now.

"So he will tell the Muwardis?"

"I don't think so," said Ammar ibn Khairan.

There was a silence. It was not a game at all.

"You killed him," said Jehane.

"A disloyal servant," said ibn Khairan, shaking his head. "A melancholy indication of the times in which we live."

"Why, Ammar?" Ishak's question this time was astonishingly clear, but it might mean many things.

This time ibn Khairan hesitated before answering. Jehane, watching closely, saw that odd expression in his face again.

He said, choosing his words, "I already carry a name through the world for something I did in my youth for Almalik of Cartada. I can live with that. Rightly or wrongly, I did it. I am...disinclined to accept the responsibility for this obscene slaughter—as he clearly intends it to fall upon me. Almalik has his reasons. I can even understand them. But at this point in my life I do not choose to indulge them. I also found Husari ibn Musa to be a clever, unassuming man and I admired your daughter's...competence and spirit. Say that it...pleases me to be on the side of virtue, for once."

Ishak was shaking his head. *"More, Ammar,"* he said, the sounds labored, dragging a little.

Again ibn Khairan hesitated. "There is always more to what a man does, ben Yonannon. Will you permit me the grace of privacy? I will be leaving Fezana myself tonight, by my own means and in my own direction. In time my motives may become clearer."

He turned to Jehane, and she saw by the candle and the light coming in through the window that his eyes were still altered and cold. He had said enough, though; she thought she knew what this was about, now.

"With the steward...unavailable," he was saying, "it is unlikely the Muwardis will come here, but there must be nothing for them to find if they do. I would advise you to forgo a meal and leave as soon as it is dark."

Jehane, grimly subdued, could only nod. With each passing moment she was becoming more aware of the danger and the strangeness of the world she had elected to enter. The morning market, the treatment rooms, all the routines of her life, seemed remote already, and receding swiftly.

"I also have a suggestion, if I may. I do not know what ibn Musa intends to do now, but you could both do worse than go north to Valledo for a time."

"You would send a Kindath to the Jaddites?" Jehane asked sharply.

He shrugged. "You lived among them during your studies abroad, and so did your father in his day."

"That was Batiara. And Ferrieres."

He made an exaggerated grimace. "Again, I am crushingly refuted. I really will have to leap out the window if you keep this up." His expression altered again. "Things are changing in the peninsula, Jehane. They may start changing very quickly. It is worth remembering that with the *parias* being paid, Valledo has guaranteed the security of Fezana. I don't know if that applies to internal...control by Cartada, but it could be argued, if ibn Musa wanted to do so. It could be an excuse. As for you, I would certainly avoid Ruenda and Jaloña if I were a Kindath, but King Ramiro of Valledo is an intelligent man."

"And his soldiers?"

"Some of them are."

"How reassuring."

She heard her father make a reproving sound behind her.

His gaze very direct, ibn Khairan said, "Jehane, you cannot look for reassurance if you leave these walls. You must understand that before you go. If you have no plans

and no direction, then serving as a doctor under the protection of Valledo is as good a course—"

"Why would you assume I have no plans?" It was curious how quickly he could anger her.

He stopped. "Forgive me."

"Where?"

She would not have answered Ammar ibn Khairan, for
any number of reasons, but she had to tell her father. He
had not spoken a word to her in four years before this
afternoon.

"Ragosa," she said quietly.

She had never even thought of it until ibn Khairan had
begun his speech, but once the name of the city was spoken it seemed to Jehane as if she had always been heading
there, east towards the shores of Lake Serrana, and the
river and the mountains.

"Ah," said ibn Khairan, thoughtfully. He rubbed his
smooth chin. "You could do worse than King Badir, yes."

"And Mazur ben Avren."

She said it too defiantly. He grinned. "The Prince of the
Kindath. Of course. I'd be careful there, Jehane."

"Why? You know him?"

"We have exchanged letters and verses over the years.
Books for our libraries. Ben Avren is an extremely subtle
man."

"And so? That is a bad thing in the principal advisor to
the king of Ragosa?"

He shook his head. "Tonight you are asking that particular question of the wrong man, actually. Just be careful if
you do get there. Remember I told you." He was silent a
moment, half-turned to the window. "And if you *are* to get
anywhere, not to mention myself, we must bring an end to
this encounter. I believe I hear voices below. Husari and
Velaz, we'd best hope."

She heard the sounds now, too, and did recognize both
voices.

"I'll leave the way I came, Ser Ishak, with your permission." Ibn Khairan moved past Jehane to take her father's

hand again. "But I do have one question of my own, if I may. I've wondered about something for four years now."

Jehane felt herself go still. Her father slowly tilted his head up towards ibn Khairan.

Who said, "Tell me, if you will, did you *know* what you risked when you delivered Almalik's last child in the way you did?"

In the stillness that followed Jehane could hear, from the courtyard below, her mother's calm voice inviting ibn Musa into their house, as if he were no more than an awaited dinner guest on an ordinary night.

She saw her father nod his head, a sound emerging from the ruined mouth like the release of a long burden. Jehane felt herself suddenly on the edge of tears again.

"Would you do it again?" ibn Khairan asked, very gently.

No delay, this time. Another affirmative nod.

"Why?" asked Ammar ibn Khairan, and Jehane could see that he truly wanted to understand this.

Ishak's mouth opened and closed, as if testing a word. "*Gareeruh*," he said finally, then shook his head in frustration.

"I don't understand," ibn Khairan said.

"*Gareeruh*," Ishak said again, and this time Jehane saw him place a hand over his heart, and she knew.

"The Oath of Galinus," she said. It was difficult to speak. "The Physician's Oath. To preserve life, if it can be done."

Ishak nodded once, and then leaned back in his chair, as if exhausted by the effort to communicate after so long. Ammar ibn Khairan was still holding his hand. Now he let it go. "I would need time to think, more time than we have, before I would presume to offer any reply to that," he said soberly. "If my stars and your moons allow, I would be honored to meet with you again, Ser Ishak. May I write to you?"

Ishak nodded his head. After a moment ibn Khairan turned back to Jehane.

"I believe I did say I had two reasons for coming," he murmured. "Or had you forgotten?" She had, actually. He saw that, and smiled again. "One was a warning of danger, the other was to bring you something."

He walked past her, back to the window. He swung up on the sill and reached out and around the side to the ledge. Without stepping down again he turned and offered something exquisite to Jehane.

"Oh dear," she said. "Oh dear."

It was, of course, her urine flask. Her father's flask.

"You did leave in rather a hurry from ibn Musa's," ibn Khairan said mildly, "and so did Velaz and Husari. I thought you might want the flask, and perhaps make better use of it than the Muwardis when they arrived."

Jehane swallowed and bit her lip. If they had found this...

She stepped forward and took the flask from his hand. Their fingers touched. "Thank you," she said.

And remained motionless, astonished, as he leaned forward and kissed her on the lips. The scent of his perfume briefly surrounded her. One of his hands came up and lightly touched her hair.

"Courier's fee," he said easily, leaning back again. "Ragosa is a good thought. But do mention Valledo to ibn Musa—he may do better with King Ramiro."

Jehane felt the rush of color to her face already beginning to recede. What followed, predictably, was something near to anger. Her father and mother, Velaz, Ser Rezzoni—everyone who knew her well—had always warned her about her pride.

She took a step forward and, standing on tiptoe, kissed Ammar ibn Khairan in her turn. She could feel his sharply intaken breath of surprise. That was better: he had been much, much too casual before.

"Doctor's fee," she said sweetly, stepping back. "We tend to charge more than couriers."

"I *will* fall out of the window," he said, but only after a moment.

"Don't. It's a long way down. You haven't said, but it seems fairly obvious you have your own plan of vengeance to pursue in Cartada. Falling from a window would be a poor way to begin." She was gratified to see that he hadn't been prepared for that either.

He paused a second time. "We shall meet again, I dare hope."

"That would be interesting," Jehane said calmly, though her heart was beating very fast. He smiled. A moment later she watched him climb down the rough wall to the courtyard. He went through an archway towards the gates without looking back.

She would have thought she'd won that last exchange, but the smile he'd offered, just before turning to climb down, made her less certain, in the end.

"*Care, Jehaa. Care,*" her father said, from behind her, echoing her own thoughts.

Feeling frightened again, by many things, Jehane went back to his chair and knelt before it. She put her head in his lap. And after a moment she felt his hands begin to stroke her hair. That had not happened for a long time.

They were like that when Velaz came for her, having already packed for the road—for both of them. He had arrived, of course, at his own decision on this matter.

Some time later, when Jehane was gone, and Velaz, and Husari ibn Musa, the silk merchant who had become, however improbably, a declared conspirator against the Lion of Cartada, strange sounds could be heard emanating from the study of Ishak ben Yonannon, the physician.

His wife Eliane stood in the corridor outside his closed door and listened as her husband, silent as death for four long years, practised articulating the letters of the alphabet, then struggled with simple words, like a child, learning what he could say and what he could not. It was fully dark outside by then; their daughter, their only child, was somewhere beyond the walls of civilization and safety, where women almost never went, in the wilderness of the wide world. Eliane held a tall, burning candle, and by its light someone watching could have seen a taut anguish to her still-beautiful face as she listened.

She stood like that a long time before she knocked and entered the room. The shutters were still folded back and the window was open, as Jehane had left them. At the end of a day of death, with the sounds of grief still raw beyond the gates of the Quarter, the stars were serene as ever in the darkening sky, the moons would rise soon, the white one first tonight, and then the blue, and the night breeze would still ease and cool the scorched summer earth where men and women breathed and walked. And spoke.

"*Eyyia?*" said her husband, and Eliane bet Danel heard the mangling of her name as music.

"You sound like a marsh frog," she said, moving to stand before his chair.

By the flickering light she saw him smile.

"Where have you been," she asked. "My dear. I've needed you so much."

"*Eyyia,*" he tried again, and stood up. His eyes were black hollows. They would always be hollows.

He opened his arms and she moved into the space they made in the world, and laying her head against his chest she permitted herself the almost unimaginable luxury of grief.

At approximately the same time, their daughter was just outside the city walls negotiating with a number of whores for the purchase of three mules.

Jehane had known, in fact, of several hidden exits in the city walls. Some of them were too tenuous for a man of Husari's girth, but there was a place in the Quarter itself, at the northwestern end, where a tree hid a key to a low passage through the stone of the city wall. It was, in the event, a near thing, but Husari was able to squeeze through with help from Velaz.

As they came out and stood up on the grassy space before the river a woman's voice—a familiar voice, in fact—said cheerfully in the darkness, "Be welcome, pilgrims. May I lead you to a Garden of Delights such as Ashar only offers to the Dead?"

"He doesn't offer it at all to the Kindath," Jehane replied. "Tonight you could almost tempt me, Jacinto."

"*Jehane?* Doctor?" The woman, scented and gaudily bejewelled, stepped closer. "Forgive me! I didn't recognize you. Who called for you tonight?"

"No one, actually. Tonight I need *your* help. The wadjis may be after me, and the Muwardis."

"Plague rot them all!" the woman named Jacinto said. "Haven't they had enough blood for one day?" By now Jehane's eyes were accustomed to the night, and she could make out the slender figure in front of her, clad only in the thinnest, most revealing wisps of cloth. "What do you need?" Jacinto asked. She was fourteen years old, Jehane knew.

"Three mules, and your silence."

"You'll have them. Come, I'll bring you to Nunaya."

She had expected that. If anyone exerted any sort of control over this community of women and boys outside the walls it was Nunaya.

Nunaya was not someone who wasted time, or words. Men in a hurry knew this, too, or they learned it soon enough. A client who came to visit her was likely to be back inside Fezana's walls within a very short span of time, relieved of certain urges and a sum of money.

The purchase of the mules was not a difficult transaction. For several years now Jehane—the only woman doctor in Fezana—had been the trusted physician of the whores of the city. First in their district inside the eastern wall and then out here to the north, after they had been pushed by the wadjis beyond the city gates and into one of the straggling suburbs by the river.

That event had been but one in a series of sporadic outbursts of pious outrage that punctuated the dealings between the city and those who traded in physical love. The women fully expected to be back inside the walls within a year—and probably back outside them again a year or two after that.

Given, however, that the women and boys one could

buy were now mostly to be found outside the walls, it was not surprising that hidden exits had been established. No city with citizens—legitimate or otherwise—dwelling beyond its walls could ever be completely sealed.

Jehane knew a good many of the whores by now, and had, on more than one occasion, slipped out to join them for an evening of food and drink and laughter. Out of courtesy to the doctor who delivered their children and healed their bodies of afflictions or wounds, clients were not welcome at such times. Jehane found these women—and the wise, bitter boys—better company than almost anyone she knew in the city, within the Kindath Quarter or outside it. She wondered, at times, what that suggested about herself.

It was far from a serene world out here among the dilapidated houses that straggled beside the moat and river, and as often as not Jehane had been urgently summoned to deal with a knife wound inflicted by one woman on another. But although the three religions were all present here, it was obvious to her that when quarrels arose it had nothing to do with whether sun or moons or stars were worshipped. And the wadjis who had forced them out here were the common enemy. Jehane knew she would not be betrayed by these people.

Nunaya sold them three mules without so much as a question in her heavy-lidded, heavily accentuated eyes. This was not a place where personal questions were asked. Everyone had their secrets, and their wounds.

Jehane mounted up on one of the mules, Velaz and Husari took the others. A lady was supposed to ride sidesaddle, but Jehane had always found that silly and awkward. Doctors were allowed to be eccentric. She rode as the men did.

It was summer, the flow of the river was lazy and slow. Moving across, holding her mule on a tight rein, Jehane felt a heavy drifting object bump them. She shivered, knowing what it was. The mule pulled away hard and she almost fell, controlling it.

They came up out of the water and started north

towards the trees. Jehane looked back just once. Lanterns burned behind them in watchtowers along the walls and in the castle and the tall houses of Fezana. Candles lit by men and women sheltered behind those walls from the dangers of the dark.

There were headless bodies in the castle moat and the river. One hundred and thirty-nine of them.

The one hundred and fortieth man was beside her now, riding in what had to be acute discomfort but uttering no sound of complaint.

"Look ahead," Velaz said quietly. It was very dark now all around them under the stars.

Jehane looked where he was pointing and saw the red glow of a fire in the distance. Her heart thumped hard. An unshielded campfire on the grasslands could mean many different things, obviously, but Jehane had no way of deciding what. She was in an alien world now, on this exposed plain at night, with an aging servant and a plump merchant. Everything she knew and understood lay behind her. Even the ragged suburb of whores next to the city walls seemed a secure, safe place suddenly.

"I think I know what that light must be," said Husari after a moment. His voice was calm, the steady sureness of his manner a continuing surprise. "In fact, I'm certain of it," he said. "Let us go there."

Jehane, weary for the moment of thinking, having got them out safely and mounted, was content to follow his lead. It did cross her mind that this adventure, this shared pursuit of vengeance, might end rather sooner than any of them had anticipated. She let her mule follow Husari's towards the fire burning on the plain.

And so it was that the three of them rode—not long after, just as the white moon was rising—straight into the encampment of Rodrigo Belmonte, the Captain of Valledo, and the fifty men he had brought with him to collect the summer *parias*, and Jehane came to realize that a very long day and night were not yet done.

Chapter IV

∾

The small-farmers of Orvilla, twelve of them, had come to the city together with their laden mules and they left Fezana together when the market closed at midday. One or two might have been inclined to stay and gawk at the soldiers strolling arrogantly about the town, but that would have meant travelling back to the village without the protection of the larger group. In unsettled country so near to the no-man's-land, and in unsettled times, the pleasures of loitering in the city—or, in the case of some of the men, visiting an interesting suburb just outside the northern walls—could not outweigh the real need for the security of numbers.

Well before the sundown prayers they had all been safely back in Orvilla with the goods they had obtained at the market in exchange for their weekly produce. As a consequence, none of them had any knowledge of what happened in Fezana that day. They would learn of it later; by then it would matter rather less. They would have a catastrophe of their own to deal with.

The raiders from the north—even ignorant villagers could recognize Jaddite horsemen—swept down upon Orvilla at precisely the moment the blue moon rose to join the white one in the summer sky. It was too precisely calculated not to be a deliberate timing, though to what purpose no one could imagine, after. Perhaps a whim. There was nothing whimsical about what happened when the horsemen—at least fifty of them—broke through or leaped over the wooden fence that encircled the houses and out-buildings of the village. Some twenty families lived in Orvilla. There were a handful of old swords, a few rusting spears. A number of mules. One ox. Three horses. Aram ibn Dunash, whose house was by the water mill on the stream, had a bow that had been his father's.

He was the first man to die, trying to nock an arrow with shaking hands as a screaming rider bore down upon him. The horseman's pike took Aram in the chest and carried him into the wall of his own home. His wife, unwisely, screamed from inside. The horseman, hearing that, leaped from his mount and strode into the tiny house. He was already unbuckling his belt as he ducked through the low door.

A number of houses were quickly fired, and the communal barn. There was straw in the barn and in midsummer it was dry. The structure went up in flames with a roar. The fire must have been visible as far away as Fezana.

Ziri ibn Aram, who liked to sleep on the roof of the barn in summer, leaped down just in time. The barn was on the far side of the village from the mill and the stream. He was spared seeing his father die. Nor had he observed the horseman striding into the home where his pregnant mother and sisters were. Ziri was fourteen years old. He would have tried to kill the man with his hands. He would have died, of course. As it was, he landed awkwardly at the feet of a laughing Jaddite who was using the flat of his sword to round up all those not killed in the first moments of the attack. There weren't very many of them, Ziri realized, looking desperately around for his family amid the smoke. Perhaps twenty people, in all, seemed to be still alive, from a village of more than twice that number. It was difficult to tell amid the flames. Orvilla was being consumed in an inferno of fire.

For the raiders, it was a disappointing exercise in some ways. There was, predictably, no one worth ransoming, not even a country wadji, who might have fetched a price. Even the brief flurry of combat had been laughable. The

pathetically armed farmers had offered nothing in the way
of opposition or training for battle. There were women of
course, but one didn't have to ride this far in the heat of
summer to find peasant women for sport. Only when one
man suggested spread-eagling the surviving men—the
women were being taken back north, of course—did the
prospect of a diversion belatedly emerge. This was, after
all, Al-Rassan. The half-naked wretches herded together
like cattle or sheep were infidels. This raid could almost
be seen as an act of piety.

"He's right!" another man shouted. "Spread the bas-
tards on their own beams, then spread their women another way!" There was laughter.

With some speed and even a measure of efficiency
amid the chaos of fire the raiders began gathering and
constructing wooden beams. The night had begun to show
promise of entertainment. They had plenty of nails. Meant
for shoeing any horses they took on the raid, they would
do as well for hammering men to wood.

They had just selected the first of the peasants for nailing—a blank-faced boy who would doubtless have grown
up to kill innocent men and women north of the *tagra*
lands—when someone shrieked a grievously tardy warning.

A whirlwind of men on horses thundered in among
them, twisting between the fires, carrying swords and
using them. Most of the raiders had dismounted by then,
many had laid down their weapons to prepare the diagonal beams for nailing the Asharites. They were easy prey.
As easy as the villagers had been for them.

The raiders were men of breeding though, not lice-
ridden outlaw brigands. They knew how these things were
done, even in Al-Rassan. Peasants were one thing—on both
sides of the no-man's-land—but men of means and status
were another. All over the hamlet of Orvilla, Jaddites
began throwing up their hands in submission and loudly
voicing the well-known cry: *"Ransom! Ransom!"*

Those who were killed in the first sweep of the new
horsemen must have died in astonished disbelief. This was

not supposed to happen. If, before they were dispatched, they realized who had come, that astonishment would likely have been redoubled, but these are not things one can know, with any certainty, of the dead.

Alvar hadn't given the matter any real thought, but he had certainly never imagined that the first man he killed in Al-Rassan would be from Valledo. The man wasn't even on his horse at the time. In a way, that didn't feel right, but Laín Nunez's instructions had been precise: kill them until you hear the order to stop. Every man was fair game except the stocky, black-haired one who would be leading them. He was to be left for the Captain.

The Captain was in a terrifying state. He had been from the moment the three riders from Fezana came into the camp with their story. The fat merchant—Abenmuza, he called himself—had told them what the king of Cartada had ordered done in Fezana that day. Searching for clues as to how to react, Alvar had looked to his leaders. If Laín Nunez had seemed indifferent to the bloody tale, almost as if he'd expected such foul deeds here in Al-Rassan, Ser Rodrigo's expression told a different story. He'd said nothing, though, when the merchant finished, save to ask the doctor—her name was Jehane—if she had ever served with a military company.

"I have not," she'd murmured calmly, "though I'd consider it some other time. For now, I have my own route to follow. I'm happy to leave Husari ibn Musa"—which was evidently the right way to say the name—"in your company to pursue his affairs and perhaps your own. I'll be away, with your leave, in the morning."

That unhurried answer, elegantly spoken, went some ways to breaking Alvar's heart. He was already half in love before she spoke. He thought the doctor was beautiful. Her hair—what he could see of it beneath the blue stole wrapped about her shoulders and head—was a rich, dark brown. Her eyes were enormous, unexpectedly blue in the firelight. Her voice was the voice Alvar thought he would like to hear speaking when he died, or for the rest of his life. She was worldly, astonishingly poised, even here in the darkness with fifty riders from the north. She would think him a child, Alvar knew, and looking at her, he felt like one.

They never knew what the Captain would have replied to her, or even if he had been intending a serious invitation that she join them, because just then Martín said sharply, "There's fire. To the west!"

"What will be there?" the Captain said to the three Fezanans as they all turned to look. The flames were spreading already, and they weren't very far away.

It was the woman doctor, not the merchant, who answered. "A village. Orvilla. I have patients there."

"Come then," said the Captain, his expression even grimmer than before. "You will have more now. Leave the mule. Ride with Laín—the older one. Alvar, take her servant. Ludus, Mauro, guard the camp with the merchant. Come on! That crawling maggot Garcia de Rada is here after all."

At least half of the Jaddite raiders were slain in a matter of moments before Jehane, sheltering with Velaz at the side of one of the burning houses, heard the man the others called the Captain say clearly, "It is enough. Gather the rest."

The Captain. She knew who this was, of course. Everyone in the peninsula knew who was called by that name alone, as a title.

His words were echoed quickly by two other riders, including the older one who had ridden here with her. The killing stopped.

There was an interval of time during which the raiders were herded towards the center of the village, an open grassy space. Some of Rodrigo Belmonte's men were filling buckets at the stream, trying to deal with the fires alongside a handful of the villagers. It was hopeless, though; even to Jehane's untutored eye it was obviously wasted effort.

"Doctor! Oh, thank the holy stars! Come quickly, please!"

Jehane turned, and recognized her patient—the woman who brought her eggs every week at the market.

"Abirab! What is it?"

"My sister! She has been terribly hurt. By one of the men. She is bleeding, and with child. And her husband is dead. Oh, what are we to *do*, doctor?"

The woman's face was black with soot and smoke, distorted with grief. Her eyes were red from weeping. Jehane, frozen for a moment by the brutal reality of horror, offered a quick inner prayer to Galinus—the only name she truly worshipped—and said, "Take me to her. We will do what we can."

Ziri ibn Aram, standing on the far side of the circle, still did not know what had happened to his father or mother. He saw his aunt approach a woman who had come with the new men. He was about to follow them, but something held him where he was. A few moments ago he had been preparing to die nailed to a beam from the barn. He had spoken the words that offered his soul as a gift to the stars of Ashar. It seemed the stars were not ready for his soul, after all.

He watched the brown-haired commander of the new arrivals remove a glove and stroke his moustache as he looked down from his black horse at the leader of those who had destroyed Ziri's village. The man on the ground was stocky and dark. He didn't seem at all, to Ziri's eyes, like someone who feared his approaching death.

"You have achieved your own destruction," he said with astonishing arrogance to the man on the horse. "Do you know who your louts have killed here?" His voice was high-pitched for a man, almost shrill. "Do you know what will happen when I report this in Esteren?"

The broad-shouldered, brown-haired man on the black horse said nothing. An older man beside him, extremely tall and lean, with greying hair, said sharply, "So sure you are going back, de Rada?"

The stocky man didn't even look at him. After a

moment, though, the first horseman, the leader, said very quietly, "Answer him, Garcia. He asked you a question." The name was used as one might admonish a child, but the voice was cold.

For the first time Ziri saw a flicker of doubt appear in the face of the man named Garcia. Only for a moment, though. "You aren't a complete fool, Belmonte. Don't play games with me."

"Games?" A hard, swift anger in the mounted man's voice. He swept one hand in a slashing arc, indicating all of Orvilla, burning freely now. Nothing would be saved. Nothing at all. Ziri began looking around for his father. A feeling of dread was overtaking him.

"Would I play a game in the midst of this?" the man on the black horse snapped. "Be careful, Garcia. Do not insult me. Not tonight. I told your brother what would happen if you came near Fezana. I assume he told you. I must assume he told you."

The man on the ground was silent.

"Does it matter?" said the grey-haired one. He spat on the ground. "This one is offal. He is less than that."

"I will remember you," said the black-haired man sharply, turning now to the speaker. He clenched his fists. "I have a good memory."

"But you forgot your brother's warning?" It was the leader once more, the one called Belmonte. His voice was calm again, dangerously so. "Or you chose to forget it, shall we say? Garcia de Rada, what you did as a boy on your family estates was no concern of mine. What you do here, as someone who passes for a man, unfortunately is. This village lies under the protection of the king of Valledo whose officer I am. The *parias* I am here to collect was paid in part by the people you have butchered tonight. You have taken the promises of King Ramiro and made him a liar in the eyes of the world." He paused, to let the words sink in. "Given that fact, what should I do with you?"

It was evidently not a question the man addressed had been expecting. But he was not slow of wit. *"Given that fact*," he mocked, imitating the tone. "You ought to have been a lawyer not a soldier, Belmonte. A judge in your eastern pastures, making rulings about stolen sheep. What is this, your courthouse?"

"Yes," said the other man. "Now you begin to understand. That is exactly what it is. We await your reply. What should I do with you? Shall I give you to these people to be spread-eagled? The Asharites nail people to wood as well. We learned it from them. Did you know that? I doubt we'd have trouble finding carpenters."

"Don't bluster," said Garcia de Rada.

Jehane, walking back towards the knot of men in the midst of the burning village, with a little girl's hand in each of hers and a black rage in her heart, saw only the blurred motion of Rodrigo Belmonte's right arm. She heard a crack, like a whip, and a man cried out.

Then she realized it *had* been a whip, and saw the black line of blood on Garcia de Rada's cheek. He would be scarred for life by that, she knew. She also knew she wanted his life to end tonight. The fury in her was as nothing she had ever felt before; it was huge, terrifying. She felt she could kill the man herself. It was necessary to breathe deeply, to try to preserve a measure of self-control.

When her father had been marred in Cartada it had come to Jehane and her mother as rumor first and then report, and then they had lived with the knowledge for two days before they were allowed to see what had been done and take him away. What she had just seen in the one-room hut by the river was raw as salt in an open sore. Jehane had wanted to scream. What was medicine, what was all her training, her oath, in the face of an atrocity such as this?

Anger made her reckless. Leading the two children, she walked straight in to stand between Rodrigo Belmonte and the leader of the Jaddite raiders, the man he'd called Garcia and had just scarred with a whip.

"Which one was it?" she said to the children. She pitched her voice to carry.

There was abruptly a silence around them. A young man, fourteen, fifteen perhaps, began hurrying towards her. The two girls had said there might be an older brother still alive. The mother's sister, Abirab, who used to request endless salves and infusions of Jehane at the market for foot pains or monthly cramps or sleeplessness, was still in the hut trying to do something impossible—to smooth the horror of a dead, viciously mutilated woman and the still-born child that had spilled from her.

The young man rushed up to them and knelt beside his sisters. One of them collapsed, weeping, against his shoulder. The other, the older, stood very straight, her face grave and intent, looking around at the raiders. "He wore a red shirt," she said quite clearly, "and red boots."

"There, then," said the man called Laín Nunez after a moment, pointing. "Bring him forward, Alvar."

A younger member of the band, the one with the oddly high stirrups on his horse, leaped from his mount. From the ranks of the surviving raiders he pushed someone into the open space. Jehane was still too consumed by her rage to give more than a brief thought to how they had all stopped what they'd been doing, for her.

It wasn't for her. She looked down at the boy kneeling with his weeping sister in his arms. "Your name is Ziri?"

He nodded, looking up at her. His dark eyes were enormous in a white face.

"I am sorry to have to tell you your mother and father are dead. There is no easy way to say it tonight."

"A great many people are dead here, doctor. Why are you interrupting?" It was Belmonte, behind her, and it was a fair question, in its way.

But Jehane's anger would not let her go. This man was a Jaddite, and the Jaddites had done this thing. "You want me to say it in front of the children?" She did not even look back at him.

"No one here is a child after tonight."

Which was true, she realized. And so Jehane pointed to the man in the red shirt and said, though later she would wish she had not, "This man raped the mother of these children, near to term with another child. Then he put his sword inside her, up inside her, and ripped it out, and left her to bleed to death. When I arrived the child had already spilled out of the wound. Its head had been almost severed. By the sword. Before it was born." She felt sick, speaking the words.

"I see." There was a weariness in Rodrigo Belmonte's voice that caused her to turn back and look up at him. She could read nothing in his features.

He sat his horse for a moment in silence, then said, "Give the boy your sword, Alvar. This we will not accept. Not in a village Valledans are bound to defend."

Where would you accept it? Jehane wanted to demand, but kept silent. She was suddenly afraid.

"This man is my cousin," the man called Garcia de Rada said sharply, holding a piece of grimy cloth to his bleeding face. "He is Parazor de Rada. The constable's cousin, Belmonte. Remember who—"

"Keep silent or I will kill you!"

For the first time Rodrigo Belmonte raised his voice, and Garcia de Rada was not the only man to flinch before what he heard there. Jehane looked again into the face of the man they called the Captain, and then she looked away. Her fury seemed to have passed, leaving only grief and waves of sickness.

The young soldier, Alvar, came obediently up to the boy who was still kneeling beside her, holding both his sisters now. Alvar offered his sword, hilt foremost. The boy, Ziri, looked past Jehane at Rodrigo Belmonte on his black horse above them.

"You have this right. I grant it to you before witnesses."

Slowly the boy stood up and slowly he took the sword. The man called Alvar was as ashen-faced as Ziri, Jehane saw—and guessed that tonight would have been his own first taste of battle. There was blood on the blade.

"Think what you are doing, Belmonte!" the man in the red shirt and boots suddenly cried hoarsely. "These things *happen* in war, on a raid. Do not pretend that your own men—"

"*War?*" Rodrigo's voice knifed in savagely. "What war? Who is at war? Who ordered a raid? Tell me!"

The other man was still a long moment. "My cousin Garcia," he finally said.

"His rank at court? His authority? His reason?"

No answer. The crackle and crash of the fires was all around them. The light was lurid, unholy, dimming the stars and even the moons. Jehane heard weeping now, the keening sounds of grief, from shadows at the edges of the flames.

"May Jad forgive you and find a place for your soul in his light," said Rodrigo Belmonte, looking at the red-shirted man, speaking in a very different voice.

Ziri looked up at him one last time, hearing that, and evidently saw what he needed to see. He turned and stepped forward, with the unfamiliar blade.

He will never have held a sword in his life, Jehane thought. She wanted to close her eyes, but something would not let her do that. The red-shirted man did not turn or try to flee. She thought it was courage, at the time, but later decided he might have been too astonished by what was happening to react. This simply did not *happen* to noblemen playing their games in the countryside.

Ziri ibn Aram took two steady steps forward and then thrust the borrowed blade—awkwardly, but with determination—straight through the heart of the man who had killed his mother and his father. The man screamed as the blade went in, a terrible sound.

Too late, Jehane remembered the two girls. She ought to have turned their faces away, covered their ears. Both had been watching. Neither was crying now. She knelt and gathered them to her.

I caused this death, she was thinking. With rage no longer driving her, it was an appalling thought. She was abruptly mindful of the fact that she was out here beyond the walls of Fezana with the purpose of causing another.

"I will take them now, doctor."

She looked up and saw the boy, Ziri, standing beside her. He had given the sword back to Alvar. There was a bleakness in his eyes. She wondered if, later, it would help him at all to have taken his revenge. She had to wonder that.

She released the two girls and watched their brother lead them away from the open space. She didn't know where they were going amid all the fires. She doubted he did either. She remained kneeling on the ground, looking at Garcia de Rada.

"My cousin was a pig," he said calmly, turning from the dead man to look up at Rodrigo Belmonte. "What he did was disgusting. We are well rid of him, and I will say as much when we all return home."

There was a bark of disbelieving laughter from Laín Nunez. Jehane could hardly believe the words, herself. Somewhere inside she was forced to acknowledge that the man had courage of a sort. He was a monster, though. A monster from the tales used by mothers to fright their children into obedience. But here in Orvilla the monster had come, after all, and children had died. One had been stabbed by a sword before entering the world.

She looked over her shoulder again, and saw Rodrigo Belmonte smiling strangely as he looked down at de Rada. No one in the world could have taken any comfort in that expression.

"Do you know," he said, his voice quiet again, almost conversational, "I have always thought you poisoned King Raimundo."

Jehane saw a startled apprehension in the craggy face of Laín Nunez. He turned sharply to Rodrigo. This, clearly, had not been expected. He moved his horse nearer to the Captain's. Without turning to him, Rodrigo lifted a hand and Laín Nunez stopped. Turning back the other way, Jehane saw Garcia de Rada open his mouth and then close it again. He was clearly thinking hard, but she could see no fear in the man, not even now. Blood was dripping from the wound on his face.

"You would not dare say such a thing in Esteren," he said at length.

His own voice was softer now. A new thread of tension seemed to be running through all the Jaddites. The last king of Valledo had been named Raimundo, Jehane knew that. The oldest of the three brothers, the sons of Sancho the Fat. There had been rumors surrounding Raimundo's death, a story involving Rodrigo Belmonte, something about the present king of Valledo's coronation. Ammar ibn Khairan could have told her, Jehane suddenly thought, and shook her head. Not a useful line of thinking.

"Perhaps I might not," Rodrigo said, still mildly. "We aren't in Esteren."

"So you feel free to slander anyone you choose?"

"Not anyone. Only you. Challenge me." He still had that strange smile on his face.

"Back home I will. Believe it."

"I do not. Fight me now, or admit you killed your king."

Out of the corner of her eye Jehane saw Laín Nunez make a curiously helpless gesture beside Rodrigo. The Captain ignored him. Something had altered in his manner and Jehane, for the first time, found herself intimidated by him. This issue—the death of King Raimundo—seemed to be his own open wound. She realized that Velaz had come up quietly to stand protectively beside her.

"I will do neither. Not here. But say this again at court and observe what I do, Belmonte."

"Rodrigo!" Jehane heard Laín Nunez rasp. "Stop this, in Jad's name! Kill him if you like, but stop this now."

"But that is the problem," said the Captain of Valledo in the same taut voice. "I don't think I can."

Jehane, struggling for understanding amid the rawness of her own emotions, wasn't sure if he meant that he couldn't kill, or he couldn't stop what he was saying. She had a flashing sense that he probably meant both.

With a roar, another of the houses collapsed. The fire had spread as far as it could. There was no more wood to ignite. Orvilla would be cinder and ash by morning, when the survivors would have to attend to the dead and the process of living past this night.

"Take your men and go," Rodrigo Belmonte said to the man who had done this thing.

"Return our horses and weapons and we ride north on the instant," said Garcia de Rada promptly.

Jehane looked back and saw that Rodrigo's cold smile was gone. He seemed tired now, drained of some vital force by this last exchange. "You sued for ransom," he said. "Remember? There are witnesses. Full price will be settled at court by the heralds. Your mounts and weapons are a first payment. You are released on your sworn oaths to pay."

"You want us to *walk* back to Valledo?"

"I want you dead," said Rodrigo succinctly. "I will not murder a countryman, though. Be grateful and start walking. There are five hundred new Muwardi mercenaries in Fezana tonight, by the way. They'll have seen these fires. You might not want to linger."

He was going to let them go. Privileges of rank and power. The way the world was run. Dead and mutilated farmers could be redeemed by horses and gold for the rescuers. Jehane had a sudden image—intense and disorienting—of herself rising smoothly from the brown, parched grass, striding over to that young soldier, Alvar, and seizing his sword. She could almost feel the weight of the weapon in her hands. With eerie clarity she watched herself walk up to Garcia de Rada—he had even turned partially away from her. In the vision she heard Velaz cry "*Jehane!*" just as she killed de Rada with a two-handed swing of the Jaddite sword. The soldier's blade entered between two ribs; she heard the dark-haired man cry out and saw his blood spurt and continue to spill as he fell.

She would never have thought such images could occur to her, let alone feel so urgent, so necessary. She was a doctor, sworn to defend life by the Oath of Galinus. The same oath her father had sworn, the one that had led him to deliver a child, aware that it could cost him his own life. He had said as much to ibn Khairan, earlier this same day. It was hard to believe it *was* the same day.

She was a physician before she was anything else, it was her holy island, her sanctuary. She had already caused one man to be killed tonight. It was enough. It was more than enough. She stood up and took a single step towards Garcia de Rada. She saw him look at her, register the Kindath-style drape of the stole about her head and shoulders. She could read contempt and derision in his eyes. It didn't matter. She had sworn an oath, years ago.

She said, "Wash that wound in the river. Then cover it with a clean cloth. Do that every day. You will be marked, but it might not fester. If you can have a doctor salve it soon, that will be better for you."

She would never have imagined it would be so difficult to speak such words. At the perimeter of the open space, half in the ruined shadows, she suddenly saw her patient, Abirab, with the two little girls held close to her. Their brother, Ziri, had stepped forward a little and was staring at her. Enduring his gaze, Jehane felt her words as the most brutal form of betrayal.

She turned away and, without looking back, without waiting for anyone, began walking from the village, between the burning houses and then out through a gap in the fence, feeling the heat of the fires on her face and in her heart as she went, with no prospect of anything to cool her grief.

She knew Velaz would be following. She had not expected to hear, so soon, the sound of a horse overtaking her.

"The camp is too far to walk," said a voice. Not Laín Nunez this time. She looked up at Rodrigo Belmonte as he slowed the horse beside her. "I think we each did something that cut against our desire back there," he said. "Shall we ride together?"

She had been awed by him at first, by the scale of his reputation, then, briefly, afraid, then angry—though unfairly so, perhaps. Now she was simply tired, and grateful for the chance to ride. He leaned over in the saddle and lifted her up, effortlessly, though she wasn't a small woman. She arranged her skirts and undertunic and swung a leg across the horse behind him. She put her arms around his waist. He wasn't wearing armor. In the silence of the night, as they left the fires behind, Jehane could feel the beating of his heart.

They rode in that silence for a time and Jehane let the stillness and the dark merge with the steady drumming of the horse's hooves to guide her back towards a semblance of composure.

This is my day for meeting famous men, she thought suddenly.

It could almost have been amusing, if so much tragedy had not been embedded in the day. The realization, though, was inescapable. The man she was riding behind had been known, for almost twenty years—since the late days of the Khalifate—as the Scourge of Al-Rassan. The wadjis still singled him out by name for cursing in the temples at the darkfall prayers. She wondered if he knew that, if he prided himself upon it.

"My temper is a problem," he said quietly, breaking the silence in remarkably unaccented Asharic. "I really shouldn't have whipped him."

"I don't see why not," Jehane said.

He shook his head. "You kill men like that or you leave them alone."

"Then you should have killed him."

"Probably. I could have, in the first attack when we arrived, but not after they had surrendered and sued for ransom."

"Ah, yes," Jehane said, aware that her bitterness was audible, "The code of warriors. Would you like to ride back and look at that mother and child?"

"I have seen such things, doctor. Believe me." She did believe him. He had probably done them, too.

"I knew your father, incidentally," said Rodrigo Belmonte after another silence. Jehane felt herself go rigid.

"Ishak of the Kindath. I was sorry to learn of his fate."

"How...how do you know who my father is? How do you know who *I* am?" she stammered.

He chuckled. And answered her, astonishingly, in fluent Kindath now. "Not a particularly difficult guess. How many blue-eyed Kindath female physicians are there in Fezana? You have your father's eyes."

"My father has no eyes," Jehane said bitterly. "As you know if you know his story. How do you know our language?"

"Soldiers tend to learn bits of many languages."

"Not that well, and not Kindath. How do you know it?"

"I fell in love once, a long time ago. Best way to learn a language, actually."

Jehane was feeling angry again. "When did you learn Asharic?" she demanded.

He switched easily back into that language. "I lived in Al-Rassan for a time. When Prince Raimundo was exiled by his father for a multitude of mostly imagined sins he spent a year in Silvenes and Fezana, and I came south with him."

"You *lived* in Fezana?"

"Part of the time. Why so surprised?"

She didn't answer. It wasn't so unusual, in fact. For decades, if not centuries, the feuds among the Jaddite monarchs of Esperaña and their families had often led noblemen and their retinues to sojourn in exile among the delights of Al-Rassan. And during the Khalifate not a few of the Asharite nobility had similarly found it prudent to distance themselves from the long reach of Silvenes, dwelling among the Horsemen of the north.

"I don't know," she answered his question. "I suppose because I'd have expected to remember you."

"Seventeen years ago? You would have been little more than a child. I think I might even have seen you once, unless you have a sister, in the market at your father's booth. There's no reason for you to have remembered me. I was much the same age young Alvar is now. And about as experienced."

The mention of the young soldier reminded her of something. "Alvar? The one who took Velaz with him? When are you going to let him in on the stirrup joke you're playing?"

A short silence as he registered that. Then Rodrigo laughed aloud. "You noticed? Clever you. But how would you know it was a joke?"

"Not a particularly difficult guess," she said, mimicking his phrase deliberately. "He's riding with knees high as his waist. They play the same trick on new recruits in Batiara. Do you want to cripple the boy?"

"Of course not. But he's a little more assertive than you imagine. It won't harm him to be chastened a little. I intended to let his legs down before we went into the city tomorrow. If you want, you can be his savior tonight. He's already smitten, or had you noticed?"

She hadn't. It wasn't the sort of thing to which Jehane had ever paid much attention.

Rodrigo Belmonte changed the subject abruptly. "Batiara, you said? You studied there? With Ser Rezzoni in Sorenica?"

She found herself disconcerted yet again. "And then at the university in Padrino for half a year. Do you know *every* physician there is?"

"Most of the good ones," he said crisply. "Part of my profession. Think about it, doctor. We don't have nearly enough trained physicians in the north. We know how to kill, but not much about healing. I was raising a serious point with you earlier this evening, not an idle one."

"The moment I arrived? You couldn't have known if I was a good doctor or not."

"Ishak of Fezana's daughter? I can allow myself an educated guess, surely?"

"I'm sure the celebrated Captain of Valledo can allow himself anything he wants," Jehane said tartly. She felt seriously at a disadvantage; the man knew much too much. He was far too clever; Jaddite soldiers weren't supposed to be at all like this.

"Not *anything*," he said in an exaggeratedly rueful voice. "My dear wife—have you met my dear wife?"

"Of course I haven't," Jehane snapped. He was playing with her.

"My dear wife has imposed strict limitations on my behavior away from home." His tone made his meaning all too plain, though the suggestion—from what she knew of the northerners—was improbable in the extreme.

"How difficult, for a soldier. She must be fearsome."

"She is," said Rodrigo Belmonte, with feeling.

But something—a nuance, a new shade of meaning in the night—had been introduced now, however flippantly, and Jehane was suddenly aware that the two of them were alone in the darkness with his men and Velaz far behind and the camp a long way ahead yet. She was sitting up close to him, thighs against his and her arms looped around him, clasped at his waist. With an effort she resisted the urge to loosen her grip and change position.

"I'm sorry," he said after a silence. "This isn't a night for joking, and now I've made you uncomfortable."

Jehane said nothing. It seemed that whether she spoke or kept silent, this man was reading her like an illuminated scroll.

Something occurred to her. "Tell me," she said firmly, ignoring his comment, "if you lived here for a time, why did you have to ask what was burning, back in camp? Orvilla has been in the same place for fifty years or more."

She couldn't see his face, of course, but somehow she knew he would be smiling. "Good," he said at length. "Very good, doctor. I shall be even sorrier now if you refuse my offer."

"I *have* refused your offer, remember?" She wouldn't allow herself to be deflected. "Why did you have to ask what was burning?"

"I didn't *have* to ask. I chose to ask. To see who answered. There are things to be learned from questions, beyond the answers to the question."

She thought about that. "And what did you learn?"

"That you are quicker than your merchant friend."

"Don't underestimate ibn Musa," Jehane said quickly. "He's surprised me several times today, and I've known him a long time."

"What *should* I do with him?" Rodrigo Belmonte asked.

It was, she realized, a serious question. She rode for a while, thinking. The two moons were both high now; they had risen about thirty degrees apart. The angle of a journey, in fact, in her own birth chart. Ahead of them now she could see the campfire where Husari would be waiting with the two men left on guard.

"You understand that he was to have been killed this afternoon with the others in the castle?"

"I gathered as much. Why did he survive?"

"I didn't let him go. He was passing a kidney stone."

He laughed. "First time he'll ever have been grateful for that, I'll wager." His tone changed. "Fine, then. He was marked by Almalik to die. What should I do?"

"Take him back north with you," she said at length, trying to think it through. "I think he wants to do that. If King Ramiro has any thoughts of taking Fezana for himself one day—"

"*Wait!* Hold, woman! What kind of a thing is that to say?"

"An obvious one, I should have thought," she said impatiently. "At some point he has to wonder why he's only exacting *parias* and not ruling the city."

Rodrigo Belmonte was laughing again, and shaking his head. "You know, not *all* obvious thoughts need be spoken."

"You asked me a question," she said sweetly. "I am taking it seriously. If Ramiro has any such thoughts—however remote and insubstantial they may be, of course—it can only help to have the sole survivor of today's massacre with him."

"Especially if he makes sure everyone knows that man came straight to him from the slaughter and asked him to intervene." Rodrigo's tone was reflective; he didn't bother responding to her sarcasm.

Jehane felt suddenly weary of talking. This was a day that had started at dawn in the market, in the most ordinary of ways. Now here she was, after the slaughter in the city and the attack on Orvilla, discussing peninsular politics in the darkness with Rodrigo Belmonte, the Scourge of Al-Rassan. It began to seem just a little too much. She was going to set out on her own path in the morning, and morning was not far off. "I suppose you are right. I'm a doctor, not a diplomat, you know," she murmured vaguely. It would be nice to fall asleep, actually.

"Much the same, at times," he replied. Which irritated her enough to pull her awake again, mostly because Ser Rezzoni had said precisely the same thing to her more than once. "Where are you riding?" he asked casually.

"Ragosa," she answered, just before remembering that she hadn't planned to tell anyone.

"Why?" he pursued.

He seemed to assume he had a right to an answer. It must come with commanding men for so long, Jehane decided.

"Because they tell me the courtiers and soldiers there are wondrous skilled in lovemaking," she murmured, in her throatiest voice. For good measure, she unlinked her hands and slid them from his waist to his thighs and left them there a moment before clasping them demurely again.

He drew a long breath and let it out slowly. She was sitting very close, though; try as he might to hide a response, she could feel his heartbeat accelerate. At about the same moment, it occurred to her that she was playing the most brazen sort of teasing game with a dangerous man.

"This," said Rodrigo Belmonte of Valledo plaintively, "is distressingly familiar. A woman putting me in my place. Are you *sure* you've never met my wife?"

A moment later, very much against her will and any reasonable expectations, Jehane began to laugh. And then, perhaps *because* she was laughing, genuinely amused, she remembered again what she'd seen in that small hut in Orvilla, and then it came back to her that her father had spoken his first words in four years tonight, and she was leaving him and her mother, perhaps forever.

She *hated* crying. Laughter and tears, Ishak used to say, were the nearest of kin. It wasn't a physician's observation, that one. His mother had told him that, and her mother had told her. The Kindath had survived a thousand years; they were laden with such folk wisdom, carrying it like their travelling baggage, well-worn, never far from reach.

So Jehane fought against her tears on Rodrigo Belmonte's black horse, riding east under moons that spelled a journey for her, against the backdrop of the summer stars, and the man with whom she rode kept blessedly silent until they reached the camp and saw that the Muwardis had been there.

For Alvar, a good part of the considerable strain of that night came from feeling so hopelessly behind what was happening. He had always thought of himself as clever. In fact, he *knew* he was intelligent. The problem was, the events unfolding tonight in Al-Rassan were so far outside the scope of his experience that cleverness was not nearly enough to show him how to deal with what was taking place.

He understood enough to know that with his share of the ransom to be negotiated for Garcia de Rada and his surviving men he was already wealthier than he had ever imagined becoming in his first year as a soldier of the king in Esteren. Even now, before any further negotiations took place, Alvar had been assigned a new horse and armor by Laín Nunez—and both of them were better than his own.

This was how soldiers rose in the world, if they did, through the plunder and ransom of war. Only he had really not expected to take that wealth from fellow Valledans.

"Happens all the time," Laín Nunez had said gruffly as they divided the spoils in the village. "Remind me to tell you of the time Rodrigo and I served as privately hired mercenaries of the Asharites of Salos downriver. We raided into Ruenda for them more than once."

"But not into Valledo," Alvar had protested, still troubled.

"All one back then, remember? King Sancho was still on the throne of united Esperaña. Three provinces of one country, lad. Not the division we've got now."

Alvar had thought about that on the way back to the camp. He was struggling with so many difficult things—including his own first killing—that he didn't even have a chance to enjoy his spoils of battle. He did notice that Laín Nunez was careful to allocate a substantial share of the ransomed weapons and mounts to the survivors of the village, though. He hadn't expected that.

Then, back at the camp, where the Captain and the Kindath doctor were waiting for them, Alvar saw the chests and sacks and barrels, and came to understand that this was the summer *parias* from Fezana, delivered by the Muwardis—the Veiled Ones—out here at night on the plain.

"The merchant?" Laín Nunez asked urgently, swinging down from his horse. "They came for him?" And Alvar abruptly remembered that the plump Asharite had been marked to die in Fezana's castle that day.

The Captain was shaking his head slowly. "The merchant," he said, "is no more."

"Rot their souls!" Laín Nunez swore violently. "By Jad's fingers and toes, I hate the Muwardis!"

"Instead of the merchant," the Captain went on placidly, "we appear to have a new outrider to join Martín and Ludus. We'll have to work some weight off him before he's much use, mind you."

Laín Nunez gave his sharp bark of laughter as a ponderous figure rose from the far side of the fire, clad—barely—in the garb of a Jaddite Horseman. Husari ibn Musa seemed, improbably, quite at ease.

"I've been a wadji already today," he said calmly, speaking passable Esperañan. "This is no more of a stretch, I suppose."

"Untrue," the Captain murmured. "Looking at Ramon's clothing on you, I'd call it a big stretch." There was laughter.

The merchant smiled, and patted his stomach cheerfully.

Alvar, joining uncertainly in the amusement, saw the Kindath doctor, Jehane, sitting on a saddle blanket by the fire, hands about her drawn-up knees. She was looking into the flames.

"How many of the desert dogs were here?" Laín Nunez asked.

"Only ten, Martín says. Which is why they didn't come to Orvilla."

"He told them we were dealing with it?"

"Yes. They are obviously under orders to give us our gold and hope we leave quickly."

Laín Nunez removed his hat and ran a hand through his thinning grey hair. "And are we? Leaving?"

"I think so," the Captain said. "I can't think of a point to make down here. There's nothing but trouble in Fezana right now."

"And trouble heading home."

"Well, walking home."

"They'll get there eventually."

Rodrigo grimaced. "What would you have had me do?"

His lieutenant shrugged, and then spat carefully into the grass. "We leave at first light, then?" he asked, without answering the question.

The Captain looked at him closely for a moment longer, opened his mouth as if to say something more, but in the end he merely shook his head. "The Muwardis will be watching us. We leave, but not in any hurry. We can take our time about breaking camp. You can pick a dozen men to ride back to Orvilla in the morning. Spend the day working there and catch us up later. There are men and women to be buried, among other things."

Alvar dismounted and walked over to the fire where the doctor was sitting. "Is there...can I help you with anything?"

She looked very tired, but she did favor him with a quick smile. "Not really, thank you." She hesitated. "This is your first time in Al-Rassan?"

Alvar nodded. He sank down on his haunches beside her. "I was hoping to see Fezana tomorrow," he said. He wished he spoke better Asharic, but he tried. "I am told it is a city of marvels."

"Not really," she repeated carelessly. "Ragosa, Cartada...Silvenes, of course. What's left of it. Those are the great cities. Seria is beautiful. There is nothing marvellous about Fezana. It has always been too close to the *tagra* lands to afford the luxury of display. You won't be seeing it tomorrow?"

"We're leaving in the morning." Again, Alvar had the unpleasant sense that he was struggling to stay afloat in waters closing over his head. "The Captain just told us. I'm not sure why. I think because the Muwardis came."

"Well, of course. Look around you. The *parias* gold is here. They don't want to open the gates tomorrow, and they particularly won't want Jaddite soldiers in the city. Not with what happened today."

"So we're just going to turn around and—"

"I'm afraid so, lad." It was the Captain. "No taste of decadent Al-Rassan for you this time." Alvar felt himself flushing.

"Well, the women *are* mostly outside the walls this year," the doctor said, with a demure expression. She was looking at Ser Rodrigo, not at Alvar.

The Captain swore. "Don't tell my men that! Alvar, you are bound to secrecy. I don't want anyone crossing the river. Any man who leaves camp walks home."

"Yes, sir," Alvar said hastily.

"Which reminds me," the Captain said to him, with a sidelong glance at the doctor, "you might as well lower your stirrups now. For the ride back."

And with those words, for the first time in a long while, Alvar felt a little more like his usual self. He'd been waiting for this moment since they'd left Valledo behind.

"Must I, Captain?" he asked, keeping his expression innocent. "I'm just getting used to them this way. I thought I'd even try bringing them up a bit higher, with your approval."

The Captain looked at the doctor again. He cleared his throat. "Well, no, Alvar. It isn't really...I don't think..."

"I thought, if I had my knees up high enough, really high, I might be able to rest my chin on them when I rode, and that would keep me fresher on a long ride. If that makes sense to you, Captain?"

Alvar de Pellino had his reward, then, for uncharacteristic silence and biding his time. He saw the doctor smile slowly at him, and then look with arched eyebrows of inquiry at the Captain.

Rodrigo Belmonte was, however, a man unlikely to be long discomfited by this sort of thing. He looked at Alvar for a moment, then he, too, broke into a smile.

"Your father?" he asked.

Alvar nodded his head. "He did warn me of some things I might encounter as a soldier."

"And you chose to accept the stirrup business nonetheless? To say nothing at all?"

"It was you who did it, Captain. And I want to remain in your company."

The Kindath doctor's amusement was obvious. Ser Rodrigo's brow darkened. "In Jad's name, boy, were you *humoring* me?"

"Yes, sir," said Alvar happily.

The woman he had decided he would love forever threw back her head and laughed aloud. A moment later, the Captain he wanted to serve all his days did exactly the same thing.

Alvar decided it hadn't been such a terrible night, after all.

"Do you see how clever my men are?" Rodrigo said to the doctor as their laughter subsided. "You are quite certain you won't reconsider and join us?"

"You tempt me," the doctor said, still smiling. "I do like clever men." Her expression changed. "But Esperaña is no place for a Kindath, Ser Rodrigo. You know that as well as I."

"It will make no difference with us," the Captain said. "If you can sew a sword wound and ease a bowel gripe you will be welcome among my company."

"I can do both those things, but your company, clever as its men may be, is not the wider world." There was no amusement in her eyes any more. "Do you remember what your Queen Vasca said of us, when Esperaña was the whole peninsula, before the Asharites came and penned you in the north?"

"That was more than three hundred years ago, doctor."

"I know that. Do you remember?"

"I do, of course, but—"

"Do *you?*" She turned to Alvar. She was angry now. Mutely, he shook his head.

"She said the Kindath were animals, to be hunted down and burned from the face of the earth."

Alvar could think of nothing to say.

"Jehane," the Captain said, "I can only repeat, that was three hundred years ago. She is long dead and gone."

"Not gone! You dare say that? Where is she?" She glared at Alvar, as if he were to blame for this, somehow. "Where is Queen Vasca's resting place?"

Alvar swallowed. "On the Isle," he whispered. "Vasca's Isle."

"Which is a shrine! A place of pilgrimage, where Jaddites from all three of your kingdoms and countries beyond the mountains come, on their *knees*, to beg miracles from the spirit of the woman who said that thing. I will make a wager that half this so-clever company have family members who have made that journey to plead for blessed Vasca's intercession."

Alvar kept his mouth firmly shut. So, too, this time, did the Captain.

"And you would tell me," Jehane of the Kindath went on bitterly, "that so long as I do my tasks well enough it will not matter what faith I profess in Esperañan lands?"

For a long time Ser Rodrigo did not answer. Alvar became aware that the merchant, ibn Musa, had come up to join them. He was standing on the other side of the fire listening. All through the camp Alvar could now hear the sounds and see the movements of men preparing themselves for sleep. It was very late.

At length, the Captain murmured, "We live in a fallen and imperfect world, Jehane bet Ishak. I am a man who kills much of the time, for his livelihood. I will not presume to give you answers. I have a question, though. What, think you, will happen to the Kindath in Al-Rassan if the Muwardis come?"

"The Muwardis are here. They were in Fezana today. In this camp tonight."

"Mercenaries, Jehane. Perhaps five thousand of them in the whole peninsula."

Her turn to be silent. The silk merchant came nearer. Alvar saw her glance up at him and then back at the Captain.

"What are you saying?" she asked.

Rodrigo crouched down now beside Alvar and plucked some blades of grass before answering.

"You spoke very bluntly a little while ago about our coming south to take Fezana one day. What do you think Almalik of Cartada and the other kings would do if they saw us coming down through the *tagra* lands and besieging Asharite cities?"

Again, the doctor said nothing. Her brow was knitted in thought.

"It would be the wadjis, first," said Husari ibn Musa softly. "They would begin it. Not the kings."

Rodrigo nodded agreement. "I imagine that is so."

"*What* would they begin?" Alvar asked.

"The process of summoning the tribes from the Majriti," said the Captain. He looked gravely at Jehane. "What happens to the Kindath if the city-kings of Al-Rassan are mastered? If Yazir and Ghalib come north across the straits with twenty thousand men? Will the desert warriors fight us and then go quietly home?"

For a long time she didn't answer, sitting motionless in

thought, and the men around the fire kept silent, waiting
for her. Behind her, to the west, Alvar saw the white moon
low in the sky, as if resting above the long sweep of the
plain. It was a strange moment for him; looking back,
after, he would say that he grew older during the course
of that long night by Fezana, that the doors and windows
of an uncomplicated life were opened and the shadowed
complexity of things was first made known to him. Not the
answers, of course, just the difficulty of the questions.

"These are the options, then?" Jehane the physician
asked, breaking the stillness. "The Veiled Ones or the
Horsemen of Jad? This is what the world holds in store?"

"We will not see the glory of the Khalifate again,"
Husari ibn Musa said softly, a shadow against the sky.
"The days of Rahman the Golden and his sons or even ibn
Zair amid the fountains of the Al-Fontina are gone."

Alvar de Pellino could not have said why this saddened
him so much. He had spent his childhood playing games
of imagined conquest among the evil Asharites, dreaming
of the sack of Silvenes, dreading the swords and short
bows of Al-Rassan. Rashid ibn Zair, last of the great khalifs, had put the Esperañan provinces of Valledo and
Ruenda to fire and sword in campaign after campaign
when Alvar's father was a boy and then a soldier. But here
under the moons and the late night stars the sad, sweet
voice of the silk merchant seemed to conjure forth reso-
nances of unimaginable loss.

"Could Almalik in Cartada be strong enough?" The doctor was looking at the merchant, and even Alvar, who
knew nothing of the background to this, could see how
hard this particular question was for her.

Ibn Musa shook his head. "He will not be allowed to
be." He gestured to the chests of gold and the mules that
had brought them into the camp. "Even with his mercenaries, which he can scarcely afford, he cannot avoid the payment of the *parias*. He is no lion, in truth. Only the
strongest of the petty-kings. And he already needs the
Muwardis to keep him that way."

"So what you intend to do, what I hope to do…are simply things that will hasten the end of Al-Rassan?"

Husari ibn Musa crouched down beside them. He smiled gently. "Ashar taught that the deeds of men are as footprints in the desert. You know that."

She tried, but failed, to return the smile. "And the Kindath say that nothing under the circling moons is fated to last. That we who call ourselves the Wanderers are the symbol of the life of all mankind." She turned then, after a moment, to the Captain. "And you?" she asked.

And softly Rodrigo Belmonte said, "Even the sun goes down, my lady." And then, "Will you not come with us?"

With a queer, unexpected sadness, Alvar watched her slowly shake her head. He saw that some strands of her brown hair had come free of the covering stole. He wanted to push them back, as gently as he could.

"I cannot truly tell you why," she said, "but it feels important that I go east. I would see King Badir's court, and speak with Mazur ben Avren, and walk under the arches of the palace of Ragosa. Before those arches fall like those of Silvenes."

"And that is why you left Fezana?" Ser Rodrigo asked.

She shook her head again. "If so, I didn't know it. I am here because of an oath I swore to myself, and to no one else, when I learned what Almalik had done today." Her expression changed. "And I will make a wager with my old friend Husari—that I will deal with Almalik of Cartada before he does."

"If someone doesn't do it before either of us," ibn Musa said soberly.

"Who?" Ser Rodrigo asked. A soldier's question, pulling them back from a mood shaped of sorrow and starlight. But the merchant only shook his head and made no reply.

"I must sleep," the doctor said then, "if only to let Velaz do so." She gestured and Alvar saw her old servant standing wearily a discreet distance away, where the firelight died in darkness.

All around them the camp had grown quiet as soldiers

settled in for the night. The doctor looked at Rodrigo. "You said you are sending men to attend to the dead of Orvilla in the morning. I will ride with them, to do what I can for the living, then Velaz and I will be on our way."

Alvar saw Velaz gesture to Jehane, and then noticed where the servant had made up a pallet for her. She walked over towards it. Alvar, after a moment, sketched an awkward bow she did not see, and went the other way, to where he usually slept near Martín and Ludus, the outriders. They were wrapped in their blankets, asleep.

He unfolded his own saddle blanket and lay down. Sleep eluded him. He had far too many things chasing and tumbling through his mind. He remembered the pride in his mother's voice the day she recounted the details of her first pilgrimage to seek Blessed Vasca's intercession for her brave son as he left home for the world of warring men. He remembered her telling how she had gone the last part of the journey on her hands and knees over the stones to kiss the feet of the statue of the queen before her tomb.

Animals, to be hunted down and burned from the face of the earth.

He had killed his first man tonight. A good sword blow from horseback, slicing down through the collarbone of a running man. A motion he had practised so many times, with friends or alone as a child under his father's eye, then drilled by the king's foul-tongued sergeants in the tiltyard at Esteren. Exactly the same motion, no different at all. And a man had fallen to the summer earth, bleeding his life away.

The deeds of men, as footprints in the desert.

He had won himself a splendid horse tonight, and armor better by far than his own, with more to come. The beginnings of wealth, a soldier's honor, perhaps an enduring place among the company of Rodrigo Belmonte. He had drawn laughter and approval from the man who might truly become his Captain now.

Nothing under the circling moons is fated to last.

He had crouched by a fire on this dark plain and heard

an Asharite and a Kindath woman of beauty and intelligence far beyond his experience, and Ser Rodrigo himself, as they spoke in Alvar's presence of the past and future of the peninsula.

Alvar de Pellino made his decision then, more easily than he would ever have imagined. And he also knew, awake under the stars and a more perceptive man than he had been this same morning, that he would be permitted to do this thing. Only then, as if this resolution had been the key to the doorway of sleep, did Alvar's mind slow its whirlwind of thought enough to allow him rest. Even then he dreamed: a dream of Silvenes, which he had never seen, of the Al-Fontina in the glorious days of the Khalifate, which were over before he was born.

Alvar saw himself walking in that palace; he saw towers and domes of burnished gold, marble columns and arches, gleaming in the light. He saw gardens with flower beds and splashing fountains and statues in the shade, heard a distant, otherworldly music, was aware of the tall green trees rustling in the breeze, offering shelter from the sun. He smelled lemons and almonds and an elusive eastern perfume he could not have named.

He was alone, though, in that place. Whatever paths he walked, past water and tree and cool stone arcade, were serenely, perfectly empty. Passing through high-ceilinged rooms with many-colored cushions on the mosaic-inlaid floors he saw wall hangings of silk and carvings of alabaster and olive wood. He saw golden and silver coffrets set with jewels, and crystal glasses of dark red wine, some filled, some almost empty—as if they had only that moment been set down. But no one was there, no voices could be heard. Only that hint of perfume in the air as he went from room to room, and the music—ahead of him and behind, tantalizing in its purity—alluded to the presence of other men and women in the Al-Fontina of Silvenes, and Alvar never saw them. Not in the dream, not ever in his life.

Even the sun goes down.

PART II

Chapter V

∽

"There's trouble coming," said Diego, as he ran past the stables and looked in briefly on the open stall. A soft rain was falling.

"What is it?" his mother asked, glancing quickly over her shoulder. She stood up.

"Don't know. A lot of men."

"Where's Fernan?"

"Gone to meet it, with some of the others. I told him already." Diego, having said what seemed necessary, turned to go.

"Wait!" his mother called. "Where's your father?"

Diego's expression was withering. "How would I know? Heading for Esteren, I guess, if he isn't there already. They must have got the *parias*, by now."

His mother, feeling foolish, and irritated because of that, said, "Don't use that tone with me. You sometimes do know, Diego."

"And when I do, I tell you," he said. "Got to run, Mother. Fernan will need me. He said to lock the gates and get everyone up on the walls."

With the swift, lethal grin that left her almost help-less—his father's smile—Diego was gone.

I am being ordered about by my sons now, thought Miranda Belmonte d'Alveda. Another adjustment in life, another measure of time passing. It was odd; she didn't *feel* old enough for this to be happening. She looked over at the frightened groom who was helping her with the mare.

"I'll finish here. You heard what he said. Tell Dario to get everyone up on the wall-walk. Including the women. Bring whatever weapons you can find. Build up the kitchen fires, we'll want boiling water if this is an attack." The old groom nodded anxiously and went off, moving as quickly as he could on a bad leg.

Miranda ran the back of a muddy hand across her forehead, leaving a streak of grime. She turned again, already murmuring to the laboring mare in the stall. The birth of a colt on a Valledan ranch was not a matter that could be superseded. It was the cornerstone of their fortune and their lives, of their whole society, really. The Horsemen of Jad, they were called, and with reason. A moment later the woman said to be the most beautiful in Valledo was on her knees again in the straw, her hands on the mare's belly, helping to bring another stallion of Belmonte's breed into the world.

She was distracted and worried, however. Not surprisingly. Diego was seldom wrong in his warnings, and almost never so when the vision had to do with trouble close to home. They had learned that, over the years.

When he'd been younger, still a child, and these foreknowings had begun it had been hard, even for him, to tell them apart from nightmares or childhood fears.

Once, memorably, he had awakened screaming in the middle of the night, crying that his father was in terrible danger, threatened by ambush. Rodrigo had been campaigning in Ruenda that year, during the bitter War of the Brothers, and everyone in the ranch house had sat awake the rest of a long night watching a shivering, blank-eyed boy, waiting to see if any further visions were vouchsafed him. Just before dawn, Diego's features had relaxed. "I was wrong," he'd said, gazing at his mother. "They aren't fighting yet. He's all right. I guess it was a dream. Sorry." He'd fallen fast asleep with the last apologetic word.

That sort of incident didn't happen any more. When Diego said he'd seen something, they tended to treat it as absolute truth. Years of living with a boy touched by the god would quell the skeptic in anyone. They had no idea how his visions came and they never spoke of them outside the family or the ranch. Neither his parents nor his brother had anything resembling this...this what? Gift or burden? Miranda had not, to this day, been able to decide.

There were tales of such people. Ibero, the family cleric, who presided over services in the new chapel Rodrigo had put up even before he'd rebuilt and expanded the ranch house, had heard of them. *Timewalkers*, he called those with such a vision. He named Diego blessed of Jad, but the boy's parents both knew that at different times and in different places, those visionaries had been burned, or nailed alive to wooden beams as sorcerers.

Miranda tried to concentrate on the mare, but her calming words, for the next little while, consisted of repeated, eloquent, curses directed at her absent husband. She had no idea what he'd done this time to bring danger to the ranch while his company was quartered at Esteren and the best of the band were south in Al-Rassan.

The boys can deal with trouble, his last letter had said breezily, after reporting a grim parting exchange with Count Gonzalez de Rada. Nothing about sending some of the soldiers to her for reinforcement. Of course not. Miranda, taught by Ibero in the first years of her marriage, prided herself on being able to read without assistance. She could also swear like a soldier. She had done so, reading that letter—to the messenger's discomfiture. She was doing so now, more carefully, not to disturb the mare.

Her boys were still boys, and their blithe, careless father and his men were far away.

By Jad's grace the foal was born healthy not long after that. Miranda waited to see if the mare accepted him, then she left the stall, grabbed an old spear propped in a corner of the stable, and hurried out into the rain to join the women and their half a dozen ranch hands on the wall-walk behind the wooden barricade.

As it turned out, it was just the women, Ibero the cleric and lame old Rebeño the groom that she joined. Fernan had already taken the ranch hands with him outside the walls. For an ambush, one of the house women said, hesitantly. Miranda, with no precious horses nearby, permitted herself a stream of entirely unmitigated profanity. Then she swiped at her brow again and climbed the wet steps to the high walk along the western side of the wall, to watch and wait. Someone offered her a hat to keep the rain from her eyes.

After a while she decided the spear was a waste of time, and exchanged it for a bow and a quiver full of arrows, taken from one of the six small guard shelters along the wall. There were no guards in the shelters. All the soldiers were in Esteren, or with Rodrigo.

The boys can handle trouble, he had written. Blithely.

She imagined seeing her husband riding home just then, emerging from the trees into the wide, grassy space before their walls. She imagined shooting him as he rode up.

The land around the Belmonte ranch was level and open in all directions, save to the west and southwest where Rodrigo's father and his grandfather before him had left a stand of oak and cedar undisturbed. Rodrigo hadn't touched the trees, either, though for a different reason.

There were holy associations with that wood, and with the pool in the midst of it, but young Fernan Belmonte had been taught by his father years ago, when he could first ride a proper horse, that the forest was deceptively useful for defense, as well.

"Think about it," he could remember his father saying. "If you wanted to attack this place unseen, which way would you approach?"

Fernan had looked around at the exposed grassland stretching in all directions. "Have to come through the trees to get close," he'd said. It was an easy answer.

"So we can be almost certain any attack will come that way, because otherwise, if our outriders aren't asleep, we'll be able to observe anyone's approach, won't we?"

"Or if Diego sees something," Fernan had added, "even if they come through the woods."

"That's true," his father had agreed briefly, though not happily.

In those early days his father and mother were still struggling to come to terms with what Diego could see and do. Fernan didn't have any such problems, but he knew Diego best of all, of course.

Years later, on a morning of soft, unseasonable summer rain he was with two of their friends and the six ranch hands in the twin gullies on either side of the natural exit from the woods. The gullies weren't natural, of course. Rodrigo's soldiers had hollowed them out in the grassy plain to make a place where they could lie unseen and watch anyone coming out of the trees.

Fernan had four other boys with bows posted halfway between the ranch buildings and the southern pastures where the mares and foals were that morning. There were two messengers with these four, to bring word if anyone appeared from the south. A last horseman was alone east of the ranch, just in case.

Diego, riding up breathlessly a few moments before, reported that he'd relayed instructions to their mother, who would be up on the wall, then, with the other women. She knew what to do. They were as ready as they could be. Fernan turned up his collar against the rain and sat in the gully under the wide brim of his hat, waiting.

There were two possibilities. If someone was approaching Rancho Belmonte with ill intent, they might be coming for the ranch compound and the people inside the walls or, more likely, they were here for the horses. Or both, Fernan corrected himself. But that would mean quite a lot of men, and in that case they might actually be in trouble. He didn't think that was the case. He wasn't much worried, in fact. He was thirteen years old.

"I have them," he heard his brother say softly. "They just entered the trees. I know who this is," Diego said.

"De Rada?" Fernan asked calmly. "The younger one?"

Diego nodded. They had both read their father's last letter.

Fernan swore. "That means we can't kill him."

"Don't see why not," said Diego matter-of-factly.

"Bloodthirsty child," Fernan grinned.

An identical grin on an identical face showed through the softly falling rain. Fernan was fifteen minutes older. He liked reminding Diego of that. Diego was hard to tease, however. Very little seemed to bother him.

"About twenty men," he said. "They're on the path in the woods now."

"Of course they are," said Fernan. "That's why the path is there."

꙳

He had lost his hat at some point, and during the period of walking north one of Garcia de Rada's boots had split at the heel. He was, accordingly, wet at crown and sole, riding through the copse of trees west of the Belmonte ranch compound. There seemed to be a rough trail leading through the wood; the horses were able to manage.

Despite his discomfort, he was fiercely happy, with a red, penetrating joy that made the long journey here seem as nothing now. His late, unlamented cousin Parazor had been a pig and a buffoon, and far too quick to voice his own thoughts on various matters. Thoughts that seemed all too frequently to differ from Garcia's own. Nonetheless, during the trek north from Al-Rassan, Garcia had been sustained in his spirit by a sense of gratitude to his slain cousin. Parazor's death at the hands of a lice-ridden Asharite peasant boy in a hamlet by Fezana was the event that would deliver Miranda Belmonte d'Alveda into Garcia's hands. And not only his hands.

Once Rodrigo Belmonte had recklessly ordered a de Rada of rank to be executed by a peasant child, against all codes of conduct among gentlemen in the three Jaddite kingdoms of Esperaña, he had exposed himself—and his family—to the response that blood demanded for such an insult.

The king could and would do nothing, Garcia was certain, if the de Rada took their just measure of revenge for what Rodrigo had done. The just measure was easy enough to calculate: horses for their own horses taken, and one woman taken in a rather different way for the execution of a de Rada cousin after he had sued for ransom. It was entirely fair. There were precedents in the history of Esperaña for a great deal more, in fact.

Garcia had resolved upon his course even while walking and stumbling north through darkness after the raid on Orvilla. Blood dripping from his torn cheek, he had kept himself going by visualizing the naked figure of Miranda Belmonte twisting beneath him, while her children were made to watch their mother's defilement. Garcia was good at imagining such things.

Twenty-four of his men survived Orvilla, with a dozen knives and assorted other small weapons. They took six mules late the next day from another hamlet, and a broken-backed nag from a small-farmer in an imprudently isolated homestead. Garcia claimed the horse, miserable as it was. He left the Asharite farmer and his wife and daughter for his companions. His own thoughts were a long way north and east already, over the border in Valledo, in the lands between the River Duric's source and the foothills of the Jaloña mountains.

There lay the wide rich grasslands where the horse herds of Esperaña had run wild for centuries until the first ranchers came and began to tame and breed and ride them. Among those ranchers the most famously arrogant, though far from the largest or wealthiest, were the Belmonte. Garcia knew exactly where he was going. And he also happened to know, from his brother, that the Captain's troops were quartered at Esteren this summer, nowhere near the ranch.

There ought to have been little danger for Belmonte in leaving his home unguarded. The Asharites had launched no raids north for twenty-five years, since the last brief flourishing of the Khalifate. The army of King Bermudo of

Jaloña had been beaten back across the mountains by the Valledans three years before and were still licking their wounds. And no outlaws, however rash or desperate, would dream of provoking the ire of the celebrated Captain of Valledo.

The ranch ought to have been perfectly safe behind its wooden stockade wall, even if guarded by boys with unbroken voices and a cluster of ranch hands deemed unworthy or too old for a place in the fighting company. On the other hand, Rodrigo Belmonte ought not to have ordered the death of a cousin of the de Rada. He ought not to have whipped the constable's brother. Such actions changed things.

When Garcia and his men had finally stumbled into Lobar, the first of the forts in the *tagra* lands, he had demanded and received—though with insolent reluctance—mounts and swords for all of them. The sweating commander of the garrison had advanced some feeble excuse about being left without sufficient weapons or horses for their own duties or safety, but Garcia had brooked none of that. The constable of Valledo, he'd said airily, would send them swords and better horses than the swaybacked creatures they were being given. He was in no mood for debate with a borderland soldier.

"That might take a long time," the commander had murmured obstinately. "All the way from Esteren."

"Indeed it might," Garcia had replied frigidly. "And if so?"

The man had bitten his lip and said nothing more. What could he have said? He was dealing with a de Rada, the brother of the constable of the realm.

The garrison's doctor, an ugly, raspy-voiced lout with a disconcerting boil on his neck, had examined Garcia's wound and whistled softly. "A whip?" he'd said. "You're a lucky man, my lord, or else someone extremely skillful was trying only to mark you. It is a clean cut and nowhere near your eye. Who did this?" Garcia had only glared, saying nothing. It was pointless, speaking to certain people.

The man prescribed an evil-smelling salve that stung like hornets, but did cause the swelling on Garcia's face to recede over the next few days. It was when he looked in a reflecting glass for the first time that Garcia decided that appropriate vengeance required the death of the Belmonte children, as well. After they had been forced to watch him with their mother.

It was the fierce anticipation of revenge that had driven him on from the *tagra* fort, with only a single day's rest. He sent four men north to Esteren, to report to his brother and to lay formal complaint before the king. That was important. If what he purposed to do was to have legal sanction, such a complaint had to be lodged against Rodrigo. Garcia was going to do this properly, and he was going to do it.

Two days after his main troop had parted from the four messengers he remembered that he'd forgotten to tell them to have weapons and horses sent back down for the garrison at Lobar. He briefly considered sending another pair of men north, but remembered the commander's insolence and elected not to bother. There would be time enough to pass on that word when he arrived in Esteren himself. It would do the pampered soldiers good to be short of weapons and mounts for a time. Perhaps someone else's boot might split at the heel.

Ten days later, in a wood on the land of Rancho Belmonte, rain was falling. Garcia's stocking was sopping wet through his cracked boot, and so were his hair and scratchy new beard. He'd been growing the beard since Orvilla. He would have to wear it for the rest of his life he'd realized by now; that, or look like a branded thief. Belmonte had intended that, he was certain of it.

Miranda Belmonte, he remembered, was very beautiful; all the d'Alveda women were. Rodrigo, that common mercenary, had made a far better marriage than he deserved. He was about to have visited upon him exactly what he did deserve.

Anticipation made Garcia's heart pound faster. Soon,

now. Boys and stable grooms were the guardians of this ranch. Rodrigo Belmonte was no more than a jumped-up fighting man who had been put back in his proper place since the ascension of King Ramiro. He had lost his rank of constable in favor of Garcia's brother. That had been only the beginning. He would learn now the cost of a feud with the de Rada. He would learn what happened when you marked Garcia de Rada as a common outlaw. Garcia touched his cheek. He was still using the salve, as instructed. The smell was ferociously unpleasant, but the swelling had subsided and the wound was clean.

The trees were very close together throughout the wood, but the curiously smooth path seemed to wind easily through them, wide enough in places for three men to ride abreast. They passed a pool of water on their right. In the grey afternoon the rain fell gently through the leaves, making droplets and ripples in the still surface of the water. It was said to be a holy place, for some reason. A few men made the god's sign of the disk as they rode by.

When the first horse fell and lay screaming on the ground with a broken leg, it seemed a malign accident. After two more such accidents, one of which left a rider with a dislocated shoulder, such an interpretation became less certain.

The path curved north through the sodden, dripping trees, and then, a little further on, swung back to the east again. In the grey, pale distance Garcia thought he could see an end to the trees.

He felt himself falling, while still in the saddle.

He had time to throw a startled glance upwards and see the bellies of the two horses that had been pacing on either side of his a moment ago. Then his mount crashed into the bottom of the pit that had been concealed in the center of the path and Garcia de Rada found himself scrambling about trying to dodge the thrashing hooves of a crippled, terrified horse. One man, quicker than the others, dropped to the ground and leaned over the edge of the pit. He extended an arm, and Garcia grabbed it and hauled himself up and out.

They looked down at the flailing horse a moment, then an archer released two arrows and the hooves stopped.

"This is no natural path," the archer said, after a moment.

"How very clever of you," said Garcia. He walked past the man, his boots squelching in the mud.

A trip wire claimed two more horses and cracked the skull of one thrown rider, and another pit took down a third stallion before they had reached the eastern end of the woods. They made it, though, and one had to expect *some* casualties on a raid of this sort.

Open grass lay before them. In the middle distance they could see the wooden wall that surrounded the ranch buildings. It was high but not high enough, Garcia saw. A skilled rider standing on the back of his mount could scale it; so could a foot soldier boosted by another. Only with a proper garrison could the ranch be defended from an attack launched by competent men. As they paused there at the edge of the trees the rain stopped. Garcia smiled, savoring the moment.

"How's that for an omen from the god?" he said to no one in particular.

He looked up pointedly at the horseman beside him. After a moment the man took his meaning and dismounted. Garcia swung up on the horse. "Straight for the ranch," he ordered. "First man over the wall has his choice of the women. We'll get their horses after. They owe us more than horseflesh."

And then, like the thundering, heroic ancestors of his lineage, Garcia de Rada drew his borrowed sword, thrust it high over his head, and kicked the horse from Lobar into a gallop. Behind him his companions gave a shout and streamed out of the woods into the greyness of the afternoon.

Six died in the first volley of arrows, and four in the second. No arrows came anywhere near Garcia himself, but by the time he was halfway to the walled enclosure of the ranch there were only five riders behind him and five others on foot running desperately across the wet and open grass.

Given such a sobering development it began to seem less and less prudent to be galloping furiously, well ahead of the others, towards the compound walls. Garcia slowed his horse and then, when he saw one of the running men shot in the chest, he reined his mount to a stop, too stupefied to give voice to the rage in his heart.

To his right, south, six horsemen now appeared, riding quickly. He looked back again and saw another group rise up, like wraiths, from two depressions he had not noticed in the level plain. These figures, armed with bows and swords, began walking steadily towards him, not hurrying. On the wall-walk of the ranch he saw a dozen or so people appear, also armed.

It seemed a good time to sheath his sword. The four horsemen left to him hastily did the same. The remaining runners straggled up, one clutching an injured shoulder.

The bowmen from the hollows surrounded them as the six riders drew near, and Garcia saw then, with disgust, that they were mostly boys. It gave him a flicker of hope, though.

"Dismount," said a well-built, brown-haired boy.

"Not until you say why you have just killed visitors without provocation," Garcia temporized, his voice stern and repressive. "What sort of conduct is that?"

The boy so addressed blinked, as if in surprise. Then he nodded his head briefly. Three archers shot Garcia's horse from under him. Kicking his feet out of the stirrups, de Rada leaped free just in time to avoid being crushed by the falling horse. He stumbled to one knee in the wet grass.

"I don't like having to kill horses," the boy said calmly. "But I can't remember the last time visitors approached us unannounced at full gallop with swords drawn." He paused, then smiled thinly. The smile was oddly familiar. "What sort of conduct is that?"

Garcia de Rada could think of nothing to say. He looked around. They had been bested by children and stable hands and it hadn't even been a fight.

The boy who was evidently leader here glanced at Garcia's riders. With unbecoming celerity they threw down their weapons and sprang from their mounts.

"Let's go," said a second boy.

Garcia glanced over at him, and then quickly back at the first one. The same face, exactly. And now he realized where he had seen that smile before.

"Are you Belmonte's sons?" he asked, trying to control his voice.

"I wouldn't bother with questions, were I you," said the second boy. "I'd spend my time preparing answers. My mother will want to speak with you."

Which was an answer to his question, of course, but Garcia decided it would be unwise to point that out. Someone gestured with a sword and Garcia began walking towards the compound. As he approached he realized, belatedly, that the figures on the wall holding bows and spears were women. One of them, wearing a man's overtunic and breeches, with mud stains on her cheeks and forehead, came along the wall-walk to stand above them, looking down. She had long, dark brown hair under a leather hat. She held a bow with an arrow nocked.

"Fernan, please tell me who this sorry figure is." Her voice was crisp in the grey stillness.

"Yes, Mother. I believe it is Ser Garcia de Rada. The constable's brother." It was the first of the boys who answered, the leader.

"Is it so?" the woman said icily. "If he is indeed of rank I will consent to speak with him." She looked directly at Garcia.

This was the woman he had been imagining pinned and naked beneath him since they'd left Orvilla. He stood in the wet grass, water seeping through his split boot, and looked up at her. He swallowed. She was indeed very beautiful, even in man's garb and stained with mud. That was, for the moment, the least of his concerns.

"Ser Garcia, you will explain yourself," she said to him. "In few words and very precisely."

The arrogance was galling, bitter as a wound. Garcia de Rada had always been quick-witted though, nor was he a coward. This was a bad situation, but no worse in its way than Orvilla had been, and he was back in Valledo now, among civilized people.

"I have a grievance with your husband," he said levelly. "He took horses belonging to my men and myself in Al-Rassan. We were coming to square that account."

"What were you doing in Al-Rassan?" she asked. He hadn't expected that.

He cleared his throat. "A raiding party. Among the infidels."

"If you met Rodrigo you must have been near Fezana, then."

How did a woman know these things? "Somewhat near," Garcia agreed. He was becoming a little uneasy.

"Then Rodrigo was dealing with you as the king's officer responsible for protecting that territory in exchange for the *parias*. On what basis do you claim a right to steal our horses?"

Garcia found himself unable, for the moment, to speak.

"Further, if you were captured and released without your mounts you will have given him your parole in exchange for a ransom to be determined by the heralds at court. Is that not so?"

It would have been pleasant to be able to deny this, but he could only nod.

"Then you have broken your oath by coming here, have you not?" The woman's voice was flat, her gaze implacable.

This was becoming ridiculous. Garcia's temper flared. "Your husband ordered a cousin of mine slain, *after* we surrendered and sued for ransom!"

"Ah. So it is more than horses and armor, is it?" The woman on the wall smiled grimly. "Would it not be the

king's task to judge whether his officer exceeded authority, Ser Garcia?" Her formality, in the circumstances, felt
like mockery. He had never in his life been so spoken to
by a woman.

"A man who slays a de Rada must answer for it," he
said, glaring up at her, using his coldest voice.

"I see," the woman said, undisturbed. "So you came
here to make him answer for it. How?"

He hesitated. "The horses," he replied finally.

"Just the horses?" And abruptly he realized where this
questioning was going. "Then why were you riding
towards these walls, Ser Garcia? The horses are pastured
south of us; they are not hard to see."

"I am tired of answering questions," Garcia de Rada
said, with as much dignity as he could manage. "I have
surrendered and so have my men. I am content to let the
king's heralds in Esteren determine fair ransom."

"You already agreed to that in Al-Rassan with Rodrigo,
yet you are here with drawn swords and ill intent. I regret
to say I cannot accept your parole. And tired or not, you
will answer my question. Why were you riding towards
these walls, young fellow?"

It was a deliberate insult. Humiliated, seething with
rage, Garcia de Rada looked up at the woman on the wall
above him, and said, "Your husband must learn that there
is a price to be paid for certain kinds of action."

There was a murmur from the boys and ranch hands.
It fell away into silence. The woman only nodded her head,
as if this was what she had been waiting to hear.

"And that price was to have been exacted by you?" she
asked calmly.

Garcia said nothing.

"Might I guess further, that it was to have been exacted
upon myself and my sons?"

There was silence in the space before the walls.
Overhead the clouds were beginning to lift and scatter as a
breeze came up.

"He had a lesson to learn," said Garcia de Rada grimly.

She shot him then. Lifting the man's bow smoothly, drawing and releasing in one motion, with considerable grace. An arrow in the throat.

"A lesson to learn," said Miranda Belmonte d'Alveda, thoughtfully, looking down from the wall at the man she had killed.

"The rest of you may go," she added, a moment later. "Start walking. You will not be harmed. You may give report in Esteren that I have executed an oath-breaker and a common brigand who threatened a Valledan woman and her children. I will make answer directly to the king should he wish me to do so. Say that in Esteren. Diego, Fernan, collect their mounts and arms. Some of the horses look decent enough."

"I don't think Father would have wanted you to shoot him," Fernan ventured hesitantly.

"Be silent. When I wish the opinions of my child I will solicit them," his mother said icily. "And your father may consider himself fortunate if I do not loose a like arrow at him when he ventures to return. Now do what I told you."

"Yes, Mother," said her two sons, as one.

As the boys and ranch hands hastened to do her bidding and Garcia de Rada's surviving companions began stumbling away to the west, the afternoon sun broke through the clouds overhead and the green grass grew bright, wet with rain in the branching light.

Chapter VI

∾

Esteren was a catastrophe of carpenters, masons, brick-layers and laborers. The streets were nearly impass-able, certainly so for a horse. The palace and the square in front of it resounded to the sounds of hammers, saws and chisels, shouted curses and frantic instructions. Complex, dangerous-looking equipment was being swung overhead or carried this way and that. It was widely reported that five workers had already died this summer. Nor was it overlooked by even the marginally observant that at least half of the project supervisors were Asharites brought north from Al-Rassan for this endeavor, at considerable cost.

King Ramiro was expanding his capital and his palace.

There had been a time, not very long ago, in fact, when the precarious kings of Esperaña—whether it was a whole country or divided as it now was again—ruled on the move. Cities were little more than hamlets; palaces a mockery of the name. Horses and mules, and heavy carts on the better-preserved of the ancient roads, were the trappings of monarchy as the courts settled in one town or castle after another through the round of the year. For one thing, the kings were constantly putting out brush-fires of rebellion, or hurrying to try at least to limit the predatory incursions of Al-Rassan. For another, resources in the hard-pressed Jaddite kingdoms in the glory years of the Silvenes Khalifate were scarcely such as to allow the monarchs to feed themselves and their retinues without spreading the burdens imposed by their presence.

Much had changed in twenty years; much, it was evident, was still changing here in Valledo, wealthiest and most fertile of the three kingdoms carved out of Esperaña for his sons by King Sancho the Fat. The current frenzy of construction in the royal city was only a part of it, funded by the infusion of *parias* money and, equally important, the absence of raiding from the south. It seemed that King Ramiro was now pursuing an entirely new definition of monarchy. Over and above everything else, this past year he had made it clear that he expected all the major nobility and clerics to show up in Esteren twice a year for his assizes, when law and policy were to be resolved and promulgated. It was rapidly becoming evident, as the new city walls grew higher, that Esteren was going to be more than merely the most established of his court residences.

And this business of *assizes*—a foreign word, Waleskan apparently—was more than slightly galling. Without his standing army it was unlikely in the extreme that Ramiro would have been able to compel attendance from his country nobility. But the army *was* here, well-paid and well-trained, and this particular summer almost every figure of importance in Valledo had elected to follow the path of prudence and show up.

Curiosity, among other things, could lead a man to travel. So could the promise of wine and food at court, and women for hire in increasingly urbanized Esteren. The dust and noise and the symbolism of a public submission to Ramiro's will were the prices to be paid. Given the turbulent and usually brief tenures of kings in Esperaña there was some reason to believe that the ambitions of King Sancho's most complex son might not trouble the world for too much longer.

In the meantime, it had to be conceded that he was offering entirely adequate entertainment. On this particular day Ramiro and his court and the visiting country lords were hunting in the king's forest southwest of Esteren, within sight of the Vargas Hills. Tomorrow they were all to attend the assizes at Ramiro's court of justice. Today they rode in summer fields and forests killing deer and boar for sport.

There was nothing, short of actual warfare, that the nobility of Esperaña could be said to enjoy more than a good hunt on a fair day. Nor could it be overlooked that the king, for all his modern, unsettling notions, was among the best of the riders in that illustrious company.

Sancho's son, after all, men could be overheard murmuring to each other in the morning sunshine. *Stands to reason, doesn't it?*

When King Ramiro dismounted to plant first spear in the largest boar of the day as it charged from the thicket where they had tracked it, even the most independent-minded and aggrieved of the rural lords could be seen banging swords or spears in approval.

When the boar was dead, the king of Valledo looked up and around at all of them. Covered in blood, he smiled. "As long as we are all gathered here," he said, "there is one small matter we might as well attend to now, rather than as part of the assizes tomorrow."

His courtiers and the country lords fell silent, looking sidelong at each other. Trust Ramiro to do something devious like this. He couldn't even let a hunt be a hunt. Looking around, a number of them realized, belatedly, that this clearing seemed carefully chosen, not merely a random place where a wild beast had gone to ground. There was space enough for all of them, and even a conveniently fallen log to which the king now strode, removing bloodied leather gloves and casually sitting down, very much as if on a throne. The outriders began dragging the boar away, leaving a smeared trail of blood on the crushed grass.

"Will Count Gonzalez de Rada and Ser Rodrigo Belmonte be so good as to attend upon me?" Speaking these words, King Ramiro used the language of high court formality, not of hunt and field, and with that the tenor and shape of the morning changed.

The two men named could be seen dismounting.

Neither betrayed, by so much as a flicker of expression, whether this development had been anticipated, or whether it was as much a surprise to them as to those assembled.

"We have all the witnesses we require," the king murmured, "and I am loath to submit men such as yourselves to a court hearing in the palace. It seems fitting to me that this affair be dealt with here. Does anyone object? Speak, if so."

Even as he was talking, two court officials could be seen approaching the tree trunk upon which the king was seated. They carried satchels and when these were opened parchments and scrolls were set down near the king.

"No objection, my liege," said Count Gonzalez de Rada. His smooth, beautiful voice filled the clearing. Servants were moving about now, pouring wine from flasks into what appeared to be genuine silver drinking goblets. The hunters exchanged glances yet again. Whatever else might be said of him, Ramiro was not stinting on the largess appropriate to a royal host. Some dismounted and handed their reins to the grooms. Others preferred to remain on horseback, reaching down for their wine and drinking in the saddle.

"I would never dream," said Rodrigo Belmonte, "of putting so many of the king's people to such a deal of preparation without acceding to whatever the king proposed." He sounded amused, but he often did, so that meant little.

"The allegations," said the king of Valledo, ignoring Ser Rodrigo's tone, "are substantial." King Ramiro, tall, broad-shouldered, prematurely greying, now wore an expression appropriate to a monarch faced with lethal hostility between two of the most important men in his realm. The festive, careening mood of the morning was gone. The gathered aristocracy, as they gradually came to terms with what was happening, were more intrigued than anything else; this sort of possibly mortal conflict provided the best entertainment in the world.

In the open space before the king's fallen tree Belmonte

and de Rada stood side by side. The former constable of the realm and the man who had succeeded him when Ramiro took the throne. The two men had placed themselves a careful distance apart. Neither had deigned to glance at the other. Given what was known about what had happened earlier this summer, the possibility of bloodshed was strong, whatever efforts the king might expend to avoid it.

A good many of those in attendance, especially those from the countryside, were rather hoping King Ramiro would fail in his attempt at resolution. A trial by combat would make this a memorable gathering. Perhaps, some thought optimistically, that was why this was taking place away from the city walls.

"It need hardly be said that Ser Rodrigo is responsible, in law, for the actions of his wife and children, given that they have no legal standing or capacity," the king said soberly. "At the same time, the sworn and uncontested statements of Ser Rodrigo indicate that the constable was formally put on notice here in Esteren that his brother would not be permitted to do harm in lands paying *parias* to us. In giving this notice," the king added, "Ser Rodrigo was acting properly, and as our officer."

More than one rancher or baron in that forest clearing found this entirely too legalistic for his taste. Why, they wondered, didn't Ramiro just let them fight it out here under the sun of Jad in the open spaces that best became a man—and have done with this dry-mouthed, dusty verbiage?

Such a pleasing possibility seemed to be becoming less likely with each passing moment. The smug expressions of the three yellow-robed clerics who had moved to stand behind the king indicated as much. Ramiro wasn't known for his close relations with the clerics of Jad, but these three certainly looked happy enough.

This, a number of the lords of Valledo thought, was what happened when a king became too full of himself, when he started making *changes*. Even that new throne room back in the palace, with its veined marble pillars:

didn't it look more like something designed for a decadent court in Al-Rassan than a Jaddite warrior hall? What was *happening* here in Valledo? It was an increasingly urgent question.

"Having considered the words of both parties and the depositions that have been rendered, including one by the Asharite silk merchant Husari ibn Musa of Fezana, we will be brief in our judgment."

The king's expression continued to match his stern words. The blunt fact was, if Belmonte and de Rada chose to pursue a blood feud Valledo was likely to be torn apart in the choosing of sides, and Ramiro's sweeping changes would fall like butchered bodies.

"It is our decision that Garcia de Rada—may his soul reside with Jad in light—violated both our laws and our obligations in his attack upon the village of Orvilla by Fezana. Ser Rodrigo's interruption of that attack was entirely proper. It was his duty, given the *parias* being paid to us for protection. It is also our judgment that ordering the death of Parazor de Rada was reasonable, if unfortunate, given the need to demonstrate both our fairness and our authority in Fezana. No blame or criticism falls to Ser Rodrigo for these things."

Count Gonzalez stirred restlessly, but grew still under the king's flat gaze. Light fell through the trees, dappling the clearing in bands of brightness and shadow.

"At the same time," King Ramiro went on, "Ser Rodrigo had no right to wound Garcia de Rada after accepting his surrender. It was not a deed that becomes a man of rank." The king hesitated and shifted a little on his tree trunk. Rodrigo Belmonte was looking straight at him, waiting. Ramiro met his gaze. "Further," he said, his voice quiet but extremely clear, "the public accusation he is reported to have made with respect to the death of my lamented brother King Raimundo is a slander beneath the dignity of both a nobleman and an officer of the king."

A number of men in that forest clearing caught their breath at this point. They had reached a matter that touched perilously near to Ramiro's position on the throne itself. The extremely abrupt death of his brother had never been satisfactorily explained.

Ser Rodrigo did not move, nor, at this juncture, did he speak. In the slanting sunlight his expression was unreadable, save for the frown of concentration as he listened. Ramiro picked up a parchment from the trunk beside him.

"That leaves us with an attack on women and children at Rancho Belmonte, and then the killing of a man who had sheathed his sword." King Ramiro looked down at the parchment for a moment and then back up. "Garcia de Rada had formally surrendered in Orvilla, and accepted terms of ransom to be determined. His obligation by his oath was to come straight here to Esteren and await the ruling of our royal heralds. Instead he recklessly stripped our defenses in the *tagra* lands to pursue a personal attack on Rancho Belmonte. For this," said the king of Valledo, speaking slowly and carefully now, "I would have ordered his public execution."

There came a swiftly rising sound of protest between the trees. This was new, a prodigious assertion of authority.

Ramiro went on, unruffled. "Dona Miranda Belmonte d'Alveda was a frail woman with no men to guard her, fearing for the lives of her young children in the face of an attack by armed soldiers." The king lifted another document from the tree trunk beside him and glanced at it. "We accept the deposition of the cleric Ibero that Ser Garcia specifically indicated to Dona Miranda that his purpose had been to exact vengeance upon herself and her sons, and not merely to claim horses from Rancho Belmonte."

"That man is a servant of Belmonte's!" the constable said sharply. The splendid voice was a shade less controlled than it had been before.

The king looked at him, and those in attendance, observing that glance, were made abruptly mindful that Ramiro was, in fact, a warrior when he chose to be. Cups of wine were raised and men drank thoughtfully.

"You were not invited to speak, Count Gonzalez. We have carefully noted that none of your brother's surviving men have contradicted this deposition. They appear to confirm it, in fact. We also note that by all accounts the attack was against the ranch itself, not the pastures where the horses were grazing. We are capable of drawing conclusions, especially when supported by the sworn word of a servant of the god. Given that your brother had already broken his parole by attacking the ranch, it is our judgment that Dona Miranda, a frightened, defenseless woman, is not to be censured for killing him and thus protecting her husband's children and possessions."

"You bring shame upon us with this," said his constable bitterly.

When Ramiro of Valledo was angry his face grew white. It did so now. He stood up, taller than almost every man in that clearing. Papers scattered beside him; a cleric hurried to collect them.

"Your brother brought you shame," the king said icily, "by refusing to accept your own authority, or ours. We do no more than rule upon his actions. Hear us, Gonzalez"— no title, the listeners realized, and wine goblets were lowered all about the clearing—"there will be no feud to follow from this. We forbid it. We make the following decree before these high-born of Valledo: Count Gonzalez de Rada, our constable, will stand surety with his own life for the next two years for the lives and safety of the family of Ser Rodrigo Belmonte. Should death or grievous harm befall any of them from any source during this time we will execute mortal judgment upon his body."

A buzzing again, and this one did not subside. Nothing remotely like this had ever been heard before.

"Why two years?"

It was Rodrigo. The first time the Captain had spoken since the hearing had begun. The angle of the sun had changed now; his face was in shadow. The question brought a silence, as the king's gaze turned to Belmonte.

"Because you will not be able to defend them," Ramiro

said levelly, still on his feet. "Officers of the king have a responsibility to exercise control both over their weapons and their words. You failed us twice over. What you did to Ser Garcia, and what you said to him, are direct causes of his death and this hard trouble in our kingdom. Rodrigo Belmonte, you are condemned to a term of exile from Valledo of two years. At the end of such time you may present yourself before us and we will rule upon your case."

"He goes alone, I take it?" It was Count Gonzalez, reacting quickly. "Not with his company?"

It mattered, all the listeners knew. Rodrigo Belmonte's company comprised one hundred and fifty of the finest fighting men in the peninsula.

Rodrigo laughed aloud, the sound almost shocking, given the tension among the trees. "You are most welcome," he said, "to try to stop them from following me."

King Ramiro was shaking his head. "I will not do so. Your men are yours and blameless in this. They may go or stay as they please. I will ask only for one undertaking from you, Ser Rodrigo."

"After exiling me from my home?" The question was pointed. Rodrigo's face was still in shadow.

"Even so." It was interesting how calm the king was. A number of men reached the same conclusion at the same time: Ramiro had anticipated almost every point of this exchange. "I do not think you can truly quarrel with our ruling, Ser Rodrigo. Take your company, if you will. We ask only that they not be used in warfare against us."

Silence again, as every man struggled to think through the implications. It could be seen that Rodrigo Belmonte was staring down at the forest floor, his forehead creased with thought. The king gazed upon him, waiting.

When Rodrigo looked up his brow had cleared. He lifted his right hand towards the sky overhead, and shaped the sun circle of the god with thumb and fingers. "I swear by holy Jad," he said formally, "that I will never lead my company in warfare into the lands of Valledo."

It was almost what the king had asked. Almost, but not

quite, and Ramiro knew it.

"And if you find a Valledan army beyond our borders?" he asked.

"I can swear no oath," Rodrigo said quietly. "Not an honorable one. Not if I am forced to take service elsewhere for my livelihood and that of my company. My lord, this is not," he added, meeting the king's gaze squarely, "a departure of my choosing."

A long stillness.

"Do not take service with Cartada," said the king at length, his voice extremely soft.

Rodrigo stood motionless, visibly thinking.

"Really, my lord? You will begin so soon? Within two years?" he asked cryptically.

"It may be so," Ramiro said, no less ambiguously.

Men were struggling to understand, but the two of them seemed to be in the midst of a private exchange.

Rodrigo was nodding his head slowly. "I suppose. I will regret being elsewhere if it does happen." He paused. "I will not serve Almalik of Cartada. I don't like what he did in Fezana. I will not serve him there, or anywhere else."

Fezana.

At the mention of the name a few men began to nod their heads, looking at their tall, proud king. A glimmering of what this seemed to be about began to come to them, like shafts of the god's sunlight falling into the clearing. Ramiro wasn't a jurist or a cleric, after all, and there might be more than hunting in the days to come.

"I accept your oath," said the king of Valledo calmly. "We have never found you lacking in honor, Ser Rodrigo. We see no reason to doubt it now."

"Well, I am grateful for that," said the Captain. It was impossible to tell if there was mockery in his voice. He took a step forward, fully into the light. "I do have a request of my own."

"Which is?"

"I will ask Count Gonzalez to swear before the god to guard my family and possessions as if they were his own while I am away. That is enough for me. I need no binding of his death. The world is a dangerous place, and the days to come may make it more so. Should accident befall a Belmonte, Valledo could ill afford to lose its constable as well. I am content with his sworn word, if it pleases the king."

He was looking at the constable, as he spoke. It could be seen that de Rada was taken by surprise.

"Why?" he asked softly; an intimate question in a very public space. The two men faced each other for the first time.

"I believe I just told you," Rodrigo replied. "It isn't so difficult. Valledo has enemies in all directions. With your life in bond someone might strike at this kingdom through my family. I would not want the king bound to your death in such a cause. I think it places them more at risk, not less. I need not like you, de Rada, to trust your word."

"Despite my brother?"

The Captain shrugged. "He is being judged by Jad."

It wasn't an answer, and yet it was. After another brief silence, in which the sound of birdsong could clearly be heard from the trees around, the constable raised his right hand in the same gesture Rodrigo had used.

"Before Jad, and before my lord the king of Valledo, and before all men here, I make oath that the family of Rodrigo Belmonte shall be as my own from this day until his return from exile. I take this upon my honor and that of my lineage." The sonorous voice filled and defined the forest space.

Both men turned back to the king. Unsmiling, standing very tall, he looked down upon them. "I am unused to having my decrees superseded by the parties involved," he murmured.

"Only you can do that," Rodrigo said. "We merely offer an alternative for the king to accept or reject."

And now it could be seen that Ramiro smiled at the man he had just condemned to exile. "So be it," he said. "We accept these oaths."

Both men bowed. Rodrigo straightened and said, "Then, with your permission, my lord, I will make immediate arrangements to depart, much as I might enjoy continuing to hunt with you."

"One moment," said the king. "Where *will* you go?" His voice betrayed, for the very first time, a shadow of doubt.

Rodrigo Belmonte's grin, caught by the falling sunlight, was wide, and unmistakably genuine. "I haven't the least idea," he said. "Though on my way to wherever I go I'll have to stop and deal with a frail and terrified woman first." His smile faded. "You might all pray for me," said the Captain of Valledo.

Then he turned, collected his horse's reins from a groom, mounted up and rode alone from the clearing back the way they had come through the trees.

༄

Ines, the queen of Valledo, was clasping a well-worn sun disk and listening, eyes devoutly closed, as her favorite cleric read aloud from the Book of the Sons of Jad—the passage about the end of the world, as it happened—when her husband's messenger arrived and indicated the king would presently be with her.

Apologetically, she bade her religious counsellor suspend his reading. The man, not unused to this, marked her Book and laid it aside. With a sigh, a pointed glance and a bow to the queen he withdrew from the chamber through an inner doorway. It was well known that King Ramiro was uneasy with intensities of faith, and the queen's best efforts over many years had done nothing to amend this unfortunate circumstance.

It had everything to do, Ines had long since decided, with the time when he had lived among the infidels. All three of the difficult, ambitious sons of King Sancho had spent time exiled among the Asharites, but only Ramiro seemed to have come back with a taste for the ways of Al-Rassan and a suspicious softness in matters of faith. It was perhaps an irony, and perhaps not, that his father had arranged a marriage for him with the pious younger daughter of the king of Ferrieres across the mountains to the east.

Ines, whose childhood aspiration had been to be accepted among the Daughters of Jad in one of the great retreats, had accepted her betrothal only upon the advice of her spiritual counsellors, including the High Clerics of Ferrieres. It was a great opportunity, they had told her. A chance to be of service to the god and to her country, both. The young man she was marrying would likely one day rule a part, at least, of Esperaña, and Ines could use her position to influence the path of worship in that troubled land.

The clerics had looked entirely prescient when Ramiro was named ruler of mountainous Jaloña in the three-way division of his father's last testament. And then even more so when, after the mysterious death of his brother Raimundo, her husband had quickly moved west and claimed the crown of Valledo as well. He hadn't been able to hold both kingdoms—not yet, at least—for his uncle Bermudo had promptly risen in Jaloña and seized that throne, but Valledo, as everyone knew, was the greater prize.

What the clerics hadn't told her—because they hadn't known—was that the young man she was marrying was fiercely intelligent, ambitious, luridly imaginative in carnal acts and so much a pragmatist in what ought to have been firm doctrines of holy faith that he might as well have been an infidel.

As if on cue to this distressing line of thought, the king appeared in her doorway, his hair and clothing still damp as further evidence of her last reflection: what self-respecting man bathed as often as King Ramiro did? Not even the Asharites in their far-off eastern homelands did so. Self-indulgent bathing rituals were characteristic only of the sybaritic courts of Al-Rassan, where they had not even the decency to observe the ascetic strictures of their own faith.

Too much time in the courts of the south, Queen Ines thought again, and at a point in life when he had been young and impressionable. She glanced sidelong at her husband, not wishing to encourage him with a fuller appraisal. It was a very handsome man who filled her doorway, no one could deny that much. Tall, well-built, square-jawed. If his hair was greying early, his moustache was yet black and there was no evidence of faltering reserves of martial or political stamina or subtlety.

Or of faltering in more private dimensions either.

With a brief gesture, if a courteous one, the king dismissed her maidservants and slaves and the two guards by the doors. Ramiro waited until they had all taken their leave then strode across the new carpet to stand before Ines's low seat. He was grinning. She knew that smile.

"Come, my wife," he said. "Events of this morning have made me amorous."

Ines refused to meet his eyes. Almost everything made him amorous, she had learned. Clutching her sun disk like a small shield, she murmured, "I'm sure it was a comely boar you slew. But was there no one of my lord's concubines who might have assuaged his appetites before he came to trouble me?"

Ramiro laughed. "Not today. Today I have a desire to see and touch the body of my life's own companion as consecrated by our most holy god. Come, Ines, let us make sport, then after I will tell you what happened in the wood."

"Tell me now."

Her problem, as she had all too often been forced to admit to her intimate counsellors, was that Ramiro was a difficult man to deny. They had urged her to use his desire for her as a means of drawing him towards a truer faith but, to the queen's endless chagrin, the effect of such encounters was rather the opposite: whether it was his natural fervor or the skills he had learned—most probably among the courtesans of Al-Rassan—Ramiro was dismayingly adept at subverting her best intentions.

Even now, in the middle of a hot summer's day, with

carpenters hammering and a barrage of shouting outside, and with the stern words of the world's end still echoing in her ears, Queen Ines found herself breathing a little more quickly at the images her husband's presence had conjured forth within her. After almost twenty years and with the full knowledge of the impious evil of his ways, this was still true. And Ramiro could read it in her as easily as her clerics could read from Jad's most holy Books. He reached down now, not ungently, and plucked the god disk from her clasp.

"Hold me like that," he murmured, laying the disk aside and lifting her to her feet with his strong hands. "Love me the way you love the god." Then he slipped his arms around her and drew her close so that she was made inescapably aware that the king of Valledo was wearing nothing at all beneath his white silk robe. And that pressing awareness, as he tilted her head to meet his kiss, brought back for Ines all the wildly disturbing sensations she always felt when this happened.

I will have to atone, she told herself as their lips met.

He began unravelling the cloth that bound the coils of her red hair. She would seek holy counsel and support later. Her own hands, unbidden, as if bearing weights, came up along his robe, feeling the hard body beneath. Ramiro drew back, then lowered his head again hungrily. He bit at the corner of her lip.

There would surely be wise, consoling thoughts from her advisors of the soul later, the queen told herself. Her fingers seemed now to be laced behind his head. She pulled his hair, not gently at all. The king laughed. He smelled of some eastern spice. That, too, was unsettling. It was unfair. She would need such a great deal of help to guide her back to the pure realm of the spirit. For the moment, though, as her husband smoothly lifted and then carried her over to the wide couch he'd had brought into her new suite of rooms, the queen of Valledo was rather more preoccupied, to her great and enduring confusion, with increasingly explicit matters of the flesh.

At one point she cried his name aloud, and at another, suffused with her eternal mixture of desire and shame, she found herself riding above his supine form, knowing that this mode of congress was yet another decadent legacy of Al-Rassan, but unable to stop herself from gasping aloud with the pleasure it gave her. Pleasure of the world, she told herself, somewhat desperately, moving up and down upon him while his fingers teased and circled her breasts. Of the world. *Only* of the world. The realm of the god was otherwise. It was eternal, holy, golden, transcendent, shining, not bound to the mortal bodies of frail—

"*Oh my!*" said the queen of Valledo then, as if in great surprise, and held herself extremely still.

The second cry that escaped her a moment later was, in its own way, an admission.

"Tell me about what happened," she said, some time after.

He liked to lie with her, entangled indecently, after congress. That much, at least, she was able to deny him. Ines had donned a robe and had forced him to clothe himself as well, before summoning one of her women with refreshments. Amused, satiated, Ramiro had obeyed.

The woman brought ale for him and a pear infusion for the queen and then withdrew. Now Ramiro lay indolently upon the couch while Ines sat on a nearby bench, needlework in hand. She was making a new pouch for her sun disk, to hang from her belt.

"It went surprisingly well," Ramiro said, turning on his side, his head propped on one hand. He looked at her with such frank admiration it brought color to her cheeks again. "Thank you, by the way. I do prefer it when you leave your hair down," he said.

She hadn't intended to. An oversight. She was wrongfully proud of her hair, and as a penance kept it tied tightly back almost all the time. Self-consciously she pushed a strand from her eyes. He would laugh at her if she began binding it up now, she knew.

"This morning," she said firmly. "We are talking about

this morning."

He grinned. Sipped from his flagon. The noise outside and below stairs continued. Among other things, he was expanding the palace baths, after the Al-Rassan fashion, with hot and cold pools, and a massage room. It was a scandal.

"They both accepted my judgment," he said. "There was a bit of noise when I said I would have executed Garcia, but no one actually spoke out. Count Gonzalez is now bound by oath to defend Belmonte's family for two years. No blood feud. He has sworn it in public."

"You announced he would die if they died?" He had discussed this with her some days before. In fairness, she had to concede that he was never reluctant to confide in her. They had even discussed, all those years ago, his move into Valledo from Jaloña. He spent a fair bit of time in her rooms, telling her his thoughts. Certainly more than her father had ever confided in her mother.

In fact, Ines suddenly realized, looking at the man on her couch, if he hadn't been so much an infidel in the most important matters, she might have been able to name her husband a paragon among men.

Her expression must have softened. He looked amused again. "I meant to tell you earlier. I love looking at your breasts from below," he said. "They change from pears to melons, did you know?"

"I really hadn't noticed," she said tartly. "Must we expound upon it? Is the constable to die if a Belmonte does?"

Ramiro shook his head. "I proclaimed it, and the count would have accepted, I think, but then Rodrigo asked me to withdraw that sanction. Said if Gonzalez swore to their defense it was enough for him. I wonder...could he be tired of his wife, do you think? They've been married a long time."

"Less long than we have," Ines replied. "And if you think he's tired of her you are a great fool. It is simply that Ser Rodrigo Belmonte is a pious man, a believer in the power of the god, and he was willing to trust to Jad's will and Gonzalez's public oath. It doesn't seem surprising to me at all."

Ramiro made no reply for a moment. "Actually, what he said was that he didn't want our enemies able to force me to execute the constable by harming Rodrigo's family. I hadn't thought of that."

Neither had Ines. She'd had years of this sort of dialogue, though. "He just said that because you wouldn't have listened if he offered a reason to do with faith."

"Probably not," Ramiro agreed, far too placidly. He looked at her happily. "I still think he may be tired of his wife. He asked us to pray for him because he had to go home."

"You see?" said Ines swiftly. "He believes in the power of prayer."

The king spoiled her triumph by laughing aloud.

Outside, the banging and rumbling noises of construction continued unabated. Esteren's castle was being turned into a veritable palace, fashioned, all too clearly, after the courts of the south. In a way it was an insult to the god. She did like the plans for her expanded quarters though.

"Again, my lady?" the king of Valledo asked his wife.

She bit at her lip. "If you come to chapel with me, after."

"Done," he said, rising from the couch.

"And speak the prayers aloud with me," she added quickly.

"Done." He came over to stand above her seat, but then he sank to his knees before her, reaching up with one hand to touch her hair.

"And you will not make any clever comments about the liturgy."

"Done. Done. Done, Ines."

It seemed a fair bargain for a summer's day. She laid her needlework aside. She even granted him a smile. The work of Jad here in Esperaña had turned out to be long and unexpectedly complex. It had led her down paths she could never have foreseen back at home in Ferrieres twenty years ago, a girl dreaming at night not of a man but a god. She slid from the bench to join her husband on the newly carpeted floor. She liked the carpet, too. It had come all the way north from Seria, in Al-Rassan.

∽

Somewhat rashly, in view of all the circumstances, Rodrigo Belmonte elected to ride on alone through the last night in order to arrive home at dawn, ahead of his company, which had travelled with him from Esteren.

He was one of the most formidable fighting men in the peninsula, and the country here was about as safe as any open country was in thinly populated Valledo, which is to say it was not, in fact, particularly safe at all.

Both of the wandering moons the Kindath named as sisters of the god were in the sky, and both were close to full. In the far distance, beyond the ranches and the rising foothills, the faint outline of the mountains of Jaloña could be seen. Given bright moonlight and a brilliantly clear sky, Rodrigo would have been easily visible from a long way off as he rode alone over the grazing lands where the the horses of Valledo still ran wild.

Of course that meant he should have been able to see trouble coming from equally far off, and his black horse was able to outrun anything on that plain. If anyone was foolish enough to attack him, once they realized who he was.

Someone, therefore, would have had to have been almost insanely reckless, and the Captain uncharacteristically lost in night thoughts, for him to be ambushed by moonlight so near to home.

They waited until his horse was in the middle of the stream—the Carriano—that formed the western boundary of Rancho Belmonte. He was, in fact, almost on his own land.

In late summer the stream ran shallow, not even up to the black horse's withers at the deepest point. They were walking across, not swimming. But when bowmen rose up, like ghosts of the dead, from the reeds at the river's edge, Rodrigo knew that someone had given thought to this. Swift as his mount was, the water was going to slow him for the first few seconds. Against archers that would be enough.

With the first words spoken his thought was confirmed.

"We will shoot the horse, Ser Rodrigo. Do not try to run."

He didn't want them to shoot the horse.

He looked around. A dozen men, all with kerchiefs pulled up and hat brims low to disguise their faces. He couldn't see their mounts. Downstream probably.

"Dismount. In the water." The same man spoke again, his voice muffled behind the kerchief.

"If you know my name you know you are dead if you pursue this folly," Rodrigo said softly. He didn't get off his horse yet, but nor did he let it move.

"Your horse is dead if you remain astride. Get down."

He did so, swinging forward deliberately, where it was shallower. The water was up to his waist.

"Throw your sword on the bank."

He hesitated.

"We will not shoot you, Ser Rodrigo. We will kill the horse. Throw your sword."

"There are close to one hundred and fifty men behind me," Rodrigo said levelly, but he was removing his sword belt as he spoke.

"They are half a night's ride behind you."

The speaker seemed remarkably well informed. Rodrigo tossed his sword and belt into the grass, carefully clear of the stream. He marked where they landed, but then someone moved to pick them up, so it didn't matter.

"Now walk. Towards us. Leave the horse where he is. Someone will take him."

"He won't take kindly to another hand," Rodrigo warned.

"That is our difficulty, then," the spokesman said. "We are accustomed to dealing with horses. Come."

He went, sloshing out of the stream and through the reeds to the grass. They took him, insultingly, further east onto his own lands. There was no one about, however, not at the very perimeter of the estate, and not in the middle of the night. They led him for several hundred paces, bows levelled constantly, though at the horse not at him. Someone was clever here.

They came to one of the range huts. Like all the huts it was small, unfurnished, no more than a primitive shelter for the herders from rainstorms or the snows that sometimes came in winter.

Someone lit a torch. They pushed him inside. Six of them came with him, faces hidden, not speaking save for the leader. They took both his knives: the one in his belt and the one in his boot. They bound his hands in front of him, and then someone hammered a stake into the packed earth floor of the hut and they forced him to lie down and pulled his bound hands up over his head and looped the thongs through the stake. They pulled off his boots and tied his ankles together the same way. Another stake was driven and the cord that bound his feet was looped across this. He was unable to move, hands high over his head, legs bound together and pinned to the earth.

"What do you think will happen," Rodrigo said, breaking the silence, "when my company comes to this ranch tomorrow and learns I have not arrived?"

The leader, standing by the doorway watching all that was being done, merely shook his head. Then he gestured to the others. The long torch was planted in the ground and they left him there in the hut, trussed like a sacrifice.

He heard footsteps receding, then the sound of horses coming up and then being ridden away. Pinned helplessly to the earth on his own land, Rodrigo Belmonte lay in silence for a few moments, listening to the horsemen riding off. And then, helplessly, but in an entirely different sense, he began to laugh. It was difficult to catch his breath with his hands pulled up so high; he whooped, he gasped, tears streamed from his eyes.

"The god burn you, Rodrigo!" said his wife storming into the hut. *"How did you know?"*

He went on laughing. He couldn't stop. Miranda carried, of all things, an arrow in one hand. She was dressed in black, in the mannish clothing that was her custom on the ranch. She glared at him in fury as he howled. Then she stepped closer and stabbed him in the thigh with her arrow.

"Ouch!" exclaimed the Captain of Valledo. He looked down and saw blood welling through the rip in his trousers.

"I hate when you laugh at me," she said. "Now, how did you know? Tell me, or I'll draw blood again."

"I have no doubt," Rodrigo said, struggling to regain his self-control. He had not seen her in almost half a year. She looked unfairly magnificent. She was also, quite evidently, in a substantial rage. He concentrated, for his own safety, on her question.

"The boys did well, actually. A few things. Corrado heard other horses as we came up to the stream. I didn't, their mounts were left far enough away to avoid that, but a war-horse can be trained to give warning."

"What else?"

"Two men let their shadows show in the water. With doubled moonlight one has to be careful."

"Anything else?" Her voice had grown even colder.

He considered it, and decided that two things were enough. He was still trussed up, and she still had an arrow. The other matters could wait.

"Nothing, Miranda. I told you, they did very well."

She stabbed him again, hard, in the other leg.

"Jad's light!" he gasped. "Miranda, will you—"

"Tell truth. What else?"

He drew a breath. "I recognized the whicker of Fernan's horse when they brought him up outside. They knew too well where my boot knife was. They were too gentle when they tied me. And this whole affair was too precisely located along the stream to be an improvised ambush. It had to be Diego seeing me and knowing which way I was coming. Is that enough, Miranda? May I get up now? May I kiss you?"

"Yes, no, and possibly later," said his wife. "Have you any idea how angry I am, Rodrigo?"

Bound and bleeding on the earth, Rodrigo Belmonte was able to say, quite truthfully, "Some idea, yes."

His expression must have been diverting, because his wife, for the first time, showed an indication of being amused.

She suppressed it quickly. "Armed men came for us, you uncaring bastard. You left me with children and range hands thirty years past their usefulness."

"That isn't just," he said. "I'm truly sorry you were frightened. You know I am. I didn't think even Garcia de Rada would do anything so stupid as an attack here, and I did think you and the boys were equal to whatever might come. I told you that."

"*I told you that*," she mimicked. "How thoughtful of you."

"If the boys are going to follow me," he said levelly, "they will have to learn to handle matters of this sort, Miranda. You know it. They'll be marked as my sons the minute they join a company—mine or anyone else's. They'll be pushed, and challenged. I can't do anything about that except help make them equal to those challenges when they come. Unless you want them both to take vows and join the clerics?"

"Twenty-four horsemen attacked us, Rodrigo. What if Diego hadn't seen them?"

He said nothing. The truth was, he'd been having nightmares about that since word of the raid had come to them in Esteren. He didn't want to say it, but there must have been more in his expression than he thought, because Miranda abruptly tossed her arrow aside and knelt on the earth beside him.

"I see," she said quietly. "You were frightened, too. All right. Half a mistake, half testing the boys. I can live with that."

"I'm not sure if I can," he said, after a moment. "If anything had happened..."

"That's why I shot him. I know you wouldn't have done it. I know it wasn't very honorable, but a man who would do what he did...He wouldn't have stopped, Rodrigo. He would have come back. Better I killed him than that you had to, *after* he'd done something to us."

He nodded his head. It wasn't easy, bound as he was. She made no movement to release him.

"I'm sorry you had to kill someone."

She shrugged. "Given who it was, it was easier than I would have thought. The boys had to kill men, too."

"In the world they are growing into, that was bound to happen."

"I would have preferred it not be so soon, Rodrigo."

He said nothing. She settled back a little, looking at him, still making no move to untie his bonds.

"The king called you a frail woman."

She smiled at that. "You didn't disagree?"

"I did, actually. I asked them to pray for me because I had to go home and tell you what has happened."

"We heard. You sent the messenger so I'd have time to calm down, I suppose."

His mouth crooked. "It doesn't seem to have worked very well. Untie me, Miranda. I'm stiff and both my legs are bleeding."

She made no movement. "Two years' exile? It could have been worse, I suppose. Where will you go?"

"Is this the way to discuss such matters?"

"It will do well enough. Where will you go, Rodrigo?"

He sighed. "Not Jaloña, obviously, and I still wouldn't be welcome in Ruenda. I could take the company out of the peninsula to Ferrieres or Batiara but I won't. Things might be starting to happen here, and I don't want us to be too far away. South, then. Al-Rassan again."

"Where?" She was concentrating. There seemed to be a rock under the small of his back.

"Ragosa, I think. King Badir can use us. He's hard-pressed between Cartada and Jaloña and outlaws raiding from the south. There's money to be made."

"Isn't Ragosa where your doctor went?"

He blinked. "Good for you. She isn't my doctor, but yes, it is where she went. I still want to try to enlist her."

"I'm sure. She's very pretty, didn't you say?"

"I said nothing remotely resembling such a thing. Am I a complete idiot?"

"Yes. Is she?"

"What?"

"Is she pretty?"

Rodrigo drew another careful breath, not easy given his position. "Miranda, I am married to the most beautiful woman I know. I am not a man to fairly judge such things in others. She's comely enough. Blue eyes, rare for a Kindath."

"I see. You noticed them?"

"Miranda."

"Well, you did." Her expression was deceptively mild. He had learned to mistrust that expression. The rock under his back seemed, improbably, to have grown larger.

"I am trained to notice things, Miranda. About men and women. If I had been better trained fifteen years ago I would have noticed you were a cruel and ungenerous woman."

"Perhaps," she said placidly. "Too late now. Tell me, what do I always say when you go away?"

"Oh, Jad! Don't start again. I *know* what you always—"

"Say it. Or I'll find my arrow again. I promised myself I'd put an arrow in you the day I shot Garcia de Rada. Two pinpricks hardly count."

"Yes they do," he said. "And those weren't pinpricks." He stopped at what he read in her expression, then said quietly, "I know what you tell me. That if I bed another woman you'll either bed another man or kill me."

She was smiling, as if encouraging a child's display of memory. "Good. And since I don't want to bed another man...?" she prompted.

Rodrigo sighed. "You'll kill me. Miranda, I *know* this. Will you let me up?"

She seemed to be thinking about it at least, which was

a positive development.

"No," she said, at length. "Not yet. I think I like you this way."

"What does that mean?" he asked, alarmed.

But she had shifted forward from where she was, beside him on her knees. She looked appraisingly down at him a moment, then calmly tore open his shirt. His eyes widened. Her hands seemed to be busy with the points and drawstrings of his trousers. It became difficult to breathe.

"Miranda," he said, "there's a rock under my back."

"Oh well," she murmured with exaggerated solicitude, "we can't have that, can we?" But she did reach under to remove what turned out to be a laughably small stone.

"Untie me, love. We'll do better if I'm free."

"No, we won't," said his joy, his torment, his wife, the fierce bright light of his days. "We'll do very well with you exactly as you are."

She had finished with his garments. She began removing her own.

"See what I mean?" she said, smiling down at his sex. As she spoke, she slipped off her black tunic. She was wearing nothing beneath. Her small breasts were smooth and firm in the torchlight.

"You see?" she said again. He did, of course.

Eventually he closed his eyes, but not before an interval had passed during which a number of movements on her part took place, bringing him to a point where he couldn't have judged the passage of time, or anything else for that matter.

The torch had burned out by then, he knew that much. There was nothing to see. Only to feel. Mouth and fingers. Her teeth, in unexpected places. The close, perfect shelter of her sex after so long.

"Shall I let you go?" she asked eventually, a breath in his ear.

"Never," said Rodrigo, eyes still closed.

Still later, the white moon, descending, slanted through a wide chink in the wall boards and a beam of light fell upon them both. He lay with Miranda upon him, her head on his chest, her dark hair loose, cloaking them both. He felt the rise and fall of her breathing, and drew in the scent and the feel of her—intoxicating as unmixed wine.

"Oh, well," she murmured, as if continuing a dialogue. "I suppose we *could* use a good doctor."

"*I* certainly could," he said, with feeling.

That made her laugh. At some point, though it was hard to mark the change, the laughter turned to tears. He could feel them falling on his chest.

"Two years is a long time," she said. "Rodrigo, am I being unfair to you?"

"I don't expect to be two years without you," he said. "One way or another."

She said nothing. Her tears fell in silence. He hesitated, then finally brought down his arms—he had worked free of the bonds in the first moments after being tied—and wrapped them around her.

"Oh, burn you, Rodrigo," she whispered, when she realized what he'd done, but she didn't say it severely this time. A moment later, she murmured, dealing with the hardest sorrow of time passing, "They are so young."

He stroked her hair, down and down her back.

"I know," he whispered gently. "I know, my love."

He had killed his own first man when he was twelve. He didn't tell her that. Not now.

∽

"Are they still in the hut?" Fernan asked.

"Uh-huh," said Diego.

"What do you think they're doing?"

"Now, now," said Ibero the cleric hastily. "That isn't a proper question!"

"I couldn't answer it, anyhow," said Diego, laughing. "Ibero, you look genuinely formidable, by the way."

Their longtime cleric's expression was uncertain for a moment, then guardedly pleased. He was indeed remarkably altered: his face daubed with mud under a black hat, garbed like an outlaw, with inserts in new riding boots to make him taller.

Fernan had made Ibero practise speaking in deep tones and walk around in those boots for days, to get used to the speech and the movement. Their cleric and tutor had been, improbably, the leader of the band that captured Rodrigo. The boys had remained out of sight, downriver with the horses. The other outlaws had been ranch hands, disguised as Ibero had been, under orders not to speak a word. They had gone back to the compound already. Now the three of them, two boys and a holy man, sat together on the dark grass under two moons and the stars of the summer night.

"You really think we deceived him?" the cleric asked.

"What? Papa? Don't be silly," said Fernan, with an amused glance.

"He'll have figured it out from at *least* half a dozen things we missed," said Diego happily. The boys smiled at each other.

The cleric's face fell. "He will have known us? Then what was the point of the deception?"

"He'll tell us the half a dozen things. We'll know better next time," Fernan explained.

"Besides," said Diego, "Mother wanted to stab him with an arrow."

"Ah," said the cleric. "That's right. I forgot." He had been with this family a long time.

They decided to ride back to the ranch house. There was no telling how long Rodrigo and Miranda would remain in that hut. On the way back Fernan began, predictably, to sing. He had an atrocious voice, normally cause for decisive quelling, but neither of the others complained that night. Under the two moons the huge darkness was eased and made welcoming. They could see the mountains far in the distance and the wide stretch of the plain to north and south and rolling west behind them and then, a little later, they caught sight of the torches left burning on the wall around the compound, to bring them all home from the night.

PART III

Chapter VII

༄

"Well then," said Almalik of Cartada, the Lion of Al-Rassan, "where is he?"

The king was angry. The signs were obvious to those in the vast and vaulted chamber. Beneath the horseshoe arches with their red and amber interplay of stone, men exchanged uneasy glances. Courtiers and artists in attendance upon a monarch known for his changing moods learned quickly how to read those changes. They watched as the king snatched an orange from a basket held by a slave and began rapidly peeling it himself with his large, capable hands. Those same hands had swung the sword that killed Ishlik ibn Raal not three months ago in this very room, spattering the poet's blood across the mosaic tiles and marble pillars and the clothing of those standing too close that day.

The young, increasingly acclaimed Tudescan poet had made the mistake of inserting two lines from another man's writing in his own verse, and then denying that he'd done so deliberately. Almalik of Cartada, however, knew his poetry and prided himself upon that. In the Al-Rassan of the city-kings after the fall of the Khalifate a distinguished poet could confer anxiously sought credibility upon a monarch.

And for fifteen years, Almalik's principal counsellor, and then the formally declared advisor and guardian of his eldest son and heir, had been that paragon of many arts, Ammar ibn Khairan of Aljais. Who had written, most unfortunately for Ishlik ibn Raal, the two stolen lines in

question. And of whom, at this precarious moment, three
months after, the king was speaking.

"Where is he?" Almalik asked again.

The attendant court figures, some thirty of them on
this particular morning, found much to interest them in
the geometries of the ceiling decoration or the mosaics of
the floor. No one in the room was looking directly at the
king, or at the man to whom he spoke. Only the one
woman there, sitting among brightly colored cushions
arranged near those of the king's dais, preserved an unper-
turbed demeanor, lightly plucking at her lute.

The stocky, white-haired commander of the Cartadan
army, a man who had seen almost forty years of warfare
under the khalifs and after their fall, remained on his
knees, his own gaze fixed on the carpet before the dais.

The carpet was magnificent, as it happened, woven and
dyed by artisans in the Soriyyan homelands centuries ago,
rescued by Almalik from the looting of the Al-Fontina in
Silvenes fifteen years before. The echo of the khalifs'
imperial splendor here in Cartada was, of course, entirely
deliberate.

Despite his efforts to hide the fact, the kneeling general
was visibly afraid. The plagiarizing poet was not the only
man to have been killed by the king in his audience chamber, he was only the most recent. Almalik had been a military leader before he was a governor and then a monarch; it
was not a thing he allowed his people to forget. The blade
that rested in its sheath by the dais was no ornament.

Without lifting his head, the kneeling ka'id murmured,
"He is not in Fezana, Magnificence. No man has seen him
since...the disciplining in that city."

"You just told me that," Almalik of Cartada said, his
voice close to a whisper now. This was a bad sign, one of
the worst. None of the courtiers ranged near the dais or
standing between the pillars dared even glance at each
other now. "I asked a different question, ibn Ruhala. I asked
the supreme ka'id of all my armies where one exceedingly
well-known figure is at this moment. Not where he is not.

Am I deficient in expressing myself, of late?"

"No, Magnificence! Not at all. Never. The deficiency is mine. I have sent my personal cadre of guards and the best of the Muwardis throughout the country, Magnificence. We have put the most extreme questioning to all who might be privy to ibn Khairan's whereabouts. Some of these people have died, Magnificence, so zealous were their interrogations. But no one knew, no one knows. Ammar ibn Khairan has disappeared...from the face of the earth."

There was a silence.

"What a dreadfully tired phrase," said the Lion of Al-Rassan.

Morning sunlight entered the chamber through the high windows, spilling down past upper galleries through the dancing motes of dust. It could be seen that the woman on the pillows smiled at the king's remark, and that Almalik noted her smile and was pleased. One or two courtiers drew slightly deeper breaths at that. One or two risked smiles of their own, and approving nods.

"Forgive me, Magnificence," murmured the ka'id, head still lowered. "I am only an old soldier. A loyal, plain man of the battlefield, not an artist with a tongue for honeyed phrases. I can say only what I have found to be true, in the simplest way I know."

"Tell me," the king said, biting into a wedge of the orange, "has Prince Almalik been put to the extreme questioning you mentioned?"

The ka'id's white head went straight down to the floor. It could be seen that his hands had begun to tremble. The woman on the pillows looked up at the dais, her expression grave. Her fingers hesitated upon the strings of the lute and then resumed their movement, though with less attentiveness than before.

There was not a man in the room who did not know that if Prince Almalik were no longer the king's heir, the two young children of this woman would be living in greatly enhanced circumstances. With Hazem ibn Almalik, the king's second son, given over to religious extremes and disgraced there would be, effectively, no one between the older of the two boys and succession to the kingship.

"We have asked...aid of the prince," the general stammered into the carpeting. "Of course he was treated with the utmost deference and he...he told us what he could. He expressed a great hope that the lord Ammar ibn Khairan would soon be found and returned, that he would be among us all once more. As he had been...among us in the past."

The ka'id's babbling was manifestly unsuitable for a man of his rank. This was no mere field soldier, this was the commander of the army of Cartada. No one in the room imagined, however, that he would have acquitted himself with greater aplomb in the same circumstances. Not at this juncture. Not in response to *that* particular question. Those who had smiled were urgently praying to their birth stars that their expressions of levity had passed unnoticed.

Only the four Muwardis, two by the entrance doors and two behind the dais, appeared undisturbed behind their half-veils, watching everything and everyone with inimical eyes, despising them all, not troubling to hide the fact.

The king bit into another section of his orange. "I ought to have the prince summoned," he said thoughtfully. "But I am certain he knows nothing. Ibn Khairan wouldn't bother telling such a fool of his plans. Is his eye still dropping like a leper's, by the way?"

Another silence. Evidently the ka'id ibn Ruhala was nursing a vain hope that someone else might reply to this. When the stillness continued, the general, only the back of his head visible to the king on his dais, so prostrate was he, said, "Your most noble son still suffers, alas, from that affliction, Magnificence. Our prayers are with him."

Almalik made a sour face. He dropped the remaining section of orange beside his pillows and held up his fingers delicately. The slave, swift and graceful, appeared before the dais with a muslin towel to wipe the juice from the king's fingers and mouth.

"He looks ridiculous," Almalik said when the slave had withdrawn. "Like a leper," he repeated. "He disgusts me with his weakness."

The woman was no longer even pretending to play at her lute. She watched the king with careful attention.

"Get up, ibn Ruhala," Almalik said abruptly. "You are becoming an embarrassment. Leave us."

With unseemly alacrity, the old general scrambled to his feet. He was crimson-faced from keeping his head lowered for so long. He made the quadruple obeisance and began retreating hastily backwards, still bowing, towards the doors.

"Hold," said Almalik absently. Ibn Ruhala froze, half-bent, like a grotesque statue. "You have made inquiries in Ragosa?"

"Of course, Magnificence. From the moment we began searching in summer. King Badir of Ragosa was our first thought."

"And south? In Arbastro?"

"Our very second thought, Magnificence! You will know how difficult it is to obtain information from those who live in the lands menaced by that dung-eating outlaw Tarif ibn Hassan. But we have been diligent and uncompromising. It does not appear that anyone has seen or heard of ibn Khairan in those places."

There was silence again. The woman on the pillows by the dais held her lute but did not play. The room was very still. The colored water in the great alabaster bowl in the central aisle showed not a ripple of movement. Only the dust was dancing, where the slanting sunlight fell.

"Diligent and uncompromising," the king repeated thoughtfully. He shook his head, as if in sorrow. "You have thirty days to find him, ibn Ruhala, or I will have you castrated and disembowelled and your odious face stuck on a pike in the middle of the market square."

There was a collective intaking of breath, but it was as if this had been expected; the necessary finale to the scene just played.

"Thirty days. Thirty. Yes. Thank you, Magnificence. Thank you," said the ka'id. He sounded absurd, fatuous, but no one could think of what else he might have said.

In silence, as ever, the two Muwardis opened the double doors and the general withdrew, facing the dais, still bowing. The doors swung closed. The sound echoed in the stillness.

"The poem, Serafi. We will hear that verse again." Almalik had taken another orange from the attendant slave and was absently peeling it.

The man addressed was a minor poet, no longer young, honored more for his recitations and his singing voice than for anything he himself had ever written. He stepped hesitantly forward from where he had been standing, half-hidden behind one of the fifty-six pillars in the room. This was not a moment when one wished, particularly, to be singled out for attention. In addition to which, "that poem" was, as everyone knew by now, the last communication to the king from the notorious and celebrated man the ka'id was so unsuccessfully seeking across the whole of Al-Rassan. Under the circumstances, Serafi ibn Dunash would have greatly preferred to be elsewhere at that moment.

Fortunately, he was sober; not a reliable state of affairs for ibn Dunash. Alcohol was forbidden to Asharites of course, but so were Jaddite and Kindath women, boys, dancing, non-religious music and a variety of excellent foods. Serafi ibn Dunash did not dance any more. He relied on that to serve him in good stead with the wadjis, should any of them upbraid him for the laxity of his morals.

It wasn't the wadjis he was afraid of at the moment, however. In the Cartada of King Almalik it was the secular arms of power that were more greatly to be feared. The secular arms, at the moment, rested lightly on the king's knees as he awaited Serafi's recitation. The verses were not flattering, and the king was in an evil mood. The omens were not even remotely auspicious. Nervously, the poet cleared his throat and prepared to begin.

For some reason the slave with the basket of oranges chose this moment to move towards the dais again. He stood directly between Serafi and the king, and then knelt before Almalik. Serafi's view was blocked, but others in the room now noticed what the slave seemed to have been the first to discern: the king appeared to be in sudden and intense distress.

The woman, Zabira, quickly laid aside her instrument and stood up. She took one step towards the dais and then remained extremely still. The king, in that same moment, slipped awkwardly sideways among his cushions and ended up propping himself up on one hand. His other hand was spasmodically clenching and squeezing over his heart. His eyes were wide open, staring at nothing. The slave, nearest to him by far, seemed paralyzed, frozen in position directly in front of Almalik. He had laid aside the basket of oranges but made no other motion. The king opened his mouth; no sound came out.

It is, in fact, a well-known characteristic of the poison *fijana* that it locks shut the throat just before it reaches the heart. As a consequence, no one in the room save the man kneeling directly in front of him was able to say, afterwards, if the dying king of Cartada realized, before he lost consciousness and life and went to join Ashar among the stars, that the slave who had been offering him oranges all morning had remarkably blue, quite distinctive eyes.

The king's arm suddenly buckled and Almalik, mouth gaping wide, fell soundlessly amid a scatter of bright pillows. Someone screamed then, the sound echoing among the columns. There was a babble of terrified noise.

"Ashar and the god are merciful," said the slave, rising from his position and turning to face the courtiers and the stupefied poet in front of the dais. "I really didn't want to hear that poem again." He gestured apologetically. "I wrote it in a great hurry, you see, and there are infelicities."

"*Ammar ibn Khairan!*" stammered Serafi somewhat unnecessarily.

The erstwhile slave was calmly unwinding his saffron-colored headcloth. He had darkened his skin but had essayed no further disguise: no one ever looked closely at slaves.

"I do hope he recognized me," said ibn Khairan in a musing tone. "I think he did." He dropped the slave's head-cloth among the pillows. He seemed utterly relaxed, standing before the dais on which the most powerful monarch in Al-Rassan lay sprawled in slack-jawed, untidy death.

As one, in that moment, the courtiers looked to the Muwardis by the doors, the only men in the room bearing arms. The veiled ones had remained inexplicably motionless through all of what had just taken place. Ibn Khairan noticed the direction of the glances.

"Mercenaries," he said gravely, "are mercenaries."

He did not add, but might have, that the tribesmen of the desert would not be sparing any moments of prayer for the secular, degenerate worse-than-infidel who had just died. As far as the Muwardis were concerned, *all* of the kings of Al-Rassan merited approximately the same fate. If they all killed each other the starlit visions of Ashar might yet be fulfilled in this land.

One of the veiled ones did come forward then, moving towards the dais. He passed near to the woman, Zabira, who had remained motionless after rising. Her hands were at her mouth.

"*Not quite*," he said softly, but the words carried, and were remembered.

Then he ascended the dais and removed the Muwardi veil from the lower part of his face and it could be seen by all assembled in the room that this was, indeed, the princely heir of Cartada's realm, Almalik ibn Almalik, he of the nervous eyelid, who his father had said looked like a leper.

He looks rather more like a desert warrior at the moment. He is also, as of this same moment, the king of Cartada.

The other three Muwardis now draw their swords, without moving from where they stand by the doors. One might have expected an outcry from the court, but stupefaction and fear impose their restraints upon men. The only sound in the audience chamber for a frozen instant is the breathing of terrified courtiers.

"The guards on the other side of the doors are mine as well, by the way," says young Almalik mildly. His afflicted eyelid, it can be seen, is not drooping or twitching at this time.

He looks down upon the toppled body of his father. After a moment, with a swift, decisive movement of one foot, he rolls the dead king off the dais. The body comes to rest at the feet of the woman, Zabira. The son sits down smoothly among the remaining pillows of the dais.

Ammar ibn Khairan sinks to his knees in front of him.

"May holy Ashar intercede with the god among the stars," he says, "to grant you long life, O great king. Be merciful in your grandeur to your loyal servants, Magnificence. May your reign be crowned with everlasting glory in Ashar's name."

He proceeds to perform the quadruple obeisance.

Behind him, the poet Serafi suddenly comes to his senses. He drops to the mosaic tiles as if smitten behind the knees and does the same. Then, very much as if they are grateful for this cue as to how to proceed, the men in the audience chamber all perform full obeisance to the new king of Cartada.

It is seen that the only woman in the room, the beautiful Zabira, does so as well, touching the floor with her forehead beside the body of her dead lover, graceful and alluring as always in the movements of her homage to the son.

It is also observed that Ammar ibn Khairan, who has been searched for through the whole of Al-Rassan, now rises to his knees and stands, without invitation from the dais.

It is a source of belated, devastating wonder to those now imprisoned in the room by the drawn swords of the Muwardis, how they could have failed to identify him before. No one looks quite like ibn Khairan, with those unconscionably blue eyes. No one moves like him. No one's arrogance quite matches his. With the headcloth removed his signature earring gleams—with amusement one could be forgiven for thinking. He will have been here in Cartada for a long time, it now becomes clear. Perhaps in this very room. A number of men in the audience chamber begin rapidly scanning their memories for remarks of an injudicious sort they might have made about the disgraced favorite during his presumed absence.

Ibn Khairan smiles and turns to survey them all. His smile is vividly remembered, if no more comforting than it has ever been.

"The Day of the Moat," he says, to no one in particular, "was a mistake in a great many ways. It is never a good idea to leave a man with no real alternatives."

For Serafi the poet this is incomprehensible, but there are wiser men than he standing among the columns and beneath the arches. Ibn Khairan's remark will be recollected, it will be expounded upon. Men will hasten to be the first to elucidate its meaning.

Ibn Khairan, they will say, whispering in bathhouses or courtyards, or in the Jaddite taverns of the city, *was meant to bear the responsibility for the executions in Fezana. He had grown too powerful in the king's eyes. He was to be curbed by this. No one would ever trust him again.* Heads will nod knowingly over sherbet or forbidden wine.

With this one cryptic sentence, the dialogues of the next days have been set in motion, or so it seems.

It is an old truth, however, that events, whether large or small, do not always follow upon the agendas of even the most subtle of men.

Behind ibn Khairan, the new king of Cartada finishes arranging the pillows of the dais to his satisfaction and says now, quietly, but very clearly, "We are indulgent of all of your obeisances. No man of you need fear us, so long as he is loyal." No mention of the woman, a number of them note.

The king continues, as ibn Khairan turns back to him. "We have certain pronouncements to make at this commencement of our reign. The first is that all formal rites of mourning will be observed for seven days, in honor of our tragically slain king and father."

The men of the Cartadan court are masters of reading the smallest nuances of information. None of them see any hint of surprise in the features or the bearing of ibn Khairan, who has just killed the king.

He planned this too, they decide. *The prince would not have been so clever.*

They are wrong, as it happens.

A great many people are about to be proven wrong about Almalik ibn Almalik in time to come. The first and foremost of them stands now, directly in front of the young king and hears the new monarch, his ward and disciple, say, in that same quiet, clear voice, "The second pronouncement must be, lamentably, a decree of exile for our once-trusted and dearly loved servant, Ammar ibn Khairan."

No sign, no motion, no slightest indication of discomfiture from the man so named. Only one raised eyebrow—a characteristic gesture that might mean many things—and then a question calmly broached: "Why, Magnificence?"

In the mouth of someone who had just killed a king, with the still-warm body lying not far away, it seems a question of astonishing impudence. Given that the killing has doubtless been effected with the countenance and involvement of the young prince, it is also a dangerous query. Almalik II of Cartada looks to one side and sees his father's sword beside the dais. He reaches out, almost absently, and takes it by the hilt. It can be seen that his unfortunate affliction of the eye has now returned.

"For sins against morality," the young king says finally. And flushes.

In the rigid silence that follows this, the laughter of Ammar ibn Khairan, when it comes, echoes from column to arch to the high vaulted ceiling. There is an edge to his amusement though—the discerning can hear it. This is *not* part of what had been arranged, they are certain of it. And there is an extreme subtlety here, the most quick-minded of them realize. The new king needs to swiftly distance himself from regicide. If he had spoken of murder as a cause of exile that distance would be lost—for his own presence, disguised, in this chamber speaks all that needs to be spoken of how his father's death has been achieved.

"Ah," says ibn Khairan now, into the silence, as the echoes of his laughter fade, "moral failings again. Only those?" He pauses, smiles. Says bluntly, "I feared you might speak of killing a king. That dreadful lie some might even now be spreading through the city. I am relieved. Might I therefore live in hope of the king's forgiving kiss upon my unworthy brow one day?"

The king flushes a deeper shade of crimson. Serafi the poet abruptly remembers that their new monarch is still a young man. And Ammar ibn Khairan has been his closest advisor and friend, and there have been certain rumors for a number of years...He decides that he now understands matters more clearly. *The king's forgiving kiss.* Indeed!

"Time and the stars and the will of Ashar determine such things," the young king says with determined, formal piety. "We have...honored you, and are grateful for your past services. This punishment...comes not easily to us."

He pauses, his voice alters. "Nevertheless, it is necessary. You have until first starlight to be gone from Cartada and seven nights to quit our lands, failing which any man who sees you is free to take your life and is commanded to do so as an agent of the king." The words are crisp, precise, not at all those of a young man who is anxious and unsure of himself.

"Hunted? Not again!" says Ammar ibn Khairan, his sardonic tones restored. "But, really, I'm so *tired* of wearing a saffron headcloth."

The tic in the king's eye is quite distracting, really. "You had best be gone," young Almalik says sternly. "What we have now to say are words for our loyal subjects. We shall pray that Ashar guides you towards virtue and enlightenment."

No wavering, the possibly loyal subjects in the room note. Even faced with mockery and what could be seen as a threat from the subtlest man in the kingdom, the young king is standing his ground. He is doing more than that, they now realize. With a slight gesture the king motions the two Muwardis by the double doors at the far end of the chamber to come forward.

They do so, swords drawn, until they stand on either side of ibn Khairan. He spares them only a brief, amused glance.

"I should have remained a poet," he says, shaking his head ruefully. "Affairs such as this are beyond my depth. Farewell, Magnificence. I shall live a sad, dark, quiet life of contemplation, awaiting a summons back to the brightness of your side."

Flawlessly he makes the four obeisances again, then rises. He stands a moment, as if about to add something more. The young king looks at him, waiting, his eyelid twitching. But Ammar ibn Khairan only smiles again and shakes his head. He leaves the room, walking between the graceful columns, across the mosaic tiles, beneath the last arch and out the doors. Not a man there believes his final words.

What the one woman is thinking, watching all of this from where she still stands beside the body of the dead king, her lover, the father of her children, no one can tell. The face of the slain monarch is already turning grey, a known effect of *fijana* poisoning. His mouth is still open in that last, soundless contortion. The oranges remain in their basket where it was set down by ibn Khairan, directly before the dais.

༅

It had been, he realized, one of those miscalculations for which a younger man might never have forgiven himself. He was no longer a young man, and his amusement was nearly genuine, his mockery almost all directed inward.

There were other elements in play here, though, and gradually, as he rode east from Cartada late in the day, Ammar ibn Khairan could feel his sardonic detachment beginning to slip. By the time he reached his country estate an afternoon's easy ride from the city walls a companion might have seen a grave expression on his face. He had no companions. The two servants following on mules some distance behind him, carrying a variety of goods—clothing and jewelry and manuscripts, mostly—were not, of course, privy to his thoughts and could not have seen his countenance. Ibn Khairan was not a confiding man.

There was a safe interval yet before first starlight when he reached his home. It would have been undignified to hasten from Cartada in the morning after Almalik's decree, but equally it would have been showy and provocative to linger to the edge of dusk—there were those in the city who might have been willing to kill him and then claim they'd seen a star some time before the first one actually appeared. He was a man with his share of enemies.

When he reached his estate two grooms came running to take his horse. Servants appeared in the doorway and others could be seen scurrying about within, lighting lanterns and candles, preparing rooms for the master. He had not been here since the spring. No one had known where he was.

His steward was dead. He had learned that from the prince some time ago: one of the closely questioned figures the ka'id had mentioned this morning.

They ought to have known better, he thought. They probably had, actually: no one, not even the Muwardis, could really have imagined he'd have told the steward who managed his country home where he was hiding. Ibn Ruhala had needed dead bodies, though, evidence of zeal in his search. It occurred to him that, ironically, the ka'id was someone who probably owed him his life now, with the death of the king. Another possible source of amusement. He really couldn't seem to summon up his usual manner today, however.

It wasn't the unexpected exile, the prince's turning upon him. There were reasons for that. He'd have been happier had he been the one to plan and implement this twist, as he'd planned all the others, but truth was, however he felt about it, the new king was not about to be a puppet, for Ammar ibn Khairan or anyone else. Probably a good thing, he thought, dismounting in the courtyard. A tribute to my own training, that I'm banished from the country by the man I've just made king.

That ought to have been diverting, too. The problem was, he finally acknowledged, looking about the forecourt of the home he most loved, diversion and amusement were going to be a little hard to come by for the next while. Memories, and the associations they brought, were rather too insistent just now.

Fifteen years ago he had killed the last khalif of Al-Rassan for the man he'd killed today.

Wasn't it the Jarainids of the farthest east, beyond the homelands, who believed that a man's life was an endlessly repeating circle of the same acts and deeds? It wasn't a philosophy that commended itself to him, but he was aware that after this morning his own life might fairly be held up as an illustration of their creed. He didn't much like the idea of being a ready example of anything. It was too uninspired a role, and he considered himself a poet before anything else.

Though that, too, was a half-truth, at best. He walked into the low, sprawling house he'd built with the generous income Almalik had always allowed him. *Never leave a man without an alternative,* he'd said carefully in the audience chamber this morning, to make certain the cleverest among those assembled would begin to spell out the tale as he wanted it told.

But there *had* been alternatives. There almost always were. Almalik had indeed administered a stringent, deeply humiliating rebuke to his son's independence and ibn Khairan's pride on the Day of the Moat. The prince had been rendered a hapless observer of butchery, no more than a symbol of his father's watchfulness, and Ammar...?

Ammar ibn Khairan, who, on behalf of the ambitious governor of Cartada fifteen years ago, had not scrupled to murder a man named khalif in the holy succession of Ashar—and who had been branded by that deed ever since—had been defined anew for the peninsula and the world as the coarse, blood-sodden architect of an ugly slaughter.

What he had seen in that Fezanan castle courtyard in the broiling heat of summer had sickened him—and he was a man who had seen and decreed death in a great many guises in the service of Cartada. He detested excess though, and the degree of it in that courtyard was appalling.

Over and above all this, of course, there was pride. There was always pride. He might loath what had been done to the citizens of Fezana but he loathed, just as much, what had been done to his own name, to his image and place in the world. He knew he was the servant of a king, however lofty his titles. Kings could rebuke their servants; they could strip them of their worldly goods, kill them, exile them. They could not take a man—if the man was Ammar ibn Khairan—and present him to the whole of Al-Rassan and the world beyond mountain and sea as an agent of...ugliness.

No alternative?

Of course there had been alternatives, had he wanted them badly enough. He could have left the world of power and its atrocities. He could even have left this beloved, diminished land of Al-Rassan and its puffed-up petty-kings. He could have gone straight from Fezana to Ferrieres across the mountains, or to any of the great cities of Batiara. There were cultivated, princely courts there where an Asharite poet would be made welcome as a glittering enhancement. He could have written for the rest of his days in luxury among the most civilized of the Jaddites.

He could even have gone farther east, taking ship all the way back to Soriyya, to visit the stone tombs of his ancestors, which he had never seen, perhaps even rediscover his faith at Ashar's Rock, make a vigil under the god's stars in the desert, finish his life far from Al-Rassan.

Of course there had been alternatives.

Instead he had taken revenge. Had disguised himself and come back to Cartada. Made himself known to the prince and then bribed a palace steward to admit him into the retinue of the court as a slave. The largest single bribe he had ever given in his life. And he had killed the king today, with *fijana* smeared on a muslin cloth.

Twice now, then. Twice in fifteen years he had murdered the most powerful monarch in the land. A khalif and a king.

I am increasingly unlikely to be best remembered, ibn Khairan decided ruefully, entering his home, *for my poetry.*

"You have a visitor, Excellence," the under-steward said, hovering inside the doorway. Ibn Khairan sat on the low bench by the door and the man knelt to help remove his boots and replace them with jewelled slippers.

"You had someone admitted without my presence?"

The man was now the steward, actually. New to his duties in a terrible time, he looked down at the ground. "I may have erred, Excellence. But she was insistent that you would see her."

"She?"

But he already knew who this had to be. Amusement briefly resurfaced before being succeeded by something else. "Where have you put her?"

"She awaits you on the terrace. I hope I acted rightly, Excellence?"

He rose and the steward did the same. "Only, ever, admit a woman this way. Have dinner prepared for two and a room readied for a guest. You and I will speak later; there is much to be done. I am leaving Cartada for a time, by the king's decree."

"Yes, Excellence," the man said expressionlessly.

Ammar turned to go within. He paused. "The new king. The old king is dead," he added. "This morning."

"Alas," said his steward, with no evident sign of surprise.

A competent man, ibn Khairan decided. Dropping his riding gloves on a marble table, he walked a sequence of corridors to the wide terrace he'd had built on the west side of the house where his own chambers were. He had always preferred sunset to sunrise. The view overlooked red hills and the blue curve of the river to the south. Cartada was invisible, just beyond the hills.

The woman, his visitor, was standing with her back to him, admiring that view. She was barefoot on the cool flagstones.

"The architect didn't want to build this for me," he said, coming to stand beside her. "'Open spaces go *inside* a house,' he kept telling me."

She glanced up at him. She would have been veiled for the ride here, but the veil was lifted now. Her dark, accented eyes held his a moment and then she turned away.

"It does feel exposed," she said quietly.

"But see where we are. From what am I hiding here in the country, I asked my architect and myself."

"And what did you answer yourself?" she asked, looking at the terraced slopes towards the river and the setting sun. "And your architect?" She was extremely beautiful, in profile. He remembered the day he had first seen her.

"Not this," he said, after a moment, gesturing at the land stretching before them. She was clever, he would do well to remember that. "I will admit I am surprised, Zabira. I am seldom surprised, but this is unexpected."

The foremost lady of King Almalik's court, the courtesan who was the mother of his two youngest children, effectively the queen of Cartada for the past eight years, looked back at him again and smiled, her small, perfect teeth showing white.

"Really?" she said. "On a day when you kill a king and are exiled from your home by your own disciple, a simple visit from a lady is what disconcerts you? I don't know whether to be flattered."

Her voice was exquisite, there seemed to be music beneath it. It had always been thus. She had broken hearts and mended them when she sang. She smelled of myrrh and roses. Her eyes and fingernails had been carefully painted. He wondered how long she had been here. He ought to have asked the steward.

"There is nothing simple about either the lady or the

visit," he murmured. "Will you take refreshment?"

A servant had appeared with a tray bearing pomegran-
ate juice and sherbet in tall glasses. He took the drinks
and offered her one. "Will I offend you if I also suggest a
cup of wine? There is a Jaddite vineyard north of us and I
have an arrangement with them."

"You would not offend me in the least," Zabira said,
with some measure of feeling.

Ammar smiled. This was the most celebrated beauty in
Al-Rassan, and young still, though perhaps a little less
youthful after this morning. Ibn Khairan was only one of
the myriad poets who had extolled her over the years. He
had been the first, though, there would always be that. He
had met her with Almalik. Had been there when it began.

> The woman we saw at the Gate of the Fountain,
> As twilight stole down upon the city walls
> Like a cloaked thief of the day's light,
> Wore the first holy stars of Ashar
> As ornaments above the dark fall of her hair.
> What shall be the name of their beauty
> If it be not her name?

Sacrilege, of course, but Al-Rassan after the Khalifate's
fall—and long before—had not been the most devout place
in the Asharite world.

She had been seventeen years old that evening when the
king and the lord ibn Khairan, his closest friend and advisor, had ridden back into Cartada from a day's hunting in
the western forests and had seen a girl drawing water from
a fountain in the last of the autumn light. Eight years ago.

"Really, Ammar, why would you be surprised?" the
same woman asked him now, infinitely sophisticated, eyeing him over the rim of the glass. Ibn Khairan gestured at
the servant, who withdrew to bring wine. "What do you
imagine Cartada might hold for me now?"

Carefully, for he was conscious that what he had done
this morning had turned her world upside-down and put

her life in peril, he said, "The son is son to the father, Zabira, and much of your own age."

She made a wry face. "You heard what he said to me this morning."

Not quite, the prince had murmured. They had all heard that. Zabira had been careful, always, but it was hardly a secret that with Hazem the second son entangled hopelessly with the most zealous of the wadjis, her own older child was the only real alternative to Prince Almalik—provided the king had lived long enough for the boy to come of age. He had not. Ammar wondered, suddenly, where the two children were.

"I heard what he said. Despite that, Almalik ibn Almalik has a nature not immune to enticement," he replied, still being cautious. In its own way he was making an appalling suggestion, though by no means an unprecedented one. Royal sons succeeded fathers, in more ways than the one.

She gave him a sidelong glance. "A man's enticement, or a woman's? Perhaps you could enlighten me as to that?" she said sweetly. Then went on before he could reply: "I know him. I've had him watched a long time, Ammar. He will be immune to whatever charms I yet retain. He is too afraid. For him, I will carry the shadow of his father wherever I go, in bed or in court, and he isn't ready to deal with that." She sipped from her drink again and looked out at the gleaming curve of the river and the reddening hills. "He will want to kill my sons."

Ammar had been thinking the same thing, actually.

He decided it was better, in the circumstances, not to ask where the boys were, though it would have been useful knowledge for later. The servant returned with two more glasses, water and wine in a beautifully crafted decanter. He had spent a small fortune on glass over the years. More things to leave behind.

The tray was set down and the servant withdrew. Ibn Khairan mixed water and wine for the two of them. They drank, not speaking. The wine was very good.

The image of two small boys seemed to hang in the air

in the gathering twilight. Suddenly, for no good reason, he thought of Ishak of Fezana, the Kindath doctor who had attended upon Zabira for both those boys—and had lost his eyes and tongue after the delivery of the second. He had gazed with an infidel's eyes upon the forbidden beauty of the woman whose life he had saved. The woman now standing here, her scent vivid and distracting, her white skin flawless. He wondered if she knew what had happened to Ishak ben Yonannon, if Almalik had ever told her. That led to another unexpected thought.

"You really did love the king, didn't you?" he asked at length, uncharacteristically awkward. He didn't feel entirely in control of this situation. Murdering someone left you vulnerable to certain things; he had almost forgotten that lesson over the course of fifteen years. How *was* one to proceed with the lover of a man one had slain?

"You know I did," she said calmly. "That isn't a difficult or even a real question, Ammar." She turned and stood facing him for the first time. "The difficult truth is that you loved him as well."

And that he had not expected.

He shook his head quickly. "No. I respected him, I admired his strength, I enjoyed the subtlety of his mind. His foresight, his cunning. I had hopes of the son, as well. In a way, I still do."

"Otherwise your teaching was wasted?"

"Otherwise my teaching was wasted."

"It was," said Zabira flatly. "You'll see, soon enough. And though I heard a denial of love, I am afraid I do not believe it."

She set down her empty glass and looked up at him thoughtfully, standing very near. "Tell me something else," she said, her voice changing timbre. "You suggested the new king was not immune to enticement. Are you, Ammar?"

He was, perhaps, the least easily startled man in Al-Rassan, but this, following hard upon the last remarks, was entirely unexpected. Hilarity, intense and swift, rose within him and as swiftly subsided. He had killed her lover that morning. The father of her children. The hope of her future.

"I have been accused of many things, but never that," he said, parrying for time.

She granted him none. "Good, then," said Zabira of Cartada, and rising on her toes, she kissed him upon the lips, slowly and with considerable expertise.

Someone else did this to me, not long ago, ibn Khairan thought, before all such associations were chased away. The woman on the terrace with him stepped back, but only to begin—silk sleeves falling away to reveal the white skin of her arms—unbinding her black hair.

He stared, mesmerized, words and thoughts scattering in disarray. He watched her hands descend to the pearl buttons of her overtunic. She undid two of them, and paused. It was not an overtunic. She wore nothing beneath. In the extremely clear, soft light he glimpsed the pale, pear-like curves of her breasts.

His throat was suddenly dry. His voice husky in his own ears, ibn Khairan said, "My rooms are just here."

"Good," she said again. "Show me."

It did occur to him just then that she might have come here to kill him.

It did not occur to him to do anything about it. He had, truly, never been accused of being immune to enticement. He lifted her up; she was small-boned and slender, no real weight at all. The scent of her surrounded him, dizzying for a moment. He felt her mouth at the lobe of one ear. Her fingers were about his neck. His blood loud within him, ibn Khairan carried her through a doorway and into his bedchamber.

Is it the possibility of dying that does this? he wondered, his first and last such clear thought for some time. *Is that what excites me so?*

His bed, in a large room hung with Serian tapestries, was low to the ground, covered with cushions and pillows in a diversity of shapes and sizes, as much for love-play as for color and texture. Crimson-dyed squares of silk hung from copper rings on the wall above the bed and set into the carved wooden foot. Ammar preferred freedom of movement in his lovemaking, the slide and traverse of bodies, but there had been those among his guests in this room who derived their keenest pleasures otherwise, and over the years he had earned a reputation as a host solicitous of all of his guests' desires.

Even so, even with almost twenty years of nuanced experience in erotic play, ibn Khairan was swiftly made aware—though not, in truth, with any great surprise—that a woman trained as Zabira had been knew some things he did not. Even, it began to emerge, things about his own nature and responses.

Unclothed among the pillows some time later, he felt her fingers teasing and exploring him, winced at a bite and felt his sex grow even more rigid amid the growing shadows of the room as her mouth came back to his ear and she whispered something quite shocking in the exquisite, celebrated voice. Then his eyes grew wide in the darkness as she proceeded to perform precisely what she had just described.

All the training mistresses and castrates of Almalik's court had come over the wide seas from the homelands of the east, where such skills had been part of courtly life for hundreds of years before Ashar's ascetic vigil in the desert. It was possible, Ammar's drifting thoughts essayed, that a journey to Soriyya might have more to offer than he'd imagined. He felt a breathless laugh escape him.

Zabira slipped further downward, her scented skin gliding along his, her fingernails offering counterpoint where they touched. Ibn Khairan heard a sigh of helpless pleasure and realized that, improbably, he had made that sound himself. He attempted to rise then, to turn, to begin the sharing, the flowing back-and-forth of love, but he felt her hands, delicately insistent, pushing him down. He surrendered, closed his eyes, let her begin, her voice exclaiming in delight or murmuring in commentary, to minister to him as he had ministered to so many people in this room.

It went on, astonishingly varied and inventive, for some

time. The sun had set. The room was encased in darkness—they had paused to light no candles here—before his sensibilities began, as a swimmer rises from green depths of the sea, to reassert themselves. And slowly, feeling almost drugged with desire, ibn Khairan came to understand something.

She was beside him just then, having turned him on his side. One of her legs was wrapped about his body, she had him enclosed within her sex, and her movements were indeed those of sea tides in their insistent, unwavering rise and fall. He brushed a nipple with his tongue, testing his new thought. Without pause in her rhythm—which was, intuitively, his own deepest rhythm—she caressed his head and tilted it away.

"Zabira," he whispered, his voice distant and difficult.

"Hush," she murmured, a tongue to his ear again. "Oh, hush. Let me carry you away."

"Zabira," he tried again.

She shifted then, sinuous and smooth, and was above him now, more urgently, his manhood still within her, sheathed in liquescence. Her mouth descended, covered his. Her breath was scented with mint, her kisses a kind of threading fire. She stopped his speech, her tongue like a hummingbird. Her nails raked downward along his side. He gasped.

And turned his head away.

He lifted his hands then, with some effort, and grasped her by the arms; gently, but so she could not twist away again. In the darkness he tried to see her eyes but could discern only the heart-shaped shadow of her face and the curtain of her black hair.

"Zabira," he said, an utterly unexpected kind of pain within him, "you need not punish yourself, or hold back sorrow. It is all right to mourn. It is allowed."

She went stiff with shock, as if slapped. Her body arched backwards in the first uncontrolled movement she had made all evening. For a long moment she remained that way, rigid, motionless, and then, with real grief and a simultaneous relief, Ammar heard her make one harsh, unnatural sound as if something had been torn in her throat, or in her heart.

He drew her slowly down until she lay along the length of him, but in a different fashion from all their touchings of before. And in the dark of that room, notorious for the woven patterns of desire it had seen, Ammar ibn Khairan held the woman beloved of the man he'd killed, and offered what small comfort he could. He granted her the courtesy and space of his silence, as she finally permitted herself to weep, mourning the depth of her loss, the appalling disappearance, in an instant, of love in a bitter world.

A bitter, ironic world, he thought, still struggling upwards as through those scented, enveloping green waters. And then, as if he had, truly, broken through to some surface of awareness, ibn Khairan confronted and accepted the fact that she had, indeed, been right in what she'd said on the terrace as the sun set.

He'd killed a hard, suspicious, brilliant, cruelly ambitious man today. And one whom he had loved.

> *When the Lion at his pleasure comes*
> *To the watering place to drink, ah see!*
> *See the lesser beasts of Al-Rassan*
> *Scatter like blown leaves in autumn,*
> *Like air-borne seedlings in the spring,*
> *Like grey clouds that part to let the first star*
> *Of the god shine down upon the earth.*

Lions died. Lovers died, or were slain. Men and women moved in their pride and folly through deeds of pity and atrocity and the stars of Ashar looked down and did or did not care.

The two of them never left his room that night. Ammar had trays brought again, with cold meats and cheeses and figs and pomegranates from his own groves. They ate by candlelight, cross-legged upon the bed, in silence. Then they removed the trays and blew out the candles and lay down together again, though not in the movements of desire.

They were awake before dawn. In the grey half-light that slowly suffused the room she told him, without his asking, that at the end of the summer her two sons had been quietly sent for fostering, after the old fashion, to King Badir of Ragosa.

Ragosa. She had made that decision herself, she said quietly, immediately after ibn Khairan's poem had arrived in Cartada, lampooning and excoriating the king. She had always tried to stay ahead of events, and the poem had offered more than a hint of change to come.

"Where will you go?" she asked him. Morning light had entered the chamber by then. They could hear birds outside and from within the house the footsteps of busy servants. She was sitting up, cross-legged again, wrapped in a light blanket as in a shepherd's cloak, her face paint streaked with the tracks of her night tears, hair tumbling in disarray.

"I haven't, to be honest, had time to think about it. I was only ordered into exile yesterday morning, remember? And then I had a somewhat demanding guest awaiting me when I came home."

She smiled wanly, but made no movement, waiting, her dark eyes, red-rimmed, fixed on his.

He truly *had* not thought about it. He had expected to be triumphantly home in Cartada as of yesterday morning, guiding the policies and first steps of the new king and the kingdom. A man could make plans, it seemed, but he could not plan for everything. He hadn't even allowed himself, through the course of the night just past, to think much about Almalik ibn Almalik, the prince—the king, now—who had so decisively turned on him. There would be time for that later. There would have to be.

In the meantime, there was a whole peninsula and a world beyond it full of places that were not Cartada. He could go almost anywhere, do so many different things. He had realized that much yesterday, riding here. He was a poet, a soldier, a courtier, a diplomat.

He looked at the woman on his bed, and read the question she was trying so hard not to ask. At length he smiled, savoring all the ironies that seemed to be emerging like flower petals in the light, and he accepted the burden that came not from killing, but from allowing someone to take comfort with him when no comfort had been expected or thought to be allowed. She was a mother. He had known that, of course, but had never given any thought to what it might mean for her.

"Where will I go? Ragosa, I suppose," he said, as if carelessly, and was humbled by the radiance of her smile, bright as the morning sunlight in the room.

Chapter VIII

❧

Ivories and throngs of people, these were the predomi-
nant images Alvar carried after three months in Ragosa.

He had been born and raised on a farm in the far north.
For him, a year before, Esteren in Valledo had been fearfully
imposing. Esteren, he now understood, was a village. King
Badir's Ragosa was one of the great cities of Al-Rassan.

He had never been in a place where so many people
lived and went about their business, and yet, amid the bustle and chaos, the swirling movements, the layers of sound,
somehow still a sense of grace hovered—a stringed instrument heard in an archway, a splashing fountain half-
glimpsed beyond the flowers of screening trees. It was true,
what he had been told: the Star-born of Al-Rassan inhabited
an entirely different world than did the Horsemen of Jad.

Every second object in the palace or the gracious homes
he had seen seemed to be made of carved and polished
ivory, imported by ship from the east. Even the handles of
the knives used at some tables. The knobs on the palace
doors. Despite the slow decline of Al-Rassan since the fall
of Silvenes, Ragosa was a conspicuously wealthy city. In
some ways it was *because* of the fall of the khalifs, actually.

Alvar had had that explained to him. Besides the celebrated workers in ivory there were poets and singers here,
leather workers, woodcarvers, masons, glassblowers,
stonecutters—masters of a bewildering variety of trades—
who would never have ventured east across the Serrana
Range in the days when Silvenes was the center of the

western world. Now, since the Khalifate's thunderous fall, every one of the city-kings had his share of craftsmen and artists to exalt and extol his virtues. They were *all* lions, if one could believe the honey-tongued poets of Al-Rassan.

One couldn't, of course. Poets were poets, and had a living to earn. Kings were kings, and there were a score of them now, some foundering in the ruin of their walls, some festering in fear or greed, a few—a very few—conceivably heirs to what Silvenes had been. It seemed to Alvar, on little enough experience, that King Badir in Ragosa had to be numbered among those in the last group.

Amid all the strangeness surrounding him—the unknown, intoxicating smells from doorway and courtyard and food stall, the bells summoning the devout to prayer at measured intervals during the day and night, the riot of noise and color in the marketplace—Alvar was grateful that here in Al-Rassan they still measured the round of the year by the white moon's cycling from full to full as they did back home. At least *that* hadn't changed. He could say exactly how long he'd been here, in another world.

On the other hand, it felt like so much more than three months, when he paused to look back. His year in Esteren seemed eerily remote, and the farm almost unimaginably distant. He wondered what his mother would say, could she have seen him in his loosely belted, flowing Asharite garb during the summer past. Actually, he didn't wonder: he was fairly certain he knew. She'd have headed straight back to Vasca's Isle, on her knees, in penance for his sins.

The fact was, though, summer was hot here in the south. One *needed* a headcovering in the white light of midday, one less cumbersome than a stiff leather hat; and the light-colored cotton tunics and trousers of Al-Rassan were far more comfortable in the city streets than what he had been wearing when they arrived. His face was darkened by the sun; he looked half Asharite himself, Alvar knew. It was an odd sensation, gazing in a glass and seeing the man who looked back. There were mirrors everywhere, too; the Ragosans were a vain people.

Autumn had come in the meantime; he wore a light brown cloak over his clothing now. Jehane had picked it out for him when the weather began to change. Twisting and pushing—expertly now—through the crowds of the weekly market, Alvar could hardly believe how little time had really passed since the two of them and Velaz had come through the mountain pass and first seen the blue waters of the lake and the towers of Ragosa.

He had been at pains to conceal his awe that day, though looking back from his newly sophisticated vantage point he suspected that his two companions had simply been generous enough to pretend not to notice. Even Fezana had intimidated him from a distance. Ragosa dwarfed it. Only Cartada itself now—with Silvenes of the khalifs looted and gutted years ago—was a more formidable city. Next to this high-walled, many-towered magnificence, Esteren was as the hamlet of Orvilla, where Garcia de Rada had come raiding on a night in summer.

Alvar's life had forked like a branch that night, his path in the morning running east through Al-Rassan and across the Serrana Range to these walls with Jehane bet Ishak, instead of north and home with the Captain.

His own choice, too, endorsed by Rodrigo and accepted, if grudgingly at first, by Jehane. She would need a guard on the road, Alvar had declared in the morning after a memorable campfire conversation. A soldier, he'd added, not merely a servant, however loyal and brave that servant might be. Alvar had offered to be that guard, with the Captain's permission. He would see her settled in Ragosa then make his way home.

He hadn't told them he was in love with her. They wouldn't have let him come if they had known, he was sure of that much. He was also ruefully certain Jehane had realized the truth early in their journey. He wasn't particularly good at hiding what he felt.

He thought she was beautiful, with her dark hair and her direct, unexpectedly blue gaze. He knew she was clever, and more than that: trained, accomplished, calmly professional. Amid the fires of Orvilla he had seen her courage, and her anger, holding the two young girls in her arms. She was a woman entirely outside the range of his life. She was also a Kindath, of the Wanderers, the god-diminishing heretics the clerics thundered against as loudly as they cursed the Asharites. Alvar tried not to let that matter, but the truth was, it did: it made her seem mysterious, exotic, even a little dangerous.

She wasn't, actually. She was sharp and practical and direct. She'd taken him to her bed for one single night, not long after their arrival in Ragosa. She had done it kindly, without guile or promise. She had almost certainly intended that such a matter-of-fact physical liaison would cure him of his youthful longings. Alvar, clever in his own right, was quite clear about that. She allowed him no candlelit illusions at all about what a night together meant. She felt kindly towards him, Alvar knew. Though the journey had proved uneventful, she'd been grateful for his company, found him reliable and trustworthy, his energy diverting. He had come to understand, being observant in his own way, that she, too, was embarking on something new and strange without being sure of her way.

He also knew she did not love him at all, that beyond the physical act, the night's harmony of two young bodies far from their homes, their union made no sense. But far from purging him of love, that night in her room had set a seal, as in heated wax, on his feelings.

In the old stories the kitchen women used to tell around the fire after the evening meal on the farm, brave Horsemen of the god loved endangered maidens on first sight and for life. It wasn't supposed to happen that way in the fallen, divided world in which they really lived. It had, for Alvar de Pellino.

He didn't make a great issue of it. He loved Jehane bet Ishak, the Kindath physician. It was a fact of existence, as much as where the god's sun rose in the morning, or the proper way to parry a left-handed sword stroke towards one's knees. Walking the crowded streets of Ragosa, Alvar felt much older than he had when he rode south with Rodrigo Belmonte to collect the summer *parias.*

It was autumn now. The breeze from the north off Lake Serrana was cool in the morning and sometimes sharply cold at night. All the soldiers wore cloaks, and two layers of clothing under them if they were on duty after sunset. Not long ago, at dawn after a night on the northwestern wall, Alvar had seen the masts and spars of the fishing boats in the harbor rimed with pale frost under the full blue moon.

In the first sunlight of the next morning the leaves of the oaks in the eastern forests had gleamed red and gold, a dazzle of brilliance. To the west, the Serrana mountains that guarded Ragosa from Cartada's armies and had screened her from Silvenes in the days of the Khalifate had been capped with snow on the higher slopes. The snow would last until spring. The pass through which he and Jehane and Velaz had come was the only one open all year. Friends had told him these things in the Jaddite taverns of the city or the food stalls of the marketplace.

He had friends here now. He hadn't expected that, but shortly after their arrival it had become obvious that he was far from the only Jaddite soldier in Ragosa. Mercenaries went where there was money and work, and Ragosa offered both. For how long, no one knew, but that summer and fall the city on Lake Serrana was home to an eclectic array of fighting men from Jaloña and Valledo, and further afield: Ferrieres, Batiara, Karch, Waleska. Blond, bearded Karcher giants from the far north mingled—and frequently brawled—with lean, smooth-shaven, dagger-wielding men from the dangerous cities of Batiara. One heard half a dozen languages in the marketplace of a morning. Alvar's Asharic was increasingly fluent now and he could swear in two Karcher dialects.

Walking a little distance aside with him on the day they had parted, Ser Rodrigo had told Alvar that he need not hurry home. He gave him leave to linger in Ragosa, with orders to post letters of report with any tradesmen heading towards Valledo.

A captain of King Badir's army had summoned Alvar on the third day after their arrival. It was a well-run, highly disciplined army, for all its diversity. He had been marked as soon as they passed through the gates. The horse and armor he'd won at Orvilla were too good for him not to be noted. He was closely interviewed, enlisted at a salary and placed in a company. He was also, after a few days, permitted to leave the barracks and live with Jehane and Velaz in the Kindath Quarter, which surprised him. It wouldn't have happened in Esteren.

It was because of Jehane's position. She had been immediately installed at court, newest of the physicians to the king and his notorious Kindath chancellor, Mazur ben Avren. Her formal place in a palace retinue—in Ragosa, as everywhere else in the world—carried with it certain perquisites.

None of which had stopped Alvar from being embroiled in three fights not of his choosing during the first fortnight after he left the barracks and went to live in their house. That much was also the same everywhere: soldiers had their own codes, whatever royal courts might decree, and young fighting men granted special privileges had to be prepared to establish their right to those.

Alvar fought. Not to the death, for that was forbidden in a city that needed its mercenaries, but he wounded two men, and took a cut on the outside of his sword arm that had Jehane briefly worried. The sight of her concern was worth the wound and the scar that remained when it healed. Alvar expected wounds and scars; he was a soldier, such things came with his chosen course of life. He was also here in Ragosa as a known representative of Rodrigo Belmonte's company, and when he fought it was with a consciousness that he was upholding the pride of the Captain's men and their eminence among the companies of the world. It was a role he shouldered alone, with an anxious sense of responsibility.

Until, at the very end of that same summer, Ser Rodrigo had come himself through the pass to Ragosa on his black horse with one hundred and fifty soldiers and a silk merchant, the banners of Belmonte and Valledo flapping in the wind as they rode up to the walls along the shore of the lake.

Things changed then. Things began to change everywhere.

"By the eyeteeth of the holy god," Laín Nunez had cackled in horror when Alvar reported to them that first day, "will you look at this! The boy's gone and converted himself! What will I tell his poor father?"

The Captain, scrutinizing Alvar's clothing with amusement, had said only, "I've had three reports. You appear to have done well by us. Tell me exactly how you were wounded and what you would do differently next time."

Alvar, grinning for all he was worth, a warm glow rising in him as from drinking unmixed wine, had told him.

Now, some time later, running through the market under the blue skies of a crisp autumn morning to find Jehane and give her the day's huge tidings, he knew himself to be recognized, envied, even a little feared.

No one challenged him to duels any more. The celebrated Ser Rodrigo of Valledo, in exile, had accepted a huge contract with King Badir, with the full year paid in advance, which was almost unheard-of.

Rodrigo's men were soldiers of Ragosa now, the vanguard of a fighting force that was to enforce order in city and countryside, to hold back newly ambitious Jaloña, and Cartada, and the worst incursions of the outlaw chieftain ibn Hassan from his southern fortress of Arbastro. Life was complex in Ragosa, and dangers many-faceted.

Life seemed an entirely splendid affair to young Alvar de Pellino that morning, and the brilliant, cultured Ragosa of King Badir was—who would dream of denying it?—the most civilized place in the world.

Alvar had been to the palace with Jehane, and several times with Rodrigo. There was a stream running right through it, watering some of the inner gardens and courtyards and passing, by a means Alvar could not grasp, through the largest of the banquet rooms.

At the most sumptuous of his feasts King Badir—sensuous, self-indulgent, undeniably shrewd—liked to have the meal floated along this stream in trays, to be collected from the water by half-naked slaves and presented to the king's guests as they reclined on their couches in the ancient fashion. Alvar had written a letter to his parents mentioning this; he knew they wouldn't believe him.

He usually tried to avoid running through the streets these days—it was too youthful, too undignified—but the news of the morning was enormous and he wanted to be the one to tell Jehane.

He skidded around a leather-goods stall and grabbed for the awning pole to help him turn. The pole rocked, the canopy tilted dangerously. The artisan, a man he knew, cursed him routinely as Alvar shouted an apology over his shoulder.

Jehane and Velaz would be at their own stall in the market. She had been following her father's practice and her own from Fezana. Even though handsomely rewarded at the palace, she was always at the booth on the country market morning, and in her consulting rooms two afternoons a week. A physician needed to be known outside the chambers of the palace, she had told Alvar. Her father had taught her that. A doctor could as easily go out of fashion at court as come into it. It was never wise to be cut off from other sources of patients.

It had been Velaz who had told Alvar what had happened to Jehane's father.

In the time before Rodrigo's arrival the two men had taken to having dinner together some evenings when Jehane was at court and Alvar free of watch or patrol duties. The night he heard the story of Ishak ben Yonannon and King Almalik's youngest son, Alvar had dreamed, for the first time but not the last, of killing the king of Cartada and coming back through the mountain pass to Jehane in Ragosa with word that her father had been avenged for his dark, silent pain.

This morning's news had ended that particular dream.

She was not at the booth. Velaz was alone at the back, closing up early, putting away medicines and implements. She must have just left; there were patients still milling about in front of the stall. A buzz of excitement and apprehension animated the whispered conversations.

"Velaz! Where is she? I have news!" Alvar said, breathing hard. He had sprinted all the way from the western gate.

Velaz looked at him over his shoulder, his expression difficult to read. "Alvar. We heard, from the palace. Almalik's dead. Zabira of Cartada's here. Jehane's gone to court."

"Why?" Alvar asked sharply.

"Mazur wanted her. He likes her with him now, when things are happening."

Alvar knew that, actually. It didn't bring him any pleasure at all.

ை

Jehane derived a healthy enjoyment from the extremely rare occasions when she engaged in the act of lovemaking.

She also had an equally healthy sense of self-respect. The universally acknowledged truths that Mazur ben Avren the chancellor of Ragosa was the most illustrious member of the Kindath community in Al-Rassan, the most sagacious, the most subtle and the most generous, did not negate the equally fundamental fact that he was the most sexually rapacious man she'd ever encountered or even heard of, outside of royalty with its harems.

He *was* royalty, in a sense, and he might as well have had a harem. Ben Avren was known as the Prince of the Kindath throughout Al-Rassan, and though he actively disavowed the name—a prudent act given the malevolent watchfulness of the wadjis—there was truth to that title, too.

Royalty or not, Jehane resisted being bedded by a man who clearly expected to do so as a matter of right.

She had made that point as emphatically as she could the first night he'd invited her to dine in his private quarters in the palace. There had been two musicians in the room. It became evident that they were expected to linger after the meal and continue playing while the chancellor and his current companion disported themselves.

Jehane was otherwise inclined.

Mazur ben Avren, seeming amused more than anything else, had contented himself with sharing sweet wine and small cakes after their meal, offering anecdotes about her father whom he had known well, and culling her own thoughts—comprehensively—about the likely course of events in Fezana now, among the Kindath community and the city at large. He was the chancellor of Ragosa before all else, he made that clear.

He made it equally obvious, however, that he expected her resistance to him to be temporary, and regarded it as an affectation more than anything else. He was fifty-seven years old that year, trim and fit, with a full head of grey hair under a soft blue Kindath cap, a neatly barbered, perfumed beard, a modulated, meditative voice, and a mind that could move without hesitation from poetry to military planning. He also bore the unmistakable look, in his dark brown, heavy-lidded eyes, of a man accustomed to pleasing and being pleased by women.

There had been days and nights in the period that followed when Jehane had asked herself whether her resistance to him *was*, in fact, merely an impediment of pride. Most of the time she didn't think so. Ben Avren, stimulating and gracious as he was with her, bestowed the exact same appraising glance upon too many women. Upon *all* women, in fact. He certainly wasn't waiting for her favors in chaste frustration. In a certain way, one had to admire his omnivorous hunger. Not many men at his age could harbor—let alone implement—such an appetite.

His amusement at her refusal did not fade; neither did his witty, elegant courtesy or the invitation that always lay just beneath that courteousness. There was never even a hint of anger, or force. This was, after all, one of the most cultivated men in Al-Rassan. He asked her opinions, flatteringly. She was careful about what she had to say, and not too quick to answer.

She began noticing changes in herself as time passed, in the way she thought about things. She found herself anticipating what Mazur's questions might be, considering her answers in advance. He always appeared to listen to her, which was something rare in Jehane's experience.

It came to be accepted that the chancellor was being regularly attended upon by the court's new doctor, in the audience hall and elsewhere. Everyone at court, even King Badir, seemed to be aware that ben Avren was persistently wooing her. It was, evidently, a source of amusement for them. She was a woman of his own faith, which made the entire, extremely public dance even more diverting, as summer gave way to autumn and the code of dress in the palace changed with the changing leaves in the gardens and in the forests beyond the walls.

Jehane didn't much like being a source of diversion for anyone, but she couldn't deny it was pleasant to be attending at a court as sophisticated as this one. Nor could she complain about being afforded less than complete respect professionally. Her father's name had ensured that at the beginning, and her own unfussy competence in a number of matters had consolidated it, after.

Then Rodrigo Belmonte had arrived, with his full company, exiled from Valledo in the wake of events she knew. The Day of the Moat and the burning of Orvilla had altered lives other than her own, it seemed.

Things began to change again. Alvar went to live in the barracks with the rest of Rodrigo's company, leaving her alone with Velaz. His departure was a source of both relief and regret for Jehane. The second emotion surprised her a little. His feelings for her were too obvious, and too obviously more than what she'd hoped they were: the transitory passion of a young man for his first love.

There was more to Alvar de Pellino than that, however,

and Jehane had to admit that during the time of her steady siege by the chancellor, when pride kept her from his bed, it had occurred to her to take refuge with her Jaddite soldier again. He wasn't *her* soldier, though, and he deserved better of her. Alvar might be young, but Jehane could see clear signs of what had led Rodrigo Belmonte to bring him south and then let him accompany her alone to Ragosa. But had she wanted a domestic life she could have had it in Fezana by now with a number of Kindath men, not with a Jaddite from the north.

There might be a day when she regretted decisions made and the ones not made, the paths that had led her to be well past her prime marrying years now, and alone, but that day had not yet come.

Their small house and treatment rooms seemed quiet and empty after Alvar left. She had grown into a habit of discussing the events of the day with him. *How very domestic*, she'd thought wryly more than once. But the truth was that many times the thoughts she'd later relayed to the chancellor had been Alvar's, over a late-night cup of wine.

Even Velaz seemed to miss the young Jaddite; she hadn't expected a friendship to develop there. Singing the sun god's exultant chants of triumph, the Jaddites of Esperaña had slaughtered the Kindath through the centuries or, in generations slightly less bloodthirsty, had forced them to convert or made them slaves. Easy friendships, perhaps even less than love, did not readily emerge from such a history.

It was hard to attach that long, stony bitterness to Alvar de Pellino, though. Or to Rodrigo Belmonte, for that matter. The Captain still wanted her as physician to his band; he had made that clear as soon as he'd arrived. Had said it was one of the reasons he was here. She didn't believe that, but he'd said it, nonetheless, and she did know how important a good doctor was to a fighting company, and how hard they were to find.

She remembered the night ride with him across the land north of Fezana and the river, Orvilla burning behind them, the bodies of the dead lying on the grass. She remembered words spoken around the campfire later. He remembered them too; she could see that in his grey eyes. Rodrigo was still unlike anything she might have expected him to be.

She had teased him on that solitary ride under the two moons, letting her hands slide down to his thighs. She had been irritated, deliberately provocative. She didn't think she would risk that again. She couldn't believe she had done it in the first place. It was reported by Alvar that the Captain was married to the most beautiful woman in Valledo.

Rodrigo had spoken of his wife that night near Fezana as if she was an unholy terror. He had an odd sense of humor. Alvar worshipped him. All his company did. It was obvious, and it said a great deal.

They had spoken seldom since he'd arrived, and only in public. It was among a number of people, including ben Avren, the chancellor, at a reception in a palace courtyard, that Rodrigo had again declared his intention of recruiting her. Mazur had been watching them. The chancellor had arched his expressive eyebrows but he hadn't raised the matter later when they were alone. Neither had Jehane.

Rodrigo was usually outside the walls through the autumn's early, mild days, leading his company—or parts of it—on a sequence of minor, overdue expeditions designed to deal with outlaw bands to the northeast, and then making a show of strength in the small, important city of Fibaz, by the pass leading to Ferrieres. Ragosa controlled Fibaz, and drew taxes from it, but King Bermudo of Jaloña had increasingly obvious designs upon the town.

He had already made his first tribute demand, the *parias* gold being exacted from Fezana by his nephew in Valledo serving as an example. The Jaddites were growing bold. Remembering that moonlit conversation by a campfire, Jehane asked Mazur once how long he thought Al-Rassan's city-kings could survive. He hadn't answered that question.

Rodrigo had made it explicit that he wanted Jehane to come as physician with his company on those early expeditions. She knew he saw them as a test for both of them.

It wasn't entirely her decision, in a way. She could have accepted or refused, but did not, waiting to see what would happen. King Badir promised his newest mercenary leader that he would consider the matter, and then promptly increased Jehane's duties at court. Mazur was controlling that, she knew. She was uncertain whether to be vexed or amused. By the terms of her engagement she was free to leave if she wanted, but they were determined to make it difficult. Rodrigo, in and out of the city through the autumn, bided his time.

Husari ibn Musa rode with him on several of those expeditions. Jehane's former patient was almost unrecognizable. No longer the portly, soft merchant he had been, he had lost a great deal of weight in a season. He looked a younger, harder man now. The kidney stones no longer vexed him, he said. He could ride all day, and had been learning to handle a sword and bow. He wore a wide-brimmed Jaddite leather hat now, even in the city. Jehane had said teasingly that he and Alvar appeared to have exchanged cultures. When the two men first saw each other they laughed, and then grew thoughtful.

The leather Jaddite hat was an emblem of sorts for Husari, Jehane decided. A reminder. He, too, had sworn an oath of vengeance, and the recollection of that served to modify her surprise at the changes in him. He was still actively doing business, he told her one night when he came for dinner in the Kindath Quarter, as he used to come to her father's house. His factors were busy all over Al-Rassan, even here in Ragosa, he added, as the servant Velaz had hired poured wine for them. There were, simply, other priorities for him now, Husari said. Since the Day of the Moat. She'd asked, cautiously, what affairs he was pursuing in Cartada, but that question he had deflected.

It was interesting, Jehane thought, lying in bed that night: all these men who trusted her had certain questions they would not answer. Except Alvar, she supposed. She was fairly certain he would answer anything she asked him. There was something to be said for straightforwardness in a world of oblique intrigue. She had Velaz for directness, though. She'd always had Velaz. More of a blessing than she deserved. She remembered that it was her father who had made her take Velaz when she left home.

Amid all of this, the king's three other court physicians actively hated her. That was to be expected. A woman, and a Kindath, and preferred by the chancellor? Openly coveted by the most celebrated Jaddite captain for his company? She was lucky they hadn't poisoned her, she wrote in a letter to Ser Rezzoni in Sorenica. She asked him to continue writing her father. She said there was reason to believe there might now be a reply. She wrote home herself twice a week. Letters came back. Her mother's careful handwriting, in slanted Kindath script, but her father's dictation now, some of the time. Small, good things, it seemed, still happened in the world.

She didn't make that jest about being poisoned to them, of course. Parents were parents, and they would have been afraid for her.

On the autumn morning when Mazur's messenger brought her tidings from Cartada and bade her follow him to court that jest didn't seem particularly witty any more.

Someone *had* been poisoned, it appeared.

In the palace of Ragosa, as Jehane arrived and made her way to the Courtyard of the Streams where the king was awaiting the newly arrived visitor, no one's thoughts or whispered words were of anything else.

Almalik of Cartada, the self-styled Lion of Al-Rassan, was dead, and the lady Zabira—more his widow than anything else—had arrived unannounced this morning, a supplicant to King Badir. She had been accompanied only by her steward in her flight through the mountains, someone whispered.

Jehane, who had made the same journey with only two companions, wasn't impressed by that. But neither was she even remotely close to sorting out how she felt about the larger tidings. She was going to need a long time for that.

For the moment she could only grasp the essential fact that the man she had vowed to kill was somehow dead at Ammar ibn Khairan's hand—the story was not yet clear—and the woman who had birthed a living child and had herself survived only because of Jehane's father was soon to enter through the arches at the far end of this garden.

Beyond these two clear facts confusion reigned within her, mingled with something close to pain. She had left Fezana with a sworn purpose, and had proceeded to spend the past months in this city enjoying her work at court, enjoying—if she was honest—the flattering attentions of an immensely civilized man, enjoying the determined skirmishing for her professional services. Taking pleasure in her life. And doing nothing at all about Almalik of Cartada and the promise she'd made to herself on the Day of the Moat.

Too late now. It would always be too late, now.

She stood, as was her custom, on the margin of one bank of the stream, not far from Mazur's position at the king's right shoulder on the island. Wind-blown leaves were falling into the water and drifting away. As many times as she'd been in this garden, by daylight and under torches at night, Jehane was still conscious of its beauty. In autumn only the late flowers still bloomed, but the falling leaves in the sunlight and those yet clinging to the trees were brilliant, many-colored. She was aware of the effect this garden could have on someone seeing it for the first time.

The Courtyard of the Streams had been designed and contrived years ago. The same stream that ran through the banquet hall had been further channelled to pass through this garden and to branch into two forks, creating a small islet in the midst of trees and flowers and marble walkways beneath the carved arcades. On the isle, reached by two arched bridges, the king of Ragosa now sat on an ivory bench with his most honored courtiers beside him. Flanking the gently curving path that approached one of the bridges members of Badir's court waited in the autumn sunshine for the woman who had come to Ragosa.

Birds flitted in the branches overhead. Four musicians played on the far bank of the stream that ran behind the isle. Goldfish swam in the water. It was cool, but pleasant in the sun.

Jehane saw Rodrigo Belmonte on the other side of the garden, among the military men. He had returned from Fibaz two nights before. His eyes met hers, and she felt exposed by the thoughtful look in them. He had no right, on so little acquaintance, to be regarding her with such appraisal. She abruptly remembered telling him, by that fireside on the Fezana plain, that she intended to deal with Almalik of Cartada herself. That made her think of Husari, who had also been there that night, who had shaped the same intention...who would be experiencing much the same difficult tangle of thoughts and emotions that she was.

If someone doesn't do it before either of us, he had said that night. Someone had.

Husari wasn't here now. He had no status at court. She hoped there would be a chance to talk with him later. She thought of her father in Fezana, and what had been done to him by the king now slain.

Between coral-colored pillars at the far end of the garden a herald appeared, in green and white. The musicians stopped. There was a brief silence then a bird sang, one quick trilling run. Bronze doors opened and Zabira of Cartada was announced.

She entered under the arches of the arcade and waited between the pillars until the herald moved aside. She had arrived without ceremony, with only the one man, her steward, two steps behind her for escort. Jehane saw, as the woman approached along the walkway, that there had been nothing at all exaggerated in the reports of her beauty.

Zabira of Cartada was, in a sense, her own ceremony. She was an exquisite supplicant in a crimson-dyed, black-bordered gown over a golden undergown. She had jewelry at wrist and throat and on her fingers, and there were rubies set in the soft, night-black silken cap she wore.

They gleamed in the sunlight. With only one man to guard her, it appeared that she had carried an extraordinary treasure through the mountains. She was reckless then, or desperate. She was also dazzling. Fashions, thought Jehane, were about to change in Ragosa if this woman stayed for long.

Zabira moved forward with effortless, trained grace, betraying no wonder at all in this place, and then sank down in full obeisance to Badir. This was not, evidently, a woman for whom a garden or courtyard, even one such as this, held the power to awe. She wouldn't even blink at the stream running through the banquet room, Jehane decided, just before something took her thoughts in another direction entirely.

Most of the court was staring at Zabira in frank admiration. King Badir had ceased doing so, however, in the moment she lowered herself to the ground before the arched bridge leading to his isle. So, too, even before the king, had his chancellor.

A high cloud slid briefly across the sun, changing the light, lending a swift chill to the air, a reminder that it was autumn. At this moment the newest physician in Ragosa, following the king's narrowed glance past the kneeling woman, encountered a difficulty with her breathing.

Nor, as it happened, was Zabira of Cartada continuing to hold the attention of the newest and most prominent of the mercenary captains at King Badir's court.

Rodrigo Belmonte admired beauty and poise in a woman and evidence of courage; he had been married for almost sixteen years to a woman with these qualities. But he, too, was looking beyond Zabira now, gazing instead at the figure approaching the bridge and the isle, two dutiful steps behind her, preserving a palpable fiction for one more moment.

The sun came out, bathing them all in light. Zabira of Cartada remained on the ground, an embodiment of beauty and grace amid the falling leaves. She hardly mattered now.

The woman's companion, her sole companion, the man

who had been announced as her steward, was Ammar ibn Khairan.

For a handful of extremely subtle people in that garden further elements of the death of King Almalik were now explained. And for them, although the woman might be the most celebrated beauty in Al-Rassan, clever and gifted in herself and the mother of two enormously important children, the man was who he was, and had done—twice now, it seemed—what he had done.

He was undisguised, the signature pearl gleaming in his right ear, and Rodrigo knew him by the report of that. The black steward's robe only accentuated his natural composure. He was smiling—not very deferentially, not very much like a steward—as he scanned the assembled court of King Badir. Rodrigo saw him nod at a poet.

Ibn Khairan bowed to the king of Ragosa. When he straightened, his gaze met the chancellor's briefly, moved to Jehane bet Ishak—as the smile returned—and then he appeared to become aware that one of the Jaddite mercenaries was staring at him, and he turned to the man and knew him.

And so did Ser Rodrigo Belmonte, the Captain of Valledo, and the lord Ammar ibn Khairan of Aljais stand in the Courtyard of the Streams of Ragosa on a bright morning in autumn and look upon each other for the first time.

Jehane, caught in the whirlwind of her own emotions, was there to see that first look exchanged. She turned from one man to the other and then she shivered, without knowing why.

Alvar de Pellino, just then entering through a door at the far end of the arcaded walkway—sanctioned by his link to both the Captain and Jehane and a hasty lie about a message for Rodrigo—was in time to see that exchange of glances as well, and though he had not the least idea who the black-robed Cartadan steward with the earring was, he knew when Rodrigo was roused to intensity, and he could see it then.

Narrowing his eyes against the sun's brightness, he

looked for and found Jehane and saw her looking back and forth from one man to the other. Alvar did the same, struggling to understand what was happening here. And then he, too, felt himself shiver, though it wasn't really cold and the sun was high.

Back home, on their farm in the remotest part of Valledo, the kitchen women and the serving women, most of whom had been still half pagan, so far in the wild north, used to say that such a shiver meant only one thing: an emissary of death had just crossed into the realms of mortal men and women from the god's own lost world of Fiñar.

In silence, unaccountably disturbed, Alvar slipped through the crowd in the garden and took his place among the mercenaries on the near bank of the stream before the island.

Rodrigo and the black-clad Cartadan steward still had not taken their eyes from each other.

Others began to notice this now—there was something in the quality of the stillness possessing both of them. Out of the corner of his eye Alvar saw Mazur ben Avren turn to look at Rodrigo and then back to the steward.

Still trying to take his bearings, Alvar looked for anger in those two faces, for hatred, respect, irony, appraisal. He saw none of these things clearly, and yet elements of all of them. Hesitantly he decided, in the moment before the king of Ragosa spoke, that what he was seeing was a kind of recognition. Not just of each other, though there had to be that, but something harder to name. He thought, still minded of the night tales told at home, that it might even be a kind of foreknowing.

Alvar, a grown man now, a soldier, amid a gathering of people on a very bright morning, suddenly felt fear, the way he used to feel it as a child at night after hearing the women's stories, lying in his bed, listening to the north wind, rattling at the windows of the house.

"You are most welcome to Ragosa, lady," the king of Ragosa murmured.

If he had sensed any of this growing tension, he did not

betray it. There was genuine appreciation in his voice and manner. King Badir was a connoisseur of beauty in all shapes and guises. Alvar, struggling with his sudden dark mood and protected by the simple fact of love, thought the Cartadan lady fetching but overly adorned. She was flawless in her manner, however. Only after Badir spoke did she rise gracefully from the walkway and stand before the king's isle.

"Is this a mother's visit?" Badir went on. "Have you come to judge our royal care of your children?"

The king knew it was more than that, Alvar realized, having learned a great deal himself in three months. This was a gambit, an opening.

"There is that, Magnificence," said Zabira of Cartada, "though I have no fears regarding your attentiveness to my little ones. I am here, though, with more import to my visit than a mother's fond doting." Her voice was low but clear, a musician's, trained.

She said, "I have come to tell a tale of murder. A son's murder of his father, and the consequences of that."

There was near silence in the garden again; only the one bird still singing overhead, the breeze in the leaves of the trees, the steady lapping of the two streams around the isle.

In that quiet, Zabira said, "By the holy teachings of Ashar it is given to us as law that a murderer of his father is eternally unclean, to be shunned while alive, to be executed or driven from all gatherings of men, accursed of the god and the stars. I ask the king of Ragosa: shall such a man reign in Cartada?"

"Does he?" King Badir was a sensualist, known to be self-indulgent, but no one had ever impugned the quality of his mind.

"He does. A fortnight ago the Lion of Cartada was foully slain, and his murdering son now bears the scepter and the glass, and styles himself Almalik II, Lion of Cartada, Defender of Al-Rassan." There was a sound in the garden then, for all the details were news: she had crossed the mountains faster than messengers. Zabira drew herself up straight and raised her voice with deliberate intent. "I am come here, my lord king, to beg you to free the people of my dear city from this father-killer and regicide. To send your armies west, fulfilling the precepts of holy Ashar, to destroy this evil man."

Another ripple of sound, like the breeze through the leaves.

"And who then shall reign in glorious Cartada?" Badir's expression gave away nothing at all.

For the first time the woman hesitated. "The city is in peril. We have learned that the usurper's brother Hazem is away to the south across the straits. He is a zealot, and seeks aid and alliance from the tribes in the Majriti deserts. He has been in open defiance of his father and was formally disinherited years ago."

"That last we know," Badir said softly. "That much all men know. But who then should reign in Cartada?" he asked again. By now even Alvar could see where this was going.

The woman had courage, there was no denying it. "You are guardian here in Ragosa of the only two loyal children of King Almalik," she said, with no hesitation now. "It is my formal petition that you take that city in the god's name and place there as king his son, Abadi ibn Almalik. And that you lend to him all such aid and support as you may during the time of his minority."

It was said, then. Openly. An invitation to take Cartada, and the cloak of right under which to do it.

Jehane, listening with fierce attention, looked beyond the woman in crimson and black and saw that Alvar had managed to obtain admittance here. She turned again to the king.

But it was the chancellor who now spoke, for the first time, the deep voice measured and grave. "I would know, if I might, is this also the thought and desire of the steward you bring with you?"

Looking quickly back to Zabira, Jehane realized that the

woman did not know the answer to that question; that she had played a card of her own, and was waiting on what would follow.

She played the next, necessary card. "He is not my steward," Zabira said. "You will know, I believe, who this man is. He has been gracious enough to escort me here, a woman without defenders or any recourse at home. I will not dare presume to speak for Ammar ibn Khairan, my lord chancellor, my lord king. No one alive would do that."

"Then perhaps the man who appears before us in the false garb of a steward might presume to speak for himself?" King Badir betrayed the slightest tension in his voice now. It wasn't surprising, Jehane thought. The woman had raised the stakes of the game extraordinarily high.

Ammar ibn Khairan, whom she had kissed—amazingly—in her father's study, turned his gaze to the king of Ragosa. There was a measure of respect to be seen in him, but no real deference. For the first time Jehane realized just how difficult a man this one could be, if he chose. He had also, she reminded herself again, killed a khalif and now a king.

He said, "Most gracious king, I find myself in a troubling circumstance. I have just heard words of open treason to my own kingdom of Cartada. My course ought to be clear, but I am doubly constrained."

"Why? And why doubly?" King Badir asked, sounding vexed.

Ibn Khairan shrugged gracefully. And waited. As if the issue was a test, not for him, but for the assembled court of Ragosa in that garden.

And it was Mazur the chancellor who said, "He ought to kill her, but will not attack a woman, and he may not draw a weapon in your presence." There was irritation in his voice. "In fact you ought not to even *have* a weapon here."

"This is true," ibn Khairan said mildly. "Your guards were...courteous. Perhaps too much so."

"Perhaps they saw no reason to fear a man of your...repute," the chancellor murmured silkily.

A dagger of sorts there, Jehane thought, chasing nuances as quickly as she could. Ibn Khairan's reputation encompassed many things, and it included a new dimension as of this morning's news. He could not, on the face of things, be said to be a harmless man. Perhaps especially not for kings.

Ammar smiled, as if savoring the innuendo. "It has been long," he said, with apparent inconsequentiality, "since I have had the privilege of exchanging words with the estimable chancellor of Ragosa. Whatever our jealous wadjis might say, he remains a credit to his people and the great king he serves. In my most humble view."

At which point the king mentioned appeared to lose patience. "You were asked a question," Badir said bluntly, and those assembled in that garden were made sharply aware that whatever poise or subtlety might be here on display, only one man ruled. "You have not answered it."

"Ah. Yes," said Ammar ibn Khairan. "That question." He clasped his hands loosely before him. Alvar de Pellino, watching closely, found himself wondering where the hidden weapon was. If there was one. Ibn Khairan said, "The lady Zabira, I will confess, has surprised me. Not for the first time, mind you." Alvar saw the woman glance away at the flowing water.

"I was of the impression, innocently, that she wished to be escorted here to see her children," said the man garbed as her steward, "and because there was no haven for her in Cartada. Being of a regrettably short-sighted nature I thought no further on these matters."

"These are games," said the king of Ragosa. "We may or may not have time for them later. You are the least short-sighted man in this peninsula."

"I am honored by your words, my lord king. Unworthy as I am, I can only repeat that I did not expect to hear what I heard just now. At the moment my position is delicate. You must appreciate that. I am still sworn to allegiance to the kingdom of Cartada." His blue eyes flashed. "If I speak with some care, perhaps that might be indulged by a king as august and wise as Badir of Ragosa."

It occurred to Jehane just about then that ibn Khairan might easily be killed here today. There was a silence. The king glared, and shifted impatiently on his bench.

"I see. You have already been exiled by the new king of Cartada. Immediately after you did his killing for him. How extremely clever of the young man." It was Mazur again, and not a question.

Badir glanced at his chancellor and then back to ibn Khairan; his expression had changed.

Of course, Jehane thought. That had to be it. Why else was the prince's advisor and confidant here with Zabira instead of controlling the transfer of power in Cartada? She felt like a fool for missing the point. She hadn't been alone, though. Throughout the garden Jehane saw men— and the handful of women—nodding their heads.

"Alas, the chancellor in his wisdom speaks the sad truth. I am exiled, yes. For my many vices." Ibn Khairan's voice was calm. "There appears some hope of my being pardoned, after I purge myself of sundry unspeakable iniquities." He smiled, and a moment later, quite unexpectedly, one man's laughter was heard, the sound startling amid the tension of the garden.

The king and his chancellor and Ammar ibn Khairan all turned to stare at Rodrigo Belmonte, who was still laughing.

"The king of Ragosa," Rodrigo said, greatly amused, "had best be careful, or every exile in the peninsula will be beating a path to his palace doors." Ibn Khairan, Jehane noticed, was no longer smiling as he looked at him.

Rodrigo chuckled again, highly amused. "If I may be forgiven, perhaps a soldier may help cut a path through the difficulty here?" He waited for the king to nod, before going on. "The lord ibn Khairan appears in a situation oddly akin to my own. He stands here exiled but with no offered allegiance to supersede the one he owes Cartada. In the absence of such an offer, he cannot possibly endorse or even honorably be asked to comment upon what the lady Zabira has suggested. Indeed, he ought properly to kill her with the blade taped to the inside of his left arm. Make him," said Rodrigo Belmonte, "an offer."

A rigid stillness followed this. The day seemed almost too bright now, as if the sunlight were at odds with the gravity of what was happening here below.

"Shall I become a mercenary?" Ibn Khairan was still gazing at the Jaddite captain, as if oblivious to those on the isle now. Again Jehane felt that odd, uncanny chill.

"We are a lowly folk, I concede. But there are lower sorts." Rodrigo was still amused, or he appeared to be.

Ibn Khairan was not. He said carefully, "I had nothing to do with the Day of the Moat." Jehane caught her breath.

"Of course you didn't," said Rodrigo Belmonte. "That's why you killed the king."

"That's why I *had* to kill the king," said ibn Khairan, grave in his black robe. Another murmur of sound rose and fell away.

It was the chancellor's turn to sound irritated. Deliberately breaking the mood, Mazur said, "And are we to offer a position here to a man who slays whenever his pride is wounded?"

Jehane realized, with an unexpected flicker of amusement, that he was irked because Rodrigo had pieced together this part of the puzzle first. *On the subject of wounded pride*, she thought...

"Not whenever," said ibn Khairan quietly. "Once in my life, and with regret, and for something very large."

"Ah!" said the chancellor sardonically, "with *regret*. Well, that changes everything."

For the first time Jehane saw ibn Khairan betray an unguarded reaction. She watched his blue gaze go cold before he lowered his eyes from ben Avren's face. Drawing a breath, he unclasped his hands and let them fall to his sides. She saw that he wasn't wearing his rings. He looked up again at the chancellor, saying nothing, waiting. Very much, Jehane thought, like someone braced for what further blows might be levelled against him.

No blows fell, verbal or otherwise. Instead, it was the

king who spoke again, his equanimity restored. "If we should agree with our Valledan friend, what could you offer us?"

Zabira of Cartada, nearly forgotten in all this, turned and looked back at the man who had come here as her steward. Her dark, carefully accentuated eyes were quite unreadable. Another fringe of cloud trailed past the sun and then away, taking the light and giving it back.

"Myself," said Ammar ibn Khairan.

In that exquisite garden no one's gaze was anywhere but upon him. The arrogance was dazzling, but the man had been known, for fifteen years and more, not only as a diplomat and a strategist, but as a military commander and the purest swordsman in Al-Rassan.

"That will be sufficient," said King Badir, visibly diverted now. "We offer you service in our court and armed companies for a term of one year. On your honor, you will not take or offer service elsewhere in that time without our leave. We shall allow our advisors to propose and discuss terms. Do you accept?"

An answering smile came, the one Jehane remembered from her father's chamber.

"I do," said ibn Khairan. "I find I rather like the idea of being bought. And the terms will be easy." The smile deepened. "Exactly those you have offered our Valledan friend."

"Ser Rodrigo came here with one hundred and fifty horsemen!" said Mazur ben Avren, with the just indignation of a man tasked with monitoring purse strings in difficult times.

"Even so," said ibn Khairan, with an indifferent shrug. Rodrigo Belmonte, Jehane saw, was smiling. The other captains were not. A palpable ripple of anger moved through them.

One man stepped forward. A blond giant from Karch. "Let them fight," he said, in thickly accented Asharic. "He says he is worth so much. Let us see it. Good soldiers here are paid much less. Let Belmonte and this man try swords for proof."

Jehane saw the idea spark and kindle through the garden. The novelty, the hint of danger. The testing. The king looked at the Karcher soldier speculatively.

"I think not."

Jehane bet Ishak would always remember that moment. How three voices chimed together, as in trained harmony, the same words in the same moment.

"We cannot afford to risk such men in idle games," said ben Avren the chancellor, first of the three to continue.

Rodrigo Belmonte and Ammar ibn Khairan, each of whom had also spoken those words, remained silent, staring at each other again. Rodrigo was no longer smiling.

Mazur stopped. The stillness stretched. Even the captain from Karch looked from one to the other and took a step backwards, muttering under his breath.

"I think," said ibn Khairan finally, so softly Jehane had to lean forward to hear, "that if this man and I ever cross swords, it will not be for anyone's diversion, or to determine yearly wages. Forgive me, but I will decline this suggestion."

King Badir looked as if he would say something, but then, glancing over at his chancellor, he did not.

"I do have a thought," Rodrigo murmured. "Though I have no doubt at all that the lord ibn Khairan is worth whatever the king of Ragosa chooses to offer him, I can appreciate why some of our companions might wish to see his mettle. I should be honored to fight beside him for the king's pleasure against our friend from Karch and any four men he would like to have join him in the lists this afternoon."

"No!" said Mazur.

"*Done*," said King Badir of Ragosa. The chancellor checked himself with an effort. The king went on, "I should enjoy such a display. So would the people of my city. Let them applaud the valiant men who defend their liberty. But as to the contract, I accept your terms, ibn Khairan. The same wages for both my exiled captains. That amuses me, in truth."

He did look pleased, as if having discerned a path through the thicket of nuances that had been woven in the garden. "My lord ibn Khairan, it is past time to begin earning your fee. We shall require your presence immediately to consider certain matters raised here this morning. You will do battle for our pleasure this afternoon. We shall then require something further." He smiled with anticipation. "A verse to be offered after the banquet we will have prepared in the lady Zabira's honor and your own tonight. I have agreed to your terms, frankly, because I am also acquiring a poet."

Ibn Khairan had been looking at Rodrigo at the beginning of this, but by the end the king had his steady, courteous regard. "I am honored to be of service in any capacity at all, my lord king. Have you a preferred subject for tonight?"

"I do, with the king's gracious permission," said Mazur ben Avren, one index finger stroking his beard. He paused for effect. "A lament for the slain king of Cartada."

Jehane had not actually known he could be cruel. She abruptly remembered that it had been ibn Khairan, in her father's chambers, who had warned her to be careful with Mazur. And with the thought she realized that he was looking at her. She felt herself flush, as if discovered at something. His own expression thoughtful, Ammar turned back to the chancellor.

"As you wish," he said simply. "It is a worthy subject."

The poem he offered them that night, after the banquet dishes and cups had been cleared away, after the afternoon's extraordinary encounter in the lists beneath the city walls, was to travel the length and breadth of the peninsula, even on the bad roads of winter.

By spring it had made people weep—more often than not against their will—in a score of castles and as many cities and towns, notwithstanding the fact that Almalik of Cartada had been the most feared man in Al-Rassan. It is an old truth that men and women sometimes miss what they hate as much as what they love.

On the night that lament was first offered, in the banquet room of Ragosa by a man who still preferred to name himself a poet before anything else, it had already been decided that war with Cartada would be premature, whatever the dead king's woman might desire for her sons. There was no real dissent. Winter was coming; not a time for armies. Spring would doubtless open a course of wisdom to them, much as flowers would open in the gardens and the countryside.

Guarding Zabira's two boys had become rather more important than hitherto; everyone agreed on that as well. Princes were useful, especially young ones. One couldn't have too many royal pawns. It was another old truth.

At the very end of that extremely long day and night— after the meeting, after the passage of arms, after the banquet, after the verses and the toasts and the last lifted glasses of wine in the splendid room where the stream ran—two men remained awake, speaking together in the king of Ragosa's private chambers with only the servants, lighting candles, in the room with them.

"I don't feel easy at all," said Mazur ben Avren to his king.

Badir, leaning back in a low chair—an exquisite thing, Jaddite in style but made of Tudescan redwood, with ivory legs in the shape of lions' feet—smiled at his chancellor and stretched out his legs upon a stool.

The two men had known each other a long time. Badir had taken a huge risk at the very outset of his reign in appointing a Kindath chancellor. The texts of Ashar were explicit: no Kindath or Jaddite could hold sovereign authority of any kind over the Star-born. No Asharite could even be employed by them. The penalty, if one followed the desert code, was the death by stones.

Of course no one who mattered in Al-Rassan followed the desert code. Not during the Khalifate, not after. The glass of wine in the king's hand was the most current evidence of that. Even so, a Kindath chancellor had been a

very large thing—a gamble that the wadjis would complain
as usual but be able to do no more. There was a chance
that roll of dice might have cost Badir his newly claimed
crown and his life if the people had risen in righteous
wrath. In return for that risk taken, Mazur ben Avren, the
so-called Prince of the Kindath, had made Ragosa not only
independent, but the second most powerful kingdom in
Al-Rassan in the turbulent years after the Khalifate's fall.
He had guided the city and her king through the dangerous shoals of a swiftly changing world, had kept Ragosa
free and solvent and proud.

He had ridden with the army himself in the first years,
in campaigns to the south and east, and had directed it in
the field, triumphantly. His mount had been a mule, not a
forbidden horse; Mazur knew enough to offer the wadjis
their necessary symbols of deference. Nonetheless, the
simple truth was that Mazur ben Avren was the first
Kindath to command an army in the western world in five
hundred years. Poet, scholar, diplomat, jurist. And soldier.
More than anything else, those early military triumphs had
ensured his survival and Badir's. Much could be forgiven if
a war went well and an army came home with gold.

Much *had* been forgiven, thus far. Badir ruled, ben
Avren beside him, and together they had shared another
dream: a desire to make Ragosa beautiful as well as free. A
city of marble and ivory and gardens of exquisite detail. If
Cartada to the west under the hated and feared Almalik
had inherited the larger portion of the power of the khalifs, Ragosa on Lake Serrana was an emblem of other things
Silvenes once had been in the lost days of splendor.

They were an old team by now, the king and his chancellor, deeply familiar with each other, without illusions.
Each of them knew that an ending could come at any time,
from any number of directions. The moons waxed and
waned. The stars could be hidden by clouds, or burned
away by the sun.

If Silvenes and the Al-Fontina could fall, if that city and
palace could be sacked and fired and left as nothing more

than wind-borne ashes of glory, any city, any kingdom could be brought down. It was a lesson learned by all who claimed any measure of power in the peninsula after the death of the last khalif.

"I know you're uneasy," King Badir said, glancing up at his chancellor. He gestured. "For one thing, you haven't touched your glass. You don't even know what I've poured for us."

Mazur smiled briefly. He picked up his golden wine, looked at it in the candlelight and then sipped, eyes closed.

"Wonderful," he murmured. "Ardeño vineyards, and a late growth, surely? When did this come?"

"When do you think?"

The chancellor sipped again, with real pleasure. "Of course. This morning. Not from the woman, I'd imagine."

"They said it was."

"Of course they did." There was a silence.

"That was a remarkable poem we heard tonight." The king's voice, resuming, was low.

Ben Avren nodded. "I thought so."

King Badir looked at his chancellor for a moment. "You've done as well, in your time."

Mazur shook his head. "Thank you, my lord, but I know my limits there." Another pause. Mazur stroked his carefully trimmed beard. "He's an extraordinary man."

The king's gaze was direct. "Too much so?"

Ben Avren shrugged. "On his own, perhaps not, but I'm not entirely sure of being able to control events through a winter with the two of them here."

Badir nodded, sipped his wine. "How are those five men from this afternoon?"

"All right, I am told. Jehane bet Ishak is looking after them tonight. I took the liberty of asking her to do that in your name. One broken arm. One who is apparently uncertain of his name or where he is." The chancellor shook his head ruefully. "The one from Karch who proposed the challenge is the one whose arm was fractured."

"I saw that. Deliberate?"

The chancellor shrugged. "I couldn't say."

"I'm still not certain how that was done to him."

"Neither is he," ben Avren said.

The king grinned and after a moment so did his chancellor. The two attendant servants had finished with the candles and the fire by now. They stood, motionless as statues, by the doors to the room.

"They fought as if they had been together all their lives," Badir said musingly, setting down his glass. He looked at his chancellor. Mazur gazed back without speaking. A moment later the king said, "You are thinking about how best to use them. About Cartada?"

The chancellor nodded. Their glances held for a long time. It was as if they had exchanged a dialogue without words. Mazur nodded again.

The king's expression was sober in the candlelight. "Did you see how they stared at each other this morning, in the garden?"

"That would have been difficult to miss."

"You think the Valledan's a match for ibn Khairan?"

Mazur's finger came up and stroked his beard again. "Very different men. You saw them, my lord. He may be. He may actually...I don't know *what* I think about that, my lord, to be honest. I do know there's too much power gathering here, and I don't think the wadjis, among others, will like *any* of it. Jaddite soldiers from Valledo now, to go with those from across the mountains, the princely sons of a courtesan, a female Kindath doctor to go with a Kindath chancellor, and now the most notoriously secular man in Al-Rassan..."

"I thought *I* was that last," King Badir said with a wry expression.

Mazur's mouth quirked. "Forgive me, my lord. The *two* most notorious, then."

Badir's expression grew reflective again. He'd had a great deal of wine, without evident effect. "Zabira said Almalik's second son had gone across the straits. To speak with the Muwardi leaders, she said."

"Hazem ibn Almalik, yes. I knew that, actually. He went some time ago. Stopped for a while in Tudesca with the wadjis there."

Badir absorbed this. The range and depth of ben Avren's information was legendary. Not even the king knew all his sources.

"What do you make of it?"

"Nothing good, my lord, to be truthful."

"Have we sent our gifts to the desert this year?"

"Of course, my lord."

Badir lifted his glass and drank. Then his mouth twitched again, the same wry amusement as before. "There was never an assurance of anything good from the time we began, was there? We've had a long run, my friend."

"It isn't over."

"Nearly?" The king's voice was soft.

The chancellor shook his head grimly. "Not if I can help it."

Badir nodded, relaxed in his chair, sipping the good wine. "It will be as the stars dispose. What do we do, in the meantime, with these...lions in my city this season?"

"Send them out, I think."

"In winter? Where?"

"I do have an idea."

The king laughed. "Don't you always?"

They smiled at each other. King Badir raised his glass and silently saluted his chancellor. Mazur rose and bowed, setting down his own wine.

"I will leave you," he said. "Good night, my lord. The stars and Ashar's spirit guide you safely through to dawn."

"And your moons ease the dark for you, my friend."

The chancellor bowed a second time and went out. The nearer of the servants closed the door after him. The king of Ragosa did not go immediately to bed, however. He sat in his chair for a long time, unmoving.

He was thinking of how kings died, of how their glory came and lingered a while, and went. Like the taste of this good wine, he thought. This gift of Ammar ibn Khairan, who had killed his own king a little time ago. What did a king leave behind? What did *anyone* leave behind? And that led him circling back to the words they'd heard recited after dinner, while lying at ease on their couches in the banquet room with the tame stream running through it, rippling quietly, a murmurous background to the spoken words.

> *Let only sorrow speak tonight.*
> *Let sorrow name the moons.*
> *Let the pale blue light be* loss
> *And the white one* memory.
> *Let clouds obscure the brightness*
> *Of the high, holy stars,*
> *And shroud the watering place*
> *Where he was wont to slake his thirst.*
> *Where lesser beasts now gather*
> *Since the Lion will come no more...*

Badir of Ragosa poured, deliberately, the last of the sweet, pale wine and drank it down.

∽

Someone else was late to bed in the palace of Ragosa, for all that it had been an eventful day and night, even for a man accustomed to such things.

Caught in the difficult space between physical fatigue and emotional unrest, the lord Ammar ibn Khairan finally left the elegant quarters assigned him for the night to go out into the streets long after dark.

The night guards at the postern doors knew him. Everyone seemed to know him already. Nothing unusual there. He was a man who needed to be disguised to pass unnoticed in Al-Rassan. Anxious and overexcited, they offered him a torch and an escort. He declined both with courtesy. He wore a sword for protection, which he showed them. He made a jest at his own expense; they laughed eagerly. After the afternoon's engagement they could hardly doubt his ability to defend himself. One of them, greatly daring, said as much. Ibn Khairan gave him a silver coin and then, with a smile, offered the same to the other two guards. They almost fell over each other opening the doors.

He went out. He had wrapped himself in a fur-lined cloak over his own clothing. He wore his rings again. No point to the steward's disguise any more. That had served its purpose on the road, in the inns between Cartada and here. They had been travelling with a kingdom's worth of gems in the two coffers he had allowed Zabira; over the years Almalik had not been less than generous with the woman he loved. It had been necessary therefore, travelling here, to appear both unconcerned and unimportant. It was not necessary any more.

He wondered where Zabira was tonight, then dismissed the thought as unworthy. She would captivate someone here soon enough—the king, the chancellor, perhaps both—but not yet. Tonight she would be with her sons. The young princes. Pieces on the board in the new, larger game. That much had been decided at the meeting before the challenge in the lists. He had begun, during that crisp discussion, to grasp precisely how shrewd Mazur ben Avren was. Why Badir had risked so much to keep his Kindath chancellor by him. There had been a reputation, of course. One formal encounter. Letters exchanged, over the years, and clever poems read. Now he had met the man. A different sort of challenge. Much to think about. It had been a fully engaged day, truly.

It was cold after dark in Ragosa, this late in the year with a wind blowing. He wanted that cold. He wanted solitude and starlight, the bite of that wind off the lake. His footsteps led him that way, past shuttered shops, then the warehouses, and then, beyond them, walking alone and in silence, to a long pier by the water's edge. He stopped there finally, breathing deeply of the night air.

Overhead, the stars were very bright, and the moons. He saw how the city walls reached out into the water here like two arms, almost meeting, enclosing the harbor. In the moonlight he watched the single-masted fishing boats and the smaller and larger pleasure craft tossed up and down on the dark, choppy waters of the lake. The slap and surge of waves. Water. What was it about water?

He knew the answer to that.

They came from the desert, his people. From shifting, impermanent dunes and sandstorms and harsh, bleak, sculpted mountains; from a place where the wind could blow forever without being checked or stayed. Where the sun killed and it was the night stars that offered promise of life, air to breathe, a breeze to cool the blistering fever of the day. Where water was...what? A dream, a prayer, the purest blessing of the god.

He had no memory of such places himself, unless it was a memory that had come with him into the world. A tribal memory bred into the Asharites, defining them. Ammuz and Soriyya, the homelands, as a presence in the soul. The deserts there. Wider sands, even, than those of the Majriti. He had never seen the Majriti, either. He had been born in Aljais, here in Al-Rassan, in a house with three splashing fountains. Even so, he was drawn to water when distressed, when something within him needed assuaging. Far from the desert, the desert lay inside him like a wound or a weight, as it lay inside them all.

The white moon was overhead, the blue just rising, a crescent. With the city lights behind him the stars were fierce and cold above the lake. Clarity, that was what they meant to him. That was what he needed tonight.

He listened to the waves striking against the pier beneath his feet. Once, a pause, again. The surging rhythm of the world. His thoughts were scattered, bobbing like the boats, refusing to coalesce. He was in some discomfort physically but that wasn't important. Weariness mostly, some bruises, a gash on one calf that he had simply ignored.

The afternoon's challenge in the lists had been effortless, in fact. One of the things with which he was having trouble.

There had been five against the two of them, and the Karcher had chosen four of the best captains in Ragosa to join him. There was a visible anger in those men, a grimness, the need to prove a point and not just about wages. It had been contrived as a display, an entertainment for court and city, not to-the-death. But even so, eyes beneath helms had been hard and cold.

It ought never to have been so swift, so much like a dance or a dream. It was as if there had been music playing somewhere, almost but not quite heard. He had fought those five men side-by-side and then back-to-back with Rodrigo Belmonte of Valledo, whom he had never seen in his life, and it had been as nothing had ever been before, on a battlefield or anywhere else. It had felt weirdly akin to having doubled himself. To fighting as if there were two hard-trained bodies with the one controlling mind. They hadn't even spoken during the fight. No warnings, tactics. It hadn't lasted long enough for that.

On the pier above the cold, choppy waters of Lake Serrana, ibn Khairan shook his head, remembering. He ought to have been elated after such a triumph, perhaps curious, intrigued. He was deeply unsettled instead. Restless. Even a little afraid, if he were honest with himself.

The wind blew. He stood facing into it, looking north across the lake. On the farther shore lay the *tagra* lands where no one lived, with Jaloña and Valledo beyond. Where the Horsemen of Jad worshipped the golden sun the Asharites feared in their burning deserts. Jad. Ashar. Banners for men to gather beneath.

He had spent his life alone, whether in play or at war. Had never sought a company to command, a coterie of subcommanders, or even, truthfully, a friend. Companions, hangers-on, acolytes, lovers, these had always been a part of his life, but not real friendship—unless one named the man he had poisoned in Cartada.

Ibn Khairan had come over the years to see the world as a place in which he moved by himself, leading men into battle when necessary, evolving plans and courses for his monarch when asked, crafting his verses and songs whenever the patterns of life allowed space for that, linking and unlinking with a succession of women—and some men.

Nothing for very long, nothing that went too deep. He had never married. Had never wanted to, or been pressured to do so. His brothers had children. Their line would continue.

If pressed, he would probably have said that this cast of mind, this steady, ongoing need for distance, had its origin on a summer's day when he had walked into the Al-Fontina in Silvenes and killed the last khalif on a fountain rim for Almalik of Cartada.

The old, blind man had praised his youthful verses. Had invited him to visit Silvenes. An aged man who had never wanted to ascend the khalif's dais. Everyone knew that. How should a blind poet rule Al-Rassan? Muzafar had been only another piece on the board, a tool of the court powers in corrupt, terrified Silvenes. Dark days those had been in Al-Rassan, when the young ibn Khairan had walked past bribed eunuchs and into the Garden of Desire bearing a forbidden blade.

It was not hard, even now, to make a case for what he had done, for what Almalik of Cartada had ordered done. Even so. That day in the innermost garden of the Al-Fontina had marked ibn Khairan. In the eyes of others, in his own eyes. *The man who killed the last khalif of Al-Rassan.*

He had been young then, rich with a sense of his own invulnerability and a dazzled awareness of all the shimmering possibilities the world held in store. He wasn't young any more. Even the cold, this keen wind off the water, knifed into him more sharply than it would have fifteen years ago. He smiled at that, for the first time that night, and shook his head ruefully. Maudlin, unworthy thoughts. An old man in a blanket before the fire? Soon enough, soon enough. If he lived. The patterns of life. What was allowed.

Come, brother, Rodrigo Belmonte of Valledo had said today as five hard men with swords had walked forward to encircle the two of them. *Shall we show them how this is done?*

They had shown them.

Brother. A golden disk of Jad on a chain about his throat. Leader of the most dangerous company in the peninsula. One hundred and fifty Horsemen of the god. A beautiful wife, two sons. Heirs to be taught, even loved perhaps. Pious and loyal, and deadly.

Ibn Khairan knew about that last, now. Only stories before. Nothing like it, ever, in a lifetime of combat. Five men against them. Trained, magnificent fighters, the best mercenaries in Ragosa. And in no time at all, really, they were down, it was over. A dance.

Usually he could remember each individual movement, every feint and parry and thrust of a battle for a long time afterwards. His mind worked that way, breaking down a larger event into its smaller parts. But this afternoon was already a blur. Which was a part of why he was so unsettled now.

He had looked at Belmonte after, and had seen—with relief and apprehension, both—a mirror image of that same strangeness. As if something had gone flying away from each of them and was only just coming back. The Valledan had looked glazed, unfocused.

At least, Ammar had thought, *it isn't only me.*

There had been uncontrolled noise by then, delirious, deafeningly loud. Screaming from up on the walls and from the royal stand by the lists. Hats and scarves and gloves and leather flasks of wine sailing through the air to land about them. It had all seemed to be coming from a long way off.

He had tried, out of habit, to be sardonic. "Shall we kill each other for them now, to set a seal on it?" he'd said.

The men they'd defeated were being helped to their feet, those who could rise. One man, the Karcher, had a broken arm from the flat of a sword. Another was unable to stand; they were carrying him away on a litter. A woman's pale blue scarf, drifting down through the sunlight, had fallen across his body. Ammar could only vaguely remember having faced the man with the broken arm. It had been at the very outset. He could not clearly recall the blow, the sequence of it. Too strange, that was.

Rodrigo Belmonte had not laughed at his attempted jest, or smiled, standing beside him amid that huge and distant noise.

"Do we want a seal on it?" he'd asked.

Ammar had shaken his head. They had stood alone in the middle of the world. A small, still space. Dreamlike. Clothing, flowers now, more wine flasks, flying through the autumn air. So much noise.

"Not yet," he'd said. "No. It may come, though. Whether we want it or not."

Rodrigo had been silent a moment, the grey eyes calm beneath an old helm with the figure of an eagle on it. From the king's stand a herald was approaching, formally garbed, gracious, deeply deferential.

Just before he reached them, the Valledan had said softly, "If it comes, it comes. The god determines all. I never did anything like this, though, in all my life. Not fighting beside another man."

A star fell into the darkness of the hills west of the lake. Ibn Khairan heard footsteps behind him. They paused, and then withdrew. One person. A watchman. No danger. There wouldn't be danger here, in any case.

He was very tired, but his mind would not allow him rest. The high white moon laid a shining, rippled track on the water, the blue crescent cast a faint one from the east. They met where he stood. This was a property of water at night. Light flowed along it to where one stood.

I earned a goodly portion of my wages today, he thought. Wages. He was a mercenary soldier now, in the service of a king who would be happy to see Cartada in ruins. Who might decide to send an army west to achieve that in the spring. Ammar, by his contract, would be a part of that army, a leader of it. He wasn't used to such shiftings of allegiance.

He had killed Almalik. Twenty years' companion. The slow rise and then the swift rise to power together. Men changed over the years. Power ebbed and flowed, and did things to them. Time and the stars turned and men changed.

The man he'd slain was the only person he could ever have called a friend in the world, even though one didn't use that word of kings. He'd sung his lament tonight. Mazur ben Avren's request, meant to wound. A subtle mind, that. But he'd already been working on the verses during the ride east with Zabira. Had offered them this evening to a banquet hall of Cartada's enemies. A room with a stream running through it. Water again. Ashar's dream amid the desert sands. It was an affectation, that banquet room, but impressive nonetheless, and tastefully done. He could come to like Badir of Ragosa, he told himself, could respect Mazur ben Avren. There was a life beyond Cartada, with scope and sweep.

Where lesser beasts now gather...

He shook his head. Turned away from the lake and started back, with the wind and the moons behind him now.

From the shadows by the oak-timbered wall of a warehouse she saw him leave the water's edge and the out-thrust arms of the city walls. She had retreated here to wait, after walking almost to the pier. As he approached she saw—her eyes by now adjusted to the moonlight—an odd, inward look to his face and she was half-inclined to let him pass. But even as that thought formed she realized that she had stepped forward into the street after all.

He stopped. His hand moved to his sword and then she saw that he knew her. She expected something ironic, a jest. Her heart was beating rapidly.

"Jehane bet Ishak. What are you doing abroad at night?"

"Walking," she said. "The same as you."

"Not the same at all. It isn't safe for a woman. There's no point to being foolish."

She felt a useful flare of anger. "I do wonder how I've survived this long in Ragosa without your guidance."

He was silent. He still had that strange look to him. She wondered what had driven him to the lake. She hadn't come out to quarrel, although she couldn't have said why she *had* come. She changed her tone. "I am known here," she murmured. "There is no real danger."

"In the dark? On the waterfront?" He raised his eyebrows. "You could be killed for your cloak or merely because of your religion. Where's your servant?"

"Velaz? Asleep, I hope. He's had a long day and night."

"And you?"

"Long enough," she said. "Where you injured I tried to heal. I've come from the infirmary." What was it, she asked herself, that kept causing her to challenge him?

He looked at her. The steady, unrevealing gaze. The pearl in his ear gleamed palely in the moonlight. He said, "It's too cold to stand here. Come." He started walking again, back towards the center of the city.

She fell into stride. The wind was behind them, cutting through her cloak. It *was* cold, and despite what she'd implied, Jehane was unused to being abroad this late. In fact, the last time had been the night of the day she met this man. The Day of the Moat. She had thought it had been his savage device, that slaughter of innocent men. All of Al-Rassan had thought so.

She said, "I remember what you said in Fezana. That it was none of your doing."

"You didn't believe me."

"Yes, I did."

He glanced at her. They continued walking.

She had seen him go by earlier, from the doorway of the infirmary. Her two patients had been sleeping, one drugged against the pain of a shattered arm, the other still deeply confused, a contusion the size of an ostrich egg on the side of his head. Jehane had left instructions that he be awakened after each of the night bells. Too deep a sleep tonight carried a risk.

She had been standing near the open doorway, breathing the night air, struggling against fatigue, when ibn Khairan went past. She had put on her cloak and followed him, without thinking about it, no reason save impulse for justification.

They had done something astonishing that day, he and Rodrigo Belmonte. Two men against five and had she not known better it might have seemed that the five had consented to be cut down, so swift and crisply defined and elegant had it been. She *did* know better, though. She was treating two of the five tonight. The Karcher with the broken arm was struggling to deal with what had happened. He was bitter, humiliated. Not a man accustomed to losing battles. Not that way, at any rate.

Stepping out into the street after ibn Khairan Jehane had been awkwardly aware that there were other kinds of women who did this sort of thing, especially after what had happened today. She half-expected to see some of them trailing behind the man, adorned, perfumed. Pursuing the hero of the moment, approaching to touch— to be touched by—glory, the shimmer that clung to fame. She had nothing but contempt for such women.

What she'd done in following him was not remotely the same thing, she told herself. She wasn't young or bedazzled; she wore a plain white cloth cap to keep her hair from her eyes while she worked, no jewelry, mud-stained boots. She was level-headed, a physician, and observant.

"Weren't you hurt this afternoon?" she said, glancing sideways and up at him. "I thought I saw you take a sword in the leg."

He looked dryly amused, an expression she remembered. "A scratch, truly. One of them caught me with his blade when he fell. It is kind of you to ask, doctor. How are your patients?"

She shrugged. "The broken arm will be all right. It set easily enough. The Batiaran that Ser Rodrigo felled was still having trouble remembering his mother's name before he fell asleep."

Ibn Khairan grinned, the white teeth flashing. "Now that is serious. If it were his father's name, of course, I'd call that normal for Batiara."

"Go ahead and jest," she said, refusing to laugh. "You don't have to deal with it." A silly thing to say.

"I'm so sorry," he murmured, all solicitude. "Did I add to your burdens today?"

She winced. She'd asked for that. It was important to watch what one said with this man. He was as sharp as Mazur was. At least as sharp.

"How is your father?" he said, changing tone. She glanced over in surprise and then away. She had a clear memory, as they walked through the dark streets, of this man on his knees before Ishak last summer, their hands clasped together.

"My parents are well enough, I thank you. My father...has dictated some letters to me since that night in Fezana. I believe that...speaking with you was of help to him."

"I am honored that you think so."

No irony in the voice now. She had heard his lament tonight. He had slain a man she herself had sworn to destroy. Had made her own vain, childish oath the meaningless thing it always had been. She had actually been close to grief, hearing the cadenced verses. The sorrow behind the sword.

She said, "I had intended to kill Almalik myself. For my father. That's why I left Fezana." As she spoke the words, as she told him, Jehane understood that this was why she had come out into the cold of the night.

"I am not surprised," he murmured, after a pause. A generous thing to say. Taking her seriously. A Kindath woman. A child's rash vow. "Are you angry that I forestalled you?"

She hadn't expected that either. She walked beside him a while in silence. They turned a corner. "I'm a little ashamed," she said. "I did nothing at all for four years, then came here and did nothing again."

"Some tasks take longer than others. As it happens, it was a little easier for me."

Disguised as a slave. She had heard the tale from Mazur just before the banquet this evening. Poison on a towel. The royal son entirely complicitous, then exiling ibn Khairan. There had to be pain there.

They turned another corner. Two lights shone ahead of them now at the end of the street, outside the infirmary. Another memory rising suddenly, against her will. That same summer's night in Fezana, the same room. Herself with this man at the window, rising on her toes to kiss him. A challenge.

I must have been mad, she thought. She stopped at the entrance to the infirmary.

And as if he could actually trace the course of her thoughts, Ammar ibn Khairan said, "Was I right about the chancellor, by the way?" A revealed edge of amusement again, infuriatingly.

"Right about what?" she temporized.

He would have seen where she had been placed tonight, at the banquet. He would have duly noted the fact that she was there at all. She hoped, fiercely, that he could not see her flushing. She almost regretted now that she had come.

He laughed softly. "I see," he said. And then, mildly, "Are you looking in on your patients, or going home?"

She glared up at him. Anger again. Useful. "What does *that* mean?" she said coldly. In the light from the torches she could see his face clearly now. He regarded her with composure, but she thought she saw laughter lingering in his eyes. "What does 'I see' mean?" she demanded.

A brief silence. "Forgive me," he said gravely. "Have I offended?"

"With that tone you did, yes," she said sturdily.

"Then I shall have to chastise him for you."

The voice was behind her, and known. She wheeled, but

not before she saw ibn Khairan's gaze shift beyond her and his expression change.

In the doorway to the infirmary Rodrigo Belmonte stood in a spill of candlelight, wearing the same overtunic and vest he'd worn to the banquet, with his sword on one hip.

"I am always being chastised by someone," ibn Khairan complained.

Rodrigo gave a snort of amusement. "I doubt that," he said. "But you ought to know, if you don't already, that Mazur ben Avren's lack of success with our doctor here has been the talk of Ragosa for months."

"It has?" said Ammar politely.

"It *has?*" said Jehane in a very different tone.

"I'm afraid so," Rodrigo replied, looking at her. He, too, was amused now, a certain wryness to the expression beneath the full moustache. "I must confess I've made a sum of money in this matter."

"You've been *wagering* on me?" Jehane heard her voice swirling upwards.

"I have great confidence in all the members of my company," Rodrigo said.

"I am *not* a member of your company!"

"I continue to live in hope," he murmured blandly.

Behind her, ibn Khairan laughed aloud. She wheeled on him. He held up his hands in a quick, warding gesture. Jehane was silent, speechless in fact. And then, resisting all the way, she felt her own amusement welling up. She began to laugh, helplessly.

She leaned in the doorway, wiping at her eyes, looking from one man to the other. From within the infirmary the two night attendants looked disapprovingly towards the three of them. Jehane, who had to give the attendants firm instructions in a moment, struggled for composure.

"She can't join us," said Ammar ibn Khairan. He had moved into the entranceway, out of the cutting wind. "Ben Avren will never let her leave the city."

"*Us?*" said Rodrigo.

"*Leave the city?*" said Jehane, in the same moment.

The handsome, smooth-shaven face turned from one of them to the other. He took his time before speaking.

"Some things do seem obvious," said ibn Khairan, looking at the Valledan. "King Badir will be exceedingly nervous about having both of us in Ragosa this winter without gainful activity. We will be sent somewhere. Together. I'll place a wager on that. And given what you have just told me about the chancellor's entirely understandable interest in our splendid physician he is not going to permit her to leave Fezana with two such irresponsible men."

"I am *not* an irresponsible man," said Rodrigo Belmonte indignantly.

"I beg to dissent," Ammar said calmly. "Jehane told me that you caused a Batiaran mercenary—a fine man, a doughty soldier—to forget his own mother's name this afternoon! Deeply irresponsible, I call that."

"His mother's?" Rodrigo exclaimed. "Not his father's? If it was his father's name—"

"You could understand it. I know," said Jehane. "The high lord ibn Khairan has already made that feeble jest. Among other things the two of you appear to share the same childish humor."

"Other things? What other things? I may now be offended." Ibn Khairan's expression belied the words. He didn't look weary or unfocused any more, she noted. The physician in her was pleased with that. She chose to ignore the question.

"I am the one offended, remember? And you haven't apologized yet. Nor have *you*," she said, turning upon Belmonte. "Wagering on my conduct! And how dare you assume that the chancellor of Ragosa—or anyone else— dictates where and when I travel?"

"Good!" said Rodrigo. "I have been waiting a long time to hear you say that! A winter campaign will be an excellent trial for all of us."

"I didn't say—"

"*Won't* you come?" he said. "Jesting aside, Jehane, I badly need a good doctor, and I still remember something you said, about working among Esperañans. Will you give us a chance to prove a point about that?"

Jehane remembered it too. She remembered that night extremely well. *Even the sun goes down, my lady.* She turned her mind from that thought.

"What?" she said, sardonically. "Are there no pilgrims heading to blessed Queen Vasca's Isle this year?"

"Not from my company," said Rodrigo quietly.

There was a silence. He had a way of stilling you, she thought.

"You might also consider that a campaign outside the city would give you a respite from ben Avren's attentions," said ibn Khairan, a little too casually.

She spun to glare at him. His hands came up again, defensively. "Assuming, of course, you want a respite," he added quickly. "He's a remarkable man. A poet, a chancellor, a genuine scholar. Prince of the Kindath. Your mother would be proud."

"If I let him bed me?" she asked sweetly.

"Well no, not that, I suppose. I was thinking of something more formal, of course. Something ..."

He stopped, having registered the look in her eyes. His hands came up for a third time, as if to block an assault. His rings glittered.

Jehane glared at him, her own fingers curled into fists. The problem was, she kept wanting to laugh, which made it difficult to cling to outrage. "You are in grave trouble if you happen to get sick on this campaign," she said grimly. "Did no one ever warn you not to offend your doctor?"

"Many people, many times," Ammar admitted ruefully. "I'm just not a responsible man, I fear."

"I am," said Rodrigo cheerfully. "Ask anyone!"

"Only," she snapped over her shoulder, "because you're terrified of your wife. You told me so!"

Ibn Khairan laughed. A moment later, so did Belmonte, his color high. Jehane crossed her arms, refusing to smile, scowling at both of them.

She felt extraordinarily happy, though.

The temple bells chimed, beyond the rooftops south of them, bright and clear in the cold night, to awaken the devout for prayer.

"Go home," said Jehane to both men, looking into the infirmary. "I have patients to check on."

They glanced at each other.

"And leave you here alone? Would your mother approve?" asked ibn Khairan.

"My father would," Jehane said crisply. "This is a hospital. I am a doctor."

That sobered them. Ibn Khairan bowed, and Belmonte did the same. They left, walking together. She watched them go, standing in the doorway until they were swallowed up by the night. She stood for another moment there, staring at the darkness before going into the infirmary.

The Karcher with the fractured arm still slept. It was what he needed. She had given him absinthe for pain, and her father's mixture to help him rest. She woke the other man gently, with the attendants on either side of his pallet. Sometimes they were violent when awakened. These were fighting men. The Batiaran knew her, though, which was good. She had them hold up a torch for her and she looked at his eyes: cloudy still, but better than before and he followed her finger when she moved it before his face. She put a hand behind his head and helped him drink: cloves, myrrh and aloes, for what had to be a brutal headache.

She changed the dressing on his wound, then withdrew to the other side of the room while the attendants helped him pass water into a beaker for her. She poured the urine into her father's flask and studied it against the candlelight. The top layer, which told of the head, was mostly clear now. He was going to be all right. She told him as much, speaking in his own language. He sank back into slumber.

She decided to snatch a short rest in the infirmary after all. They made up one of the beds for her and drew a screen in front of it for privacy. She removed her boots and lay down in her clothing. She had done this many times. A doctor had to learn to sleep anywhere, in whatever brief snatches of time were allowed.

Just before she dropped off, a thought came to her: she had, it seemed, just agreed to leave the comforts of city and court to go out on a winter campaign—wherever that expedition turned out to be going. She hadn't even asked them. *Nobody* went on winter campaigns.

"*You idiot*," she murmured aloud, aware that she was smiling in the darkness.

In the morning the Batiaran remembered his mother, knew where he was, the day of the week and the sub-commanders of his company. When she asked, a trifle unwisely, about his father's name, he flushed a vivid crimson.

Jehane took pains to show no reaction at all, of course. She swore a silent oath to herself, on the spot, in the name of Galinus, father of all physicians, that she would die before telling Ammar ibn Khairan or Rodrigo Belmonte about this.

That oath, at least, she kept.

Chapter IX

∽

The wind was north. Yazir could taste salt in the air, though they were half a day's ride across the Majriti sands from the sea. It was cold.

Behind him he could hear the flapping of the tents as the wind caught and tugged at them. They had come this far north and set up a camp to meet with their visitor.

On the coast, out of sight beyond the high, shifting dunes, lay the new port of Abeneven, whose walls offered shelter from the wind. Yazir ibn Q'arif would rather be dead and with Ashar among the stars than winter in a city. He shrugged deeper into his cloak. He looked up at the sky. The sun, no menace now at the brink of winter so far to the north, was a pale disk in a sky of racing clouds. There was a little time yet before the third summons to prayer. They could continue this discussion.

No one had said a word, however, for some time. Their visitor was clearly unsettled by that. This was good, on the whole; unsettled men, in Yazir's experience, revealed more of themselves.

Yazir looked over and saw that his brother had pulled down the veil that covered the lower half of his face. He was breaking beetle shells and sucking at the juices inside. An old habit. His teeth were badly stained by it. Their guest had already declined the offered dish. This, of course, was an insult, but Yazir had gained some insight into the manners of their brethren across the straits in Al-Rassan, and was not unduly perturbed. Ghalib, his brother,

was a more impetuous man, and Yazir could see him dealing with anger. The visitor would not be aware of this, of
course. Their guest, miserably cold, and obviously unhappy with the smell and feel of the camel hair cloak they had
presented him as a gift, sat uncomfortably on Yazir's
meeting blanket and sniffled.

He was ill, he had told them. He talked a great deal,
their visitor. The long journey to Abirab and then along the
coast to this wintering place of the Muwardi leaders had
afflicted him with an ailment of the head and chest, he had
explained. He was shivering like a girl. Ghalib's contempt
was obvious to Yazir, but this man from across the straits
would not see that either, even with Ghalib's veil lowered.

Yazir had long ago realized—and had tried to make his
brother understand—that the softness of life in Al-Rassan
had not only turned the men there into infidels, it had also
made them very nearly women. Less than women, in fact.
Not one of Yazir's wives would have been half so pathetic
as this Prince Hazem of Cartada, his nose dripping like a
child's in the face of a little wind.

And this young man, lamentably, was one of the devout
ones. One of the true, pious followers of Ashar in Al-
Rassan. Yazir was forced to keep reminding himself of
that. The man had been corresponding with them for
some time. Now he had come himself to the Majriti, a long
way in a difficult season, to speak his plea to the two leaders of the Muwardis, here on a blanket before flapping
tents in the vast and empty desert.

He had probably expected to meet them in Abirab, or
Abeneven at worst, Yazir thought. Cities and houses were
what the soft men of Al-Rassan knew. Beds with scented
pillows, cushions to recline upon. Flowers and trees and
green grass, with more water than any man could use in
his lifetime. Forbidden wine and naked dancers and painted Jaddite women. Arrogant Kindath merchants exploiting
the faithful and worshipping their female moons instead
of Ashar's holy stars. A world where the bells summoning
to prayer were occasion for a cursory nod in the direction

of a temple, if that much.

Yazir dreamed at night of fire. A great burning in Al-Rassan and north of it, among the kingdoms of Esperaña, where they worshipped the killing sun in mockery of the Star-born children of the desert. He dreamed of a purging inferno that would leave the green, seductive land scorched back towards sand but pure again, ready for rebirth. A place where the holy stars might shine cleanly down and not avert their light in horror from what men did below in the cesspools of their cities.

He was a cautious man, though, Yazir ibn Q'arif of the Zuhrite tribe. Even before the foul murder of the last khalif in Silvenes wadjis had been coming across the straits to him and his brother, year after year, beseeching that the tribes sweep north across the water to a burning of infidels.

Yazir didn't like boats; he didn't like water. He and Ghalib had more than enough on their hands controlling the desert tribes. He had elected to roll small dice only behind his veil—akin to a cautious play in the ancient bone game of the desert—and had allowed some of his soldiers to go north as mercenaries. Not to serve the wadjis either, but the very kings they opposed. The petty-kings of Al-Rassan had money, and paid it for good soldiers. Money was useful; it bought food from north and east in hard seasons, it hired masons and shipbuilders—men Yazir had reluctantly come to realize he needed, if the Muwardis were to have any more permanence than the drifting sands.

Information was useful, too. His soldiers sent home all their wages, and with these sums came tidings of affairs in Al-Rassan. Yazir and Ghalib knew a great deal. Some of it was comprehensible, some was not. They learned that there were courtyards within the palaces of the kings, and even in the public squares of cities, where water was permitted to burst freely from pipes through the mouths of sculpted animals—and then to run away again, unused. This was almost impossible to credit, but the tale had been reported too many times not to be true.

One report—this one a fable, obviously—even had it

that in Ragosa, where a Kindath sorcerer had bewitched
the feeble king, a river ran through the palace. It was said
that there was a waterfall in the sorcerer's bedchamber,
where the Kindath fiend bedded helpless Asharite women,
ripping their maidenheads and laughing at his power over
the Star-born.

Yazir stirred restlessly within his cloak; the image filled
him with a heavy rage. Ghalib finished cracking beetles,
pushed the earthenware dish away, pulled up his veil and
mumbled something under his breath.

"I'm sorry?" the Cartadan prince said, leaping at the
sound. He sniffled. "My ears. I'm sorry. I failed to hear.
Excellence?"

Ghalib looked at Yazir. It was increasingly evident that
he wanted to kill this man. That was understandable, but
it remained a bad idea, in Yazir's view. He *was* the older
brother. Ghalib would follow him, in most things. He narrowed his eyes in warning. Their visitor missed this of
course; he missed everything.

On the other hand, Yazir abruptly reminded himself,
Ashar had taught that charity towards the devout was the
highest deed of earthly piety, short of dying in a holy war,
and this man—this Hazem ibn Almalik—was as close to
being truly devout as any prince of Al-Rassan had been in
a long time. He was here, after all. He had come to them.
They had to take note of that. If only he wasn't such a
sorry, emasculated excuse for a man.

"Nothing," Yazir grunted.

"What? I beg—"

"My brother said nothing. Do not trouble yourself so."
He tried to say it kindly. Kindness did not come naturally
to him. Neither did patience, though that he had been at
pains to teach himself over the years.

His world was different now from when he and Ghalib
had led the Zuhrites out of the west and swept all the
other tribes before them, leaving the sands blood-red
where they passed. More than twenty years ago that was.
They had been young men. The khalif in Silvenes had sent

them gifts. Then the next khalif, and the next, until the
last one was slain.

There was still blood on the sands, most years. The
tribes of the desert had never taken easily to authority.
Twenty years was a very long time to have held sway. Long
enough even to build two cities on the coast, with shipyards now and warehouses, and three more settlements
inland, with markets, where the gold of the south could be
assembled and dispersed in the long caravans. Yazir hated
cities, but they mattered. They were marks of endurance
on the shifting face of the desert. They were a beginning
to something larger.

The next stage of permanence for the Muwardis, though,
lay beyond the sands. That much was becoming more and
more clear to Yazir as the seasons and the stars turned.

Ghalib flatly rejected the very thought of leaving the
desert life he knew, but not the idea of a holy war across
the straits. That idea he liked. Ghalib was good at killing
people. He was not a man well-suited to leading the tribes
in peacetime, or to building things that might remain after
him, for his sons and his sons' sons. Yazir, who had come
out of the west those long years ago with a string of camels
and a sword, with five thousand warriors and a bright,
hard vision of Ashar, was trying to become such a man.

Ibn Rashid, the ascetic, the wadji who had come to the
westernmost Zuhrite tribes bearing the teachings of Ashar
from the so-called homelands none of the Muwardis had
ever seen, would have approved, Yazir knew that much.

The wadji, gaunt and tall, with his unkempt white
beard and hair and his black eyes that read souls, had settled with six disciples in a cluster of tents among the
wildest people of the desert. Yazir and his brother, the
sons of the Zuhrite chieftain, had come one day to laugh
at this new, harmless madman in his settlement, where he
preached the visions of another madman in another desert
in a far land named Soriyya.

Their lives had changed. The life of the Majriti had
changed.

Ashar's truths had been moving through the desert for some time before ibn Rashid came west, but none of the other tribes had accepted those truths and pursued them as resolutely as the Zuhrites were to do when Yazir and Ghalib led them east—all of them veiled now like ibn Rashid—in holy, cleansing war.

Yazir had spent almost half of his life trying to earn his wadji's approval, even after ibn Rashid had died and only his rattling bones and skull accompanied Yazir and Ghalib in their journeys. He still tried to measure his deeds by what the wadji's eyes would have seen in them. It was difficult, trying to change from a simple warrior, a son of the desert and stars, to a leader in a slippery world of cities and money, of diplomats and emissaries from across the straits or far to the east. It was very difficult.

He needed scribes now, men who could decipher the messages brought him from those other lands. In scratchings on parchment lay the deaths of men and the fulfillment or rejection of Ashar's starry visions. That was a hard thing to accept.

Yazir often envied his brother his clear approach to all things. Ghalib had not changed, saw no reason to change. He was a Zuhrite war leader still, direct and unblunted as a wind. This man sitting before them, for example. For Ghalib he was less than a man, and he sniffled, and insulted them by refusing to eat food they offered. He ought, therefore, to be slain. He would provide some amusement then, at least. Ghalib had a number of ways of killing men. This one, Yazir thought, would probably be castrated then given to the soldiers—or even the women—to be used. Ghalib would see such a death as an obvious one.

Yazir, a son of the hard desert himself, half-inclined to agree, continued his long struggle towards a different view of things. Hazem ibn Almalik was a prince from across the water. He could rule Cartada if circumstances changed only slightly. He was here to ask Yazir and Ghalib to change those circumstances. That would mean, he had told them, a true believer on the dais of the most powerful kingdom in Al-Rassan. He would even don the half-veil of the Muwardis, he told them.

Yazir didn't know what a dais was, but he did under-stand what was being asked of him. He was fairly certain his brother understood as well, but Ghalib would have a different attitude. Ghalib would hardly care who ruled Cartada in Al-Rassan. Whether this man adopted the veil ibn Rashid had ordained for the tribes—to screen and hold back impieties—would be a matter of uttermost indiffer-ence to Ghalib. He would simply want the chance to go to war again in the name of Ashar and the god. War was good, a holy war was the best thing in the world.

Sometimes, though, a man striving to shape a divided, tribal people into a nation, a force in the world, something more than drifts of sand, had to try to hold back his desires, or rise above them.

Yazir, on his blanket in the north wind, with winter coming, felt a deep uncertainty gnawing at his vitals. No one had ever warned him that leadership, this kind of leadership, was bad for the stomach.

He had begun losing his hair years ago. His scalp, though usually covered, had burned the same hue as the rest of his face over the years. Ghalib, with no concerns save how to keep his warriors killing enemies and not each other, still had his long dark mane. He wore it tied back, to keep it from his eyes and he still wore his thong about his neck. Men sometimes asked about that. Ghalib would smile and decline to answer, inviting speculation. Yazir knew what the thong was. He was far from a squeamish man, but he didn't like thinking about it.

He looked up at the wan sun again. There remained only a little time before prayers. There was information their visitor lacked. He had been a long time journeying here; others had left after him and come before. Yazir was still unsure how to make use of this.

"What about the Jaddites?" he asked, by way of a begin-ning.

Hazem ibn Almalik jerked like a snared creature at the

words. He flashed Yazir a startled, revealing glance. It was the first concrete question either of the brothers had put to him. The wind whistled, sand blew.

"The Jaddites?" the man repeated blankly. He was, Yazir concluded, very nearly simple-minded. It was a pity.

"The Jaddites," Yazir repeated, as if to a child. Ghalib glanced at him briefly and then away, saying nothing. "How strong are they? We are told Cartada allows payment of tribute to the Horsemen. This is forbidden by the Laws. If such tribute is paid there must be a reason. What is the reason?"

Hazem wiped at his dripping nose. He used his right hand, which was offensive. He cleared his throat. "That tribute is one reason I am here, Excellence. Of course it is forbidden. It is a blasphemy, among so many others. The arrogant Horsemen see no danger in the weak kings of Al-Rassan. Even my father cringes before the Jaddites, though he calls himself a Lion." He laughed bitterly. Yazir said nothing, listening, observing through hooded eyes. The sand blew past them, tent cloths flapped in the camp. A dog barked.

Their visitor babbled on. "The Jaddites make their demands, and are given all they ask, despite the clear word of Ashar. They take our gold, they take our women, they ride laughing through our streets looking down upon the faithful, mocking our feeble leaders. Little do they know that their danger comes not from godless rulers, but from the true heirs of Ashar, the pure sons of the desert. Will you not come? Will you not cleanse Al-Rassan?"

Ghalib grunted, pulled down his veil, and spat.

"Why?" he said.

Yazir was surprised. His brother was not inclined to demand reasons for war. The prince from over the water seemed more confident suddenly; he sat up straighter on the blanket. It was as if he had needed only their questions. All those who had come to them from Al-Rassan over the years, the wadjis and emissaries, were great talkers. They wore no veils, perhaps that was part of it. Poets, singers, heralds—words ran like water in that land. It was silence that made them uneasy. It was quite clear by now that their visitor did not know his father was dead.

"Who else is there?" Hazem of Cartada asked, and gestured excessively with his hands, almost touching Yazir's knee. "If you come not, the Horsemen of Jad will rule. In our lifetime. And Al-Rassan will be lost to Ashar and the stars."

"It is lost already," Ghalib muttered, surprising Yazir again.

"Then regain it!" said Hazem ibn Almalik quickly. "It is there for you. For us."

"Us?" Yazir said softly.

The prince visibly checked himself. He looked briefly afraid. He said, "For all of us who grieve for what is happening. Who bear the heavy burden of what Jaddites and Kindath and false, fallen kings are doing to a land once strong in the will of Ashar." He hesitated. "There is water there, orchards and green grass. Tall grain grows in the fields, rain falls in the spring and ripe, sweet fruits can be plucked wild from the trees. Surely your soldiers have told you this."

"They have told us many things," Yazir said repressively, stirred in spite of himself. He believed little of it, in fact. Rivers running through palaces? Did they think he was a fool? He could not even conceive of what kind of a fruit might grow freely, untended, to be taken at will by any man with a thirst. Such things were promised in Paradise, not to men on the sands of earth.

"You sent soldiers to serve my father," Hazem ibn Almalik said shrilly. "Why will you not lead them to serve Ashar?"

This was offensive. Men had been flayed for less. They had been staked alive in the sun with their skin peeled away.

"Your father has been killed," Yazir said quickly, before Ghalib could do anything irreversible. "Your brother rules in Cartada."

"What?" The young man scrambled to his feet, fear and

amazement imprinted on his pallid, exposed features.

Ghalib reached for the spear planted beside him. He swung it with one hand, almost casually, so that the shaft smote the prince behind the knees. There was a cracking sound, swallowed by the empty spaces around them. Hazem ibn Almalik crumpled to the ground, whimpering.

"You do not rise before my brother does," Ghalib said softly. "It is an insult." He spoke slowly, as if to someone deficient in his faculties.

He planted his spear again. The handful of warriors who had accompanied them here from the encampment had glanced over at the flurry of movement. Now they looked away again. This talk was boring for them; most things had been boring of late. Autumn and winter were a difficult time for discipline.

Yazir again considered giving the Cartadan to his brother and the soldiers. The prince's death would offer a diversion and the men needed that. He decided against it. There was more at stake here than an execution to quiet restless warriors. He had the feeling even Ghalib knew that. The shaft of a spear along the back of the knees was an extremely mild response for his brother.

"Sit up," Yazir said coldly. The prince's moaning was beginning to grate on him.

It was amusing how quickly the sounds stopped. Hazem ibn Almalik swung himself up to a sitting position. He wiped at his nose. His right hand again. Some men had no idea of manners. But if they denied the god and the visions of Ashar, why should they be expected to know polite, proper behavior? He reminded himself, again, that this man was among the devout.

"It is time for prayers," Yazir said to the Cartadan prince. "We will go back to the camp. After, we will eat. Then you will tell me all you know about your brother."

"No, no. No! I must go back home now, Excellence. As quickly as possible." The man showed a surprising amount of energy for the first time. "With my father dead there is an opportunity. For me, for *all* of us who serve Ashar and the god. I must write to the wadjis of the city! I must—"

"It is time for prayers," Yazir repeated, and rose.

Ghalib did the same, with a warrior's grace. The prince scrambled upright. They began walking back. Hazem limped along, still talking, trying to keep pace.

"This is wonderful!" he said. "My accursed father is dead. My brother is weak, with a corrupt, godless advisor—the evil man who killed the last khalif! We can take Cartada easily, Excellence. The people will be with us! I will go home to Al-Rassan, and tell them you are following. Don't you see, Ashar has given us a gift from the stars!"

Yazir stopped. He didn't like being distracted as he readied himself for prayer, and this man was clearly going to be a vexing distraction. There was also the distinct possibility that Ghalib would be irked enough to kill him out-of-hand.

Yazir said, "We go to pray. Be silent now. But understand me: we travel nowhere in winter. Neither do you. You will remain with us. You are our guest for this season. In spring we will take counsel again. For the rest of the winter I do not want to hear you speak unless addressed by one of us." He paused, tried to sound gentle, soothing. "I say this for your safety, do you understand? You are not in a place where things are as you know them."

The man's jaw had dropped open. He reached forward with a hand—his right hand, alas—and clutched at Yazir's sleeve.

"But I *cannot* stay!" he said. "Excellence, I *must* go back. Before the winter storms. I must be—"

He said no more. He was looking downwards, a blank incredulity in his face. It was very nearly amusing. Ghalib had cut off the offending hand at the wrist. He was already sheathing his sword. Hazem ibn Almalik, prince of Cartada, looked at the bleeding stump where his right hand had been, made a strangled sound in his throat, and fainted.

Ghalib looked down at him expressionlessly.

"Shall I cut out his tongue?" he asked. "We will never

endure a winter of his words. He will not survive, brother. Someone will kill him."

Yazir considered it. Ghalib was almost certainly right. He sighed, shook his head. "No," he said reluctantly. "We do need to speak with him. We might have need of this man."

"Man?" Ghalib said. Lowering his veil, he spat.

Yazir shrugged and turned away. "Come. It is time for prayers."

He turned to walk on. Ghalib looked as if he would protest. In his mind's eye Yazir could almost see him severing the man's tongue. The prospect of silence was appealing. He imagined Ghalib kneeling, knife drawn, the Cartadan's head lifted to rest on his left knee, the tongue pulled out as far as it could go, the blade...Ghalib had done this many times. He was good at it. Yazir very nearly changed his mind. Nearly, but not quite.

He didn't look back. A moment later, he heard his brother following. Most of the time Ghalib still followed. Yazir gestured, and three of the warriors moved to bring the Cartadan. He might die of his wound, but it was unlikely. They knew how to treat such injuries in the desert. Hazem ibn Almalik would live. He would never realize that his life and speech were Yazir's gift to him. Some people you just couldn't help, no matter how you tried.

He joined their wadji and the tribesmen in the compound. They had waited for him. The bell was rung, the sound small and fragile in the wind. They lowered their veils and prayed then in the open spaces to the one god and his beloved servant Ashar, their exposed faces turned to where Soriyya was, so far away. They prayed for strength and mercy, for purity of heart and mortal body, for the fulfillment of Ashar's starlit visions, and for access, at the end of their own days among the sands of earth, to Paradise.

∽

He had been forewarned, but not sufficiently. King Ramiro of Valledo, sitting upon his throne set before the triple arches in his newly completed audience chamber, was sharply aware of trouble the moment the visitors entered the hall.

He glanced briefly at his wife and noted the heightened color in her face, which only confirmed his instinct. Ines had taken great pains with her appearance this morning. Not a surprise; these were guests from Ferrieres, which had been her home.

On his other side, one step back from the throne, his constable, Count Gonzalez de Rada, displayed only his customary arrogance to their guests. That was fine, but Ramiro was almost certain that de Rada was oblivious to what these men might actually mean for Valledo.

No real surprise there, either. Gonzalez had a good mind and a direct way of achieving things, but his perceptions extended no further than the three kingdoms of Esperaña. He could make shrewd observations about what King Ramiro's brother in Ruenda or his uncle in Jaloña might intend, and propose measures to balk them, but clerics from countries across the mountains held no interest for him and therefore shared no part of his thought.

Which was why the warning had been insufficient. Five men of the god, one of them high-ranking, were stopping here at the queen's invitation, en route to the shrine on Vasca's Isle. What could that possibly signify? Gonzalez had hardly given it a thought. Neither, to his own swiftly growing regret, had the king.

Betraying no hint of these emerging apprehensions, Ramiro of Valledo gazed politely at the man proceeding down the carpeted approach to the throne, a few telling steps ahead of his fellows. Some men alerted you with their very presence that something of substance was afoot. This was one such.

Geraud de Chervalles, High Cleric of Ferrieres, was tall enough to look down on every man in that room, including the king. His face was shaved smooth as a baby's, with grey hair swept straight back from his brow, making him seem even taller. His eyes, even at a distance from the throne, were a penetrating blue, set beneath straight eyebrows and above a long nose and a thin, wide mouth. His bearing was patrician, courtly, the manner of an ambassador to a lesser court, not that of a servant of the god appearing before a monarch. Garbed in the blue robes of the Ferrieres clerics, fringed and belted with yellow for the sun, Geraud de Chervalles was an undeniably imposing man.

The king saw no deference at all in that aristocratic face. Nor did he find it—sparing a quick glance—in the expressions of the four lesser clerics who had now come to a halt behind de Chervalles. No hostility or aggression, nothing as ill-bred as that, but clerics didn't have to be hostile to cause a world of trouble, and Ramiro now, belatedly, had a sense that trouble was what had arrived beneath his arches to stand upon the newly laid carpets and mosaics this cold and drizzly morning in autumn.

It didn't help to know that his wife had requested their presence.

He pulled his fur-collared robe more closely about himself. Out of the corner of one eye he saw Gonzalez make a discreet gesture and servants hastened to build up the fires. His constable was endlessly solicitous of the king's comforts in such small matters. Unfortunately he had missed something large here. On the other hand, so had Ramiro himself, and he was not a man to task others for failings he shared.

"Be welcome to Valledo," he said calmly, as the tall cleric stopped a proper distance before the throne. "In the holy name of Jad."

Geraud of Ferrieres bowed then—not before, Ramiro noted. The bow was proper, though, a full, formal salutation. He straightened.

"We are honored, my lord king." The High Cleric's voice was rich and cultured. He spoke Esperañan flawlessly, even to the patrician lisp. "Honored by the invitation from our own beloved Ines, your most devout queen, and by your royal welcome. Only the prospect of a winter's comfort here at Esteren's much-celebrated court could have drawn us forth upon the roads and through the mountains so late in the year."

No bones about it then. His very first remarks. They were staying. Not really a surprise, though they *might* have been intending to push on to Ruenda. That would have been pleasant. Ramiro was aware of Ines beaming beside him, elegant and desirable. She had been looking forward to this for a long time.

"We shall offer what comforts we may," the king said, "though we fear we cannot match the fame of Ferrieres for the delights of the flesh." He smiled, to make clear it was a jest.

The High Cleric shook his head. There was an unwelcome hint of admonition in his expression. Already. "We live simple lives, your grace," he murmured. "We will be well content with any meager space and amenities you are able to spare. Our delight and sustenance will come from the presence of the god in this mighty stronghold of Jad in the west."

Ramiro schooled his features. He was aware that Ines had already allocated and sumptuously furnished a suite of connecting rooms for the Ferrieres clerics in the new wing of the palace, in the event that they elected to linger for more than a short time. There was even a chapel there, at her insistence. Geraud de Chervalles would not be forced to deal with any meager spaces here. The king was also aware of the detailed exchange of letters between his queen and the clerics of her birthplace. It would be unseemly, of course, to betray knowledge of this. He felt like being unseemly.

"We are certain our dearly beloved queen has been at pains to comply with every point of your instructions regarding what accommodations would be adequate for your needs. The hot water has been arranged for your rooms, your personal masseur for each afternoon. The food as stipulated. The requested Farlenian wine."

He smiled genially. Ines stiffened beside him. Geraud de Chervalles looked briefly discomfited, then sorrowful, in the manner of all clerics. He had, however, no easy reply. It was useful, Ramiro thought, to bring them up short early, like a horse in the breaking, before all the smooth, rolling phrases began to pour endlessly forth. He doubted, though, that this man was susceptible to being checked. A moment later this was confirmed.

"I do regret that my advancing years have made it necessary to beg certain solicitous favors from those who honor us with a request to visit. Especially in winter, I fear. Your majesty is young yet, in the flush of your god-granted vigor. Those of us who have begun our mortal decline can only look to you as our stern arm of support, under the holy sun of Jad."

As expected. Not someone who could be quelled as he had managed to quell the yellow-garbed clerics here over the years. Erratic men, ambitious, but without leadership or force. Without looking he could picture the smug expressions on their faces. They had a champion now, and things might be about to change. Well, he ought to have known this was coming. He ought to have given it more thought. He had no one to blame but himself for agreeing to Ines's request that they invite one of the High Clerics from her own country to stop here on his way to the Isle, for the comfort of her soul.

He'd known the name of de Chervalles, known he was a figure of power. Beyond that he had not concerned himself. A weakness. He didn't like thinking about clerics. He did have a vague memory of the afternoon she'd asked his permission to invite the man. He had been lulled and languorous in the aftermath of lovemaking. His queen, thought Ramiro of Valledo, looking straight ahead, knew him altogether too well.

He forced himself to smile again at the tall, grey-haired man in the luxurious blue and yellow robe. "You are unlikely to need defending here in winter. Except against cold and boredom, perhaps. We will do what we can to make you comfortable during your brief time with us." He allowed his tone to hint at dismissal. Perhaps this first encounter, at least, could be kept short. That would give him time to think things through a little.

De Chervalles's expression grew dark, troubled. "The god knows our fears are not for ourselves or our own comfort, gracious king. We come hither on the hard roads heavy with thoughts of the Children of Jad who live not beneath the benevolent rule of the kings in the lands of Esperaña. This, I confess, is what will make the coming winter hard for me."

Well, that had been a vain thought: that they might keep the first meeting brief. And trouble lay ahead now like a thicket of spears. Ramiro said nothing. It was still possible he might deflect the worst of this, for the moment. He really was going to need time to think.

"What can you mean, most holy sire?" Ines's question was transparently earnest. Her hands were clasped together, holding the sun disk in her lap, her face betrayed anxious concern. The king of Valledo swore inwardly, but refused to permit any flicker of emotion to cross his face.

"How can I *not* think of all our pious brethren of the god who must endure yet another winter under the cruel torments of the infidels of Ashar," said Geraud de Chervalles. Said it smoothly, flowingly, sorrowfully. Loudly enough for the whole court to hear.

It was upon him, Ramiro thought grimly. It had arrived, with this assured, dangerous man from Ferrieres. De Chervalles had come here to say this one thing. Say it this morning, and then again, and again, until he made kings and riders and farmers from the fields dance to his tune and die.

Despite his earlier resolutions, Ramiro felt a flicker of anger against his constable. Gonzalez ought to have been alert to this. Was that not part of his office? Did Ramiro have to plan and prepare for *everything* of importance? He knew the answer to that, actually.

No one to blame but himself. The king thought of Rodrigo Belmonte, far away in Al-Rassan. Exiled among the infidels. They weren't even certain where he'd gone yet. He had promised not to attack Valledo with anyone; promised that much but no more. He had been Raimundo's man: his boyhood friend then his constable. Not entirely trusted by Ramiro, or trusting him, if it came to that. Raimundo's death. The shadows around it. Too much history there. And Belmonte was too proud, too independent a man. Needed, though; badly needed, in fact.

"But most holy sire, what can we do?" Ines asked, lifting her clasped hands to her breast. "Our hearts are heavy to hear your words." Her golden disk shone in the muted light falling down through the new windows. It had begun to rain outside; the king could hear it on the glass.

Had he not known better, Ramiro would have thought his queen had been given her words by de Chervalles, so patly did they lead to the High Cleric's next speech. The king wanted to close his eyes, his ears. Wanted urgently to be away from here, riding a horse in the rain. The words came, entirely predictable, but sonorous and compelling nonetheless.

"We can do what those charged by Jad with his holy mission on earth can do—that, and no more or less, most revered queen. The accursed Khalifate of the Asharites is no more," said Geraud of Ferrieres, and paused, suggestively.

"Now there's news," said Gonzalez de Rada sarcastically, his own beautiful voice cutting into the mood. "More than fifteen years old." He glanced at the king. Ramiro understood: the count had finally grasped where this was heading, and was trying to steer it aside.

Too late, of course.

"But there is fresher news, I understand," the tall cleric from Ferrieres said, undeterred. "The vicious king of Cartada is also dead now, summoned to the black judgment Jad visits upon all unbelievers. Surely there is a message here for us! Surely with the leader of the jackals gone it is a time to act!"

The voice had risen, modulating smoothly towards a first crescendo. Ramiro had heard this sort of thing before, but never from such a master. In a kind of horrified admiration, he waited.

"To act? Now?" Gonzalez didn't bother to mask his irony. "A trifle cold is it not?"

Another good effort, the dry tone as much as the words, but Geraud de Chervalles overmastered it. "The fires of the god warm those who serve his will!" His gaze as he looked at the constable was scornful and unyielding. Gonzalez de Rada was unlikely to tolerate this, the king knew from experience, and wondered if he ought to intervene before something serious happened.

But then, unexpectedly, the cleric smiled, much as any man might smile. His stern features relaxed, he lowered his voice. "Of course I do not speak of a winter war. I hope I am not so foolish as that. I know these matters take time, much planning, the right season. These are issues for brave men of the sword such as the valiant kings of Esperaña and their legendary Horsemen. I can only try, in my small way, to help light a fire, and to offer tidings that may aid and inspire you."

He waited. There was a silence. Rain drummed on the windows. A log shifted in one of the fires, then fell with a crash and a flurry of sparks. Ramiro expected Ines to ask the awaited question, but she had fallen unexpectedly silent. He looked at her. She had lowered the sun disk to her lap and was staring at the cleric, biting her lip. Her expression was unreadable now. Inwardly, the king shrugged. The game had begun, it was going to have to be played out.

"What tidings?" he asked politely.

Geraud de Chervalles's smile became a radiant thing. He said, "I thought it might be so. You have not yet heard." He paused, raised his voice. "Hear, then, news to cause all hearts to exult and offer praise: the king of Ferrieres and both counts of Waleska, the mightiest lords of the Karch Lowlands and most of the nobility of Batiara have come together to wage war."

"*What?* Where?" Gonzalez this time, the sharp words pulled from him.

The cleric's smile grew even more triumphant. His blue eyes shone.

"In Soriyya," he whispered into the stillness. "In Ammuz. In the desert homelands of the infidels, where Jad is denied and his life-bringing sun is cursed. The army of the god is assembling even now. It will winter south by the sea in Batiara and take ship in the spring. Already, though, a first battle has been fought in this holy war; we heard the tidings before we left to come to you."

"Where was this battle?" Gonzalez again.

"A city called Sorenica. Do you know it?"

"I do," said Ramiro quietly. "It is the Kindath city in the south of Batiara, granted them as their own long ago, for aid given the princes of Batiara in peace and war. What Asharite armies were there, may I ask?"

Geraud's smile faded. There was a coldness in his eyes now. The belated recognition of a possible foe. *Be careful,* Ramiro told himself.

The cleric said, "Think you the so-called Star-born of the desert are the only infidels we must face? Do you not *know* the rites the Kindath practise on the nights of two full moons?"

"Most of them," said Ramiro of Valledo calmly. It seemed he was not going to be careful, after all. His slow, deep anger was beginning to rise. He feared that anger, but not enough to resist it. He was aware that his wife was looking at him now. He stared at the cleric from Ferrieres. "I've given thought to inviting the Kindath back, you see. We need their industry and their knowledge in Valledo. We need all kinds of people here. I wanted to know as much as I could about Kindath beliefs before I proceeded further. There is nothing I've ever heard, or read, to suggest blood or desecration are part of their faith."

"Invite them back?" Geraud de Chervalles's voice had lost its modulated control. "At the very time when all the kings and princes of the Jaddite world are joining together to cleanse the world of heresy?" He turned to Ines. "You told us nothing of this, my lady." The words were an accusation, stiff and grim.

Ramiro lost his temper. This was too much.

But before he could speak, his queen, his holy, devout queen from Ferrieres said, "Why, cleric, would I tell you such a thing?" Her tone was astringent, royal, shockingly cold.

Geraud de Chervalles, utterly unprepared for this, took an involuntary step backwards. Ines went on: "Why would the plans of my dear lord and husband for our own land be a part of any communication between you and me with regard to your pilgrimage? I think you presume, cleric. I await your apology."

Ramiro was as shocked as the man addressed. Support from Ines against a High Cleric was not something he'd ever have expected. He dared not even look at her. He knew this ice-cold voice of hers extremely well; most often it had been used against him, for one sin or another.

Geraud de Chervalles, his color heightened now, said, "I beg forgiveness, of course, for any offense the queen has perceived. But I will say this: there are no internal, private affairs of any Jaddite kingdom, not when it comes to the infidels, Asharite *or* Kindath. They are a matter for the clerics of the god."

"Then burn them yourselves," said Ramiro of Valledo grimly. "Or if you seek men to die and women to be put at risk of losing all they have in your cause, speak a little more softly, especially at a royal court where you are a guest."

"I have a question," Ines added suddenly. "If I may?" She looked at the king. Ramiro nodded. He still couldn't believe what had happened to her. She asked, "Who is it has mounted this war? Who summoned the armies?"

"The clerics of Jad, of course," said Geraud, his color still high, the easy smile gone. "Led by those of us in Ferrieres, of course."

"Of course," said Ines. "Then tell me, why are you here, cleric? Why are you not with that mighty army in Batiara, preparing to make the long journey to those distant, dangerous eastern lands?"

Ramiro had never seen his wife like this. He looked at

her again in frank astonishment. His own surprise, he saw, was as nothing compared to that of the man addressed.

"There are infidels nearer to home," Geraud said darkly.

"Of course," Ines murmured. Her expression was guileless. "And Soriyya is so far, and sea voyages so tedious, and war in the desert so chancy. I think I do begin to understand."

"I don't think you do. I think—"

"I am fatigued," Queen Ines said, rising. "Forgive me. A woman's weakness. Perhaps we might continue this another time, my lord king?" She looked at Ramiro.

Still unable to believe what he was hearing, the king rose. "Of course, my lady," he said. "If you are unwell..." He extended a hand, she took it. He felt, unmistakably, a pressure of her fingers. "Count Gonzalez, will you be so good as to see to our distinguished guests..."

"A great honor," said Gonzalez de Rada.

He snapped his fingers. Eight men came forward to flank the clerics from Ferrieres. Ramiro nodded his head politely and waited. Geraud de Chervalles, still red-faced, had no choice but to bow. Ramiro turned, Ines swinging around him, still holding his hand, as in the steps of a dance—though she never danced—and they went out through the new bronze doors behind the throne.

The doors closed behind them. It was a small retreat they entered, graciously appointed, with carpeting and new-bought tapestries. There was wine on a table by one wall. Ramiro walked quickly over and poured for himself. He drained a glass, poured another, drained it.

"Jad curse that insufferable man! Might I have just a little of that?" his queen said.

The king wheeled around. The servants had withdrawn. They were alone. Ines's expression was not one he could ever remember seeing. Covering his confusion, he quickly poured for her, mixed water, brought her the glass.

She took it, looked up at him. "I'm sorry," she said. "I brought this upon us, didn't I?"

"An unpleasant guest?" He managed a smile. He felt

oddly buoyant, looking at her. "We've dealt with such before."

"He's more than that, though, isn't he?" He watched her sip from the glass. She made a face, but took another sip. His sudden high spirits faded as quickly as they'd surged.

"Yes," he said, "he is more than that. Or, not him alone, but the tidings he's brought."

"I know that. A holy war. All those armies together. They will want us to join the cause, won't they? In Al-Rassan?"

"And my soldiers will want it."

"You don't want to go south." It was not a question.

There was a discreet knock. The king spoke and Gonzalez de Rada entered. He was very pale, his expression somber. Ramiro went back to the table and poured another glass for himself. This one he watered. It was not a time for indulgence.

"Do I want to wage a holy war in Al-Rassan?" He framed Ines's question again for the constable. "Truthful answer?" He shook his head. "I do not. I want to go south on my own terms in my own time. I want to take Ruenda from my feckless brother, Jaloña from Uncle Bermudo—may his fingers and toes rot—take Fezana from those butchering Cartadans, and *then* look further afield, or let my sons look further afield when I am dead and troubling you no longer." He smiled briefly at Ines. She did not smile back.

"If an army of kings is sailing to Ammuz and Soriyya," Gonzalez said, "it will be hard for us not to go south in the spring. Every cleric in the three kingdoms of Esperaña will be threatening from his chapel that we endanger our souls if we do not."

"I know that," Ramiro murmured. "Pour yourself some wine. It will ease your endangered soul."

"This is my fault," said Ines. "I brought him here."

The king put down his wine. He went to her and claimed her glass and set it down. He took her hands. She did not pull away. All of this was very new.

"He would have come, my dear. He and others. If all the

lords east of the mountains are dancing for them now, why should we be allowed to live free of the yoke? You may be sure there are men like this one in Jaloña already, and on the way to Ruenda if not there by now. They will demand a winter meeting between the three of us. Wait for it. They will *order* us to meet, on pain of banning in the chapels, of losing our immortal places in the god's light. And we will have to listen to them. We will meet, Uncle Bermudo and brother Sanchez and I will sit together, and hunt. They will watch every move I make, and I will do the same with them. We will swear a holy truce amongst ourselves. The clerics will sing our praises in rapture. And we will almost certainly be riding to war in Al-Rassan by spring."

"And?"

She was direct, his queen. Clever and surprising and direct.

Ramiro shrugged. "No sober man ever speaks with certainty about war. Especially not this kind of war, with three armies that hate each other on one side, and twenty that fear each other opposing them."

"And the Muwardis across the straits," said Count Gonzalez softly. "Do not forget them."

Ramiro closed his eyes. He could still hear the rain. Ferrieres, Waleska, Karch, the cities of Batiara...all gathered together in holy war. Despite himself, despite all his sober instincts, there was something undeniably stirring in the image. He could almost see the assembled banners, all those mighty lords of war brought together. How could any man of spirit *not* want to be there, not want to share in such an enterprise?

"The world is a different place than it was this morning," Ramiro of Valledo said gravely. He became aware that he was still holding his wife's hands, that she was allowing him to do so. "Do you know what I would like to do?" he added suddenly, surprising himself.

She looked up at him, waiting. He knew what she was thinking. He always wanted the same thing when he spoke to her like that. Well, she wasn't the only person here who could offer the unexpected. And this new feeling was strong.

"I would like to pray," said the king of Valledo. "After what we have just learned, I think I would like to pray. Will you both come with me?"

They went to the royal chapel together, the king and his queen and their constable. The palace cleric was there, having just arrived from the audience chamber in great dismay. He was as astonished as might have been expected at the sight of the king, which was extremely so. He took his place hastily at the altar before the disk.

Each of them signified the symbol of the god's sun with their right hand over their heart and then sank down upon their knees on the stone of the floor. The light in the royal chapel was muted. There were windows but they were old, and smaller, and rain was falling upon them.

They prayed in that simple, unadorned space to the one god and the life-giving light of his sun, their faces turned to where an emblem of that sun was set upon the wall behind the altar stone. They prayed for strength and mercy, for purity of heart and mortal body, for the fulfillment of Jad's bright visions, and for access, at the end of their own days among the fields of earth, to Paradise.

PART IV

Chapter X

〜

Nino di Carrera, young, handsome and adept, the
most favored courtier of King Bermudo of Jaloña
and concurrently the latest of the furtive lovers of
Bermudo's demanding queen, Fruela, was in a condition of
anxious perplexity.

In fact, he hadn't the least idea what to do.

Confusion made him angry. Anger was compounded by
the increasing embarrassment of what was presently taking place. Nino swept off his iron helmet and shook out
his yellow mane of hair, the envy and desire of most of the
women at Bermudo's court in Eschalou. His breath and
that of the two scouts and all of their horses made white
puffs in the frigid early-morning air.

Behind him his company had come to a halt in this high
valley ringed with hills. They were well-trained, his own
men. The horses had been turned outward and the mules
with their chests of gold from Fibaz were in the center of
the formation. Six chests. A year's *parias* from an infidel
city in Al-Rassan. The first-ever such tribute payment to
Jaloña. A promise of wealth, of power and of much more
to come. The horse thieves of Valledo were not the only
ones who could whip Asharites to heel like the mongrels
they were. And he, Nino di Carrera, had been entrusted
with claiming this first treasure and bringing it back to
Eschalou before the winter snows. The king had promised
him much upon his return; the queen...the queen had
already given him a reward, the night before he left.

My golden one, she'd called him, lying in her bed after
their frenzy. A phrase more apt than ever now. He was
bringing back gold, six chests of it, to the greater glory of
Jad and Jaloña—and of Count Nino di Carrera, who was
soaring like a golden falcon now. And who knew how high
that might be before all was done and spoken before the
god?

But all that—that shining, lofty future—was dependent
on whether he could get these six chests safely home and,
more to the immediate point, whether he could silence the
woman's voice that kept echoing down upon them in this
supernaturally resonant highland valley he wished they
had never entered.

*"Nino, Nino, Nino! Oh, my darling! It is I, Fruela, your
queen! Come to me, my love!"*

The plangent summons, high and clear, rang like a bell,
filling the valley with sound over and over again. Nino di
Carrera was, among other things, aware that his color had
risen: a lifelong affliction that came with fair skin. It was
not—of *course* it wasn't!—Queen Fruela's voice they were
hearing, but it *was* a woman, fluent in Esperañan, and her
tone was urgent with desire.

*"Come, Nino! Take me. Take me here on the hills! Make
me yours!"*

It was not, in any conceivable way, useful for a rising
figure at King Bermudo's court to have this sort of request
publicly uttered. By anyone. Anywhere. And the words were
very public here. They were soaring all about them, echoing endlessly. Someone was amusing themselves at Nino di
Carrera's expense. Someone was going to pay for that.

He was careful not to glance back at his company, but
as the woman's voice, ripe with longing, continued to offer
explicit variations on the same theme, Nino heard—unmistakably—ripples of suppressed laughter behind him.

*"Oh, my rampant stallion, I must have you! Make me
yield to your mastery, my love!"*

Sound carried absurdly well in this place. It was unnatural, that was what it was! And not only did the words

carry, they echoed, so that each yearning proclamation of his name, each vividly proposed activity, resonated as if sung by a choir in chapel.

The two outriders were ashen-faced, refusing to meet his eyes. No trace of amusement there. They wouldn't have dared, in any event, but the tidings they had brought precluded levity. The woman wailing with desire was an offense, even a mortal one; armed men waiting in ambush ahead were something else.

Reckless as his appearance and youth might suggest him to be, Nino di Carrera was a careful commander of a good company, and his outriders, in particular, were excellent. The odds were, in fact, that few companies would have received this advance warning. Most leaders would have felt blithely secure in the presence of almost a hundred mounted men. Nino had been too conscious of how important this *parias* mission was, however: to Jaloña, to himself. He'd had outriders ahead and behind, and on both flanks until the hills forced those men back in. The pair up front had spotted the carefully laid ambush at the northern exit from this valley.

"Nino! I burn for you! Oh, my love, I am a woman before I am a queen!"

It was almost impossible to concentrate with that voice filling the valley bowl. But concentration had become vital now: whoever had laid this trap *had* to know exactly how many men the Jaddites had. Which meant that they weren't fazed by the numbers. Which meant serious trouble. They *couldn't* be from Fibaz: that would be absurd, to give them the gold and then attack them for it. And King Badir of Ragosa, who controlled the small, wealthy city of Fibaz, had authorized this *parias* payment himself, however grudgingly. Why release it from behind defended walls, then attack in open country? Why agree to pay in the first place, if you felt secure enough to attack?

None of it made any sense. And therefore, obviously, the ambush ahead had been laid by outlaws. Nino was pleased he could still think clearly enough—the woman on the hills was now intimating that her clothing was being removed in anticipation of his presence—to sort this through.

There were still problems, though; what was happening *still* didn't seem conceivable. It was almost impossible to imagine any outlaw band large enough and well-equipped enough to try to waylay a hundred trained Horsemen of Jad.

Something occurred to Nino di Carrera then. He narrowed his eyes. He scratched his jaw. Unless, unless...

"I throb, I yearn, I die. Oh, Nino, come to me with the short sword of your loins!"

The short sword?

One of the outriders coughed abruptly and turned his head sharply away. Unmistakable sounds could now be heard from behind, where the company had halted.

That did it. That was enough.

"Edrique! To me! Now!" Di Carrera barked the command without looking back. Immediately he heard a horse cantering up.

"My lord?" His burly, competent second-in-command, unusually ruddy-faced, appeared at his side.

"I want that woman silenced. Take five men."

Edrique's expression was carefully neutral. "Of course, my lord. At once."

"My stallion, come! Let me ride you to Paradise!"

Edrique's turn to cough, averting his crimson features.

"When you are sufficiently recovered," said Nino icily, "go about your business. You might be interested to know there is an ambush laid at the neck of this valley."

That sobered the man quickly enough.

"You think the woman is connected with—"

"How in Jad's name would I know?" Nino snapped. "Deal with her, whoever she is, and get back, quickly. Bring her with you. I want her alive. In the meantime, we're going to double back south and loop around this valley, however far it takes us out of our way. I hate this place!" He said it with more feeling than he'd intended. "I won't ride into a narrow space where the enemy knows the ground."

Edrique nodded and clapped spurs to his horse. They heard him rattling off names to accompany him. Nino remained motionless a moment, thinking as best he could with a feverish woman crying his name so that it rang through the valley.

He'd had an important thought, a moment ago. It was gone now.

But doubling back was the right decision, he was sure of it, much as it gnawed at him to retreat from Asharite scum. If these outlaws were confident enough to have set a trap, it made no sense to ride into it, however strong his company might be. Pride had to be swallowed here. For the moment. Revenge, as his people said, was a wine to be slowly savored.

He heard horses approaching. The outriders looked quickly past him. Nino turned. The two men he had assigned to cover their rear were galloping up. They pulled their horses rearing to a halt before him.

"My lord! There is a company of men behind us! They have closed the south end of this valley!"

"My rampant one, my own king! Take me! I burn for you!"

"What is that accursed woman *doing?*" Nino snarled.

He fought to control himself. He had to *think*, to be decisive, not angry, not distracted. He looked at the outriders for a blank moment then turned back north to gaze towards the end of the valley. There was a darkness there, where the hills came together in a long neck and the sunlight died. An ambush ahead, and men now closing the space behind. They would be pincered here if they waited. If the enemy was in strength. But how *could* they be in strength? It made no sense!

"How many back there?" he snapped over his shoulder to the second pair of scouts.

"Hard to say, my lord. A first group of twenty-five or so. There seemed to be others behind them."

"On foot?"

"Of course, my lord. Outlaws would not have—"

"If I want opinions I will ask!"

"Yes, my lord!"

"Ask of me anything, oh my true king! I am your slave. I am naked, awaiting your mastery! Command me to your will!"

Cursing, Nino pushed a hand roughly through his hair. They were bottled up here! It was unbelievable. How could there be so many bandits in this place? He saw Edrique, with his five men, beginning to mount the slope to the east, after the wailing woman. They would only be able to take the horses partway, then they'd have to go on foot. She'd see them coming, all the way.

He made his decision. It was a time for a leader's decisiveness.

"Edrique!" he roared. The captain turned his horse. "Get back here!"

He waited, four outriders anxious-faced beside him, for his second-in-command. Edrique picked his way back down then galloped up.

"Forget her!" Nino rasped. "We're going north. There are men behind us now. If there are outlaws at each end we push forward. They will have balanced their forces. No point going back now. I have changed my mind. I will not retreat before Asharite bandits."

Edrique smiled grimly. "Indeed no, my lord. We shall teach them a lesson they will never forget." He wheeled back to the company, barking commands.

Nino clapped his helmet firmly on his head. Edrique was good, no question about it. His calm, sure manner gave confidence and support to his leader. The men would see that, and respond to it. It was a fine company he had, superbly mounted, every man of them proud to have been chosen for this mission. Whoever these Asharite scavengers might be, they would have cause to regret their presumption today.

For this provocation, Nino decided, it would be necessary to burn them. Right here in the valley. Let the screaming echo. A message. A warning. Future companies coming south for the *parias* would thank him for it.

"Nino, my shining one, it is your own Fruela! I am dying for you!"

The woman. The woman would have to wait. If she was burning and dying, well, there would be a flame for her as well, soon enough, and for whoever had put her up to this humiliating charade.

And so, focused in anger, did Nino di Carrera banish confusion and doubt. He drew his sword. His company had already wheeled into position behind him. He looked back, saw Edrique nod crisply, his own blade uplifted.

"To Jaloña's glory!" cried Nino then. "Ride now! Ride, in the holy name of Jad!"

They started north, moving quickly, but in tight formation, the mules with their gold still safely in the center of the company. They traversed the valley, shouting in battle fever now, in anticipation. There was no fear. They knew what they were and could do. They rode through bright sunlight over frosted grass and came to the shadows where the hills closed in. They thundered into the dark defile, screaming the god's name, one hundred brave, trained Horsemen of Jad.

Idar ibn Tarif, who had command of the forty men on the western side of the gorge, had been swearing without surcease and with considerable inventiveness since the Jaddite advance scouts had been spotted above them on the slopes. They had been shot at and briefly pursued, to no avail.

They had been discovered! Their trap was exposed. The long hunt was over. Who would ever have imagined a Jaddite commander would be so timorous as to send scouts! The man had a hundred Horsemen! He was supposed to be arrogant, reckless. In Ashar's star-bright name, what was he doing being so cautious?

Across the narrow, sharply angled canyon at the north end of the valley his brother and father were still waiting, oblivious to the disaster that had just taken place, readying their archers for a feathered volley of death against unsuspecting men. Idar, sick at heart, had been about to slip across the shadowy ground to tell them about the scouts when he heard the woman's voice begin, up on the eastern ridges of the Emin ha'Nazar—the echoing valley where the stinking, dog-faced Horsemen had halted.

On this side of the defile beyond the valley the high voice could be clearly heard. Idar was far from fluent in Esperañan, but he knew enough to be suddenly arrested in his purpose. Wondering—and even amused in spite of the catastrophe that had befallen them—he decided to await events.

The Jaddites were going to double back. It was evident to anyone with half a mind. If they had spotted the ambush they would draw all the obvious conclusions. They were swine and unbelievers, but they knew how to wage war. They would circle back out of the Emin ha'Nazar and take the longer way around to the west.

And there was no other place of entrapment between here and the *tagra* lands that would allow eighty unevenly equipped men—a mix of bowmen, cut-throats, some riders, he and his brother and their notorious father—to have any hope of defeating so many soldiers. Gold was worth a great deal of risk, and so was glory, but neither, in Idar's view, justified certain death. He despised the Jaddites, but he was not so foolish as to underestimate how they could fight. And his father had based his long career on never giving battle save on ground of his own choosing.

It was over then, this uncharacteristic chance they had taken, so far north, so late in the year. Well, it had always been that: a gamble. They would wait for the Jaddites to clear the valley and head west. Then they would start back south themselves and begin the long journey home. If the season had not been so close to the winter rains and mud, they might have been able to take their time and find some solace in raiding through Ragosan lands along the way.

Solace, Idar thought glumly, was unlikely to be found before they got back to their own stone walls. He wanted a drink right now, actually, but his father would forbid that. Not for religious reasons of course, but as a commander on a raid. A rule of forty years, that one. Idar would have balked at the old man's strictures save for two things: he loved him, and he feared him more than anyone alive.

"*Look!*" whispered one of the archers beside him. "In the name of Ashar's Paradise, *look!*"

Idar looked. He caught his breath. They were coming. The god had driven the Jaddites mad, or perhaps the woman's voice had done so. Who knew what made men do such things as this? What Idar did know was that he and his brother and father and their men were about to be in a battle such as they hadn't known in years. Their ambush had been uncovered, and the Horsemen were still coming.

The Jaddites approached the defile, one hundred riders, with six mules laboring in their midst. They were riding too fast. They would be blind, Idar knew, the moment they entered the shadows where the steep slopes hid the sun. They were making a terrible mistake. It was time to make them pay for that.

His was one of the first arrows. He launched another, and a third, then he started running and sliding down the slope to where Jaddites and their horses were screaming now in the pits that had been dug, hurled upon each other in a mangling of limbs, falling on the sharp spears planted in the cold ground for killing.

Fast as he moved, Idar saw that his father was ahead of him.

Jehane had been affronted at first by Rodrigo's suggestion, then amused, and finally inspired to inventiveness. In the midst of the exercise she discovered that it was unexpectedly stimulating to be crying aloud in feverish, explicit desire for the whole of the valley below them to hear.

The two men beside her were nearly convulsed in silent hilarity as she offered increasingly flamboyant variations on the theme of her anguished physical yearning—as Queen Fruela of Jaloña—for the golden-haired count who had come to claim the *parias* from Fibaz. She had to concede that it was partly her pleasure at their helpless mirth, their unstinting approval of her performance, that led her on to wilder flights of suggestive fantasy.

They were high on the eastern slopes of the hills that ringed the valley bowl of Emin ha'Nazar, the well-known Place of Many Voices. Well-known, that is, save to the Jaddites who had entered the valley this morning. Even Rodrigo hadn't heard of the place before today, but ibn Khairan had not only known of it, he had anticipated that this might be the place where a trap would be laid for the gold of Fibaz.

The Emin ha'Nazar was known for more than echoes. Among the ghostly voices said to resonate in the valley at night were those of men slain here in battles going back for centuries.

The first such encounter had involved Jaddites as well, in the great wave of the Khalifate's initial expansion, when the boundary between Ashar and Jad had been pushed as far north as it was ever to go. Where it remained now, in fact, just south of the River Duric and the mountains that screened Jaloña.

That savage long-ago campaign had begun—in the endless paradox of things—the centuries-long splendor of Al-Rassan. A brilliant succession of khalifs in the growing Al-Fontina of Silvenes had chosen to name themselves for what they achieved in war: The Conqueror, The Destroyer, Sword of the Star-born, Scourge of the Unbelievers.

They had been those things, there was no hubris in the naming. Those khalifs and their armies, following upon the first reckless, astonishingly successful thrust northward across the straits from the Majriti more than three hundred years ago, had carved and hewed a glorious realm in this peninsula, driving the Esperañans into the farthest north, raiding them twice a year for gold and grain and slaves, and for the sheer pleasure and great glory of doing so in Ashar's ever-bright name.

It had been called a Golden Age.

Jehane supposed that, as such things were measured, it had been. For the Kindath, treading lightly at all times, the expanding world of the khalifs had offered a measure of peace and fragile security. They paid the heretics' tax, as did the Jaddites who dwelt in Al-Rassan; they were to worship the god and his sisters in their fashion only behind closed doors; they were to wear blue and white clothing only, as stipulated in Ashar's Laws. They were forbidden to ride horses, to have intimate congress with Believers, to build the roofs of their sanctuaries higher than any temple of the Asharites in the same city or town...there were rules and laws that enclosed them, but there was a life to be found, and the enforcement of laws varied widely through the passing centuries.

A Golden Age. Now gone. The moons waxed and the moons waned. Silvenes was fallen; the petty-kings bristled and sparred against each other. And now the Jaddites were coming south again, on the magnificent horses they bred in the north. Valledo claimed tribute from Fezana. Ruenda was making overtures towards Salos and the towns north of it along the coast, and here now, below them in this valley, was the first *parias* party from Jaloña, come to share in the banquet, to bring Fibaz gold back to King Bermudo in his drafty castle in Eschalou.

If they could.

High on the slopes above the valley, Jehane lifted her voice again and cried out in Esperañan, in a tone she hoped would convey uncontrollable desire:

"Nino, my golden king, it is Fruela! I am afire for you!"

Screened behind cedar and pine, they saw the young Jaddite commander look up again. He hesitated, then clapped his helmet back on his head.

"That's it," said Rodrigo softly. He had stopped laughing. "I think you've done it, Jehane."

"He's calling back the party he sent up here," Ammar said, also quietly.

"*What* have I done?" Jehane asked, careful to whisper now. Neither of them had yet bothered to explain. They had simply asked her to come up here and pretend to be helpless with desire. It had seemed amusing at the time.

"Goaded him," Rodrigo murmured, not taking his eyes from the valley below. The Horsemen were beginning to move, shifting alignment, turning north. "Nino di Carrera is vain but not a fool. He had outriders ahead and behind. Given a calm space in which to think he would do the intelligent thing and double back. You've been taking space and calm away from him. He is not thinking properly because he is humiliated and angry."

"He is dead," said Ammar ibn Khairan flatly. He, too, had never stopped scanning the valley. "Look what they're doing."

The Jaddites had begun to ride, Jehane saw. High up among the trees in the wind she heard their voices lift in cries of menace and exaltation. Their massed formation looked terrifying to her. The huge thundering of hooves carried up to where they watched. She saw Nino di Carrera lead his company into the shadows at the valley's end and she lost them there.

"Too fast," said Rodrigo.

"Much. There will be a spear pit where the canyon bends," Ammar said grimly.

"And arrows as the horses pile up."

"Of course. Messy."

"It works," said Rodrigo.

A moment later Jehane heard the screaming begin.

The two men looked at each other. They had shaped events to achieve exactly this, Jehane understood that much. *What* they were striving towards, she did not yet know. There were deaths involved, though; she could hear men dying.

"First part done," Ammar said calmly. "We ought to go down."

She looked from him to Rodrigo, who had been the one to suggest the performance as Queen Fruela. "You aren't going to explain this, are you?"

"Later, Jehane, I promise," Rodrigo said. "No leisure

now. We need our own swords to be ready, and then a doctor's labors, I fear."

"There's Laín already," ibn Khairan said, pointing to the other end of the valley bowl. Jehane saw their own men coming up from the south towards the shadows where the Jaloñans had disappeared.

"Of course," Rodrigo said. She detected a note of complacency. "He knows how to do this. What do you think we are?"

Ammar grinned at that, the white teeth flashing. "Valiant Horsemen of Jad," he said. "The same as the ones being butchered down below."

"Not quite," Rodrigo replied, refusing to be baited. "Not quite the same. You'll see. Come on, Jehane. Can you control your smoldering enough to get down from here?"

She would have hit him with something, but by then the sounds of men and their horses in the darkness beyond the north end of the valley were appalling and she followed her two companions down in silence.

"We kill anyone who comes out from the defile," Laín Nunez said flatly when he gave the command to ride. "No surrender accepted. Treat both parties as enemies. We are seriously outnumbered here."

Alvar was intimidated by the grimness in the old warrior's face as he gave his orders. It was no secret that Laín had always thought this intricate, many-layered plan to be foolish and unworkable. But with Mazur ben Avren in Ragosa, Ser Rodrigo and Ammar ibn Khairan all vying to outdo each other in subtlety the scheme had acquired so many nuances as to be almost incomprehensible. Alvar had long ago given up trying to follow what was happening.

He understood no more than the essence: they had made certain that a notorious outlaw leader knew about the Fibaz gold. They *wanted* him to come after the *parias*. King Badir had delayed agreeing to payment of the gold to Jaloña until as late in the year as possible to give this outlaw time to act, if he chose.

Then, after a lone messenger had arrived from the south one night, Rodrigo and ibn Khairan had led fifty of the Valledans out from Ragosa the next morning in a cold rain on the brink of winter. No banners, no identifying emblems, not even their own horses—they rode nondescript mounts from Ragosa. They had passed like ghosts through the countryside, heading east, twenty of them at any time scattering to watch for the movement of companies of men.

It was Martín, predictably, who had spotted the outlaw band coming north. The Captain and ibn Khairan had smiled then; old Laín had not. From that point on the bandit chieftain's progress had been carefully monitored all the way to this valley. He had about eighty men.

The Jaloñans, led by a Count Nino di Carrera—not a name Alvar knew—were already in Fibaz, east and south of where the outlaws waited. Di Carrera had a hundred men, superbly mounted, by report.

When word came of where the ambush was being laid, Ammar ibn Khairan had smiled again. Rain had been falling that day too, dripping from hat brims and into the collars of overtunics and cloaks. The cart roads and fields were already turning to winter's thick mud, treacherous for the horses.

"The Emin ha'Nazar? That old fox," ibn Khairan had said. "He *would* do it in the valley. Truly, I shall be a little sorry if we must kill him."

Alvar was still not sure how he felt about the lord Ammar ibn Khairan.

Jehane liked him, he was fairly certain of that—which complicated matters. Her presence on this ride was complication enough. He worried about her in the cold and the rain, sleeping in a tent on damp or frozen ground, but she said nothing, offered no complaint, rode a horse—normally forbidden the Kindath, of course—surprisingly well. She had learned in Batiara, he discovered. It appeared that in Batiara any number of normally forbidden things could be done.

"What is that valley?" Rodrigo had asked ibn Khairan.

"Tell me all you know about it."

The two of them had walked off together into the mist, talking quietly, so Alvar heard no more. He had happened to be watching Laín Nunez's face, and from the older man's expression had grasped a part of why Laín was so unhappy on this winter expedition. Alvar wasn't the only man here feeling displaced by recent developments.

Nonetheless, Laín's disapproval seemed unwarranted in the end. Even with all the complexity and the need for absolute secrecy of movement, it had all come together after all, here at this strange, high, echoing valley. There was even sunshine today; the air bright and very cold.

Alvar had been part of the first small group that had run up—no horses allowed, by ibn Khairan's orders—to close the southern entrance to the valley after the Jaloñans had gone through. They were posing as outlaws, he understood that much: as part of the same band lying in ambush to the north. And they were meant to be seen by the Jaloñan outriders.

They were. Martín spotted the two scouts in plenty of time to have killed them had they wanted to. They didn't want to. For whatever reason in this indecipherable scheme, they were to allow the scouts to see them and then race back into the valley to report. It was very hard to puzzle out. It was made even harder for Alvar because all through the tense movements of the morning he had been forced to listen to Jehane's voice from high on the slopes as she moaned her desire for the yellow-haired Jaloñan commander in the valley ahead of them. He didn't like that part at all, though most of the others seemed to find it killingly funny.

By the time Laín Nunez gave the order to ride—the horses had been brought up the moment the two scouts left—Alvar was in a mood to do injury to someone. It did cross his mind, as they galloped north in the wintry sunlight, that he was about to kill Jaddites in an Asharite cause. He tried not to let that bother him. He was a mercenary, after all.

Nino was wearing good armor. One arrow hit his chest and was turned away, another grazed his unprotected calf, drawing blood. Then his horse, moving too quickly, trod on emptiness and fell into a pit.

It screamed as it impaled itself upon the forest of stakes below. The screaming of a horse is a terrible sound. Nino di Carrera, lithe and desperate, hurled himself from the saddle even as the horse was falling. He grabbed for the near wall of the pit, clutched, held, and hauled himself out. Just in time to be nearly trampled by the mount of one of his men, veering frantically around the death pit.

He took a kick in the ribs and sprawled on the frozen ground. He saw another horse coming and rolled, agonizingly, away from flailing hooves. He fought for air. The breath had been knocked out of him and his ears were ringing, but Nino found that all limbs were intact. Gasping, wheezing, he could move. He scrambled to his feet, only to discover that he'd lost his sword in the pit. There was a dead man beside him with an arrow in his throat. Nino seized the soldier's blade, ignoring the pain in his ribs, and looked around for someone to kill.

No shortage of candidates. Outlaws were pouring down from the slopes on either side of the defile. At least thirty of Nino's men—probably more—were down, dead or crippled by the spear trap and the volley of arrows. That still left a good number of Horsemen, though, and these were Asharite bandits opposing them, offal, dogs, food for dogs.

Holding a hand to his side, Nino roared his defiance. His men heard him and cheered. He looked around for Edrique. Saw him battling three men, fighting to maneuver his horse in the narrow space. Even as Nino watched, one of the bandits ducked in under the legs of Edrique's mount and stabbed upwards. A peasant's way to fight, knifing horses from below. It worked, though. Edrique's stallion reared up on its hind legs, screaming in pain as the man with the short sword scrambled away.

Nino saw his second-in-command beginning to slide in the saddle. He was already sprinting towards him. The second outlaw, waiting for Edrique to fall, never knew what killed him. Nino's swinging sword, white rage driving it, hewed the man's unhelmed head from his shoulders. It landed in the grass a distance away and rolled like a ball. The blood that fountained from the headless torso spattered them all.

Nino roared in triumph. Edrique swung his feet free of the stirrups to fall free of the maimed horse. He was up on his feet instantly. The two men exchanged a fierce glance then fought together, side by side in that dark defile, two of Jad's holy warriors against legions of the infidels.

Against bandits, really, and as he swung his sword again and again and strove to carve a space to advance, Nino abruptly reclaimed the thought he had found and then lost earlier.

It chilled him, even amid the clotted, sweating chaos of battle: whoever his outriders had seen coming up south of the valley *couldn't* have been part of this ambush. It was so obvious. Where had his mind been? *No one* laid a death trap like this and then split his forces.

Struggling for understanding again, Nino tried to get some sense of what was happening, but the narrow ground between the steep slopes meant that the fighting was desperately close, hand-to-hand, fists and knives and shoulders as much as swords. No chance to step back and evaluate anything. They were spared the arrows now. With their own men entangled with the Jaddites, the bandits could not shoot.

The mules! Nino suddenly remembered the gold. If they lost that there was no point to anything else. He hammered his metal-clad forearm into a bandit's face and felt bones crunch with the blow. With a moment's respite he looked quickly around and spotted a cluster of his men ringing the gold. Two of the mules were down: the cowards had shot at the animals again.

"Over there!" he shouted to Edrique, gesturing. "Fight over that way!"

Edrique nodded his head and turned. Then he fell.

Someone jerked a sword out from his ribs.

In the space where his second-in-command had stood a moment before, a brave, competent, living man, Nino saw an apparition.

The man who had killed Edrique had to be at least sixty years old. He was built like an ox, though, massive and thick-muscled, broad-shouldered, heavy-browed, a huge, ugly head. He was dripping with blood. His long, snarled white beard was dyed and clotted with it; blood streamed from his bald head and had soaked the dun-colored clothing and leather armor he wore. The man, eyes wild with battle lust, levelled his red sword at Nino.

"*Surrender or you will die!*" he roared in crude Esperañan. "We grant ransoming if you yield!"

Nino glanced past the outlaw. Saw the ring of his men still holding around the mules. Many dead, but more of their foes fallen in front of them—and his company were soldiers, the best Jaloña had. The old man was bluffing, taking Nino for a coward and a fool.

"*Jad rot you!*" Nino screamed, his throat scraped raw. He cut viciously on the backhand against the other man's blade and drove the blood-soaked figure back a step with the sheer force of his rage. Another outlaw rushed up on Nino's left; Nino twisted under his too-high sword stroke and swept his own blade back across and down. He felt it bite into flesh. A red joy filled him. His victim made a sloppy, wet sound and fell to the frosted earth.

The white-bearded outlaw froze for a moment, screaming a name, and Nino used that hesitation to ram straight into him and then past, as the man gave way, to where most of his remaining men were ferociously defending the gold. He stumbled into their ranks, greeted with glad, fierce cries, and he turned, snarling, to fight again.

Surrender? To these? To be ransomed by the king from Asharite bandits, with the *parias* lost? There were worse things than dying, far worse things.

This is not war as I dreamed it, Alvar was thinking.

He was remembering the farm, childhood, an eager boy, a soldier's only son, with a wooden sword always by his bed at night. Images of glory and heroism dancing beyond the window in the starry dark after the candles had been blown out. A long time ago.

They were waiting in pale cold sunlight at the north end of the valley.

Kill anyone who comes out, Laín Nunez had said. Only two men had. They had been battling each other, grappled together, grunting and snorting like animals. Their combat had carried them right out of the defile, tumbling and rolling, fingers clawing at each other's eyes. Ludus and Martín, efficient and precise, had moved their horses over and dispatched both men with arrows. The two bodies lay now, still intertwined, on the frosted grass.

There was nothing remotely heroic or even particularly dangerous about what they were doing. Even the night sweep into the burning hamlet of Orvilla last summer had had more intensity, more of a sense of real warfare, than this edgy waiting while other men killed each other out of sight in the dark space north of them.

Alvar glanced over his shoulder at a sound and saw the Captain riding up, with Jehane and ibn Khairan. Jehane looked anxious, he thought. The two men appeared calm, unconcerned. Neither spared a glance for the two dead men on the grass. They cantered their horses up to Laín Nunez.

"It goes well?" Rodrigo asked.

Laín, predictably, spat before answering. "They are killing each other for us, if that is what you mean."

Ammar ibn Khairan grinned at the tone. Rodrigo offered a level glance at his second-in-command. "You know what this is about. We've had our real battles and we'll have them again. We're trying to achieve something here."

Laín opened his mouth to reply, then shut it firmly. The expression in the Captain's face was not conducive to argument.

Rodrigo turned to Martín. "Take a quick look. I need

the numbers in there. We don't want the Jaloñans to win, of course. If they are, we'll have to move in, after all."

Alvar, vainly trying to follow, was made edgy again by his ignorance. Laín might know what was going on, but no one else did. Was it always this way in war? Didn't you usually know that your enemy was ahead of you and your task was to be braver and stronger? To kill before you were killed? He'd a feeling Laín felt the same way.

"He's already been in there," Laín said sourly. "I do know what I'm doing. It is balanced, about thirty of each left. The outlaws will break soon."

"Then we have to go in."

It was ibn Khairan who spoke, looking at Rodrigo. "The Jaloñans are good. You said they would be." He glanced at Laín. "You get your battle, after all."

Jehane, beside him, still looked worried. It was difficult to relate her expression to the intoxicated words Alvar had heard her crying from among the trees.

"Your orders, Captain?" Laín was staring at Rodrigo. His tone was formal.

For the first time Rodrigo Belmonte looked unhappy, as if he'd rather have heard different tidings from the defile. He shrugged his shoulders, though, and drew his sword.

"Not much choice, though this won't be pretty. We've wasted our time if di Carrera fights free or the outlaws break."

He lifted his voice then, so fifty men could hear him. "We're going in. Our task is exact: we are joining the bandits. Not a man of the Jaloñans leaves that defile. No ransom. Once they see us and know we are here we have no choice about that. If even one of them makes it back to Eschalou and reports our presence this has all been for nothing and worse than that. If it helps at all, remember what they did at Cabriz in the War of Three Kings."

Alvar did remember that. Everyone in Valledo did. He had been a bewildered child, watching his father weep when tidings came to the farm. King Bermudo had besieged the city of Cabriz, promised amnesty on surrender, then slaughtered every Valledan fighting man when they rode out under the banner of truce. The Asharites were not the only ones with a grasp of savagery.

Even so, this was still not war as he had imagined it. Alvar looked towards Jehane again. She had turned away. In horror, he thought at first, then saw that she was gesturing to someone near the back of their ranks. Velaz came forward, calm and brisk as ever, with her doctor's implements. Alvar felt ashamed: she wasn't reacting emotionally, as a woman; she was simply readying herself, physician of a company about to go into battle. He had no business doing less than the same. No one had ever said a soldier's life was designed to give fulfillment to a child's dreams.

Alvar drew his sword, saw others doing the same. A few shaped the sign of the sun disk as they did, whispering the words of the soldier's invocation: *Jad send us Light, and let there be Light waiting for us.* The archers fitted arrows to strings. They waited. Rodrigo looked back at them, nodded his approval. Then he lifted and dropped his hand. They rode out of the sun into the defile where men were killing each other in the cold.

Nino di Carrera knew that he was winning. There came a moment in every battle when one could sense the rhythm changing and he had felt it now. The outlaws had needed to defeat them quickly, with the chaos of the spear pit and the shock of their archers' ambush. Once those had been survived—if barely—this became a clash of roughly even forces and could have only one result. It was only a question of time before the Asharites broke and fled; he was mildly surprised they hadn't done so by now. Even as he fought, shoulder to shoulder with his men in the ring around the gold, Nino was beginning to calculate his next course of action.

It would be pleasant to pursue this rabble when they ran, exceedingly pleasant to burn them alive for the deaths of so many men and so many purebred horses. There was the woman, too, if she could still be found on the slopes. A

burning would go a long way towards addressing the
grievances of this morning.

On the other hand, he was likely to emerge from this
evil place with no more than twenty men and a long way
yet to travel through hostile country with the gold of
Jaloña's future. He simply could not afford to lose any
more soldiers after this. They were going to have to travel
at speed, Nino realized; no rest except what was utterly
necessary, riding by night as well. They could travel with
two horses, at least, for each man left, which would spare
the beasts, if not the riders.

That would be the only course until they reached the
tagra lands where he might assume there would be no
forces large enough to trouble twenty mounted men.
There will be time for revenge, he told himself, battling.
There will be years and years for the taking of revenge.
Nino might be young, but he knew exactly what this first
installment of the *parias* meant. Almost contemptuously
he blocked an outlaw's slash and drove the man stagger-
ing back with a counterblow.

It was all beginning here, with him and this small company. The men of Jaloña would be coming back south once
more, again and again. The long tide of centuries was turning, and it was going to sweep all the way through Al-
Rassan to the southern straits.

First, though, there was this matter of bandits in a defile.
They ought to have broken by now, Nino thought again.
Grimly he hacked and chopped, with more space to move
now, and even, at moments, room to advance a few paces.
They were brave enough, these outlaws from the south, but
Jaddite iron and Jaddite courage were going to prevail.

Someone fell with a grunt beside him; Nino pivoted and
thrust his sword deep into the guts of the man who had
just killed one of his soldiers. The bandit shrieked; his eyes
bulged. Nino twisted his blade deliberately before hauling
it free. The fellow's hands clutched at his oozing, slippery
intestines, trying to keep them from spilling out.

Nino was laughing at that, as it happened, when the

fifty new riders swept into the defile.

They were Jaddites, he saw that much in the first astonished glance. Then he saw—and tried desperately to understand—that their mounts were small, nondescript horses of Al-Rassan. Then he realized, with a cold pressing of blackness against his heart, that they had come not to aid him but to kill.

It was in that frozen moment of revelation that Nino recognized the first of these riders by the image of an eagle on the crown of his old-fashioned helmet.

He knew that emblem. Every fighting man in Esperaña knew of that helmet and the man who wore it. There was a paralyzing weight of disbelief in Nino's mind. He experienced an appalling sense of the unfairness of things. He raised his sword as the eagle-helmed horseman came straight towards him. Nino feinted, then swung savagely for the man's ribs. His blow was parried, casually, and then, before he could right himself, Nino saw a long, bright, final blade come scything and he left the world of living men and fell down into the dark.

Idar, fighting beside his father, had been struggling to summon the courage to suggest retreat.

It had never happened before that his father had persisted this long with what was clearly a failed assault. They had established their name, their fortune, their castle at Arbastro, by knowing when to engage and when—as now, surely!—to withdraw and fight another time.

It was his brother's wound, Idar knew, laboring with his sword in the trammelling press. Abir was dying on the hard ground behind them and their father was out of his head with grief. One of their men was beside Abir on his knees, cradling his head, two others stood by to defend him should any of the accursed Jaddites break free of their tight circle.

Their father was a wild, terrifying figure beside Idar, frenzied in his attacks on the ring of their enemies, oblivious to circumstance and need, to the devastating fact that more than half their number were dead. There were barely thirty men doing battle now with almost as many of the dung-eating Horsemen. Their weapons and armor were less good, their style of combat was not and never had been this kind of savage face-to-face confrontation.

The ambush had almost succeeded but it had not quite been enough. It was time to break free, to run south, to accept that a huge risk had nearly worked, but had not. They had a desperately long way to go to get home to Arbastro, on evil winter paths, through mud and rain, and with the wounded to slow them. It was past time to pull out while they could, while some of them yet lived.

As if to mark the truth of his thought, Idar was forced in that moment to duck swiftly down and to one side as a burly Jaddite with a studded mace stepped forward and hammered a sideswung blow at his face. The Jaddite was armored from head to calves, Idar wore a leather helm and a light chain breastpiece. What were they *doing* fighting face to face?

Twisting under the lethal mace, Idar chopped sharply at the back of the Jaddite's ankle. He felt his sword bite through the boot and into flesh. The man screamed and fell to one knee. They would say it was a coward's way to fight, Idar knew. They had their armor and their iron. The men of Arbastro had decades of experience in the tactics of cunning and entrapment. When it came to killing or dying there were no rules; his father had drilled that into them from the beginning.

Idar killed the fallen giant with a slicing blow to the neck, where the helmet did not quite meet his body armor. He thought about grabbing the mace, but decided it would be too heavy for him, especially if they had to run.

And they *did* have to run, or they were going to die in this defile. He watched his father, still wild with rage, pounding his blade over and again against a Jaddite shield. The Jaddite withdrew, one pace and then another, but the shield arm held, steady and resilient. Just beyond his father Idar saw the Jaddite captain, the yellow-haired one, dispatch another of their men. They were going to die here.

It was in that moment that the second wave of Jaddites came galloping up behind them, the hooves of their horses like sudden thunder in the defile.

Idar wheeled about, aghast. *Too late now*, he thought, and in his mind he saw a swift, vivid image of a white-faced, black-haired maiden coming for him, her long fingernails reaching for his red heart. And then, a pulsebeat later, Idar realized that he understood nothing at all of what was happening here today.

The leader of this new wave of Horsemen came sweeping through the outlaw line. He rode straight up to where the yellow-haired man wielded his heavy sword. Leaning in the saddle, he blocked a thrust and then, curbing his horse tightly, swept his own long blade down with incisive mastery and killed the other Jaddite where he stood.

Idar became aware that his mouth was gaping open. He closed it. He looked desperately towards the red-smeared figure of blood and grief and fury that was his father and he saw the sharp-eyed clarity that he remembered—that he *needed*—suddenly return.

"We have been used," his father said to him then, quiet amid the roiling chaos of new horses and dying men in front of them. He had lowered his sword. "I am in my dotage. Too old to be allowed to lead men. I ought to have died before today."

And, amazingly, he sheathed his blade and stepped back, seemingly indifferent, as the new Jaddites killed the first ones without mercy or respite, even though swords were being thrown down in the circle around the gold and men were crying aloud for ransom.

No one's surrender was accepted. Idar, who had killed many men in his time, watched in silence from where he and his father had withdrawn beside his dying brother.

The men from Jaloña, who had come south for a fortune in *parias* gold, who had ridden foolishly into a trap and then survived it by main courage and discipline, died that morning, every one of them, in that dark place.

Afterwards it was quiet, save for the moaning of injured outlaws. Idar realized that some of the new Jaddite archers were shooting the wounded horses, which is why those sounds had stopped. The animals' screaming had been going on so long he had almost blocked it out. He watched as the undamaged horses were rounded up. They were magnificent stallions; no mounts in Al-Rassan could match those from the ranches of Esperaña.

Idar and his father and the others laid aside their weapons, as ordered: there was no point resisting. They numbered barely more than twenty, all exhausted and many wounded, with nowhere to run, facing fifty mounted warriors. On the ground beside them, his head now pillowed on a saddle cloth, Abir breathed raggedly, dealing with pain. The wound in his thigh was too deep, Idar saw; it was still bleeding despite the knot tied above it. Idar had seen that kind of wound before. His brother was going to die. There was a kind of blankness in Idar's mind because of that, an inability to think properly. He remembered, quite suddenly, the vision he had had when the new Horsemen had appeared: death as a woman, her nails raking for his life.

It wasn't his life, after all. He knelt and touched his younger brother's cheek. He found that he could not speak. Abir looked up at him. He lifted a hand so their fingers touched. There was fear in his eyes but he said nothing at all. Idar swallowed hard. It would not do to cry. They were still on a battlefield. He squeezed Abir's hand and stood up. He walked a few steps back to stand beside their father. The old man's blood-smeared head was high, his shoulders straight as he looked up at the new men on their horses.

Tarif ibn Hassan of Arbastro, captured at last after almost forty years.

The outlaw who had become more a king—and who had always been more a lion—than any of the myriad pretenders to royalty since Silvenes fell. The numbness in Idar extended to this as well. Their world was ending in this defile. A new legend to go with the old ones about the haunted Emin ha'Nazar. His father betrayed no expression at all. For more than three decades a series of khalifs and then half a dozen of the petty monarchs of Al-Rassan had vowed to cut off his fingers and toes one by one before they allowed him to die.

The leaders of the new company sat astride their horses, gazing down upon him. They looked undisturbed, as if nothing of note or consequence had taken place. Their own weapons had been sheathed. One of them was an Asharite. The other was Jaddite, as were all of the soldiers. The Jaddite wore an old-fashioned helm with a bronze eagle on the crown. Idar didn't know either man.

His father said, not waiting for them, "You are mercenaries from Ragosa. It was Mazur the Kindath who planned all of this." He did not put it as a question.

The two men looked at each other. Idar thought he saw a trace of amusement in their expressions. He felt too hollow to be angered by that. His brother was dying. His body ached, and his head hurt in the silence after the screaming. It was in his heart, though, that the real pain lay.

The Asharite spoke. A courtier's voice. "A measure of self-respect requires that we accept some of the credit, but you are correct in the main: we are from Ragosa."

"You arranged for us to know about the *parias*. You drew us north." Tarif's voice was flat. Idar blinked.

"That is also correct."

"And the woman on the slopes?" Idar said suddenly. "She was yours?" His father looked at him.

"She travels with us," the smooth-featured man said. He wore a pearl in one ear. "Our doctor. She's a Kindath, too. They are very subtle, aren't they?"

Idar scowled. "That wasn't her doing."

The other man, the Jaddite, spoke. "No, that part was ours. I thought it might be useful to have di Carrera distracted. I'd heard some rumors from Eschalou."

Idar finally understood. "You drove them into us! They thought you were part of our company, or they would never have ridden into the trap. They had sent spies, I saw them. They knew we were here!"

The Jaddite brought a gloved hand up and touched his moustache. "Correct again. You laid your ambush well, but di Carrera is—was—a capable soldier. They would have doubled back and around the valley. We gave them a reason not to. A chance to make a mistake."

"We were supposed to kill them for you, weren't we?" Idar's father's voice was bitter. "I do apologize for our failure."

The Asharite smiled and shook his head. "Hardly a failure. They were well trained and better armed. You came close, didn't you? You must have known this was a gamble from the moment you set out."

There was a silence.

"Who are you?" Idar's father asked then, staring narrowly up at the two of them. "Who are you both?" The wind had picked up. It was very cold in the defile.

"Forgive me," the smooth one said. He swung down from his horse. "It is an honor to finally meet you. The fame of Tarif ibn Hassan has spanned the peninsula all my life. You have been a byword for courage and daring. My name is Ammar ibn Khairan, late of Cartada, currently serving the king of Ragosa."

He bowed.

Idar felt his mouth falling open again and he shut it hard. He stared openly. This was...this was the man who had slain the last khalif! And who had just killed Almalik of Cartada!

"I see," said his father quietly. "Some things are now explained." His expression was thoughtful. "You know we had people die in villages near Arbastro because of you."

"When Almalik was searching for me? I did hear about that. I beg forgiveness, though you will appreciate that I had no control over the king of Cartada at that point."

"And so you killed him. Of course. May I know who your fellow is, who leads these men?"

The other man had taken off his helm. It was tucked under one arm. His thick brown hair was disordered. He had not dismounted.

"Rodrigo Belmonte of Valledo," he said.

Idar actually felt as if the hard ground had suddenly become unstable beneath his feet, as in an earth tremor. This man, this Rodrigo, had been named by the wadjis for years to be cursed in the temples. The Scourge of Al-Rassan, he had been called. And if these were his men...

"More things," Idar's father said gravely, "are now explained." For all the blood that smeared and stained Tarif ibn Hassan's head and clothing, there was a remarkable dignity and composure to him now. "One of you ought surely to have been enough," he murmured. "If I am to be finally defeated and slain, I suppose it will at least be said in years to come that it took the best men of two lands to do it."

"And neither man would claim to be better than you."

This fellow, ibn Khairan, had a way with words, Idar thought. Then he remembered that the Cartadan was a poet, to go with everything else.

"You aren't going to be slain," Rodrigo Belmonte added. "Unless you insist upon it." Idar stared up at him, keeping his mouth firmly closed.

"That last is unlikely," Idar's father growled. "I am old and feeble but not yet tired of life. I *am* tired of mysteries. If you aren't going to kill us, tell me what it is you want." He said it in a tone very nearly of command.

Idar had never been able to keep up with his father, to match or encompass the raw force in him; he had long since stopped trying. He followed—in love, in fear, very often in awe. Neither he nor Abir had ever spoken about what would happen when their father was gone. It did not bear thinking about. There was an emptiness that lay beyond that thought. The white-faced, dark-haired woman with her nails.

The two mercenaries, one standing before them, the other still on horseback, looked at each other for a long moment. An agreement seemed to pass between them.

"We want you to take one mule's worth of Fibaz gold and go home," said Rodrigo Belmonte. "In exchange for that, for your lives and that measure of gold, you will ensure that the world hears of how you successfully ambushed the Jaloñan party and killed them all and took all the *parias* gold back to Arbastro."

Idar blinked again, struggling. He folded his arms across his chest and tried to look shrewd. His father, after a moment, laughed aloud.

"Magnificent!" he said. "And whose is the credit for *this* part of the scheme?"

The two men before him glanced again at each other. "This part," said ibn Khairan a little ruefully, "is indeed, I am sorry to have to say, the thought-child of Mazur ben Avren. I do wish I had thought of it. I'm sure that I would have, given time."

The Valledan captain laughed.

"I have no doubt," Tarif ibn Hassan said dryly. Idar watched his father working through all of this. "So that is why you killed them all?"

"Why we had to," Rodrigo Belmonte agreed, amusement gone as swiftly as it had come. "Once they saw my company, if any of di Carrera's party made it home the story would never hold. They would know we had the gold back in Ragosa."

"Alas, I must beg your forgiveness again," Tarif murmured. "We were to do your killing for you and we failed miserably. What," he asked quietly, "would you have done if we had taken them for ransom?"

"Killed them," said Ammar ibn Khairan. "Are you shocked, ibn Hassan? Do you fight by courtly rules of war like the paladins of the old tales? Was Arbastro built with treasure won in bloodless adventures?" There was an edge to his tone, for the first time.

He didn't like doing this, Idar thought. *He may pretend otherwise, but he didn't like it.*

His father seemed satisfied by something. His own manner changed. "I have been an outlaw most of my life, with a price on my head. You know the answer to your own questions." He smiled thinly, his wolf's expression. "I have no objection to taking gold home and receiving the acclaim for a successful raid. On the other hand, once I am back in Arbastro, it might please me to embarrass you by letting the truth be known."

Ammar ibn Khairan smiled, the edge still there. "It has pleased a number of people over the years to embarrass me, one way or another." He shook his head sorrowfully. "I had hoped that a loving father's concern for his sons in Ragosa might take precedence over the pleasure of distressing us."

Idar stepped quickly forward, but his father, without glancing at him, extended a hand and held him back. "You would stand before a man whose youngest child is dying as we speak and propose to take away his other son?"

"He is far from dying. What sort of medical care are you accustomed to?"

Idar wheeled around. Beside Abir now, on her knees, was a woman. They had said their doctor was a woman. A servant was with her, and she had a cloth full of implements already opened. Idar hadn't even seen her walk around them to Abir, so intense was his focus on the two men. She was unexpectedly young, pretty for a Kindath; her manner was crisp and precise though, almost curt.

She said, looking at his father, "I ought to be able to save his life, though I am afraid it is going to cost him the leg. It will need to be taken off above the wound, the sooner the better. I need the place and time of his birth, to see if it is proper to do surgery now. Do you know these things?"

"I do," Idar heard himself saying. His father was staring at the woman.

"Good. Give them to my assistant, please. I will offer your brother the best care I can here, and I will be pleased to look after him when he returns with us to Ragosa. With luck and diligence he ought to be able to move about with sticks before spring." Her eyes were extremely blue, and quite level as her gaze rested on Idar's father. "I am also confident that having his brother as a companion will speed his recovery."

Idar watched his father's face. The old warrior's expression moved from relief to fury to a gradual awareness that he had no resources here. Nothing to do in the presence of these people but accede. It was not a role he had ever played happily in his life.

He managed another thin, wolf's smile. Turned from the Kindath doctor back to the two men. "Do help an old man's faltering grasp of things," he said. "Was this elaborate scheme truly worth a single season's delay? You must know that King Bermudo will send again to Fibaz in the spring, demanding *parias*, almost certainly a doubled sum."

"Of course he will," said ibn Khairan. "But this happens to be an important season and this gold can be put to better use than arming Jaloña for the coming year." The pearl in his right ear gleamed. He said, "When next he comes Fibaz might refuse him tribute."

"Ah!" said Idar's father then. He pulled a bloody hand slowly through his beard, smearing it even further. "I am illuminated! The spirit of Ashar allows me sight at last." He bowed mockingly to both men. "I am humbled to be even a small part of so great an undertaking. Of *course* it is an important season. Of *course* you need the gold. You are going after Cartada in the spring."

"Good for you!" said Ammar ibn Khairan, encouragement in his voice and the blue eyes. He smiled. "Wouldn't you like to come with us?"

A short time later, back in the sunlight of the valley, Jehane bet Ishak prepared to saw off the right leg of Abir ibn Tarif, assisted by Velaz and the strong hands of Martín and Ludus, and with the aid of a massive dose, administered by saturated sponge, of her father's strongest soporific.

She had performed amputations before, but never on open ground like this. She didn't tell them that, of course. Ser Rezzoni again: *Let them always believe you do nothing but this procedure, day after day.*

The wounded man's brother hovered impotently nearby, begging to be of assistance. She was struggling to find polite words to send him away when Alvar de Pellino materialized beside the man with an open flask.

"Will I offend you if I offer wine?" he asked the white-faced bandit. The look of grateful need was answer enough. Alvar led the man to the far side of their temporary camp. The father, ibn Hassan, was conversing there with Rodrigo and Ammar. He betrayed his distraction by glancing in their direction with regularity. Jehane noted that, then put all such matters from her mind.

Amputations in the field did not have a high success rate. On the other hand, most military doctors had no real idea what they were doing. Rodrigo had known that very well. It was why she was here. It was also why she was nervous. She could have asked the moon sisters and the god for an easier first procedure with this company. For almost anything else, in truth.

She let none of this show in her face. She checked her implements again. They were clean, laid out by Velaz on a white cloth on the green grass. She had consulted her almanac and cast the moons: those of the patient's birth hour were in acceptable harmony with today's. She would only have delayed if faced with the worst possible reading.

There was wine to pour into the wound and the cauterizing iron waited in the fire, red-hot already. The patient was dazed with the drugs Velaz had given him. Not surprisingly: the sponge had been steeped in crushed poppies, mandragora and hemlock. She took his arm and pinched it, as hard as she could. He didn't move. She looked into his eyes and was satisfied. Two strong men, used to battlefield surgery, were holding him down. Velaz—from whom she had no secrets—offered her a reassuring glance, and her heavy saw.

No reason, really, to delay.

"Hold him," she said, and began to grind through flesh and bone.

Chapter XI

∾

"Where's Papa now?"

Fernan Belmonte, who had asked the question, was lying in clean straw in the loft above the barn. Most of him was buried for warmth, only the face and brown, tousled hair showing.

Ibero the cleric, who had reluctantly acceded to the twins' morning lessons taking place up here today—it *was* warmer in the barn above the cows, he'd had to concede—opened his mouth quickly to object, but then shut it and looked with apprehension towards where the other boy lay.

Diego was completely invisible under the straw. They could see it shift with the rise and fall of his breathing, but that was all.

"Why does it matter?" His voice, when it came, seemed disembodied. A message from the spirit-world, Ibero thought, then surreptitiously made the sign of the sun disk, chiding himself for such nonsense.

"Doesn't really," Fernan replied. "I'm just curious." They were taking a brief rest before switching courses of study.

"Idle child. You know what Ibero says about curiosity," Diego said darkly from his cave of straw.

His brother looked around for something to throw. Ibero, used to this, quelled him with a glance.

"Well, is he allowed to be rude?" Fernan asked in an aggrieved tone. "He's using you as authority for impolite behavior to his older brother. Will you let him? Doesn't that make you a party to his action?"

"What's impolite about it?" Diego queried, muffled and unseen. "Do I have to answer every question that comes into his empty head, Ibero?"

The little cleric sighed. It was becoming increasingly difficult to deal with his two charges. Not only were they impatient and frequently reckless, they were also ferociously intelligent.

"I think," he said, prudently dodging both queries, "that this particular exchange suggests that our rest is over. Shall we turn to the matter of weights and measures?"

Fernan made a ghastly, contorted face, pretended he was strangling, and then pulled straw over his head in unsubtle protest. Ibero reached for and found a buried foot. He twisted, hard. Fernan yelped and surfaced.

"Weights and measures," the cleric repeated. "If you won't apply yourself properly up here we'll just have to go down and inform your mother what happens when I'm tolerant of your requests."

Fernan sat up quickly. Some threats still worked. Some of the time.

"He's somewhere east of Ragosa," Diego said. "There's a fight of some kind."

Ibero and Fernan looked quickly at each other. The matter of weights and measures was, for the moment, abandoned.

"What does *somewhere* mean?" Fernan demanded. His tone was sharp now. "Come on, Diego, do better than that."

"Near some city to the east. There's a valley."

Fernan looked to Ibero for help. The straw on the other side of the cleric shifted and disgorged a blinking thirteen-year-old. Diego began brushing straw from his hair and neck.

Ibero was a teacher. He couldn't help himself. "Well, he's given us some clues. What's the city east of Ragosa. You both ought to know."

The brothers looked at each other.

"Ronizza?" Fernan hazarded.

"That's south," Ibero said, shaking his head. "And on

what river is it?"

"The Larrios. Come on, Ibero, this is important!" Fernan had the capacity to seem older than his years when military matters were being discussed.

But Ibero was equal to this challenge. "Of course it's serious. What sort of commander relies on his cleric to help him with geography? Your father knows the name and size and the terrain surrounding every city in the peninsula."

"It's Fibaz," Diego said suddenly. "Beneath the pass to Ferrieres. I don't know the valley, though. It's north and west of the city." He paused and looked away again. They waited.

"Papa killed someone," Diego said. "I think the fighting is stopping."

Ibero swallowed. It was difficult with this child. It was almost impossibly difficult. He looked closely at Diego. The boy seemed calm; a little distracted, but it was impossible to see from his face that he was registering events unimaginably far away. And Ibero had no doubt—not after so many trials—that Diego was reporting them truly.

Fernan had none of that calm just now. Grey eyes gleaming, he stood up. "I'll bet you anything this has to do with Jaloña," he said. "They were sending a *parias* party, remember?"

"Your father wouldn't attack other Jaddites for the infidels," Ibero said quickly.

"Of course he would! He's a mercenary, he's being paid by Ragosa. The only promise he made was not to come with an army into Valledo, remember?" Fernan looked confidently from Ibero to Diego. His whole being was afire now, charged with energy.

And it was Ibero's task—as tutor, guardian, spiritual counsellor—to somehow control and channel that force. He looked at the two boys, one feverish with excitement, the other seeming a little unfocused, not altogether present, and he surrendered yet again.

"You are both going to be useless for the rest of the morning, I can see that much." He shook his head darkly.

"Very well, you are released." Fernan whooped: a child again, not a commander-in-waiting. Diego hastily stood up. Ibero had been known to change his mind.

"One condition," the cleric added sternly. "You will spend time with the maps in the library this afternoon. Tomorrow morning I am going to have you mark the cities of Al-Rassan for me. Major ones, smaller ones. This matters. I want you to know them. You are your father's heirs and his pride."

"Done," said Fernan. Diego just grinned.

"Then go," said Ibero. And watched them hurtle past him and down the ladder. He smiled in spite of himself. They were good boys, both of them, and he was a kindly person.

He was also a devout man, and a thoughtful one.

He knew—who in Valledo did not, by now?—of the holy war being launched this coming spring from Batiara, an armada of ships sailing for the eastern homelands of the infidels. He knew of the presence in Esteren, as a guest of the king and queen, of one of the highest of the clerics of Ferrieres, come to preach a war of the three kingdoms of Esperaña against Al-Rassan. The Reconquest. Was it truly to come now, in their lifetime, after so many hundreds of years?

It was a war every devout man in the peninsula was duty-bound to support and succor with all his being. And how much more did that apply to the clerics of holy Jad?

Sitting alone in the straw of the barn loft, listening to the milk cows complaining below him, Ibero the cleric of Rancho Belmonte began a hard wrestling match within his soul. He had been with this family most of his life. He loved them all with a fierce, enduring passion.

He loved and feared his god with all his heart.

He remained up there, thinking, for a long time, but when he finally came down the ladder his expression was calm and his tread firm.

He went directly to his own chamber beside the chapel and took parchment and quill and ink and composed then, carefully, a letter to the High Cleric Geraud de Chervalles at the king's palace in Esteren, writing in the name of Jad and humbly setting forth certain unusual circumstances as he understood them.

∽

"When I sleep," said Abir ibn Tarif, "it feels as if I still have my leg. In my dreams I put my hand down to my knee, and I wake up, because it isn't there." He was reporting it, not complaining. He was not a man who complained.

Jehane, changing the dressing on his wound, nodded her head. "I told you that might happen. You feel tingling, pain, as if the leg were still attached?"

"That is it," Abir said. Then, stoutly, "The pain is not so great, mind you."

She smiled at him, and across the infirmary bed at his brother, who was always present when she visited. "A lesser man would not say that," she murmured. Abir looked pleased. She liked both of them, these sons of an outlaw chieftain, hostages in Ragosa for the winter. They were gentler men than she might have expected.

Idar, who had developed an attachment to her, had been telling stories through the winter of Arbastro and their father's courage and cunning. Jehane was a good listener, and sometimes heard more than the teller intended. Physicians learned to do that.

She had wondered before about the price paid by the sons of great men. This winter, with Idar and Abir, she addressed the question again. Could such children move out from under that huge shadow into their own manhood? She thought of Almalik II of Cartada, son of the Lion; of the three sons of King Sancho the Fat of Esperaña; indeed, of Rodrigo Belmonte's two young boys.

She considered whether the same challenge confronted a daughter. She decided it didn't, not in the same way. She wasn't in competition with her father, she was only trying, as best she could, to be worthy of his teaching and his example; deserving of the flask she carried as heir to his reputation.

She finished with Abir's dressing. The wound had healed well. She was pleased, and a little proud. She thought her father would have approved. She'd written to him soon after their return to Ragosa. There were always some hardy travellers who could carry messages back and forth through the winter pass, though not swiftly. Her mother's neat handwriting had conveyed Ishak's reply: *This will be too late to be useful, but in cases when you operate in the field you must watch even more carefully for the green discharge. Press the skin near the wound and listen for a crackling sound.*

She had known about this. Such a sound meant death, unless she cut again, even higher—and few men survived that. But Abir ibn Tarif's wound did not turn green and his endurance was strong. His brother seldom left his side and the men of Rodrigo's company seemed to have taken a collective liking to the sons of ibn Hassan. Abir did not lack for visitors. Once, when Jehane had come to attend upon him, she caught a lingering trace of the scent favored by the women of a certain neighborhood.

She had sniffed the air elaborately and tsked her disapproval. Idar laughed; Abir looked shamefaced. He was well on the road to recovery by then, however, and secretly Jehane was pleased. The presence of physical desire, Ser Rezzoni had taught, was one of the clearest signs of returning good health after surgery.

She checked the fitting of the new dressing a last time and stepped back. "Has he been practising?" she asked Idar.

"Not enough," the older of the brothers replied. "He is lazy, I told you." Abir swore in quick protest, then apologized even more quickly.

This was a game, in fact. If he wasn't watched carefully, Abir was likely to push himself to exhaustion in his efforts to learn how to get about with the shoulder sticks Velaz had fashioned for him.

Jehane grinned at both of them. "Tomorrow morning,"

she said to her patient. "It looks very good, though. By the end of next week I expect you can leave this place and go live with your brother." She paused a moment, for effect. "It will surely save you money on bribes here, when you have company after dark."

Idar laughed again. Abir turned red. Jehane gave his shoulder a pat and turned to leave.

Rodrigo Belmonte, booted and cloaked, leather hat in one hand, was standing by the fire on the far side of the room. From the expression on his face she knew something had happened. Her heart thumped.

"What is it?" she said quickly. "My parents?"

He shook his head. "No, no. Nothing to do with them, Jehane. But there are tidings you ought to know."

He crossed towards her. Velaz appeared from behind the screen where he made his salves and tinctures.

Jehane straightened her shoulders and held herself very still.

Rodrigo said, "I am presuming in a way, but you are, for the moment, still my company physician, and I wanted you to hear this from me."

She blinked. *For the moment?*

He said, "Word has just come from the southern coast, one of the last ships in from the east. It seems a great army from several Jaddite lands has gathered in Batiara this winter, preparing to sail to Ammuz and Soriyya in the spring."

Jehane bit her lip. Very large news indeed, but...

"This is a holy army," Rodrigo said. His face was grim. "Or so they call themselves. It seems that earlier this autumn several companies attacked and destroyed Sorenica. They set fire to the city and put the inhabitants to the sword. All of them, we are told. Jehane, Velaz, I am so sorry."

Sorenica.

Mild, starry nights in winter. Spring evenings, years ago. Wine in the torchlit garden of her kinfolk. Flowers everywhere, and the breeze from the sea. Sorenica. The most beautiful sanctuary of the god and his sisters that Jehane had ever seen. The Kindath High Priest with his sweet, laden voice intoning the liturgy of the doubled full moons. White and blue candles burning in every niche that night. So many people gathered; a sense of peace, of calm, of a home for the Wanderers. A choir singing, then more music after, in the winding torchlit streets outside the sanctuary, beneath the round, holy moons.

Sorenica. Bright city on the ocean with its vineyards above. Given to the Kindath long ago for service to the lords of Batiara. A place to call their own in a hostile world.

To the sword. An end of music. Trampled flowers. Children?

"All of them?" she asked in a faint voice.

"So we have been told," Rodrigo said. He drew a breath. "What can I say, Jehane? You said you could not trust the Sons of Jad. I told you that you could. This makes a liar of me."

She could see genuine distress in the wide-set grey eyes. He would have hurried to find her as soon as he heard the tidings. There would be an emissary from court waiting at her home, or coming here even now. Mazur would have sent. Shared faith, shared grief. Should it not have been another Kindath who told her this? She could not answer that. Something seemed to have shut down inside her, closing around a wound.

Sorenica. Where the gardens were Kindath gardens, the blessings Kindath blessings, the wise men and women filled with the learning and the sorrow of the Wanderers, century upon century.

To the sword.

She closed her eyes. Saw a garden in her mind's eye, and could not look at it. Opened her eyes again. She turned to Velaz and saw that he, who had adopted their faith the day her father made him a free man, had covered his face with both hands and was weeping.

She said, carefully, to Rodrigo Belmonte of Valledo, "I cannot hold you responsible for the doings of every man or woman of your faith. Thank you for bringing these tidings so speedily. I think I will go home now."

"May I escort you there?" he asked.

"Velaz will do so," she said. "Doubtless I shall see you at court later in the day. Or tomorrow." She didn't really know what she was saying.

She could read the sorrow in his face, but she had nothing in her to offer to that. She could not assuage. Not this moment, not now.

Velaz wiped at his eyes and lowered his hands. He was not a man she had ever seen weep before, save for joy, the day she came home from her studies in Batiara.

Batiara, where bright Sorenica had been.

Whichever way the wind blows...

It was fire, this time, not rain that had come. She looked around for her cloak. Idar ibn Tarif had picked it up and was holding it for her. Wordlessly he helped her into it. She turned and walked to the doorway, past Rodrigo, following Velaz.

At the very last moment, being what she was—her father's daughter, trained to ease pain where she saw it—she reached out a hand and touched his arm as she went by.

᠂᠆᠄

Winter in Cartada was seldom unduly harsh. The city was sheltered from the worst of the winds by forests to the north and the mountains beyond them. Snow was unheard-of, and mild bright days not at all unusual. There was also rain of course, churning market squares and alleys to mud, but Almalik I and now his son and successor had allocated substantial resources to keeping the city clean and functioning, and the winter produce market flourished.

The season was an inconvenience, not the serious hardship it could be further north or to the east where it seemed to rain all the time. Winter flowers flecked the celebrated gardens with color. Fish thrived in the Guadiara, and boats still came upstream from Tudesca and Silvenes and went back down.

Since Cartada had shaped a kingdom of its own after the fall of the Khalifate, the inns and cook shops had never suffered a shortage of food, and plenty of wood was brought into the city from the forests for the hearth fires.

There were also winter entertainments of esoteric variety, as befitted a city and court that claimed aesthetic as well as military pre-eminence in Al-Rassan.

The Jaddite taverns were always crowded in winter, despite the imprecations of the wadjis. At court, in the taverns, in the better homes, poets and musicians vied for patronage with jugglers, acrobats and animal trainers, with women who claimed to converse with the dead, Kindath fortune tellers who would read one's future in the moons, or with itinerant artisans settled for the season in premises on the perimeter of the city. This winter the fashion was to have one's portrait done in miniature by an artist from Seria.

There were even some entertaining wadjis to be found in the smaller out-of-the-way temples, or on street corners on the mild days, pronouncing their warnings of doom and Ashar's wrath with fiery eloquence.

Many of the higher-born women of Cartada enjoyed attending upon these ragged, wild-eyed figures in the morning, to be pleasingly frightened by their prophecies of the fate awaiting Believers who strayed from the true path Ashar had decreed for the Star-born children of the sands. The women would repair from such an outing to one gracious home or another to sip from delicately mulled concoctions of wine and honey and spice—forbidden, of course, which only added piquancy to the morning's adventure. They would appraise the latest flamboyant invective much as they discussed the declamations of the court poets or the songs of the musicians. Talk by the warming fire would usually turn then to the officers of the army, many of them quartered in town for the winter—with diverting implications.

It was not at all a bad place to be in the cold season, Cartada. This remained true, the longer-lived and more thoughtful of the courtiers at the palace agreed, even in this year of a change of monarchs.

Almalik I had governed Cartada for the khalifs of Silvenes for three years, and then reigned as king for fifteen. A long time to hold power in a turbulent peninsula. Younger members of the court couldn't even remember a time when someone else had governed, and of course there never *had* been another king in proud Cartada.

Now there was, and the prevailing view seemed to be that the son was beginning well. Prudent where he needed to be, in defense and in minimizing disruption to the civil service and court; generous where a powerful monarch ought to be generous, with favor shown to artists and those courtiers who had taken risks for him in the days when his succession was...problematic, to put the matter discreetly. Almalik II might be young, but he had grown up in a clever, cynical court and seemed to have learned his lessons. He'd had an exceptionally subtle tutor, some of the courtiers noted, but that remark was offered quietly and only among friends.

Nor was the new king a weakling, by all early appearances. The twitch above one eye—a legacy of the Day of the Moat—remained, but it seemed to be no more than an indicator of the king's mood, a useful clue for a cautious courtier. Certainly there were no signs of indecisiveness in this monarch.

A number of the more visibly corrupt of the officials had already been dealt with: men who had allowed their long association with the last king to...override their integrity, and had been engaged in a variety of fiscal improprieties. Several were involved in the dyeing monopoly that was the foundation of Cartada's wealth. In the valley south of the city the *cermas* beetle made its home, feeding on the white *illixa* flower and then producing, dutifully, the crimson dye that Cartada exported to the world. There were fortunes to be made from supervising that trade, and where great wealth went, as the old saying ran, the desire for more would follow.

There were some of this sort at every court. It was one of the reasons one *came* to court. And there were, of course, risks.

Those apprehended officials who were not yet castrates had been gelded before execution. Their bodies were hung from the city walls with dead dogs on either side of them. The castrates of the court, who really ought to have known better, were flayed and skinned and then staked out on the cleared ground beyond the Silvenes Gate. It was too cold for the fire ants, but the animals were always hungry in winter.

New officials were appointed from the appropriate families. They swore all the proper oaths. Some poets and singers left for different courts, others arrived. It was all part of the normal course of events. One could tire of an artist, and a new monarch needed to put the stamp of his own taste on a great many things.

The harem, long dominated by Zabira, the late king's favorite, went through a predictably unsettled phase as the women maneuvered viciously for their opportunity with the young king. The stakes were extreme. Everyone knew how Zabira had begun, and how very high she'd risen. There were knifings, and one attempt at poisoning, before the harem-mistresses and the castrates managed to reassert a measure of control.

One cause of the turmoil was that so little was known about the new king's preferences, though rumor was always willing to oblige with guesses. There *had* been tales, especially those concerning the disgraced Ammar ibn Khairan of Aljais, the king's former guardian and mentor—but shortly after Almalik II's ascension word from certain of the less discreet supervisors in the harem put the more scandalous of these stories to rest.

The women, it was reported, were being kept extremely busy. The young king appeared to have an entirely conventional orientation in matters of love, and an appetite that—by one of the oldest omens for the outset of a reign in Asharite lands—presaged well for his prowess in other matters.

The auspices were good in a great many ways. Fezana had been subdued, rather violently it would always be remembered. Silvenes was quiescent, as usual: only broken, dispirited men still lingered in and about the sad ruins of the Al-Fontina. Elvira on the coast had seemed inclined to offer some signs of unwonted independence when Almalik I died, but these flickerings had been quickly snuffed out by the new ka'id of the army, who made a symbolic journey south with a company of Muwardis just before winter came.

The old ka'id was dead, of course. As a much-applauded gesture of courtesy the king had allowed him to take his own life rather than face public execution. This death, too, was only normal: it was not considered a wise idea for new monarchs to allow generals to continue in power, or even remain alive. It was one of the inherent risks that came with accepting a position of high command in an army in Al-Rassan.

Even the outlaw Tarif ibn Hassan, the terror of merchants on the southern roads and all lawful tax collectors, seemed to have decided to turn his attentions elsewhere this season. He had eschewed his chronic, debilitating raids from impregnable Arbastro into the Cartadan hinterlands in favor of a genuinely spectacular action in Ragosan territory to the north.

Talk of that affair continued through the winter as hardy travellers and merchants straggled into the city with newer versions of the story. It appeared that ibn Hassan had actually managed to seize the first-ever *parias* tribute from Fibaz to Jaloña, slaughtering the entire Jaddite party in the process. An astonishing coup in every respect. Another strand to the forty-year legend.

The embarrassment to Ragosa—since King Badir had authorized the payment in the first place—was extreme, and so were the economic and military implications. Some of the more free-spoken of those drinking in the taverns of Cartada that winter offered the view that the Jaloñans might even ride south in numbers come spring, to teach

Fibaz a lesson. Which meant, to teach Badir of Ragosa a lesson.

That was someone else's problem, the drinkers agreed. For once ibn Hassan had caused real trouble elsewhere. Wouldn't it be nice if the aged jackal obligingly died soon? Wasn't he old enough, already? There was good land around Arbastro, where a loyal courtier of the new king of Cartada might one day find himself with, say, a small castle and a crown-bestowed estate to manage and defend.

Winter was a time for dreaming, among other things.

The new king of Cartada had neither the leisure nor the disposition to share in such dreams. An edgy, precise man, very much the son of his father—though both would have denied that—Almalik II knew too much that his citizens did not and his own winter, accordingly, encompassed little of the optimism of theirs.

Not that this was unusual for kings.

He knew his brother was with the Muwardis in the desert, with the blessings and hopes of the wadjis accompanying him. He knew with certainty what Hazem would be suggesting. He had no way of knowing how the proposals would be received by Yazir ibn Q'arif. The transition from a strong king to his successor was always a dangerous time.

He made a point of pausing in his business to pray each time the bells rang during the day. He summoned the most prominent of the wadjis of Cartada and listened to their list of complaints. He lamented with them that his beloved father—a Believer of course, but a secular man— had let their great city slip some distance from the Laws of Ashar. He promised to take regular counsel with them. He ordered a notorious street of Jaddite prostitutes to be cleared immediately and a new temple built there, with gardens and a residence for the wadjis.

He sent gifts, substantial ones, to Yazir and his brother in the desert. It was all he could do, for the moment.

He also learned, early in the winter before the flow of

news from abroad slowed to a trickle, that a holy war was being readied in Batiara, with armies from four Jaddite lands massed to sail to Ammuz and Soriyya in the spring.

That was potentially the most momentous news of all, but not his immediate problem, and it was difficult to imagine that after a bored, fractious winter together such a disparate force would ever really sail. In another way, though, whether they did or didn't embark, the mere assembling of that army represented the gravest danger imaginable.

He dictated a message of warning to the Grand Khalif in Soriyya. It would not arrive before spring, of course, and there would be other warnings sent, but it was important to add his voice to the chorus. They would ask him for soldiers and gold, but it would take time for that request to make its way back.

Meanwhile it was more important to decipher what the Jaddites in the north of this peninsula might be contemplating in the wake of these tidings of war, which they too would have by now. If four Jaddite armies were massing to sail east, what might the Esperañans be considering, with Asharites so near to hand and an example of holy war? Would not their holy men be preaching to the kings even now?

Could the three rulers of Esperaña even gather in the same place without one of them killing another? Almalik II doubted it, but he took counsel with his advisors and then sent certain gifts and a message to King Sanchez of Ruenda.

The gifts were princely; the message took carefully worded note of the fact that Fezana, which Cartada controlled and which currently paid *parias* to arrogant Valledo, not Ruenda, was at least as close to the latter kingdom, and at least as much potentially subject to Ruendan protection. He besought, respectfully, King Sanchez's thoughts on these thorny matters.

There were divisions to be sown in the north, and it was not especially hard to sow them among the successors of Sancho the Fat.

Jaloña in the northeast was not, for the moment, of concern to him. They were more likely to cause difficulty for Ragosa, and that was useful, so long as it didn't amount to more than that. It occurred to him more than once that he really ought to be exchanging counsel with King Badir this winter, but he balked at that. Any interaction with Badir meant dealing, now, with Ammar ibn Khairan, who had fled to Cartada's principal rival the day after his exiling.

It had been a cowardly thing to do, Almalik had decided. It even bordered on the treasonous. All Ammar would have had to do was withdraw discreetly somewhere for a year, write some poems, maybe make a pilgrimage east, even fight for the Faith in Soriyya this coming year, in Ashar's name...and then Almalik could have welcomed him back, a contrite, chastened courtier who had done a decent time of penance. It had seemed so obvious.

Instead, ibn Khairan, prickly and contrary as ever, had stolen away with Zabira straight to Badir and his wily Kindath chancellor in dangerous Ragosa. Very dangerous Ragosa, in fact, because Almalik's sources then informed him, belatedly, that the woman had apparently sent her two sons—his own half-brothers—to Badir during the summer, immediately after the Day of the Moat.

That was news he ought to have had sooner, before his father died. He was compelled to make an example and execute two of his men: it was perilous to be receiving such important tidings so late. Those two boys represented a threat to his tenure on this throne almost as great as Hazem in the desert.

Superfluous brothers, the new king of Cartada decided, were best disposed of swiftly. Look at what had happened among the Jaddites, for example. Ramiro of Valledo, for all his vaunted prowess, had only begun to flourish after the abrupt passing of his brother Raimundo. And though there had been rumors from the moment of that death, they hadn't impeded Ramiro's steady ascent at all.

A lesson to be learned there. Almalik summoned two

men known to him and gave them careful instructions and explicit promises and sent them east, equipped as spice merchants, to cross the mountains to Ragosa while the pass was still open to legitimate traders. He was sobered, and more than a little shaken, to learn later in the winter that they had both died in a tavern brawl the very evening of their arrival in Badir's city.

Badir was clever, his father had always said so. The Kindath chancellor was extremely clever. And now Ammar was with them, when he ought to have been *here*, or at least waiting quietly somewhere for permission to return.

Almalik II, seeking transitory solace one windy night in his father's harem, which was now his own, felt very much alone. He rubbed absently at his irritating eyelid while an extremely tall yellow-haired woman from Karch ministered eagerly to him with scented oils and supple hands, and he considered certain facts.

The first was that Ammar ibn Khairan was not going to be amenable to a swift return to Cartada, even with a promise of restored honor and immense power. He knew this with certainty. His carefully thought-out exiling of ibn Khairan on the day of his father's demise had begun to seem a less judicious course of action than it had at the time.

Angrily, he confronted and accepted the fact that he *needed* Ammar. Too many things were happening this winter, too many disparate events needed to be addressed and responded to, and the men around him were not equal to that. He had need of good counsel and the only man he trusted to provide it was the one who had always treated him with the amused condescension of a master towards a pupil. He was king of Cartada now; it could not be the same way again, but he *had* to get Ammar back.

He arranged the woman on her hands and knees and entered her. She was extraordinarily tall; it was briefly awkward. Her immediate sounds of rapture were patently exaggerated. They were all like that, desperately anxious to win favor. Even as he moved upon the Karcher woman he found himself wondering what the delicate, subtle Zabira had been like, with his father in this same bed. The woman beneath him moaned and gasped as if she were dying. He finished quickly and dismissed her.

Then he lay back alone among the pillows, and began to give careful thought to how to regain the one man he needed before the threats from so many directions burst into flame like bonfires to consume him.

In the morning, at first pale light, he sent for a spy he had used before. The young king of Cartada received this man alone, without even his bedchamber slaves in the room.

"I want to know," he said, without greeting or preamble, "everything you can discover about the movements of the lord Ammar ibn Khairan in Fezana on the Day of the Moat."

⁓

On their way of a midwinter morning to their booth in the market, Jehane and Velaz were abducted so smoothly that no one in the street around them was even aware of what was happening.

It was a grey day; sliding clouds, lighter and darker. Wind and some rain. Two men came up to them; one begged a moment of her attention. Even as he spoke a knife was against her ribs, screened by his body and fur-lined cloak.

"Your servant dies if you open your mouth," he said pleasantly. "You die if he does." She looked quickly over: Velaz was engaged in identical circumstances by the second man. They appeared, to anyone casually glancing at them, to be doing no more than converse.

"*Thank you, doctor,*" the man beside her said loudly. "The rooms are just this way. We are most grateful."

She went where he guided her. The knife pricked her skin as they moved. Velaz had gone white, she saw. She knew it was rage, not fear. There was something about these men, a quality of assurance, that made her believe they would kill, even in a public place.

They came to a door, opened it with a heavy key, entered. The second man locked it behind them with one hand. The other hand held the knife against Velaz. She saw him drop the key into a purse at his belt.

They were in a courtyard. It was empty. The windows of the house beyond were shuttered. There was a fountain basin full of dead leaves, empty of water. The statue in the center had lost its head and one arm. The courtyard looked as if it had not been used for a long time. She had passed this doorway a score of mornings. How did a place such as this become the setting for what might be the end of one's life?

She said, keeping her voice as firm as she could manage, "You invite death and you must know it. I am a court physician to King Badir."

"Now that is a relief," said the first man. "If you were not, we might have had a problem."

He had a dry, precise voice. No accent she could identify. He was Asharite, a merchant, or dressed like one. They both were. Their clothing was expensive. One of them wore a fragrant perfume. Their hands and nails were clean. These were no tavern louts, or if they were, someone had been at pains to conceal the fact. Jehane drew a deep breath; her mouth was dry. She could feel her legs beginning to tremble. She hoped they could not see that. She said nothing, waiting. Then she noticed blood on Velaz's tunic, where his own cloak fell away, and her trembling abruptly stopped.

The second man, taller and broader than the first, said calmly, "We are going to bind and gag your servant and leave him in this place. His clothing will be removed. No one ever comes here. Look around if you wish to satisfy yourself of that. No one knows where he is. He will die of exposure if we do not return to release him. Do you understand what I am saying to you?"

Jehane stared at him, contempt in her eyes disguising fear. She made no reply. The man looked briefly amused; she saw the muscles in his forearm flex, just before the knife moved. Velaz made a small, involuntary sound. There was a real wound now, not a cut.

"If he asks a question you had best answer it," the first man said mildly. "He has an easily affronted nature."

"I understand you," Jehane said, through her teeth.

"Excellent," the bigger man murmured. With a sudden motion he ripped off Velaz's blue cloak and dropped it on the ground. "Remove your clothes," he said. "All of them." Velaz hesitated, looking at Jehane.

"We have other ways of doing what we are here to do," the first man said briskly to Velaz, "even if we have to kill you both. It will cause us no distress to do so. Believe me in this. Take your clothes off, you disgusting Kindath offal. Do it now." The savage insult was the more chilling for the utterly calm tone in which it was spoken.

Jehane thought then of Sorenica. Of those who had died there at autumn's end: burned, decapitated, babies cut in half by the sword. There had been more stories after that first messenger, each one worse than the one before. Did two more deaths matter? Could the god and his sisters possibly care?

Velaz began to disrobe. His face was expressionless now. The second man moved a few steps away to the far side of the fountain basin and retrieved a coil of rope and a square of heavy cloth. It started to rain again. It was very cold. Jehane began trying to calculate how long a man could survive, lying naked and bound here.

"What is it you want of me?" she asked, against her will. She was afraid now.

"Patience, doctor." Her captor's voice was bland; the knife never left her ribs. "Let us deal with your surety first."

They did so. Velaz was not even allowed his undergarments. Utterly naked, looking small and old in the damp grey chill, he was trussed hand and foot. A cloth was tied tightly about his mouth. Then the bigger man lifted him and dropped him into the fountain basin. Jehane winced. The wet stone would be as ice on his exposed flesh. Velaz had not said a word, of protest or appeal. He was unable to do so now. He lay on his back, helpless; his eyes were on hers, though, and what she saw still was a burning anger, not fear.

He was indomitable, he always had been. His courage gave her back her own.

"Once more," she said, moving a deliberate step away from the knife. "What is it you want?" The man did not follow her. He seemed indifferent to her defiance.

He said calmly, "It is our understanding that as physician to the court you know where the two sons of the Lady Zabira are lodged. This has proven to be difficult information to obtain. You will take us to that place and gain us admission. You will remain with us for a time there, and then you are free to return here and release your servant."

"You expect me to simply walk you into that place?"

The second man had turned away again. From another large satchel he began removing items of clothing. Two white tunics, two blue robes fringed in white, two small soft blue caps.

Jehane began to understand.

"We are your kindred, dear lady. Physicians of your own faith from Fezana, come to study with you. We have too little knowledge in the diseases of children, alas, and you are widely known for such expertise. The two boys are past due for a routine examination. You will take us there, introduce us as doctors you know, and bring us into their presence. That is all."

"And what will happen?"

The second man smiled from by the fountain; he was donning the white and blue Kindath garments. "Is that a question you really want answered?"

Which was, of course, an answer.

"No," she said. "I will not do it."

"I am sorry to hear that," the first man said, undisturbed. "Personally I do not like gelding men, even when provoked. Nonetheless, you will note that your servant is securely gagged. When we cut off his organs of sex he will naturally try to scream. No one will hear him."

Jehane tried to breathe normally. Sorenica. They would have done this in Sorenica. "And if I scream now?" she asked, more to gain time than anything else.

Nothing seemed to perturb them. The one by the fountain was fully garbed as a Kindath now, the first one removed his fur-trimmed robe, preparing to do the same.

He said, "There is a locked door here and a high wall. You will have noted these things. You would both be dead and we would be out through the house and a back passageway and lost in the city long before anyone broke through that door to find a castrated man and a dead woman with her intestines spilling out. Really, doctor, I had hoped you would not be foolish about this."

Inwardly then, and quite unfairly, Jehane began to curse all the men she knew here in Ragosa. Mazur. Ammar. Rodrigo. Alvar and Husari. With so much prowess surrounding her, how had this come to be?

The answer, of course, was her own insisted-upon independence, and their willingness to grant her that—which is what made the cursing unfair. Under the circumstances, she decided, fairness didn't matter in the least: one of them, *somehow*, ought to have been here to prevent this.

"Why do you want the children?" she asked.

"You really are better off not asking too many questions, doctor. We are not unwilling to let you both live after this is done, but you will appreciate that we are moderately exposed to risk here, and must not allow you to increase that."

But even as he spoke Jehane realized that she knew. She could confront them with that knowledge but she was thinking clearly enough to know that that might mean her death warrant, and Velaz's, here in the abandoned courtyard. She kept silent.

It was Almalik II in Cartada, she was certain of it. Seeking to destroy the young boys, his brothers, who were threats to his throne by their very existence. Kings and their brothers; an ancient story, retold in every generation, including hers now.

The two men had completed their disguises. Each of them picked up a small satchel and took out a urine flask: emblems of their assumed profession. Velaz had been carrying Jehane's implements and her flask. The larger of the assassins gestured and Jehane, after a moment, picked them up herself.

"I am going to be next to you the whole way," the smaller man said. "You can cry out, of course. You will die when you do, and so, of course, will your servant here, unrescued. We might also be killed, but you have no certainty of that, for we are skilled at our trade. I wouldn't advise an attempt at disruption, doctor. Where are we going?"

There really were no options. Not yet. Not until she was out from this courtyard. She looked back towards Velaz, but she couldn't see him now, over the fountain rim. The wind had picked up and the rain was falling harder, slanting in cold, stinging drops. There wasn't much time. Bleakly, she named the house. Then she put up her hood and went out with them.

The residence where the two small children of Zabira of Cartada were lodging, occasionally in the presence of their mother, more often not, was close to the palace quarter. It was an affluent district, and a quiet one.

Any hopes Jehane might have nourished of being seen by someone who knew her were quickly abandoned. Her two captors knew Ragosa well—either from previous visits, or from quick study. They took her by a winding route that bypassed the market and palace squares entirely. They were not in a hurry now.

They did go past one of the infirmaries where Jehane had patients too ill to be left at home, but the assassins evidently knew this as well: they kept to the far side of the street and did not break stride. She remembered, as they went by the door, seeing Rodrigo Belmonte and Ammar ibn Khairan disappear together one night around the same corner where she now passed with two men who were using her to kill children.

They walked closely together, the men simulating intense conversation on either side of her: to all the world, three Kindath physicians with their implements and flasks, attending upon some patient wealthy enough to afford them. In the neighborhood into which they passed, this was not cause for note or comment. In the wet cold morning few people were abroad to take notice in any case. Even the weather seemed to be conspiring against her, Jehane thought. She had an appalling image of Velaz, naked and shivering under the needle-like rain in that empty courtyard.

They came to the house she had named.

For the first time Jehane thought specifically about the children who lived here. She had only seen them twice, summoned for the treatment of minor illnesses. She had even thought about refusing, she remembered. The younger of these two was the cause of her father's darkness and his silence. Thinking about Ishak, though, knowing what he would have done, had caused her to attend as requested. The children were not to be blamed. The children were entitled to her care, to the strict observance of her Oath of Galinus.

Which raised a terrible question about what she was doing now. She knocked on the door.

"Ask for the mother," the bigger man muttered quickly. He betrayed, for the first time, a tension in his voice. In a curious way, that calmed Jehane. They were not quite so unruffled as they seemed. *Kindath offal*, he had named Velaz. She wanted these men dead.

The door opened. A steward stood in the entrance, a well-lit hallway behind him and an inner courtyard beyond. It was a gracious house. She remembered the steward from before; an innocuous, earnest man. His eyes widened in surprise.

"Doctor? What is it?"

Jehane took a deep breath. Unseen beneath the cloaks, a knife pressed against her back. "The Lady Zabira? She is waiting for me?"

"But no, doctor." The steward looked apologetic and anxious. "She is at court this morning. She left no word about your visit."

The smaller of the two men with Jehane offered a dry chuckle. "A typical mother! Only when the little ones are gravely ill do they wait for us. We made an appointment two days ago. Jehane bet Ishak has been kind enough to allow us to attend upon her visits to her younger patients. We are studying to improve our own skills with the young ones." He lifted his flask slightly.

The steward looked uncertainly at Jehane. The knife pressed; she felt the point fret through her clothing against her skin.

"This is so," she said, despairing. "Did your mistress leave no word at all?"

"Not with me, doctor." He was still apologetic. Were he a sterner man, she thought, he would now close the door upon them and tell them to come back when Zabira was in residence.

"Well then," Jehane tried, "if she left no—"

"But doctor, I do know you, and I know she trusts you. It must have been an oversight. The boys are making mischief, I'm afraid, but please come in." The steward smiled ingratiatingly. One of the men with her gave him a kindly glance and a silver coin. Too much money, in fact; it ought to have warned a good servant something was amiss. The steward palmed it and bowed them in. Jehane would have happily dissected him.

"Go right upstairs, doctor," he murmured to Jehane. "Shall I have hot drinks prepared? It is bitter this morning."

"That would be wonderful," the smaller assassin said, removing his cloak and then, courteously, Jehane's. The knife was nowhere to be seen for a moment but then, as the steward hastily claimed all three outer garments, Jehane felt the blade against her side.

From upstairs the sound of laughing children could now be heard, and the protests of an evidently overmatched servant. Something fell with a reverberating crash. There was a moment of silence, then renewed high-pitched laughter.

The steward looked anxious again.

"Sedatives may be called for," one of her abductors murmured suavely, and smiled to let the man see it was a jest.

They moved to the stairway and started up. The steward watched for a moment then turned away to give his orders for their refreshments.

"They are only children," Jehane said softly. There was a hammering in her breast and a growing fear, colder than anything outside. She was becoming aware that it was not going to be possible for her to do this.

At the top of the stairs, she thought. Last chance. She prayed there might be someone there.

"Children die all the time," the man with the knife beside her murmured. "You are a physician, you know this. One of them ought never to have been born. You know this too. They will not suffer pain."

They reached the top of the stairs.

Corridors in two directions, ahead and to the right; the hallways wrapped around the inner courtyard of the house. She saw elaborate, glass-paned doors opening out to the ambulatory overlooking the garden. Other doorways led into the rooms. The laughter had ceased now. It was very quiet. Jehane looked both ways, a little frantically. Death was here, in this house, and she was not ready for it.

No aid, though, no answers to anything. Only one young servant, little more than a boy himself, could be seen, hurriedly sweeping with a broom at the shards of what had evidently been a large display urn.

He looked up, saw them. Dropped the broom in dismay.

"Doctors! Holy Ashar, forgive us! An accident...the children." He nervously picked up and then laid aside the broom. He hurried anxiously forward. "May I assist you? The steward—"

"We are here to see the children," the bigger man with her said. His tone was crisp, but again with its inflection of tension. "Take us to them."

"Of course!" the young servant smiled, eagerly. Why were they all so eager here? Jehane's heart was a drum in her breast. She could stand here, walk with them, let this happen, probably live.

She could not do that.

The boy stepped forward, one hand extended. "May I take your satchels for you, doctors?"

"No, no, that is fine. Just lead on." The nearer man withdrew his bag slightly.

It will take them time to find the boys, Jehane thought. *There are many rooms. Help might come in time.* She drew breath to scream, knowing it meant her death.

In that same moment she thought, absurdly, that she recognized this servant. But before the memory could coalesce into something more, he had continued his reaching motion, stumbled slightly, and bumped into the small man who was holding the blade against her side. The assassin grunted; a surprised sound. The boy straightened, withdrawing his right hand, and shoving Jehane hard with his left.

Jehane stumbled, falling—and cried out then, at the top of her voice: *"Help! They are killers! Help us!"*

She dropped to her knees, heard something shatter. She turned back, expecting a blade, her death, the soft dark presence of the sisters of the god.

Tardily, she saw the stiletto that had materialized in the boy's hand. The smaller assassin was on the floor, clutching with both hands at his belly. Jehane saw blood welling between his fingers, and then much more of it. The bigger man had turned, snarling, balancing his own drawn blade. The boy stepped back a little, ready for him.

Jehane screamed again, at the top of her voice.

Someone had already appeared down the corridor straight ahead. Someone, unbelievably, carrying a bow. The big man saw this, turned swiftly back towards the stairway.

The steward was standing there, holding a sword, no longer smiling or innocuous.

The assassin pivoted again, ducked, and without warning sprang at Jehane. The young servant shouted with alarm, lifting his blade to intervene.

Before the knives engaged there came a clear sound, a note of music almost, and then Jehane saw an arrow in the assassin's throat, and blood. His hands flew upwards, the knife falling away. He clattered to the floor. His flask shattered on the tiles.

There was a stillness, as after thunder has come and rolled away.

Struggling for self-control, Jehane looked back down the hall. The man with the bow, walking forward now, was Idar ibn Tarif, whose brother she had saved and then tended. He was smiling in calm reassurance.

Jehane, still on her knees, began to tremble. She looked at the boy beside her. He had sheathed his knife; she couldn't tell where. The first assassin made a sudden rattling sound in his throat and slid sideways beside the larger one. She knew that sound. She was a doctor. He had just died.

There was broken glass all around them, and blood staining the sand-colored tiles of the floor. A trickle of it ran towards her. She rose to her feet and stepped aside.

Broken glass.

Jehane turned and looked behind her. Her father's flask lay shattered on the floor. She swallowed hard. Closed her eyes.

"Are you all right, doctor?" It was the boy. He could be no more than fifteen. He had saved her life.

She nodded her head. Opened her eyes again. And then she knew him.

"*Ziri?*" she said, incredulously. "Ziri, from Orvilla?"

"I am honored, doctor," he said, bowing. "I am honored that you remember me."

"What are you doing here?"

She had last seen this boy killing a Jaddite with Alvar de Pellino's sword amid the burning of his village. Nothing made any sense at all.

"He's been guarding you," said a voice she knew. She looked quickly over. In an open doorway, a little distance down the hall, stood Alvar himself, that same sword in his hand.

"Come," he said. "See if you can quiet two impossible children." He sheathed the sword, walked forward, took both her hands. His grip was steady and strong.

As if in a trance, surrounded by these calm, smiling men, Jehane went down the corridor and entered the indicated room.

The two boys, one seven, the other almost five years old, as she knew very well, weren't being particularly loud, in fact. There was a fire burning on the hearth, but the windows above each of the two beds had been shuttered so the room was mostly dark. Candles had been lit opposite the fire and using those for light Ammar ibn Khairan, dressed in black and gold, his earring gleaming palely, was energetically making shadow-figures on the far wall for the boys' entertainment. Jehane saw his sword, unsheathed, on a pillow by his side.

"What do you think?" he said over his shoulder. "I'm proud of my wolf, actually."

"It is a magnificent achievement," Jehane said.

The two boys evidently thought so too; they were raptly attentive. The wolf, even as she watched, stalked and then devoured what was presumably meant to be a chicken.

"I'm not impressed by the fowl," Jehane managed to say.

"It's a pig!" ibn Khairan protested. "*Anyone* should be able to see that."

"May I sit down?" Jehane said. Her legs seemed to be failing her.

A stool materialized. Idar ibn Tarif smilingly motioned for her to sit.

She did, then sprang to her feet again.

"*Velaz!* We have to free him!"

"It is done," said Alvar from the doorway. "Ziri told us

where the courtyard is. Husari and two others have gone to release him. He'll be safe by now, Jehane."

"It is over," said Idar gently. "Sit, doctor. You are all safe now."

Jehane sat. Odd, how the worst reactions seemed to occur after the danger had passed.

"*More!*" the elder of Zabira's boys cried. The younger one simply sat cross-legged on the floor, staring at the shadow-figures on the wall, his eyes wide.

"There *is* no more, I'm afraid," said the lord Ammar ibn Khairan. "Once the wolf eats the pig, or the fowl, whichever, there is no more to see."

"Later?" the older child asked, with some deference.

"Later, indeed," said ibn Khairan. "I will come back. I must practise my pigs, and I'll need your help. The doctor thought it was a chicken, which is a bad sign. But for now, go with the steward. I believe he has chocolate for you?"

The steward, in the doorway behind Alvar, nodded his head.

"The bad man have gone?" It was the smaller one, speaking for the first time. The one her father had delivered through his mother's belly.

"The bad man have gone," said Ammar ibn Khairan gravely. Jehane was aware that she was close to crying. She didn't want to cry. "It is as if they never came looking at all," ibn Khairan added gently, still addressing the smaller child. He looked over then, to Alvar and the steward by the door, eyebrows raised in inquiry.

Alvar said, "Nothing out there. Some stains on the floor. A broken urn."

"Of course. The urn. I'd forgotten." Ibn Khairan grinned suddenly. Jehane knew that grin by now.

"I doubt the owner of this house will forget," Alvar said virtuously. "You chose a destructive way of signalling their arrival."

"I suppose," said ibn Khairan. "But the owner of this house has some answering to do to the king for the absence of any proper security here, wouldn't you say?"

Alvar's manner altered. Jehane could see him tracking the thought, and adjusting. She had made that sort of adjustment herself many times, during the campaign to the east. Ammar ibn Khairan almost never did anything randomly.

"Where is Rodrigo?" she asked suddenly.

"Now we *are* offended," Ammar said, the blue gaze returning to her. It was brighter in the room; Idar had drawn back the shutters. The two boys had left with the steward. "All these loyal men hastening to your aid, and you ask only about the one who is obviously indifferent to your fate." He smiled as he said it, though.

"He's on patrol outside the walls," Alvar said loyally. "And besides, it was Ser Rodrigo who had Ziri watching you in the first place. That's how we knew."

"In the first place? What does *that* mean?" Jehane, reaching for something normal, tried to grab hold of indignation.

"I came here some time ago," Ziri said softly. She was trying, unsuccessfully, to glare at him. "After I was certain my sisters were all right with my aunt, I went to your mother in Fezana and learned where you had gone. Then I came through the mountains after you." He said it with the utmost simplicity, as if it was nothing at all.

It was, though. He had left his home, what was left of his family, all of the world he knew, had crossed the country alone, and...

"You went to my...you *what?* Why, Ziri?"

"Because of what you did in my village," he said, with the same simplicity.

"But I didn't do anything there."

"Yes, you did, doctor. You made them allow me to execute the man who killed my mother and my father." Ziri's eyes were very dark. "It would not have happened without you. He would have lived, ridden back to Jaddite lands to tell that tale as a boast. I would have had to walk there after him, and I fear I would not have been able to kill him there."

His expression was grave. The story he was telling her was almost overwhelming.

"You would have gone to Valledo after him?"

"He killed my parents. And the brother I have never had."

No more than fifteen, Jehane thought. "And you have been following me here in Ragosa?"

"Since I arrived. I found your place in the market. Your mother said you would have a booth there. Then I sought out the Captain, Ser Rodrigo. And he remembered me, and was pleased that I had come. He gave me a place to sleep, with his company, and instructed me to watch you whenever you were not at court or with his men."

"I *told* you all I didn't want to be watched or followed," Jehane protested.

Idar ibn Tarif reached down and squeezed her shoulder. He wasn't much like any outlaw she'd heard about.

"You did, indeed, tell us that," Ammar said, without levity. He was sitting on one of the small beds now and was regarding her carefully. The candlelight burnished his hair and was reflected in his eyes. "We all apologize, in a measured degree, for not obeying. Rodrigo felt, and I agreed, that there was some chance you were at risk, because of your rescue of Husari from the Muwardis among other things."

"But how could you know I wouldn't recognize Ziri? I *should* have recognized him."

"We couldn't know that, of course. He was urged to be cautious in how he followed you, and had a story to tell if you did see him. Your parents approved of this, by the way."

"How would you know that?"

"I promised your father I would write him. Remember? I try to keep my promises."

It seemed to have been quite thoroughly worked out. She looked at Ziri. "Where did you learn to use a knife like that?"

He looked both pleased and abashed. "I have been with

the Captain's men, doctor. They have been teaching me. Ser Rodrigo himself gave me my blade. The lord ibn Khairan showed me how to conceal it inside my sleeve and draw it down."

Jehane looked back at Ammar. "And Velaz? What if he had known him, even if I didn't?"

"Velaz did know him, Jehane." Ibn Khairan's voice was gentle; rather like the tone in which he'd spoken to the younger boy. "He spotted Ziri some time ago and went to Rodrigo. An understanding was achieved. Velaz shared our view that Ziri was a wise precaution. And so he was, my dear. It was Ziri who was on top of the wall of that courtyard this morning and heard the men from Cartada tell you their purpose. He found Alvar, who found me. We had time to be here before you."

"I feel like a child," Jehane said. She heard Alvar's wordless protest behind her.

"Not that," said ibn Khairan, rising from the bed. "Never that, Jehane. But just as you may have to care for us, if arrow or blade or illness comes, so we must, surely, offer our care to you? If only to set things in balance, as your Kindath moons balance the sun and stars."

She looked up at him. "Don't be such a poet," she said tartly. "I'm not distracted by images. I am going to think about this, and then let you all know exactly how I feel. Especially Rodrigo," she added. "He was the one who promised I would be left alone."

"I was afraid you would remember that," said someone entering from the corridor.

Rodrigo Belmonte, still in boots and winter cloak, with his sword on and the whip in his belt, strode into the room. He had, incongruously, a cup of chocolate in each hand.

He offered one to Jehane. "Drink. I had to promise this was for you and no one else. The older one downstairs is greedy and wanted it all."

"And what about *me?*" Ibn Khairan complained. "I did damage to my wrists and fingers making wolves and pigs for them."

Rodrigo laughed. He took a sip from the other cup. "Well, if you must know the truth, this one *was* for you as a reward, but I didn't actually promise, and the chocolate is good and I was cold. You've been inside and warm for a while." He lowered the cup and smiled.

"You've chocolate on your moustache," Jehane said. "And you are supposed to be outside the walls. Defending the city. Much good you are to anyone, arriving now."

"Exactly," Ammar said with a vigorous nod of his head. "Give me my chocolate."

Rodrigo did so. He looked at Jehane.

"Martín fetched me. We weren't far away. Jehane, you'll have to choose between being angry with me for having you guarded, or for not being here to defend you myself."

"Why?" she snapped. "Why can't I be angry for both?"

"Exactly," said Ammar again, sipping the chocolate. His tone was so smugly pleased it almost made her laugh. He does nothing by chance, she reminded herself, struggling for self-possession. Ziri and Idar were grinning, and so, reluctantly, was Alvar.

Jehane, looking around her, came to accept, finally, that it was over. They had saved her life and Velaz's, and the lives of the two children. She was being, perhaps, just the least bit ungrateful.

"I am sorry about the broken promise," Rodrigo said soberly. "I didn't want to argue with you back then, and Ziri's arrival seemed a stroke of fortune. You know he came through the pass alone?"

"So I gather." She *was* being ungrateful. "What will be done about those two men?" she asked. "Who were they?"

"Two that I know of, as it happens." It was Ammar. "Almalik used them several times. It seems his son remembered that. They were the best assassins he had."

"Will this cause a scandal?"

Ammar shook his head and looked at Rodrigo. "I don't think it has to. I think there is a better way to deal with this."

"No one knows they came so close but the servants

here," Rodrigo said thoughtfully. "They can be trusted, I think."

Ammar nodded. "That is my thought. I believe I heard," he said carefully, "that two merchants from Cartada were unfortunately murdered in a tavern quarrel shortly after they arrived here. I think the appropriate Guild ought to send apologies and condolences to Cartada. Let Almalik believe they were discerned the moment they came. Let him feel that much more anxious."

"You know the man," Rodrigo said.

"I do," ibn Khairan agreed. "Not as well as I once thought, but well enough."

"What will he do next?" Jehane asked suddenly.

Ammar ibn Khairan looked at her. His expression was very sober now. He had laid down the cup of chocolate. "I believe," he said, "he will attempt to win me back."

There was a brief stillness.

"Will he succeed?" Rodrigo was as blunt as ever.

Ammar shrugged. "I'm a mercenary now, remember? Just as you are. What would your answer be? If King Ramiro summoned you tomorrow would you abandon your contract here and go home?"

Another silence. "I don't know," said Rodrigo Belmonte at length. "Though my wife would stab me if she heard me say that."

"Then I suppose I am in a better circumstance than you, because if I give the same answer, no woman is likely to kill me." Ibn Khairan smiled.

"Don't," said Jehane, "be quite so sure."

They all looked at her uncertainly, until she smiled.

"Thank you, by the way," she said, to all of them.

Chapter XII

∽

Towards the end of winter, when the first wildflowers were appearing in the meadows, but while snow still lay thick in the higher plateaus and the mountain passes, the three kings of Esperaña gathered near Carcasia in Valledo to hunt elk and boar in the oak woods where the smells were of rebirth and the burgeoning of spring could be felt along the blood.

Though even the best of the ancient straight roads were little more than muddy impediments to travel, their queens were with them and substantial retinues from their courts, for hunting—pleasurable as it might be—was merely a pretext for this meeting.

It had been Geraud de Chervalles, the formidable cleric from Ferrieres who, together with colleagues wintering at Eschalou and Orvedo, had prevailed upon three men who hated and feared each other to come together early in the year to hold afternoon converse after chases in field and wood.

A greater hunt was near to hand, the clerics had declared in the court of each king; one that redounded both to the glory of Jad and the vastly increased wealth and fame and power of each of the three lands that had been carved from what was left of Esperaña.

The glory of Jad was, of course, an entirely good thing. Everyone agreed on that. Wealth and power, and certainly fame, were prospects worth a journey. Whether these things were also worth the associated company remained, as yet, to be seen.

Two days had passed since the Ruendans, last to arrive, had joined the others within Carcasia's walls. No untoward incidents had yet transpired—little of note either, though King Bermudo of Jaloña had proven himself still the equal of his nephews on horseback and with a boar spear. Of the queens, the accolades had gone to red-haired Ines of Valledo, daughter of the hunting-mad king of Ferrieres, clearly the best rider of the women there—and better than most of the courtiers.

For a man known to be clever and ambitious, her husband appeared preoccupied and inattentive much of the time, even during the afternoon and evening discussions of policy and war. He left it to his constable to raise questions and objections.

For his part, Bermudo of Jaloña hunted with fury in the mornings and spoke during the meetings of vengeance against the cities of Ragosa and Fibaz, which had defaulted on his first-ever *parias* claim. He accepted condolences on the death of a favored courtier, the young Count Nino di Carrera, ambushed by outlaws in a valley in Al-Rassan. No one was quite clear how a party of one hundred trained and well-mounted Horsemen could have been slaughtered by a mere outlaw band, but no one was unkind or impolitic enough to raise that question directly. Queen Fruela, still a handsome woman, was seen to grow misty-eyed at the mention of the slain young gallant.

King Sanchez of Ruenda drank steadily from a flask at his saddle horn, or a brimming cup at the afternoon meetings or the banquet hall. The wine had little evident effect on him, but neither did he hunt with notable success. His arrows of a morning were surprisingly erratic, though his horsemanship remained impeccable. Say what you liked about the hot-headed king of Ruenda, but he could ride.

The two brothers never even looked at each other, and they regarded their uncle with evident contempt. All, however, appeared to have taken due note of the implications of the army now assembled in Batiara, ready to sail with the first fair winds. They wouldn't be here had they not given thought to that.

The three High Clerics from Ferrieres, schooled in dealing with royalty, and beginning to comprehend—if belatedly—the depths of distrust they had to contend with here, carried the discussion for the kings. There was a movement abroad in the world, and the men in this room were privileged to be reigning at such a time, Geraud of Ferrieres declaimed ringingly on the first afternoon. The carrion dogs of Ashar in Al-Rassan, he said, were ready to be swept back across the straits. The whole peninsula was there to be retaken. If only they would act together the great kings of Valledo and Ruenda and Jaloña might ride their stallions into the southern sea by summer's end, in the glorious name of Jad.

"How would you divide it?" King Bermudo asked bluntly. Ramiro of Valledo laughed aloud at that, his first sign of animation all day. Sanchez drank and scowled.

Geraud of Ferrieres, who had been ready for this question, and had spent time with maps over the winter, made a suggestion. None of the kings bothered to reply. They all rose instead, without apology—moving in unison for the first time—and walked quickly from the room. Sanchez carried his flask with him. The clerics, left behind, looked at each other.

On the third day they flew falcons and hawks at small birds and rabbits in the wet grass for the delight of the ladies of each court. Queen Ines carried a small eagle, caught and trained in the mountains near Jaloña, and loosed it to triumphant effect.

Younger than Fruela, undeniably more accomplished than Bearte of Ruenda, the queen of Valledo, her red hair bound up in a golden net, her eyes flashing and her color high in the cool air, rode between her husband and the High Cleric from her homeland and was the focus of all men's eyes that day.

Which made it the more disturbing, afterwards, that no one was able to identify with certainty the source of the

arrow that struck her shortly after the dogs had flushed a
boar at the edge of the forest. It seemed obvious, however,
that the arrow was either a terrible accident, having been
intended for the boar beyond her—or that it had been
aimed at one of the two men beside her. There was, it was
generally agreed, no evident reason for anyone to desire
the death of the queen of Valledo.

It did not appear at first to be a deadly wound, for she
was struck only on the arm, but—despite the standard
treatment of a thick mud-coating, followed by bleedings,
both congruent and transverse—Ines of Valledo, clutching
a sun disk, took a marked turn for the worse, feverish and
in great pain, before the sun went down that day.

It was at this point that the chancellor of Valledo was
seen entering the royal quarters of the castle, striding past
the grim-faced guards, escorting a lean man of loutish
appearance.

She had never been injured in such a fashion in her life.
She had no idea how it was supposed to feel.

It felt as if she were dying. Her arm had swollen to
twice its normal size—she could see that, even through
the coating of mud. When they bled her—working through
a screen for decency—that, too, had hurt, almost unbear-
ably. There had been a quarrel between the two physicians
from Esteren and her own longtime doctor from Ferrieres.
Her own had won: they had given her nothing for pain.
Peire d'Alorre was of the view that soporifics dulled the
body's ability to fight injury caused by sharp edges. He
had lectured on the subject in all the universities.

Her head was on fire. Even the slightest movement of
her arm was intolerable. She was dimly conscious that
Ramiro had hardly left her side; that he was holding her
good hand, gripping it steadily, and had been doing so
since she had been brought here, withdrawing only when
the doctors compelled him to, for the bleeding. The odd
thing was, she could see him holding her hand, but she
couldn't really feel his touch.

She was dying. That seemed clear to her, if not yet to them. She had caused a sun disk to be brought for her. She was trying to pray, but it was difficult.

In a haze of pain she understood that someone new had entered the room. Count Gonzalez, and another man. Another doctor. His features—a long, ugly face—swam into view, very close. He apologized to her and the king, and then laid a hand directly upon her forehead. He took her good hand from Ramiro and pinched the back of it. He asked her if she felt that. Ines shook her head. The new doctor scowled.

Peire d'Alorre, behind him, said something cutting. He was prone to sardonic remarks, especially about the Esperañans. A habit he had never shaken in all his years here.

The new man, whose hands were gentle, if his face was not, said, "Do we have the arrow that was removed? Has anyone thought to examine it?" His voice rasped like a saw.

Ines was aware of a silence. Her vision was not good, just then, but she saw the three court physicians exchange glances.

"It is over here," said Gonzalez de Rada. He approached the bed, swimming into view, holding the arrow gingerly near the feathers. The doctor took it. He brought the head up to his face and sniffed. He grimaced. He had an awful face, actually, and a large boil on his neck. He came back to the queen and, again apologizing, he shifted the covers at the bottom of the bed and took one of her feet.

"Do you feel my touch?" he asked. Again, she shook her head.

He looked angry. "Forgive me, my lord king, if I am blunt. It may be I have spent too long in the *tagra* lands for courtly company. But these three men have come near to killing the queen. It may be too late, and I will have to lay hands and, I fear, more than hands upon her, but I will try if you allow me."

"There is poison?" she heard Ramiro ask.

"Yes, my lord king."

"What can you do?"

"With your permission, my lord, I must clean this...disgusting coating from her arm to prevent more of the substance from entering the wound. Then I will have to administer a compound I will prepare. It will be...difficult for the queen, my lord. Extremely unpleasant. It is a substance that may make her very ill as it combats the poison in her. We must hope it does so. I know of no other course. Do you wish me to proceed? Do you wish to remain here?"

Ramiro did, both things. Peire d'Alorre ventured an acerbic, unwise objection. He was unceremoniously ushered by Gonzalez de Rada to a far corner of the room, along with the other two doctors. Ramiro, following part of the way, said something to them that Ines could not hear. They were extremely quiet after that.

The king came back and sat once more beside the bed holding her good hand in both of his. She still couldn't feel his touch. The new doctor's coarse features appeared close to hers again. He explained what he was about to do, and apologized beforehand. When he spoke softly, his voice was not actually unpleasant. His breath was sweetly scented with some herb.

What followed was worse than childbirth had been. She did scream, as he carefully but thoroughly cleaned the mud from her wounded arm. At some point the god mercifully granted her oblivion.

They revived her, though. They had to. She was made to drink something. What ensued was even worse. The queen, racked with spasms in the belly and sweating with fever, found that she could not even bear the muted light of the candles in the room. All sounds hurt her head amazingly. She lost track of time, where she was, who was there. She heard her own voice at one point, speaking wildly, begging for release. She couldn't even pray, or hold properly to her disk.

When she swam back towards awareness, the doctor insisted that she drink more of the same substance, and she sank back into fever and the pain.

It went on for an unimaginably long time.

Eventually it ended. She had no idea when. She seemed to be still alive, however. She lay on the sweat-soaked pillows of the bed. The doctor gently cooled her face and forehead with damp towels, murmuring encouragement. He asked for clean linens; these were brought and, while the men turned away, Ines's ladies-in-waiting changed her garments and the bedding. When they had finished the doctor came back and very gently anointed and then bandaged Ines's arm. His movements were steady and precise. The king watched intently.

When the doctor from the forts was done, he ordered the room cleared of all but one of the queen's ladies. He spoke now with the authority of a man who had assumed command of a situation. More diffidently, he then asked permission to speak in private with the king. Ines watched them withdraw to an adjacent room. She closed her eyes and slept.

"Will she live?" King Ramiro was blunt. He spoke as soon as the door was closed behind them.

The doctor was equally direct. "I will not know until later tonight, my lord king." He pushed a hand through his untidy, straw-colored hair. "The poison ought to have been countered immediately."

"Why did you suspect it?"

"The degree of swelling, my lord, and the absence of any feeling in her feet and hands. A simple arrow wound ought not to have caused such responses. I have seen enough of those, Jad knows. And then I smelled it on the arrow."

"How did you know to do what you did?"

There was a hesitation, for the first time. "My lord, since being assigned the great honor of serving in the *tagra* forts, I have used the...proximity to Al-Rassan to obtain the writings from some of their physicians. I have made a course of study, my lord."

"The Asharite doctors know more than we?"

"About most things, my lord. And...the Kindath know even more, in many matters. In this instance, I was schooled by certain writings of a Kindath physician, a man of Fezana, my lord."

"You can read the Kindath script?"

"I have taught myself, my lord."

"And this text told you how to identify and deal with this poison? What to administer?"

"And how to make it. Yes, my lord." Another hesitation. "There is one thing more, my lord king. The reason I wished to speak with you alone. About the...source of this evil thing."

"Tell me."

The doctor from the *tagra* forts did so. He was asked an extremely precise question and answered it. He then received his king's permission to return to the queen. Ramiro of Valledo remained alone in that adjoining room for some time, however, dealing with a rising fury and coming, quite swiftly after long indecision, to a clear resolution.

In such a fashion, very often, had the course and destiny of nations both lesser and greater than Valledo been shaped and devised.

The doctor gave Ines his compound one more time. He explained that the body expelled it more swiftly than the poison it fought. Painful as it was, the substance was the only thing that might save her. The queen nodded her understanding, and drank.

Again she swam towards oblivion, but it wasn't quite so bad this time. She always knew where she was.

In the middle of the night her fever broke. The king was dozing in an armchair by the bed, the lady-in-waiting on a pallet by the fire. The doctor, unsleeping, was attending upon her. When she opened her eyes his harsh features seemed beautiful to her. He reached for her good hand and pinched it.

"Yes," the queen said. The doctor smiled.

When King Ramiro woke it was to see his wife gazing at him by the light of several candles. Her eyes were clear. They looked at each other for a long time.

"I had a sun disk, at one point," she said finally, a pale

whisper, "but what I also remember, when I remember anything, is you beside me."

Ramiro moved to kneel beside the bed. He looked a question across it at the physician, whose fatigue was now evident.

"I believe we have passed through this," the man said. The long, unfortunate face was creased by a smile.

Ramiro said, huskily, "Your career is made, doctor. I do not even know your name, but your life is made by this. I was not ready to let her go." He looked back at his queen, his wife, and repeated softly, "I was not ready."

Then the king of Valledo wept. His queen lifted her good hand, hesitated a moment, and then lowered it to stroke his hair.

Earlier that same night, as King Ramiro lingered by the bedside of his queen, harsh words had been exchanged at dinner by the men of the Valledan court with those who served King Sanchez of Ruenda. Accusations, savage and explicit, were levelled. Swords were drawn in the castle hall.

Seventeen men died in the fighting there. Only the courageous intervention of the three clerics from Ferrieres, striding unarmed and bare-headed into the midst of a bloody melee, their sun disks held high, prevented worse.

It was remembered, afterwards, that the party from Jaloña had dined by themselves that evening, conspicuously absent from the scene of the affray, as if anticipating something. Wholesale slaughter among the courtiers of the other two kings could only be of benefit to King Bermudo, it was agreed sourly. Some of the Valledans offered darker thoughts, but there was nothing to substantiate these.

In the morning Bermudo of Jaloña and his queen sent a herald to King Ramiro with a formal leavetaking and their prayers for the survival of the queen—word was, she had not yet passed to the god. Then they rode towards the rising sun with all their company.

The king and queen and surviving courtiers of Ruenda had already left—in the middle of the night, after the fighting in the hall. Stealing guiltily away like horse thieves, some of Ramiro's courtiers said, though the more pragmatic noted that they had been on Valledan ground here and in real peril of their lives. It was also pointed out, by some of the most level-headed, that hunting accidents were a fact of life and that Queen Ines was far from the first to be wounded in this fashion.

A majority, however, among the courtiers of Valledo were ready to pursue the Ruendan party west along the Duric's banks as soon as the word was given—but the constable gave no such order, and the king was still closeted with his queen and her new physician.

Those who attended upon them reported that the queen appeared much improved—that she was likely to survive. There was, however, a new report that poison had been used on the arrow.

All things considered, King Ramiro's ensuing behavior—it was three days before he showed his face outside the queen's bedchamber or the adjoining room, which he used as a temporary counsel chamber—was viewed as erratic and even unmanly. It was clearly time to order a pursuit of the Ruendan party before they reached the nearest of their own forts. Notwithstanding the presence of the clerics, there was enough, surely, to suggest that Ruendan fingers had drawn that bow, and holy Jad knew that revenge needed little excuse in Esperaña.

Among other things, it had come to light by then—no one was certain how—that King Sanchez had had the audacity to draft a letter asserting authority over and demanding tribute from Fezana. That letter had not, apparently, been sent yet—winter had barely ended, after all—but rumor of the demand was rife in Carcasia in the days following the Ruendan departure. The city of Fezana paid *parias* to Valledo and every person in the castle knew the implications of a counter-demand.

It was also pointed out by observant men that King Sanchez himself—known to be one of the finest archers in the three kingdoms—had been conspicuously errant with his own arrows for the two days before the morning of falconry. Could that unwonted incompetence have been a screen? A deliberate contrivance, in the event someone did trace a lethal arrow back to him?

Had the arrow been meant for his brother? Had those days of poor shooting produced a last aberrant flight when a true one had finally been intended? It would not, the most cynical found themselves thinking, necessarily have been the first time one of the sons of Sancho the Fat had slain another. No one voiced that particular thought, however.

The untimely death of Raimundo, the eldest son, was not something that could yet be forgotten. It was remembered that among a grimly silent gathering of courtiers that day long ago, the hard questions raised by young Rodrigo Belmonte, Raimundo's constable, had been specific and shocking.

Ser Rodrigo was far away now, exiled among the infidels. His well-born wife and young sons had, in fact, been invited to be among the Valledan company here, but Miranda Belmonte d'Alveda had declined, pleading distance and responsibilities in the absence of her lord. De Chervalles, the cleric from Ferrieres, had expressed some disappointment at this news when it came. He was said to be a connoisseur of women and Ser Rodrigo's wife was a celebrated beauty.

Jad alone knew what the Captain would have said and done today had he been here. He might have told the king this injury to the queen was the god's punishment for Ramiro's own evildoing years ago. Or he might as easily have pursued the king of Ruenda—alone, if necessary—and brought his head back in a sack. Rodrigo Belmonte had never been an easy man to anticipate.

Neither was Ramiro of Valledo, mind you.

When the king finally emerged from his meetings with Geraud de Chervalles and Count Gonzalez and a number of his military captains anticipation ran wild in Carcasia. Finally, they might be going after the Ruendan scum. The provocation was there: even the clerics could be made to see that. It was past time for Valledo to move west.

No commands came.

Ramiro appeared from those meetings with a sternly resolute expression. So did the men with whom he had been speaking. No one said a word, though, as to what had transpired. It was noted that de Chervalles, the cleric, shocked and sobered as he might be by what had happened, did not look censorious.

King Ramiro seemed subtly changed, with a new manner that unsettled his courtiers. He appeared to be reaching inward for strength or resolution. Perhaps he was nurturing the desire for bloodshed, someone suggested. Men could understand that. Spring was the time for war in any case, and war was where a brave man found his truest sense of life.

Still no one was certain what was afoot. The king showed no signs of leaving Carcasia for Esteren. Messengers went out in all directions. A single herald was sent west along the river towards Ruenda. Only a herald. No army. Men cursed in the taverns of Carcasia. No one knew what message he carried. Another small party set out east. One of them told a friend they were bound for the ranching lands where the horses of Valledo were bred. No one knew what to make of that either.

Through the ensuing days and then weeks, the king remained inscrutable. He hunted most mornings, though in a distracted fashion. He spent a great deal of time with the queen, as if her passage near to death had drawn the two of them closer. The constable was a busy man, and he too offered no hint, by word or expression, of what was happening. Only the High Cleric from Ferrieres could be seen to be smiling when he thought he was unobserved, as if something he'd thought lost had been unexpectedly found.

Then, as the spring ripened and flowers bloomed in the meadows and the forest clearings, the Horsemen of Valledo began to ride into Carcasia.

They were the finest riders in the world, on the finest horses, and they came armed and equipped for war. As more and more of them appeared, it slowly became apparent, to even the dullest courtier in Carcasia, what was taking place.

An air of disbelief mingled with a trembling excitement began to pervade the city and castle as the soldiers continued to gather, company after company. Men and women who had been markedly lax in their observances for some time, if not all their lives, began to be seen at the services in Carcasia's ancient chapel, built in those long-ago days when Esperaña had ruled all of the peninsula, not just the northlands.

At those services, frequently led by the High Cleric from Ferrieres, the king of Valledo and, after she was allowed to leave her rooms, his queen were present, morning and evening, kneeling side by side in prayer, sun disks of the god clasped in their hands.

Over a span of centuries, the golden, fabulously wealthy khalifs of Al-Rassan had led their armies thundering north, irresistible as the sea, to raid and enslave the Jaddites cowering at the hard fringes of a land that had once been their own. Year after year after year, back beyond the memories of men.

The last, weak puppet khalif in Silvenes had been slain, though, nearly sixteen years ago. There were no khalifs any more. It was time to start rolling back the tide the other way, in Jad's fierce, bright, holy name.

ↄ

Eliane bet Danel, wife to a physician and mother of one, was not unused to strangers speaking to her in the street. She was known in the city, and her husband and daughter had both had a great many patients over the years here in Fezana. Some might wish to express gratitude, others to seek a speedy or a less expensive access to the doctor. Eliane had learned to deal briskly with both sorts.

The woman who stopped her on a cool market morning in the early spring of that year fell into neither category. In fact, Eliane was later to reflect, this marked the first time in her life she'd ever been accosted by a prostitute of either sex.

"My lady," the woman said, without stepping from the shaded side of the lane, and speaking much more politely than was customary for an Asharite addressing a Kindath, "might I have a moment only of your time?"

Eliane had been too surprised to do more than nod and follow the woman—a girl, truly, she realized—further back into the shadows. A small alleyway ran off the lane. Eliane had come this way twice a week for much of her life and had never noticed it. There was a smell of decay here, and she saw what she hoped were small cats moving quickly about further along the alley. She wrinkled her nose.

"I hope this isn't where you do business," she said in her crispest tones.

"Used to be, up above," the girl said carelessly, "before they moved us outside the walls. Sorry about the smell. I won't keep you long."

"I'm sure," Eliane said. "How may I help you?"

"You can't. Your daughter has, though, most of us, one way or another. That's why I'm here."

Eliane liked things to be as clear as possible. "Jehane, my daughter, has treated you medically, is that what you are saying?"

"That's it. And she's been good to us, too. Almost a friend, if that doesn't shame you." She said it with a youthful defiance that touched Eliane unexpectedly.

"It doesn't shame me," she said. "Jehane has good judgment in whom she befriends."

That surprised the girl. As Eliane's eyes adjusted further to the darkness here, she saw that the woman with whom she spoke was thin-boned and small, no more than fifteen or sixteen years old, and that she was wrapped only in a torn shawl over a faded green knee-length tunic. Not nearly enough for a day this cold and windy. She almost said something about that, but kept silent.

"I wanted to tell you, there's trouble coming," the girl said abruptly. "For the Kindath, I mean."

Eliane felt something icy slide into her. "What does that mean?" she said, involuntarily looking over her shoulder, back where the sunlight was, where people were moving, and might be listening.

"We're hearing things, outside. From the men that come. There's been sheets posted on walls. A nasty poem. A...what do they call it...an allegation. About the Kindath and the Day of the Moat. Nunaya thinks something's being planned. That the governor may be under orders."

"Who is Nunaya?" Eliane realized that she had begun to shiver.

"Our leader. Outside the walls. She's older. Knows a lot." The girl hesitated. "She's a friend of Jehane's. She sold her mules when Jehane left."

"You know about that?"

"I took her to Nunaya myself that night. We wouldn't have let Jehane down." Defiance again, a note of pride.

"Thank you, then. I'm sure you wouldn't have let her down. I told you, she knew where to choose her friends."

"She was always good to me," the girl said, with a shrug, trying to seem indifferent. "Don't see what's so wrong with calling the moons sisters, anyhow, myself."

Eliane had to be careful not to smile, despite the fear in her. Fifteen years old. "Some disagree with you, unfortunately," was all she said.

"I know *that*," the girl replied. "Jehane's all right?"

"I think so." Eliane hesitated. "She's in Ragosa, working there."

The girl nodded, satisfied. "I'll tell Nunaya. Anyhow, that's all I wanted to say. Nunaya says you should be careful. Think about leaving. She says people here are nervous again because of this claim by that other king in the north...from Ruensa?"

"Ruenda," Eliane said. "About the *parias?* Why should that affect the Kindath?"

"Now you're asking the wrong person, aren't you?" The girl shrugged again. "I hear things, but I don't know much. Nunaya thinks there's something funny about it, that's all."

Eliane stood in silence for a moment, looking at the girl. That shawl really wasn't at *all* warm enough for this time of year. Impulsively, surprising herself again, she took off her own blue cloak and draped it over the girl. "I have another," she said. "Will this be stolen from you?"

The girl's eyes had widened. She fingered the warm, woven cloak. "Not unless someone wants to wake up dead," she said.

"Good. Thank you for the warning." Eliane turned to go.

"My lady."

She stopped and looked back.

"Do you know the toy-maker's shop, at the end of the Street of Seven Windings?"

"I have seen it."

"Just past it, by the city wall, there's a linden tree. There's bushes behind it, along the wall. There's a way out there. It's a small gate, and locked, but the key is hanging from a nail on the tree, on the back side, about my height." She indicated with her hand. "If you ever need to get out that's one way that will bring you to us."

Eliane was silent again, then she nodded her head.

"I am glad my daughter has such friends," she said, and went back into the sunlight, which did not warm her now, without her cloak.

She decided to forgo the market this morning, though it normally gave her pleasure. One of the servants could go. She was cold. She turned back towards the Kindath Quarter and the house that had been her home for thirty years.

Think about leaving. Just like that.

The Wanderers. They were always thinking about leaving. Moving like the moons against the fixed and gleaming stars. But brighter, Ishak had liked to say. Brighter than the stars and gentler than the sun. And he and she had had their home here in Fezana for so long now.

She decided to say nothing to him about this.

The very next day a Jaddite leather worker approached her as she walked out in the morning to buy a new cloak— her old one was distinctly frayed, it turned out.

The man had been waiting just outside the guarded gates to the Quarter. He came up as soon as she turned the corner. He was respectful, and evidently afraid. He wasted little time, which was fine with Eliane. His message was the same as that of the girl the day before. He, too, had been a patient of Jehane's—or his young son had been. Eliane gathered that Ishak's absinthe dilution, offered for a nominal fee, had broken a dangerous fever the summer before. The man was grateful, had not forgotten. And told her it might be wise for them to leave Fezana for a time, before the spring was much further advanced. Men were talking in the taverns, he said, about matters that did not bode well.

There was anger, he said. And the more fiery of the street corner wadjis were not being kept under control the way they usually were. She asked him directly if he was leaving with his family, if the same dangers applied to the Jaddites. He said he had decided to convert, after resisting for many years. At the first branching of streets he walked away from her without looking back. She never learned his name.

She bought herself a cloak from a small, reliable shop in the Weavers' Lane, someone she had done business with for a dozen years or more. It might have been her imagination, but the merchant seemed cool, almost brusque with her.

Perhaps business was simply bad, she tried to tell herself. Certainly Fezana had endured grief and then real hardship this past year, with almost all of those who were central to the life of the city dead in the moat last summer.

But to drive the Kindath away because of that?

It made no sense. The taxes paid by the unbelievers— Kindath and Jaddite, both—went a long way towards supporting the wadjis and the temples, fortifying the walls and supplying the *parias* Fezana sent north to Valledo. Surely the new young king in Cartada understood that, or his advisors did? Surely they were aware of the economic impact if the Kindath Quarter of Fezana was emptied by a migration to some other city?

Or by something worse than that.

This time she told Ishak about the warnings. She thought she knew exactly what he would say, in the mangled sounds she had learned to understand since last summer.

He surprised her, though. After all these years he could still surprise her. It was the tidings from Sorenica, he explained, laboring to be clear. Something to be read in that: a new mood in the world, a swinging again, like a pendulum. Change in the air, in the winds.

The two of them, with their household, began quietly preparing to leave for Ragosa, and Jehane.

They weren't quite fast enough, however.

∽

Their daughter, in the same week her mother received these warnings of danger—which was the same week Ines of Valledo nearly died—was, with more anticipation than she liked to admit, preparing for Carnival in Ragosa.

Alvar de Pellino, off duty and walking up to meet her on a crowded street corner one morning, with Husari beside him and trailed by the watchful figure of young Ziri, privately decided that Jehane had never looked more beautiful. Husari, to whom he had impulsively confided his feelings about her one night, had warned him that springtime did this sort of thing to young men.

Alvar didn't think it was the season. Much had changed in his life since the summer before, and changes were still taking place, but what he had felt for Jehane before the end of that first night by the campfire north of Fezana had not altered, and was not about to. He was quietly certain of that. He was aware that there was something strange about such certainty, but it was there.

Physician to a court and a military company, Jehane bet Ishak was surrounded by brilliant and accomplished men. Alvar could deal with that. He had few expectations of any kind. So long as he was able to play a role, to be nearby, he would be content, he told himself.

Most of the time that was true. There were nights when it wasn't, and he'd had to admit—though not to pragmatic Husari—that the return of the spring flowers and the gentling of the evening breezes off the lake had made those nights more frequent. Men were singing in the streets now at night under the windows of women they desired. Alvar would lie awake listening to the music as it spoke of longing. He was aware at such times of how far he had come from a farm in the northlands of Valledo. He was also aware—how could he not be?—that he would be going back north one day, when the Captain's exile ended.

He tried not to dwell upon that.

They came up to Jehane and greeted her, each in his fashion: Husari with a grin and Alvar with his rapidly improving Asharite court bow. He'd been practising, for amusement.

"In the name of the moons, look at the two of you!" Jehane exclaimed. "You look as if you're already in costume. What would your poor mothers say?"

The two men regarded each other complacently. Alvar was dressed in a wide-sleeved linen overshirt, ivory-colored, loosely belted at the waist, over hose of a slightly darker shade and Asharite city slippers, worked with gold thread. He wore a soft cloth cap, crimson-colored, bought in the market the week before. He rather liked the cap.

Husari ibn Musa, silk merchant of Fezana, wore a plain brown Jaddite soldier's shirt under a stained and well-worn leather vest. There were knives tucked into his wide belt on both sides. His horseman's trousers were tucked into high black boots. On his head he wore, as always, a brown, wide-brimmed leather hat.

"My sadly departed mother would have been diverted, I hope," Husari said. "She had a gift of laughter, may Ashar guard her spirit."

"*Mine* would be appalled," Alvar said in his most helpful voice. Husari laughed.

Jehane struggled not to. "What would *any* rational person say, looking at you two?" she wondered aloud. Ziri had drifted apart from them; he did his guarding from a distance.

"I think," Husari murmured, "such a person—if we could find one in Ragosa this week—might say we two represent the best this peninsula has to offer. Brave Alvar and my poor self, as we stand humbly before you, are proof that men of different worlds can blend and mingle those worlds. That we can take the very finest things from each, to make a new whole, shining and imperishable."

"I'm not actually sure that vest of yours is the very finest Valledo has to offer," Alvar said with a frown, "but we'll let that pass."

"And I'm not sure I wanted a serious answer to my question," Jehane said. Blue eyes narrowed thoughtfully, she looked closely at Husari.

He grinned again. "Did I give you one? Oh, dear. I was trying my pedant's manner. I've been asked to give a lecture on the ethics of trade at the university this summer. I'm in training. I have to give long, sweeping answers to *everything.*"

"Not this morning," Jehane said, "or we'll never do what we have to do." She began walking; the men fell into step on either side of her.

"*I* thought it was a good answer," Alvar said quietly.

They both glanced at him. There was a little silence.

"So did I," said Jehane, finally. "But we shouldn't be encouraging him."

"Encouragement," Husari said grandly, striding along in his black boots, "never matters to the true scholar, filled with zeal and vigor in his pursuit of truth and knowledge, his solitary quest, on roads apart from the paths trod by lesser men."

"See what I mean," Jehane said.

"Let's try," said Alvar, "to find him a better vest."

They turned a corner, into a street they'd been told to look for, and then all three of them stopped in their tracks. Even Husari, who had seen many cities in his time.

Ragosa was always vibrant, always colorful. When the

sun shone and the sky and the lake were blue as a Kindath cloak the city could almost be said to gleam in the light: marble and ivory and the mosaics and engravings of arch and doorway. Even so, nothing in half a year had prepared Alvar for this.

Along the length of the narrow, twisting laneway temporary stalls had been hastily thrown together, scores of them, their tables laden with masks of animals and birds, real and fabulous, in a riot of colors and forms.

Jehane laughed in delight. Husari shook his head, grinning. On the other side of the laneway, young Ziri's mouth hung open; Alvar felt like doing the same thing.

He saw a wolf's head, a stallion, a saffron-bright sunbird, an extraordinarily convincing, appalling fire ant mask—and these were all on the first table of the lane.

A woman approached them, walking the other way, beautifully dressed and adorned. A slave behind her carried an exquisite creation: a leather and fur mask of a mountain cat's head, the collar encrusted with gems. There was a loop on the collar for a leash; the woman was carrying the leash, Alvar saw: it looked like beaten and worked gold. That ensemble must have cost a fortune. It must have taken half a year to make. The woman slowed as she came up to the three of them, then she smiled at Alvar, meeting his eyes as she went by. Alvar turned to watch her go. Ibn Musa laughed aloud, Jehane raised her eyebrows.

"Remember that mask, my friend!" Husari chortled. "Remember it for tomorrow!" Alvar hoped he wasn't blushing.

They had met on this mild, fragrant morning to buy disguises of their own for the night when torches would burn until dawn in the streets of Ragosa. A night when the city would welcome the spring—and celebrate the birth day of King Badir—with music and dancing and wine, and in other ways notably distant from the ascetic strictures of Ashar. And from the teachings of the clerics of Jad, and the high priests of the Kindath, too, for that matter.

Notwithstanding the clearly voiced opinions of their spiritual leaders, people came to Ragosa from a long way off,
sometimes travelling for weeks from Ferrieres or Batiara—
though there was still snow in the passes east—to join the
Carnival. The return of spring was always worth celebrating,
and King Badir, who had reigned since the Khalifate fell,
was a man widely honored, and even loved, whatever the
wadjis might say about him and his Kindath chancellor.

They strolled through the thronged lane, twisting and
turning to force a passage. Alvar kept a hand on the wallet
at his belt. A place such as this was Paradise on earth for a
cut-purse. At the first mask-maker's stall at which they
stopped, Alvar picked up an eagle's visage, in homage to
the Captain. He donned it and the craftsman, nodding vigorous approval, held up a seeing glass. Alvar didn't recognize himself. He looked like an eagle. He looked dangerous.

"Excellent," Jehane pronounced. "Buy it."

Alvar winced, behind the mask, at the quoted price, but
Husari did the bargaining for him, and the cost came
down by half. Husari, amused and witty this morning, led
them onward, elbowing through the crowd, and a little further along he pounced with a cry upon a spectacular ren-
dition of a peacock's head and plumage. He put it on, not
without difficulty. People had to press backwards to make
room. The mask was magnificent, overwhelming.

"No one," said Jehane, stepping back to get a better
look at him, "will be able to get anywhere close to you."

"I might!" a woman cried from the cluster of onlookers.
There was a roar of ribald laughter. Husari carefully
sketched a bow to the woman.

"There *are* ways around such dilemmas, Jehane,"
Husari said, his voice resonating oddly from behind the
close-fitting headpiece and spectacular feathers. "Given
what I know about this particular festival."

Alvar had heard the stories too. The barracks and taverns and the towers of the night watch had been full
of them for weeks. Jehane tried, unsuccessfully, to look
disapproving. It was hard to disapprove of Husari, Alvar

thought. The silk merchant seemed to be one of those men whom everyone liked. He was also a man who had entirely changed his life this past year.

Once portly and sedentary, and far from young, ibn Musa was now fully accepted in Rodrigo's company. He was one of those with whom the Captain took counsel, and gruff old Laín Nunez—Jaddite to the tips of his fingers, for all his profane impieties—had adopted him as a highly unlikely brother.

With the assistance of the artisan, Husari removed the mask. His hair was disordered and his face flushed when he emerged.

"How much, my friend?" he asked. "It is an almost passable contrivance."

The artisan, eyeing him closely, quoted a price. Ibn Musa let out a shriek, as of a man grievously wounded.

"I think," Jehane said, "that this particular negotiation is going to take some time. Perhaps Ziri and I will proceed alone from here, with your indulgence? If I'm going to be disguised it does seem pointless for everyone to know what I'm wearing."

"We aren't *everyone*," Husari protested, turning from the opening salvos of the bargaining session.

"And you know our masks already," Alvar added.

"I do, don't I?" Jehane's smile flashed. "That's useful. If I need either of you during the Carnival I'll know to look in the aviary."

"Don't be complacent," Husari said, wagging a finger. "Alvar may well be in a mountain cat's lair."

"He wouldn't do that," Jehane said.

Husari laughed. Jehane, after a brief hesitation, and a glance at Alvar, turned and walked on. Clutching his eagle visage, Alvar watched her go until she and Ziri were swallowed by the crowd.

Husari, after a negotiating exercise so animated it drew another cluster of people around them for the entertainment, bought the peacock mask at a sum that represented most of a year's income for a professional soldier. The artisan agreed to deliver it later, when the crowds had thinned.

"I believe I need a drink," ibn Musa declared. "Holy Ashar forgive us all our sins in this world."

Alvar, for whom it wasn't a sin, decided he wanted one too, though it was early in the day for him. They had several flagons, in the event, before leaving the tavern.

"Mountain cats," Husari said musingly at one point, "are said to be ferocious in their coupling."

"Don't *tell* me things like that!" Alvar groaned.

Husari ibn Musa—silk merchant, soldier, Asharite, friend—laughed and ordered another flask of the good red wine.

Walking alone through the crowd past the mask-makers' stalls, Jehane told herself sternly that the deception was minor and that she'd every right to her privacy. She didn't like dissembling, however, and she cared for both men very much. She'd even surprised herself with a twinge of what was unmistakably jealousy when that long-legged Asharite creature with the mountain cat mask had smiled at Alvar in a way that left little room for ambiguity.

Still, it really wasn't any of Alvar's business or Husari's that she already had a mask for the Carnival, courtesy of the chancellor of Ragosa. She was wearied and irritated by the constant speculation that surrounded their relationship. The more so since the arrival of the alluring figure of Zabira of Cartada had rendered Mazur's pursuit of Jehane almost entirely ritualized.

It was inconsistent to be as bothered by his largely abandoned attempts at conquest as she had been by his earlier assumption that her surrender was merely a matter of time, but Jehane was acutely conscious that this was exactly how she felt.

She sighed. She could imagine what Ser Rezzoni in Batiara would have said about all of this. Something about the essential nature of womankind. The god and his sisters knew, they'd argued about *that* often enough during her years in Batiara. She'd written him since learning the news of Sorenica. No reply, as yet. He was there most of the time, but not always. He often took his family north with him, while he lectured at some of the other universities. He might be dead, though. She tried very hard to avoid thinking about that.

Looking around, she spotted Ziri moving through the crowd a short distance away. For a time after she and Velaz had been abducted in the attempt on the life of the two children, Jehane had had to stave off a flicker of anxiety every time she went into the streets. She had come to realize, quickly enough, that Ziri was *always* nearby; her lithe shadow, learning—far too young—how to hide knives on his person and use them to deadly effect. He had killed a man to save her life.

They'd summoned her to the barracks one night to attend to Ziri. He'd appeared deathly ill when she first saw him: white-faced, vomiting convulsively. It had only been wine, though. Rodrigo's men had taken him to a tavern for the first time. She'd chided them angrily for that, and they'd allowed her to do so, but in truth, Jehane knew they were initiating him into a life that offered so much more than the one he would have had in Orvilla. Would it be a better fate, a happier one? How could a mortal answer that?

You touched people's lives, glancingly, and those lives changed forever. That was a hard thing to deal with sometimes.

Ziri would realize soon enough, if he hadn't already, that she wasn't really buying a mask this morning. That didn't matter. He would be torn apart between stallions before he said a word to a living soul that might betray anything he knew about her.

Jehane was learning to accept that people besides her mother and father might love her, and do certain things because of that. Another hard lesson, oddly enough. She had not been beautiful or particularly endearing as a child; contrary and provocative were closer to the truth. Such people didn't discover young how to deal with being loved, she thought. They didn't get enough practice.

She slowed to admire some of the handiwork on display. It was remarkable how even the most unlikely masks—a badger, a boar, a whiskered grey mouse's head made of softest leather—were crafted in such a fashion as to be sensuous and attractive. How could the head of a boar be sensuous? She wasn't sure, but she wasn't an artisan, either. The masks would be even more alluring, she realized, tomorrow night under torchlight and the risen moons, with wine running in the streets and lanes of the city, mingling anonymity with desire.

Mazur had invited her to dine with him the evening before, for the first time in a long while, and at the end of the meal had presented her, courteous and assured as ever, with a gift.

She'd opened the offered box. Even the container was beautiful: ivory and sandalwood, with a silver lock and key. Inside, lying on crimson silk, had been the mask of a white owl.

It was the doctor's owl, Jehane knew, sacred to the white moon and the pursuit of knowledge, a pale light flying down the long paths of the dark. Galinus, father of all physicians, had had an owl carved at the head of his staff. Not many people knew about that. Mazur, evidently, was one who did.

It was a generous, thoughtful gift, from a man who had never been less than generous or thoughtful with her.

She looked at him. He smiled. The problem with Mazur ben Avren, she had decided in that moment, was that he always *knew* he was being perceptive; that when he offered a gift it was the precise gift that ought to be offered. There was no uncertainty in him, no waiting to see if approval might come.

"Thank you," she said. "It is beautiful. I will be honored to wear it."

"It should become you," he said gravely, reclining at ease on the couch opposite hers, a glass of wine in one hand. They were alone; the servants had been dismissed when the meal was done.

"Tell me," Jehane added, closing the box and turning the delicate key in its lock, "what have you chosen for the Lady Zabira? If the question is not over-bold?" Contrary, provocative. Why should one be expected to change? And it was always a pleasure—such a rare pleasure—to cause this man to blink and hesitate, if only for a moment. Almost childish, she knew, but surely not everything child-like was a bad thing?

"It would be ungracious of me to reveal her disguise, would it not? Just as it would be wrong for me to tell her what I have offered you."

He did have a way of making you feel foolish.

Her response to that, though, was much the same as it had been all her life. "I suppose," she said lightly. "How many of us will you have personally disguised for Carnival, so no one but you knows who we are?"

He hesitated again, but not from discomfiture this time. "Two, Jehane. You and Zabira." The pale wine in his glass caught the candlelight. He smiled ruefully. "I am not so young as I once was, you know."

He was not above duplicity in this sort of thing, but she had a sense he was speaking the truth here. She was touched, and a little guilty.

"I'm sorry," she said.

He shrugged. "Don't be. Five years ago, even two years ago, I would have deserved that." He smiled again. "Though I must say, no other woman would have asked the question."

"My mother would be horrified to hear you say that."

He shook his head slightly. "I think you malign her. I think she would be pleased her daughter was a match for any man."

"I'm hardly that, Mazur. I'm just prickly. It gets in the way, sometimes."

"I know," he said, making a face. "That I do know."

She smiled, and stood up then. "It is late for a working doctor," she'd said. "May I thank you again, and take my leave?"

He'd risen as well, still graceful, save for the hip that sometimes troubled him in rain. Not nearly so old and infirm as he might want, for the moment, to suggest. There was always a purpose to what Mazur said. Ammar ibn Khairan—who was, of course, exactly the same in this—had warned her about that.

Sometimes one didn't want to track through all the layers of meaning or implication. Sometimes one wanted to simply *do* a certain thing. Jehane walked towards Mazur and kissed him softly upon the mouth for the first time.

And *that* surprised him, she realized. He didn't even lift his arms to hold her. She'd done the same thing to ibn Khairan once, in Fezana. She was a terrible woman.

"Thank you," she'd said to the chancellor of Ragosa, withdrawing. "Thank you for my mask."

Walking home, with an escort, she realized that she'd forgotten to ask what *he* would be wearing at Carnival.

Amid the morning sunlight and the crowds, thinking about that evening, Jehane discovered that she had reached the end of the long street of stalls. She turned left, towards the lake, where it was quieter. Knowing that Ziri was following unobtrusively behind her, she strolled, without real purpose or destination.

She could go back to the infirmary. She had three patients there. There was a woman near her delivery time who could be looked in on at her home. None of them needed her particularly this morning, however, and it was pleasant to be abroad in springtime without immediate responsibilities.

It occurred to her then that what she really lacked here in Ragosa was a woman to befriend. She was surrounded by so many accomplished, even brilliant men, but what she missed just now was the chance to go outside the walls on this bright morning filled with birdsong to sit beside a tumbledown hut with Nunaya and some of the other street women, drinking something cool and laughing at their ribald, caustic stories. Sometimes you needed to be able to laugh at men and their world, Jehane thought.

She had spent—what was it, much of a year?—being serious and professional in a man's world. Sleeping in a tent in winter in the midst of a military company. They had respected her for that, had accepted her skills, trusted her judgment, and some of them even loved her, Jehane knew. But there were no other women with whom she could simply laugh, or shake her head in shared bemusement at the follies of soldiers and diplomats. Or perhaps even confide certain night-time struggles, when she lay awake in bed listening to stringed music played for other women from the dark streets below.

For all its pleasures and satisfactions there had been unexpected stresses to this life away from home, beyond the ones that might have been predicted. Perhaps, thought Jehane, it wasn't such a bad thing that this notorious Carnival was coming, when no one but Mazur ben Avren would know for certain who she was. An edge of excitement came with that thought, and, inevitably, some anxiety. It would have been nice to have Nunaya to talk to today. Nunaya understood more about men than anyone Jehane knew.

Unaware that she was doing so, she gave her characteristic small shrug and walked on. She wasn't good at meandering. She walked too briskly, as if there was a pressing engagement awaiting her and she was late for it.

She was twenty-eight years old, and nearing the moments that would mark her life forever.

First, though, passing along a quieter laneway, she glanced into an open doorway and saw someone she knew. She hesitated, and then, in part because she hadn't spoken privately with him since learning the tidings of Sorenica, Jehane walked in to where Rodrigo Belmonte stood alone, his back to the doorway, fingering samples of parchment in a scribe's shop.

He was concentrating on what he was doing and didn't see her enter. The shopkeeper did, and came out from around his counter to greet her. Jehane motioned him to silence. The man smiled knowingly, winked and withdrew to his stool.

Why, Jehane wondered, did all men have that same smile? She was irked by the shopkeeper's assumption and so her words when she spoke were cooler than she'd meant them to be.

"And what will you use this for?" she asked. "Ransom demands?"

Rodrigo was another difficult man to surprise. He glanced back and smiled. "Hello, Jehane. Isn't this beautiful? Look. Gazelle skin parchment, and sheepskin. And have you seen the *paper* this splendid man has?" The scribe beamed. Rodrigo took two steps towards another bin and lifted, carefully, a creamy scroll of flax paper.

"He has linen, as well. Come see. And some of it dyed. Here's crimson. *That* would do for ransom notes!" He grinned. There was unfeigned pleasure in his voice.

"More money for Cartada," Jehane said. "The dye comes from the valley south of them."

"I know that," said Rodrigo. "But I can't begrudge it to them, if they make something so beautiful with it."

"Would the esteemed Captain wish to purchase some of the linen, then?" the merchant asked, rising from his stool.

"The Captain cannot, alas, indulge himself in anything so extravagant," Rodrigo said. "Even for ransom notes. I'll take the parchment. Ten sheets, some ink, half a dozen good quills."

"Will you wish to avail yourself of my own services?" the man asked. "I have samples of my writing for you to view."

"Thank you, no. I'm sure it is impeccable, judging from the taste you display in your materials. But I enjoy writing letters when I have the leisure, and people claim they can decipher my hand." He smiled.

His spoken Asharic, Jehane thought, had always been excellent. He might have been a native, though unlike Alvar and some of the other northerners, Rodrigo had maintained his style of dress. He still carried his whip in his belt, even when he walked out, as now, without a sword.

"Are they really for ransom notes?" she asked.

"To your father," he murmured. "I've tired of having a physician who's even sharper with me than Laín is. What will he give me for you?"

"Laín?"

"Your father."

"Not much, I fear. He also thinks I'm too sharp."

Rodrigo took a silver coin from his purse and paid the man. He waited for his purchases and accepted his change, counting it.

Jehane walked out with him. She saw him assess the street, instinctively, and note the presence of Ziri in a doorway halfway down. It must be odd, she thought suddenly, to have a view of the world that made such appraisals routine.

"Why," he asked, beginning to walk east, "do you think you are so astringent towards those who genuinely like you?"

She hadn't expected to be immediately in this sort of conversation, though it jibed with where her thoughts had been going before.

She gave her quick shrug. "A way of coping. You all drink together, brawl, train, swear at each other. I have only my tongue, and a manner with it, sometimes."

"Fair enough. Are you having trouble coping, Jehane?"

"Not at all," she said quickly.

"No, really. You're a member of my company. This is a captain's question, doctor. Would you like some time off duty? There will be little chance once the season changes for good, I should warn you."

Jehane bit back a quick retort. It *was* a fair question. "I'm happiest working," she said at length. "I wouldn't know what to do with time away. It wouldn't be safe to go home, I don't think."

"Fezana? No it wouldn't," he said. "Not this spring."

She picked up on the intonation. "It is coming soon, you think? Will Badir really send the army west?"

They turned a corner, walking north now. The crowds were thinning out, nearing midday. The lake was ahead of them and the curved arms of the walls, reaching out over the water. Jehane could see the masts of fishing boats.

Rodrigo said, "I think a number of armies will be moving soon. I believe ours will be one of them."

"You *are* being careful," she said.

He glanced at her. Grinned suddenly beneath the thick moustache. "I'm always careful with you, Jehane."

She left a silence, not responding. He went on, "If I knew more for certain I'd tell you. Laín is quite sure this rumored gathering of all three northern kings will lead to one army coming down. I doubt it, myself, but that doesn't mean there won't be three Jaddite kings riding, each with his own little holy war." His tone was dry.

"And where," she asked, stopping by a bench outside a large warehouse, "would that leave Rodrigo Belmonte of Valledo?" It was a trait of hers: when uncertain she tended to be most direct. To cut through, like a surgeon.

He put a booted foot on the stone bench and set down his package. He gestured and she sat. There was a plane tree for shade. It was warmer now, with the sun high. She caught a glimpse of Ziri perched on a fountain rim, playing with his knife, looking for all the world like an apprentice off duty for an hour, or dawdling on the way back from an errand.

Rodrigo said, "I have no easier answer to that than I did in the winter. Remember, ibn Khairan asked me the same thing?"

She did remember: the morning she had nearly died, with two small boys who'd committed no sin other than to be the half-brothers of a king.

"Would the money you are earning here truly come before loyalty to Valledo?"

"Put that way, no. There *are* other ways to put it, Jehane."

"Tell me."

He looked at her, the grey eyes calm. Very little ruffled him. It almost made you want to try. But this man, she thought suddenly, spoke to her exactly as to a trusted officer. No concessions, no condescension. Well, almost none. She wasn't sure he teased Laín Nunez in the same way.

"Should loyalty to my own idea of honor outweigh a duty to my wife and the future of my sons."

There was a breeze now, nearer the water. Jehane said, "Will you explain that?"

"Laín and Martín are both afraid we might miss a real chance, being exiled this particular year. They've been urging me to petition Ramiro to allow me to return and then break my contract here if he does. I've chosen not to do so. There are some things I won't do."

"Which? Break a contract or petition for return?"

He smiled. "Both, actually. The second more than the first. I could return my salary, I certainly haven't spent it. But Jehane, think about this. The larger point. If Valledo moves south through the *tagra* and besieges Fezana, what men do you think Ramiro will give land to, should he succeed?" He looked at her. "Do you see?"

Being quick, and her father's daughter, she did. "You could be riding around Ragosa chasing bandits for a salary when there are kingdoms to be won."

"Not quite kingdoms, perhaps, but something substantial, certainly. Much more than a salary, however generous. So, you tell me, doctor? Do I owe my two boys a chance to be the heirs of, say, the king's governor of Fezana? Or of a tract of newly conquered land between there and Carcasia, with permission to build a castle?"

"I can't answer that. I don't know your boys."

"Doesn't matter. They are boys. The question is, what should a man *strive* for, Jehane? Honorably?" His eyes were direct and even a little intimidating now. Ser Rezzoni used to have a look like that sometimes. She tended to forget, until reminded, as now, that Rodrigo was a teacher, besides being one of the most feared fighting men in the peninsula.

"I still can't answer," she said.

He shook his head, impatient for the first time. "Do you think I go to war and kill, order surrendering foes to be slain, women burned alive—I have *done* that, Jehane—out of some simple-minded battle-lust?"

"You tell me."

She felt a little cold now, in the shade. This was not what she'd expected from a morning walk through the city.

"There is pleasure in warfare, yes." He was measuring his words. "I would never deny that. For good or ill, I feel most alive in the presence of death. I need danger, comradeship, pride of mastery. The chance to win honor, glory, even fortune—all of which matter in this world, if not in Jad's Paradise of Souls. But it takes me away from those I love and leaves them exposed to danger in my absence. And surely, surely, if we are not simply animals that live to fight, there must be a *reason* for bloodshed."

"And the reason is? For you?"

"Power, Jehane. A bastion. A way to be as secure as this uncertain world allows, with a chance to build something for my sons to hold on to after I die."

"And you all want this? This is what drives you?"

He thought about it. "I would never speak for all men. For some the sweet excitement is enough. The blood. Some do kill for the love of it. You met some of that sort at Orvilla. But I'd wager...I'd wager that if you asked Ammar ibn Khairan he would tell you he is here in this city because he hopes to govern Cartada for King Badir before summer's end."

Jehane stood up abruptly. She resumed walking, thinking hard now. Rodrigo collected his small package and caught up, falling into stride beside her. They walked in silence past all the warehouses until they came to the end of a long pier and stood above the blue water. The fishing boats were being decorated for Carnival. There were lanterns and banners in the riggings and on the masts. The sun was overhead now; few people were about in the middle of the day.

"You can't both win those things, can you?" she said finally. "You and Ammar. Or not for long. Ramiro can't conquer Fezana and hold it if Badir takes Cartada and holds it."

"They *could*, I suppose. But no, I don't think both things will happen. And certainly not if I stay here."

He was not a vain man, but he knew his own worth. She looked up at him. He was gazing out at the water.

"You do have a problem, don't you?"

"As I told you," he said quietly. "There will be armies moving soon, and I don't know what will be the result. Also, you may have forgotten, but there is another set of players."

"No, I haven't," said Jehane. "I never forget about them." Out on the lake one late boat was turning now, white sails bright in the sun, heading back to harbor with the morning's catch. "Will the Muwardis allow your people to begin conquering in Al-Rassan?"

"Reconquering, we say. But no, I doubt they will," said Rodrigo Belmonte.

"Will they come too, then? This summer?"

"Possibly. If the northern kings do."

They watched the gulls swoop and dart above the water. White clouds, swift as birds, raced by overhead.

Jehane looked at the man she was with.

"This summer ends something then, doesn't it?"

"We could say that every year each season ends something."

"We could say that. Are you going to?"

He shook his head. "No. I have felt for some time we are nearing a change. I don't know what it will be. But it is coming, I think." He paused. "Of course, I have been wrong about such things."

"Often?"

He grinned. "Not very, Jehane."

"Thank you for your honesty."

He continued to look at her. The direct gaze. "Pure self-protection, doctor. I dare not dissemble with you. You may have to bleed me one day. Or cut off a leg."

She realized that she didn't like thinking about that.

"Have you a mask for the Carnival?" she asked, inconsequentially.

He smiled again, crookedly. "Actually, I do. Ludus and Martín, who like to think they are amusing, bought me something elaborate. Perhaps I'll wear it, to humor them, and walk about early for a while, but I don't think I'll stay out."

"Why not? What will you do? Sit in a blanket by the fire?"

He lifted the small parcel he carried. "Write letters. Home." He hesitated. "To my wife."

"Ah," said Jehane. "Stern duty summons. Even during Carnival?"

Rodrigo colored slightly, for the first time she could ever remember, and looked away. The last fishing boat was in now. The sailors were unloading their catch.

"Not duty," he said.

And Jehane realized then, belatedly, something important about him.

He walked her home. She invited him in for a midday meal, but he declined, graciously. She ate alone, fish and fruit, prepared by the cook Velaz had hired for them.

Thoughtfully, she went to look in on her patients later in the day, and thoughtfully she came home at twilight to bathe and dress for the banquet at the palace.

Mazur had sent jewelry for her, another generous act. It was a notoriously elegant occasion, she had learned, the king's banquet on the eve of Carnival. Husari had presented her with her gown, crimson dyed, edged in black. He had flatly refused payment—one argument she had lost, resoundingly. She looked at the gown in her room. It was exquisite. She had never worn anything like it in her life.

The Kindath were supposed to wear blue and white only, and without ostentation. It had been made clear, however, that for tonight—and most certainly for tomorrow—such rules were suspended in King Badir's Ragosa. She began to dress.

Thinking about Husari, she remembered his speech of the morning. The pompous, lofty style of a mock-scholar. He had been jesting, he said.

But he hadn't been, or not entirely.

At certain moments, Jehane thought, in the presence of men like Husari ibn Musa or young Alvar, or Rodrigo Belmonte, it was actually possible to imagine a future for this peninsula that left room for hope. Men and women could change, could cross boundaries, give and take, each from the other...given enough time, enough good will, intelligence.

There was a world for the making in Esperaña, in Al-Rassan, one world made of the two—or perhaps, if one were to dream, made of three. Sun, stars and the moons.

Then you remembered Orvilla, the Day of the Moat. You looked into the eyes of the Muwardis, or paused on a street corner and heard a wadji demanding death for the foul Kindath sorcerer ben Avren, who drank the blood of Asharite infants torn from their mothers' arms.

Even the sun goes down, my lady.

Rodrigo had said that.

She had never known a man like him. Or no, that was not quite so. One other, met on the same terrible day last summer. They were like a bright golden coin, those two, two sides, different images on each, one value.

Was that true? Or did it just *sound* true, like the words of one of those pedagogues Husari mocked, all symmetry, no substance?

She didn't know the answer to that. She missed Nunaya and the women outside the walls of Fezana. She missed her own room at home. She missed her mother.

She missed her father very much. He would have liked to have seen her looking as she did now, she knew. He would never see her again, never see anything again. The man who had done that to him was dead. Ammar ibn Khairan had killed him, and then written his lament. Jehane had been near to tears, hearing that elegy, in the palace where they were dining again tonight, in a room with a stream running through it.

It was very hard, how many things in life you never discovered the answers to, no matter how much you tried.

Jehane stood before her seldom-used looking glass and put on Mazur's jewelry. She stayed there, looking at herself, for a long time.

Eventually, she heard music approaching outside, and then a knocking at the door downstairs. She heard Velaz going to answer. Mazur had sent an escort for her; strings and wind instruments, it sounded like. She had made him feel guilty last night, it seemed. She ought to be amused by that. She remained motionless another moment, staring at her image in the glass.

She didn't look like a doctor serving with a military company. She looked like a woman—not young with the extreme freshness of youth, but not so old, either, with quite good cheekbones and blue eyes accentuated now by paint and Mazur's lapis lazuli at ears and throat. A court lady, about to join a glittering company at a palace banquet.

Looking at the figure in the glass, Jehane offered her small shrug. That, at least, she recognized.

The mask, her real disguise, lay on the table beside the glass. That was for tomorrow. Tonight, in the palace of King Badir, however altered she might seem, everyone would still know she was Jehane. Whatever that meant.

Chapter XIII

❧

"Were you pleased?" the king of Ragosa asked his chancellor, breaking a companionable silence.

Mazur ben Avren glanced up from the cushions where he reclined. "I ought to be asking you that," he said.

Badir smiled in his deep, low chair. "I am easily pleased," he murmured. "I enjoyed the food and the company. The music was splendid tonight, especially the reeds. Your new musician from Ronizza is a discovery. Are we paying him well?"

"Extremely well, I'm sorry to say. There have been other offers for his services."

The king sipped from his glass, held it to the nearest candle flame and looked, thoughtfully. The sweet wine was pale: as starlight, the white moon, a northern girl. He tried briefly but failed to think of a fresher image. It was very late. "What did you think of the verses tonight?"

The verses were an issue, as it happened.

The chancellor took his time before answering. They were alone again, in the king's chambers. It occurred to ben Avren to wonder how many times over the years the two of them had sat like this at the end of a night.

Badir's second wife had died six winters ago, giving birth to his third son. The king had never remarried. He had heirs, and no single overriding political interest had emerged to dictate an obvious union. It was useful at times for a secure monarch to be unattached: overtures came, and negotiations could be spun out a long while. Rulers in three countries had reason to believe their daughter might one day be queen of wealthy Ragosa in Al-Rassan.

"What did *you* think of the verses, my lord?"

It was unlike the chancellor to deflect a question back. Badir raised one eyebrow. "Are you being careful, old friend? With me?"

Mazur shook his head. "Not careful. Uncertain, actually. I may be...prejudiced by my own aspirations in the realm of poetry."

"That gives me most of an answer."

Mazur smiled. "I know."

The king leaned back and put his feet up on his favorite stool. He balanced his wine on the wide arm of the chair.

"What do I think? I think most of the poems were indifferent. The usual run of images. I also think," he added, "that our friend ibn Khairan betrayed a conflict in his verse—either deliberately, or something he would rather have kept hidden."

The chancellor nodded slowly. "That seems exact. You will think I am flattering, I fear." King Badir's glance was keen. He waited. Mazur sipped from his wine. "Ibn Khairan's too honest a poet, my lord. He might dissemble in speech and act, but not easily in verse."

"What do we do about it?"

Mazur gestured gracefully. "There is nothing to do. We wait and see what he decides."

"Ought we to try to influence that decision? If we know what our own desires are?"

Mazur shook his head. "He knows what he can have from you, my lord."

"Does he?" Badir's tone sharpened. "I don't. What is it he can have from me?"

The chancellor laid his glass down and sat up straighter. They had been drinking all night—during the banquet, and now alone. Ben Avren was weary but clear-headed. "It is, as ever, yours to decide, my lord, but it is my view that he can have whatever it is he wants, should he choose to remain with us."

A silence. It was an extraordinary thing to have said. Both men knew it.

"I need him so much, Mazur?"

"Not if we choose to stay as we are, my lord. But if you wish to have more, then yes, you need him that much."

Another reflective stillness.

"I do, of course, wish to have more," said King Badir of Ragosa.

"I know."

"Can my sons deal with a wider realm when I'm gone, Mazur? Are they capable of such?"

"With help, I think so."

"Will they not have you, my friend, as I have?"

"So long as I am able. We are much the same age, as you know, my lord. That," said the chancellor of Ragosa, "is actually the point of what I am saying."

Badir looked at him. He held up his almost empty glass. Mazur rose smoothly and went to the sideboard. He took the decanter and poured for the king and then, at a gesture, for himself. He replaced the decanter and returned to his cushions, subsiding among them.

"It was an *extremely* short poem," said the king of Ragosa.

"It was."

"Almost…perfunctory."

"Almost. Not quite." The chancellor was silent a moment. "I think he was giving you a compliment of an unusual kind, my lord."

"Ah. How so?"

"He let you *see* that he is struggling. He did not hide the fact behind some bland, elaborate homage."

The king's turn to be silent again. "Let me understand you," he said at length. There was a trace of irritation in his voice now, a rare thing. He was tired. "Ammar ibn Khairan, asked to offer a verse for my birth day, recites a quick little piece about there always being water from a pool or wine in my cup. That is all. Six lines. And my chancellor, my poet, says this is to be construed as a compliment?"

Mazur looked undisturbed. "Because he could so easily have done more, my lord, or at the least, have claimed his inspiration was inadequate to the magnitude of the occasion. He is too experienced not to have done so, had he felt the slightest need to play a courtier's game. Which means he wanted you—and me, I suppose—to understand that he is being and will be honest with us."

"And that is a compliment?"

"From a man such as this, I believe it is. He is saying he believes we are thoughtful enough to read that message in his six lines, and wait for him."

"And we *will* wait for him, Mazur?"

"It is my counsel, my lord."

The king stood up then, and so the chancellor did the same. Badir strode, in jewelled slippers on the carpet and the marble floor, to a window. He turned the latch and pushed open both panes of beautifully etched glass. He stood overlooking a courtyard with almond and lemon trees and a fountain. Torches had been left burning below to light the play of water.

From beyond the palace the streets of the city were quiet. They would not be tomorrow night. In the distance, faintly, could be heard the sound of a stringed instrument, and then a voice, yearning. The blue moon was overhead, shining through the open window and upon the splashing fountain and the grass. Stars glittered around the moon and through the branches of the tall trees.

"You think a great deal of this man," King Badir said finally, looking out at the night.

"What I think," said his chancellor, "if you will allow me to pursue a poet's conceit and imagine men as bodies in the heavens, is that we have the two most brilliant comets in the sky here in Ragosa this spring."

Badir turned back to look at him. After a moment, he smiled.

"And where would you put yourself, old friend, in such a glittering firmament?"

And now the chancellor, too, smiled.

"That is easy, in truth. I am a moon at your side, my good lord."

The king thought about that. He shook his head. "Inexact, Mazur. Moons wander. Your people are named for that. But you have not. You have been steadfast."

"Thank you, my lord."

The king crossed his arms, still musing. "A moon is also brighter than comets in the dark," he said. "Though being familiar, perhaps it occasions less note."

Mazur inclined his head but said nothing.

"Will you be going abroad tomorrow night?"

Mazur smiled. "I always do, my lord. For a little time. Carnival is useful, to walk about unknown, and gauge the mood of the city."

"And it is solely duty that takes you out, my friend? You find no pleasure in the night?"

"I would never say that, my lord."

The two men shared the smile this time.

After a moment, Badir asked, bemusedly, "Why plain water from a pool, though, Mazur. In his verse. Why not just a rich red wine?"

And this, too, his chancellor explained to him.

A little later, Mazur ben Avren took leave of his king. When, at length, he reached his own quarters in the palace, the Lady Zabira was waiting.

She had been very much present at the banquet, of course, and had all the questions of someone who understood royal courts well and wished to rise in this one. She also displayed, gracefully, a continuing desire to minister to whatever needs the chancellor of Ragosa might have—in a fashion that might surpass anyone who had come before her.

As it happened, she had been doing just that through the winter, to his pleasure and surprise. He had thought he was too old for such a thing to happen.

Later that night, when he was drifting towards the shores of sleep, feeling her youthful nakedness against his body, soft as a cat, warm as a pleasant dream, Mazur heard her ask one last question. "Did the king understand what ibn Khairan meant in his poem tonight? About the water at the drinking place?"

She was clever too, this lady from Cartada, sharp as a cutting edge. He would do well to remember that. He was getting old, must not allow it to render him vulnerable. He had seen that happen to other men.

"He understands it now," he murmured, eyes closed.

He heard her laugh then, softly. Her laughter seemed to ease him wonderfully, a caressing sound. One of her hands slid across his chest. She turned herself a little, to fit more closely to him.

She said, "I was watching Ammar tonight. I have known him for many years. I believe he is troubled by something beyond...divided loyalty. I don't think he understands it himself yet. If I am right, it would be amusing, in truth."

He opened his eyes and looked at her, waiting. And then she told him something he would never have even contemplated. Women, Mazur ben Avren had long thought, had an entirely different way of seeing the world. It was one of the reasons he enjoyed their company so much.

Soon after that she fell asleep. The chancellor of Ragosa lay awake for a long time, however, considering what she had said, turning it over and over in his mind, as a stone in the hand, or the different possible endings for a verse.

∽

> For the bright lord of Ragosa,
> Long-tenured on his dais,
> Much-loved, and deservedly,
> May there always be in times to come
> Cool water from the moonlit pool
> And wine in the drinking glass.

He could perhaps have said, *alone by the pool*, Ammar ibn Khairan reflected, but that would have had a flavor of sycophancy, however subtle, and he wasn't ready—so soon

after the elegy for Almalik—to give so much to Badir of
Ragosa in a verse. Almost, but not quite. That was the
problem.

It was lions, of course, who were alone when they came
down to the water to drink.

He wondered if the king had been offended by his
brevity, which would be a pity. The banquet tables had
barely settled themselves to silence when ibn Khairan,
given pride of place, first recital, had already finished
speaking his brief verse. The lines were as simple as he
could make them, more a well-wishing than an homage.
Save for the hint...the moonlit waters. If Badir understood.
He wondered.

I am too old, Ammar ibn Khairan said to himself, justi-
fying, to abuse my craft.

Any of your crafts?

The inner voice always had the hard questions. He was
a soldier and a diplomat as well as a poet. Those were the
real crafts of his living here in Ragosa, as they had been in
Cartada. The poetry? Was for when the winds of the world
died down.

What ought a man honorably to do? To aspire towards?
Was it the stillness of that pool—dreamed of, and written
about—where only the one beast dared stalk from the
dark trees to drink in the moonlight and under the stars?

That stillness, that single image, was the touchstone of
verse for him. A place out of the wind, for once, where the
noise of the world and all the brilliant color—the noise
and color he still loved!—might recede and a deceptively
simple art be conjured forth.

Standing, as he had stood one night before—the night
he'd first come here—by the waters of Lake Serrana, ibn
Khairan understood that he was still a long way from that
dark pool. Water and water. The dream of the Asharites.
The water that nourished the body and the waters the soul
craved. If I am not careful, he told himself, I'll end up
being good for nothing but mumbled, cryptic teachings
under some arch in Soriyya. I'll let my beard and hair

grow, walk barefoot in a torn robe, let my students bring me bread and water for sustenance.

Water the body needed, waters the soul desired.

There were lanterns in the rigging of all the fishing boats, he saw by the blue moonlight. They were not yet alight. That would come tomorrow. Carnival. Masks. Music and wine. Pleasures of torchlight. A brilliance until dawn.

Sometimes the darkness needed to be pushed back.

Beloved Al-Rassan, the thought came to him in that moment, sharp and unexpected as a blade from beneath a friend's cloak, *shall I live to shape your elegy as well?*

In that innermost, jewel-like garden of the Al-Fontina those long years ago the last blind khalif of Silvenes had greeted him as a welcome visitor, before the blade—from beneath a friend's cloak—had ended him.

Ammar ibn Khairan drew a breath and shook his head. It might have been useful to have a friend here tonight, but that had never been the way he'd ordered his life, and it would be a weakness to dwell upon it now. Almalik was dead, which was a part, a large part, of the present difficulties.

It had been decided two nights ago—though not yet made generally known—that in two weeks' time, when the white moon was full, the mercenary army of Ragosa would set out for Cartada to wrest that city from a parricide. They would march and ride in the name of a small boy, Zabira's elder son, who had besought the shelter and support of King Badir and the intercession of the holy stars.

Ibn Khairan stood motionless for another moment, then turned away from the water and the boats to walk back. The last time he had been here by the lake late at night Jehane bet Ishak had been waiting by the warehouses and they had met Rodrigo Belmonte at the infirmary and he and Belmonte had left her there, laughing, and gone off to get unexpectedly drunk together. The night of the day he had arrived, the day they had fought side by side.

Something too close there, deeply unsettling.

Jehane had looked remarkably beautiful in the banquet

room tonight, he thought, inconsequentially. His steps echoed on the planks of the wharf. He came to the first warehouses and continued on. The streets were empty. He was quite alone.

She'd been gowned in crimson silk, extravagantly, with only lapis jewelry and a white shawl as gestures towards the Kindath clothing laws. It would have been Husari who provided that dress for her, Ammar thought, and ben Avren, probably, the jewels.

Her hair adorned with gems, and the lapis at ears and throat adding brilliance to her eyes, the doctor had caused a palpable stir when she entered the banquet room, though she'd been a fixture here, pragmatic and unpretentious, from the day she arrived. Sometimes, he thought, people reached a point where they wanted to say something different about themselves.

He had teased her this evening, about trying to catch the king's glance. Alleged she was harboring aspirations to be the first Kindath queen in Al-Rassan. If they start wagering on me again, she'd answered dryly—quick as ever—do let me know: I wouldn't mind making a little money this time.

He'd looked for her later, after the meal, after the music and all the verses, including his own, but she had already gone. So had Rodrigo Belmonte, it now occurred to him. An idle thought, wispy as a blown cloud across the moon, drifted into his mind.

The two of them, he realized, walking towards the center of the city, were the only people in Ragosa with whom he might have wanted to speak just now. Such an odd conjunction. Jaddite soldier, Kindath woman and physician.

Then he corrected himself. There was a third, actually. One more. He doubted the chancellor of Ragosa was alone, however, and greatly doubted he would be disposed to discuss nuances of poetry just then, so late at night, with Zabira in his bed, accomplished and alluring.

He was both right and wrong, as it happened. He went home alone, in any event, to the house and garden he had leased at the edge of the palace quarter with a small part of the great wealth he had earned in the service of the last king of Cartada.

⌒

In the horse-breeding lands of Valledo the next day—the morning of the Carnival of Ragosa, in fact—they came for Diego Belmonte at the ranch of his family where he had lived all his short life.

His mother was away at the time, riding the eastern perimeter of Rancho Belmonte, supervising the spring roundup of new foals. This absence on the part of the lady of the estate had not been planned by those who arrived at the ranch house, but they regarded it, nonetheless, as a highly fortuitous circumstance. The lady was known to be headstrong and even violent. She had killed a man here not long ago. Put an arrow through him, in fact. Nor was it assumed by those who arrived that day charged with a particular and delicate mission that Miranda Belmonte d'Alveda would regard them and their task with favor.

Mothers were chancy, at best.

There had not, in fact, been any great press of volunteers in Carcasia for this task, when word came from the castle that one of the sons of Ser Rodrigo Belmonte was to be brought west to join the army as it assembled just north of the *tagra* lands.

This absence of enthusiasm was accentuated when it became clear that the request for the presence of the young fellow came not from the king directly, but from the Ferrieres cleric Geraud de Chervalles. It was de Chervalles who wanted the boy, for some reason. A messy business, the soldiers agreed, getting tangled in the affairs of foreign clerics. Still, the king had endorsed the request and orders were orders. A company of ten men had been mustered to ride east along the muddy roads to Rancho Belmonte and bring back the lad.

Many of them, it emerged in campfire discussions along the way, had had their own first taste of warfare—

against the Asharites or the pigs from Jaloña or Ruenda—
at fourteen or fifteen years of age. The boy was said to be
almost fourteen now, and as Rodrigo Belmonte's
son...well, Jad knew, he *ought* to be able to fight. No one
knew why the army of Valledo needed a boy, but no one
put that question openly.

They came to Rancho Belmonte, riding beneath the
banner of the kings of Valledo, and were met in a cleared
space before the wooden compound walls by several
household officials, a small, nervous cleric and two boys,
one of whom they were there to claim.

The lady of the household—who would, in fact, have
cheerfully killed the lot of them had she been present to
learn of their mission—was elsewhere on the estate, the
cleric informed them. The leader of the troop showed him
the king's seal and his command. The cleric—Ibero was his
name—tore open the seal, read the letter then surprised
them by handing it over to the two boys, who read it
together.

They were utterly identical, Ser Rodrigo's two sons. A
few of the horsemen had already made the sign of Jad,
discreetly. Magic and witchcraft were said to attend upon
such mirrored twins.

"But of course," said one of the boys, looking up as he
finished reading. It was evident that they *could* read. "If
the king believes my...gift may be of use, if he wishes me
to come, I am honored to do so."

The captain of the company didn't know anything
about a gift. He didn't much care; he was simply relieved
to find things going smoothly.

"And I," said the other brother quickly. "Where Diego
goes, I also go."

This was not expected, but it didn't seem to pose a
great problem, and the captain agreed. If the king didn't
want this other brother in Carcasia, for whatever reason,
he could send him back. With someone else. The two boys
glanced at each other and flashed identical smiles before
dashing off to get ready. Some of the soldiers glanced at

each other with ironic expressions. Youngsters, everywhere, looked forward to war.

They *were* very young, and not especially prepossess-
ing either. Still, it was not a soldier's place to dwell upon
orders, and these *were* the sons of Rodrigo Belmonte. The
riders were offered refreshments, which they accepted,
and a night's lodging, which they courteously declined. It
would be imprudent, their captain decided, to push the
luck that had caused the lady of Rancho Belmonte to be
absent this day. They took a cold lunch, fed and watered
the horses, and provisioned themselves.

Ten men, escorting two boys and a squire of little more
than the boys' age, rode west from the ranch house
towards mid-afternoon of that same day, passing to the
south of a copse of trees, and crossing the stream at a
place Rodrigo's sons suggested. The ranch dogs followed
them that far and then went loping back.

∾

Ibero di Vaquez had lived an uneventful, even a sedate life,
given the turbulent times into which he had been born. He
was fifty-two years old. Raised in what was now Jaloña, he
had come west to Esteren to study with the clerics there
when quite young. Thirteen years old, in fact.

He was a good acolyte, attentive and disciplined. In his
early twenties, he had been sent as part of a holy mission
bearing relics of Queen Vasca to the High Clerics in
Ferrieres and had lingered there, with permission, for two
years, spending most of his time in the magnificent
libraries of the great sanctuaries there.

Upon his return to Esperaña he had been assigned—
and had cheerfully accepted—the short-term position of
cleric to the Belmontes, a moderately important ranching
family in the breeding lands of the southeast. The possibilities for advancement were certainly greater in Esteren
or one of the larger sanctuaries, but Ibero was not an
ambitious man and he had never had much appetite for
courts or the equally faction-riven retreats of Jad.

He was a quiet man, somewhat old before his years, but not without a sense of humor or an awareness of how the stern precepts of the god had, at times, to be measured against an awareness of human frailty and passions. The short-term position had turned, as sometimes happened without one's noticing, into a permanent one. He had been with the Belmontes now for twenty-eight years, since the Captain himself had been a boy. They had built a chapel and a library for him, and then expanded both. He had taught young Rodrigo his letters, and then his wife, and later his sons.

It had been a good, gentle life. Pleasures came from the books he was able to obtain with the sums allocated him; from his herb garden; from correspondents in many places. He had taught himself a little of medicine, and had a reputation for extracting teeth efficiently. Excitement— not inconsiderable—arrived home at intervals with the Captain and his company. Ibero would listen in the dining hall to the tales of warfare and intrigue they brought with them. He'd formed an unlikely friendship with gruff old Laín Nunez, whose profanity masked a generous spirit, in the little cleric's view.

For Ibero di Vaquez the stories he heard were enough turbulence for him, and more than close enough to real conflict. He liked the seasonal rhythms of existence here, the measured routine of the days and years.

His first intervention on the wider stage of the world, seven years ago, had been a brief, respectful essay on a doctrinal clash between the clerics of Ferrieres and Batiara on the meaning of solar eclipses. That clash, and the battle for precedence it represented, was still unresolved. Ibero's contribution appeared to have been ignored, so far as he could tell.

His second intervention had been to write a letter, in the late autumn of last year, to the holy person of Geraud de Chervalles, High Cleric of Ferrieres, dwelling in Esteren.

A company of men had arrived this morning in response to that. They had come and had gone, with the boys. And now Ibero, late that same afternoon, stood with his head bowed and trembling hands clasped before him, learning that he, too, was to quit this house. Leave chapel, library, garden, home. After almost thirty years.

He was weeping. He had never been spoken to, in all his life, in the tones with which he was being addressed by Miranda Belmonte in her small sitting room, as the sun went down.

"Understand me perfectly," she was saying, pacing before the fire, her face bloodless, unheeded tears sparkling on her cheeks. "This was a traitor's betrayal of our family. The betrayal of a confidence we had reposed in you, regarding Diego. I will not kill you, or order your death. I have known you, and loved you, for too long." Her voice caught. She stopped her pacing.

"Rodrigo might," she said. "He might find you, wherever you go, and kill you for this."

"He will not do that," the little cleric whispered. It was difficult to speak. It was also hard for him, now, to imagine what he had expected her response might be, back in the autumn, when he wrote that letter to Esteren.

She glared at him. He found it impossible to sustain her glance. It wasn't the fury, it was the tears.

"No," Miranda Belmonte said, "no, you're right, he won't. He loves you too dearly. He will simply tell you, or write to you, how you have wounded him."

Which would break Ibero's heart. He knew it would.

He tried, again, to explain. "Dearest lady, this is a time of holiness, of men riding beneath the god's banner. They will be taking ship in Batiara for the east soon. There is hope they may be riding south here, in the name of Jad. In *our* time, my lady. The Reconquest may begin!"

"And it could begin and continue *without my children!*" She had clenched her fists at her sides like a man, but he saw that her lips were trembling. "Diego's is a special gift, a frightening one. Something we have kept to ourselves all his life. You know—you *know*, Ibero!—that clerics have *burned* such people. *What have you done to him?*"

He swallowed hard. He said, "The high lord Geraud de Chervalles is an enlightened man. The king of Valledo is the same. It is my belief that Diego and Fernan will be welcomed with honor into the army. That if Diego is able to help in this holy cause he will win renown in his own name, not simply his father's."

"And be named a sorcerer all his life?" Miranda swiped at the tears on her face. "Had you thought of *that*, Ibero? Had you? What price renown, then? His own, or his father's?"

Ibero swallowed again. "It will be a holy war, my lady. If he aids in the cause of Jad—"

"Oh, Ibero, you innocent fool! I could kill you, I swear I could! It is *not* a holy war. If it happens, this will be a Valledan campaign to take Fezana and expand south into the *tagra*. That is all. King Ramiro has been thinking about this for years. Your precious High Cleric simply showed up at the right time to put a gloss on it. Ibero, this is no Reconquest by a united Esperaña. There *is* no Esperaña any more! This is just Valledo expanding. Ramiro is as likely to turn west and besiege his brother in Orvedo as anything else before autumn comes. What does your holy god say to that?"

She was blaspheming, now, and her soul was in his care, but he feared to chide her. It was also possible that she was right about much of this. He *was* an innocent man, he would never have denied that, but even so...

"Kings may err, Miranda, my lady. So may humble clerics. I do what I do, always, in the name of Jad and his holy light."

She sat down, abruptly, as if the last of her strength had given out. She looked as if she had been physically injured, he saw, and there seemed to be a lost place in her eyes. She had been alone, without Ser Rodrigo, for a long time. His heart ached.

Labelled a sorcerer all his life.

It might be true. He had thought only of the triumph, the glory Diego might accrue should he help the king in battle with his gift of sight.

Miranda said, her voice low now, uninflected, "You were here at Rancho Belmonte to serve Jad and this family. For all these years there has been no conflict in that. Here, for once, it seems there was. You made a choice. You chose, as you say, the god and his light over the needs and the trust of the Belmonte. You are entitled to do so. Perhaps you are required to do so. I don't know. I only know that you cannot make such a choice and remain here. You will be gone in the morning. I will not see you. Goodbye, Ibero. Leave me now. I wish to cry alone, for my sons."

He tried, heartsick, to think of something to say. He could not. She would not even look at him. He left the room. He went to his own chambers. He sat in his bedroom for a time, desolate, lost, and then went next door to the chapel. He knelt and prayed, without finding any comfort.

In the morning he packed a very few belongings. In the kitchen, when he went there to say farewell, they gave him food and wine to begin his journey. They asked for his blessing, which he gave, making the sign of the god's disk over them. They were weeping; so was he. Rain was falling when he went back out; the good, much-needed rain of spring.

Outside the stables there was a horse saddled for him. By the lady's orders, he was given to understand. She was true to her word, however. She did not come out to see him ride away in the rain.

◊

His heart hammering the way it had in battle, Alvar watched as the grey *iguarra* spider approached him slowly. The *iguarra* was poisonous, sometimes fatally so. The son of one of the farm workers had died of a bite. He tried to move, but could not. The spider came up and kissed him on the lips.

Alvar, twisting, managed to free his arms in the press of people and put them around the spider. He kissed her back as best he could from behind his eagle mask. He was improving, he thought. He had learned a great deal since sundown.

The spider stepped back. Some people seemed to have a knack of finding space to maneuver in the crowd. That trick, Alvar hadn't learned yet.

"Nice. Find me later, eagle," said the *iguarra*. She reached downwards and gave him a quick squeeze on his private parts. Alvar hoped the others hadn't seen.

Not much chance of that.

A hard, bony elbow was driven into his ribs as the spider drifted away. "What I'd give," cackled Laín Nunez, "to be young and broad-shouldered again! Did she hurt you, child?"

"What do you mean *again?*" roared Martín, on Alvar's other side. He was a fox for the Carnival; it suited him. "You were never built like Alvar, except in your dreams!"

"I assume," said Laín, with dignity, "that you are speaking of his shoulders, and not elsewhere?"

There was a raucous whoop of laughter in response to that. Not that the noise level could possibly get much higher, Alvar thought. Just ahead of them—he *had* to walk ahead of them, given his spectacular mask—Husari ibn Musa carefully turned around and gave Laín a gesture of encouragement. The normally dour old warrior waved back jauntily. He was a red and green rooster.

They had been drinking since the first stars had come out. There was food everywhere and the smells of cooking: chestnuts roasting, grilled lamb, small-boned fish from the lake, cheeses, sausages, spring melons. And every tavern, thronged to bursting, had opened its doors and was selling wine and ale from booths on the street. Ragosa had been transformed.

Alvar had already been kissed by more women than he'd ever touched in his life. Half a dozen of them had urged him to find them later. The night was becoming a blur already. He was trying to stay alert, though. He was looking for Jehane, however she might be disguised, and, though he certainly wouldn't tell this to the others, for a certain jungle cat mask. He was sure he'd recognize it, even by torchlight and in the press; there was the golden leash, for one thing.

Jehane was beginning, just a little, to regret that she'd insisted on anonymity and on walking the streets alone tonight.

It was fascinating, certainly, and there was an undeniable excitement to being masked and unknown amid a crowd of similarly unrecognizable people. She didn't really like drinking so much, though, and couldn't claim to be thrilled by the number of men—and one or two women— who had already used the license of Carnival to put their arms around her and claim a kiss. No one had really abused the privilege—it was early yet, and the crowds were dense—but Jehane, responding as best she could in the spirit of the night, wouldn't have said it was a *pleasure*, either.

Her own fault, if so, she told herself. Her own choice, not to be walking about with Rodrigo's men, safely escorted through the chaos of the streets. Out for a while, and then home like a good girl, to bed alone.

Her own choice, indeed. No one knew her, unless someone recognized her walk or tilt of head in the flickering of torches. Martín might, she thought, or Ludus: they were good at such things. She hadn't spotted any of the soldiers yet. She'd know Husari at a distance, of course. There would only be one peacock like that in Ragosa tonight.

She was approached and enveloped by a brown bear. She submitted, good-humoredly, to the bone-crushing hug and a smack on the lips.

"Come with me!" the bear invited. "I *like* owls!"

"I don't think so," Jehane said, gasping for breath. "It's too early in a long night for broken ribs."

The bear laughed, patted her on the head with gloved hand, and lumbered on. Jehane looked around, wondering if Ziri was somewhere in the crowd swirling past beneath the wavering torches. He didn't know her mask, though, and she had exited her house through the back door into the dark.

She couldn't have said why it was so important to her to be alone tonight. Or no, she probably could have if she demanded an honest answer of herself. She wasn't about to do that. Carnival wasn't a time for inward searching, Jehane decided. It was a night for doing the things one only dreamed about all the rest of the year. She looked around. A grey she-wolf and a horse were improbably entwined not far away.

A stag, seven-tined, emerged out of the tumult in front of her. He was holding a leather flask. He offered it to Jehane with a slight bow. A deeper inclination of his head might have impaled her.

"Thank you," Jehane said politely, holding out a hand for the wine.

"A kiss?" The voice was muffled, soft.

"Fair enough," said Ishak ben Yonannon's daughter. It was Carnival. She stepped forward, kissed him lightly, accepted the flask, and drank. There seemed to be something familiar about this man, but Jehane didn't pursue the thought: there had been something familiar about half the men who'd kissed her tonight. Masks and imagination and too much wine did that to you.

The stag moved on without speaking again. Jehane watched him go, then realized he'd left her the flask. She called after him but he didn't turn. She shrugged, looked at the flask, drank again. This wine was good, and scarcely watered, if at all.

"I am going to have to start being careful," she said aloud.

"*Tonight?*" said a brown rabbit, laughing beside her. "How absurd. Come with us instead. We're going down to the boats." There were four of them, all rabbits, three women and a man with his arm around two of them. It seemed a reasonable thing to do. As reasonable as anything else. And better, after all, than wandering alone. She shared the leather flask with them on the way to the lake.

Behind the mask, which alone made tonight possible, eyes watched from the shadows of a recessed doorway as a stag was briefly kissed by a white owl and then stalked gracefully away, leaving a flask of wine behind.

The owl hesitated visibly, drank again from the flask, and then went off in another direction with a quartet of rabbits.

The rabbits didn't matter at all. The stag and the owl were known. The watching one—disguised, on a whim, as a lioness—left the shelter of the doorway and followed the stag.

There were surviving pagan legends, in countries now worshipping either Jad or the stars of Ashar, about a man changed into a stag. In those lands conquered by the followers of the sun god, the man had been so transmuted for having abandoned a battlefield for a woman's arms. In the east—in Ammuz and Soriyya, before Ashar had changed the world with his visions—the ancient tale was of a hunter who had spied upon a goddess bathing in a forest pool and was altered on the spot.

In each tale, the stag—once a man—was fair game for the hunting dogs and was torn apart in the heart of a dark wood for his sin, his one unforgivable sin.

In the years since Ragosa's Carnival had begun a number of traditions had emerged. License, of course, was one—and to be expected. Art, its frequent bedfellow, was another.

There was a tavern—Ozra's—between the palace and the River Gate to the south. Here, under the benevolent eye of the longtime proprietor, the poets and musicians of Ragosa—and those who, masked, wished to be numbered among them, if only for a night—would gather to offer anonymous verse and song to each other and to those who paused in their torchlit careen to listen at the door.

Carnival was quieter in Ozra's, though not the less interesting for that. The masks led people to perform in ways they might never have ventured, exposed as themselves.

Some of the most celebrated artists of the city had, over the years, come to this unassuming tavern on Carnival night to gauge the response their work might elicit with the aura of fame and fashion removed.

They had not always been pleased with the results. Tonight's was a difficult, sophisticated audience and they, too, were masked.

Amusing things happened, sometimes. It was still remembered how, a decade ago, one of the wadjis had taken the performer's stool, disguised as a crow, and chanted a savage lampoon against Mazur ben Avren. An attempt, clearly, to take their campaign against the Kindath chancellor to a different level.

The wadji had had a good voice, and even played his instrument passably well, but he'd refused the customary performer's glass of wine far too awkwardly, and he had also neglected to remove the traditional sandals of the wadjis, modelled on those Ashar had worn in the desert. From the moment he'd sat down everyone in the tavern knew exactly what he was, and the diversion the knowledge offered had quite removed the sting from the lampoon.

The next year three crows appeared in Ozra's, and each of them wore wadjis' sandals. They drank in unison, however, and then performed together and there was nothing devout about that performance. The satire, this time, was directed at the wadjis—to great and remembered success.

Ragosa was a city that valued cleverness.

It also respected the rituals of this night, though, and the performer now taking his place on the stool between the four candles in their tall black holders was granted polite attention. He was effectively disguised: the full-face mask of a greyhound above nondescript clothing that revealed nothing. No one knew who he was. That was, of course, the point.

He settled himself, without an instrument, and looked around the crowded room. Ozra di Cozari, once of Eschalou in Jaloña, but long since at home here in Al-Rassan, watched from behind his bar as the man on the

stool appeared to notice someone. The greyhound hesitated, then inclined his head in a greeting. Ozra followed the
glance. The figure so saluted, standing by the doorway,
had come in some time ago, remaining near the entranceway. He must have had to duck his head to enter, because
of the branching tines of his horns. Beneath the exquisite
stag mask that hid his eyes and the upper part of his face,
he appeared to smile in return.

Ozra turned back to the greyhound between the candles, and listened. As it happened, he knew who this was.
The poet began without title or preamble.

> *Shall we linger in Ragosa amid spring flowers,*
> *Between the white diamond of the lake*
> *And the blue necklace of the river*
> *Sliding away south to the sea,*
> *As pearls run through a woman's fingers?*
> *Shall we linger to sing the praises of this city?*
> *And shall we not remember as we do*
> *Silvenes in the time of lions?*
>
> *In the fountains of the Al-Fontina, it is told,*
> *Twenty thousand loaves of bread fed the fish*
> *Each and every day.*
> *In Silvenes of the khalifs,*
> *In the fountains of the Al-Fontina.*

There was a stir in the tavern. This was something
unexpected, in structure and in tone. The poet, whoever he
was, paused and sipped from the glass at his elbow. He
looked around again, waiting for stillness, then resumed.

> *Shall we linger here amid this fragile beauty,*
> *Admiring the fall of light on ivory?*
> *Shall we ask ourselves*
> *What will become of Al-Rassan,*
> *Beloved of Ashar and the stars?*

What has become of Silvenes?
Where are the centers of wisdom and the teachers?
Where are the dancing girls with slender ankles,
And where the music beneath the almond trees?
Where is the palace whence the khalifs of all-fame
Thundered forth with armies?
What wild beasts wander now at will
Between the ruined pillars?
Wolves are seen by white moonlight there.

Another stir, quickly suppressed, for the poet had not paused this time.

Ask in stern-walled Cartada for news of Silvenes,
but ask here in Ragosa about Al-Rassan.
Ask of ourselves, between river and lake,
if we will suffer the stars to be blotted out.
Ask of the river, ask of the lake,
ask of the wine that flows tonight
between the torches and the stars.

The poet ended. He rose without ceremony and stepped down from the dais. He could not avoid the applause, however, the sound of genuine appreciation, nor the speculative glances that followed him to the bar.

Ozra, following tradition here as well, offered him a glass of his best white wine. He usually made a quip at this time, but could think of nothing to say.

Ask of the wine that flows tonight.

Ozra di Cozari was seldom moved by what was read or sung in his tavern, but there was something about what he had just heard. The man in the greyhound disguise lifted the glass and saluted him briefly, before drinking. It was with no great surprise that Ozra noticed, just then, that the stag had come in from the doorway and was standing beside them.

The greyhound turned and looked at him. They were of a height, the two men, though the horns of the stag made him seem taller.

Very softly, so that Ozra di Cazari was almost certain he was the only other man to hear, the seven-tined stag said, "'*Beloved of Ashar?*'"

The poet laughed, quietly. "Ah, well. What would you have me do?"

Ozra didn't understand, but he hadn't expected to.

The other man said, "Exactly what you did do, I suppose." His eyes were completely hidden behind his mask. He said, "It was very fine. Dark thoughts for a Carnival."

"I know." The greyhound hesitated. "There is a darker side to Carnivals, in my experience."

"In mine, as well."

"Are we to have a verse from you?"

"I think not. I am humbled by what I have just heard."

The greyhound inclined his head. "You are far too generous. Are you enjoying the night?"

"A pleasant beginning. I gather it has only begun."

"For some."

"Not you? Will you not come wandering? With me?"

Another hesitation. "Thank you, no. I will drink a little more of Ozra's good wine and listen to the verses and the music a while before bed."

"Are we expecting any crows tonight?"

The greyhound laughed again. "You heard about that? We never expect anything at Carnival, and so hope never to be disappointed and never greatly surprised."

The stag lifted its head. "We differ there, at least. I am always, endlessly, hoping to be surprised."

"Then I wish it for you."

They exchanged a glance, then the stag turned away and found a passage to the doorway and out into the street. A black bull had taken the dais now, holding a small harp.

"I think," said the greyhound, "I will have another glass, Ozra, if you will."

"Yes, my lord," said Ozra, before he could stop himself. He'd said it softly though, and didn't think anyone had heard.

As he poured the wine he saw the first of the women approaching the poet where he stood at the bar. This always happened, too, at Carnival.

"Might we talk a moment in private?" asked the lioness softly. The greyhound turned to look at her. So did Ozra. It was not a woman's voice.

"Private speech is difficult to arrange tonight," the poet said.

"I'm certain you can manage it. I have some information for you."

"Indeed?"

"I will want something in return."

"Imagine my astonishment." The greyhound sipped from his wine, eyeing the newcomer carefully. The lioness laughed, a deep disconcerting sound beneath the mask.

Ozra felt a flicker of unease. From the tone of this, this man masked as a woman knew exactly who the poet was, which posed more than a measure of danger.

"You do not trust yourself with me?"

"If I knew who you were, I might. Why have you worn a mask to change your sex?"

Only the briefest hesitation. "It amused me. There is no beast more fierce, in the legends, in defense of her young."

The greyhound carefully laid down his glass.

"I see," he said finally. "You are very bold. I must say, I *am* surprised, after all." He looked at Ozra. "Is there a room upstairs?"

"Use mine," said the innkeeper. He reached beneath the counter and handed across a key. The greyhound and the lioness moved together across the room and up the stairs. A number of eyes watched them go, as the black bull on the dais finished tuning his instrument and began to play.

"How did you find me?" Mazur ben Avren asked, removing the greyhound mask in the small bedchamber.

The other man struggled with his own mask a moment, then pulled it off. "I was led to you," he said. "I had a choice of two people to follow, and made the right choice.

The stag brought me here."

"You knew him?"

"I tend to know men by how they move as much as how they look. Yes, I knew him," said Tarif ibn Hassan, scratching at his chin where the full white beard had been shaved away. He smiled.

So, too, after a moment, did the chancellor of Ragosa.

"I had not ever thought to meet you," he said. "You know there is a price on your life here?"

"Of course I do. I am offended by it: Cartada has offered more."

"Cartada has suffered more."

"I suppose. Shall I rectify that?"

"Shall I let you leave the city?"

"How would you stop me if I killed you now?"

The chancellor appeared to be considering that. After a moment, he moved to a small table and picked up a beaker of wine sitting there. There were glasses, as well. He gestured with the wine.

"As you will perhaps have realized, I have an arrangement here with the innkeeper. We are private, but not entirely alone. I hope you will not require me to demonstrate."

The outlaw looked around then and noted the inner door ajar and another door to the balcony. "I see," he said. "I ought to have expected this."

"I suppose so. I do have responsibilities, and cannot be entirely reckless, even tonight."

Ibn Hassan accepted the glass the chancellor offered. "If I wanted to kill you I could still do it. If you wanted to take me, you could have done so by now."

"You mentioned tidings. And a price. I am curious."

"The price you ought to know." Ibn Hassan looked pointedly over at his discarded mask.

"Ah," said the chancellor. "Of course. Your sons?"

"My sons. I find I miss them in my old age."

"I can understand that. Good sons are a great comfort. They are fine men; we enjoy having them with us."

"They are missed in Arbastro."

"The sad fortunes of war," said ben Avren calmly. "What is it you have to tell me?"

Tarif ibn Hassan drank deeply and held out his glass. The chancellor refilled it.

"The Muwardis have been building boats all winter. In the new shipyards at Abeneven. Hazem ibn Almalik is still with them. He has lost a hand. I don't know how, or why."

Mazur's turn to drink, thoughtfully. "That is all?"

"Hardly. I try to offer fair coinage when I make a request. Almalik II of Cartada has been seeding rumors about the Kindath of Fezana. I do not know to what purpose. There is growing tension there, however."

The chancellor set down the beaker of wine. "How do you know this?"

Tarif shrugged. "I know a good deal of what happens in lands controlled by Cartada. They have a large price on my life, remember?"

Mazur looked at him a long moment. "Almalik is anxious," he said finally. "He feels exposed. But he is clever and unpredictable. I will admit I have no great certainty about what he will do."

"Nor I," the outlaw chieftain agreed. "Does it matter? If it comes to armies?"

"Perhaps not. Have you anything more? Brighter coinage?"

"I have given good weight already, I think. But one more thing. Not brighter, though. The Jaddite army in Batiara. It is sailing for Soriyya after all. I never thought it would. I thought they would feed on each other over the winter and fall apart."

"So did I. It is not so?"

"It is not so."

There was a silence.

It was the outlaw, this time, who refilled both glasses. "I heard your verse," he said. "It seemed to me, listening, that you had a knowledge of these things already."

Ben Avren looked at him. "No. An apprehension perhaps. My people have a custom—a superstition, really. We voice our fears as a talisman: by bringing them into the open, we hope to make them untrue."

"Talismans," said Tarif ibn Hassan, "don't usually work."

"I know," said the chancellor. His voice turned brisk. "You have given, as promised, good weight. In truth, it hardly matters if you reveal the tale of the Emin ha'Nazar now. I can't readily imagine you would, in any case. The offer made to you there still stands: do you want to be part of the army that takes Cartada?"

"That tries to take Cartada."

"With your aid, I have great hopes that we would."

The old chieftain stroked the stubble of his chin. "I fear I will have little enough choice. Both my sons want to do this thing, and I have not the strength to overrule them together."

"That I do not believe," Mazur smiled. "But if you wish to put it in this way, it is no matter to me. Meet us north of Lonza. I will send heralds to you to arrange the exact timing, but we ride from here at the white full moon."

"So soon?"

"Even more urgently now, with what you have told me. If other armies are setting forth, we had best be first in the field, don't you think?"

"Are you covered at your back? In Fibaz?"

"That's where I spent the money the world thinks you stole from the *parias* party."

"Walls?"

"And soldiers. Two thousand from Karch and Waleska."

"And they will be loyal against Jaddites?"

"If I pay them, I believe they will be."

"What about Belmonte? Is Ser Rodrigo with you?"

Mazur looked thoughtful again. "He is, for now. If Ramiro of Valledo takes the field, I will not say I am sure of him."

"A dangerous man."

"Most useful men are dangerous." The chancellor's smile was wry. "Including beardless outlaws who want their sons back. I will send for them. Right now, in fact. It might be safest if you left tonight."

"I thought the same. I took the precaution of finding them before I looked for you. They are waiting for me outside the walls."

Mazur looked startled for the first time. He set down his glass. "You have them already? Then why...?"

"I wanted to meet you," the bandit chieftain said. His smile was grim. "After so many years. I also have a dislike for breaking my sworn word, though that might surprise you. They were granted their lives by ibn Khairan and Belmonte on our oath to accept their being hostages. Abir's life was given back to him by their physician."

"My physician," said the chancellor quickly.

Tarif raised his eyebrows. "As you please. In any case, I would have been unhappy to simply steal them away. It might have confirmed your worst thoughts of me."

"And instead?"

Ibn Hassan laughed. "I have probably confirmed your worst thoughts of me."

"Pretty much," said the chancellor of Ragosa. After a moment, though, he extended his hand. Ibn Hassan took it. "I am pleased to have spoken with you," Mazur said. "Neither of us is young. It might not have happened."

"I'm not planning on making an end soon," said ibn Hassan. "Perhaps next year I'll offer a verse here, at Carnival."

"That," said ben Avren, a hand at his own beard, "might be a revelation."

He sat alone for some time after the chieftain from Arbastro had donned his mask and left. He had no intention of telling anyone, but the news about the army sailing east struck him as almost unimaginably bad.

And rumors being spread about his Kindath brethren in Fezana—that was terrifying. He had literally no idea what Almalik II of Cartada had in mind, but it was clear that the man felt frightened and alone and was lashing out. Frightened men were the hardest of all to read, sometimes.

Ibn Hassan had asked about Rodrigo Belmonte, but not about the other one. The other one was just as much at issue, and in a way, he mattered even more.

"I wish," muttered Mazur ben Avren testily, "that I really *were* a sorcerer, whatever that is."

He felt tired suddenly, and his hip was bothering him again. It seemed to him that there ought to be orders to give to the bowmen on the balcony or the guards in the adjacent room, but there weren't.

It was Carnival. He could hear the noise from the street. It overwhelmed the harp music from below. The night was growing louder, wilder. Shouts and laughter. The sharp, high whirring of those noise-makers he hated. He wondered, suddenly, where the stag had gone.

Then he remembered what Zabira had told him, in bed the night before.

Chapter XIV

∽

In fact, it was the cat that found Alvar, late in the wild night, well after the blue moon had risen and was shining down, a wandering presence among the stars.

He had separated from the others some time before. Laín had been dragged off, protesting unconvincingly, by a cluster of field mice. Their giggling gave them away: they were the girls who served at the tables in the favorite tavern of Rodrigo's men. Bristling old Laín had been the object of their teasing—and warnings about his fate tonight—for some time.

Ludus, endlessly curious, had lingered at a street corner to watch a wolf swallowing fire—trying to decipher the trick of it—and had never caught up with the rest of them. Alvar wasn't sure where and when he had lost Martín or how the peacock regalia that flamboyantly disguised a certain silk merchant had somehow managed to disappear. It was very late. He'd had more to drink than was good for any man.

He hadn't seen Jehane anywhere. He'd thought earlier that he might know her by her walk, but as the night continued and the streets grew more frenzied it even became difficult at times to tell if someone passing in the dark was a man or a woman. He reminded himself that she knew his mask; that if he kept moving she might find him in the crowd to offer a greeting, share laughter. A kiss, perhaps, in this altered, wavering night. Although that was a dangerous channel for his thoughts.

There was too much license surrounding him, too

charged and wanton a mood in the streets of Ragosa now. Alvar found himself almost aching with desire, and with something more complex than that.

Alone and far from home in a foreign land at night, amidst animals and birds and fabulous creatures that had never been, passing food stalls and wine sellers and musicians playing by the orange and amber light of candles and torches beneath the blue moon and the stars of spring, Alvar wandered the streets, a leather flask at one hip, and longed for comfort, for a sharing of what this difficult, mutable world offered to men and women.

He found something very different.

A leash, to be precise.

It was slipped over his eagle mask and around his neck as he stood watching dancers in a square not far from the barracks. The dancers had their hands all over each other, and the women were being lifted and swung about in a way he had never seen before. He tried to imagine himself joining in, then dismissed the thought. Not a soldier's son from a farm in the north of Valledo.

It was in that moment that the leash was dropped over him from behind and tightened about his throat. Alvar turned quickly. A passing torch was briefly too close; he couldn't see for a moment, and then he could.

"I will have to decide how offended I am," said the sleek jungle cat he had seen in the street the morning before. "You were to have found me, Valledan. Instead..."

She wore the necklace that had come with her mask and much other jewelry. Not a great deal of clothing, however, as if to compensate. What she was wearing clung to the lines of her body. The voice beneath the mask was remarkably near to a feline purr.

"I was looking!" Alvar stammered, then flushed beneath his own disguise.

"Good," she murmured. "That earns you some redress. Not all, mind you. I ought not to have had to be the huntress tonight."

"How did you know me?" he asked, struggling for self-possession.

He heard her laugh. "A man of your build wearing Asharite slippers? Not hard, my northern soldier." She paused, tugged a little on the golden leash. "You *are* mine now, you understand? For whatever I choose tonight."

Alvar discovered that his mouth had gone dry. He didn't answer. He didn't really have to. He saw her smile, beneath the mask. She began walking and he followed her, wherever she was taking him.

In one way, it was not far at all: just around the corner, a house fronting on the same wide square as their barracks, near the palace. They passed through an imposing double doorway, crossed a torchlit courtyard and climbed a flight of stairs. It was an elegantly appointed house. Servants dressed in black, masked as small forest creatures, watched them pass, in silence.

In another sense, though, what ensued when they came to the room where she led him—with its balcony over the square, and its enormous fireplace, and the wide, canopied bed—marked one of the longest journeys of Alvar's life.

∾

Jehane was alone again. She had left the four brown rabbits by the water, a little reluctantly, because they were amusing, but she wasn't inclined to become too much a part of their visibly growing intimacy, and at one point she had simply slipped off the fishing boat where they had been, and moved quietly back to the pier and into the crowd.

She still had the wine flask the stag had left her, but she'd stopped drinking. She felt clear-headed now, almost unsettlingly so. She was discovering, as she moved through the late-night streets, that Carnival, for all its disguises, was a difficult night in which to hide from the self after all.

At one point she caught a glimpse of Husari in his spectacular mask. The silk merchant was dancing, part of a group of figures. In fact, he was in the center of a ring, turning in neat-footed movements while the laughing crowd applauded him. Jehane paused a short distance

away, smiling behind her owl face, long enough to see a
woman masked as a vixen step from the circle to come up
to the peacock and loop her arms around his neck, careful
of the feathers. They began moving together, gracefully.

Jehane watched for another moment and then moved
on.

It might have seemed as if her wandering was aimless,
carrying her with the swirling movements of the crowd
past entertainments and food vendors, to pause outside
tavern windows listening to the music floating out, or to
sit for a time on the stone bench outside one of the larger
homes and watch the people flowing past like a river in
the night.

It wasn't so, however. Her movements were not, in the
end, random. Honest with herself, tonight and most
nights, Jehane knew where her steps were drawing her,
however slowly, by whatever meandering paths through
the city. She couldn't claim to be happy, or easy in her
soul about this, but her heartbeat grew steadily quicker,
and the doctor in her could diagnose that, at least, without difficulty.

She rose from a last bench, turned a corner and walked
down a street of handsome mansions near the palace.
Passing elegant, formal façades, she saw the door of one
house closing behind a man and a woman. She caught a
glimpse of a leash. That stirred a memory, but then it
drifted away.

And so it was that she found herself standing outside a
very large building. There were torches set along the wall
at intervals but very little ornament and the windows
above were all dark save for one, and she knew that room.

Jehane stood against a rough stone wall across the
street, oblivious now to the people passing by her in the
square, and gazed up at the highest level of that building,
towards the solitary light.

Someone was awake and alone, very late at night.

Someone was writing, on newly bought parchment. Not
ransom demands; letters home. Jehane looked up past the

smoke of the passing torches and those fixed in the walls, and struggled to accept and make sense of what lay within her heart. Overhead, shining along the street and down upon all the people in the square, the blue moon bathed the night in its glow. The sliver of the white moon had just risen. She had seen it by the water. She could not see it here. In the teachings of the Kindath, the white moon meant clarity; the blue one was mystery, secrets of the soul, complexities of need.

A small man, amusingly disguised beneath a blond wig and the thick yellow beard of a Karcher, staggered past her, carrying a long-legged woman in the veiled guise of a Muwardi from the desert. "Put me down!" the woman cried, unconvincingly, and laughed. They continued along the street, lit by torches and the moon, and turned the corner out of sight.

There would be a guard by the door of the barracks. Someone who had drawn one of the short straws and been posted, complaining, on duty for a part of tonight. Whoever it was, he would let her pass. They all knew her. She could identify herself and be allowed to enter. And then go up the first circling flight of stairs and then the second one, and then down a dark hallway to knock on that last door behind which a candle burned.

His voice would call out, not at all alarmed. She would say her name. There would be a silence. He would rise from his desk, from his letter home, and cross to open the door. Looking up into his grey eyes, she would step into his room and remove her mask, finally, and find, by the steady light of that candle...what?

Sanctuary? Shelter? A place to hide from the heart's truth of tonight and all nights?

Standing alone in the street, Jehane shook her head a little and then, quite unconsciously, gave the small shrug those who knew her best could always recognize.

She squared her shoulders and drew a deep breath. It was Carnival in Ragosa. A time for hiding from others, perhaps, but not from the self. It was important to have come here, she understood. To have stood gazing up at that window and pictured herself ascending a winding stair towards the man in that room. Important to acknowledge certain truths, however difficult. And then, having done so, it was as important to turn away and move on. Truly wandering now. Alone in the frenzy of the night streets, searching again—but, more truly, waiting to be found.

If, indeed, it was to happen. If, somewhere between moon and torchlight and dark, this would be.

As she stepped away from the stone wall and turned her back on that room with its pale glow of light far above, another figure also moved, detaching from shadow, following her.

And a third figure followed that one, unnoticed in the loud streets of Ragosa, as this dance, one among so many in the whirling night and the sad, sweet world, moved towards its beginning and its end.

She was outside the palace, watching two jugglers toss wheels of flame back and forth, when the voice from behind spoke to her.

"I believe you have my wine flask." The tones were low, muffled by a mask; even now, she wasn't entirely certain.

She turned. It was not the stag.

A lion stood before her, golden-maned, imperial. Jehane blinked and took a step backwards, bumping into someone. She had been reaching to her hip for the leather flask, now she let it fall again.

"You are deceived," she said. "I do have someone's flask, but it was a stag who left it with me."

"I have been a stag," the lion said, in oracular tones. The voice changed, "I can assure you I will never be one again."

Something in the inflection. Not to be mistaken. She knew, finally. And the hard, quick hammering was in her pulse.

"And why is that?" she asked, struggling to keep her voice steady. She was grateful for darkness, for fitful, passing light, for her own mask.

"Plays all havoc in doorways," said the lion. "And I ended up collecting ridiculous things on the horns, just walking. A hat. A flask. A torch once. Almost set myself on fire."

She laughed, in spite of herself.

The voice changed again. "It is late now, Jehane," said this man who seemed to have found her in the night after all. "It may even be too late, but shall we walk together a while, you and I?"

"How did you know me?" she asked, not answering the question, nor asking the harder one he'd invited. Not yet. Not quite yet. Her heart was loud. She felt it as a drumbeat in the dark.

"I think," said Ammar ibn Khairan of Aljais, very slowly, "that I should know you in a pitch black room. I think I would know you anywhere near me in the world." He paused. "Is that answer enough, Jehane? Or too much of one? Will you say?"

She heard, for the first time ever, uncertainty in his voice. And that, more than any other thing, was what made her tremble.

She asked, "Why might it be too late? The blue moon is still high. The night has a distance to run."

He shook his head. Left a silence. She heard laughter and applause behind her. The jugglers had done something new.

Ibn Khairan said, "My dear, I have been other things in my time, besides a stag at Carnival."

She understood. For all the wit and edge and irony, there was this grace to him, always, an allowance for her own intelligence. She said, honestly, "I know this, of course. It is a part of why I'm afraid."

"That is what I meant," he said simply.

All the stories. Through the years a young girl hearing, against her will, gossip by the well in Fezana, or at the shallow place by the river where the women washed their clothes. And then, a woman herself, home from studies abroad, hearing the same stories again. New names, new variations, the same man. Ibn Khairan of Aljais. Of Cartada.

Jehane looked at the man in the lion mask and felt something lodge, hard and painful, in the place where her heart was drumming.

He had killed the last khalif of Al-Rassan.

Behind the mask, in the flickering passage of torches all around where they were, she could just glimpse his eyes. They would be blue if he removed the disguise, if they stood in brighter light. She became aware that he was waiting for her to speak.

"Ought I to be afraid?" she asked, finally.

And he said, gravely, "No more than I, Jehane, in this."

Which was what she had needed to hear. Exactly what she needed, and Jehane, still wondering, still incredulous, took his hand in hers, saying, "Let us walk."

"Where would you like to go?" he asked, carefully, adjusting his stride to her pace.

"Where we can be alone," she said steadily, her grip firm, coming home at last to where her heart had been waiting since a summer's day in Fezana. "Where we can set aside owl and lion, apt as they might be, and be what we are."

"Flawed as we might be?" he asked.

"How otherwise?" she replied, discovering with surprise that her heartbeat had slowed the moment she had taken his hand. Something occurred to her, unexpectedly. She hesitated, and then, being what she was, asked, "Were you with me earlier, when I stopped outside the barracks?"

He didn't answer for a moment. At length he said, "Cleverest of women, you do your father and mother proud with every word you speak. Yes, I was there. I had already decided I could not approach you tonight before you made that choice on your own."

She shook her head, and gripped his hand more tightly. A thread of fear; she might so easily have gone up those stairs. "It wasn't the choice you may have thought it. It was a matter of hiding, or not."

"I know," he said. "Forgive me, my dear, but I know that."

His own honesty, risking her ruffled pride. But she did forgive him this, because the hiding had ended now, on a night of masks, and it was all right that he understood this. He had approached. He had found her.

They came to the house he leased. It was nearer the palace than the quarters she shared with Velaz. He opened the door to the street with his own key: the steward and servants had been dismissed for the night to their pleasures. They went inside.

On the street behind them, a figure watched them enter. He had been following Jehane, and he knew who the lion was. He hesitated, then decided it was all right to leave her now. He considered staying out for a while longer but decided against that. He was tired, and wasn't at all sure how he felt about the alleged delights of Carnival.

Ziri went back to the barracks, spoke briefly with the man on duty in the doorway, then went into the dormitory and to bed. He was asleep almost immediately, alone in the large room. All the others were still in the streets.

In Ammar ibn Khairan's house, the servants had left two torches burning to light the entrance hall, and there were candles in the wall sconces. Before going up the stairs they removed their masks and set them aside and Jehane saw his eyes by the burning of those lights.

This time it was he who stepped towards her and this time, when they kissed, it was not the same—not at all the same—as it had been in her father's room, by the open window the summer before.

And so she discovered that her heartbeat, which had steadied and slowed while they walked, wasn't quite so steady any longer, and the trembling had returned.

They went up the stairs, and they kissed again, slowly, outside his bedroom door, where a spill of candlelight showed in a line along the floor. She felt his hands around her, strong and sure, drawing her close. Desire was within her, an ache of need, deep and wide and strong as a river rising in the dark.

His mouth moved from hers, and went to one ear.

Softly he whispered, "*There is someone in my room. The candles would not have been left burning there.*"

Her heart thudded once, and seemed actually to stop for a moment before starting to beat again.

They had been silent ascending the stairs, and now here. Anyone in the bedroom would have heard the front door open, though, and known Ammar was in the house, alone or accompanied. She asked the question with her eyes only. His mouth came back to her ear. "They want me to know they're here. I have no idea. To be safe, go along to the next room. There's a balcony, shared with mine. Listen there. Be careful."

She nodded. "And you," she murmured, no more than a breath. "I want you healthy, after."

She felt his soundless laughter.

Afterwards, she would remember that: how utterly unafraid he had been. Diverted, intrigued, challenged, perhaps. But not at all frightened, or even disconcerted. She wondered what woman he had thought might be waiting. Or what man.

She went along the corridor. Opened the next door, silently passed within into a dark bedchamber. Just before she closed the door behind her, she heard Ammar call out, raising his voice, "Who is here? Why are you in my house?"

And then she heard the reply.

The door to the street would have been easy enough to unlock, and with the servants gone and candles helpfully burning it must have been no trick to find his bedroom.

Ibn Khairan, all his senses still oriented towards the feel and scent of the woman who had just slipped down the corridor, called out to the intruder, his mind struggling to sort through possibilities. Too many. Tonight and all nights there were too many people who might be waiting for him in his room.

Even so, even with twenty years of experience in such mysteries, he was not, in fact, prepared.

The door swung open, almost as soon as he called out.

A man stood there, unmasked, in the spill of candlelight from the room.

"*Finally*," said King Almalik II of Cartada, smiling. "I had begun to fear a journey wasted."

It took an extreme effort, all his celebrated poise, but ibn Khairan managed a return smile, and then a bow. "Good evening, 'Malik. My lord king. This is a surprise. A long journey, it must have been."

"Almost two weeks, Ammar. The roads were not good at all."

"Were you extremely uncomfortable?" Polite questions. Buying time for thoughts to begin to organize themselves. If Almalik of Cartada was taken in Ragosa, the balance of power in Al-Rassan would change, at a stroke.

"Tolerably." The young man who had been his protégé for three years smiled again. "You never allowed me to grow soft, and I haven't been king long enough for that to change." He paused, and Ammar saw, in that hesitation, that the king wasn't quite as composed as he might want to appear. "You understand that I could only do this tonight."

"I wouldn't have thought you could do it at all," ibn Khairan said frankly. "This is a rather extreme risk, 'Malik."

He found himself offering thanks to all possible deities that Jehane was out of sight, and praying she could keep quiet enough. Almalik could not possibly afford to be reported here, which meant that anyone who saw him was in mortal danger. Ibn Khairan deferred, for a moment, the question of where this left him.

He said, "I'd best join you inside."

The king of Cartada stepped back and Ammar walked into his own room. He registered the two Muwardis waiting there. There was an air of unreality to all of this. He was still trying to absorb the astonishing fact that Almalik had come here. But then, suddenly, as he turned to face the king, he grasped what this had to be about and disorientation spun away, to be replaced by something almost as unsettling.

"No one but you," said the king of Cartada quietly, "calls me 'Malik any more."

"Forgive me. Old habits. I'll stop, of course. Magnificence."

"I didn't say it offended me."

"No, but even if it doesn't...you *are* the king of Cartada."

"I am, aren't I?" Almalik murmured. He sank down into the northern-style armchair by the bed; a young man, not particularly graceful, but tall and well-made. "And, can you believe it, the first act of my reign, very nearly, was to exile the man I most needed."

Which made it all quite explicit.

He had not changed in this, ibn Khairan noted. A capacity for directness was something Almalik had always had, even as a boy. Ammar had never resolved within himself whether it marked a strength, or a tactic of the weak: forcing stronger friends to deal with his declared vulnerabilities. His eyelid was moving, but that was something one hardly noticed after a while.

"You hadn't even been crowned," ibn Khairan said softly.

He really wasn't prepared for this conversation. Not tonight. He had been readying himself, in an entirely different way, for something else. Had stood watching in the street, holding his breath like a boy, while Jehane bet Ishak had gazed upwards at a high, candlelit window, and he had only begun to breathe normally again when she gave the shrug he knew and moved on, a stillness seeming to wrap itself about her amid the tumult of the night.

He had never thought it might require courage to approach a woman.

"I am surprised to find you alone," Almalik said, a little too lightly.

"You shouldn't be," ibn Khairan murmured, being careful now. "Tonight's encounters lack a certain...refinement, wouldn't you say?"

"I wouldn't know, Ammar. It seemed lively enough. We spent some time looking for you, and then I realized it was hopeless. It was easier to buy the location of your house and wait."

"Did you really come to Ragosa expecting to find me in the streets at Carnival?"

"I came here because I could see no other way to speak with you quickly enough. I had only hope, and need, when we set out. There is no company of men with me, by the way. These two, and half a dozen others for safety on the road. No one else. I have come to say certain things. And to ask you to come back to me."

Ibn Khairan was silent. He had been waiting for this, and latterly, had been afraid of it. He had been the guardian and mentor of this man, the named heir to Cartada's throne. Had put a great deal of effort into making of Almalik ibn Almalik a man worthy of power. He did not like admitting failure. He wasn't even certain he *had* failed. This was going to be ferociously difficult.

He crossed to the sideboard, deliberately brushing past one of the Muwardis. The man did not move, or even spare a glance. They hated him; all of them did. His whole life was a sustained assault upon their grim piety. It was a sentiment he returned: *their* way of life—single-minded faith, single-minded hatred—affronted all his sensibilities, his perception of what life ought to be.

"Will you take a glass of wine?" he asked the king of Cartada, deliberately provoking the Muwardis. Unworthy, perhaps, but he couldn't help this.

Almalik shrugged, nodded his head. Ibn Khairan poured for both of them and carried the glasses over. They saluted each other, top of glass touching bottom, then bottom to top.

"It took courage for you to do this," Ammar said. It was right that he acknowledge this.

Almalik shook his head, looking up at him from the chair. In the candlelight it could be seen how young he still was. And standing more closely now, ibn Khairan could see the marks of strain.

"It took only an awareness that if you do not return I

do not know what I will do. And I understand you very well, Ammar, in some things. What was I to do? Write you pleading letters? You would not have come. You know you would not."

"Surely the king of Cartada is surrounded by men of wisdom and experience?"

"Now you are jesting. Do not."

Quick anger flared, surprising him. Before it could be suppressed, ibn Khairan snapped, "It was you who exiled me. Be so good as to remember that, 'Malik."

A raw wound: the pupil turning upon the teacher in the moment of shared ascendancy. An old story, in truth, but he had never thought it would happen to him. First the father, and then the son.

"I do remember it," Almalik said quietly. "I made a mistake, Ammar."

Weakness or strength, it had always been hard to tell. This trait might even be, at different times, a sign of both. The father had never, in twenty years together, admitted to an error.

"Not all mistakes can be undone." He was stalling, waiting for something to make this clearer for him. Behind, beneath all these words lay a decision that had to be made.

Almalik stood up. "I know that, of course. I am here in the hope that this was not one such. What is it you want, Ammar? What must I say?"

Ibn Khairan looked at him a moment before answering. "What is it I want? To write in peace, I could answer, but that would be dissembling, wouldn't it? To live my life with a measure of honor, and be seen by the world to be doing so. That would be true enough, and that, incidentally, is why I had to kill your father."

"I *know* that. I know it better than anyone." The king hesitated. "Ammar, I believe the Jaddites will be coming south this summer. My brother is with Yazir ibn Q'arif in the desert, still. We have learned they are building ships. In Abeneven. And I don't know what King Badir intends."

"So you tried to kill the boys?"

Almalik blinked. It was an unfair thrust, but he was a clever man, very much his father's son. He said, "Those two men weren't killed in a tavern brawl, then? I wondered about that." The king shrugged. "Am I the first ruler in Al-Rassan to try to strengthen himself by dealing with siblings? Were you not my teacher of history, Ammar?"

Ibn Khairan smiled. "Did I criticize?"

Almalik flushed suddenly. "But you stopped them. You saved the boys. Zabira's sons."

"Others did. I was a small part of it. I am exiled here, Almalik, remember? I have signed a contract in Ragosa, and have been honoring it."

"With my enemies!" A young man's voice now, the control slipping, a boy's words.

Ibn Khairan felt something twist within him like a soft blade. He knew this part of the man. Of the king. He said, "It seems we live in a world where boundaries are shifting all the time. This makes it more difficult for a man to do what is right."

"Ammar, no. Your place is in Cartada. You have *always* served Cartada, striven for it." He hesitated, then set down his glass and said, "You killed a khalif for my father, can you not at least come home for me?"

It seemed that with understanding there so often came sadness. This one was measuring himself, still, against a dead man, just as he had when his father lived. He would probably do this all his life, whether long or short. Testing. Comparing allotments of love. Demanding to be cared for as much, and more.

It occurred to ibn Khairan, for the first time, to wonder how the young king had reacted to the lament Ammar had written for his father. *Where lesser beasts now gather...* He also realized, in that same moment, that Zabira had been right: 'Malik would not have suffered the concubine who had loved his father to live.

"I don't know," he said, answering the question. "I do not know where my place is now."

Somewhere inside him though, even as he spoke those

words, a voice was saying: *This is a lie, though once it might have been true. There is something new. The world can change, so can you. The world has changed.* And in his mind, amazingly, he could hear her name, as if in the sound of bells. There was a momentary wonder that no one else in the room seemed to notice this.

He went on, straining to concentrate. "May I take it that this visit is intended to convey a rescinding of my exile and an invitation to return to my position?"

He made his words deliberately formal, to pull them back from the raw place where the king's question had taken them. *Can you not come home for me?*

The young king opened his mouth and closed it. There was hurt in his eyes. He said, stiffly, "You may take it as such."

"What position, precisely."

Another hesitation. Almalik had not been prepared for a negotiating session. That was fine. Ammar had not been prepared for any of this.

"Chancellor of Cartada. Of course."

Ibn Khairan nodded. "And your formally declared successor, pending marriage and legitimate heirs?" The thought—monstrous thought!—had only come to him in this moment.

One of the Muwardis shifted by the fireplace. Ibn Khairan turned and looked at him. The man's eyes locked on his this time, black with hatred. Ammar smiled affably and drank slowly from his glass without looking away.

Almalik II of Cartada said, softly, "Is this your condition, Ammar? Is it wise?"

Of course it wasn't wise. It was sheerest folly.

"I doubt it," ibn Khairan said carelessly. "Leave that in reserve. Have you begun negotiations for a marriage?"

"Some overtures have been made to us, yes." Almalik's tone was awkward.

"You had best accept one of them soon. Killing children is less useful than begetting them. What have you done about Valledo?"

The king picked up his glass again and drained it before answering. "I am receiving useless advice, Ammar. They agonize, they wring their hands. They advise doubling the *parias*, then delaying it, then refusing it! I took some measures of my own to stir up Ruenda and...we have a man there, do you remember him?"

"Centuro d'Arrosa. Your father bought him years ago. What of him?"

"I instructed him to do whatever he had to do to cause a mortal breach between Ruenda and Valledo. You know they were all to be meeting this spring. They may have done so by now."

Thoughtfully, ibn Khairan said, "King Ramiro doesn't need his brother's aid to menace you."

"No, but what if he is induced to ride against Ruenda, instead of against me?" Almalik's expression was that of a schoolboy who thinks he has passed a test.

"What have you done?"

King Almalik smiled. "Is it my loyal chancellor who asks?"

After a moment, ibn Khairan returned the smile. "Fair enough. What about Fezana itself, then? Defenses?"

"As best we can. Food storage for half a year. Some of the walls repaired, though money is an issue, as you will know. The additional soldiers in the new wing of the castle. I have allowed the wadjis to stir up anger against the Kindath."

Ammar felt a coldness as if a wind had come into the room. A woman was hearing this, out on the balcony.

"Why that?" he asked, very quietly.

Almalik shrugged. "My father used to do the same thing. The wadjis need to be kept happy. They inspire the people. In a siege that will matter. And if they do push some of the Kindath out, or kill a few, a siege will be easier to withstand. That seems obvious to me."

Ibn Khairan said nothing. The king of Cartada looked at him, a close, suspicious glance. "It has been reported to me that you spent time on the Day of the Moat with a

Kindath physician. A woman. Was there a reason?"

It seemed that answers to the hardest questions life offered might come in unexpected ways. In the strangest fashion, that cold, narrowed gaze came as a relief to ibn Khairan. A reminder of what had always kept him from truly loving the boy who had become this man, despite a number of reasons for doing so.

"You had my movements traced?"

The king of Cartada was unfazed. "You were the one who taught me that all information helped. I wanted you back. I was searching for ways to achieve it."

"And spying out my activities seemed a good method of enlisting my willing aid?"

"Aid," said the king of Cartada, "can come for many reasons and in many guises. I could have kept this a secret from you, Ammar. I have not. I am here in Ragosa, trusting you. Now your turn: *was* there a reason, Ammar?"

Ibn Khairan snorted. "Did I want to bed her, you mean? Come on, 'Malik. I went to find that doctor because she was the physician of someone invited to the ceremony. A man who said he was too ill to come. I had no idea who she was until later. She was, incidentally, Ishak ben Yonannon's daughter. You'll know that by now. Does it mean anything to you?"

Almalik nodded. "My father's physician. I remember him. They blinded him when Zabira's last child was born."

"And cut out his tongue."

The king shrugged again. "We have to keep the wadjis happy, don't we? Or if not happy, at least not preaching against us in the streets. They wanted the Kindath doctor to die. My father surprised me then, I remember." Almalik gestured suddenly with both hands. "Ammar, I have no weapons against you here. I don't *want* a weapon. I want *you* as my sword. What must I do?"

This had gone on too long, ibn Khairan realized. It was painful, and there was greater danger the longer it lasted. He carried no blade either, save the usual one taped to his left arm. However calm Almalik seemed, he was a man

who could be pushed to rashness, and the Muwardi tribesmen would dance under the desert stars if they learned
that Ammar ibn Khairan of Aljais had died.

He said, "Let me think on this, 'Malik. I have a contract
that ends at the beginning of autumn. Honor may be
served by then."

"By autumn? You swear it? I will have you—"

"I said, let me think. That is all I will say."

"And what should I do in the meantime?"

Ibn Khairan's mouth quirked with amusement. He
couldn't help it. He was a man who found many things in
life inexpressibly ironic. "You want me to tell you how to
govern Cartada? Here and now? In this room, during
Carnival?"

After a moment, Almalik laughed, and shook his head.
"You would not believe how badly I am served, Ammar."

"Then find better men! They exist. All over Al-Rassan.
Put your labors into that."

"And into what else?"

Ibn Khairan hesitated. Old habits died very hard. "You
are probably right: Fezana is in danger. Whether the Jaddite
army in Batiara sails this spring or not, there is a changed
mood in the north. And if you lose Fezana, I do not think
you can hold your dais. The wadjis will not allow it."

"Or the Muwardis," said Almalik, with a glance at the
guards in the room. The veiled ones remained impassive.
"I have already done one further thing about this. Tonight,
actually, here in Ragosa. You will approve."

Odd, odd and sometimes frightening, how a lifetime's
instincts could put the soldier in one on such instanta-
neous alert.

"Approve of what?" he asked, keeping his voice calm.

Later, he would realize that he had somehow known,
though, even before the king of Cartada answered him.

"As I told you, six others came with me. I've had them
find and kill the Valledan mercenary Belmonte. He is too
dangerous to be permitted to go back to King Ramiro from
his own exile. It seems he never left his room tonight; they

know where he is, and there is only one guard at the street door." Almalik of Cartada smiled. "It is a useful blow, Ammar. I hurt Badir and Ramiro both, very badly, by taking this man away from them."

And me, Ammar ibn Khairan was thinking then, but did not say. *And me. Very badly.*

They had defeated five men together, in a display last autumn. Rodrigo would have been alone tonight, however, and not expecting an assault. There were people costumed as Muwardis all over the city. Six silent killers, one frustrated guard at the street door. He could picture how it would have been. It would be over by now.

Even so, there were things one did, movements shaped without actual thought. The drive towards action as a blocking of pain. Even as the king of Cartada finished speaking, ibn Khairan had spun back to the door of his room, and was pulling it open. As he did so, in the same smooth movement, he ducked down low, so the blade thrown at his back embedded itself instead in the dark wood of the door.

Then he was out, running down the corridor, taking the stairs three and then four at a time, knowing that if Almalik had told him about this it was much too late already, but running, running.

Even in his haste, he remembered to do one thing before hurtling out the door and back into the street.

"Fool!" Jehane heard the king of Cartada shout. "What were you doing with that knife? I want him *with* us, you worm!"

"He will not be."

The other man, the Muwardi, had a desert accent and a voice deep as an old grave. She could see none of them. Just out of sight on the double balcony, Jehane felt a grief heavy as a smith's anvil pulling on her heart. She clenched her fists, nails biting into palms. She could do nothing. She had to wait for them to leave. She wanted to scream.

"He *will* come back," she heard the young king rasp.

"He is upset about the Valledan, a comrade-at-arms. I thought he might be, but ibn Khairan is not a man who makes decisions based on such things. He would have been the first to *tell* me to plan a stroke such as this."

"He will not be with you," the other man said again, blunt, quiet, sure.

There was a short silence.

"Kill this man," said Almalik II of Cartada calmly. "This is a command. You were under orders not to harm ibn Khairan. These orders were violated with that blade. Execute him. Now."

Jehane caught her breath. Then, more quickly than she could have imagined, she heard a grunting sound. Someone fell.

"Good," she heard the king of Cartada say, after a moment. "At least some of you are loyal. Leave his body. I want Ammar to know I had him killed." Jehane heard footsteps. The king's voice came from farther away. "Come. It is time to leave Ragosa. I have done what I could. We can do nothing but wait on Ammar now."

"You can kill him," the second Muwardi said in a soft, uninflected tone. "If he refuses you, why should he be permitted to live?"

The king of Cartada made no reply.

A moment later, Jehane heard them going out, and then down the stairs.

She waited until she heard the front door open and close again, and then she raced to follow—through the second bedroom, and out into the corridor. She spared one quick glance into Ammar's chamber. There was a man lying on the floor. The doctor in her compelled a pause; for too many years this had been an instinct. She rushed in, knelt beside him, felt for a heartbeat. He was, of course, dead. No blade remained, but the wound was in his throat. The Muwardis knew how to kill.

Rodrigo would have been at his desk. Writing a letter home. Expecting carousing friends, if any knock had come.

Jehane scrambled to her feet and sped down the stairs

into the entranceway. She looked for her mask on the small table. It was not there. She froze.

Then she understood. Ammar had taken it: that the Cartadans not see an owl mask and surmise the presence of a woman here. For all she knew, King Almalik might even have understood the symbol of the owl as physician: he had been Ammar's pupil, hadn't he?

Which was a part of the grief that now lay like a stone at the center of a spinning night. She pushed open the door and ran out, unmasked now, into the roiling street. She began forcing her way through the crowd towards the barracks. Someone groped for her, playfully. Jehane twisted away and kept moving. It was difficult, people were everywhere, amid torches and smoke. It took her a long time to get through.

Afterwards, she realized that it was the silence that had warned her.

When she came back into the square before the barracks, she saw that the huge crowd had grown unnaturally still and had forced itself back towards the perimeter of the square, away from a place where someone lay on the ground.

By the torches and the one moon, she saw Ammar standing there, unmasked, ashen-faced, with a number of other men she knew extremely well. She pushed her way through the murmuring onlookers and knelt beside the wounded man on the cobblestones. It only took one glance. It was too late for a doctor's art here. Heartsick, too shocked to speak, she began, helplessly, to weep.

"*Jehane,*" whispered the dying man. His eyes had opened and were locked on hers. "Jehane...I...so very..."

She put her fingers gently to his lips. Then laid her hand against his cheek. There was a Muwardi knife embedded in his chest, and a hideous, pouring sword wound deep in his collarbone, and that was what was going to kill him.

A moment later, it did. She watched him reach for a last, inadequate breath and then close his eyes, as if in weariness. This was one of the ways men died. She had seen it so many times. Her fingers were still against his cheek when he went away from all of them, to whatever lay in wait beyond the dark.

"My dear," she said, brokenly. "Oh, my dear."

Was it always like this? That one thought of all the things one so much wanted to say, endlessly too late?

Above her the circle of soldiers parted. Someone passed between them and sank to his knees on the other side of the body, heedless of the dark blood soaking the cobblestones. He was breathing quickly, as if he'd been running. Jehane didn't look up, but then she saw him reach forward and take the dead man by the hand.

"May there be light waiting for you," she heard him say, very softly. "More and gentler light than any of us can dream or imagine."

She did look up then, through her tears.

"Oh, Jehane," said Rodrigo Belmonte. "I am so sorry. This should never have happened. He saved my life."

∽

At some point, with all the unmixed wine he had drunk, and the heady smell of incense burning in the room, and the many-colored candles everywhere, and the useful pillows on bed and woven carpet, and the extraordinary ways it seemed that a slender golden leash could be used, Alvar lost track of time and place.

He moved with this unknown woman, and upon her, and at times beneath her urgency. They had removed their masks when they entered the house. It didn't matter: she was still a hunting cat tonight, whatever she was by daylight in the customary round of the year. He had raking scratches down his body, as if to prove it. With some dismay he realized that she did, too. He couldn't remember doing that. Then, a little later, he realized he was doing it again. They were standing, coupled, bending forward against the bed then.

"I don't even know your name," he gasped, later, on the carpet before the fire.

"And why should that matter tonight, in any possible way?" she had replied.

Her fingers were long, the painted nails sharp. She was wondrously skilled with her hands, among other things. She had green eyes and a wide mouth. He gathered, through various signs, that he was giving pleasure as well as taking it.

Some time afterwards she chose to blow out all the candles and leash him in a particularly intimate fashion. They went out together, naked, with the marks of their lovemaking on both of them, to stand on the dark balcony one level above the teeming square.

She leaned against the waist-high balustrade and guided him into her from behind. Alvar was almost convinced by then that something had been put into his wine. He ought to have been exhausted by this point.

The night breeze was cool. His skin felt feverish, unnaturally sensitive. He could see past her, look down upon the crowd. Music and cries and laughter came up from below and it was as if they were hovering here, their movements almost a part of the dancing, weaving throng in the street. He had never imagined that lovemaking in such an exposed fashion could be so exhilarating. It was, though. He would be a liar to deny it. He might want to deny many things tomorrow, Alvar thought suddenly, but he was not capable of doing so just now.

"Only think," she whispered, tilting her head far back to whisper to him. "If any of them were to look up...what they would see."

He felt her tug a little on the leash. He had put it about her, earlier. It was on him again. Very much so. His hands, which had been gripping the balustrade beside her, came up and encircled her small breasts. A man was playing a five-stringed lute directly below them. A ring of dancing figures surrounded him. In the center of the ring a peacock was dancing. The peacock was Husari ibn Musa.

"What do you think?" Alvar heard, tongue at his ear again, the long neck arched backwards. So much like a cat.

"Shall we bring a torch out here and carry on?"

He thought of Husari looking up, and winced. But he didn't think he was going to be able to deny this woman anything tonight. And he knew, without yet having tested the limits of it, that she would refuse him nothing he might ask of her between now and dawn. He didn't know which thought excited or frightened him more. What he did know, finally understanding, was that this was the dark, dangerous truth at the heart of the Carnival. For this one night, all the rules of the circling year were changed.

He drew a long breath before answering her. He looked up from the crowd below them to the night sky: only the one moon, blue among the stars.

Still within her, moving steadily in their merging rhythms, Alvar looked down again, away from the distant lights in the sky to the nearer ones lit by mortal men and women to chase away the dark.

Across the square, between torches set into the wall of the barracks, he saw Rodrigo Belmonte falling.

∽

He had indeed been sitting at the writing desk, parchment before him, ink and quills, a glass of dark wine at one elbow, trying to think of what more there was to say—of tidings, counsels, apprehensions, need.

He was not the sort of man who could write to his wife about how much he longed to have her in this room with him. How he would unbind her hair, strand by strand, and slip his arms about her and draw her near, after so long. Allow his hands to travel, and then, his own clothing gone, how they might...

He could not write these things. He could think them, however, a kind of punishment. He could sit alone at night in a high room and listen to the sounds of revelry drifting up through the open window and he could picture Miranda in his mind, and imagine her here now, and feel weak with his desire.

He had made a promise years before, and had renewed

it over and again—to her, but more to himself. He was not the kind of man who broke promises. He defined himself, in large part, by that. A man found his honor, Rodrigo Belmonte thought—and his self-respect, and certainly pride—on many different kinds of battlefield. He was on one, or hovering above one, tonight in Ragosa. He didn't write that to Miranda, either.

He picked up a quill again and dipped it into the black ink and prepared to resume: something for the boys, he thought, to take his mind from these unsettling channels.

The boys. Love there, too, sword-sharp; fear and pride as well. Almost men now. Too soon. Riding with him? Would that be best? He thought of the old outlaw Tarif ibn Hassan, in that echoing valley. A cunning, ferocious giant of a man. He had thought about him often since that day in the Emin ha'Nazar. Two sons there, as well. Kept beside him. Both of them fine men, capable and decent, though the one had lost his leg now, which was a misfortune. Alive though, thanks to Jehane. No longer young, either of them. And neither, it could be seen, would ever break free of the father's wide shade into his own defining sunlight, to cast his own shadow. Not even after Tarif died. It could be seen.

Would he do that to Fernan and Diego?

He became aware that he had been holding the pen for a long time over the smooth pale parchment. Writing nothing. Chasing thoughts. The ink had dried. He laid the quill down again.

There came a knocking at his door.

Later, tracking events backwards, he would realize what had put him—very slightly—on the alert.

He had not heard footsteps. Any of his own company come calling—as many of them had promised, or threatened, to do—would have warned him by their noisy progression up the stairs and along the corridor. The Muwardis were too schooled to silence. The stillness of the desert, at night under stars.

Even so, it was only a partial warning, because he *had* been expecting some of the men to come up tonight, with more wine, and stories from the streets. He'd even been wondering, feeling a little sorry for himself, what was taking them so long.

So he called out an easy greeting, and pushed his chair back, rising to let them in.

And the door burst open.

He had no weapon to hand: his sword and the rancher's whip lay across the room, by the bed where he always left them. Moving by sheerest instinct, triggered by that half-doubt at the back of his mind, he twisted desperately away from the first flung dagger. He felt it graze his arm. In the same wrenching motion he seized and hurled the candle from the desk into the face of the first man into the room.

There were two more behind that one, he had time to see. The sword was hopeless; he would never get to it.

He heard a cry of pain, but he had already turned. Hurtling straight over the desk, expecting a knife in his back any moment, Rodrigo Belmonte went out the open window.

The third-floor window. Much too far above the ground for a man to survive a fall to the street.

He had no intention of falling.

Laín had taught him a trick years and years ago. Whenever he spent a night in a room well above the ground, whether in castle or palace or barracks hall, Rodrigo would hammer a spike into the wall outside his window and tie a length of rope to that spike. A way out. He always wanted a way out. It had saved his life twice. Once here in Al-Rassan, with Raimundo in the time of exile, once on the Jaloñan campaign.

He gripped the window ledge as he went through, and used that grip to turn his body to where he knew the rope to be. He let go of the ledge and reached for it.

The rope wasn't there.

Rodrigo fell, knees scraping along the wall. Even as he plummeted, fighting a blind panic, he realized that they must have scouted the location of his room earlier, while he was out, dining with the company. Someone with extremely good eyesight, and equally good with a bow, had shot and severed the coiled rope.

Figuring this out did nothing whatsoever to break his fall.

Something else did: the fact that Laín Nunez—with the privileges of age and rank—had taken the corner room directly below him, and had done the same thing outside his own chamber.

They hadn't bothered to shoot the lower rope. Hurtling down between moon and torches, Rodrigo reached out as he saw Laín's window rush up towards him and he clutched for, and found, the rope tied to a spike outside it.

It tore through his hands, shredding his palms. But it held, and he held on at the bottom, though his shoulders were almost pulled from their sockets. He ended up swinging back and forth between two torches on the barracks wall, one flight above the crowded square. No one seemed even to have noticed.

Or, no one not actually watching for him from below.

Rodrigo took a knife in the left arm, flung up from the street. No chance to quietly maneuver into a first-floor room. He let go, jerking the Muwardi dagger out as he fell. He landed hard, rolling immediately—and so went under the sword sweeping at him.

He rolled again on the cobblestones and then was up and spinning. A veiled Muwardi appeared before him, sword up. Rodrigo feinted left and then cut back the other way. The descending blade missed him, striking sparks on the stones. Rodrigo pivoted, swinging his knife at the back of the Muwardi's head. It sank into his neck. The man grunted and toppled over. Rodrigo grappled for the sword.

He ought to have died in that moment.

For all his celebrated prowess, his valor and experience, he ought to have died and left the world of men to meet his god behind the sun.

He was armed with only a knife, wounded already, and without armor. The assassins in the square had been hand-picked from among the desert warriors in Cartada for the task of killing him.

He would have died in Ragosa that night, had someone in that square not looked up to see him falling along the wall, and known him, and reacted to the sight of an upward-flung dagger in the night.

The third Muwardi, rushing up as Belmonte reached for that life-preserving sword, had his weapon out and slashing to kill.

His blade was intercepted and deflected by a wooden stave. The Muwardi swore, righted himself and received a hard blow on the shin from the staff. He wheeled, ignoring pain as a warrior had to and, raising the sword high, towards the holy stars, brought it sweeping downwards against the accursed interloper.

The man before him, alert and balanced, moved to parry this. The stave came up, crosswise, in precisely the right fashion. It was light wood, though, only part of a Carnival costume, and the descending Muwardi sword was real as death. The blade sheared through the staff as if it wasn't there and bit deep into the intruder's collarbone in the same moment that another dagger, flung by the third of the assassins, sank into the man's breast.

The nearer Muwardi grunted with satisfaction, ripped his sword roughly free, and died.

Rodrigo Belmonte, with that moment's respite granted—one of those moments that defined, with precision, the narrow space between living and lying dead on stone— had a Muwardi blade in his hand and a black rage in his heart.

He drove the sword straight into the chest of the Muwardi, tore it out, and turned to confront the third man. Who did not run, or visibly quail, though there was reason now to do both. They were brave men, however. Whatever else there was to say about them, the warriors of the sands were as courageous in battle as any men who walked the earth. They had been promised Paradise if they died with a weapon in hand.

The two swords met with a grinding and then a quick, clattering sound. A woman suddenly screamed, and then a man did the same. The crowd around them began frantically spilling away from this abrupt, lethal violence.

It didn't last long. The Muwardi had been chosen for his skill in causing other men to die, but he was facing Rodrigo Belmonte of Valledo on even terms in a cleared space, and Belmonte had not been bested in single combat since he crossed out of boyhood.

Another clanging of metal, as Belmonte drove hard for the other man's knees. The Muwardi parried, retreated. Rodrigo feinted on the backhand, high, moving forward with a long stride. Then he dropped swiftly, unexpectedly, to one knee and slashed his sword into the Muwardi's thigh. The man cried out, staggered sideways, and died as the sword bit a second time, cleanly in his throat.

Rodrigo turned, without pausing. He saw what he had expected to see: three more of them—the ones who had burst into his room—racing out the door of the barracks, fanning apart. He knew that whichever of his men had drawn the short straw for this watch was dead in that doorway. He didn't know who it had been.

The deaths of his men enraged him beyond any words.

He went forward to meet these three alone, to slake rage with retribution, grief with hard and deadly movement. He *did* know who had died, behind him in the square, saving his life. Rage, a great grief. He moved to face the assassins.

Others were there before him.

An entirely naked man, with something trailing along the ground from his waist, had seized the sword of one of the fallen Muwardis. He was already engaging the first of the new ones. From the other side, the spectacle of a peacock wielding a shepherd's crook presented itself. Even as Rodrigo ran forward he saw the peacock bring that crook down from behind upon the head of one of the Muwardis. The desert warrior crumpled like a child's soft toy. The peacock scarcely hesitated: he brought the staff savagely down again on the fallen man's skull.

The naked man—and now Rodrigo realized it was Alvar de Pellino, and that the trailing object was not, in fact, tied to his waist—faced his Muwardi, crashing straight into him, screaming at the top of his voice as he drove the man back. He began dealing and receiving swordstrokes, heedless of his naked vulnerability. Rodrigo, sprinting past them towards the last man, gave Alvar's foe a quick slash to the back of the calf. This was battle, not courtly display. The man made a high-pitched sound, fell, and Alvar killed him with a stroke.

The last man was Rodrigo's.

Again he was brave, no hint of surrender or flight. Again he was skilled with his sword, defiant in his aggression, seeing the man he had come here to kill standing alone before him. None of these things extended his tenure on life under the blue moon or the torches or the stars he worshipped. Belmonte was enraged, and his fury was always cold and controlling in battle. The sixth Muwardi fell to a heavy, driving, backhand stroke to his collarbone—very much, in fact, like the blow that had killed the man with the staff.

It was over. As so many such battles had ended through the years—seemingly as swiftly as it had begun. He had an extreme facility for combat such as this. It defined him, this skill, in the eyes of the world in which he lived. In which he still lived, though he should have died tonight.

Rodrigo turned, breathing rapidly, and looked towards Alvar and the peacock, who turned out, improbably, to be Husari. Ibn Musa had torn off his mask and stood, white-faced, over the body of the man he'd just clubbed to death. First killing. A new thing for him.

Alvar, in the stillness after combat, seemed to become aware of his condition—and his sole item of golden adornment. In any other circumstance at all Rodrigo would have laughed in delight.

There was no laughter in him. In any of them. A number of the other men of the company were hurrying up.

One of them, without comment, threw Alvar his own cloak. Alvar wrapped himself in it and untied the leash.

"You are all right?"

It was Martín, speaking to Rodrigo, eyeing him closely.

Belmonte nodded. "Nothing to speak of."

He said no more, walking past them all, six dead Muwardis and the men of his company and the milling, frightened people in the square.

He came to where Laín Nunez crouched beside the small figure that lay breathing shallowly on the stones, his life seeping away from the deep wound in his throat. Laín had folded his cloak as a pillow for the fallen man. Ludus had seized a torch and was holding it above them. Someone else brought up another light.

Rodrigo took one glance, and then had to close his eyes for a moment. He had seen this many times; it ought to have become easier by now. It never had. Not with people you knew. He knelt on the blood-soaked stones and gently slipped off the token eye-mask the little man had worn as a concession to the rites of Ragosa's Carnival.

"Velaz," he said.

And found he couldn't say anything more. This was not—it was so profoundly not—the proper ending for such a man as this. He ought not to be dying here, with a knife in his chest and this hideous, pouring wound. The *wrongness* of it was appalling.

"They...dead?" The dying man's eyes were open; fierce, clear, fighting pain.

"All of them. You saved my life. What words can I say to you?"

Velaz swallowed, tried to speak again, then had to wait as a hard high wave of pain crashed over him.

"Care...her," he whispered. "Please?"

Rodrigo felt sorrow threaten to overwhelm him. This oldest, endless sorrow of mankind, and new every single time. Of *course* this would be what Velaz of Fezana needed to ask before he died. How did the world in which they lived cause such things as this to happen? Why hadn't

Laín, or Ludus, Martín...any of a dozen soldiers...been nearest when Rodrigo fell to the ground among enemies? Any one of so many men who would have been bitterly mourned, but whose death in this fashion could have been seen as something embedded—a known and courted risk—in the life they had chosen?

"We will take care of her," he said quietly. "On my oath. She will be cherished, as you cherished her."

Velaz nodded his head, satisfied. Even that small movement caused a pumping of blood in his terrible wound.

He closed his eyes again. There was no color in his face at all. He said, eyes still closed, "Can...find?"

And this, too, Rodrigo understood. "I will. I'll find her for you."

He rose then, and strode away, blood soaking his clothes, moving swiftly, purposefully, to try to do a thing that was, in fact, beyond him or any man that night: to find a single, masked woman in the careening dark of Carnival.

Which is why he was not in the square, but hammering at the door of her house and then doubling back through the streets, shouting her name at the top of his voice in a world of noise and laughter, when first Ammar and then Jehane herself came running up, fearing to find Rodrigo dead, only to discover it was Velaz lying on the stones under torches held by silent soldiers.

∽

Jehane had never realized how much affection had been won from a company of Valledan soldiers by the little man who had served her father and then herself all these years. It ought not, perhaps, to have been such a surprise. Military men recognized competence and inner strength and loyalty, and Velaz had embodied these things.

Alvar, in particular, was taking this death very badly, almost blaming himself for it. It appeared that he had been the second man to arrive when Rodrigo was attacked. Jehane didn't know where he'd come from, but she gathered he'd been with a woman not far away.

Her thinking wasn't really very clear. The night was nearly done. The thin crescent of the white moon was overhead now, but there already appeared to be a hint of grey through the open windows east. They were in the barracks, the dining room on the ground floor. The streets seemed quieter now, but that may have been an illusion, behind these walls. Jehane wanted to tell Alvar there was nothing inappropriate about having been with a woman at Carnival, but she couldn't seem to be able to manage any words yet.

Someone—Husari, she thought—had brought her a cup of something warm. She gripped it in both hands, shivering. Someone else had draped a cloak over her. Another cloak lay over Velaz, on one of the tables not far away. A third covered the soldier who had died in the doorway when the Muwardis burst in. The door had been unlocked. It seemed he had been watching the dancing in the square.

She had been crying, off and on, for a long time. She felt numb, hollow, light-headed. Very cold, even beneath the cloak. In her mind she tried to begin a letter to her mother and father...and then stopped. The process of forming those necessary words threatened to make her weep again.

He had been a part of the world all her life; if not at the very center, then never far away. He had not ever, as best she knew, done a violent or a hurtful thing to any man or woman until tonight when he had attacked a Muwardi warrior and saved Rodrigo's life.

That made her remember, much too late, something else. She looked over and saw that Rodrigo's wounds were being cleaned and dressed by Laín Nunez. *I ought to be doing that*, a part of her said inwardly, but she couldn't have. She could not have done it tonight.

She realized that Ammar had come up and was crouched on his heels beside her. She also realized, belatedly, that it was his cloak she was wearing. He looked at her searchingly, then took her hand, not speaking. How to comprehend that this same night they had kissed? And he had said certain things that opened up new horizons in the world.

Then the king of Cartada.

Then Velaz on the cobblestones.

She had not told anyone about Almalik. A man she loved was here—she could use that word now in her mind, admit it to herself—and that part of this night's dark spinning was his to tell, or to preserve in silence.

She had heard enough from the balcony to understand a little of what lay between Ammar and the young, frightened king of Cartada. The king who had nonetheless been calculating enough to send killers from the desert after Rodrigo Belmonte. He had also ordered the execution of the warrior who'd thrown a blade at Ammar. There was something complex and hurtful here.

She could not seek her vengeance for Velaz by setting these men on the track of the Cartadan king. It was Rodrigo he had tried to kill, and mercenary soldiers, passing back and forth across the *tagra* lands and the boundaries of Jad and Ashar, lived lives that made that likely, even probable.

Velaz had not. Velaz ben Ishak—he had taken her father's name when he adopted the Kindath faith—had lived a life that ought to have ended in a kind and cared-for old age. Not on a table in a barracks hall with that sword wound in his neck.

It occurred to Jehane then—in the dreamy way thoughts were coming—that she, too, had decisions to make in the days that lay ahead. The divided loyalties were not only Ammar's or Rodrigo's. She was physician to a band of Valledan mercenaries and to the court of Ragosa. She was also a citizen of Fezana, in Cartadan lands. Her home was there and her family. It was her own king, in fact, who was riding away from these walls tonight, with one companion only on a dangerous journey home. The man he had ordered killed was a Valledan, a Jaddite enemy, the Scourge of Al-Rassan.

A man who might, through his valor and his company's,

achieve the conquest of her own city if he were to rejoin King Ramiro and the assault upon Fezana became a reality. The Jaddites of Esperaña had burned the Kindath, or enslaved them. The island tomb of Queen Vasca remained a place of holiest pilgrimage.

Ammar was holding her hand. Husari came back. His eyes were red-rimmed. She lifted her free hand and he took it in his. Good men all around her in this room; decent, caring men. But the most decent, the most caring, the one who had loved her from the day she was born, was dead on a table under a soldier's cloak.

Somewhere within her grieving soul Jehane experienced a tremor then, an apprehension of pain to come. The world of Esperaña, of Al-Rassan, seemed to her to be rushing headlong towards something vast and terrible, and the deaths of Velaz and of Rodrigo's man at the barracks door, and even of seven desert warriors tonight—all these were merely prelude to much worse to come.

She looked around the large room and by the light of the torches saw men she liked and admired, and some she loved, and she wondered—in the strange, hollowed-out mood she had passed into—how many of them would live to see the next Ragosa Carnival.

Or if there would be another one a year from now.

Rodrigo came over, shirtless, a neat, efficient bandage covering his most serious wound. His upper body and arms were hard and muscled, laced with scars. One more now, when this healed. She would have a look at it later in the day. Work was sometimes the only barrier there was between life and the emptiness beyond.

His expression was strange. She hadn't seen him look this way since...since the night she'd met him and they had watched a hamlet burn north of Fezana. There was that same anger now, and a kind of hurt that didn't sort easily with his profession. Or perhaps that wasn't true: perhaps Rodrigo was good at what he did because he knew the price exacted by the deeds of soldiers at war?

Odd, how her mind was drifting. Questions for which

there were no answers. Much like death. The emptiness. The physician's implacable adversary. A sword wound deep into the collarbone. There was no answer for that.

She said, clearing her throat, "Did he clean it...before he put the dressing on?"

Belmonte nodded. "With a whole flask of wine. Didn't you hear me?"

She shook her head. "It looks like a proper dressing."

"Laín's been doing this for years."

"I know."

There was a little silence. He knelt in front of her, beside Ammar. "His last words to me were to ask that we take care of you. Jehane, I swore that we would."

She bit her lip. Said, "I thought I'd been hired to take care of all of you."

"It goes both ways, my dear." That was Husari. Ammar said nothing, only watched. His fingers were cool, holding hers.

Rodrigo looked at him, registering the linked hands, and said, "Muwardi assassins suggests Cartada." He stood up.

"I would think so," Ammar said. "In fact, I know it was. There was an emissary who found me, as well. A different kind of mission."

Rodrigo nodded slowly. "He wants you back?"

"He does."

"We assumed that, didn't we?"

"I think Almalik wanted to make certain I knew it."

"What was the offer?"

"All the things one might expect." The tone was cool.

Rodrigo registered that, too. "My apologies. I ought not to have asked."

"Perhaps. But you did. Ask the next question?" Ammar released her hand. He rose to his feet.

The two men gazed at each other, grey eyes and blue. Rodrigo nodded his head, as if accepting a challenge. "Very well. What did you tell them?"

"That I didn't know my answer, whether I would return or not."

"I see. Was that true?"

"At the time."

A silence. "Not so long ago, if it was tonight."

"It was. Some things have intervened."

"I see. And what would you answer if the same question were asked of you now?"

A small, deliberate hesitation. "That I am well content with the company in which I find myself." There was a nuance there, Jehane realized. A moment later she saw that Rodrigo had also caught it.

He gestured around the room. "We are that company?"

Ibn Khairan inclined his head. "A part of it." The two men were of a height; the Valledan was broader across the shoulders and chest.

"I see."

"And you?" Ammar asked, and now Jehane understood why he had permitted—even invited—the questions. "Where will the men of Rodrigo Belmonte be serving this summer?"

"We ride against Cartada soon. With the army of Ragosa."

"And if King Ramiro should also be riding? Against Fezana's walls? What then, O Scourge of Al-Rassan? Will we lose you? Will we live to fear the sight of your banner again?"

Some of the company had come over and were listening. It was quiet in the room and there was, indeed, light coming in from the east. Sunrise soon.

Rodrigo was silent a long while. Then, "I, too, am well content with where I find myself."

"But?"

The anger in Belmonte's eyes was gone. The other thing was still there. "But if the armies of Esperaña come through the *tagra* lands, I think I must go to them."

Jehane let out her breath. She hadn't been aware that she'd been holding it.

"Of course you must," Ammar said. "You have lived your life for this."

Rodrigo looked away for the first time and then back. "What do you want me to say?"

Ammar's tone was suddenly hard, merciless. "Oh, well...how about, *'Die, Asharite dogs! Kindath swine!'* Something of that sort?"

There was a sound from the soldiers. Rodrigo winced and shook his head. "Not from me, Ammar. Not from those who ride with me."

"And from those who will ride all around you?"

Rodrigo shook his head again, almost doggedly. "Again, what can I say to you? They will be much as the Muwardis are, I suppose. Driven by hatred and holiness." He made a curious gesture, both hands opening and then closing again. "You tell me. What shall good men do in such a war, Ammar?"

Ammar's answer came, as Jehane had feared and known it would: "Kill each other, until something ends in the world."

Alvar and Husari took her home as the sun was rising over the strewn and empty streets. They all needed sleep very badly. Alvar took his old room on the ground level, the one he'd used when she and he and Velaz had first come through the pass to Ragosa. Husari took Velaz's bed beside the chamber where Jehane saw her patients.

She bade them good night, though the night was done. She went up the stairs to her room. She opened the window and stood there watching the eastern sky grow brighter beyond the roofs of houses.

It was going to be a beautiful morning. The dawn wind brought the scent of almond trees from the garden across the way. It was quiet now. The streets were empty. Velaz would not see this morning come.

She tried, again, to think how she could tell this to her mother and father, and again backed away from that. She thought of something else: it would be necessary to arrange for burial, a Kindath service. Avren would help. Perhaps she would ask him to do this? Find someone to chant the ancient words of the liturgy: *One sun for the god. Two moons for his beloved sisters. Uncountable stars to shine in the night. Oh, man and woman, born to a dark path, only look up and the lights shall guide you home.*

She cried again, the tears spilling down her cheeks, falling on the window sill.

After a time she wiped her face with the backs of her hands and lay down on the bed, not bothering to undress, though there was blood on her clothing. The tears had stopped. An emptiness, pushing outwards from her heart, took their place. She lay there but could not sleep.

A little later she heard the sound from outside. She had been waiting for that sound.

Ammar swung up and onto the window ledge. He stayed there, motionless, regarding her a long while.

"Will you forgive me?" he asked finally. "I needed to come."

"I would not have forgiven you, ever, had you not," she said. "Hold me."

He jumped down to the floor and crossed the room. He lay on the bed beside her and she laid her head on his chest. She could feel his heartbeat. She closed her eyes. His hand came up and touched her hair.

"Oh, my love," he said softly. "Jehane."

She began, again, to cry.

This passed as well, though not soon. When she had been quiet for a time he spoke again. "We can lie like this, as long as you like. It is all right."

But there was an emptiness in her, and it needed not to be empty any more.

"No we can't," she said, and lifted her head and kissed him. Salt. Her own tears. She brought her hands up and laced them in his hair and kissed him again.

Much later, with both of them unclothed, she lay wrapped in his arms under the bedcovers and fell into desperately needed sleep.

He did not. He was much too aware of what was to come, later this same day. He had to leave Ragosa, before nightfall. He would urge that she remain here. She would refuse. He even knew who would insist upon coming with them. There was a darkness looming in the west, like a high-piled thundercloud. Above Fezana. Where they had met.

He lay awake, holding her in his arms, and became aware of a great irony, observing how the newly risen sun poured in through the eastern window and fell upon them both, as if someone or something wished to cloak them in a blessing made entirely of light.

PART V

Even the Sun Goes Down

Chapter XV

༄

The governor of Fezana was a watchful and a cautious man. If he occasionally remembered that the lamented King Almalik I, the Lion of Cartada, had begun his own ascent to glory from the position of governing that city for the khalifs of Silvenes, he more often reminded himself of his extreme good fortune in having been the only important city governor to survive the transition from father to son in Cartada.

When unsettled by dreams of loftier position he had learned to allow himself an evening of distraction: a quantity of Jaddite wine, dancers, encounters—watching or participating—involving slaves of both sexes in varying combinations. He had discovered that the release afforded by such activities served to quell the disturbances of inappropriate dreams for a time.

In truth, it wasn't merely good fortune that had ensured his continuance in Fezana. During the last years of the reign of the elder Almalik, the governor had taken pains, quietly, to establish cordial relations with the son. Though the tension between the king and the prince was evident, the governor of Fezana nonetheless judged that the young man was likely to survive and succeed his father. His reasoning was simple in the extreme: the alternatives were untenable, and the prince had Ammar ibn Khairan for his guardian.

The governor of Fezana had been born in Aljais.

He had known ibn Khairan from the poet's boyhood in

that city. Concerning a number of the tales emerging from that reckless, not-too-distant time he had a first-hand awareness. It was his own considered judgment that any prince being counselled by the man that boy had become was someone a prudent administrator would do well to cultivate.

He had been proved right, of course, though he was greatly unnerved when the young king had promptly sent ibn Khairan into exile. When he learned that the exiled courtier was in Ragosa he conveyed, by indirect means, his good wishes to him there. At the same time, he continued to serve the younger Almalik with the diligence he had applied to the father's interests. One remained in office— and wealthy, and alive—by such competence as much as by luck or scenting shifts in the wind. He stole very little, and with discretion.

He was also careful not to make assumptions. So when the unexpected, indeed startling, *parias* demand from Ruenda arrived by royal herald early in the spring, the governor sent it on to Cartada without comment.

He might form conjectures as to how this demand had emerged, and even admire the subtlety that had produced it, but it was not his place, unless invited by his king, to offer opinions about any of this.

His tasks were more pragmatic. He fortified and rebuilt Fezana's walls and defenses as best he could, given a dispirited populace. Having spent years dealing with a dangerously rebellious city, the governor judged he could cope with enervated depression for a time. The additional Muwardis in the new wing of the castle were not especially good at wall-building—desert warriors could hardly be expected to be—but they were being well paid and he had no compunctions about putting them to work.

He was aware of the religious broadsides being posted about the city that winter, as he was aware of most things in his city. He judged that the wadjis of Cartada were being allowed some leeway by the new king as a conciliatory gesture, and that this was spreading to the other cities of the kingdom. He had the prostitutes harassed a little more than usual. A few Jaddite taverns were closed. The governor quietly augmented his own stock of wine from the confiscations that accompanied this. Such actions were normal, though the times were not.

The Kindath were receiving rather more vituperation than was customary. This didn't particularly distress him. He didn't like the Kindath. They seemed always to have an air—even the women—of knowing things he didn't. Secrets of the world. The future mapped in their wandering moons. This made him nervous. If the wadjis chose to preach against the Wanderers more ferociously than in the recent past, it was apparently with the king's approval or acceptance and the governor was certainly not about to intervene.

He had graver concerns that year.

Fezana wasn't fortifying its walls or adding Muwardis to the garrison simply to keep soldiers busy. There was a mood in the north this season that augured ill for the future, whether mapped in the Kindath moons or not.

Even so, the governor, being deeply cautious by nature, couldn't quite believe that Ramiro of Valledo would be foolish enough to come and make war here, laying a siege so far from his own lands. Valledo was being paid *parias* from Fezana twice a year. Why would any rational man risk life and his kingdom's stability to conquer a city that was already filling his coffers with gold? Among other things, a Valledan army coming down through the *tagra* lands meant extreme vulnerability back home—to Jaloña or Ruenda.

On the other hand, the governor had heard along with everyone else tidings of that Jaddite army assembling in Batiara, due to sail east this spring for Ammuz and Soriyya. That sort of thing could set a very bad example, the governor of Fezana thought.

Spring came. The Tavares rose and subsided without undue flooding. In the temples Ashar and the holy stars of the god were ritually thanked for that. Fields made rich by the river were tilled and sown. Flowers bloomed in the gardens of Fezana and outside the walls. There were melons and cherries in the market and on his table. The governor was fond of melon.

Word came down through the *tagra* lands of a gathering of the three Jaddite kings in Carcasia.

This was not a good thing, by any measure. He relayed the information to Cartada. Almost immediately afterwards, further tidings came that the gathering had ended in violence, after an attempt on the life of either the king or queen or perhaps the constable of Valledo.

Information from the north was seldom clear; sometimes it was almost useless. This was no exception. The governor didn't know who, if anyone, had been injured or killed, or who was behind it. He passed this word along as well, however, for what it was worth.

He received swift messages back from Cartada: continue work on the walls, store up food and drink. Keep the wadjis happy and the Muwardis in good order. Post watchmen near the *tagra* lands. Be endlessly vigilant, in the name of Ashar and the kingdom.

None of this was reassuring. He did all of these things competently in an increasingly nervous city. The governor discovered that he wasn't enjoying his melon in the morning as much as he was wont to do. His stomach seemed to be vexing him.

Then the child died in the tannery.

And that very day came word that the Valledan army had been seen. South of the *tagra* lands, in Al-Rassan, banners flying.

An army. A very large army, coming swiftly. For the first time in hundreds of years the Horsemen of Jad were riding towards his city. It was folly, the governor thought agitatedly. Sheerest folly! What was King Ramiro *doing*?

And what could a prudent, diligent civil servant do when the kings of the world went mad?

Or when his own people did, that same day?

ᥬ

Sometimes events in far-distant places speak with a single

voice of a changed mood, a turning of the world towards darkness or light. It was remembered long years afterwards that the Kindath massacres in Sorenica and Fezana occurred within half a year of each other. One was achieved by Jaddite soldiers wild with boredom, the other by Asharite citizens in a frenzy of fear. The effects were not dissimilar.

In Fezana it began with a child's fever. The daughter of a tanner, one ibn Shapur, contracted an illness that spring. The poorer laborers lived nearest to the river and in the flooding season sickness was common, especially among children and the aged.

The child's parents, unable or unwilling to pay for the services of a physician, utilized instead the ancient remedy of placing her on a pallet in the tannery itself. The noxious fumes were thought to drive away the evil presence of illness. It was a healing that had been in use for centuries.

It so happened that day that a Kindath merchant, ben Mores by name, was at the tannery buying hides for export to the east by way of Salos then down the coast and through the straits.

While expertly appraising the finished and unfinished leathers in the yard he heard the crying child. Informed of what was being done, the Kindath merchant loudly and profanely began slandering the parents of the girl and proceeded to stride into the tannery and lay hands upon the child—which was forbidden. Ignoring protests, he carried her out from the healing place and into the chill of the spring air.

He was continuing to shout imprecations when ibn Shapur, observing his small daughter being dishonored and abducted by one of the Kindath, knowing that this evil people used children's blood in their foul rites, ran up and struck the merchant on the head from behind with a tanner's hook, killing him instantly. It was common agreement afterwards that ibn Shapur had never been considered a violent man.

The child fell to the ground, crying piteously. Her

father picked her up, accepted the grim congratulations of his fellows, and carried her back into the tannery. For the rest of the day the Kindath merchant's body was left where it had fallen in the yard. Flies gathered upon him in the sun. Dogs came over and licked at his blood.

The child died, just before sunset.

The Kindath's touch had cursed her, the leather workers agreed, lingering after work, angrily discussing the matter in the yard. She had been surely on the mend before that. Children died when Kindath laid hands upon them, it was a fact. A wadji arrived in the yard; no one later remembered who had summoned him. When informed of what had transpired the pious man threw up his hands in horror.

Someone pointed out at about that point, echoing a verse widely posted and recited earlier in the year, that none of the Kindath had died in the Day of the Moat—not one. Only good Asharites. They are a poison in our midst, this same man cried. They kill our children and our leaders, both.

The body of the slain merchant was dragged from the place where it had been lying. It was mutilated and abused. The wadji, watching, made no remonstration. Someone had the idea of decapitating the dead man and throwing his corpse into the moat. The head was cut off. The crowd of tanners left their yard, carrying the body, and began proceeding towards the gate nearest the moat.

While crossing the city the leather workers—quite a number of them by then—came across two Kindath women buying shawls in Weavers' Lane late in the day. It was the man who had recited the posted poem who struck one of them across the face. The other woman had the temerity to strike him in return.

An unbeliever, a *woman*, laying hands upon one of Ashar's Star-born? It was not to be endured.

Both women were bludgeoned to death in front of the shop where their purchases were still being wrapped. The weaver quietly put the two shawls back under the counter and pocketed the money that had been tendered. She then closed up shop for the day. A very large crowd had now assembled. After the briefest hesitation, the two women had their heads cut off. No one could later remember clearly who had actually wielded the blades.

The angry crowd, growing larger all the time, began streaming towards the Gate of the Moat with three headless, bleeding Kindath bodies.

On the way there they met another, even larger, gathering. This crowd was in the market square, almost filling it. It was not a market day.

They had just heard tidings from the north. Jaddites had been seen. They were almost upon them. An army from Valledo, coming to sack and burn Fezana.

Without any person ever voicing the specific suggestion—as best anyone could recall afterwards—the two crowds merged into one, and drew others to their mass, and they turned, together, in the hour before sunset and the rising of the white moon, towards the gates of the Kindath Quarter.

∽

The governor of Fezana received advice of some sort of uprising among the tanners, and violence done, at almost the same moment that the long-feared word of Horsemen thundering south, already down through the *tagra*, also reached him. He would have greatly preferred that these tidings remain his alone for a time, but this proved impossible. A third messenger reported, immediately on the heels of the first two, that there was a mob gathered in the marketplace and that they had already heard the news from the north.

The governor thus had a number of decisions to make in rapid succession. He sent two separate messengers immediately for Cartada and another to Lonza. It had been agreed that part of the Lonza garrison would be diverted northwards to the slopes of the Tavares Range if a siege actually began at Fezana—they could partly forestall Jaddite raids south of the river. Food for a besieging army, or the absence of it, was often the key to a siege.

The governor also sent an aide running for certain documents that had long since been prepared for him. More than three years ago, in fact, Almalik I of Cartada, who had been a governor before he was a monarch (the thought was an enduring distraction), had recorded with his generals and advisors some plans to be followed in the event of a siege of Fezana. Consulting these written instructions, which had not been superseded, the governor noted with trepidation the boldest element of them. He hesitated for a time, then elected to trust to the wisdom of the dead king. Orders were given to the most senior Muwardi in the room. The man's veiled face revealed nothing, of course. He left immediately, to assemble the men required.

All of this, and other associated commands, took some little while. As a consequence, by the time another messenger arrived to report that an extremely large number of people were now heading towards the Kindath Gates carrying torches, the governor was lagging uncharacteristically behind the sweep of events in his city. The torches spurred him to action, though. It was not yet dark; torches were not needed for light. What was the good of defending against the Valledans if they burned down their own city? Ashar and the stars knew, he had no love for the Kindath, but if that Quarter was fired, the whole city could go up. Wooden walls knew nothing of the boundaries of faith. The governor ordered the mob dispersed.

It was the proper thing to do, and it could possibly have even been achieved, had the order come earlier.

◦∽

Alvar never forgot that evening and night as long as he lived.

He would wake in terror from a dream that he was in Fezana again at sunset watching the mob approach. That memory marked him and stayed with him as nothing in his life ever had and only one moment after—also at sunset—was ever to do.

They had arrived that afternoon, crowding in ahead of the Jaddite dust cloud with a frightened swarm of people from the countryside. The five of them had raced all the way west from Ragosa across the hills and meadows of springtime. They had left the day after Carnival, immediately after burying Velaz with Kindath rites and the slain soldier in a Jaddite ceremony.

No time to mourn. Ibn Khairan had made that clear based on what he had learned, and Jehane, wild with fear for her parents, could not have lingered. They were out of Ragosa by mid-afternoon: Alvar, Husari, Jehane, ibn Khairan—and Rodrigo Belmonte. All of them exhausted after the night just past, all aware that in the mood of this spring something monstrous could happen.

They made the ten days' journey in six, riding into the darkness, arriving late one afternoon at a place where they could see the walls of Fezana. They had already seen the dust cloud that was the army of Valledo.

It was Rodrigo who spotted it. He had pointed, and then exchanged a long glance with ibn Khairan that Alvar could not interpret. Jehane bit her lip, gazing north. Husari said something under his breath that might have been a prayer.

For Alvar, despite weariness and anxiety, the sight of a cloud of dust stirred up by the Horsemen of Valledo in Al-Rassan stirred him deeply. Then he looked again at Jehane and Husari and back to ibn Khairan, and confusion arose once more. How did it happen that something one had desired all one's life became cause for doubt and apprehension?

"They are moving very fast," ibn Khairan had said, finally.

"Too fast," Rodrigo murmured. "They will outstrip some of the fleeing villagers. I don't understand. They *want* as many mouths in the city as possible."

"Unless this isn't to be a siege."

"What else can it be? He isn't about to storm those walls."

Ibn Khairan looked northwards again from their vantage point, high on a hill east of the city. "Perhaps just the vanguard is flying," he said. "For some reason."

"That wouldn't make sense either," Rodrigo had replied, his brow furrowed. He sounded edgy to Alvar, not exultant at all.

"Does it matter?" Jehane asked sharply. "Come on!"

She had ridden at a soldier's pace all the way. Indeed, there were times when Rodrigo or ibn Khairan had had to restrain her, lest they ruin the horses with their speed.

Her relationship with ibn Khairan had changed since Carnival. They tried not to show it too plainly on the ride, but it was there to be seen, in the man as much as in the woman. Alvar was making an effort not to let this distract him. He was only partly successful in that. It seemed that life could throw confusion and pain at you from many directions.

They came down from that height to cross the moat and enter the city. Alvar for the first time, Jehane and Husari coming home, ibn Khairan returning to where Almalik I had tried to destroy his reputation and curb his power.

And Rodrigo?

Alvar understood that the Captain was with them, disguised as an Asharite—his moustache shaved off, hair and skin darkened—because he had sworn an oath to Velaz ben Ishak to defend the woman who was here with them. He was not a man who forswore his oaths.

Jehane's parents were to be delivered from Fezana and a warning given to the other Kindath. That was the immediate task. After, they would have to turn again to sorting out loyalties and the next steps. They were all, as best Alvar understood, still to join the army of Ragosa somewhere west of Lonza, on the way to Cartada.

The dust cloud north of them had probably altered that.

With Jaddites invading Al-Rassan, did Ragosa still make war on Cartada? Asharite against Asharite with the Horsemen down through the *tagra?* And did the most renowned leader of Jaddite soldiers in the peninsula fight for Ragosa at such a time?

Alvar, one of those Jaddite soldiers, had no idea. On the ride west he had sensed an emerging distance between ibn Khairan and Ser Rodrigo. Not a coldness, certainly not opposition. It was more like...a marshalling of defenses. Each man fortifying himself against what might be coming.

Husari, normally voluble and perceptive, was no help at all in trying to sort this out. He kept his own counsel all the way here.

He had killed his first man in the square at Carnival. Jehane, in one of her few exchanges with Alvar on the ride, said she thought that might be the trouble. Husari had been a merchant not a warrior. A gentle man, a lazy, soft one, even. He had slain a Muwardi assassin that night, though, smashing his skull with a blow, spilling brains and blood on the cobblestones.

That could shake a man, Alvar thought. Not all were made for a soldier's life and what came with it.

Truth to tell—though he told no one this—Alvar wasn't certain any more if he was made for that life, either. That was frightening. If he wasn't this, what was he? But it appeared that a soldier needed to be able to see things in extremely simple terms and Alvar had come to realize that he wasn't especially good at that.

On the fourth morning he had broached this much, diffidently, with the Captain. Rodrigo had ridden in silence a long time before answering. Birds had been singing; the spring day was bright.

"You may be too intelligent to be a good soldier," Rodrigo had said, finally.

Which wasn't really what Alvar wanted to hear. It sounded like a rejection. "What about you?" he demanded. "You have been, all your life."

Rodrigo hesitated again, choosing his words. "I grew up in a different age, Alvar, though it was only a little before yours. When the khalifs ruled in Al-Rassan we lived in fear of our lives in the north. We were raided once, sometimes twice, a year. Every year. Even after the raids began to stop, we children were frightened into bed at night with warnings about the infidels coming to take us away if we were bad. We dreamed of miracles, reversals. Of coming back."

"So did I!"

"But now you *can*, don't you see? It isn't a dream any more. The world has changed. When you can do what you dreamed about, sometimes it isn't...as simple any more." Rodrigo looked at Alvar. "I don't know if that makes any sense at all."

"I don't either," Alvar said glumly.

The Captain's mouth quirked at that, and Alvar realized he hadn't been very respectful.

"Sorry," he said quickly. He remembered—it seemed an unbelievably long time ago—the day Rodrigo had knocked him from his horse just outside Esteren for such impertinence.

Rodrigo only shook his head now. The world had changed. "Try this, if it helps," he said. "How easy do you find it to think of the three people we're riding with as infidels, vile in their ways and loathsome to the god?"

Alvar blinked. "But we *always* knew there was honor in Al-Rassan."

Rodrigo shook his head. "No. Be honest. Think about this. *Some* of us did, Alvar. The clerics deny it to this day. I have a feeling your mother would. Think of Vasca's Isle. The very idea of holy war denies it: Asharites and Kindath are an attack upon Jad. Their existence wounds our god. That's what we've all been taught for centuries. No room for acknowledging honor, let alone grandeur in an enemy. Not in a war driven by such beliefs. That's what I'm trying—badly—to say. It's one thing to make war for your country, your family, even in pursuit of glory. It's another to believe that the people you fight are embodiments of evil and must be destroyed for that. I want this peninsula back. I want Esperaña great again, but I will not pretend that if we smash Al-Rassan and all it has built we are doing the will of any god I know."

It was so difficult. Amazingly difficult. Alvar rode without speaking for a long while. "Do you think King Ramiro feels that way?"

"I have no idea how King Ramiro feels."

The answer came too quickly. The wrong question to have asked, Alvar realized. It ended the conversation. And none of the others seemed inclined to talk.

He kept thinking about it, however. He had time to think as they passed west through springtime. Nothing emerged clearly.

What had happened to the sunlit world one dreamed of as a child: when all one wanted was a part in the glory of which Rodrigo had spoken, an honorable role in the battling of lions and a share of pride?

The battling of lions. A child's dreaming. How did that fit in with what Valledan men had done in Orvilla last summer? Or with Velaz ben Ishak—as good a man as Alvar had ever known—dead on the stones of Ragosa? Or, indeed, with what they themselves had done to a Jaloñan party in a valley northwest of Fibaz? Was there glory there? Was there any way to say there was?

He still wore his cool, loose garb of Al-Rassan. Husari had not removed his leather Valledan hat or vest or leggings. Alvar wasn't sure why, but that meant something to him. Perhaps in the absence of real answers men needed their emblems more?

Or perhaps he *did* spend too much time on thoughts such as these ever to be a proper soldier. It was a little reassuring to see the Captain struggling as well. But that didn't resolve anything.

On a hilltop east of Fezana in Al-Rassan, watching a dust cloud stirred up by the horses of his countrymen, in the moments before the five of them rode down towards the city, Alvar de Pellino decided that glory—the fierce, bright purity of it—was hopelessly hard to come by, in fact.

And then, that same evening, he found it after all and a signing of his future as if branded in the burning sky.

Ammar took control when they approached the Gate of the Moat. Jehane had seen it before, on the campaign near Fibaz, how he and Rodrigo seemed to have an effortless interchange of authority as situations altered. This was, she had come to realize, one of the sorrows she was carrying: whatever bond had evolved, whatever unspoken awareness they shared across two worlds, it was going to be severed now.

A Jaddite army in Al-Rassan made certain of that. The two of them were aware of it. Nothing had been said on the hill, watching the dust, but it was known. They were here to take her parents away from danger, and after that...? After that, whatever it was that had begun that autumn day in Ragosa in a symbolic battle beneath the ramparts would come to an end.

She wanted to talk with Ammar. She *needed* to talk with him; about this, and so many other things. About love, and whether something could truly begin in a time of deaths, with endings all around in the world they had known.

Not on this ride, though. They had spoken with glances and the briefest exchanges. Whatever was to be resolved, whatever diminished or expanded possibilities the future might encompass in the mingled signs of their stars and moons, would have to be considered afterwards. If time and the world allowed.

She had no doubts of him. It was astonishing in a way, but she'd had none at all from those first moments in the street at Carnival. Sometimes the heart's arrow found its way to certainty despite the cautionings of a careful nature.

He was what he was and she knew something about that. He had done what he had done, and the stories ran the length of the peninsula.

And he had said he loved her and she believed him, and there was no need for fear. Not of him. Of the world, perhaps; of darkness, blood, fire; but not of this man who was, it seemed, amazingly, the destination of her soul.

They entered Fezana in the midst of a milling, terrified mass of people from the countryside fleeing the advance of the Jaddite army. Wagons and pushcarts clogged the road into the city and the bridge before the wall, blocking the gates. They were enmeshed among crying children, barking dogs, mules, chickens, shouting men and women; Jehane saw all the signs of a general panic.

Ammar looked over at Rodrigo. "We may be just in time. There could be violence here tonight." He said it quietly. Jehane felt fear, like the pounding of a drum inside her.

"Let's get inside," Belmonte said.

Ammar hesitated. "Rodrigo, you may be trapped in a city your army is besieging."

"My army is in Ragosa, preparing to set out for Cartada, remember?" Rodrigo's voice was grim. "I'll deal with changes as they arise."

The other man hesitated again, as if about to add something, but merely nodded his head. "Cloak yourself, then. You'll be slain on the spot if they know you for a Valledan." He looked over at Alvar and then, improbably, flashed the grin they all knew. "You, on the other hand, look more like a native than I do."

Alvar returned the smile. "Worry about Husari," he said in effortless Asharic. "He'll get us all killed with his hat." He looked over at Jehane and smiled. "We'll get them out."

She managed to nod her head. It was extraordinary what the passage of less than a year had done to him. Or perhaps not so: there had been steel and a mind in Alvar de Pellino from the beginning and he had spent much of this year in the company of two of the most exceptional men in their world. He was on the way, Jehane thought suddenly, to becoming something out of the ordinary himself.

Husari and Ammar led them, urging their horses steadily through the crowd. Stumbling out of their path, men swore at them, but not loudly. They were armed and mounted, and that was enough. They forced a way through.

There were guards at the gate but they were overwhelmed by the clamor and chaos. No one took note of them, no one stayed their course. Late in the afternoon of the day the Valledans arrived, Jehane came back into the city where she had been born and raised.

They reached the Kindath Quarter just ahead of the mob bearing weapons and brands of fire.

Since Ishak had begun to talk again, Eliane had discovered that her husband's hearing was extremely good. It was he who first heard the sounds from outside the Quarter and drew her attention to them. She could understand him almost perfectly now: the mangled words, because they were his, were to her as water in a dry place.

She put down the letter she had been reading him— Rezzoni ben Corli had written from Padrino where he was living now with his family. He had sent news of Batiara in the aftermath of the massacre in Sorenica.

She was to remember, later, that this was what she had been reading when Ishak said he heard a noise outside. Crossing to the window, Eliane opened it and stood listening. An angry sound, a crowd in the distant streets.

The window of Ishak's study overlooked a common courtyard shared by a dozen of the larger homes in the Quarter. Looking down, Eliane saw a number of people below, talking nervously, gesticulating. Someone ran into the courtyard: her friend Nasreh bet Rivek's younger son.

"*They are coming!*" he shouted. "They've killed Mezira ben Mores! They are coming for us with fire!"

Someone screamed from a window across the way. Eliane closed her eyes, clutching the ledge. She was briefly afraid she would fall. She had been warned of this, explicitly. They had been making plans to leave, hard as it was to abandon a home at their age. It seemed they had waited too long.

There was a scraping sound as Ishak rose from his chair behind her. Eliane opened her eyes and looked out, drawing a ragged breath. Faces appeared at windows, people ran into the courtyard. The sun was westering, the cobblestones sliced by a diagonal line of shadow. Frightened men and women crossed in and out of the light. Someone appeared carrying a spear—Nasreh's older son. Frenzied movement in a once-quiet place, a babble of sound. The huge noise was nearer now. Was this, then, how the world ended?

Ishak spoke her name. She started to turn back to him, but in that moment, blinking in disbelief, she realized that one of the people running into the courtyard below was her daughter.

☙

Jehane had known the guards at the iron gates to the Quarter. They let her enter with the men accompanying her. They had heard and seen the mob gathering by the market square. The Kindath guards were armed—against regulations—and composed. No signs of panic that Alvar could see. They knew what was coming. They knew about the Jaddites too.

Jehane hesitated just inside the gates. Alvar saw her look at Ammar ibn Khairan. And in that moment—not before, in fact—he finally understood something. He felt a quick, hard pain, much like a blade, then it was gone. A different feeling lingered, nearer to sorrow.

He had never really imagined she might be for him.

"Ser Rodrigo, you take her in," ibn Khairan said quickly. "You're still a danger if you are seen. Husari and Alvar and I will help out at this gate. We may be able to do something. We can gain you time, if nothing else."

If nothing else. Alvar knew what that meant.

Jehane said, "Ammar, it isn't just my parents any more."

"I know that. We'll do all we can. Go get them. I know the house. Be downstairs. If we can, we'll be with you." He turned to Rodrigo. "If you hear we've broken, get them out." He paused, blue eyes on grey in the light of late afternoon. "I charge you with this," he said.

Belmonte said nothing. Only nodded.

Jehane and the Captain left them. No time for more

words, of farewell or otherwise. It didn't seem as if the
world was allowing any space for such things. The noise
from the streets was louder now. Alvar felt fear touch him
then, a quick finger beneath the skin. He had never dealt
with a mob, he had never even seen one.

"They have already killed three of us," one of the
Kindath guards said grimly.

The gates to the Kindath Quarter were recessed into a
narrow laneway. The crowd would be channelled and
backed up here when they arrived. That would have been
deliberate, Alvar realized. The Kindath had experience with
these things. A terrible truth. It occurred to him that
Queen Vasca, whom his mother worshipped as holy, would
have been urging on the people that were coming now.

Eyes on the open space before the gates, Alvar lifted
the round shield from his back, looped his left arm
through the strap and drew his sword. Ammar ibn Khairan
did the same. Husari touched his weapon, then let it go.

"Give me a moment, first," he said, his words were
quiet, scarcely audible over the rising volume of sound
from beyond. Husari stepped out from behind the gates
into the open space.

Seeing him do so, Alvar instinctively did the same—in
the precise moment Ammar ibn Khairan also moved forward and out.

"Lock your gates," ibn Khairan said over his shoulder.

The guards didn't need instructions. Alvar heard the
clang of metal behind him, and a key turning. He looked
back and up: four more Kindath guards stood on a platform above and behind the double gates. They had bows
to hand, nocked with arrows. All weapons were forbidden
to the Kindath in Al-Rassan. He didn't think these men
were greatly concerned with such laws at this moment.

He stood with Husari and Ammar ibn Khairan, exposed
and alone in the narrow lane. The gates were locked
behind them; there was nowhere to run. Ibn Khairan
glanced at Husari and then at Alvar. "This," he said lightly,
"may not be the most intelligent thing we have ever done."

The rumble became a roar and then the mob was there.

The first things Alvar registered, sickeningly, were the three severed heads on spears. The noise was huge, a wall of sound that did not seem entirely human. The howling, screaming press of people spilled around the corner into the space before the gates, and then, seeing three men standing there, the vanguard drew to a skidding halt, pushing back hard against those behind them.

There were half a hundred torches. Alvar saw swords and pikes, wooden cudgels, knives. Faces were contorted, filled with hatred, but what Alvar sensed was fear more than rage. His gaze kept returning to those severed, dripping heads. Terror or anger: it didn't much matter, did it? This crowd had already killed. After the first deaths others would come easily.

In that moment Husari ibn Musa stepped forward, moving from the shadow of the gates into the last of the afternoon sunlight. He lifted both hands, showing them empty. He still wore his Jaddite hat, recklessly.

There was a gradual spilling backwards of silence. They were going to let him speak, it seemed. Then Alvar caught a glint of sunlight on a moving blade. He moved, without conscious thought.

His shield, thrust in front of Husari, blocked the flung knife, a butcher's heavy blade. It fell with a clatter to the stones. There was blood on that knife, Alvar saw. He heard a flurry of shouts, and then stillness again.

"Are you a complete fool, Mutafa ibn Bashir?"

Husari's voice was sharp, clear, mocking, it filled the space before the gates. "It's ibn Abazi, right beside you, that your wife's sleeping with, not me!"

In the shocked stillness that followed this, someone actually laughed. A thin, nervous sound, but it was laughter.

"Who are you?" another voice cried. "Why do you stand before the gates of those who kill children?"

"Who *am* I?" Husari exclaimed, spreading his arms wide. "I am insulted and offended. Among other things, you owe me money, ibn Dinaz. How *dare* you pretend not to know me!"

Another pause, another subtle shifting of mood. Alvar could see those near the front relaying rapid explanations backwards. Most of the huge crowd was still around the corner, out of sight of this.

"*It's Husari!*" someone exclaimed. "It's Husari ibn Musa!"

Husari promptly swept off the leather hat and offered an elaborate bow. "And a bolt of good cloth goes to you tomorrow morning, ibn Zhani. Am I so changed that even my friends do not know me? Not to mention my debtors?"

He *was*, of course. He was very greatly changed. He was also, Alvar realized, buying them as much time as he could. Next to Alvar, Ammar ibn Khairan murmured out of the side of his mouth, "Sword down, look easy. If he holds them long enough the governor will have troops here. He can't afford a fire tonight."

Alvar obeyed, trying to find a balance between watchfulness and the appearance of calm. It was hard to feign ease with those bobbing, severed heads on pikes in front of him. Two of them were women.

"Husari!" someone cried. "Have you heard? The Jaddites are coming!"

"So they are," ibn Musa agreed soberly. "Our walls have held against worse in their time. But in Ashar's holy name, are we madmen, to riot in our own city when an enemy appears?"

"The Kindath are in league with them!" someone shouted thickly. It was the man who'd thrown the knife. There was a quick rumble of agreement.

Husari laughed then. "Ibn Bashir, count the blessings of your birth stars that a butcher needs no more brains than the meat he carves. The Kindath fear the Jaddites more than we do! They are slaves in the north! Here they live freely, and pay half our taxes for us, *and* buy your stringy meat, even with your fat thumb on the scale!" Alvar saw someone smile at that.

"None of them died on the Day of the Moat!" Another voice, harsh as the butcher's. Alvar felt a movement beside him, then realized he was standing alone.

"And what," said Ammar ibn Khairan, stepping forward into the sunlight, "would have been the point of that?" He made a production of sheathing his magnificent sword, giving them time to look at him.

He was known. Immediately. Alvar could see it happen. He saw shock, confusion, fear again, a measure of awe. Whispers ran backwards like water down a hill.

Ibn Khairan looked out over the crowd in the laneway, taking his time. "The last king of Cartada wished to eliminate the leading citizens of this city last year as a message to all of you. Which man here would name a Kindath as one such? A leading citizen? One of the Kindath? It is," said Ammar ibn Khairan, "an amusing thought."

"You were exiled!" one brave person shouted. "It was proclaimed last summer!"

"And revoked this spring," Husari said calmly. "The man beside me—I see you know him—has been sent by King Almalik II to take charge of our defense against the rabble from the north."

Someone cheered, then more people did. There was a perceptible brightening of countenances, another shift of mood. Alvar drew a breath.

"Why is he *here* then, why not with the governor?"

"With that stuffed pork chop?" ibn Khairan said indignantly.

Another ripple of laughter. The governor would not be well-liked; governors seldom were. Ammar shook his head. "Spare me, please! I'd far rather be with ibn Bashir's wife, if you want to know the truth. But if I'm charged with your defense, I can hardly let the city be fired, can I?"

"Oh! Oh! My heart! I'm here, my lord! I'm right here!"

A woman's hands could be seen waving vigorously, part of the way up the lane. Ibn Bashir, the butcher, turned to look, his face reddening. General laughter now.

"You do know," Ammar said gravely, as the amusement

subsided, "that the Muwardis are coming here even as we speak. They have orders to quell any disturbance. I'm afraid my control over them is not perfect yet. I have just arrived. I do *not* want anyone killed here this afternoon. It might spoil my pleasure in what I have planned for tonight." He grinned slyly.

"Here, my lord! Why wait for tonight?" A different woman this time. And suddenly there were more than a dozen waving hands and imploring female voices through the crowd.

Ibn Khairan threw his head back and laughed aloud. "I am honored," he said, "and exhausted by the very thought." A ripple of amusement again, a further softening of mood. The westering sun left most of the lane in shadow now.

Ibn Khairan's tone changed. "Good people, go to your homes before the veiled ones come. Put out your torches. We must not do the Jaddites' work for them. Our walls are strong, the king of Cartada has sent me to you and others are coming even now. We have food and water in plenty and the Valledans are far from their homes in a land they do not know. We need only fear weakness in ourselves, or folly. This gathering has been folly. It is time to go home. See, the sun is setting, the prayer bells will be ringing soon. It is a good evening for prayer, my friends, an evening to be as pure as we can be, in the sight of Ashar and beneath his stars when they appear."

The beautiful voice had become lyric, cadenced, soothing. He was a poet, Alvar remembered. Jehane had told him once that ibn Khairan still thought of himself as such, over and above anything else.

The crowd in the laneway seemed to have been lulled. Alvar saw one of the men holding a spear with a severed head look up at what he carried, and he saw repugnance and dismay cross the man's features. These were frightened people, not evil ones. Leaderless and under assault, they had turned to the nearest, most accessible targets to purge their own terror. It seemed that the presence of a strong clear voice before them had blunted the edge of that.

It ought to have.

It might indeed have done so, but Ammar ibn Khairan had only been seen and heard by the leading edge of that mob and the Kindath Quarter of Fezana had been designed to keep the Kindath in at night, not to protect them in any real way.

It was not particularly hard to penetrate through means other than the gates of the entrance. A few makeshift ladders, broken windows in the outer houses and someone angry and determined enough could be right in among the treacherous, child-killing—

"Fire!"

The wild shout came from one of the guards on the platform behind them. Alvar wheeled, saw black smoke. Heard a child cry from inside the Quarter, and then the screaming began. Fire was the purest terror. Fire destroyed cities.

He slung his shield on his back, took three quick, running steps towards the gates, and leaped. One of the guards reached down a hand, gripped Alvar's wrist, and pulled him up. Ammar was right beside him, and Husari too, more agile than he had ever been in his life.

Ibn Khairan turned back to the suddenly agitated crowd in the lane. "*To your homes!*" he shouted, hard authority in his voice now. "I will order the Muwardis to kill any man or woman who enters this Quarter. *We cannot have the city burn!*"

It *was* burning, though, and people would already be dying in the Kindath Quarter. Alvar didn't wait to see what happened in front of the gates. He jumped down from the platform, out of the last sunlight of the day. He stumbled and fell on the cobblestones, rose up and drew his sword.

How do you put out fires when attackers, crazed with hatred and fear, are spilling into your streets and killing you? One of those questions, Alvar thought, sprinting towards the smoke and the screaming, for which there were no answers: only the swirling images of nightmare.

The Kindath were streaming towards a part of the

Quarter where the twin domes of the sanctuary could be seen. All the twisting, narrow streets seemed to lead that way. The fires had started in the houses nearest the streets beyond the gate. The Asharites had penetrated through outer windows and torched the homes through which they passed.

Even as he ran, cutting against the flow of running people, Alvar saw an Asharite with a sickle chop at the legs of a running boy. The wickedly honed blade sheared through the child's legs as if they were stalks of grain. The boy went down in blood, screaming. Alvar veered over, not breaking stride and, shouting incoherently, brought his sword down with all his strength, killing the man who had done that thing.

Half a dozen Asharites stopped dead in their tracks just ahead of him. He must look like a wild man, Alvar realized; their faces registered gaping apprehension. It was one thing to pursue unarmed children; another to be confronted by a man wielding a sword, with that look in his eyes.

"Are you all *mad!*" It was Husari, running up, screaming at his fellow citizens. "Fezana is on fire! Get water! Now! We will destroy our own city!"

"We will destroy the Kindath!" someone shouted back. "*Then* we will deal with flames. It is the holy work of Ashar we do!"

"It is the work of evil!" Husari screamed, his face distorted with pain and grief. And then Alvar saw him step forward and thrust his sword into the belly of the man he addressed. Instinctively, Alvar advanced, covering Husari with his shield. The Asharites in front of them retreated.

"*Go!*" screamed Husari, his voice raw. "Or if you stay, get water, *now!* We give our city to the Horsemen if this goes on!"

Alvar looked back over his shoulder. Kindath men and women were running past; some of the men had turned to make a stand where the tangle of streets reached a square. It was hard to make sense of the chaos in the half-light and the black, blowing smoke.

Even as he watched another house went up in a red sheet of flame. There was screaming everywhere. He had a sudden, appalling memory of Orvilla last summer. This was worse. This was a city, with houses almost all of wood, and if one part of it caught the whole of Fezana might burn. They had to get out.

He had lost sight of ibn Khairan, and had no idea where Jehane and her family home might be. Husari would know. He seized his friend's shoulder. "Come on!" he shouted over the crashing and the screams. "Have to find Jehane!"

Husari turned, stumbling over the body of the man he'd killed. He seemed dazed, aghast; he carried his sword as if he didn't even know what it was any more. There were flames at the head of this lane now. Already. Alvar, gripping Husari by the arm, turned back. His eyes were stinging from the smoke.

In a doorway across the street he saw a girl with a wooden staff facing a pair of men armed with knives. A small boy clutched at the girl's legs from behind. He was crying desperately. The house was on fire above them. The men with knives were laughing.

It was the laughter that took Alvar past his own breaking point. Before he was aware of forming the thought, he had released Husari and was running.

Too many people in between. A thronged, roiling street. Only a dozen strides, but they were too far. The girl stood, smoke billowing around her, defending her burning home and her small brother against two men with blades.

No one else seemed to have seen them; there was too much panic all around. The nearer of the two men feinted with his blade, then drew it back to thrust as the girl over-reacted badly.

"No!" Alvar screamed, from the middle of the street, battering a path across a tide of fleeing people. *"No!"*

Then he saw, in the shadows and flame, the man's knife hand snap backwards uncontrollably. The Asharite cried out, dropped his blade.

And the whip that had caught him immediately coiled

and lashed out again, catching the second man across the throat, opening a red gash. Alvar looked up and saw Rodrigo at a window above, leaning out with his whip. Alvar didn't break stride. He came up to those two men and chopped them down like animals, a rage in his heart.

He stood there, fighting for control, and looked at the girl. She eyed him in terror. Was she twelve, thirteen?

"Where are your parents?" he gasped, trying to master his voice.

"They are dead," she replied, her voice flattened out. "Upstairs. Men came in with torches and a spear." Her eyes were too wide, opening on a world given over to horror. No tears.

She ought to be crying, Alvar thought. He looked up again. Rodrigo was shouting something, and gesturing to the next doorway: he couldn't hear the words. The child behind the girl was no more than four years old. He was crying in harsh, convulsive bursts, scarcely able to draw breath.

"Come with me," Alvar snapped, his voice sharp with urgency. He bent down abruptly and picked up the little boy and then pushed the girl out of the doorway with a hand on her back. A burly figure came rushing up to them, an axe raised. Still holding the small child, Alvar twisted away from a blow, pivoted, and thrust his reddened blade into the man's chest.

There was a huge, roaring sound behind him. He looked up. The girl's house was alight now, flames in all the upper windows. The whole of the Kindath Quarter was on fire. He carried the terrified child and guided the girl towards the doorway Rodrigo had indicated from above.

He gasped with relief when he got there. Jehane stood in the doorway with two people who had to be her parents. Rodrigo came hurtling down the stairs.

"Where's Ammar?" Jehane asked quickly. He couldn't ever remember seeing her look so frightened.

"Don't know. Think he's holding the gate with the guards."

"Husari's right over there," Rodrigo said. Alvar looked back. Ibn Musa was wielding his blade again, fighting a slow retreat in the street, letting the running Kindath stream past him towards the square.

"We have to get out. It's all going up," Alvar gasped. He was still carrying the little boy. He handed the child over to the nearest person, who happened to be Jehane's mother. "Is there a way out?"

"There is," Jehane said. "We have a long way to go to get there, though, and—*oh, thank the god and the moons!*"

Ammar ibn Khairan, bleeding from a gash in one arm, came running up. "The Muwardis are here," he snapped. "This will end soon, but we have to be gone before they round everyone up!"

Alvar, a day ago, half a day, would have been unable to conceive of how tidings of the arrival of the veiled ones could ever have brought him relief.

"Jehane, which way?" It was Rodrigo. "Past the sanctuary?"

"No. The other way! There's a place in the wall, but it's on the far side of the Quarter." She pointed past where Asharites were still streaming in pursuit of her kindred. Even as he looked, Alvar saw a running woman clubbed down from behind. The man who had felled her stopped running and began beating her where she lay. Alvar took a step towards them, but felt Rodrigo's hand grip his arm.

"We cannot save them all. We must do what we can. What we came to do." The Captain's eyes were bleak.

"Let's go," said Ammar ibn Khairan.

"These two come with us," Alvar said flatly, gesturing to the children.

"Of course they do," said Eliane bet Danel. "Can you get us through?"

"Yes we can," said Alvar, speaking before ibn Khairan, before the Captain. "No one is going to stop us." He looked at the two leaders. "I go first, with your permission."

They glanced at each other. He saw something in both faces: a kind of acknowledgment. "You lead," said ibn

Khairan. "Jehane guides. Let's go."

Alvar stepped from the doorway in the direction Jehane had indicated. They had to go straight into the stream of the attackers—those who would destroy people, small children, with sickles and axes and cudgels. With utter savagery. The Asharites were terrified themselves, he tried to remind himself. There were invaders approaching their walls.

It didn't matter.

Nuances were not for this evening. At the descent of twilight in the burning Kindath Quarter of Fezana in Al-Rassan, Alvar de Pellino went forward with a shield and a sword and an undivided heart, and he could not be stopped.

Banishing ambiguities, everything but the need to be swift and deadly and sure, he led their small party into the path of the advancing mob and he carved a way with his blade for the others to follow.

He became aware that Husari was with them now, that the merchant had sheathed his blade and was guiding the blind physician who was Jehane's father. When they reached the head of the street, Alvar felt the presence of Rodrigo at his side in the stinging smoke and the heat. He knew, without looking back, that ibn Khairan would be guarding their rear.

They dealt with a sudden swirl of assailants in the open space. Alvar blocked a blow, chopped his sword at someone's knees. Turned and cut back the other way, even as the first man was falling. He had never moved so quickly in his life.

There was a vast, cracking sound; an entire building collapsed across the way in a shower of sparks and a rush of flame. They felt the heat as a wave.

"That way!" Jehane cried.

Alvar saw where she pointed. Led them, slashing with his blade. Went through thick smoke and the heat of the fires, past the running figures of Kindath and their pursuers, forging a path against the flow. Jehane signalled again and then again, and one more time, and finally they came to a place at the other end of the Quarter, a dead-end laneway leading only to the outer walls.

Alvar looked back. No one was following through the smoke. There was blood in his eyes. He didn't think it was his own. He swiped at it with his forearm.

Rodrigo was beside him, breathing quickly but calm as ever. The Captain gave him a searching glance. "Bravely done," he said quietly. "I could have done no better. This is truth, not flattery."

"Nor I," said ibn Khairan, coming up to them. "I knew you were a soldier. I never knew how much of one. Forgive me that."

"*I'm not*," said Alvar, but he rasped it under his breath, and he didn't think they heard. With the fever gone, the white rage, it was gradually coming to him how many terrified people he had just sent to their god. He looked at his sword. It was clotted with blood.

It was quieter here. In the distance they could hear new sounds, a change in the noise. The Muwardis had come. They would care nothing for the butchered Kindath but would be ruthless in suppressing the violence. And the fires would have to be contained or Fezana would be at the mercy of the Jaddites outside.

But I'm a Jaddite, Alvar thought. He knelt and began wiping his slippery blade on a clump of weeds by the wall. *This is good for us.*

It didn't feel that way. He stood up and sheathed his weapon. He looked at the others. The little boy was quiet now, clutching the neck of Jehane's mother. She had carried him all the way here. His sister stood close by, her face white, eyes still wide, still without tears. Jehane's father was stone-faced and silent, a hand on Husari's shoulder.

It was Husari who was weeping.

Alvar felt his heart twist for his friend. This was Husari's city, he would have known so many of these maddened people, he had probably killed men he had known all his life. Alvar opened his mouth and then closed it. There was nothing he could think of to say. There were places into which words could not go. Not the words he knew.

Jehane was on her knees, scrabbling at a stone in the wall. It came loose. She reached in a hand, swore as a scorpion scurried away, and pulled out a key. She stood up.

"Over here," she gasped. She ran a short distance along the wall to a clump of raspberry bushes. Ducking in behind them, she dropped to her knees again, inserted the key and pulled, hard.

A small, low section of the stone wall swung outwards. The hinging mechanism was ingenious; they had no time to admire it.

"Is this," said Eliane, "one of the ways out your friends taught you?"

Jehane glanced up at her mother. "How do you know about them?"

Eliane's expression was bitter. "They warned me. We were too slow to move."

"Then we must not be now," said Ammar ibn Khairan. "Come."

"I'll go," Alvar said. "Wait for my signal." Who knew what lay outside in the darkness? Whatever it was, Alvar was going to be first to meet it.

"There's another key inside," Jehane said. "You need to use it to push the outer piece open."

He slipped behind the bushes and then wriggled into a hollowed-out space in the thick stone city wall. In the close blackness he found the second key by touch and then the keyhole. He inserted, turned, pushed. The outer wall piece swung away and Alvar crawled through. He felt grass, stood up and looked around, blade quickly to hand again.

Only twilight, damp earth by the river, the first stars and a rising white moon. The water rippled just ahead, reflecting the pale moonlight.

"Come on," he said, mouth to the hollow space in the stone.

The others came through then, one by one. He helped them slip out and then stand outside the wall between stone and dark water. Rodrigo, last through, dropped the key back inside and pushed the opening shut.

They crossed the water immediately, those who could swim helping the others. The river was very cold this early in the year. They climbed up on the far bank in the dark. Alvar collapsed among the high grass and the reeds, sucking in deep breaths of the clean air. His face stung; it felt raw and burnt.

He became aware of something. Slowly he rose to his feet again. Rodrigo had walked a few steps from the rest of them and was staring out into the darkness. His sword was drawn.

"Who's there?" the Captain called.

There was silence. Ammar ibn Khairan also stood up.

Then there came an answer from the dark: "A friend. Someone is here to bid you welcome, Ser Rodrigo." The speaker had a deep, calm voice.

But it wasn't the tone, it was the language spoken that caused Alvar to step forward beside Rodrigo, his heart hammering again.

He was close enough to hear the Captain draw breath.

"Light a torch, then," Rodrigo said. "Darkness offers no true welcome."

They heard a command. Flint was struck. Light blazed.

"Welcome back, truly," said the very tall, bearded man illuminated by that torch. Alvar had seen him twice in his life. He forgot to breathe.

"My lord," said Rodrigo, after a moment. "This is unexpected."

King Ramiro of Valledo, surrounded by a company of men, smiled his pleasure. "I had hoped it might be. It is rare that any of us are able to surprise you."

"How come you to be here?" Rodrigo said. His voice was controlled, but Alvar was near enough to know there was effort involved in that. He heard ibn Khairan come quietly up beside them.

King Ramiro's smile deepened. He gestured, and someone stepped from the group of men behind him.

"Hello, Papa," said a young boy, coming to stand beside the king.

Rodrigo sucked in his breath, his control gone. "*Fernan?* In Jad's name, what—"

"It was Diego," the boy said, a little too brightly. He wore light armor and a sword. "He knew where you were, this morning, and told us where to wait tonight." Rodrigo was silent. "He sometimes knows where you are, remember?" The boy's voice betrayed uncertainty. "Are you not pleased to see me, Papa?"

"Oh, Jad," Alvar heard the Captain say. And then, to the king of Valledo, "*What have you done?* Why are my sons with this army?"

"There will be time to explain," said Ramiro calmly. "This is not the place. Will you come with us? We can offer dry clothing and food."

"And those I am with?" Rodrigo's tone was ice-cold.

"They are my guests if you speak for them, whoever they may be. Come now, greet your son, Ser Rodrigo. He has been dreaming of this moment."

Rodrigo opened his mouth quickly, then closed it. Slowly he sheathed his blade.

"Come to me," he said to the boy, and with an involuntary sound, Fernan Belmonte ran forward and was gathered fiercely in his father's embrace. Alvar saw the Captain close his eyes as he gripped his son.

"Your mother," said Rodrigo, when he finally stepped back, "is going to kill all of us for this, you realize. Starting with me."

"Mother's with the queen, Papa. We haven't seen her yet but there was a message she came south and joined Queen Ines with the rest of the army following us. We tried to cut you off before you reached the city. That's why we came so fast. Why are you here, Papa? What happened to your moustache?"

"I had friends in danger. I came to get them out. Where is Diego?"

"They are taking great care of him," Fernan said. "He's

angry about it. They wouldn't let him come here. They made him stay with the food train, in some village by the river west."

"Ashar, no! Not there!"

All his days Alvar would remember those words and the expression on Ammar ibn Khairan's face, crying them. Rodrigo wheeled on him.

"What is it? *Tell me!*"

"Ambush!" snapped the other man, already moving. "The Muwardis. Almalik planned it, years ago. Pray to your god and ride!"

Rodrigo was already running towards the horses.

And so, moments later, for the second time in less than a year, Alvar de Pellino—wet and burnt and cold, pushing past exhaustion and half a dozen small wounds—found himself galloping flat-out through darkness over the plain north of Fezana towards a hamlet named Orvilla.

Ammar ibn Khairan was beside him, against all allegiances, and the king of Valledo was on his other side with Jehane and her parents and Husari and two children and a party of fifty of the king's guard streaming behind them in the cool, clear night.

Ahead of them all, whipping his mount like a madman under the stars and the white moon, was a father racing time and the turning heavens to his child.

Chapter XVI

༄

Until the very moment, under the stars and the white moon in Al-Rassan of the infidels, when the veiled ones appeared out of the darkening plain, Ibero the cleric had succeeded in persuading himself that the hand of Jad was upon his shoulder after all, guiding him.

He had shaped his plan on that first morning, riding west from Rancho Belmonte in the rain. It was possible— he'd been forced to admit it—that Miranda had been right. That in furthering the demands of holy faith Ibero had done wrong by the family he so dearly loved. If that were so, he had vowed on that grey, cold morning he would do all he could to ensure that the wrong was contained and redressed. Miranda Belmonte might have turned him away, driven him from his home, but he would not turn his back on her or her family.

He had fallen in with a company of soldiers from the ranch country, heading towards Carcasia in response to the king's summons: the same summons that had claimed the two boys. He went with the soldiers. This was a holy war, in name at least, and clerics were not unwelcome if they could keep up on the ride. Ibero knew how to handle a horse. Years with the Belmonte had made certain of that.

He found Fernan and Diego among the king's party seven days later in the plain south of Carcasia, amid the tents and banners of a war camp. Rodrigo's sons were being treated with evident respect, although the scrutiny afforded Diego by those who knew why he was here made

Ibero uncomfortable. Against his will, he was reminded of Miranda's words: those with the far-sight, or whatever name was given it, *had* been burned in the past. In the not-so-distant past. This, Ibero told himself again, was a more enlightened age.

The boys weren't entirely pleased to see him, but Ibero had a streak of stubbornness in his nature and he made it clear to all concerned, including the elegant High Cleric from Ferrieres, that where the sons of Rodrigo Belmonte went, Ibero also would go. He didn't tell the boys he had been driven from the ranch by their mother; perhaps he ought to have, but he couldn't manage to do it. That meant his presence with them involved a deception, but he trusted the god to forgive him for that. He meant well. He had always meant well.

Fernan and Diego had obviously been up to mischief on the way here and since arriving. They were high-spirited and too clever for their own good sometimes. It was judged useful to have their tutor about for discipline. There was a tale doing the rounds of the camp about the rock-laden saddlebags of one of the soldiers who had brought them here. It was quite a funny story, but Ibero was practised at not encouraging his charges with visible amusement.

Soon afterwards they rode south through the no-man's-land with the army of reconquest; with the vanguard, in fact, for Diego and Fernan were kept close to the king himself.

Ibero had never seen his king before. Ramiro of Valledo was a handsome, impressive man. Worthy, the little cleric thought humbly, to be the instrument of Esperaña's reconquest. If the god allowed. He was acutely aware that all the men in this army were a part of something momentous. The king kept speaking of a limited campaign, a tactical capture of Fezana, but even Ibero the cleric knew that once Valledo was in Al-Rassan the shape and tenor of their age would have changed forever.

The lean, elegant constable, Count Gonzalez de Rada, hovered unsettlingly close to the boys all the way south.

Ibero knew that Ser Rodrigo and this man had no love for each other, but he also remembered that de Rada had sworn to guard Belmonte's family when Rodrigo had been exiled. Ibero hoped—and prayed, each morning and when the sun went down—that the sardonic constable's proximity was a manifestation of that vow and nothing else.

South of the two small *tagra* forts the king's vanguard began to open a distance from the rest of the army, with outriders galloping back and forth to keep communications flowing.

This was how Ibero learned that Miranda Belmonte d'Alveda had also become a part of their army, joining the entourage of Queen Ines, who had chosen to come with her husband into the lands of the infidels. When he told the boys they seemed unsurprised. Ibero was disconcerted by that until he remembered the obvious.

Diego's gift was difficult to deal with at times. He would have known before the messengers came, Ibero realized. A little reluctantly, he admonished Diego.

"You ought to be telling the rest of us if you...see anything. It might be important. That is why we are here, after all."

Diego's expression had been comical. "*My mother?*" he asked. "Ibero, my mother's arrival is important to the war?"

Put that way, he did have a point. Fernan, predictably, had a different perspective entirely.

"Isn't this wonderful," he had exclaimed indignantly. "Our first campaign and everyone from home comes trotting along. Who else should we expect? The cook, our nurses from childhood? This is ridiculous! Are you here to make sure we keep warm at night?"

Diego had laughed. Ibero was too uneasy about the tidings of Miranda to be amused or chastising. Fernan's words were disrespectful, but Ibero could understand how a young man on his first campaign might feel...crowded by his tutor's arrival, and now his mother's.

Nothing for it. If the boys felt unhappy or the soldiers teased them they would have to deal with that themselves.

The truth was, they *were* too young to be here, and would not have come had Diego not been what he was. And had not Ibero sent a certain letter to Esteren.

He sent another letter—a formal message to Miranda by one of the outriders. He reported his own presence and the good health and respectful treatment of the two boys. No word came back.

They did hear, indirectly, that the queen was entirely recovered from her unfortunate accident and that she had great faith in her new physician, a doctor from one of the *tagra* forts.

The story was that he had saved Queen Ines's life at the very brink of death. Diego, in particular, was fascinated by the tale and ferreted out all the details he could from those who had been at that meeting of the three kings. Fernan was more interested in upcoming events. He managed to attach himself to the king's entourage, staying close to Count Gonzalez, in fact. It was Fernan who explained to the other two why they were leaving the Asharite farms and hamlets untouched as they rode.

They had passed a number of them since leaving the *tagra* lands. The villagers and farmers had fled into the hills with most of their belongings, but it had always been customary, in the wars of Ashar and Jad, to fire the houses and fields.

Things were different this time.

Despite a visible disagreement emanating from Geraud de Chervalles, King Ramiro was insistent on the point. This was not a raid, Fernan reported the king as saying. They were coming south to take Fezana and to stay. And if they did that, they would need Asharites to resettle these villages and farmhouses, to pay taxes and till the fields. Time and steady governance would bring Jad back into Al-Rassan, the king had declared, not burnings and destruction. Ibero wasn't entirely sure how that meshed with holy doctrine, but he kept silent in the presence of his betters.

Fernan would spend the time after twilight prayers, before dark and bed, drawing maps for his brother and the cleric, explaining what might happen when they reached Fezana, and after. Ibero noted, a little wryly, that he was entirely conversant now with the location—and the proper spelling—of all the major cities and rivers in Al-Rassan.

Four more days passed. The spring weather remained mild; they made steady progress, drumming hooves and the dust of an army moving over the grasslands of Al-Rassan.

Then Diego announced, shortly before they broke camp one morning, that he had seen his father riding west.

∽

The king and the constable and the tall cleric from Ferrieres had asked all sorts of questions he couldn't answer.

Once, such questions had made Diego feel inadequate, as if he was letting the questioners down by not being able to reply. He didn't like disappointing people. Later, though, the queries—even from his parents—had begun to irritate him, betraying, as they did, such a failure to understand the limits of his capability. Diego had made himself practise being patient at such times. The fact was, people *didn't* understand his limits; they couldn't possibly, because they didn't understand how he did what he did.

Not that Diego really understood his own gift; where it came from, why he had it, what it meant. He knew some things, of course. He knew that what he could do marked him as different from others. He knew—from his mother long ago—that there was some undefined danger associated with being different in this way, and that he was not to tell others about what he could do.

All that, of course, had changed now. Horsemen had come from the king of Valledo and taken him to war. Fernan, naturally, had come too. Fernan was the one who really wanted to go to war, but when they had reached the encampment by Carcasia's walls it had become clear—during a first intimidating meeting with the king himself and the cleric from over the mountains—that Diego was the one they wanted. He'd had to explain, shyly, what it was he could do.

Not so much, really. He could see their disappointment. At times over the years he had wondered about all the secrecy and anxiety. It wasn't a complicated gift: he could sometimes tell where his family was, even when they were far away. His father, his mother, his brother, though Fernan was never far from him and his mother very seldom was.

Also, he could sometimes sense danger coming for any of the three of them. As to that, it had almost always been his father. His father's life involved quite a lot of danger.

Fernan wanted to be exactly like their father. He dreamed of it, practised for it, had rushed through his childhood hungry for a man's weapons, and war.

Fernan was stronger and quicker, though they had been born identical. There were times when Diego thought their father preferred Fernan, but there were other times when he thought otherwise. He loved his father without reservation. Other people found Rodrigo intimidating, he knew. Diego thought that was funny. Fernan didn't; Fernan considered it useful. They differed in such small things.

It didn't much matter, really. Nothing was ever going to separate the sons of Rodrigo Belmonte; they had realized that, definitively, when they were very young.

Fernan was enjoying almost everything about the campaign they had joined. Diego thought it was an interesting place to be, certainly better than another summer on the ranch, but he had a recurrence of his old feelings of anxiety when it appeared that he was disappointing those who had brought him here to help. At that first meeting he had answered the sharp questions from the High Cleric as best he could, and a few from the constable and the king, too. He liked the king most, though he supposed it wasn't really his place to *like* the king or not.

In any case, he couldn't be much help to them and he did his best to make that clear. Some days ago he had sensed his mother's arrival among the main body of the army, half a day behind them. He had told Fernan, of course. He'd considered telling the king and the cleric from Ferrieres just to have something to offer them, but thinking about his mother led him to keep quiet. *Her* movements, surely, weren't a part of this campaign. It felt like a kind of betrayal to talk about her, and so he didn't. Besides, he knew why she had come. Fernan did, too. It made Fernan prickly and angry; Diego just felt sad. They probably ought to have waited for her to come home that day before riding off. He'd been thinking guiltily about that since they left.

He knew she would not have let them join this army had she been at the ranch when the soldiers arrived. Fernan had scoffed at that suggestion when Diego mentioned it, pointing out that their mother, forceful as she might be, was hardly likely to have defied a direct summons from the king.

Diego wasn't so sure about that. He found that he missed his mother. She was gentler with him than with most people. He knew Fernan missed her too, but his brother would deny that if Diego spoke of it, so he didn't. They talked about their father, instead. It was all right, the way Fernan saw the world, to miss their father.

Then one morning Diego woke with an image of Rodrigo in his mind. It was blurred, because his father was riding very fast, and the landscape changed too quickly for Diego to get a clear picture. But he was coming towards them from the east, and he wasn't far away.

Diego lay under his blanket for a little while, eyes closed, concentrating. He heard Fernan wake up beside him, and start to say something. Then Fernan was quiet. He could usually tell when Diego was reaching out, or reaching in. It was hard to know the right words for this.

The landscape refused to become clearer. He saw that his father was with only a few people, not a large company, and there seemed to be a river beyond him—which would make sense, if Diego remembered the maps correctly. Rodrigo would be riding along the Tavares. He seemed to be agitated about something, but Diego had no sense of immediate danger. He tried casting his mind a little away from his father, to see if he could place him more exactly. He saw the river, grasslands, hills.

Then, vividly, an image of a city and its walls. That *had* to be Fezana.

His father was going into Fezana.

Diego opened his eyes. Fernan was there, watching him. Without speaking, his brother offered him an orange, already sliced. Diego bit into it.

"Why," he asked softly, "would Papa be going into Fezana?"

Fernan's brow knitted. "No idea," he said at length. "Is he? Are you going to tell the king?"

"Guess so. That's why we're here, isn't it?"

Fernan didn't like thinking of it that way, Diego knew, but it was the truth. They told Ibero first. Then Diego and his brother and their tutor went to find King Ramiro.

A remarkably short time after that conversation they were racing, with the king and the constable and one hundred of Valledo's best Horsemen, towards Fezana, a full day's fast ride away.

"This is *very* important," the king had said to Diego. "You have justified your being here. We thank you."

"Papa isn't in trouble, is he?" Fernan had asked sharply. He was no longer shy in this company. "He isn't exiled from *here*, is he? Only Valledo."

King Ramiro had paused then, and looked at both boys. His expression had softened. "Is that what you have been fearing? Your father isn't in trouble at all. Not from me. I have to catch him before he gets to Fezana. I have no idea why he's going there, but I want to stop him and end his exile. I need him badly on this campaign. I can't afford to have my best captain trapped inside the city I'm about to besiege, can I?"

Fernan had nodded gravely, as if he'd been thinking along these same lines. Perhaps he had. Diego, different in nature and response, had looked quickly at Count Gonzalez when the king named Rodrigo his best captain. He had been able to read nothing in the constable's features, though.

They rode so rapidly through the morning that they

actually caught and passed several groups of farmers and villagers heading for Fezana, fleeing their approach. People began screaming as the Horsemen raced by, but it wasn't until noontime that the king ordered a party of Asharites killed. Their first killings in this war.

It was important, Diego was given to understand. The people streaming into Fezana, and those already waiting there, had to fear them terribly—to be made to doubt the wisdom of resistance. Walled cities as well-defended as Fezana couldn't be stormed, they had to be besieged, and the morale of those inside was critical to that. A certain number of people had to die so that word of killings might run ahead into the city.

Neither he nor Fernan was part of the contingent that peeled away from their ranks and began cutting a swath through the cluster of families the king had indicated. Diego, for his own part, was entirely happy not to be involved. He saw Fernan looking back over his shoulder as they rode, watching the slaughter. Diego didn't look at all, after his first glance. He thought his brother was secretly relieved, as well, not to be part of that group. He didn't say this, of course. But Fernan's play-battles had always been against the veiled Muwardis, where despite being hideously outnumbered, the lords Fernan and Diego Belmonte with their gallant riders had managed to prevail, breaking through the ranks of the desert-spawned to rescue their captive father and the king and earn great praise.

Chopping down farmers and small children on a dusty road was something else entirely. The king's party galloped on, outrunning the screaming. The soldiers who had been detailed to the task caught up with them a little later. Geraud de Chervalles, looking excited and happy, blessed them and their weapons. In a ringing voice Diego thought was too loud, he called what they had done a proud moment in the history of Esperaña.

The king ordered a rest after that and men slipped down from their mounts to take water and food. The sun was high, but it was still early in the year and not too hot.

Diego walked a little way apart, found some bushes for shade, sat down on the ground and closed his eyes, looking for his father. It was his task. It was why they were here. There was nothing private or personal about his gift any more. He would have to think more about that, later.

He found Rodrigo quickly this time and realized something immediately. He could see the city in the same image as his father. There was something else, too, an aura Diego recognized from many times before.

He stood up, briefly dizzy, which sometimes happened. He went to find the king. Fernan saw him going and rose to follow. Diego waited for his brother and they walked over together. King Ramiro was sitting on a saddle blanket eating food from his lap, like a soldier, and drinking from a leather wine flask. He handed the flask and his platter to a servant when he saw Diego coming. He stood up.

"What is it, lad?"

"When will we reach Fezana, my lord?"

"Sunset. A little before, if we go very fast. Why?"

"My father is already there. On a hill just east of the walls. I don't think we can reach him. And I think...I believe he's in danger now, after he gets inside."

King Ramiro looked at him thoughtfully.

"Be more *precise*, in Jad's name!" It was the cleric from Ferrieres.

"He would be if he could, de Chervalles. You must see that." The king didn't appear to much like the High Cleric. He turned back to Diego. "You can anticipate danger as well as see it happening?"

"For my father, yes, but not always, my lord."

"You still have no idea why he is going into Fezana?" Diego shook his head.

"He is not with his company? A small party, you say?" Diego nodded.

There was a nervous cough. They all turned to Ibero. Diego hadn't heard him come up. Self-conscious in the extreme, the small cleric said, "I may be able to offer a thought on this, my lord."

"Do so." Geraud de Chervalles spoke before the king. Ramiro directed a glance at him but said nothing.

Ibero said, "In his letters home, Ser Rodrigo did say that his company had retained the services of a physician. A woman. A Kindath from Fezana. Jehane bet Ishak, I believe. Perhaps...?"

The king was briskly nodding his head. "That would make sense. Rodrigo knew we might be coming. He would be guided by loyalty if she is part of his company. Would this woman still have family in Fezana?"

"I would not know, my lord."

"I do." It was Fernan, speaking with assurance. "He wrote my mother about that. Her father was a physician as well, and still lives in Fezana."

The king quickly held up a hand. "Ishak of Fezana? Is that the father? The one blinded by Almalik?"

Fernan blinked. "I don't know anything about—"

"It must be! That's the man whose treatise the queen's doctor read! That is how he saved her life!" King Ramiro's eyes gleamed. "By Jad, I see it now. I know what is happening. Ser Rodrigo is going in, but he'll be coming out with them any way he can. He needs time before we arrive."

"You *will* tell us your thinking, I hope, my lord?" Geraud de Chervalles wore an expression poised between pique and curiosity.

"As much as you need to know," the king of Valledo said agreeably. The cleric reddened. The king, appearing not to notice, turned to Gonzalez de Rada. "Constable, this is what I want done, and I want it done swiftly..."

King Ramiro seemed to be extremely good at giving orders, so far as Diego could judge. A king must spend most of his time telling people what he wanted them to do, he supposed. A number of men were seen riding back to the main body of the army soon afterwards. He and Fernan remained with the king's guard.

They slowed their pace, however. And shortly before day's end, at a place to which one of the outriders led them—a stand of trees within sight of the river and the city walls, but not too close to them—they stopped, taking shelter at the edge of the trees.

King Ramiro, riding gloves in one hand, walked over, unexpectedly alone, to where Diego and Fernan and Ibero were watering their horses. He gestured, and Diego quickly handed his horse's reins to his brother and followed. Fernan made as if to come too, but the king held up a finger and shook his head and Diego watched his brother stop, crestfallen.

It was the first time he had been alone with the king. Kings weren't alone very often, he thought.

They walked through the stand of trees—beech and oak, a few cypresses like sentries at the edge of the wood. There were small white flowers everywhere, like a carpet on the forest floor. Diego wondered how they grew in such profusion in the dark, cool shade. They came to a place near the eastern end of the woods and here the king stopped. He turned to look south and Diego did the same.

In the light of the setting sun they could see the gleam of the Tavares River. Beyond it was Fezana. River and city had been nothing more than names on a map for Diego once, tests from their tutor: *"Name the cities owing allegiance at this time to the king of Cartada. Name that king. Now write those names, and spell them correctly."*

Tavares. Fezana. Almalik. Not just names any more. He was in Al-Rassan, land of terror and legend. Here with the army of Valledo, come to conquer. To *reconquer*, for all of this had once been their own, when Esperaña was a name of power in the world, long ago.

Truth to tell, looking out at those massive stone walls the color of honey in the slanting light, Diego Belmonte found himself wondering how even this king and this army dared imagine taking such a city. Nothing in his experience—he had only seen Esteren once, and then Carcasia—could compare with this splendor. Even as he stood looking south, his image of Valledo grew smaller.

Rising behind the walls Diego could see domes gleaming in the last of the light. Places of worship, he knew.

Shrines to beliefs the clerics of Jad named foul and evil.

They looked beautiful, though, to Diego.

As if reading his thoughts or following his gaze, the king said softly, "The two nearer domes—the blue and white—are those of the Kindath sanctuary. The silver ones that shine, the larger ones, are the temples of Ashar. At sundown, soon, we ought to be able to hear the bells for prayer, even from here. I remember loving that sound."

The king had spent a year exiled in Al-Rassan, Diego knew. Just as, earlier, Raimundo and Diego's own father had been exiled by King Sancho the Fat to the cities of the infidels. That episode was part of their family history, tangled up with why Rodrigo wasn't constable of Valledo any more.

Diego, feeling he was expected to say something, murmured, "My father ought to know this city well enough. He's been here before."

"I know that, Diego. Do you think you'll be able to tell me when he is coming out, and where? There will have to be a way out through the walls. The gates will be locked by now."

Diego looked up at his king. "I'll try."

"We need some warning. I want to be there, wherever he comes out. Will you know where he's going? Which part of the city?"

"Sometimes I can do that. Not always." Diego felt guilty again. "I'm sorry, my lord. I don't...I can't tell very well what I'll see. Sometimes there's nothing. I'm afraid I'm not very—"

A hand came down on his shoulder. "You have already been a help and if Jad finds us both worthy you will be again. Believe this. I am not saying words to ease you."

"But how, my lord?" Diego knew he probably shouldn't ask this but he had been wondering about it since leaving home.

The king looked down at him for a moment. "It isn't complex, if you understand war." His brow furrowed as he reached for words. "Diego, think of it this way: you know men cannot see very well in the dark of night. Think of war as *all* taking place in darkness. During battle or before battle, a captain, a king, knows only what is happening next to him, and not even that much very clearly. But if I have you with me and I have your father commanding a wing of my army—and by Jad I hope I will soon—then *you* can tell me something of what is happening where *he* is. Anything you give me is more than I would otherwise have had. Diego, you can be my beam of light, like a gift from the god, to see by in darkness."

There was a stirring of the wind; leaves rustled. Diego, looked up at his king, swallowing hard. It was odd, but in that moment he felt both larger and smaller than he was. He looked away, abashed. But his gaze fell once more upon the mighty walls and gleaming domes of Fezana and there was no comfort there.

He closed his eyes. The familiar spinning came. He reached out a hand and braced himself against a tree.

Then he was with his father, and aware of something else in the same moment. In a stillness at the edge of a wood Diego Belmonte reached out, trying to serve his country and his king, and he found himself enmeshed in Fezana's streets. He felt danger surrounding his father like a ring of fire.

It *was* fire, he realized.

Heart pounding, eyes still closed, concentrating as hard as he could, he said, "There are torches and a large crowd. People running. Houses are burning, my lord. There is an old man with my father."

"Is he blind?" the king asked quickly.

"I cannot tell that. Everything is burning."

"You're right! I see smoke now. In Jad's name, what are they doing there? Where is your father going?"

"My lord, I cannot, I...*wait.*"

Diego struggled to orient himself. He never saw actual faces with this sight, only presences, auras, an awareness of people, with his father—or mother, or brother—at the center. He sensed tall houses, walls, a fountain. A press of running figures. Then two domes, blue and white.

Behind his father. East. He opened his eyes, fought the dizziness, looking south. He pointed.

"They are going towards a place in the walls on this side of the city. There must be a way out, as you said. There is fighting. Why is there fighting, my lord?"

He looked anxiously up at the king. Ramiro's expression was grim.

"I don't know. I can only guess. If your father is with ben Yonannon and he is fighting, then it may be the Asharites are attacking the Kindath in the city. Why, I cannot tell. But it works to our gain—*if Rodrigo gets out.*"

Which offered no comfort.

"Come!" the king said. "You have helped me again. You are my beam of light, Diego Belmonte, truly."

Even as he said this, the sun went down. Twilight descended, swift and beautiful, over the plain north of Fezana. To the west, a last glow of red suffused the sky. The gleaming of the domes was gone. Diego, looking south as they ran back towards the others, saw smoke rising from the city.

He was not allowed to go see if his father was able to get out and greet him if he did.

The king let Fernan come with him but Diego was forbidden. It was judged that there was too much danger near the walls, with only the fifty men the king took with him, quietly stealing up to the river and moat in darkness.

Diego was outraged. *He* was the reason the king knew where Rodrigo was going, he was the *only* reason Ramiro was able to do this, and he was being denied the chance to join them. There were, it emerged, disadvantages to being useful to the king of Valledo.

Fernan was elated, but sympathetic enough to try to conceal it. Diego wasn't fooled. He watched his brother leave with the king's party and he turned, grim and silent, to go with the other half of the vanguard troop. Ibero was with him, of course, and—to Diego's surprise—Count

Gonzalez de Rada.

It was possible, he mused, riding west along the river, that the constable had no desire to meet Rodrigo in this unexpected way. It was also possible that the constable was taking his oath to guard Rodrigo's family very seriously. Fernan was with the king, so Gonzalez would stay with Diego. He looked thoughtfully towards the constable but it was almost dark by then and they were riding without torches.

They didn't have far to go. They saw campfires. The white moon was rising behind them as they came up to the hamlet where the food wagons had begun assembling during the afternoon. This was, Diego was given to understand, the obvious place to locate the stores and supplies for a siege. That had been decided upon a long time ago by those who knew the terrain here.

Diego and the others entered the tiny village—it had already been abandoned by the Asharites. The hamlet lay alongside the river. There was a water mill. Almost all of the houses looked new, which was unexpected. The smell of cooking came to Diego. He discovered in that moment that he was ravenous. This was an absurd time to be thinking of food. On the other hand, he told himself, what else was there to do now, besides wait?

He dismounted between Ibero and the constable. Men came running to take their horses. Diego turned back and looked east, towards the low moon. Fernan would be at the river and the walls by now, waiting to surprise their father. It wasn't, Diego decided, fair at all.

He looked around. This hamlet had a name, of course— Fernan had marked it on one of his maps—but Diego had forgotten it. He half-expected Ibero to demand that he give the name. He was prepared to be extremely sarcastic if this happened.

They weren't far from Fezana in this cluster of huts and houses, but at night under stars the city would normally have been lost to sight. It wasn't now. Diego saw a red glow to the east and he knew Fezana was burning. His father was in there.

He put aside his anger with that thought and forgetting about hunger closed his eyes.

He touched Rodrigo's presence, was aware of him by the city walls but still inside. Just across the river he found Fernan. With relief, he realized that he had no sense of immediate danger. No fighting near either of them. On impulse Diego reached out north and found his mother—closer than he had expected.

He took comfort in knowing where she was. That they were all safe, for the moment. It even seemed they might be together soon, here with the king's army in Al-Rassan. That would be good. That would be wonderful, in fact. Diego opened his eyes, letting his mind come back to the hamlet and, reassured, he let himself think about food again.

In that moment he heard a low, hard drumming sound and the first scream, cut off. Then he saw the Muwardis.

∽

It was, in the end, as easy as might have been expected. Not that this mattered to the desert-born. If anything, it was a vexation: when war was too easy there was less glory in it.

Aziz ibn Dabir of the Zuhrite tribe, assigned to serve in Fezana by the king of Cartada—to whom he had originally been posted by his own lord, Yazir ibn Q'arif, ruler of all the desert—had taken one hundred of his men west from the city earlier that day. They had stayed on the south bank of the Tavares and then crossed at a fording place where the river curved and slowed.

At twilight they offered the sunset prayers and then, moving with extreme care, had doubled back west towards the hamlet of Orvilla.

It had been considered, years ago, by the last king of Cartada and his advisors, that if the accursed sun-worshippers ever dared to venture south with designs upon Fezana, they would be very likely to choose Orvilla as a base for their supplies during a siege. It was the obvious place and because of that the plan of Almalik I, Aziz had to concede, was a shrewd one. This was true notwithstanding that it had been devised by wine-drinkers in Al-Rassan, and not by tribesmen pure in the will of Ashar.

Still, it was the warriors of the Majriti who had been asked to perform the attack. *Of course,* thought Aziz. Who among the womanish men left in Fezana could have implemented this?

During their silent loop back to the east, Aziz had moved ahead of the company with his two best outriders. Leaving their horses out of sight, they had crawled through the grass to overlook Orvilla.

It was exactly as had been foreseen.

The Jaddites, stupid in their predictability, had indeed sent their wagons here. Whichever of their women had come south would almost certainly be arriving in Orvilla tomorrow. Secure in the notion that the people of the countryside had fled into the city, they hadn't bothered to detail more than a rudimentary force to guard those setting up camp.

Aziz heard careless laughter, saw tents being readied, smelled meat already cooking on the fires. He caught snatches of conversation in the sibilant accents of Esperaña. He didn't understand what was being said. It didn't matter. What mattered was that his tribesmen were going to achieve a slaughter here. One that ought to shake the invading northerners to their godless souls. Aziz had ideas as to how to heighten that effect. It was a shame that the women weren't here yet: that would have made things perfect. Aziz had not had a woman for some time.

Unconsciously he stroked the head of the hammer looped at his belt—his own favorite weapon. It had been his father's before him, on the legendary first ride of the Zuhrites out of the farthest west. It would one day belong to his own eldest son, if Ashar's stars allowed it to be so.

Ashar seemed to be with him in that moment. Just as Aziz was about to slip down from his vantage point and order the attack, something alerted him to danger. He held out a warning hand to his two companions and placed an ear to the ground. Hoofbeats. The other two, doing the same, looked at Aziz in the darkness.

They waited. A few moments later a company of soldiers rode up on the proud stallions of Valledo. Aziz coveted those horses almost as much as he wanted to sever the heads and sexual organs of the men who rode them. It was dark of course, but there were fires in Orvilla and Aziz was blessed with good night vision. He made out fifty riders, not more. They could deal with that, in fact he *wanted* to deal with them. This was now an attack in which glory could be found.

Timing mattered. They had been ordered to engage and then swiftly withdraw—not risk being trapped outside the city. He saw the new Horsemen enter Orvilla, riding through a gate in the low fence rebuilt since the fire of last summer. He bent his head towards one of his men and whispered his orders. Nothing very complex. There was no need for complications here.

"These men will be hungry now, and vulnerable. Get back to the others. Tell them we attack now, in Ashar's name."

The god's stars were steady above them. The new Jaddites were dismounting, even as he watched. Their horses were being led away by servants. These men would be fighters, Aziz knew, but on foot? Against one hundred of the best-trained Muwardis in Al-Rassan?

A moment later Aziz heard the sound of hooves. He stood up and looked back. He saw the curved line of his tribesmen approaching. One man came sweeping up to him, the reins of Aziz's horse in one hand. Aziz swung up onto the saddle cloth while the horses were still moving. He pulled his hammer free of his belt.

He heard a scream from one of the cookfires. The sound broke off sharply. Someone had shot an arrow. There were other cries, the desperate sounds of men caught utterly by surprise.

They reached the low fence and hurdled it. Aziz lifted his own voice then, crying Ashar's name in triumph beneath the watching, holy stars.

They did, in the darkness of night, what they had come out from Fezana to do. They killed, and more than that. A message was to be given here, and the northerners were not to be permitted to avoid that message.

There was some resistance, which offered a kind of pleasure. The fifty men who had come were soldiers, but they were outnumbered and on foot, and the Muwardis knew exactly what they were doing.

Aziz had already identified the leader of the soldiers and chosen him for his own, as a captain of the tribes had to do if he wanted to keep his honor and rank. He raced up to the man, wheeling his hammer in anticipation—but then had to rock wildly in the saddle to avoid a leaping sword blow from the northerner. The man was no longer young, but he was quick, and had very nearly been deadly. Aziz, going past, turning his horse, saw the tribesman behind him fall to a second slash of the same sword. The Jaddite commander, a dark, tall man, shoved the tribesman from the saddle and swung himself up on the horse in the same motion. The two leaders faced each other. Aziz smiled. This was life, this was what a man lived for.

The Valledan screamed something suddenly, and brandished his sword high. It was too flamboyant, he was too far away. A distraction.

Aziz turned, instinctively, and saw the boy with a blade coming towards him from behind. If his horse had been stabbed Aziz might have been in peril, but the boy disdained such tactics, swinging upwards for the Muwardi's ribs. Aziz blocked the blow and then—something he had done a hundred times, at least—brought his hammer across and down, through the feeble parrying of that sword. He smashed the boy's skull, felt it break like the shell of an egg.

"*Diego!*" the Valledan leader cried.

Aziz laughed aloud. The dark Valledan drove his seized

mount forward and chopped at the neck of Aziz's horse. The sword bit deep. The animal screamed, rearing wildly on its hind legs. Aziz fought to keep his seat, felt himself sliding, and saw the northerner's long sword coming.

Had Aziz ibn Dabir been a lesser man he would have died then. He was a Muwardi though, of the Zuhrites, hand-picked to come to Al-Rassan. He hurled his body from the saddle, away from the sweeping blade, and hit the ground on the far side of his horse.

He came up with his left shoulder hurting but his hammer ready. It wasn't necessary. Aziz saw that the Valledan had been dispatched from behind by two of the tribesmen. One sword had gone in so far it had come out through the man's breast where he lay on the ground.

Aware that he had lost more than dignity in this encounter, Aziz strode over and seized the sword from the second tribesman. Enraged, he severed the dead man's head with a blow. He spoke a command, breathing hard. One of his men leaped from his horse and pulled down the lower clothing of the dead man. Aziz, not troubling to be neat about it, castrated the Valledan. Then he seized the dead boy, flipped him on his belly, and dragged the headless, emasculated captain on top of him, as if they had been lovers butchered in congress.

It was all a matter of sending a message. Making the Jaddites brutally aware of what they faced if they remained in the lands of Ashar so far from their pastures in the north.

Aziz looked up. An outrider was racing towards them from the eastern edge of the hamlet.

"More of them!" he shouted. "Riding from Fezana."

"How many?"

"Fifty. Maybe more."

Aziz scowled. He badly wanted to stay and defeat these men as well, especially since his own disgrace, but surprise was gone now, and the new Valledans would be mounted and ready. His orders had been clear, and he understood them too well to disobey, whatever pride might desire.

He ordered the withdrawal. Dead Valledans were strewn through the camp. The food and the supply wagons were burning. They rode out to the north and crossed the river by the narrow bridge. The last men chopped it down, just to be sure.

They raced back to Fezana without incident, were known and admitted at the southern gate. Aziz made his report to the governor. Then he and his men were immediately detailed to join others in fighting the fires that had begun in their absence. It appeared that someone had chosen a poor moment to perform an entirely proper act: dealing with the Kindath of the city.

It was mid-morning before Aziz ibn Dabir fell, exhausted, into bed. His shoulder had begun to hurt quite badly during the labors of the long night. He dozed fitfully, despite his fatigue, knowing that word would be travelling south across Al-Rassan and then the straits to the desert all too soon.

Word of how Aziz ibn Dabir had been on the very brink of defeat in combat with a single Valledan and had only been saved by the intercession of men he led. Aziz was painfully aware that the extent of his own contribution to the ambush at Orvilla had been to kill a child and then mutilate a man others had slain for him—which, among the tribes, was woman's work. Yazir might tolerate this, in a captain of experience, but his brother Ghalib, who commanded the armies of the Majriti for him, was less likely to do so.

And Aziz happened to be one of those who knew the origins of the extremely unusual thong Ghalib ibn Q'arif wore about his neck.

∽

He could not remember feeling so pure a terror in all his life. His heart was pounding uncontrollably as he raced over the plain; he thought he might actually lose control of himself, fall off the horse, be trampled to death by those who followed in his wake.

That might be, thought Rodrigo Belmonte, a blessing, the way shooting a horse or a hunting dog with a broken leg was a gift of mercy.

He was a horse or a dog like that.

He was a father trying to outrun the arc of time to his son. Terror was in him, defined him, made his mind a blank of dread.

Nothing like this, ever before. Fear, yes. No honest soldier could truly say he had never known fear. Courage lay in fighting past that, through it, rising above it to do what one had to do. He had faced his own death many times, and feared it, and dealt with that fear. He had never felt what he was experiencing now, in this night of Al-Rassan, hurtling towards Orvilla for the second time in less than a year.

And with that thought, Rodrigo saw the fires burning ahead of him and knew—a soldier, a trained soldier—that he was too late.

He heard a sound in the night. A name, his own voice crying, over and over, the one name. His child's. It was dark. It was dark under the stars, and there were fires ahead.

The Muwardis—it would have been Muwardi warriors, of course—had left by the time he came racing up to the low stockade and leaped it and flung himself from his horse amid burning wagons and tents and slain, mutilated men he knew.

He found Ibero first. He had no comprehension of how the man had come to be here. The little cleric lay in a pool of his own blood, black in the light of the fires. His hands and feet had been cut off. They lay a little distance from his body, pieces of a child's torn doll.

Rodrigo smelled burning flesh. Some of their people had been thrown on the cooking fires. He stumbled towards the central green, remembering it from the summer before. Hope gone now, but with no defenses in him against this, he saw the severed head of Gonzalez de Rada and, beside it, the body of the constable, leggings torn off, sprawled obscenely atop the small, face-down figure of a boy.

Rodrigo heard himself make a sound again.

A wordless plea. For mercy, for kindness, for time to run backwards and let him be here soon enough. In time to save his child, or die with Diego if nothing else were allowed.

Sounds, sights, the smell of flesh burning faded away into a distance. He walked over to the two bodies lying there.

As in a dream, his movements impossibly slow, he knelt down and rolled Gonzalez de Rada's body off the prone figure of his son. He saw then—dreamlike, unbelieving—what else had been done to the constable of Valledo.

Then, gently, gently, as in a dream, he turned Diego over on the blood-soaked ground and saw the blow that had broken his head. He began to weep then, rocking back and forth, for the child in his arms who had gone away.

He heard, as from a distance, others coming up now. Horses. Footsteps. Running, then walking. They stopped. Somehow a thought came to him. Not looking up, unable to look up, he said, to whoever was near, "Fernan. Stop Fernan. Don't let him see this."

"It is me, Papa. Oh, Papa, is he *dead?*"

He looked up then. He forced himself. He had a living child. Twin to this one. Bonded souls. Different all their lives, but one birth, one face. Together, always, against what the world had brought them. Not any more. Fernan would be feeling a nakedness now, Rodrigo thought, an icy wind blowing right through him in the place where his brother had been.

By the light of burning wagons he saw Fernan's face. And Rodrigo Belmonte knew, in that moment, that the boy would never entirely move past this image of seeing his dead brother in his father's arms. It would shape him and define his life to come and there was nothing Rodrigo could do to alter that.

He had to stop weeping, though. He had to try.

Ammar ibn Khairan was here, just behind Fernan. His had been the warning, immediate but too late. He, too, would have seen slaughters like this in his time. Killings and desecrations meant to convey a message, a warning.

Rodrigo remembered, suddenly, the Day of the Moat and what ibn Khairan had done to the king of Cartada in the aftermath of that. Killing. An answer, of a kind.

He realized that he was close to losing all control. "Ammar, please take him away," he whispered. "He ought not to be seeing this. Go with this man, Fernan. *Please.*"

"Is he dead?" Fernan asked again, ignoring or unable to register the mute, terrible evidence of the shattered and bleeding skull.

"Come, Fernan," said ibn Khairan gently, a poet's voice. "Let us walk over to the river and sit a moment. Perhaps we can each pray, after our own fashion. Will you do that with me?"

In the distant, muffled place to which he seemed to have come, Rodrigo watched his son walk away with Ammar ibn Khairan of Aljais. An Asharite. An enemy. *Guard him*, he wanted to say to Ammar, but there was no need now, and it was too late. The damage had been done.

He looked down again at the child he was holding. Diego. Little one. Poets everywhere wrote about hearts breaking for love. He wondered if they really knew. He felt, absurdly, as if there was an actual crack running straight down through his own heart and that crack would never be mended, never become healed and whole. The world had entered in and broken him past repair.

There was an army here, with the king. An army in Al-Rassan. He wondered, vaguely, how much killing he was about to undertake, in an effort—hopeless before it ever began—to avenge and assuage this moment. This small, limp figure in his arms. Diego.

He wondered if anything would ever reach through to him again.

"*Oh, dear Jad,*" he heard someone say sharply. Ramiro, the king of Valledo. "Oh, not this, in the name of what is holy!"

Rodrigo looked over. Something in the king's voice.

New torches, more riders approaching. From the north. Not the king's party that had met them by the river and the walls. The other direction. Valledan banners, lit by flames.

They came nearer and stopped. He saw the queen of Valledo, Ines.

He saw his wife dismount to stand there, looking straight towards him, motionless. Without defense.

He had no idea why Miranda was here. Why any of them were here. He had to move, though, to try to spare her a small part of this, at least. If he could.

Gently, gently, he laid Diego down again on the cold ground and rose, stumbling, blood soaking his clothing, and went towards Miranda between the fires and slain men.

He rubbed at his eyes, his face. His hands seemed to belong to someone else. There were words needed now, but he didn't have them. It was a dream. He would never wake from this.

"Please tell me he is only hurt," his wife said very quietly. "Rodrigo, please say he is only hurt."

He opened his mouth and closed it. He shook his head.

Miranda screamed then. The name. Only the name. The same as he had done. It went into him the way a spear enters.

He reached out to take her in his arms. She went past him, running, to where Diego lay. There were other people around him now, Rodrigo saw, turning. Jehane had come up. She was kneeling beside his son. Another man from the queen's party, someone he didn't recognize, was on the other side. Miranda stopped beside them.

"Oh, please?" she said, in a small voice he had never heard before. "Please?"

She knelt beside Jehane and gathered Diego's hands between her own.

He saw Fernan coming back from the river with ibn Khairan. He would have heard his mother scream. Fernan was crying now, his face distorted. A wind, blowing right through him.

Only this morning, riding towards Fezana, Rodrigo Belmonte would have said, if asked, that the world was a hard place but an interesting one, and he would have named himself a man blessed beyond his worth by the god, with love and companionship and tasks worthy of a man.

He'd had two sons this morning, though.

He came back to where Diego lay. Someone—the king, it appeared—had placed his own cloak over the mutilated body of Gonzalez de Rada nearby. Fernan was standing behind his mother. He was not asking for comfort, Rodrigo saw. He was keeping very still, weeping, with a hand on Miranda's shoulder, looking down at his brother. He was thirteen years old.

Jehane finished what she was doing. She looked up at Rodrigo. "He isn't dead but I'm afraid he's dying." Her face was white. Her clothing was still wet from the river, he saw. It was all so dreamlike. "Rodrigo, I'm so sorry. The blow has broken his head, here. There is too much pressure. He will not wake up. It will not be long." She looked at the other woman beside her, the child's hands in hers. "He is...he is not in pain now, my lady."

He'd had a dream once in Ragosa, such a strange one, of the two of them—Miranda and Jehane—standing at sunset somewhere. Not speaking, no clear details, only standing together at the end of a day.

It was dark here, however, and they were kneeling on the ground. Miranda said nothing at all, made no movement, eyes on her child. Then she did move, freeing one of her hands and laying it, so softly, against the broken place on Diego's head.

Jehane looked up at him again, and Rodrigo saw the sorrow in her eyes, and the rage. The physician's rage at what they could not defeat, the things that claimed human lives too soon, leaving doctors helpless. She looked across Diego's body at the other man.

"You are a doctor?" she asked.

He nodded. "To the queen, formerly with the army."

"I will aid you here, then," she said quietly. "There may be others who need our services. Surely they are not all dead. There may be some we can save."

"You would do this?" the man asked. "For a Jaddite army?"

A spasm of impatience crossed Jehane's face. "As to that," she said, "I am physician to the company of Rodrigo Belmonte. After tonight, I have no idea, but for the moment I am yours to command."

"May I hold him?" Miranda, whispering, to Jehane. As if no one else had spoken.

Rodrigo took another step forward, helplessly.

"You can do no harm to him at all, my lady." Jehane's voice was as gentle as he had ever heard it. "Of course you may hold him." She hesitated, then repeated, "He is not in pain."

She made as if to rise.

"Jehane, wait." Another voice, from behind them. A woman's voice. Rodrigo turned, very slowly. "Your father wishes to examine the boy," said Eliane bet Danel.

In Al-Rassan, in Esperaña, Ferrieres, Karch, Batiara—even, in time, in the far-off eastern homelands of the Asharites—what happened that night in a burning hamlet near Fezana became legend, told so often among physicians, courts, military companies, in universities, taverns, places of worship, that it became imbued with the aura of magic and the supernatural.

It was not, of course, supernatural. What Ishak ben Yonannon did—blind under the white moon and stars and the torches brought for those who assisted him—was as precise and carefully worked out as what he had done five years before in Cartada, delivering the last child of Almalik I, and it was as wondrous as that.

Indeed, it was more than that had been. Sightless, unable to communicate except through his wife who understood every mangled syllable he spoke, handling a surgeon's blades and implements for the first time since his blinding, working by touch and memory and instinct, ben Yonannon did something even Galinus had only hinted might possibly be done.

He carved an opening in the skull of Diego Belmonte, around the place where the Muwardi blow had broken the boy's head, and he drew forth the shattered bone that had been driven down into what was shockingly exposed beneath the peeled-back scalp and the opened skull. The intruded fragment of bone that would have killed Rodrigo's son before the blue moon joined the white one in the sky.

Trepanning, it was called in the text of Galinus. Jehane knew that, and so, it appeared, did Bernart d'Iñigo, the Jaddite physician assisting them. And they both knew, as well, that it had never been done.

She would never even have tried, Jehane was aware, all through what happened. Never have *thought* to try, or dreamed it was possible. With awe, fighting back the desire to cry all the time, she watched her father's sure, steady hands probe and define the wound, circumscribe it, then wield the small saw and chisel with which he cut a hole in Diego Belmonte's head.

He gave them instructions when he needed to; her mother, standing above them, under a torch held by the king of Valledo himself, translated his words. Jehane or Bernart moved, as ordered, to offer a blade, a saw, a clamp, to sponge away the heavily flowing blood where Ishak had peeled back the skin of the boy's scalp. Diego was being held in a sitting position, that the blood might drain away and not into the wound.

It was his father who was holding him.

Rodrigo's eyes were closed most of the time, concentrating on keeping utterly still, which Ishak, through Eliane, had said was imperative. Perhaps he was praying. Jehane didn't know. She did know, moved beyond words, that Diego never budged. Rodrigo held his child rock-steady, without shifting his position once through the whole of that impossible, blind surgery on the plain.

Jehane had a strange illusion at one point: that Rodrigo could have sat like this with his child in his arms forever if need was. That he might almost *want* to do that. A stone, a statue, a father doing the one thing left for him to do, and allowed.

The shattered bone of the skull came out in one ugly, jagged piece. Ishak had Jehane probe the open wound to be sure he had it all. She found two small fragments and removed them with pincers d'Iñigo handed her. Then she and the Valledan doctor sutured the flaps of skin and bandaged the wound and when that was done they remained, on their knees, on either side of the boy.

They laid Diego down then, Rodrigo moving to stand silently above him beside Miranda. The brother—Fernan—was behind his mother. To Jehane's eyes he had an obvious need for something to make him sleep. She doubted he would accept it.

The white moon was directly overhead by then, the blue climbing in the eastern sky. The fires had been put out. Other doctors had come, summoned from the body of the army north of them. They were dealing with the survivors. There didn't appear to be very many of those.

A great deal of time seemed to have passed, Jehane realized. Ishak, guided by Eliane and Ammar, had moved a little apart, to a camp stool provided for him.

Jehane and the Jaddite doctor, d'Iñigo, looked at each other across the body of the boy. D'Iñigo had an unfortunate face but kind eyes, Jehane thought. He had been calmly competent all through what had just been done. She hadn't expected that of a Valledan physician.

He cleared his throat, struggling with fatigue and emotion.

"Whatever..." he began, and then stopped. He swallowed. "Whatever happens to me, whatever else I do, this will always be the proudest moment of my life as a doctor. To have been a small part of this. With your father, who is my...who I respect so much. In his writings, and..." He stopped, overcome.

Jehane discovered that she was overwhelmingly tired. Her father must be exhausted. It hadn't shown. If she wasn't careful she would begin remembering what had happened in Fezana before all this, and that wouldn't do. Not yet. She had to stay in control.

She said, "He may not survive. You know that."

D'Iñigo shook his head. "He will. He will survive! That is the wonder of it. You saw what was done as well as I. The bone came out! It was flawless."

"And we have *no* idea whether anyone can live through an opening up of their skull like that."

"Galinus said—"

"Galinus never did it! It was sacrilege to him. To the Asharites, the Kindath. To all of us. You know that!" She hadn't meant to raise her voice. People looked over at them.

Jehane gazed back down at the unconscious boy. He was lying now on a pallet and pillow, covered in blankets. He was utterly white, from the loss of so much blood. That was one of the dangers now. One of them. Jehane laid her fingers against his throat. The pulse was steady, if too fast. But even as she did this and studied Diego's face, Jehane realized that she, too, was certain he would live. It was unprofessional, hopelessly emotional.

It was an absolute conviction.

She looked up, at Rodrigo, and the wife he loved, the mother of this child, and she nodded her head. "He is doing well. As well as we could hope," she said. Then she rose and went to where her father and mother were. Ammar was with them, which was good. It was very good.

Jehane knelt at Ishak's feet and laid her head in his lap, the way she used to when she was a child, and she felt her father's hands—his strong, calm, steady hands—come to rest upon her head.

After a time she stood up—because she was not, in truth, a little girl any more, dwelling in her parents' house—and she turned to the man she loved among all others in the world and Ammar opened his arms for her and she let him draw away a little of what had happened to her people in the city that night, with his touch.

Chapter XVII

∽

After holding a steady torch over Diego Belmonte in the dark of that night, Alvar de Pellino watched Jehane's father walk wearily with his wife to the edge of the village and then stumble alone through the eastern gate out into the grass. There he knelt down and, rocking slowly back and forth on his knees, began to pray.

It was Husari, coming to stand with Alvar, stained with blood and ash and sweat—as Alvar knew himself to be—who murmured, softly, "This will be the Kindath lament. Under both moons. For the dead."

"In Fezana?"

"Of course. But if I know this man he is offering a part of it for Velaz."

Alvar winced. He looked back out at the shape of the man on his knees in darkness. He had, shamefully, forgotten about Velaz. Jehane's parents would only have heard those tidings tonight. Watching the old physician rocking slowly back and forth, Alvar felt an unexpected renewal, quiet and sure, of what he had begun to realize on the ride west: he was not going to be a soldier, after all.

He could kill, well enough it seemed, lacking neither in courage nor calm nor skill, but he had no heart for the butchery of war. He could not name it as the singers did: a pageantry, a contest, a glorious field whereon men could search out and find their honor.

He had no idea what the alternatives were or might be, but he knew that this wasn't the night to sort through that. He heard a sound from behind and turned. Rodrigo walked up to them.

"Alvar, I'd be grateful if you'd come with me." His tone was grave; there was a bone-weariness at the bottom of it. Diego was still unconscious; Jehane had said he would probably be so all night and into the morning. "I think I want a witness for what happens next. Are you all right?"

"Of course," Alvar said quickly. "But what is...?"

"The king has asked to speak with me."

Alvar swallowed. "And you want me to..."

"I do. I need one of my men." Rodrigo flashed the faint ghost of a smile. "Unless you have a need to urinate?"

Memory, vivid as a shaft of light.

He walked over with Rodrigo to where the king stood, conferring with outriders. Ramiro saw them approaching, raised his eyebrows briefly at Alvar.

"You wish a third man with us?" he asked.

"If you do not object, my lord. Do you know Pellino de Damon's son? One of my most trusted men." There was—Alvar heard it—an edge to Rodrigo's voice now.

"I do not," said his king, "but if you value him so highly, I hope to know him well in days to come."

Alvar bowed. "Thank you, my lord." He was conscious that he must look a fearsome sight. Like a fighting man.

Ramiro dismissed the outriders and the three of them walked towards the northern fence of the hamlet and then, as Alvar opened a gate, out onto the plain.

A wind was blowing. They carried no torches. The fires were behind them and had mostly died. The moons and the stars shone above the wide land all around them. It was too dark for Alvar to read the expressions of the other two men. He kept silent. A witness. To what, he knew not.

"I am pleased you are back. You will have questions. Ask me," said Ramiro of Valledo. "Then I will tell you some other things you do not know."

Rodrigo said coldly, "Very well. Start with my sons. How came they here? You may not be glad of my presence for long, my lord king, depending on the answers."

"Your cleric wrote a letter to Geraud de Chervalles, a High Cleric from Ferrieres, wintering with us on his pilgrimage to Vasca's Isle. He was preaching a holy war, along with his fellows in Eschalou and Orvedo. You know the army in Batiara has sailed?"

"I do. What sort of letter?"

"Explaining about your son's gift. Suggesting it might be of aid to us in a war against the infidels."

"Ibero did that?"

"I will show you the letter, Ser Rodrigo. Was it a betrayal?"

"It was."

The king said, "He has been punished."

"Not by me."

"Does it matter? He was a holy man. Jad will judge him."

There was a silence.

"Go on. The letter arrived in Esteren?"

"And de Chervalles asked my permission to send for the boy. This was after what had happened at Carcasia. You heard about that?"

Rodrigo nodded. "A little."

The king said, "In the wake of those events, I ordered the army to assemble and I sent men to fetch your son. His brother insisted on coming. Your lady wife followed, joining the queen. Am I, also, to be punished, Ser Rodrigo?"

The tone of both men was cold, precise. In the darkness, in that keen wind, Alvar had a sense that he was listening to the first notes of an exchange that had been waiting to happen for a long time.

"I don't know yet," said Rodrigo Belmonte flatly. Alvar blinked. The Captain was speaking to his anointed monarch. "What happened at Carcasia? You had best tell me about that."

"I intended to. Almalik II used a spy at the court of my brother of Ruenda to try to kill the queen. His purpose was subtle and nearly succeeded. If the queen had died and I blamed Sanchez it would have shattered any alliance and sent us to war against each other. I nearly rode against Ruenda. I would have, had she died."

"But?"

"The physician, d'Iñigo—who assisted with your boy tonight—was able to save the queen where her own doctors could not. He realized, from the nature of the wound, that there had been poison on the arrow, and provided the remedy."

"We owe him a great deal, then," said Rodrigo.

"We do. He said he learned of that poison from the writings of a certain Kindath physician in Fezana."

Another silence. Alvar saw a star fall across the sky in the west. A birth, a death. One or the other, in the folk tales at home. He was far from home.

"I see. I had intended to ask you," said Rodrigo, "whatever else happens, to look to the well-being of Ser Ishak and his family."

"You need not ask," said the king. "It is done. For the queen's sake, and your son's. Whatever else happens."

Alvar saw Rodrigo incline his head in the moonlight. A cloud drifted across the face of the white moon, deepening the darkness.

"D'Iñigo also told me something else," the king said quietly. "He said the poison used was one known only in Al-Rassan. The Ruendans would have had no ready access to it, or knowledge of it."

"I see." Rodrigo's tone changed. "You wrote to your brother of Ruenda?"

"I did. I told him what we had learned. He had fled the meeting, fearing we might attack them. As I said, I nearly did, Ser Rodrigo. If the queen had died..."

"I believe I can understand that, my lord."

"Sanchez wrote back. They had unmasked the Cartadan spy and found arrows in his home with the same poison. My brother was grateful."

"Of course. Insofar as he can be." The tone was dry.

"It went far enough. He agreed to come south at the same time I did. He is riding for Salos even now."

This was news. Alvar could see Rodrigo absorbing it.

"And Jaloña?" he asked softly. "Your uncle?"

"Is driving towards Ragosa and Fibaz. It is happening. The clerics have their holy war, after all, Ser Rodrigo."

Rodrigo shook his head. "Three wars of conquest, it would seem to me."

"Of course." The king's turn to sound wry. "But the clergy ride with us, and so far as I trust my uncle and brother not to turn back and attack Valledo, it is because of them."

"And because of them my son was brought here?"

"He was summoned because in my anger I allowed an offered weapon to be brought to me."

"He is a child, not a weapon, my lord."

"He is both, Ser Rodrigo. With respect. And our country is at war. How old were you when you first rode in my father's army beside Raimundo?"

No answer. Wind in the tall grass.

"That is my tale. Am I still to be punished?" King Ramiro asked softly. "I hope not so. I need you, Ser Rodrigo. Valledo has no constable tonight, no war leader, and we stand in Al-Rassan."

Alvar sucked in his breath sharply. Neither of the other men so much as glanced at him. He might not even have been here in the darkness with them.

"You mentioned the name," said Rodrigo, his voice suddenly no more than a whisper, "of your late brother."

Alvar shivered suddenly. He was very tired, and the night breeze was growing colder, and he had begun to feel the places where he'd been wounded, but none of these were the reason.

"I always thought," said King Ramiro, "that we would have to arrive here eventually, you and I."

He stopped, and after a moment Alvar realized that the king was looking at him, evaluating. It was for this, Alvar understood, that the Captain had wanted him here.

The king spoke again, finally, in a very different tone. "You genuinely loved him, didn't you? I could not...I could never understand why everyone loved Raimundo so much. Even our father. Obviously. Even he was seduced by my brother. He gave him Valledo. Tell me, Ser Rodrigo, answer a question for *me* this time: do you truly think Raimundo would have been a better king, had he lived, than I have been?"

"Doesn't matter," Rodrigo said, in that same stiff, difficult whisper.

"It *does* matter. Answer me."

Silence. Wind, and swift clouds overhead. Alvar heard an animal cry out far off on the plain. He looked at the Captain in the moonlight. *He is afraid*, he thought.

Rodrigo said, "I can't answer that question. He died too young. We can't know what he would have grown into. I know what you want me to say. That he had more charm than strength. That he was selfish and reckless and even cruel. He *was*. All of these things, at times. But, as Jad will judge my life when I make my end, I have only known one other man, ever, who came even close to making...the act of living through days and nights so full of richness and delight. You have been a far-sighted and a strong king, my lord. I grant you that freely. But I did love your brother, yes. We were young—exiled together and then home together in triumph—and I have always believed he was killed."

"He was," said King Ramiro.

Alvar swallowed, hard.

Rodrigo brought one hand up, involuntarily, and touched his forehead. He stayed thus a moment, then lowered his arm. "And who was it who killed him?" His voice actually cracked on the question.

"Garcia de Rada." The king's words were flat, uninflected. "You always thought so, didn't you?"

Alvar had another memory then, torchlit. This same hamlet. Rodrigo's whip lashing out, catching Garcia de Rada on the face, ripping his cheek open. Laín Nunez struggling to control the Captain's black rage. The cold, ferocious words spoken—accusation of a king's murder.

He heard Rodrigo slowly release his breath. He couldn't

make out his features clearly but he saw the Captain cross his arms on his breast, as if holding tightly to something there.

"Garcia was—what?—seventeen, eighteen that year?" Rodrigo said. "He acted on his brother's orders?"

Ramiro hesitated. "I am speaking truth, Ser Rodrigo, believe it. The answer is, I do not know. Even tonight, with Gonzalez dead, I do not know for certain. My thought has always been, he did not. I believe Count Gonzalez innocent of my brother's blood."

"I do not share your belief, I fear. Would an eighteen-year-old have killed his king, unprompted?"

"I don't know," said King Ramiro again. He paused. "Should I point out that Gonzalez de Rada died terribly tonight because he would not leave Diego's side from the time your boys joined this army."

Rodrigo was unmoved. "He swore an oath to me last year. He valued his family honor."

"Then would he have murdered his king?"

"He valued many other things, my lord. Power and wealth among them. He, too, was younger then. He might have done so, yes. I thought you could tell me."

"I have given you my belief."

"You have. Which leaves us with only the last question, doesn't it? You know what it is, my lord."

Alvar knew it as well, by now. *The last question.* What followed the last question? He wished he were somewhere else.

The king said, quietly, "I had no love for Raimundo. Or Sanchez, for that matter. Nor they for me. It was no secret, Jad knows. Our father chose a certain way to raise his three sons. But I knew I could do more for Valledo, and perhaps all of Esperaña one day, than either of my brothers ever could. I *knew* it. In my own time of exile here in Al-Rassan, when men came south to speak with me, I will not deny that I voiced anger that Valledo was probably going to be given to Raimundo when our father died. Which is what happened, of course."

The king stopped. Alvar heard the animal call out again, far off in darkness. King Ramiro said, "It is...very possible...that someone listening to me in a tavern or wine shop here might have concluded that were Raimundo to die...unexpectedly, I would not be displeased."

Clouds slid from the white moon. Alvar saw the king look at Rodrigo in the doubled moonlight. "I would not have been displeased. I *was* not, in the event. I will not lie about this. But before Jad, and on the life of my queen, and by whatever else you would wish me to swear, I did not command his murder, nor do I know how it was achieved."

"Then how," Rodrigo asked, implacable, "do you know it was Garcia?"

"He told me. He wanted to tell me more. I stopped him."

Rodrigo's hands were fists at his sides. "And that is *all* you did? Stop him from telling you? Shall I believe this? No punishment, no exposure? For the killing of a king? You made his brother constable of Valledo. You let Garcia live as he chose, doing what he wished all these years, until he nearly killed my wife and my boys?"

"I did," said Ramiro quietly. "I let him live his life. Gonzalez de Rada became constable because he was worthy of the post—do not deny that—and because you would not serve me after Raimundo died."

"After he was murdered!"

The king made a small movement of hands and shoulders. "After he was murdered. Garcia was never given rank, status, office, power...none of these things. You might consider that a moment, given what he could have expected from his birth. I thought of having him killed, frankly, because he was a risk and an embarrassment, and because I loathed the man. But I was...aware that Raimundo had been killed by him because he thought I would approve and because he had...enough reason to think so. I would not kill a man for that. Yes, I let him live. I kept the secret. I allowed Gonzalez to serve me and Valledo. Honorably. You had been my brother's man. I would not beg you for aid or approval, Ser Rodrigo, at my ascension, or after. I will not do so now. I think you were one of those blind to what Raimundo really was, and that your youth excused this, then."

Alvar heard the king's voice change. "It is no excuse now. Not any more. We are no longer young, Rodrigo Belmonte, and all these events are done with, in the past. Though I will not beg, I will ask. What I have told you tonight is truth. It is all truth. Will you be my constable? Will you command this army for me?"

Rodrigo Belmonte had a quality, Alvar had long ago observed, of being able to hold himself utterly, disconcertingly still. He was like that now, for what seemed a very long time.

"I don't think," he murmured finally, "that the past is ever really done with us." But then, in a firmer voice he asked, "Command the army to achieve what end, my lord king?"

"To take Fezana. And Cartada. And Silvenes. Lonza. Aljais. Elvira. Everything I can." The answer was decisive.

Alvar discovered that he was shivering again.

"And then?"

"And then," said King Ramiro, as bluntly as before, "I intend to occupy my uncle's kingdom of Jaloña. And then my brother's Ruenda. As you said, this campaign is a holy war in name alone. I want Esperaña back, Ser Rodrigo, and not only the land my father ruled under the khalifs' sufferance. I want *all* of this peninsula. Before I die, I intend to ride my horse into the seas to south and west and north, and up into the mountains to look down upon Ferrieres—and know that all the lands through which I rode were Esperaña."

"And then?" An odd question, in a way.

"And then," said King Ramiro, more softly, almost amused, "I will probably rest. And try to make a belated peace with Jad for all my transgressions beneath his light."

Alvar de Pellino, having struggled through a long year and a terrible day and night towards a new awareness of himself, realized that he was thrilled by this beyond words or clear thought. His skin was tingling, the hairs on the nape of his neck standing up.

It was the sheer grandeur of the vision. Lost and conquered Esperaña made whole again, one Jaddite kingdom in all the wide peninsula, with Valledo and its Horsemen at the heart of it. Alvar longed to be a part of this, to see it come to be, to ride his own horse into those oceans and up that mountain with his king. Yet, even as his heart heard this call to glory, he was aware of slaughter embedded in the sweep of the king's dream, or swooping above it like the carrion birds that followed the battlefields of men.

Will I ever, he thought, with a knifing of despair, *be at peace between these things?*

He heard Rodrigo Belmonte say then, very calmly, "You might have told me about Garcia a long time ago, my lord. I think I should have believed you. I do believe you now. I am your man, since you want me."

And he knelt before the king and held up his hands together, palms touching. Ramiro looked down upon him, unspeaking for a moment.

"You would not have believed," he said. "You would always have doubted. We needed to grow older, you and I, for me to say this and you to hear it. I wonder if your young soldier can possibly understand that."

Alvar flushed in the darkness, then heard the Captain say, "You might be surprised, my lord. He's more than a soldier, though I will tell you later what he did in Fezana this evening. If I am to be your constable I have my first request: I would ask that Alvar de Pellino be named my herald, to bear Valledo's staff and carry our words to the Star-born."

"It is an honor," the king said. "He is very young. It is also a dangerous post in this war." He motioned towards the hamlet behind them. "The Asharites may not observe the laws of heralds and their codes."

Rodrigo shook his head. "They will. That much I know. They value their own honor as much as we do ours. Even the Muwardis. In a way, *especially* the Muwardis. And Alvar will acquit himself."

Ramiro looked at Alvar, that appraising glance in the moonlight. "You wish this for yourself?" he asked. "There is less glory than might be found in battle by a courageous young man."

Alvar knelt beside Rodrigo Belmonte and lifted his joined palms. "I wish for this," he replied, discovering as he spoke that he did; that it was *exactly* what he wanted. "I, too, am your sworn man if you will have me, my lord."

The king placed his hands around those of Rodrigo, and then he touched Alvar's the same way. He said, "Let us go forward from this place and begin to reclaim our lost land."

He looked as if he would say more, but did not. They rose then, and began walking back to Orvilla. But Alvar, unable to stop the thought from coming—even now— found himself saying, inwardly, *And whose land will be broken and lost in that claiming?*

He knew the answer. It wasn't a real question. In the newest royal herald of Valledo, pride and bone-cold apprehension came together and warred for dominion.

Then, nearing the hamlet, he saw Jehane. She was standing by the northern gate waiting for them with Ammar ibn Khairan beside her. And looking at her small, straight-backed figure in the mingled light of the moons, Alvar felt love come back, too, bittersweet among the weapons and shed blood, tonight and yet to come.

∽

She saw them both kneel: Rodrigo first, and then Alvar.

Beside her, Ammar said softly, "He is being made constable now." And then, as she looked quickly up at him, "It is best for both of them, Rodrigo and the king. He ought to have been, all these years."

She took his hand. Smoke drifted behind them, though the fires were mostly out. Husari was with her parents and the two children they had saved from the Kindath Quarter. The queen of Valledo had come to them. She had said that Ishak and his family were her guests and would be, for so long as they desired. She had been gracious and well-spoken, but it was evident—to Jehane, at least—that Queen Ines had never met or talked with a Kindath before and didn't quite know how to deal with that.

That shouldn't have bothered her, perhaps, but tonight it did. She had almost wanted to ask Ines of Valledo if there were any plump babies around, to cook for a proper Kindath breakfast, but too many children had died that evening, and Jehane had nothing left in her for the force of real anger. She was very tired.

It was Bernart d'Iñigo, the doctor from the *tagra* forts, who had readied this welcome for them, she understood. It seemed he had saved the life of the queen using knowledge gained from reading Ishak's writings. He had taught himself Asharic and Kindath years ago, he confided to Jehane. The lanky, sad-faced man was a good physician, there was no denying it.

Why shouldn't he be? Jehane had thought. *If he's bothered to learn from us...*

Not a fair thought, really, but tonight she wasn't putting much stress on trying to be fair. D'Iñigo had volunteered to take the first watch beside Rodrigo's son. Diego's mother and brother were with him as well. Jehane wasn't needed. Valledan doctors were tending to the handful of people who had survived the assault. Only a handful; the rest were dead, butchered hideously.

They come from the desert, Jehane remembered, seeing the chopped-up bodies, smelling charred human flesh. Her father's words, from so long ago. *If you would understand the Star-born of Ashar...*

"Who are my enemies?" Jehane had said then, aloud, looking around the hamlet.

There must have been something in her voice; a hint of vanishing control. Ammar, without speaking, had placed an arm about her shoulders and guided her away. They had walked around the perimeter of Orvilla but Jehane, unable to be eased, had found herself both looking back at dying fires and remembering them.

Who are my enemies? The citizens of Fezana? The Muwardis here? The soldiers of a Jaddite holy army who had run wild through Sorenica? The Valledans who burned this hamlet last summer? She wanted to weep, but was afraid to let herself.

Ammar had a gash on one arm, which she examined by torchlight; it wasn't serious. He'd told her that, but she'd needed to look. She led him down to the river and cleaned the cut and bandaged it. A thing to do. On her knees, she dipped a cloth in the cold water and washed her face, looking down at the rippling lines of moonlight in the Tavares. She took a deep breath of the night air.

They had walked again, following the perimeter fence to the north. And there they saw King Ramiro with Rodrigo and Alvar out among the grasses, the dark, wide emptiness beyond them. At one point, watching, Jehane saw Rodrigo cross his arms tightly over his breast. It was very late. A wind was blowing in the night.

Whichever way the wind blows.

Then they saw Rodrigo and Alvar kneel before the king and then rise.

"Who are my enemies?" Jehane asked, at length.

"Mine, I hope," said Ammar.

"And yours are?"

"We'll know more of that soon enough, my love. Watch and listen. I will likely be made a handsome offer soon."

His tone had a coolness now, but that was as much a defense as anything else, she knew. More than anyone in the world, perhaps, she had a sense of what had come, however improbably, to bind Ammar ibn Khairan and Rodrigo Belmonte, each to the other.

There was an anticipation of partings in her now, Jehane realized: endings had come upon them tonight. As much as anything else, that was what made her want to weep.

They waited. The three men came over the dark grass and approached them by the gate. She saw that Alvar, too, was wounded. There was blood on his shoulder. Without speaking she went over to him and began carefully tearing at his loose shirt to expose the gash below. He looked at her and then away, standing quietly as she examined the cut.

"Ammar. I was hoping to find you," Rodrigo said quietly. "Have you a moment to speak?" He spoke in Esperañan.

"With you, always," ibn Khairan said gravely, in the same tongue.

"The king of Valledo has done me the honor of asking me to be his constable."

Jehane looked over at him. Ammar inclined his head. "He is equally honored if you have accepted."

"I have."

Ammar smiled thinly. "Badir of Ragosa will be distressed."

"I imagine so. I propose to give him, unfortunately, even greater cause for regret."

"How so?"

It was like a dance, Jehane thought, this formality screening things so much deeper than words could go. She stood by young Alvar, listening, and stopped even pretending to examine his shoulder. It was too dark here, in any case.

"I believe I have sufficient authority to make you a proposal on behalf of the king of Valledo."

He was right, Jehane thought. How had Ammar known, so surely? No answer to that, except to remember who and what he was. What they both were. In the wind from the north she could feel something swiftly approaching its end.

Ammar said, "I am always interested in proposals. And yours have ever been intriguing."

Rodrigo hesitated, choosing words. "As we stand here, King Sanchez of Ruenda is riding for Salos downriver, and the army of Jaloña is approaching Ragosa."

"Ah! Jaloña rides! Queen Fruela comes to avenge her dead captain?"

King Ramiro's mouth quirked sideways at that.

"Something of the sort," Rodrigo said, unsmiling. "There have been a great many dead captains over the years."

"Alas, it is true. '*War feeds like a wild dog upon the*

hearts of brave men.'"

"I know that," said the king of Valledo suddenly. "That was written by ibn Khairan of Aljais."

Ammar turned to him and Jehane knew he was surprised, however he might try to conceal it. "At your service, my lord. The line scans better in Asharic."

The king's turn to betray astonishment. He looked sharply at Rodrigo and then back to Ammar. "I had not...*you* are...?" He turned to Rodrigo again, eyebrows arched.

Calmly, Rodrigo said, "We were exiled at the same time last year in Ragosa. We have been companions since. He came here despite a death sentence in Cartadan lands to bring Ishak ben Yonannon and his wife out of Fezana. Jehane bet Ishak who stands here is physician to my company. Ibn Khairan would have been killed by the Muwardis had they known he was in the city."

"I daresay there is no love shared there," King Ramiro murmured. He was a tall, handsome man. He had also recognized a line from a poem by Ammar. "Is there any shared here?" he asked.

"I am attempting to find out," Rodrigo said. "Ammar, we have always thought that if this army and the other two moved south, Yazir ibn Q'arif would probably be in the peninsula by summer's end or next spring. Al-Rassan, as it has been, is coming to an end."

"Sorrowfully, I believe that," Jehane heard the man she loved say quietly. "Tell me, who will remember the gardens of the Al-Fontina in time to come? Or the ivories in the holy places of Ragosa?"

"I cannot answer that," Rodrigo replied. "Perhaps you will help us all remember, I do not know. I have more immediate concerns. The king has instructed me that this is to be a Valledan campaign of conquest, not a holy war, though there are clerics with us and it might appear otherwise."

"Oh, *good!*" Ammar said, too brightly. "Does that mean only those who resist you are nailed to wood or burned alive while the clerics sing paeans to Jad?"

"Something of the sort," Rodrigo said levelly.

"Almalik of Cartada is a dead man," King Ramiro interjected quietly, "for what he tried to do to the queen. And the Muwardis, when we find them, will be offered no kindness by me. Not after tonight. But my heart is not set on slaughter, either for its own sake or to make the clerics happy."

"Ah," said Ammar in his most sardonic voice, "a *gentle* conquest. Horsemen of Jad waving to happy Asharite farmers as they trot by. And to keep your brave soldiers content—what? Chop up a few Kindath on the way? No one will miss them, will they?"

Rodrigo refused to rise to the bait. "This is warfare, Ammar. Neither of us are children. It is still Ashar and Jad and there will be ugliness. After several hundred years and with that other army sailing for Soriyya there will be worse than ugliness."

"What, I wonder, is worse than ugliness?"

"You do not really mean that," Rodrigo said. "I have part of an answer, though. Worse, is when what little space there is for men to move back and forth between worlds disappears because the worlds are lost to hatred. That may happen to us yet." He hesitated. "It probably will, Ammar. I have no more illusions than you do. There will be no happy farmers where this army passes. We will conquer if we can, and do what we must do, and then we will try to govern here, as the khalifs and the city-kings have governed the Jaddites and Kindath among you."

"How...pragmatic of you," Ammar said, with an icy smile. He was angry, Jehane saw, and not trying to hide it.

Rodrigo saw it too. He said, "Are we the proper targets for your feelings right now?"

"You are adequate, failing something better."

"*What would you have me do?*" Rodrigo cried suddenly. In the silence that followed, Jehane had a sense, as once before in Ragosa, that for these two men, staring fixedly at each other now, no one else was in the world, just for a moment.

The moment came, and was briefly held, and then it passed. Jehane felt as if she could almost see it happen: something receding from the two of them, faster than any horses could run, into the dark.

"What would I have you do?" Ammar's voice had softened. He spoke Asharic now. "What you cannot do, I suppose. Go home. Breed horses, raise your sons, love your wife." He turned to the king of Valledo. "Make your country—all of Esperaña if you can unite it—into a land that understands more than only war and righteous piety. Allow space in your lives for more than battle chants to inspire soldiers. Teach your people to...understand a garden, the reason for a fountain, music."

The wind blew past them. Ibn Khairan shook his head. "Forgive me. I am being extremely foolish. I am tired and I know you are as well. These tidings you bring are not unexpected, but they do mark the death of something I have...held dear."

"I know this." Rodrigo's voice was rock-steady. "I would like you to help keep some part of Al-Rassan alive. I said I had a proposal. If the king does not disagree, I would offer you certain offices in Al-Rassan and ultimately the rank of constable of Valledo, shared with myself."

Jehane heard Alvar de Pellino gasp and saw the king make an abrupt, uncontrolled movement. Rodrigo had just proposed to cut his own position in half and give it to an Asharite.

Ammar laughed softly. He looked at the king and then back to Rodrigo. "You *do* enjoy surprising people, don't you? I thought that was my vice."

Again, Rodrigo did not smile. "It seems simple enough to me. We haven't nearly enough people to take and settle Al-Rassan. We need the Star-born—and the Kindath—to stay here, farm the land, conduct their business, pay taxes...perhaps one day become Jaddites in the same way our people have turned to Ashar here over the centuries. If this campaign succeeds, we will be a very few people in a large land. To keep the sons and daughters of Ashar calm

and well-governed we need men of their own faith. A great
many of them eventually, but at the moment there is only
one man I trust to wield so much power and strive
towards this balancing and you are that man. Will you help
govern Al-Rassan for us? So much of it as we control?"

Ammar turned to the king again. "He is eloquent when
he chooses to be, is he not? Does he persuade you?" The
cutting edge of irony was in his voice again. "Does it
sound *simple enough* to you?"

The horses were running away in the night. Jehane
could almost see them, so vivid was the image for her—
manes lifting with their speed under the moons and the
racing clouds.

"He has surprised me," said King Ramiro carefully.
"Though not more than I am surprised to discover you in
my camp. But yes, Ser Rodrigo speaks simple truths and I
can hear those as well as any man, I hope. Speaking for
myself, I also prefer a palace or a chapel with some grace
to one that merely keeps out wind and rain. I am not
unaware of what Al-Rassan has been. I have read your verses, and that of other poets here. There are those among us
who might be hoping for bonfires of flesh as we move
south. I would prefer to disappoint their expectations."

"And your brother? And your uncle?"

King Ramiro's mouth twitched again. "I would prefer,"
he murmured, "to disappoint their expectations as well."

Ammar laughed aloud. Again Rodrigo did not smile.
Absolutely self-contained, he was waiting for his answer,
Jehane understood. And he *wanted* this. She thought she
understood that too. His son had nearly died tonight.
Might yet die. Rodrigo Belmonte did not want to endure
another loss now.

Ammar's laughter stopped. Unexpectedly he looked
over at her. She held his gaze, but it was difficult to read
expressions in the moonlight. He turned back to Rodrigo.

"I *can't*," he said, with finality. In Jehane's mind the
horses were gone now, out of sight.

"It will be the Muwardis," Rodrigo said quickly. "You

know it, Ammar! Ragosa cannot even hold against Jaloña with half its army mercenaries from Jaddite lands. When High Clerics appear outside the walls and speak of holy war—"

"I *know* this!"

"And Fezana falls to us. You know that, too! Before summer's end."

"I know this city," King Ramiro interposed quietly. "I was in exile here in my youth. I observed certain things. Unless the defenses are greatly altered, I believe I can take Fezana, even with its new garrison."

"It is possible."

Rodrigo continued, with a note of desperation. "And then Yazir and Ghalib come across the straits to meet us. Al-Rassan is theirs, or it is ours, Ammar. By my god and yours, you must see that! Cartada, Ragosa, your memory of Silvenes...they *cannot* be saved. Even you cannot dance that dance between fires. And surely, Ammar, surely you know—"

"I have to try."

"What?"

"Rodrigo, I have to try. To dance that dance."

Rodrigo stopped, breathing hard, like a horse reined up too harshly.

"Your faith means so much to you?" King Ramiro's voice was thoughtful. "I had heard tales otherwise. It means so much that you would serve the veiled ones of the desert, knowing their ways and what they will bring to your land?"

"My faith? I would put it differently, my lord. I would say, my history. Not just Al-Rassan, but Ammuz, Soriyya...Ashar in the desert of the homelands under stars. Our sages, our singers, the khalifs of the eastern world." Ammar shrugged his shoulders. "The Muwardis? They are a part of that. Every people has its zealots. They come, and change, and come again in a new guise. Forgive me for saying this, but if a king of Valledo can be as reflective as you, my lord—a descendant of Queen Vasca of blessed name!—shall I be the one to deny the possibility of like grace descending upon a veiled son of the sands? Perhaps among the seductive fountains, the flowing rivers of Al-Rassan...?"

"You would rather be with them." Jehane heard the bitterness in Rodrigo's voice.

Ammar looked at him. "As companions? Friends? Am I mad? Rodrigo, do I *look* mad?" He shook his head. "But the Muwardis, what are they? Exactly the same as Queen Vasca was, as most of the people of your north still are today. Righteous, convinced, unforgiving. Terrified of anything beyond their understanding of the world. The tribes are uncivilized? I think so. But I confess I find little of value in the cities of Esperaña either. The desert is a hard place, harder even than your northlands in winter. Ashar knows, I have no bonding of spirit with the veiled ones, but I share even less with those who make pilgrimage on their knees to Vasca's Isle. Would I *rather* be with the tribesmen? Again, put it a little differently, and then leave it, Rodrigo, as my last words, lest we quarrel before we part. I suppose I would rather, if Al-Rassan is to be lost, herd camels in the Majriti than be a shepherd in Esperaña."

"No! That *cannot* be a last word, Ammar!" Rodrigo shook his head vehemently. "How do I let you ride to them? Do you know what they will do to you?"

Ammar smiled again, wryly this time. "What will they do? Take away my ink and paper? For a start, I will almost certainly be named ka'id of all Cartada's armies by Almalik II. I expect Ghalib ibn Q'arif and I will one day have a disagreement over who leads our conjoined forces, and I will politely defer to him. I am reliably informed he wears a neck thong made of the foreskins of those who do not defer to him." He let the smile fade. "After that, I truly do not know. It may come to camel herding, after all. Leave it, Rodrigo, please." He paused. "There is a question about Jehane, however."

"*No there isn't.*"

She had actually been expecting this and she was ready

when it came. The four men turned to her. "Ammar, if I can have some assurance that my parents are safe with Rodrigo and the king, then I'm afraid you must let me come with you—or I'll kill you before you leave this camp."

She saw Rodrigo Belmonte smile then for the first time that night, the remembered look softening his face. "Ah. You've met my wife, then?" he said.

Jehane turned to him. "I have. The lady Miranda is as gracious and as beautiful as I was told—by others—she would be. Would she let you leave her behind in such a circumstance as this, Ser Rodrigo?"

Ammar said quickly, "It is not the—"

"It *is* the same. Enough so as to make no difference," Jehane snapped. She was afraid weariness would make her cry again, and she didn't want that at all.

"Well now," said the king of Valledo, "I do regret having to add my voice to what seems a matter of the heart, but I need to be told why I ought to allow the self-proclaimed future ka'id of my enemies to depart."

Jehane swallowed abruptly. Her heart thudded. She hadn't even thought of this.

"You must let him leave," Rodrigo said quietly.

King Ramiro looked sharply at him, and Jehane saw that his temper was being kept in check. What he had just said terrified her. In truth, given the war that had begun, she could see no reason why he ought to let them go. Ammar had had his chance, his astonishing offer, and now...

"I *must?*" said Ramiro of Valledo. "I am never happy with the word, Ser Rodrigo."

"My lord, forgive me," said Rodrigo calmly, "but I have—*we* have—one hundred and fifty men in the army of Ragosa. Trapped there. When word comes that you are in Al-Rassan and I am with you, and that the king of Jaloña has come south as well, I believe Badir of Ragosa will receive counsel that he should eliminate my company before they are deployed against him."

Ammar's expression had grown sober. "You believe Mazur would propose this?"

Rodrigo said, "Ben Avren, or one of the others. Remember? Last autumn? Badir valued you at your named price—equal, in yourself, to me and all my company. By that measure, he does a lesser thing in destroying them than we would in killing you."

"You are playing with words. That isn't a true measure, Rodrigo."

"What is? In wartime? They are in mortal danger. I must try to deal with that. You are my best—at the moment my only way. The price of your freedom is this: you ensure, upon your oath and your honor, that my men are allowed to leave that army and come here."

"And if I cannot?"

It was the king who answered. His anger had passed. "You agree to return, on your oath and honor, and submit to my judgment. True measure, or not, if King Badir accepted such a value for your service, so will I."

It was monstrous, Jehane thought, monstrous, and somehow inevitable, as if the careless banter about mercenary wages that bright, autumn day in Ragosa had led straight to this moment on a dark plain. She heard sounds from the camp behind them, and the wind blowing.

"It is agreed," said Ammar quietly.

"You can free them *and* come back," Rodrigo added quickly. He was not a man who surrendered easily, if at all, Jehane realized. And he would not stand on pride. There was a plea in his voice.

Ammar, she saw, heard it too. He *had* to hear it. Again the two men looked at each other, but by now the horses were long gone, far apart in a too wide, too dark night. It was over.

Ammar said softly, "We refused to fight each other that day in Ragosa."

"I remember."

"It was an entertainment they proposed. It is a different place now, the world," said ibn Khairan, unwontedly awkward. "I...deeply regret to say this. More than I can tell you. Rodrigo, I could wish..." He thought for a moment, then spread his hands and fell silent.

"You have a choice," Rodrigo said. "You are making a choice tonight. You have had an offer from us."

Ammar shook his head, and when he spoke, for the first time there was something desperate in his voice, too. "Not *really* a choice," he said. "Not in this. I cannot turn my back on this land, now that it has come to such bitter grief. Don't you understand? Rodrigo, you of all men must *surely* understand." They heard his small, known, self-mocking laugh. "I'm the man who killed the last khalif of Al-Rassan."

And hearing those words, Rodrigo Belmonte bowed his neck, as if to accept the descent of a sword. Jehane saw Ammar lift a hand, as if he would touch the other man, but then he let his hand fall.

Beside her, she realized that Alvar de Pellino was weeping. She would remember that after, and love him for it.

✤

Her parents were asleep, and the two children as well, in tents provided by the queen. Jehane looked in on them briefly, and then went, as promised, to relieve Bernart d'Iñigo beside their patient. She ought to have been sleeping during this time but it was not, evidently, to be a night for sleep. Not for her.

She was used to this. Doctors often had to deal with nights of vigil beside those who depended upon them to fight back the coming of final darkness. In another way, though, this night was unlike any she had known. It marked an ending, in a real sense, to everything she *had* ever known.

Bernart d'Iñigo smiled tiredly at her as she walked up. He held a finger to his lips. Jehane saw that Fernan had fallen asleep on the ground beside his brother. So, too, on a pillow, covered by a small blanket, had his mother.

"Get some rest," Jehane whispered to the Jaddite doctor. "I'll do what's left of the night." D'Iñigo nodded and rose. He stumbled a little as he went. They were all bone-weary.

She looked down at Diego. He lay on his back, head propped on folded blankets. The doctor in her began to assert control again. She knelt and took his wrist, and was immediately encouraged. His pulse was stronger and it had slowed.

She looked up and gestured. A soldier not far away came nearer with a torch. "Hold it close," she whispered.

She lifted the boy's closed eyelids and watched how the eyes contracted in the light: equally, and both were centered. Again, good. He was extremely pale, but that was to be expected. There was no fever. The dressing was secure.

He was doing wonderfully well. Despite everything else that had happened, Jehane could not suppress another shiver of pride and disbelief. This boy, by all rights, by everything known, ought to be dead.

He would have been, if Jehane had been his physician. If Bernart d'Iñigo had; if *any* doctor she could name had been. He was alive, his pulse was firm and his breathing steady, because Ishak ben Yonannon was still—after five years in darkness—the most courageous and the most gifted surgeon alive. Who, after tonight, would deny it? Who would dare?

Jehane shook her head. False pride. Did such things matter so much, now? They didn't, and yet they did. In the presence of war, on the brink of so many deaths to come, Ishak had reclaimed a life that was lost. No physician—and certainly not his daughter—could be immune to the sense of a small, precious victory won back from the dark.

She nodded and the soldier withdrew with his torch. Jehane settled back beside the unconscious boy. She had ordered Ammar to snatch some rest before morning; she might be able to let herself doze, after all.

"He is all right?"

It was the mother. Rodrigo's wife. Jehane, looking across at her in the darkness, thought of all the elaborately bloodthirsty stories he had told of her. And now here was a small, very beautiful woman lying on the cold ground beside her child, speaking with fear in her voice.

"He is doing well. He might wake in the morning. He needs to sleep now."

Her eyes were adjusting to the dark again. She could make out the other woman a little more clearly, on the far side of Diego.

"D'Iñigo told me...that no one has ever done this surgery."

"That is true."

"Your father...he was blinded for saving someone's life?"

"Mother and infant. In childbirth. He touched an Asharite woman to do so."

Miranda Belmonte shook her head. "How is it that we do these things to each other?"

"I have no answer for that, my lady."

There was a silence.

"Rodrigo mentioned you many times," Miranda said softly. "In his letters. He had nothing but praise for you. His Kindath physician." Jehane thought she saw the ghost of a smile. "I was jealous."

Jehane shook her head. "No one loved as much as you are should ever be jealous."

"I know that, actually," said Miranda Belmonte. "It is the great gift of my life. If Diego lives, because of your father, that will be two such gifts. It is too much. I am not worthy. It makes me afraid."

There was a longer silence. A moment later Jehane realized that the other woman had drifted to sleep again.

She sat beside the sleeping boy, leaning against a heavy sack of dried goods someone kind had placed nearby. She thought of deaths and births, sight and blindness, moons and sun and stars. Ashar and Jad at war, rain falling on the Kindath as they wandered the world. She thought of love and of one day bearing a child of her own.

She heard footsteps approaching and knew who it was. She had been certain, in fact, somewhere deep within herself, that this last conversation lay waiting in the night.

"How is he?" asked Rodrigo quietly, crouching beside

her. He was looking down at his son. His face was in darkness.

"As well as we can hope. I told your wife he may wake
in the morning."

"I'll want to be here."

"Of course."

Rodrigo stood up. "Walk with me?"

She had known. How had she known? How did the
heart see what it did?

"Not far from him," she murmured, but rose and they
walked a little apart, past the soldier with the torch. They
stopped by the river, near a small hut Jehane remembered.
One of the few that hadn't burned last year. Garcia de
Rada's cousin had killed a woman here, and an unborn
child. Her life seemed to have circled back to this place.
She had met Rodrigo that night and Ammar that day. Both
of them.

It was very quiet. They listened to the river. Rodrigo
said, "You know your parents are safe with us. This
is...the best possible place for them right now."

"I believe that."

"Jehane. It is...probably the best place for you, as well."

She had known he would say that. She shook her head.
"Safest, perhaps. Not best." She left the deeper words
unsaid, but with Rodrigo they didn't have to be spoken.

Another silence. The moons had swung west, and the
slow stars. The river murmured below.

"I've asked Husari to stay with me. He has agreed. I told
the king a small lie tonight."

"I guessed. You don't really think Laín and Martín will
be unable to get the company out, do you?"

"Not really. And Husari, in his way, may be as good a
governor—in Fezana, or elsewhere—as Ammar would have
been."

"Will he do it?"

"I believe so. He will not serve the Muwardis. And he, at
least, trusts me, if Ammar does not."

She heard the bitterness. "It isn't a question of trust.

You know that."

"I suppose." He looked at her. "I wanted to be sure he could leave, if he insisted, so I made up that story about my company trapped in Ragosa."

"I know that, Rodrigo."

"I didn't want him to go."

"I know that, too."

"I don't want *you* to go, Jehane. There is no place in Al-Rassan for you, for either of you, when the Muwardis come."

"We'll have to try to make a place," she said.

Stillness. He was waiting, she realized, and so she did say it, after all. "I will not leave him, Rodrigo."

She heard him release his breath.

In the darkness by the river's steady, murmurous flow, Jehane said, looking down at the water, not at the man beside her, "I was under your window at Carnival. I stood there a long time, looking at your light." She swallowed. "I almost came up to you."

She sensed him turning towards her. She kept her gaze fixed upon the river.

"Why didn't you?" His voice had altered.

"Because of what you told me that afternoon."

"I was buying paper, I remember. What did I tell you, Jehane?"

She did look at him then. It was dark, but she knew those features by heart now. They had ridden from this hamlet the summer before on the one horse. So little time ago, really.

"You told me how much you loved your wife."

"I see," he said.

Jehane looked away. She needed to look away. They had come to a place too hard for held glances. She said softly, to the river, to the dark, "Is it wrong, or impossible, for a woman to love two men?"

After what seemed to her a very long time, Rodrigo Belmonte said, "No more so than for a man."

Jehane closed her eyes.

"Thank you," she said. And then, after another moment, holding as tightly as she could to the thing suspended there, "Goodbye."

With her words the moment passed, the world moved on again: time, the flowing river, the moons. And the delicate thing that had been in the air between them—whatever it might have been named—fell, as it seemed to Jehane, softly to rest in the grass by the water.

"Goodbye," he said. "Be always blessed, on all the paths of your life. My dear." And then he said her name.

They did not touch. They walked back beside each other to the place where Diego and Fernan and Miranda Belmonte lay asleep and, after standing a long moment gazing down upon his family, Rodrigo Belmonte went towards the king's tent where the strategies of war were being devised.

She watched him go. She saw him lift the tent flap, to be lit briefly by the lanterns from inside, then disappear within as the tent closed after him.

Goodbye. Goodbye. Goodbye.

෴

Jehane saw Diego's eyes open in the greyness before sunrise.

He was weak, and in considerable pain, but he recognized his father and mother, and managed the beginnings of a smile. It was Fernan who knelt beside him, though, gripping both his hands. Bernart d'Iñigo stood behind them all, grinning ferociously, then Ishak came out to see his patient, to take his pulse and feel the shape of the wound.

They had no need of her. Jehane used the moment to walk a little apart with her mother and tell her what she was about to do, and why. It did not greatly surprise her to discover that Eliane and Ishak had already learned most of this from Ammar.

It appeared he had been waiting outside their tent when they woke. She had a memory of him kneeling before Ishak the summer before. The two of them had known each other a long time, she'd realized that day, and Ammar ibn Khairan was not a man to ride away with their daughter without a word of his own spoken.

She wondered what had been said. What did surprise her was to encounter no protest. Her mother had never been hesitant with objections. Yet now Jehane was about to ride off through a land at war, with an Asharite, towards a future only the moons knew—and her mother was accepting that. It was, Jehane thought, another measure of how much had changed.

Mother and daughter embraced. Neither wept, but Jehane did do so when her father held her in his arms just before she mounted the horse provided for her.

She looked at Alvar de Pellino standing silently nearby, his heart in his eyes, as ever. She looked at Husari. At Rodrigo.

She looked at Ammar ibn Khairan beside her on his mount and nodded her head and they rode away together. East towards Fezana and past it, well north of the river, watching the plumes of smoke still coiling up from the city into the brightening sky.

She looked back only once, but Orvilla was already out of sight and she had stopped crying by then. She had set out on this same path a summer ago, riding with Alvar and Velaz. She had only one man with her now, but he was worth a hundred and fifty, by one measure.

He was worth infinitely more than that, by the measuring of her heart.

She moved her horse nearer to his, and held out a hand and he removed his glove and laced his fingers through hers. They rode through much of the morning like that as the clouds ahead of them slowly lifted and grey became blue towards the sun.

At one point, breaking the long silence, she said, comically, "*A camel herder in the Majriti?*" And was rewarded to hear his swift laughter fill the wide spaces around them.

Later, in a different voice, she asked him, "What did you say to my father? Did you ask his blessing?"

He shook his head. "Too much to ask. I told them I loved you, and then I asked their forgiveness."

She rode in silence, dealing with this. Finally, very quietly, she said, "How much time are we going to be allowed?"

And gravely he replied, "I truly don't know, love. I will do all I can to give us enough."

"It will never be enough, Ammar. Understand that. I will always need more time."

Their lovemaking each night, after they made camp, had an urgency Jehane had never known.

After ten days of riding they intercepted the army of Ragosa heading towards Cartada, and time, in Al-Rassan the Beloved, began to run, swift as horses, towards its end.

Chapter XVIII

In a reaction to the protracted siege of his city, King Badir of Ragosa had ordered the northern-style wooden chairs removed from his private chambers in the palace. They had been replaced by additional pillows. The king had just lowered himself—with some care for his wine glass—into a nest of cushions by the fire.

Mazur ben Avren, his chancellor, did the same, not bothering to hide a wince of pain. Personally, he regarded the king's abjuring of northern furnishings as an entirely unnecessary gesture. Descending to the floor to recline seemed a more difficult exercise every time he did it.

Badir, watching him, looked amused. "You're younger than I am, my friend. You've let yourself grow soft. How does that happen during a siege?"

Mazur grimaced as he searched for an easier position. "A touch...of something in my hip, my lord. It will ease when the rains let up."

"The rains are useful. They must be miserable out there in their tents."

"I do hope so," said ben Avren with fervor. There had been rumors of sickness in the Jaloñan camp.

He lifted a hand and the nearest servant hastily brought him a glass of wine. From ben Avren's point of view, it was an extreme relief that his monarch's rejection of things northern had not extended to the better Jaddite wines. He saluted the king, still trying to find a comfortable position. Both men were silent for a time.

It was autumn and the eastern rains had arrived early. Ragosa had been under siege since early summer. It had not fallen, nor had the walls been breached. Under the prevailing circumstances this was remarkable.

Fezana had been taken by the Valledan army in the middle of summer, and recent tidings had come by carrier pigeon that the king of Ruenda had broken through the walls of Salos at the mouth of the Tavares and had put all the adult males to the sword. Women and infants had been burned, in the name of Jad, but the city itself had not been torched: King Sanchez of Ruenda was evidently proposing to winter there. A bad sign, and Badir and his chancellor knew it.

The Valledan army, more bold, had already pushed southeast over the hills towards Lonza. Rodrigo Belmonte, once a captain in Badir's own army, did not seem inclined to rest content with only the one major city taken before winter. The Valledans were said to be meeting with resistance in the hill country, but details, for obvious reasons, were hard to come by in besieged Ragosa.

Given these developments to the west and given the fact that they'd had to release almost half their own army or risk an internal uprising—many of the Jaddite mercenaries had promptly joined the Jaloñans outside the walls—Ragosa's holding out was an achievement. A measure, as much as anything else, of the chancellor's prudent marshalling of food reserves and supplies, and the affection and confidence the people of the city vested in their king.

There were, however, limits. To food, to supplies. To support for a beleaguered monarch and his advisor. His Kindath advisor.

If they could last until winter they might survive. Or if Yazir came. There had been no word from the Majriti. They were waiting. Everyone in Al-Rassan was waiting that autumn—Jaddite, Asharite, Kindath. If the tribes came north across the straits everything in the peninsula would change.

Everything had already changed though, and both men

knew it. The city they had built together—a smaller, quieter repository of some of the same graces Silvenes had embodied under the khalifs—was already finished, its brief flowering done. However this invasion ended, King Badir's city of music and ivory was lost.

The Jaloñans or the Muwardis. One way lay a terrible burning, and the other way...?

It was very late. Rain was falling outside, a steady sound on the windows and the leaves. The two men were still in the habit of taking this last glass together; the depth and endurance of friendship marked as much in their silence as in the words.

"There was a report this morning they are building small boats now," Badir said. He sipped from his wine.

"I heard the same thing." Mazur shrugged. "They won't get in through the lake. They could never make craft large enough to carry sufficient men. We would annihilate them from the harbor towers."

"They might stop our fishing boats from going out."

The siege was failing in part because the small craft of Ragosa had been able to go out upon the lake, using care, covered by archers from the harbor walls as they came back in.

"I'd like to see Jaddites try to blockade this harbor in the autumn winds. I have swimmers who could sink any boat they send out there. I'm hoping they try."

"Swimmers? In autumn? You would send someone out with an auger?"

Mazur drank from his glass. "They would fall over themselves volunteering, my lord. We have a city disinclined to yield, I am pleased to say."

It helped that surrender wasn't really a possibility. They'd killed the king of Jaloña and one of the High Clerics from Ferrieres even before the siege had begun.

That had been ibn Khairan's doing; his last act in Ragosan employ, just before he left them for Cartada.

He'd taken a dozen of the best men in the city and slipped out one moonless night in two small boats, heading

east and north along the lake. The Jaloñans, enthusiastical-
ly burning villages and farms as they came south around
Lake Serrana, were too complacent, and it cost them.

Ibn Khairan and his men surprised a raiding party,
which had been their intention. It was purest luck—he had
always been said to be a lucky man—that the Jaloñan party
of thirty riders had included King Bermudo and the cleric.

At twilight on a spring evening ibn Khairan's men had
come upon them at a fishing village. They'd waited down
the beach, hidden by the boats. They'd had to watch villagers burned alive, and hear them scream as they were
nailed to wooden beams. When the wine flasks had emerged
among the raiding party the mood became wild and the
northerners had turned to the women and young girls.

Thirteen men from Ragosa, acting in cold rage and with
specific intent, had come up from the beach in the darkness. They were outnumbered but it didn't matter. Ibn
Khairan moved through that burning village like a dark
streak of lightning, his men said after, killing where he
went.

They slew all thirty men in that raiding party.

The king of Jaloña had been cut down by one of the
Ragosans before his identity was known. They had wanted
to throw him onto the nearest of the fires, but ibn
Khairan, swearing like a fisherman when he saw who it
was, made them carry King Bermudo's body back to the
city. He would have been far more useful alive, but there
were still things that could be done.

The cleric from Ferrieres was nailed to one of the
wooden beams he had been instrumental in having raised.
All of Esperaña was coming south, it had by then become
evident, and the Ferrieres clerics were stridently invoking
a holy war. It was not a time for ransoms or the courtesies
normally offered pious men.

There had been a brief flickering of hope in Ragosa that
the shocking disappearance of their king might lead the
enemy to withdraw. It was not to be.

Queen Fruela, who had insisted on accompanying the

invading army, took control of the Jaloñan forces with her eldest son, Beñedo. By the time that army reached the walls of Ragosa, a great many farmers and fisherfolk had been captured on sweeps through the countryside. These had not been killed. Instead, the besieging army set about mutilating them, one by one, within sight of the city, at sunrise and sundown while the Jaddites prayed to their golden god of light.

After four days of this, it was King Badir who made the decision to show the body of King Bermudo from the city walls. It was indicated by a herald that the corpse would be desecrated if the torturing continued outside. Queen Fruela, afire with holy zeal, appeared inclined to continue nonetheless but her young son, the new king of Jaloña, prevailed in this matter. The prisoners outside the walls were all killed the next morning, without ceremony. The body of King Bermudo was burned in Ragosa. The Jaddites, watching the smoke of that pyre rise up, took solace in knowing that since he had died in the midst of a war against the infidels, his soul was already dwelling with the god in light.

As a consequence of all this, it was understood from the beginning of the siege of Ragosa that a negotiated surrender was not an option. No one in the city was going to be permitted to live if it fell. In a way that made things simpler for those inside the walls. It removed an otherwise distracting possibility.

It had, in fact, been ibn Khairan who foretold this. "If it comes to an ending," he had said to Mazur ben Avren on the spring morning he rode back west with Jehane bet Ishak, "try, any way you can, to surrender to Valledo."

Unexpected words, and both the king and his chancellor saw them as such, but they became rather more explicable after the very different occupations of Fezana and Salos later that summer.

Unfortunately, there seemed no obvious way to negotiate such a surrender, and ibn Khairan himself—the ka'id of Cartada's armies now—was engaged in making life as miserable as he could for the Valledans as they approached Lonza. If King Ramiro had begun this invasion in a tolerant cast of mind, he might well be abandoning that attitude by now, under the deadly, morale-sapping raids of Cartada's brilliant commander, and with autumn and the rains coming on.

King Badir's servant built up the fire again and then deftly refilled the glasses of both men. They could still hear the rain outside. A companionable silence descended.

The chancellor felt his thoughts drifting. He found himself taking note of the trappings of this, the king's most private room. He looked, as if for the first time, at the fireplace with its mantle carved in a pattern of grapes and leaves. He gazed at the wine itself, and the beautifully worked goblets, at the white candles in their gold sconces, the tapestries from Elvira, the carved ivory figures on sideboard and mantelpiece. He smelled the incense imported from Soriyya burning in a copper dish, observed the etched windows over the garden, the gilt-edged mirror on the opposite wall, the intricately woven carpets...

In a way, Mazur ben Avren thought, all these delicate things were bulwarks, the innermost defenses of civilized man against the rain and dark, and ignorance.

The Jaddites outside the walls did not understand that. Neither, to an even greater degree, did the veiled ones from the desert—the longed-for saviors of everyone's prayers.

It was too bitter a truth even for irony. These things in Badir's room—these measures of having found the space to strive for and value beauty in the world—were seen by those to north and south as the markers of corruption, decadence, frivolity. Impiety. Dangerous earthly distractions from a properly humble, cringing appeasement of a blazing god of the sun, or a far, cold deity behind the stars.

"The lady Zabira," he said, shifting position to ease his hip, "has offered to present herself as a gift to the young king of Jaloña."

Badir looked up. He had been gazing into the fire.

"She believes she might be able to kill him," ben Avren added, by way of explanation.

King Badir shook his head. "No point. A brave offer, but that young man means little to his army. What is he, sixteen? And his mother would have Zabira torn apart before she came anywhere near the boy."

"My thought as well, my lord. I thanked her and declined, on your behalf." He smiled. "I told her she could present herself to you, instead, but that I needed her more with winter coming."

The king returned the smile, briefly.

"Do we make it to the winter?" he asked.

Ben Avren sipped his wine before answering. He had been hoping this would not be asked. "I would rather we didn't have to, to be honest. It will be a near thing. We need an army from the desert to at least land in Al-Rassan, to put the Jaloñans on warning that they are at risk of being trapped outside walls and shelter. They might withdraw then."

"They should have taken Fibaz before besieging us."

"Of course they should have. Give thanks to Ashar and I'll offer a libation to the moons."

The king didn't smile this time. "And if the Muwardis don't land?"

Ben Avren shrugged. "What can I say, my lord? No city is ever safe from betrayal. Especially as supplies begin to dwindle. And you *do* have a principal advisor who is one of the hated, evil Kindath. If the Jaloñans ever offer a measure of clemency..."

"They will not."

"But if they did? If we then had something to offer back to them, in partial redress of their king's death...?"

Badir scowled. "We have been through this. Do not vex me again. I will not accept your resignation, your departure, your sacrifice...none of these things. What am I clinging to, so desperately, that I would allow myself to lose you?"

"Life? The lives of your people?"

Badir shook his head. "I am too old to clutch like that.

If the veiled ones come, my people may survive...after a fashion. This city, as we built it, will not."

He gestured around the room. "We made this together, my friend. If it goes, one way or another, I will make an end drinking my wine with you. Do not speak of this again. I regard the subject as a...betrayal."

Ben Avren's expression was grave. "It is not that, my lord."

"It is. We find a way out together, or we do not. Are you not proud of what we have achieved, we two? Is it not a denial of our very lives to speak as you are speaking now? I will not *cling* to some miserable form of existence at the price of all we have been."

His chancellor said nothing. The king, after a pause, said, "Mazur, are there not some things we have made here, some things we have done, that are worthy to have been in Silvenes, even in the golden age?"

And Mazur ben Avren, with rare emotion in the deep voice, replied, "There has been a king here, at the least, my lord, more than worthy to have been a khalif in the Al-Fontina in those most shining days."

Another silence. King Badir said, at length, very softly, "Then speak no more, old friend, of my losing you. I cannot."

Ben Avren inclined his head. "I will speak of it no more," he said. "My lord."

They finished their wine. The chancellor rose, with some difficulty, and bade his king good night. He went down the long palace corridors, his slippers silent on the marble floors, walking under torches and past tapestries, listening to the rain.

Zabira was asleep. She had left one candle burning on a table with a flask of wine and another of water, and a glass for him, already filled. He smiled, looking down upon her—as beautiful in sleep as she was awake.

The northerners, he thought, the desert tribes: how could they even comprehend a place and time—a world—that had produced a woman such as this? She would be a symbol of corruption for them both. They would kill her or degrade her, he knew. They would have no idea what else to do with Zabira of Cartada or the music she made, moving in the world.

He sat down with a sigh in the carved, deep-cushioned wooden chair he'd commissioned from a Jaddite craftsman in the city. He drank a glass of wine, and then, eventually, another, not really sleepy, deep in thought.

No real regrets, he told himself. And realized it was true.

Before he undressed for bed he went to the inner window and opened it and looked out, breathing the night air. The rain had stopped. Water dripped from the leaves of the trees to the garden below.

∽

A long way to the south and west another man was awake that same night, beneath a very different sky.

Past the peaks of the Serrana; past Lonza, huddled and afraid behind its walls, waiting for the Valledans to come; past Ronizza whose lacework was known through all the world; past arrogant Cartada in the valley of its power where the red dye was made; past Aljais and the canals of Elvira, and Silvenes where ghosts and ghostly music were said still to drift among the ruins; past, even, Tudesca at the mouth of the Guadiara, where ships put out to sea with the wealth of Al-Rassan and brought eastern treasures home.

Past all of these and beyond the waters of the straits, outside the walls of Abirab at the northern tip of the Majriti sands, Yazir ibn Q'arif, lord of the tribes of the desert, Sword of Ashar in the West, breathed the salt air from the sea and, sitting alone on an outspread cloak, looked up at a clear sky strewn with the stars of his god.

The Zuhrites had been taught by the sage who had come to them that there were as many stars as there were sands in the desert. Twenty years ago, new to belief, Yazir used to try to comprehend what that meant. He would run grains of sand through his hand while gazing at the heavens.

He was beyond such testing now. Understanding of the god was only for one such as Ashar, worthy of the gift of vision. What could a simple warrior do but bow his head and worship before such unimaginable vastness?

Stars of the heavens like the sands of the desert? What could any man do but humble himself and serve, praying by day and night for mercy and grace, understanding that he was only a part—less than a grain in the drifting sands—of the larger, unheard purpose of the god.

How could men grow swollen with pride, nourish delusions of their worth or the worth of the frail, vain things they made, if they truly believed in Ashar and the stars? That, Yazir ibn Q'arif thought, was a question he would like to ask the kings of Al-Rassan.

The night was mild, though Yazir could sense a hint of winter to come in the wind from the sea. Not long now. Two moons were riding among the stars, the blue one waxing and the white one a waning crescent in the west beyond the last of the land.

Looking at the moons, he was thinking about the Kindath, as it happened.

He had only met one of them in all his life, a barefoot wanderer in a belted robe who had come ashore years ago at a trading station on the coast east of Abeneven. The man had asked to meet the leader of the tribes and had been brought, eventually, to Yazir.

The Kindath had not been a man as most men were; he was not even typical of his own people. He had said as much to Yazir at their first meeting on the sands. Hardened by years of travel, his skin burnt dark and weathered by wind and sun, he reminded Yazir of no one so much as ibn Rashid, the wadji who had come to the Zuhrites long ago—heretical as such a thought might have been. He had the same long, untended white beard, the same clear eyes that seemed to look at something behind or beyond what other men saw.

He was journeying through many lands, the Kindath said, writing of his travels, recording the glorious places of creation, speaking with men of all faiths and beliefs. Not to preach or cajole as the wadjis did, but to deepen his own sense of wonder at the splendor of the world. He laughed often, that Kindath traveller, frequently at himself, telling tales of his own ignorance and helplessness in countries of which Yazir had not even known the names.

He spoke, during his sojourn with Yazir's people, of the world as having been made by more than one god, and as only one dwelling place among many for the children of creation. This was heresy beyond comprehension. Yazir remembered wondering if even to *hear* it condemned him to the darkness far from Paradise when he died.

It appeared that there was a sect of the Kindath, an ancient tribe, that taught of these other worlds scattered among the stars, far beyond the moons that wandered the night.

Ashar's starry visions had been right, the traveller confided to Yazir, but so were the wiser prophets of Jad, and so, in truth, were the Kindath sages who had seen goddesses in the moons. All these teachings revealed a part—but only a part—of the mystery.

There were other deities, other worlds. There was one god above all, ruler of stars and sun and moons, of all the worlds. No man knew the name of this most high lord. Only in the world that had been made first, the world all others—including their own—had followed into Time was that name known and spoken. Only there did the Supreme One allow knowledge of himself, and there the gods did him homage.

They had broken bread together for several mornings and nights, and spoken of many things. Then the Kindath traveller had begged leave to go alone from Yazir's camp that he might travel the vast and mighty Majriti desert and worship the splendor thereof.

Ghalib, who had been listening to some of what had been said over the past days, had asked Yazir's permission—unusual, for him—to follow and kill the man because of his impieties. Yazir, torn by the burden of a host towards a guest and the spiritual duties of a leader to his people, had given his consent, reluctantly. One more transgression for which Ashar would have to grant forgiveness when Yazir's time came to be judged.

That strange man had been the only one of the Kindath he'd ever met.

Two days ago a letter had come, delivered by a tribesman crossing back to the desert from Tudesca. It had been carried before that by messengers across most of Al-Rassan. It had begun as a note tied to a pigeon's leg, carried out from besieged Ragosa.

It was from the sorcerer himself, Mazur ben Avren.

After it had been read to him, three times, by a scribe, Yazir had walked from his tent and mounted a camel and ridden into the desert alone to think.

He was still thinking, tonight under the stars. He had a decision to make—one that might shape the destiny of his people—and no more time for delay. To delay further was to decide.

Ghalib was ready to cross to Al-Rassan, Yazir knew that. Ghalib wanted to go where there was already war, to test himself and his tribesmen. To die, if it came to that, with a red sword in his hand, battling in Ashar's name. The surest path to Paradise.

The Kindath traveller, years ago, hadn't named that first world where the one true god reigned. He'd said the name was another mystery. Yazir wished he'd never heard the tale. It refused to leave him, still.

Ragosa will not hold out until winter, as matters now stand, Mazur ben Avren had written. *But if you so much as land at Tudesca, and come no further this autumn than Aljais or Cartada, the Jaloñans here will be greatly afraid and our people will take heart. I believe we can endure if this happens, and in spring we may turn them back.*

Ghalib had said the same thing. He wanted to land before winter, to let the Jaddites fear their presence and push forward no further. Yazir had been inclined to wait— for more ships, more men, and most of all, for tidings from Soriyya, towards which a Jaddite army was sailing even now.

What did a pious man do when he was asked, desperately, for aid in two different fields of holy war?

It has come to me as a thought, Mazur ben Avren's letter went on, *that one reason you hesitate to relieve us from this peril is my own presence in Ragosa. King Badir is a good man and a wise king, beloved of his people. If it will ease the burden of decision that lies upon you, know that I am ready to leave this city should you send word.*

Leave the city? One did not leave besieged cities. Unless...

I will walk into the Jaddite camp so soon as word comes from you that you have elected to cross to Al-Rassan and cleanse it of those who must be driven back lest this land be lost to Ashar and the Star-born.

It was a Kindath saying this, offering this.

Yazir imagined his reply being carried north and east, one rider after another, city to city, and then a carrier bird loosed from hills near Ragosa. He imagined that bird landing in the city, his scribe-crafted note carried to the sorcerer. Yazir pictured him reading it.

Strange, strangest thing of all: he never doubted for a moment that the man would do what he said.

The king will not take happily to my presuming to send this letter, and I beg your own forgiveness for my impertinence. Should you agree with my unworthy thoughts, O Sword of Ashar, leader of all the tribes, send only the words "It shall be as has been written," and I alone will understand and offer thanks to you and act as I have said. May whatever sins Ragosa holds in Ashar's sight and your own be deemed to rest upon my head as I walk out. My own people in this city honor their Asharite king and know their proper place. If there has been arrogance and presumption it has been my own, and I am prepared to make atonement.

The crescent of the white moon lay almost upon the sea. Yazir watched as it slipped down and out of sight. The innumerable stars were everywhere in the sky and the innumerable sands were about him.

He heard a footfall, and knew it.

"You asked me to come at white moonset," his brother said softly, crouching on his haunches beside Yazir's spread cloak. "Do we cross? Do we wait? Do we sail for the homelands?"

Yazir drew a breath. There were deaths and deaths to come. Man was born into this world to die. Best do it in the service of Ashar, essaying those things that could truly be done.

"Soriyya is too far," he said. "I do not think either of us are destined to see the homelands, my brother."

Ghalib said nothing, waiting.

"I would be happier in spring," Yazir said.

His brother's teeth showed in the darkness. "You are never happy," Ghalib said.

Yazir looked away. It was true, of late. He *had* been happy once, as a young man, without any great cares, in the Zuhrite lands south of where they were tonight. Before his feet had been placed on a path of righteousness carved in blood.

"We will cross the straits," he said. "Beginning tomorrow. We will not allow the Sons of Jad to burn any more of the Star-born, or take any more cities, however far our people may have strayed from Ashar's path. We will lead them back. It comes to me that if the city-kings lose Al-Rassan to the Jaddites, we are the ones who will be answerable before the god."

Ghalib rose to his feet. "I am pleased," he said.

Yazir saw that his brother's eyes were gleaming, like those of a cat. "And the Kindath sorcerer?" Ghalib added. "The letter that came?"

"Go to my scribe," Yazir said. "Wake him. Have him write a reply and have it carried across the water—tonight, before the rest of us depart."

"What reply, brother?"

Yazir looked up at him. *"It shall be as has been written."*

"That is all?"

"That is all."

Ghalib turned and walked back to his camel. He made it kneel and then he mounted up and rode. Yazir remained where he was. So many stars, so many, many sands, the blue moon high in the clear night.

He could still see his message crossing the straits, men riding, a bird flying. A hidden opening in the walls of Ragosa, perhaps in the grey hour before dawn. A man walking out, alone, towards the watchfires of his enemies.

Slowly, he nodded his head, picturing all this in the eye of his mind. It was Ashar's will, Ashar's law: no Kindath was to hold sway over the Star-born. It had been written. And that sorcerer in Ragosa would not be the first, nor would he be the last man—brave or otherwise—to die in the days of blood to come.

The autumn seas were mild and generous the next morning and the next as the children of the desert, veiled before the wonder of the god's creation, knelt in holy prayer and then sailed on an unfamiliar element to the redeeming of Al-Rassan.

∾

A little less than a year later two women stood, late on a windy summer's day, upon a hilltop near the sad ruins of Silvenes, in the moments before the ending of the world they both had known.

White clouds hurried overhead and laced the western horizon where the sun was low. Banners snapping and blowing, two armies lay beneath them north of the swift and gleaming Guadiara.

The forces of Ashar and Jad had finally come together after a summer and autumn and then a spring of siege and skirmish, bracketing a harsh winter with its enforced inactivity. A great many people had died that winter, of hunger and cold and the illnesses that followed on the heels of hardship and war. It had snowed as far south as Lonza and Ronizza, and Ardeño in the west.

All three cities were Jaddite now.

Rodrigo Belmonte, commanding the joined armies of Ruenda and Valledo and Jaloña, had taken them this spring. At Ardeño—first of the three to fall—he'd led the western part of the Esperañan army himself in a first engagement with the tribesmen, and he had killed Ghalib ibn Q'arif.

No man had so much as wounded Ghalib in combat since he'd ridden east beside his brother more than twenty years ago. Men had lost count of the times he had championed the Zuhrites and Ashar's visions against the best man of another tribe in the ritual combat before a battle began. There had been no such rituals at Ardeño. Rodrigo Belmonte had singled him out, though, on the difficult side-slipping ground east of the city, and he had broken Ghalib's helm and shield with a blow, and thrown him from his horse, and then, leaping down, had gashed his thigh to the bone and almost severed one arm before killing him with a swordstroke down through neck and collarbone.

No one in either army had ever seen a man fight like that.

It was understood that Ser Rodrigo's son had very nearly died in a Muwardi ambush the summer before. It was pointed out that Ardeño marked the first time the new constable of Valledo had been able to confront an army of the veiled ones on open ground.

Leaving the citizens of Ardeño, for the moment, to their fate, the Muwardis had retreated south, though in good order and doing damage to those who pursued too rashly.

They had fallen back towards Silvenes, where Yazir and the bulk of his forces—both those of Al-Rassan, and newly arriving tribesmen—were assembling.

Rodrigo Belmonte had left the king of Ruenda with the western army to pin down the Asharites there. With only his own band of one hundred and fifty men he had raced east towards Lonza and King Ramiro.

The walls of that small city were breached fifteen days after he arrived. Further east, Ronizza on the River Larrios, under siege from Jaloñan forces that had bypassed still-unconquered Ragosa, surrendered immediately when word of the fall of Lonza came. Ronizza's gates were not opened, however, until Ser Rodrigo's own herald arrived with a company of Valledans to accept their surrender. There had been lessons learned from the occupations of Fezana and Salos the year before.

The northern armies left a garrison and a governor in each city. A number of people were executed to promote order but, for the moment, the transitions were calm. There were no burnings. King Ramiro and his constable had firm control of the northern forces now. The armies of Jaloña and Valledo joined ranks and doubled back west to merge with the Ruendans north of Silvenes.

What was left of the Ruendans, that is.

The strong army on its high ground that Belmonte had left behind had been chopped to pieces by a beaten foe.

Yazir ibn Q'arif—visibly shaken by his brother's death, wearing a grey veil of mourning now—had wasted no time in naming the new leader of the Asharite forces in Al-Rassan. It was not a popular choice among the tribesmen, but Yazir had had a winter and spring to learn the way of things in this peninsula—who knew how to lead, who could be trusted, who needed to be watched—and he did not hesitate once the rites for his brother were done.

Ammar ibn Khairan, the newly named ka'id, had regrouped the Muwardis, linked to them a fresh contingent of soldiers from Cartada, and surprised the Ruendans with a two-pronged attack from south and east. The timing, on difficult ground, had had to be flawless, and it was. He had chased the northerners all the way back into Ardeño.

The Muwardis, grieving for Ghalib, had been impossible to control in that pursuit. Prisoners weren't being taken anywhere in this war, but the captured Ruendans were savagely abused before and after they were killed. When the surviving northerners were safely within the walls of Ardeño, they promptly began nailing men and women to wood and burning them, by way of response.

Rodrigo Belmonte came back west. The Asharites with-drew towards Silvenes again and reinforcements came to them from Cartada and Tudesca and up from Elvira on the coast.

Five hundred men also arrived from the fortress of Arbastro—led by Tarif ibn Hassan himself. The outlaw and his sons had stopped at Cartada to receive formal pardons from the new king. Almalik II, the parricide, had been exe-cuted by Yazir—one of his first actions upon arriving the autumn before. His brother Hazem, called One-hand, had been installed in Cartada.

The Ruendan army, what was left of it, emerged from Ardeño again and moved cautiously south, joining the rest of the Esperañan forces near Silvenes.

Silvenes. It seemed that here the seasons of war were to come to an end. Either Yazir and his army of rescue, here in response to the importunities of fleeing kings and panic-stricken wadjis, would bring Ashar back in triumph to this land, or...or the Khalifate's fall a generation ago would be as nothing compared to what came now. The necklace of Al-Rassan had been broken then, the pearls scattering. Now they could be lost.

Heralds met on the ground between two armies.

Yazir ibn Q'arif, weighing possibilities, accustomed to swift decisions, instructed his herald to make a proposal. The representative of King Ramiro, a man clearly too young for his task—he was white-faced with what he heard—car-ried that message back to Ramiro and his constable.

A short time later, grim and precise, the same young herald rode back and met his counterpart again, bearing a reply.

It was as had been expected.

There had been, in truth, no way to refuse. Not in honor, not in pride, not before a battle such as this one was to be. The weight of centuries had come down.

❧

Waking in the morning before Ammar, Jehane lay quietly,

looking at him, trying to comprehend how time and the gods had brought them to this. From outside the tent, she heard the sounds of men beginning to stir in the camp; the first prayers of the morning would soon begin.

Her last dream before waking had been of Mazur. Prince of the Kindath. Dead now, half a year ago. She was still unable to stop herself from picturing him emerging from the walls of Ragosa and walking to the Jaddite camp. Where did men find it in themselves to do such things?

The Muwardis had landed in Al-Rassan that same season. Later, in winter, they had learned how those two crossings—ben Avren through the walls to his death and Yazir ibn Q'arif across the straits—were linked to each other. Lines of movement, so far apart, joined at their source. Mazur's last gift to his king and Ragosa.

There had been terrible stories of what Queen Fruela had ordered done to the grey-haired Kindath chancellor after he had walked, unarmed, into her camp. Jehane knew that the worst of them would be true. She also knew, bitter and grieving, that the Muwardis would have done much the same, had they been the ones outside Ragosa's walls.

Who are my enemies?

How did one rise above hatred at these times?

Ammar slept still. It amazed her that he could. She was tempted to trace his features with a hand—eyes, mouth, ears, the straight nose—like a blind woman, to memorize him. She shook her head, pushing the thought away. His breathing was quiet and slow. One arm lay across his chest, oddly childlike.

He could die today. If he did not, Rodrigo would.

It had come to this. Were mortals only playthings for the gods they worshipped, to be tormented in their dying?

It had been agreed between the heralds of Ashar and Jad that leaders of each army would fight before battle, to invoke the will and the power of their gods. One of the oldest rituals of men at war.

Had they somehow guessed that this day might come, the two of them? Had that been the terrible foreknowing that lay beneath the last words they had spoken in the darkness of Orvilla? Or even earlier: in Ragosa, staring at each other that first morning in the brightness of the king's garden with the stream running through it? They had refused to fight each other. There, they could refuse. There, they could fight side by side.

Jehane made herself a promise at that moment, watching her lover sleep, hearing the camp coming awake outside: she would do all she could not to weep. Tears were an easy refuge. What was to happen today demanded more of her.

Ammar's eyes opened without warning, vivid and blue, the same color as her own. He looked at her. She watched him settle into an awareness of the day, what morning it was.

He said, first words, "Jehane, if I fall, you must go with Alvar. He can take you to your parents. There will be nowhere else, my love."

She nodded her head, not speaking. She didn't trust herself to speak. She leaned across and kissed him on the lips. Then she laid her head down on his chest, listening to the beating of his heart. When they spoke afterwards, outside, it was about inconsequential things. The absurd pretense that the world was a normal place that day.

There will be nowhere else, my love.

❧

Alternately hot and cold as the setting sun slipped behind and then out from the swift clouds in the west, Jehane stood on a windy height beside Miranda Belmonte d'Alveda, looking down on a plain between armies.

Alvar de Pellino, a herald of Valledo, garbed in white and gold, was with them as escort to Miranda. So was Husari, granted leave by King Ramiro to accompany his herald.

Husari was the governor of Fezana now, serving Valledo. Jehane did not begrudge him that. He had chosen Ramiro over the Muwardis, making his choice of evils in a time that forced such choices upon all of them. Ziri had decided otherwise, it seemed. He had not left Ragosa with Rodrigo's men. Jehane understood. He would not fight under the banners of the god whose followers had killed his parents. She had no idea what had happened to him. You lost people in war.

She looked down. The armies below were roughly balanced. The ground was even. Neither leader would have been here with his forces had it been otherwise.

The temporarily united Jaddite troops could not remain in the field another winter, and the tribesmen had no disposition for a war of siege and attrition so far from their sands. Tomorrow would see a battle on open ground. A rare thing. There might even be a decisive result, or this could go on and on. Slow, bitter years of fire and sword, disease and hunger and cold, in the breaking of a world.

But before tomorrow could come, with its armies in that plain beneath banners of blue-and-gold or silver-on-black, there had first to be this evening's sunset. Jehane reminded herself that she had vowed not to weep.

Ceremonial battles between Ashar and Jad took place at dawn or at day's end, in the balancing moments between sun and stars. There was one moon in the eastern sky—the white one, nearly full. It was, Jehane thought bitterly, irrelevant to the duality so harmoniously shaped and decreed.

A handful of soldiers from each army were on opposite sides of the slope below them. She knew the Jaddites. Rodrigo's men: Laín, Martín, Ludus. They were not really needed as guards, for Alvar was on the hill and the traditions of heralds were being honored in this campaign.

Men were like that, Jehane thought, unable to check the bitterness from rising again. This was warfare as savage as could be imagined, but the soldiers—even the Muwardis—would defer to the herald's banner and staff.

And they would watch now like boys—enraptured, overawed by the ancient symbolism—what was to happen on the plain between armies. A challenge of gods! Each faith with its great champion, its holy lion of the battlefield! Poets would write verses and songs, chant them at feasts or in taverns or in the dark under desert stars.

"Will there ever be a time when it is not a curse to be born a woman?" Miranda had spoken without turning her head. "When we can do more," she added, staring down at the plain, "than stand by and be brave and watch them die?"

Jehane said nothing. She could think of no answer that was adequate. She would not, before today, have called her own womanhood a burden, aware that she'd been luckier than most—in her family, friends, in her profession. She didn't feel very fortunate today. Today she thought she could agree with Miranda Belmonte. Standing on this windy height, it was easy to agree.

There came a new sound below them. Both armies reacting to something. Loud cries, a banging of swords on shields.

From opposite directions, north and south, two men were riding towards each other across the ground west of Silvenes.

No one escorted either man, so no one knew what it was that Rodrigo Belmonte and Ammar ibn Khairan said to each other when they stopped their horses a little distance apart, alone in the world.

Each man dismounted, however, after a moment, and each turned his horse and sent it cantering back the way he had come across the grass. Then they faced each other again and Jehane could see Ammar say one last thing, and Rodrigo reply. Then they lowered their helms.

On that watching height at day's windy end, she saw each of them take a round shield from where it hung upon his back and then each of them drew his sword.

There would be an eagle on Rodrigo's helm; Ammar's had a pattern of vine leaves. These were things she knew but could not see: she was too far away on this hill and the sun was wrong, behind the two men, and low. They were almost silhouettes against the light, standing alone. Even the horses had finished running away from them.

Is it wrong to love two men? she had asked the summer before, in darkness by the river.

Without taking her eyes from the plain below, Miranda crossed her arms over her breast as if holding tightly to something there. Jehane had seen Rodrigo use that same gesture, exactly, in the moonlight of Orvilla a year ago. She wondered, if she and Ammar were granted enough time, would they, too, come to share gestures like that? And would they ever make a child to be loved as much as the woman beside her and the man below loved their sons?

There will never be enough time, she had said to Ammar.

Looking towards the sun, she saw Rodrigo feint and then swing his blade, hard, back the other way and she watched Ammar parry that blow with a movement of his own sword, smooth as Husari's silk, as a line of verse, as a good wine tasted at the end of day. He turned the parry, seamlessly, into a driving thrust, low, and Rodrigo—fast as a dream of a hunting cat—pushed down his shield and blocked it.

The two men stepped back. They stood looking at each other from beneath their helms, motionless. It had begun. Jehane closed her eyes.

A heavy sound arose from the armies: hungry, needing, enthralled.

Opening her eyes again, Jehane saw that Husari had come to stand beside her. He was crying, without conceal-ment or pretense.

She looked at him, and then away, without speaking. She was afraid to attempt to say anything. She had made a promise to herself. Had sworn she would not weep. Until it was over. Until time had run away from them like those horses on the plain.

∽

They were a match. Both of them had always known it. In a way, the desperate exigencies required to stay alive now were a good thing: they made it harder for the heart to intervene and cripple with its sorrow.

There were reasons for staying alive. There was a woman on a hilltop east of them. There was love. He blocked a low thrust, barely, cut forward *with* the motion—a difficult thing—and was parried, elegantly. Never a swordsman like this before. Never a match. Could it be called a dance? Should they embrace? Were they not?

One let the body rule here, faster than thought; movements not even imagined, a blurring engaged by the same when blades met. The mind floating just above, out of the way except when it noticed something. A weakness, a faltering.

No faltering here at red sunset. He hadn't thought there would be.

On that hilltop to the east there was love.

Once, during their campaign for Ragosa, when they'd lured the old bandit ibn Hassan into ambushing the *parias* party for them, Jehane had joined the company by the fire one night, and had offered a Kindath song.

> *Who knows love?*
> *Who says he knows love?*
> *What is love, tell me.*
>
> *"I know love,"*
> *Says the littlest one.*
> *"Love is like a tall oak tree."*
>
> *"Why is love a tall oak tree?*
> *Little one tell me."*
>
> *"Love is a tree*
> *For the shelter it gives*
> *In sunshine or in storm."*

He stumbled unexpectedly as an attack pushed him back; swore as he felt himself falling. Too careless, distracted. He had *seen* that rock, had thought of using it.

Twisting desperately, he released his shield—behind him, the grip upwards—and blocked his fall with his freed left arm, palm braced hard on the grass, sword sweeping into position to take the other man's descending blade and turn it away.

He let himself roll with the weight of that blow to the necessary place, reclaimed the shield and was up again—all in the same smooth motion. In time to blunt the swift second stroke. Dropped to a knee then and slashed across, faster than he should have been able to. Almost got through with that one; almost buried his sword. Didn't. They were a match. Both of them had known. From first meeting in Ragosa. That garden with the tame stream.

Who knows love?
Who says he knows love?
What is love, tell me.

"I know love,"
Says the littlest one.
"Love is like a flower."

"Why is love a flower?
Little one tell me."

"Love is a flower
For the sweetness it gives
Before it dies away."

It would have been pleasant, the thought came to him, to be able to lay down their weapons on the darkening grass. To walk away from this place, from what they were being made to do, past the ruins, along the river and into the woods beyond. To find a forest pool, wash their wounds and drink from the cool water and then sit beneath the trees, out of the wind, silent as the summer night came down.

Not in this life.

He thought, then, of something he could do with his shield.

It would have been so much better had she been able to hate the man trying to kill Rodrigo. It was this man, though, who had given the warning that saved Diego's life. He hadn't had to do that. He was Asharite. He was now the commander of their army, the ka'id.

But she had never, ever heard Rodrigo speak of another man—not even Raimundo, who had died so long ago—the way he'd talked about Ammar ibn Khairan during the long, waiting winter just past. The way the man sat a horse, handled a blade, a bow, devised strategies, jested, spoke of history, geography, the properties of good wine. Even the way he wrote poetry.

"*Poetry?*" Miranda could remember saying to this last, in the voice she reserved for her most withering sarcasm.

Rodrigo had a liking for verse, an ear for what he heard. She did not, and he knew it. He used to torment her with snatches of lyrics in bed. She'd cover her head with pillows.

"Are you in love with this man?" she'd asked her husband once in Fezana that winter—more than half jealous, if truth were told.

"I suppose I am, in a way," Rodrigo had replied after a moment. "Isn't it odd?"

It wasn't, really, Miranda thought, on that hill by Silvenes. The low sun was making it difficult to see the two of them now. There were moments when she found it impossible to tell them apart. She would have thought she'd know Rodrigo beside any man on earth, but he was in armor now, and far away, a moving shadow against red light, and the two men would come together, circle and turn, very close, before disengaging. It was easy to confuse them in these movements leading to a death.

She wasn't ready to lose him. To be alone.

It was the wind that was bringing tears to her eyes. She wiped at them with the back of a hand, glancing sidelong at the other woman. Jehane bet Ishak stood dry-eyed, white-faced, never moving her gaze from what was happening below. Miranda thought suddenly: *We have had our years. I know what it is I will lose. She hasn't even had time to gather memories against the dark.*

Which was the harder loss to bear? Were there measurements for such things? Did it matter?

"*Oh, love,*" she whispered aloud. And then, to herself, a prayer, "*Do not leave me now.*"

In that moment she saw one of them throw his shield.

∽

She would never have thought there could be beauty in something so purely terrifying, but she ought to have known, remembering what they could do. Both of them.

She had seen them fight—that challenge in Ragosa, the Emin ha'Nazar, the Kindath Quarter in Fezana. She ought to have expected this.

Most of the time, eyes narrowed against the sun, Jehane could tell them apart. Not always, though, as they overlapped and merged and broke apart. They *were* silhouettes now, no more than that, against the last red disk of light.

She suddenly remembered, as if the thought had somehow been given to her, a cold night during that campaign in the east for Mazur and King Badir. She'd heard the company singing by one of the campfires, to the sound of Martín's guitar. She had come out from her tent, half asleep, wrapped in a cloak. They had made a place for her near the fire. Eventually she had sung a tune her mother used to sing to her in childhood, as Eliane's own mother had sung it for her. It was such an old song.

Both men had been watching her from across the fire that night, Jehane remembered. A strange memory now, but it had come. She remembered the night, the fire, the song.

> "*Love is a flower*
> *For the sweetness it gives*
> *Before it dies away.*"

The sun, red as a flame, dropped below the western bank of clouds, underlighting them, hanging on the rim of the world. The two men were shadow-figures against it.

They circled, came together, circled. She could truly not distinguish them now, the movements were so much the same.

One of them threw his shield.

Hurled it flat like a discus, wrong-handed, straight at the other's knees. The other man leaped to evade, almost did, was hit, fell awkwardly. Jehane caught her breath. The first one drove straight forward, hard, and they were locked again, entangled.

"*Rodrigo,*" said Miranda suddenly.

The man without a shield was above the other, who had fought to his knees. The one on the ground blocked the descent of a sword, was thrown back. Hurled himself completely over and away on the grass, letting fall his own shield to do it. They engaged, without defenses now, blades whipping and parrying. One body, almost. A creature of myth, some lost, fabulous beast of long ago. They pushed apart. Two figures again, against the sun's disk.

Jehane's hands were up before her mouth. One of the two men threw himself against the other again. Half the sun was gone now, at the end of the world. She could see the shields where they had fallen.

Someone hammered downwards, was blocked. He broke free, feinted a thrust, slashed across.

And was not parried. Not this time.

The long blade sank in. They could see it from on the hill. Jehane began to cry. The wounded man pulled free and back, somehow deflected another driving blow. Then he twisted suddenly, one arm held tight against his ribs. Jehane saw him take a quick step to the side and grip his sword in both hands. It was upon them.

> *Who knows love?*
> *Who says he knows love?*
> *What is love, tell me.*

An old song. A child's song.

And so, at the last, from far away, against the red and

failing light, she saw a good man raise his sword and she saw a good man fall.

There came a vast roaring sound from the armies. But though she was aware of this it seemed already distant to Jehane, and moving away, as if a silence was descending to cover the world.

The man who yet stood upright on the plain turned towards the hill where the women were. He let fall his own blade onto the dark, trampled grass. Holding a palm again to his wounded side, he made a gesture—a small, helpless movement—with his free hand.

Then he turned away from them to the man lying on the ground and he sank to his knees beside him as the sun went down.

Soon after that the clouds began rolling in from the west, blanketing the sky.

No sun, no moon, no stars over Al-Rassan.

EPILOGUE

The rapid resettlement of the Kindath community of Sorenica in Batiara was something that could be regarded in a number of different ways. Burned to the ground nearly twenty years before, on the eve of the disastrous Jaddite campaign against the Asharite homelands in the east, Sorenica had been rebuilt and was thriving again.

Some viewed this as a sad demonstration of the Kindath's desperate desire for roots and a home—any kind of home, however precarious. Others saw the speedy restoration of a devastated city as emblematic of endurance in the face of hardships that would have destroyed a people with a lesser heritage to sustain them.

The Kindath physician Alvar ben Pellino, who had been one of the first to settle here in his youth—he had completed his studies at the newly re-established university— had a different perspective from most, and a more pragmatic view.

Men and women of all faiths struggled to find ways to shape a life for themselves and their children. When opportunities emerged they were grasped. Sorenica's revival was simply such an opportunity being seized.

In the aftermath of their army's destruction twenty years ago, the Jaddite princes of several kingdoms had been informed by their spiritual advisors that the god had not been pleased by the brutal attack on Sorenica before the fleet sailed. The Kindath had not been the real targets of that holy war, the clerics solemnly decreed, conveniently forgetting their own role in the massacre. Sorenica's destruction, they decided, had represented a failure of piety, a deviation from proper awareness of the holy mission that lay ahead.

Jad had sent his punishments: storm winds at sea, sickness, murder among princes, deaths in battle in far-off, inhospitable lands.

Those leaders and their followers who finally came home two long years later had wearily agreed to make atonement for the Sorenica massacre. The Kindath had been invited back, royal monies were allocated for the rebuilding of their sanctuaries, markets, houses, the university, the harbor, warehouses, city walls. Taxes were remitted for all who agreed to settle there in those first years. The highest lords of Batiara—many of them the sons of men who had died in the Asharite homelands—put their seals to a long, clerkly document drawn up to attest to the assured safety of Sorenica and its inhabitants.

One did not have to *believe* such things, Alvar ben Pellino thought, striding quickly past the stalls of the market towards the harbor, to have decided that in an uncertain, violent world, Sorenica offered no more risks than anywhere else and a few benefits not otherwise available.

In his case, more than a few benefits, in that long-ago year when they'd escaped the savagery that was consuming Esperaña and Al-Rassan, tearing the peninsula apart the way wild beasts shred a carcass.

Ben Pellino was well-known and well-loved in Sorenica. Hasten as he might, his progress towards the harbor was slow. Every few steps he was forced to stop and exchange pleasantries with someone or another. A surprising number of men and women wished him the moons' blessing on his fortieth birth day. The Kindath, with their charts of birth, paid more attention to such days than his own people had: a small adjustment among larger ones.

It was his daughters, Alvar gradually understood, who had been busily informing everyone. Ruefully smiling, he acknowledged all the good wishes, agreeing with cheerful suggestions that his youth was now behind him.

He'd had a highly dramatic life in his early years and people knew something of that. He'd been a Horseman and even a royal herald in Valledo, before coming away from that peninsula, adopting the Kindath faith and beginning his training in medicine.

He was much sought after and trusted as a physician: calm, learned, reassuring. A steady hand and eye in surgery. His services had once been in demand among the mercenary armies of Batiara but he had never gone with the soldiers, ever. A season's summons to a princely court he would accept—to deliver children, attend to gout, couch cataracts—but never a position with an army in the field. Had he wanted to tread or ride a battlefield, ben Pellino said calmly to all who asked, he would still be a Horseman in the army of Ramiro the Great of Esperaña.

He was a doctor, he said, and his labor was preserving and easing life. He would not, given a choice, freely venture into death's own domain of war.

His wife did so, however. Also a physician—an even better one in the view of some, since she'd been trained from childhood by her celebrated father—she was not averse to a campaign or two among the armies. One saw injuries and ailments in the field that could only serve to broaden and deepen a doctor's knowledge. Her father had done the same thing in his day.

Alvar, disengaging from yet another well-wisher, made a mental note to chastise his daughters when he returned home. They'd no business proclaiming his advancing years to the whole community! He didn't *look* forty; everyone said as much. He wasn't ready to be venerable and sage; unless it helped in disciplining two girls hovering precariously on the brink of womanhood. In the case of his daughters Alvar rather doubted anything would greatly help.

On the other hand, they were the ones who had decided to have a celebration today, and who'd been busy all week preparing it. They'd ordered the cook out of the kitchen. They had been making the confections themselves. His wife, more sympathetic to his desire to pass the day quietly, had tried to deter them—to no avail. When the two girls acted in tandem, the idea of deterrence was naive.

Knowing he was expected home by now for the celebration, Alvar hurried along the slip where ships from all over the world were loading or off-loading cargoes. He looked for and found the one with an Esperañan flag: yellow sun on a pale blue field, Queen Vasca's crown above it.

A boy from the docks had run a message to their treatment rooms. A letter was waiting for them, entrusted to the captain. Alvar had finished with his patients first and had come to collect it.

He didn't recognize the captain who granted him permission to board the ship. They exchanged pleasantries.

He did know the writing and the seal, and he took a deep breath when he accepted the salt-stained packet from the man. It was addressed to him and Jehane both, so after offering his thanks and a silver coin and striding back down to the wooden planks of the wharf, Alvar opened it. Normally he let Jehane read their mail from Esperaña first, but today was his birth day, after all, and he allowed himself this much luxury. He was immediately sorry.

My dear Jehane, my dear Alvar, he read, *may the god and his sisters guard and preserve you and all your loved ones. We are well, though events, as you will have heard from others by now, have been turbulent this summer....*

Alvar stopped reading, his heart thudding. They hadn't heard anything from others. He turned back to the ship. He called out. The captain turned at the rail to look down at him.

"What's happened in the peninsula?" Alvar shouted up. He spoke in Esperañan. Heads turned towards him.

"You don't know?" the captain cried.

"You're the first Esperañan ship here in a month."

"Then I can be tale teller!" the captain said, visibly pleased. He brought his two hands together above his eyes, making the sign of the god's disk. "Belmonte took Cartada and Aljais this summer, and then Tudesca surrendered to him! Ramiro the Great has ridden his black horse into the sea at the mouth of the Guadiara. Jad has reconquered Al-Rassan! The peninsula belongs to Esperaña again!"

There was a babble of noise along the harbor. The news would be all over Sorenica by the time Alvar got home if he didn't hurry.

He began moving quickly, almost running, barely pausing to throw a thank you over his shoulder. He didn't want this news to come from the street. There were those at his house today who would need a warning, some shelter from this.

He needed that himself, in truth.

Even as he hurried back through the market, Alvar was remembering a long-ago night north of Fezana, when King Ramiro had told him and Ser Rodrigo of his firm intent to ride into the seas surrounding Al-Rassan and claim all the lands that touched them for his own.

He'd done it now. Ramiro the Great. Nearly twenty years after, but he'd done it. He was king of Esperaña. Of Valledo, Ruenda, Jaloña. Of Al-Rassan, though that name would be gone now. From this summer forward, that name was a word for poets and historians.

Clutching the letter, Alvar broke into a run. People looked at him curiously, but there were other running figures in the street now, carrying the same tidings. He cut along a laneway and past their treatment rooms. Closed. Everyone would be at his house by now. For the party. His happy celebration.

Alvar was aware that he would need to weep before this day was done. He wouldn't be the only one.

The outer doors of the house were open. He walked in. No one to be seen. They would all be in the courtyard, waiting for him. He paused before the looking glass, startled by his reflection. A brown-haired man, unfashionably bearded, beginning to grey. White-faced, just now. So much so that were he his own patient, Alvar would have ordered immediate rest. He'd had a blow. An extreme one.

He heard sounds from the kitchen and turned that way. In the doorway he stopped. His wife was there, still dressed for work, checking on the small cakes and pies the girls had been making. Even now, even with what had just happened to him, Alvar offered his prayer of thanksgiving to the god and the moons that he had been vouchsafed this gift of love, so unexpectedly, so profoundly undeserved.

He cleared his throat. She turned to look at him.

"You're late," she said lightly. "Dina, your darling little girl, has been threatening to—" She stopped. *"What has happened?"*

How did one say this?

"Al-Rassan has fallen." He heard himself speaking the words as in a place that echoed, like the valley of the Emin ha'Nazar. "This summer. All of the peninsula is Jaddite now."

His wife leaned back, her hands behind her, against the table by the hearth. Then, pushing herself forward, she took three steps across the stone floor and wrapped her arms around him, her head against his chest.

"Oh, my love," she said. "Oh, Alvar, this must be so hard for you. What can I say?"

"Is everyone here?"

"Almost. Oh, my dear," said Marisa bet Rezzoni, his wife, his colleague and Jehane's, daughter of his teacher, mother of his children, light of his days and nights. "Oh, Alvar, how are you going to tell them?"

"Tell them what?" Jehane asked, coming into the kitchen. "What is it? One of the children?"

"No. No, not that," Alvar said, and fell silent.

He looked at the first woman he had ever loved. He knew he would love her and in more than a way of speaking until he died. She was still, with silver in her hair and a softening to her features now, the same astonishing, courageous woman with whom he had ridden across the Serrana Range to King Badir's Ragosa all those years ago.

Another known footfall in the hallway outside. "We're in here," Alvar said, lifting his voice. "In the kitchen." In a way it was better like this.

Ammar, hardly using his stick today, paused in the doorway and then came to stand beside his wife. He looked at Jehane, at Marisa, at Alvar. He laid a hand on Jehane's shoulder and said, in his beautiful voice, "Alvar has had the same tidings I have. He is trying to think of how to shelter us. Me, mostly, I suppose."

"You, mostly," Alvar agreed quietly. "Ammar, I'm so sorry."

"Please!" Jehane said. *"What is it?"*

Her husband released her and she turned to look at him. "I was going to wait until Alvar's celebration was done, but there is no point now. A ship from Esperaña is in, my love. Fernan Belmonte took Cartada, and my own Aljais of the nightingales this summer. Tudesca opened her gates immediately after. They were the last, those three."

Alvar saw that his wife, who alone of the four of them had never even been in that beloved, tormented peninsula, was weeping. Marisa could feel for the pain she saw, could almost take it into herself. It was a part of her physician's gift, and it frightened him sometimes.

Jehane had gone white, much as he himself had appeared in the looking glass. She did not cry. She said, after a moment, "It was going to happen. There was no one to turn the tide back, and Fernan..."

"Appears to have become something close to what his father was," Ammar finished for her. "It was going to happen, yes." He smiled, the smile they had all come to know and need over the years here in Sorenica. "Have I not been trying to write a history and an elegy for Al-Rassan all this time? Would it not have been a cruel jest upon me, if—"

"Don't!" Jehane said, and stepping forward, put her arms around her husband. Ammar stopped. He closed his eyes.

Alvar swallowed, near to weeping, for reasons too complex for words. The Star-born were not his people. He was Jaddite born, Kindath by choice—even before he'd met and wooed Ser Rezzoni's youngest daughter. He had made that decision, along with a resolve to pursue a doctor's life, by the time he left Esteren, escorting Ishak ben Yonannon and his wife to their daughter on behalf of the king and queen of Valledo.

Jehane had already been in Sorenica, having come with ibn Khairan when the Muwardi tribesmen in Al-Rassan threatened revolt if Ammar continued to lead their armies. Yazir ibn Q'arif had been urged to execute him—a man, the wadjis cried, who had slain a khalif. A man more offensive in Ashar's sight than even the Jaddites were.

Yazir had yielded to the first pressure but resisted the second, surprisingly. He had exiled ibn Khairan but allowed him his life. Partly for what he had achieved as ka'id, but mostly for one evening's single combat as the named, holy sword arm of Ashar. Had he not defeated the man no one could defeat? Had he not granted them victory by Silvenes when he killed Rodrigo Belmonte, the Scourge of Al-Rassan?

And more: had he not—above all else—thereby taken blood revenge for Ghalib? Yazir ibn Q'arif, who had travelled the sands for the past twenty years with his brother at his side, would not destroy the man who had done that for him. Ibn Khairan had been permitted to leave, with his Kindath concubine.

"We've a letter from Miranda," Alvar said, clearing his throat.

Jehane looked at ibn Khairan and, reassured by what she saw, let him go. "You've read it?" she asked Alvar.

"I started. Go ahead." He handed her the envelope.

Jehane took it, unfolded the paper and began reading. Alvar walked to a sideboard and poured himself a glass of wine. He glanced at Marisa who shook her head, and at Ammar who nodded. He poured for the other man, his dearest friend in the world, and carried it over, unmixed.

Jehane was reading aloud. "*...turbulent this summer. Fernan and the king have taken the last three cities of Al-Rassan. I don't know the details, I never ask, but in two of them the slaughter was bad, it seems. I know this can bring you no joy, not even Alvar, and I know it will be a great grief for Ammar. Does he believe I bear him no ill-will, even now? Will he accept that I have an understanding of his sorrow, and that Rodrigo would have understood it as well?*

I do not think Fernan does, though Diego might. I'm not sure. I don't see them very much any more, of course. Diego and his wife have had a boy by Jad's grace, my first grandson, and the mother is well. He is named Rodrigo, but you would know that. Diego has been honored by the king with a new title, created for him: he is the first chancellor of united Esperaña. The people are saying that Fernan will win our wars and Diego will guide us in peace. I am proud of them both, of course, though could wish, as a mother, for more kindness in Fernan. I suppose we all know where he lost his gentleness, but I may be the only one who remembers when he had it.

I sound old, don't I? I have a grandchild. I am old. Most of the time I don't think I've changed so much, but I probably have. You wouldn't recognize the king, by the way—he's grown enormously fat, like his father.

They moved Rodrigo's bones this spring, before the summer campaign began. I didn't want him to leave the ranch, but both boys and the king thought he ought to be honored in Esteren and I didn't have the heart to fight them all. I used to be better at fighting. I did insist on one thing, and Diego and King Ramiro, to my surprise, agreed. The words above him are from the ones Ammar sent me so long ago.

I thought I would be the only one who felt that was proper but I wasn't. I went there for the ceremony. Esteren is greatly changed, of course—Alvar, you wouldn't know it at all. Rodrigo lies now in a bay to one side of the god disk in the royal chapel. There's a statue, in marble, done by one of

*Ramiro's new sculptors. It isn't really Rodrigo, of course—
the man never knew him. They gave him his father's eagle
helm and the whip and a sword. He looks terribly stern.
They carved Ammar's words at the base of the statue. In
Esperañan, I'm afraid, but the king did the translation himself, so I suppose that counts for something, doesn't it?*
   He did it like this:

> *Know, all who see these lines,*
> *That this man, by his appetite for honor,*
> *By his steadfastness,*
> *By his love for his country,*
> *By his courage,*
> *Was one of the miracles of the god.*

Jehane stopped reading, struggling visibly. At times
Alvar thought she would do better if she let herself cry.
Marisa had said the same thing, more than once. Jehane
had wept when her father died, and when her third child—
her daughter—was stillborn, but Alvar couldn't remember
any other times, not since a twilit hill by Silvenes.

Even now she controlled herself, laid the letter aside
and said, in a thin voice, "Perhaps I ought to finish this
after the celebration?"

As if to reinforce that, a girl's impatient voice was
heard calling from the courtyard: "Will you come on! We're
all *waiting!*"

"Let's go," Alvar said, allowing himself to take charge.
"Dina's likely to assault me if I make her wait any longer."

They went out to the courtyard. His friends were
there—quite a few of them. Eliane bet Danel, Jehane's
mother, had come to honor him and he saluted her first of
all. His daughters skittered about like a pair of long-legged
colts putting everyone in their proper places before they
bolted for the kitchen, giggling.

"You are all," said Marisa, as soon as they were out of
earshot, "on your oaths not to mention that the cakes are
burnt."

There was laughter. Alvar looked for ibn Khairan. He had taken a chair in one corner of the garden where he could stretch out his leg.

Dina and Razel came back, more decorously, bearing their enterprise on silver trays. No one said a word about the cakes. Alvar, who thought his daughters embodied all the graces of both moons, thought they were delicious, and said so. Marisa made sure his wine glass was always full.

He was toasted several times, made a few wry jests in the speech they demanded: about being ready to settle by the fire now but not being able to afford to do so until his burdens had been properly married off. The girls made faces at him.

Ammar, from his corner, declared that he and Eliane were in no way ready to surrender *their* places by the fire. Alvar would have to wait his turn.

The afternoon passed. When his friends rose to go, Alvar was touched and a little surprised by the warmth with which they embraced him. It still came as a source of wonder to him that he was a man with nearly grown daughters and a loving wife and that so many people seemed to regard him with affection. In his own mind, much of the time, he was still the same person, barely come to manhood, who had ridden from Carcasia, stirrups comically high, with Rodrigo Belmonte one morning long ago.

He seemed to have had a great deal to drink, much more than usual. Marisa's doing. She'd evidently decided it would be good for him today. He remembered kissing Eliane goodbye, holding her gently as she reached up and patted his cheek. That, too, had been a source of wonder, years ago, when he had realized that she approved of him. He looked around. The girls were gone, and Jehane and Ammar's twins. Somewhere upstairs, causing mischief almost certainly. They would probably hear a scream in due course.

It was quiet in the courtyard now, and a little cold. Marisa had brought out a shawl for herself and one for

Jehane who had taken her mother home and returned. Jehane was lighting candles. Alvar made as if to rise and help, but she motioned him back to his chair.

He sat back dutifully, but then, as a strong impulse overtook him, stood up and made his way, carrying his glass and the flask, to the seat beside Ammar. Ibn Khairan was nursing the last of his wine; Alvar filled his glass.

"Fare gently in the god, old friend," Ammar said to him, smiling gravely. "My love and good wishes, today and all days."

Alvar nodded his head. "Will you do something for me?" he asked. "I know this is a celebration. It *has* been. But the girls are upstairs with your boys, we needn't worry about disappointing them."

"A good thing," Ammar said, with a straight face.

Alvar snorted. Everyone teased him on the subject of his daughters. "But truthfully, the day will be wrong for me if we pretend nothing has happened, or changed. I can't pretend. Ammar, you've improvised for kings and khalifs, will you honor my birth day by doing so for me? Or is it too much to ask?"

Ammar's expression had changed. He set down his wine. "The honor will be mine," he said quietly. "Have you a theme?"

"You know the theme."

The two women had come nearer, and now they sat down next to each other, wrapped in their shawls, on a stone bench.

There was a silence. They watched ibn Khairan, and waited. From upstairs the sound of their children's laughter carried down to the garden through an open window.

Ammar said:

> *Ask Fezana what has become of Fibaz,*
> *And where is Ardeño, or where Lonza?*
> *Where is Ragosa, the seat of great learning,*
> *How many wise men remain there?*
> *Where is Cartada, city of towers,*

In the red valley of its power?
Or Seria where the silk was spun?
Where are Tudesca, Elvira, Aljais,
And where, in this twilight, is Silvenes?
The streams, the perfect gardens,
The many-arched courtyards of the Al-Fontina?
The wells and the fountains weep for sorrow,
As a lover does when dawn comes
To take him away from his desire.
They mourn for the passing of lions,
For the ending of Al-Rassan the Beloved,
Which is gone.

The measured, beautiful voice fell silent.

Alvar looked up at the sky. The first stars were out. The white moon would be rising soon above Sorenica. Would it shine on that peninsula west of them?

Time lay upon him like a weight. Rodrigo's two sons were grown men. They were constable and chancellor of Esperaña. Serving King Ramiro the Great. And Rodrigo lay in Esteren, under a statue, under stone.

Alvar filled his glass again, and set it down untouched, a libation, on the bench beside him. He stood up, extending a hand to Ammar, whose leg had never been the same since that other twilight by Silvenes.

"Come," he said. "It is dark and cold. I think we all need light, and the children."

He saw Jehane set her own glass down, as he had, on the table near her. Marisa led them in. She spoke a quiet word with the servants. They dined that evening, together, in a bright room with two fires amid the laughter of their sons and daughters. It was very late when Ammar and Jehane and their children took their leave and walked the short distance to their own home.

Alvar listened to Marisa and the nurse settling two overly stimulated young women. He went up to say good night to his daughters and then he and his wife went along the corridor to their own room and closed the door and drew the curtains against the night.

Outside, white moonlight shone down upon the court-yard where the day's celebration had taken place. It fell upon the water and the small, quick fish in the water. It silvered the olive and fig trees, the tall cypress by the ivy-covered wall and the late-season shrubs. And it cast its pale light upon the three glasses of wine that had each been left deliberately behind, brim-full, on a stone table, a stone bench, on the rim of the fountain there.